George Rose Emerson, David Williamson

William Ewart Gladstone

Statesman and scholar

George Rose Emerson, David Williamson

William Ewart Gladstone
Statesman and scholar

ISBN/EAN: 9783337013219

Printed in Europe, USA, Canada, Australia, Japan

Cover: Foto ©Raphael Reischuk / pixelio.de

More available books at **www.hansebooks.com**

THE RIGHT HON. WILLIAM EWART GLADSTONE.

From the portrait by Numa Blanc, taken at Cannes, in February, 1848.

WILLIAM EWART GLADSTONE:

STATESMAN AND SCHOLAR.

EDITED BY

DAVID WILLIAMSON.

WITH MANY PORTRAITS AND ILLUSTRATIONS.

TORONTO:

G. M. ROSE & SONS,

25, WELLINGTON STREET, WEST.

1898.

PREFACE.

Lord Rosebery once remarked that if an adequate biography of
Mr. Gladstone were ever written, it would be the work of a
Limited Liability Company. Certainly, the marvellous variety of
interests which absorbed Mr. Gladstone during his long life
has made the task of recording his multifarious achievements, and
of appreciating their value, well-nigh impossible. Yet it is a task
which is all the more fascinating by its very greatness and
difficulty.

Mr. Gladstone has given his own opinions on the subject of
biography : " What we want in a biography, and what, despite the
etymology of the title, we very seldom find, is *life*. The very best
transcript is a failure, if it be a transcript only. To fulfil its idea,
it must have in it the essential quality of movement ; must realise
the lofty fiction of the divine shield of Achilles, where the up-
turning earth, though wrought in metal, darkened as the plough
went on ; and the figures of the battle-pieces dealt their blows
and parried them, and dragged out from the turmoil the bodies
of their dead."

In compiling this volume the aim has been to give a careful
chronicle not only of the political career of certainly the busiest
politician of the century, but also to complete the picture of the
activities of Mr. Gladstone in other fields by recording his acts
and speeches in connection with theology, literature, and art—
interests which shared the throne with politics—" the sum of all
the sciences," as Seward called it.

One of the outstanding characteristics of Mr. Gladstone was his love of home ; and his happiness in family life was, undoubtedly, a continual support to him amid the anxieties and strains of high responsibilities. He received the affectionate interest of thousands who held none of his political views, but who reverenced the man while they disagreed with the politician. In these pages the incidents of his social and private life are not forgotten amid the more striking facts of national importance.

Three hands have had a share in the compilation of this volume —so that, unintentionally, Lord Rosebery's idea of a " Limited Liability Company " has been realised. Mr. G. R. Emerson passed away before he had the pleasure of completing the task on which he had embarked with enthusiasm and with many other qualifications of a biographer. Mr. Ronald Smith carried the record further on, with not a little of the skill of his predecessor. And finally it has fallen to the present writer to consummate what had been commenced so admirably.

CONTENTS.

vi

CONTENTS.

LIST OF ILLUSTRATIONS.

vii

WILLIAM EWART GLADSTONE:

A Tribute and an Appreciation.

"THE final lesson, the final trial"—using Mr. Gladstone's own words—has ended at last; and the world is the poorer by the death of the most renowned man in the British Empire. It will be easier to appreciate the true greatness of William Ewart Gladstone in the perspective which future days will bring; now, in this moment of loss, one may only strive to record some of the qualities and triumphs which belonged to him whose departure has left so visible a gap in our national life. Seeking for a comprehensive eulogy, I found the lines written by Dean Plumptre of Gladstone at the zenith of his career:—

> "Not thine the exile's weary lot to tread
> The stairs of others as with weary feet,
> Nor yet in lonely wanderings still to eat
> The doled-out bitter griefs of others' bread.
> Thine is it rather to have nobly led
> Where others halted, or would fain retreat;
> To steer the State, tho' fierce the storm winds beat,
> On to the wished-for haven, sails full-spread."

Mr. Gladstone lived so long and so publicly that criticism had an unending task during certainly the last sixty years of his life. Yet in each ten years there were fresh developments of interest and sentiments in the man which required an altered view for correct judgment. In the language of the geologist, there are several distinct strata in the career of Mr. Gladstone, and no verdict on them as a whole can be considered useful which does not take each into consideration. But, throughout all these changes, there was a changeless temperament. Mr. Gladstone was always serious, enthusiastic, religious, and eloquent. It was only in the varied ways in which these qualities found expression that the man altered.

ix

Dominating all his political career was his love of literature, giving him remarkable recreation at the most anxious moments, and accounting for the choice of not a few of his friends, colleagues, and subordinates. And, above his passion for literature and politics, was his interest in theology—an interest which was practical as well as speculative, and never confined to his own Church or school of thought. One of his intimates said truly, "If you want to make a request to Mr. Gladstone, talk theology first, and he will refuse you nothing afterwards." He always left most willingly the dusty road of politics for the cool glade of religion. Men as divergent in opinion as General Booth of the Salvation Army, the Archbishop of Canterbury, Dr. Guinness Rogers, or, indeed, any representative of the religious world, were sure of an interested listener in Mr. Gladstone, who would ply them with a series of sympathetic questions showing exact knowledge. It was theology that called him from politics when, nearly a quarter of a century ago, he resigned the leadership of his party; and it was to theology that he turned when he retired from the Premiership for the last time in 1894. Throughout his career his scrupulous attention to religious observances was a characteristic, and his respect for all who were set apart for the ministry never waned. For the benefit of those who shared his love of theological study Mr. Gladstone founded St. Deiniol's Hostel and Library, near the old church where he had read the Lessons on so many Sabbaths. To this Library he conveyed, often in his own hands, thousands of treasured volumes; and many a happy hour he spent arranging the books on a particular system evolved from his long experience. The memory of the famous donor of the Library will always pervade the sunny rooms with their crowded shelves of valuable volumes. I shall not soon forget a charming afternoon spent in examining the contents of St. Deiniol's Library. Mr. Gladstone's wide range of reading was reflected in the eclectic choice which he had made. Side by side with a book by a High Churchman like Liddon, Pusey, or Gore, you found one of the works of a Free Church divine like Dr. R. W. Dale. Lighter literature was represented by some standard novels, and I caught sight of " Johnny

Gibb of Gushetnouk," that classic in Doric dialect which we owe to the late Dr. Wm. Alexander. All the books are indexed on a card method, which permits of their speedy discovery. Quite close to the Library is the Hostel, presided over by Mr. Gladstone's son-in-law, the Rev. Harry Drew.

While writing of this example of Mr. Gladstone's love of books and belief in their educational value, one may allude to the omnivorous nature of his appetite for them. When absent from home it was one of the difficulties which hosts had to face; for very soon the veteran reader had mastered all the volumes within his reach. Though a student of classics, he was not one who would say, " When a new book appears, I take down an old one," for he welcomed new voices in the land of literature with almost indiscriminate enthusiasm. At one time any author who took the trouble to send his book to Mr. Gladstone received from him a courteous acknowledgment, and often a kindly remark, which enterprising publishers were not slow to reprint in advertisements. It was Disraeli's custom to reply evasively on such occasions "*I will lose no time in reading your book.*" But his great rival took time and trouble to appreciate most volumes, if pretentiousness were absent from their pages. Mr. Gladstone's exactitude revolted against any mis-statement, however trivial, and I have seen a four-page letter from him to a stranger correcting a very slight blunder. I remember his writing once late at night, from the House of Commons, a letter dealing with an intricate translation of a Latin poem. This was one of the many instances of his well-nigh infallible memory, for he was unable to refer to any book bearing on the case. On another occasion he introduced in a Parliamentary speech an unusual quotation, which baffled even the experienced members of the Press Gallery. One gentleman was deputed to ask Mr. Gladstone for the correct version of the lines. He tracked the Prime Minister from the House to the Universities' Club, only to find that he had just left for a reception at a friend's house. The weary, but undaunted, journalist went to the West End, but again just missed his quarry. It was past midnight before he arrived, almost simultaneously with Mr. Gladstone, at his house in Carlton Gardens. Hurrying up to the door, which Mr. Gladstone was already opening, he asked if he could favour him with a copy of the lines he had quoted in the House.   At once the right hon. gentleman turned and recited them slowly, while the reporter wrote from his dictation.   Then, with a courteous good-night, the statesman entered his home, as if it were the most usual thing in the world to recite Horace at midnight on one's door-step, and the journalist returned happy to his office !

A Cabinet Minister has said that when any matter was under discussion Mr. Gladstone's memory was so accurate regarding past events, that on reference to papers he was generally found to be absolutely correct.   With all his love of rhetoric he seldom allowed his fervour to carry him beyond the bare statement of facts—a rare restraint for an orator of his calibre.

Allusion has been made incidentally to his sympathy ; and much more might well be said on this point.   He preserved a wonderful sense of gratitude for any services, however slight, which had been rendered to him.   Despite all the temptations to suspicion of others which official life gives to most men, he retained to the last a singular power to think the best of most people.   There was an innocence concerning many of the baser motives of self-seekers which was perfectly astonishing in one who had seen so much of life.   Lord Melbourne used to welcome Mr. Delane, the famous editor of the *Times*, with the words, " I'm particularly glad to see you, Mr. Delane, for you are the only man *who never wants anything.*"   Mr. Gladstone welcomed most men, whether they wanted anything or not.   He suffered bores gladly, and would somehow or other manage to extract an interesting piece of information from the greatest dullard.

His omniscience gave rise to several amusing stories, probably apocryphal.   It is said that two men determined to start at dinner a topic on which Mr. Gladstone knew nothing.   They selected a most recondite subject, which they raked up from an old Review ; and in due time launched it on the sea of conversation.   For a while Mr. Gladstone could not be drawn to express his opinion.   At last some one at the table made a direct appeal to him, when he turned the tables on everybody by remarking, "I believe little has occurred in recent years to modify the opinion I expressed on this matter long ago in a certain Review!" It was the very same article with which the conversationalists had hoped to baffle Mr. Gladstone!

His philanthropy was extraordinary, especially in proportion to his income. He was conservative in supporting the same charitable societies, and many of them received subscriptions from Mr. Gladstone for fifty years in succession. It was mentioned not long ago by Lord Medway that the House of Charity had been aided by the Gladstone Family for half a century; and this continuity of interest was a characteristic of Mr. Gladstone. He was naturally concerned for the success of three or four special causes in which his wife was an active worker. The Orphanage for Working Boys, which stands within a few paces of Hawarden Castle, was visited by Mr. Gladstone very frequently, as well as by most of the distinguished guests who stayed at the Castle. Indeed, the visitors' book at the Orphanage is a remarkable collection of autographs, contributed by a wonderful variety of famous men and women. Mrs. Gladstone's Free Convalescent Home for the poor, especially of the East of London, at Woodford, and the Newport Market Refuge and Industrial School were two other institutions to which he gave generous support. To funds raised in connection with the Established Church he gave thousands of pounds; and missionary enterprises had in him a cordial friend.

His kindness to individuals who had fallen on misfortune was shown in hundreds of benevolent acts, of which only his family circle was aware. Of simple tastes himself, he had no sympathy with the display of wealth and luxury which were to be seen in so many houses. In this respect Hawarden Castle offered a strong contrast to most ancestral homes. It is furnished comfortably, but not remarkably, and no room in the whole mansion was less luxurious than Mr. Gladstone's bedroom. Beyond three or four portraits of members of the family there was little decoration in the room, and it gave one a little insight into Mr. Gladstone's character to see about fifty books of devotion lying ready to hand. Before the march of age compelled less early rising, it was his wont to set forth for prayers at the church, returning at a quick pace through the park in time for breakfast. For years this was his habit at Hawarden, and the greater the stress of political affairs the more certain was his recourse to early service—the only time in the day when the Prime Minister could ensure solitude for quiet worship. On Sundays, when he was in residence, hundreds of visitors drove over from Chester and other parts of the neighbourhood in order to catch a glimpse of Mr. Gladstone, and perhaps hear his melodious voice reading the Lessons and joining heartily in every part of the service. It was especially interesting to see the close attention with which Mr. Gladstone listened to the most ordinary sermon—another example of his reverence for the clergy. But he was a careful listener to most speakers, whether in church or in the House of Commons. It made his colleagues marvel to notice the courteous attention which Mr. Gladstone gave to almost any one addressing the House. In the days when some of the "young bloods" of the Tory party delighted to "draw Gladstone," it was pathetic to witness the ease with which they elicited a fiery oration from the Statesman on quite a minor matter. He regarded the gift of speech so highly that he accorded to every one some of the reverence he felt for the power of utterance.

That brings me to the charity of thought which was a leading feature of Mr. Gladstone's character. He disliked very few men, and then only after failing to discover anything admirable in them. As the years went on he mellowed, as an old man should ; and had no harsh words for even those who treated him with incivility among the crowds of people with whom he had met and conversed. This was not because of weak indifference, but because, as the sun was setting, he saw things in a twilight which toned down the glaring faults and foibles of those whom he disliked. Yet, any despicable action would rouse the old lion, and with burning words he would express his abhorrence. Of one man who was erstwhile a Parliamentary colleague, but who opposed Mr. Gladstone with considerable spleen and vigour, he could hardly speak with patience. But for any who had differed from him, for conscientious reasons, he had profound respect, and allowed no incautious phrase used by them to rankle in his breast. Once a friend related an action which exemplified the sharpness, rather than the good faith, of a certain prominent politican. To his astonishment Mr. Gladstone ejaculated, "I don't call that clever, I call it fiendish!" Just as strong language he used to express his abhorrence of the Armenian atrocities which sent a shudder through the Christian community in 1896. He was called from retirement, although in feeble health, to speak at Chester on the subject; and none who heard the veteran orator denounce the Turk and his evil ways will ever forget it. His passion for righteousness, his horror of cruelty, his disdain for cautious, unavailing diplomacy, made the crowded hall ring with applause. And next morning's newspapers sent his burning words echoing through the world. It was appropriate that the last political speech delivered to his countrymen should have been on a similar subject as that of the Bulgarian atrocities which first made Mr. Gladstone a national voice.

Although usually the public which crowded to see him behaved with cordial appreciation of his long services, there were a few occasions in later years when boors allowed their feelings of dislike to Mr. Gladstone to be expressed. The scene at a reception given in the Imperial Institute by the Prince of Wales showed that some in the so-called upper classes still cherished a hatred for Mr. Gladstone. The Prince was annoyed exceedingly at the insults hurled at his guest, to whom he always acted with the kindliest reverence. Prior to Mr. Gladstone's departure for Bournemouth, in the spring of 1898, the Prince called and chatted for a long while with Mr. Gladstone, who, punctilious to the last, lost no time in returning the call at Marlborough House.

There is no doubt that Mr. Gladstone had innate respect for rank, although his knowledge of humanity had taught him—

> " Rank is but the guinea's stamp,
> A man's the gowd for a' that."

. He was slow to believe that men of good family were not, in many ways, best qualified for governing their fellows. The large proportion of peers in his Ministries bears witness to this feeling on Mr. Gladstone's part.

There was, beyond all the qualities discussed in the foregoing pages, the remarkable and enduring quality of courage. One cannot apply more truthfully to any one than Mr. Gladstone the lines of Robert Browning, who sings of—

> " One who never turned his back but marched breast-forward,
> Never doubted clouds would break,
> Never dreamed, though right were worsted, wrong would triumph,
> Held we fall to rise, are baffled to fight better,
>   Sleep to wake."

All through his career he was courageous, never espousing a cause because it was likely to be successful, but because he felt it was a righteous cause ; never hesitating, even with the certainty of losing power and prestige, to lead his party into the lobby where it would be outnumbered ; and to the very last he faced pain and suffering with a bravery which inspired all those who nursed him with admiration. His religious faith sustained his physical endurance when all his political hopes were shattered, and it burned as a bright flame in the darkening hours of ill-health and restricted activity.

The dauntless old warrior has fought his " one fight more—the last, the best ; " the voice of the courageous orator has ceased to speak, save in the memories of the past ; the great religionist has passed beyond the uncertain speculations of Earth. Yet for many a year William Ewart Gladstone will be a name held in high honour by multitudes who knew and revered him, and his character, so unique and inspiring, will become a national treasure more and more to be valued as time rolls on.

INDEX.

WILLIAM EWART GLADSTONE.

CHAPTER I.

THE GLADSTONE FAMILY.

SIR BERNARD BURKE, Ulster King-at Arms, and the most trust-worthy of genealogists, claims for the Prime Minister of England direct descent, by the maternal side, from Robert Bruce, King of Scotland, and Henry the Third, King of England, through Lady Jane, or Joan, Beaufort, who married James the First of Scotland. The elaborate pedigree so carefully traced by Sir Bernard Burke may be briefly epitomised. When the young James—"the ablest of the Stuarts," as he has been styled—was a prisoner in England, he saw by chance the golden-haired beauty, Joan Beaufort, daughter of John Beaufort, Marquis of Dorset, fourth son of John of Gaunt. Her mother was also descended in a direct line from Henry the Third, so that, by both lines, Joan was a daughter of the royal house of England. James first caught sight of her when he was a captive at Windsor, and he records, in one of his poems, that he doubted whether she was

> " A worldly creature,
> Or heavenly thing in likeness of nature."

The loving young couple were married, before the departure of James for Scotland, in the old church of St. Mary Overie, at the Southwark foot of London Bridge, and James took his bride to share his Scottish throne, having given hostages for the payment to the English crown of a ransom equal in amount to forty thousand pounds of English money.

The courtship of the young couple, with its attendant poetry (for James was a poet of no mean power), is one of the prettiest episodes in the history of the Plantagenet times. For thirteen years James reigned, and never was Scotland better governed. Highly educated for the time in which he lived, James possessed great natural talents and literary taste.   He is generally credited with the authorship of a poem, " Christ's Kirk on the Green," looked upon as one of the early literary treasures of his country ; and, more certainly, with that of " The King's Quhair," a well-known and highly appreciated poem.   But at Christmas, 1437, Sir Robert Graham, who had been sentenced to banishment for treason, collected three hundred armed men, forced an entry into the King's chamber at Perth—breaking the arm of brave Catherine Douglas, who had endeavoured to secure the door by thrusting her arm into a staple, and so making it serve the purpose of a bar—and brutally murdered the King.   The Queen received two wounds in her endeavour to protect him.

Queen Joan, a disconsolate widow for a time, afterwards married Sir James Stewart, the Black Knight of Lorne, a descendant of the Bruces ; and their son was John, Earl of Athol, who married Lady Eleonora Sinclair, daughter of William, Earl of Orkney and Caithness.   Their daughter, the Lady Isabel Stewart, became (early in the sixteenth century) the wife of John Robertson of Muirton, county of Elgin.   From this pair was descended in a direct line Anne Robertson, who, in April, 1800, married John Gladstone, and became the mother of the great statesman, the subject of this biography.   One of the descendants of Isabel Stewart and John Robertson was William Robertson, the historian, Principal of the University of Edinburgh, Royal Historiographer for Scotland, and author of the famous " History of the Reign of the Emperor Charles V.," " History of America," and " History of Scotland."   Another of the line was the mother of Henry, Lord Brougham.   There must have been a strong element of intellectual vitality in a stock which produced the large-minded historian, and two such instances of versatile power and oratorical greatness as Brougham and Gladstone.

One Scotch genealogist asserts that the mother of our great statesman was also a descendant of the Mackenzies of Kintail, of the ancient Kings of Man, and other illustrious personages. We do not feel it incumbent on us to enquire very curiously into the validity of the claims set up for, not by, an eminent public man who owes the consideration he enjoys, and the high position he has attained, to his own great qualities, recognised no less by political opponents than by those who have enjoyed his friend-ship, followed his leadership, and shared his fortunes.   No ancestry, however famous, could add to his reputation ; no genealogist, however industrious and far-seeking, could discover on his behalf a greater claim on the respect and admiration of the British nation than that which his splendid abilities have secured throughout half a century of political and literary life. He is, we believe, himself well content to know that his immediate progenitors were men of high ability and character, eminent in the commercial world for intelligence and public spirit, who achieved success by their own efforts, and transmitted to their sons the heritage of an unblemished name.

Long before the union of the Scottish and English crowns, the Gledestanes, Gledstanes, or Gladstanes, were settled in the parish of Libberton, in Clydesdale, now included in Lanarkshire. The name may possibly have been derived from the Lowland *gled*, a hawk, and *stanes*, rock, and so indicate the character of the district in which the Gledstanes dwelt.

The name of Herbert de Gledestane appears as that of one of the Scots who subscribed at Berwick the oath of fealty to Edward the First of England—"hammer of the Scots"—contained in what is known as the "Ragman Roll," of 1296, or Ragimande's Roll, as no doubt it should be properly styled from the name of the papal legate in Scotland. After the defeat of David the Second at Neville's Cross in 1346, Patrick and William of Gledstanes were two of the commissioners appointed to negotiate with the victorious English. Robert the Third granted, about 1390, to "William of Gledstanes, Knight," lands known as Woodgrenynton, in the valley of Eddlestone, or Tweeddale. The fortunate knight added considerably to his possessions by marrying Margaret Trumble, of Hundleshope, near Peebles, who brought to him not only that estate, but also lands in Selkirkshire, Teviotdale, and other places. The Teviotdale estates were held by feudal tenure from the Douglas family, and thenceforth the Border lands seem to have been the scene of the principal exploits of the Gledstanes. That some of them at least were "moss-troopers" is very probable; and certainly the family residence at Ormiston was besieged by no less a person than the renowned Hotspur.

An alliance by marriage appears to have been contracted with the powerful house of Buccleuch; for Scott of Satchells, who chronicled in prose and verse the doings of Sir Walter Scott of Branxholm, "the bold Buccleuch," in the latter part of the sixteenth century, gives the names of four-and-twenty gentlemen, cadets of the Buccleuch family, who were pensioners of the house, and possessed lands in return for rendering military service on the Border. Twenty-three of these bore the name of Scott; the other was "Walter Gladstanes of Whitelaw, a near cousin of my

lord's." A ballad, quoted in the " Border Minstrelsy," tells us
that—

> " The Scotts they rode, the Scotts they ran,
>   Sae starkly and sae steadilie !
>   And aye the ower-word o' the thrang
>   Was —' Rise for Branksome readilie.'"

Probably this Walter Gladstanes, or Gledstanes, was a worthy
associate of the

> " Knights of mettle true,
>   Kinsmen to the bold Buccleuch."

He was, we infer, son of the John Gledstanes of Ormiston,
who, in 1564, subscribed, as an adherent of Buccleuch, a contract of reconciliation between the Scotts and the Kerrs.

The family property appears to have diminished—probably the
fluctuations of Border warfare were not conducive to prosperity ;
and, at the beginning of the seventeenth century, a small estate—
Arthurshiel—near the original Gledstanes, was all that was left to
the family in Clydesdale, and that was sold seventy or eighty
years afterwards by John Gledstanes.

At a later period, we find a branch of the family residing in the
town of Biggar, in Lanarkshire. The Border wars were ended
long ago, and the descendants of the steel-capped troopers had
taken to more peaceful pursuits. In 1728 there died at Biggar
William Gladstones (the family name had now assumed that
form), who had been an industrious and thriving maltster of the
town. He was the last of the family buried in the churchyard of
Libberton, where so many of his ancestors had been laid. Three
sons and one daughter were left to mourn the good old maltster.
John, one of the sons (presumably the eldest), inherited the
malt-kilns, and carried on the business with success. He was an
active man in local affairs, an elder of the Kirk, and apparently,
from the brief records of his useful life which have been preserved, a good specimen of the industrious, thrifty, God-fearing
trader of the Lowlands of Scotland; living in troublous times, but
too prudent to entangle himself in political difficulties, and well
content to plod on honestly and cautiously, and realise a modest
competence, which enabled him to purchase a small property,
and so become a laird. He ended his days in 1756, leaving behind him four sons and six daughters. The small estate, Mid-
Toftcombs, came into possession of the third son, another John
(what became of the elder brothers we cannot certainly say, but
one appears to have been for some time a schoolmaster at Leith),
who married Christian (some authorities give the name Janet)

Taverner, with whom he received a comfortable dowry. The fourth son, John, born in 1732, left the paternal home early in life, intent on seeking fortune for himself. He sett'ed at Leith as a corn-merchant, in a house on the Coalhill, that old street which skirts the harbour, but of which very little is now left except the name, the ancient houses having nearly all disappeared in the course of improvements. For more than fifty years he carried on the business, and realised a handsome fortune, which he must have needed, for sixteen children blessed his union with Helen, daughter of Mr. Walter Neilson, of Springfield; and twelve of the number grew up to maturity, and were helped into business or matrimony, or otherwise provided for out of the results of the father's thrift and industry.

The eldest son of this large family, John, born at Leith in 1763, was brought up to his father's business, and showed such aptitude that, when he had but just attained his majority, his father entrusted him with an important mission to Liverpool, to dispose of a cargo of grain which had arrived there. While there he attracted the attention of one of the leading corn-merchants of the town, who offered him a situation in his office. The paternal assent was readily given—there were other sons well qualified to carry on the Leith business—and John Gladstones became a clerk in the house of Currie and Co. Before long he was raised to the position of partner, and the firm, now Currie, Gladstone and Bradshaw, occupied a high position among the leading mercantile establishments of the great port. It will be noticed that the final "s" had disappeared from the name. What induced John Gladstones to make this alteration is not known; but later in life (February, 1835) he procured a Royal licence for the change.

The partnership continued for sixteen years, and then John Gladstone became sole head of the house. Shortly afterwards he took his brother Robert into partnership, and the business of the firm was greatly extended. A large trade with Russia was established, and, as sugar importers, with the West Indies.

In course of time all John Gladstone's six brothers were settled in Liverpool. The opening of the East India and China trades to private enterprise in 1814, offered new scope for mercantile adventure; and the first private vessel, the *Kingsmill*, despatched by English merchants to Calcutta, was jointly chartered by Mr. Gladstone and another Liverpool merchant.

In 1792 Mr. John Gladstone married Miss Hall, of Liverpool, but she died six years afterwards, leaving no children. In April,

1800, he contracted a second marriage, the bride being Miss Anne Robertson, daughter of Mr. Andrew Robertson, of Stornoway, Provost of Dingwall. This is the lady whose descent from the Royal families of England and Scotland can be traced. She is described as "a lady of great accomplishments, a fascinating woman, of commanding presence and high intellect ; one to grace any home and endear any heart." The union lasted for thirty-five years, blessed by domestic happiness and outward prosperity ; and four sons and two daughters grew up around the family table, in the spacious mansion in Rodney Street, Liverpool. The eldest son, Sir Thomas Gladstone, survives ; the second, John Neilson, who entered the Royal Navy, became a captain, and represented the Irish borough of Portarlington in Parliament, died in 1863 ; the third son, to whom was given the mother's family name, Robertson, succeeded to the headship of the mercantile house at Liverpool, and died in 1875 ; and the fourth son, William Ewart, was destined to become the most eminent of the family. The sisters, Helen Jane, and Ann M'Kenzie, died unmarried, the former as recently as December, 1879.

We must devote a brief space to the career, as merchant and politician, of John Gladstone ; for there is something of the father in the son, added to the more sensitive and excitable temperament which may have been derived from his mother's lineage. We have shown how the elder Gladstone rose to opulence by energy and ability. The acute and vigorous intellect which had made him one of the leading merchants in Liverpool, made him, too, one of the most prominent and public-spirited among the townsmen.

In 1807 the United States resisted the claim of the British Government to right of search, and adopted measures of retaliation, thus greatly interfering with, indeed, virtually suspending, the commerce between the two countries. Liverpool suffered greatly, in one year the trade declining one-fourth. The merchants engaged in the American trade called a meeting and petitioned Parliament against the obnoxious Order in Council, and one of the leading names among the requisitionists was that of Mr. Gladstone. Early in life he adopted Whig principles, but modified his opinions as time advanced, and in 1812 we see him an energetic supporter of George Canning, as chairman of a public meeting called for the purpose of inviting that brilliant politician to become a candidate for the representation of the borough. Although a friend and ally of Pitt, and professedly

a Tory, Canning held advanced views on some subjects, and
was certainly very far from being a Tory of the Eldon type. He
advocated, with all the eloquence at his command, the cause of
Catholic emancipation, was in favour of the abolition of slavery,
and, in commercial matters, exhibited a constant tendency towards the relaxation of prohibitive duties. Mr. Gladstone, who
warmly admired Canning, and enjoyed his friendship, appears to
have felt no inconsistency in supporting Brougham as a colleague in the representation of the town. Two other candidates
were in the field : Mr. Creevy, an advanced Radical, and General
Gascoyne, a Tory of the old school. Brougham thought it would
be to his advantage to make common cause with Creevy, and,
perhaps, felt a gratification, dear to his combative and jealous
nature, in appearing as an opponent rather than as a colleague
of the eloquent, satirical, many-talented Canning. His conduct
decided the course of action taken by Mr. Gladstone, who discarded Brougham and gave the support of his influence to
Gascoyne. The election proceedings were turbulent, notable
even in those stormy days of party strife, two or three men being
killed in the affrays which took place. Canning and Gascoyne
were successful, the former at the top of the poll, and were
chaired through the town, and Canning addressed the crowd
from the window of Mr. Gladstone's house. The noise of the
enthusiastic cheering perhaps reached the nursery, and who can
say what influence may not have been exerted on the mind of the
precocious, restless, eager, vigorous little boy of three years old,
William Ewart, as he listened to the shouts, or perhaps peeped
from the barred windows of the nursery upon the crowd which
surged so tumultuously into Rodney Street. When acknowledging
a congratulatory address on the occasion of his seventieth birthday,
presented by a deputation from Liverpool, he said, " I remember
the first election of Mr. Canning in Liverpool." At the banquet
given to celebrate the return of Mr. Canning, Mr. Gladstone presided.

It was natural that a man so able as Mr. Gladstone should be
invited to accept municipal office in the town where he was so
prominent a figure. But he was strongly opposed to the manner
in which the corporation was elected, and was too conscientious
to permit any consideration of personal ambition to influence his
sense of public duty. The invitations were courteously but firmly
declined; but he actively exerted himself in all public movements which he conceived to be for the local or general benefit.
In particular, it was owing to his exertions that a clause was

B

introduced into the Steamboat Act, requiring a sufficient number
of boats for passengers; a provision sadly needed to prevent
the lamentable accidents which not unfrequently occurred owing
to the reckless overloading of the passenger steamers between
Liverpool and Dublin. In 1818 he spoke at a public meeting in
favour of a resolution recommending the revision and amendment of the criminal law, the frequent executions for the offence
of passing forged one-pound notes having greatly impressed
the public mind.

In 1818 Mr. Canning was again returned for Liverpool, Mr.
Gladstone once more appearing as his most prominent supporter.
One of the election squibs of the time took the form of a parody
of Burns' "Jolly Beggars" and one of the introduced songs
ran :—

> "John Gladstone was as fine a man
>   As ever graced commercial story ;
> Till all at once he changed his plan,
>   And from a Whig became a Tory.
>
> And now he meets his friends with pride,
>   Yet tells them but a wretched story,
> He says not *why* he changed his side,
>   He *was* a Whig, he's now a Tory."

Four years afterwards in 1822, Mr. Canning accepted the office
of Governor-General of India, and had nearly completed his preparations for departure, when the suicide of Lord Castlereagh led
to a reconstruction of the Cabinet, and Canning, called on in the
emergency, resigned the splendid appointment, and accepted for
the second time the office of Secretary of State for Foreign
Affairs. Before that event, however, a farewell banquet had been
given to Canning, by the members of the Canning Club, at Liverpool, at which Mr. Gladstone presided ; and, at his residence,
Seaforth House (to which he had removed in 1818), an address
was presented to that statesman. One of the objects dear to
Mr. Canning's heart was the independence of Greece; and his
Liverpool friends shared his views on the subject. In 1824
a meeting was called to express sympathy for the cause, at which
Mr. Gladstone was one of the principal speakers. Three years
later, he attended a meeting of the townsmen and moved that an
address be presented to the King, congratulating him on the formation of a Canning administration ; the brilliant statesman
having achieved the object of his ambition—the Premiership of
Great Britain, an honour he did not long enjoy, for before the
summer of the year was over he died at Chiswick.

In October, 1824, the leading merchants and townsmen of Liverpool presented Mr. Gladstone with a magnificent service of plate, as a mark of their high sense of his successful exertions for the promotion of trade and commerce, and an acknowledgment of his most important services rendered to the town of Liverpool. In 1825 he was one of the witnesses examined before the committee of the House of Commons respecting the proposed construction of George Stephenson's line of railway between Manchester and Liverpool; and in his evidence he sketched his commercial career. He said he had been a merchant of Liverpool for thirty-eight years, and for the greater part of that time a shipowner. For the first sixteen years of that time he had been almost wholly engaged in the corn trade; and since then he had been concerned with various branches of commerce connected with the town/of Liverpool, the West Indies, the Brazils, the East Indies, and other parts of the world.

It is somewhat remarkable that Mr. Gladstone, who felt a strong interest in political matters—who was, although Scotch by birth, a typical Liverpool man, with his commercial interests centred in the borough in which he had for so many years occupied a leading position, and who certainly was not without parliamentary ambition—should not have been brought forward as a candidate to represent Liverpool in the House of Commons. He did sit in Parliament, but it was for Woodstock, a pocket borough of the Duke of Marlborough; and he was afterwards returned for Lancaster and other constituencies. An energetic, practical man, not deficient in public spirit, but sincerely attached to the old framework of the constitution, which he was not unwilling to expand in accordance with the advancing spirit of the times, he feared revolutionary tendencies, and although he gave a modified support to the cause of Reform, he in nowise desired that it should march with too rapid steps, or be unduly comprehensive. Pocket boroughs, he seems to have thought—as did many others at the time—had occasionally done good service by affording opportunities to men of talent to enter Parliament, which would be otherwise closed to them; and he had no scruple in sitting for Woodstock by favour of the Marlborough family. As a conscientious Christian man, he would have revolted at the idea of treating slaves with cruelty; but slavery, as an institution, he believed to be recognised, if not directly authorised, by Scripture; and besides, he had large commercial interests connected with the trade in sugar, and a plantation in Demerara, which could not be cultivated without negro labour. He held aloof, then,

from the agitation for emancipation, and was content to know
that his sugar estate at Vreeden Hoop was well managed and
profitable.

Generally his support was given to the Tory party; and in
1826 he supported Mr. Huskisson, a candidate for the representation of Liverpool. While sitting for Woodstock, he voted
against the Marquis of Tavistock's motion condemning the
ministers for taking proceedings against Queen Caroline; against
Mr. Plunket's motion for the appointment of a committee to
consider the laws affecting Roman Catholics (in this respect refusing to adopt the views of his old friend Canning); and
against a Bill for the repeal of the additional malt tax. Never
prominent in the House as a speaker, he occasionally gave literary utterance to his views, and was the author of several
political pamphlets of marked ability. In 1830 he published a
pamphlet on slavery in the British sugar and coffee colonies, and
the United States; and another, "Facts Relating to Slavery: A
Letter to Sir Robert Peel." In 1839 and 1846 he produced
pamphlets on the subject of the repeal of the Corn Laws, and
the probable effect on the public revenue. He was first Vice-
President of the Liverpool Institution; was Chairman of the West
India Association; and, in 1829, spoke at a public meeting, at
which resolutions were passed condemning the monopoly enjoyed
by the East India Company. The more thoughtful members of
the Tory party, Canning, Huskisson, and others, had earnestly
studied the doctrines of political economy, and made advances
in the direction of free trade principles; and it was natural that so
large-minded and clear-headed a man as John Gladstone, who
was besides so greatly interested in commercial development,
should adopt their views.

Mr. Picton, in his interesting "Memorials of Liverpool," says:
"Mr. Gladstone was one of the most eminent in the long succession of the enterprising merchants of Liverpool. Far-seeing,
sagacious, and clear-headed, his views were at once comprehensive and practical. As a mercantile man, he was looked up to
as the leader, *facile princeps*, on the Liverpool Exchange." His
large wealth was munificently employed. Warmly attached to the
Church, in 1815 he contributed funds for the erection of St.
Andrew's Church, in Renshaw Street, near his residence. The
church, completed at a cost of £12,000, has little architectural
beauty to recommend it; but at that time the revival of a taste for
ecclesiastical architecture had not commenced, and Mr. Gladstone
was satisfied with providing a large and commodious church, even

if the plain brick exterior were unattractive. The first incumbent was the Rev. John Jones, afterwards Archdeacon of Liverpool, and to whose care the preliminary education of little William Ewart Gladstone was entrusted.

Leith, the cradle of the thriving band of brothers then settled at Liverpool, was not forgotten. After the elder brother had become Sir John Gladstone, he built at the end of Sheriff Brae, near his humble birthplace on Coalhill, and close to the upper drawbridge over Leith Water, St. Thomas's Church; and adjoining it he established a valuable benevolent institution, the Asylum for Female Incurables.

In September, 1835, the amiable and beloved wife of John Gladstone died. Ten years afterwards, Sir Robert Peel conferred a baronetcy on him as Sir John Gladstone, of Fasque, Kincardineshire, and in 1851, the year of the Great Exhibition, he died, aged eighty-eight. He had amassed a noble fortune, secured "respect and memory and troops of friends," and lived to see his most gifted son represent in Parliament the University of Oxford, and rise from office to office, till he had become a member of the Cabinet as Secretary of State for the Colonies, and one of the foremost of that group of able statesmen and brilliant orators who followed the political fortunes of Sir Robert Peel.

When in January, 1843, William Ewart Gladstone—then a young statesman rising into fame, distinguished by his ardent support of Peel's free trade policy—spoke at the opening of the Liverpool Collegiate Institution, his brother, Robertson Gladstone, presiding as Mayor of the town, he said, "I have never forgotten —I never shall forget—that I am a native of this town, distinguished as is this town by everything that can ennoble a commercial community; aye, and by everything that can ennoble a Christian community; and I do trust that I may be allowed to feel a sentiment, apart from any feelings of personal vanity—a sentiment of satisfaction, in reflecting that *I have a favourable introduction to your notice in the name of my father.*"

CHAPTER II.

ABOUT a quarter of a mile from Lime Street Station, Liverpool, and reached by way of Lime Street and Mount Pleasant, or by Bold and Leece Streets, is Rodney Street, a broad thoroughfare, at the southern end of which is St. James's Cemetery. In this street are many large brick houses, once residences of well-to-do merchants; but the wealthy frequenters of the Exchange Flags, the shipowners and cotton dealers, who are the modern merchant princes of Liverpool, now select choicer localities for their residences. Rodney Street was laid out and many houses erected in the early days of the present century, and thither migrated many of the rich townsmen who had previously dwelt in Hanover Street and near Salthouse Dock. The name of the gallant Admiral George Brydges Rodney, who captured the Dutch West India Islands, and defeated the French fleet under the Count de Grasse, had not lost its popularity, or been quite overshadowed by the greater renown of Nelson, and the new line of road was named Rodney Street. Near the centre of the west side of the street, and a few doors from Leece Street, is a large house now numbered 64. When first built, it was almost detached from any other building, being connected only by small wings, used for domestic offices, with other buildings. One of these wings has been altered and converted into a separate dwelling. It is a large two-storied house, old-fashioned and unpicturesque, built flush upon the line of street, but decidedly commodious and comfortable; such a house, indeed, as may be seen in any provincial town, or in the suburbs of great cities, and which is generally tenanted by the leading doctor or lawyer of the locality. We presume that it was from the arched window on the first floor over the doorway that George Canning addressed the Liverpool electors after the chairing at the memorable election of 1812.

In this house, on the 29th of December, 1809, the future Premier of England was born. To the family name, William (that of the last Gladstone who was buried in Libberton kirkyard), was added the surname of his godfather, Mr. Ewart, a Liverpool merchant, who was one of the most intimate friends of the elder

MR. GLADSTONE'S BIRTHPLACE, IN RODNEY STREET, LIVERPOOL.

Gladstone. The son of this gentleman was the well-known Mr William Ewart, who was for many years a member of the House of Commons, and distinguished himself in Parliament by his persistent efforts to obtain the abolition of capital punishment, and the establishment of public libraries, museums, and schools of design; and to whose exertions is due in a great degree the repeal of what was generally described as the "taxes on knowledge."

In the first nine years of William Ewart Gladstone's life, Rodney Street was his home; but, in 1818, his father removed to a residence, Seaforth House, more in accordance with his position as a very wealthy merchant. The Rodney Street house was rented by Mr. John Cardwell, of Blackburn, whose son, Edward, at that time five years old, became in due time member of Parliament, a cabinet minister, and ultimately Viscount Cardwell in the British Peerage. It is certainly notable that two men who have attained such political eminence and who have been so closely allied in public life, should, without any bond of relationship, have each passed several years of childhood in the old house in Rodney Street.

William's first schoolmaster was the Rev. M⁺. Jones, who kept a small academy near the town. Probably the four sons of Sir John Gladstone received their first education there, and the manner in which he discharged his duties may have led to his selection as first incumbent of the church built by Mr. Gladstone in Renshaw Street. Stories respecting the childhood of great men are always abundantly forthcoming; and probably not very much dependence is to be placed on the legend that the Rev. Mr. Jones complained that he found it very difficult indeed to instil even the rudiments of arithmetic into the juvenile mind of William. There is a certain amount of antithesis between the dulness of the boy in matters arithmetical and the splendid financial ability developed in mature life that makes the story attractive. Probably, the precocity of an active mind ever alert for variety made plodding through the dreary pages of " Bonnycastle," or the "Tutor's Assistant," with the pedantic rules and over-elaborated methods of imparting knowledge, distasteful to the eager, restless boy.

There is another legend relating to this time, which may have better foundation. It is to the effect that William's father took great pleasure in talking with his clever little boy about the public questions of the day, especially the doings of Mr. Canning, and that William was a good and intelligent listener. We have seen that, in later life, he said he could remember the election of 1812, when he was only in his third year; and it is quite likely that that event was fixed in his mind by his father's frequent allusions to it. John Gladstone was too sensible a man, too large minded and practical, to endeavour to "manufacture" a political philosopher from a small boy, as James Stuart Mill did; but there can be little doubt that the children of his family heard more of political and commercial matters, discussed in their presence by their father and his many friends, than most children do; and that the quick intellect of William was early trained to a recognition, at least, of many important principles, and to familiarity with commercial topics which did him good service in after life.

Mr. John Gladstone, we may be tolerably certain, was not slow to discover the early promise of ability given by his fourth son, who, in September, 1821, as yet wanting three months of completing his twelfth year, was sent to Eton. He was a robust and active, as well as a clever boy, and made light of many of the hardships which have made public school life very unpleasant to weak or timid lads. Gladstone soon showed that he was well able to take his own part; and when it was found that he was not only one of the most active and successful in all school sports, but also one of the very cleverest of the boys, his popularity at Eton was assured.

He remained about six years at Eton, and there formed some lasting friendships. One of his schoolfellows, of the same age as himself, was George Augustus Selwyn, afterwards the famous missionary bishop of New Zealand, and who died Bishop of Lichfield. Francis Hastings Doyle, who in after life became Professor of Poetry at Oxford, was also at school at the time; and another of the Eton boys of Gladstone's time, but two years younger than he, was the modern Lycidas, Arthur Henry Hallam, whose friendship with Tennyson and early death produced one of the noblest poems of our time, "In Memoriam." Gladstone soon distinguished himself in the school by his success in Latin versification; and it was not likely that he would remain unaffected by the literary traditions of the school. George Canning—in the estimation of all the Gladstone family a very Admirable Crichton—had, when he was an Eton boy, contributed to a school magazine, so had John Hookham Frere—the author of the "Whistlecraft Papers" (which suggested to Byron the style of "Beppo" and "Don Juan"), and father of Sir Bartle Frere—and Winthrop Mackworth Praed. The *Etonian*, to which the latter contributed, was published at Windsor by Charles Knight, at that time a bookseller and printer in the royal town;

and so much talent was brought to light in its pages, that it was
made the basis of another magazine, to which Macaulay and
others who did not belong to Eton contributed. In the last year
of Gladstone's residence at the school, he was one of the pro-
jectors of the *Eton Miscellany*, and certainly the most prolific
contributor, young Selwyn ranking next. Thirteen papers from
the pen of William Ewart Gladstone appeared in the first volume ;
among them a poem in well-balanced heroic couplets, celebrating
the achievements of Richard Cœur de Lion, and "Guatimozin's
Death Song," for the suggestion of which he was probably indebted to his mother's relative, Principal Robertson's account of
the conquest of Mexico by Cortez. To the second volume of
the *Miscellany* he made seventeen contributions. Classical
literature was, of course, among the subjects of the papers. At
a very early period the Homeric poems appear to have powerfully
attracted his attention ; but there were also articles, professedly
humorous, in which, we imagine, he was less successful. The
title of one paper was "Eloquence," and if the youth's oratorical
powers in any adequate degree indicated those of the man, he
was assuredly competent to write effectively on such a topic.
Probably he felt a confidence that he possessed the power "the
applause of listening senates to command," and, indeed, there is
in the essay an indication of an ambition which is not unlike
Benjamin Disraeli's day-dreams of his Vivian Grey period. Both
youths were prophets, inspired by the consciousness of great
abilities and faith in themselves. "A successful *début*," wrote
Gladstone (in his eighteenth year, at school at Eton), "an offer
from the minister, a Secretaryship of State, and even the Premiership itself, are the objects which form the vista along which a
young visionary loves to look."

In 1827 he bade farewell to Eton, its school-room and playing-
fields. Few of the pupils at that famous school were so well
grounded in the classical learning chiefly valued there. He
continued his studies for about two years, as private pupil of Dr.
Turner, who was afterwards appointed Bishop of Calcutta ; and
then entered, as a student, Christ Church College, Oxford. Here
his industry was enormous, and even in the vacation he scarcely
relaxed his ardour. One writer, describing his career at this
period, says : "No matter where he was, whether in college
rooms or country mansion, from 10 a.m. to 2 p.m. no one ever
saw William Ewart Gladstone. During this interval he was invariably locked up with his books. From the age of eighteen
until that of twenty-one, he never neglected studying during these

particular hours, unless he happened to be travelling. And his evening ordeal was scarcely less severe. Eight o'clock saw him once more engaged in a stiff bout with Aristotle, or plunged deep in the text of Thucydides."

In one respect the industrious student was more prudent than many of his fellows and competitors. Throughout his long life he has recognised the natural alliance of the physical and intellectual portions of our compound being. Naturally hardy and muscular, he cultivated his bodily powers by regular active exercise, and his high moral nature preserved him from the temptation to indulge in enervating luxuriousness. Temperate and active, trained to muscular exertion, he could probably have outwalked any of the undergraduates of his college as easily as he could have surpassed most of them in mental acquirements. A brisk walk of thirty or forty miles was a small matter to the handsome, well-knit, resolute young student, who returned from it with a refreshed brain and renewed vitality to his studies. The Oxford Union, that renowned debating society where so many of our greatest statesmen, lawyers, and divines trained their oratorical powers and learned their first lessons in practical politics and philosophy, offered great attractions to Gladstone. The position of President of the Union was justly looked upon as conferring a high honour, due to acknowledged intellectual power and oratorical ability ; and it is worth noting that seven presidents were at one time united in one of the administrations of which Mr. Gladstone was the chief. He had only been a member of the university for a few months when he made his first speech at the Union, on the 11th of February, 1830. He was afterwards a frequent speaker, taking the Tory view of public questions. That his style was rather rhetorically ornate, and that he made frequent reference to classical examples and freely resorted to classical quotations, we can readily suppose ; and that he was fluent, enthusiastic, and excitable, is equally probable. He opposed the removal of Jewish disabilities, and Parliamentary Reform, but supported Catholic Emancipation. A few years since, he referred to the opinions he had held in these Oxford days : " I trace," he said, " in the education of Oxford of my own time one great defect. Perhaps it was my own fault; but I must admit that I did not learn when at Oxford that which I have learned since, namely, to set a due value on the imperishable and inestimable principles of human liberty. The temper which I think too much prevailed in academic circles was to regard liberty with jealousy."

Even before the delivery of his first speech, the new member of the Union had been warmly welcomed and recognised as an acquisition. The University of Cambridge had, as well as the sister University, its Union; and we are reminded by its proceedings of the times, glorious in the annals of the Schools, when ambitious students travelled from town to town, challenging learned professors or students to argue questions of doctrine, literature, or philosophy. The Cambridge Union sent a delegation, headed by Mr. Monckton-Milnes (now Lord Houghton), to Oxford, to maintain the proposition that Shelley was a greater poet than Byron. The author of "Queen Mab" had been then dead about seven years, and Byron about five years; and the poetical youth were divided into two parties on the subject of their respective merits. Shelley had been an Oxford man, and Byron had studied at Cambridge; nevertheless, the eager disputants of the Cambridge Union adopted the former for their champion, and deputed to the poetical young Monckton-Milnes and his associates the task of convincing the Oxonians, who were believed to favour Byron. The challenge was cordially accepted by the Dark Blues (as, perhaps, we should style them now), and the Cantabs were "formally received," when they reached Oxford after their tedious coach ride, "by Gladstone of Christ Church and Manning of Oriel." Manning of Oriel is now the Roman Catholic Cardinal Archbishop of Westminster. The debate took place, and no doubt great interest was excited. Gladstone took no part in it, but Manning did, supporting the superiority of Byron. The visitors, however, "won the match," the greater number of votes being given for Shelley.

At the Michaelmas Examination of 1831, the greatest of academical successes was attained by Mr. Gladstone, who took a first-class in *Literis Humanioribus*, and also in *Disciplinus Mathematicis et Physicis*. It is rarely that a "double first" is achieved; but on this occasion another Christ Church student, Mr. Henry Denison, was also successful.

Mr. Gladstone, who, for a short time afterwards, held a fellowship at All Souls, left the University too early to share in the great awakening of intellectual and religious activity which shortly took place. Strongly attached to the principles and formularies of the Church of England, and animated by profoundly religious sentiments, he would no doubt have been a prominent figure in the great movement which Keble, Pusey and Newman headed. In his college days the religious aspect of the University was decorous, but dull. There were active intellects, great learning, devout bearing; but as yet the wind had not

arisen which was to ruffle the ocean of controversy. The Church
was too generally regarded as a profession; there were men in
the University who before long would, with amazing ability and
earnestness, claim for its clergy the position, in its fullest sense,
of a priesthood.

In his "Chapter of Autobiography," written in 1868, when
he was devoting all his energies to the work of disestablishing
the Irish Church, Mr. Gladstone refers to the subject:—

" At the time when I resided at Oxford, from 1828 to 1831, no sign of it
[the great revival of religious activity in the Church of England] had yet
appeared. A steady, clear, but dry, Anglican orthodoxy bore sway, and
frowned this way or that, at the first indication of any tendency to diverge from
the beaten path. Dr. Pusey was at that time revered for his learning and talent, but suspected (I believe) of
sympathy with the German theology, in which he was known to be profoundly
versed. Dr. Newman was thought to have about him the flavour of what he
has now told the world were the opinions he derived in youth from the works
of Thomas Scott. Mr. Keble, the 'sweet singer of Israel,' and a true saint, if
this generation has seen one, did not reside in Oxford; the chief chair of
Theology had been occupied by Bishop Lloyd, the old tutor and the attached
and intimate friend of Peel: a man of powerful talents, and of a character
both winning and decided, who, had his life been spared, might have acted
powerfully for good on the fortunes of the Church of England, by guiding
the energetic influences which his teaching had done much to form. But he
had been hurried away, in 1829, by an early death; and Dr. Whately, who
was also, in his own way, a known power in the University, was, in 1830,
induced to accept the Archbishopric of Dublin. There was nothing at that
time in the theology, or in the religious life, of the University to indicate what
was to come."

CHAPTER III.

ENTRANCE INTO POLITICAL LIFE.

THE brilliant success at Oxford fairly entitled Mr. Gladstone to a little relaxation, and he made a short tour on the Continent, and was absent from England during the stormy times of the great Reform agitation. The Reform Act (more precisely the "Act to Amend the Representation of the People in England and Wales, 2 and 3 Wm. IV., c. 45") received the royal assent on the 7th of June, 1832, and the Scotch and Irish Reform Bills on the 17th of July and the 7th of August respectively. Preparations for the general election were carried on with the greatest ardour, but fortunately with little disturbance to the public peace. There was, indeed, something like a popular reaction. Political fury had exhausted itself in the riots at Bristol, Nottingham and elsewhere ; and personal animosity was for the time quiescent. Forty-two new boroughs had been created, to return sixty-four members ; fifty-six had been disfranchised, among them the snug pocket boroughs in which a handful of voters had returned unquestioning the nominees of a few great houses. Ambitious politicians were too busily engaged in wooing the new constituencies to have much time for "fighting their battles o'er again," and new constituencies were looking out for representatives to their taste. The great landed proprietors and heads of noble houses feared a democratic incursion into Parliament, which would attack, perhaps sweep away, certainly interfere greatly with, their privileges ; and bestirred themselves to exert the interest they still possessed in some of the boroughs which had survived the Reform Act, and which might be relied on to return "safe" men. The Established Church, the Corn Laws, the Game Laws, were threatened, and who could foresee what changes would be demanded by the host of indomitable Radicals who might find themselves in the House of Commons as representatives of constituencies which never before had had a voice in the government of the country?

It was very desirable, therefore, that the "old cause" should be supported by new champions who would contribute youthful energy and marked ability to the Tory rank and file. At such a time William Ewart Gladstone could scarcely be overlooked.

His University success had been most brilliant; he had given promise at the Union of the possession of gifts of oratory which might be most useful to the party; and the interest he had exhibited in the great questions which then occupied the political mind, had marked him out for a Parliamentary career. One of his Oxford friends was the Earl of Lincoln, son of the Duke of Newcastle, and the Duke decided that the talented son of the able and wealthy Liverpool merchant would be an excellent representative for Newark, a borough which, hitherto, the Duke had found to be particularly willing to return any candidate he might select. Mr. Gladstone was sent for, and hastily quitted Italy—not perhaps without a sigh of regret at leaving classic ground, but honourably ambitious of entering on the career opened to him.

He was not, however, destined to receive an unopposed return. Mr. Handley, a Tory, and Serjeant Wilde, a Whig (afterwards, as Lord Truro, Lord Chancellor in the Russell Administration, 1851-2), contested the seat. Mr. Gladstone issued his address on the 9th of October, and did little more than repeat the familiar creed of the Tory party; but his good taste and cultivated mind made him avoid the vituperations and asperities which then characterised political discussion. Tory though he declared himself to be—immature and inexperienced as he certainly was—his nature forbade assimilation with the narrow views of the old school, or the boisterous energy and unscrupulous vituperation of the writers in *Blackwood.* The address touched the subjects of Reform, Church and State, the Condition of the Working Classes, and the agitation for the Abolition of Slavery. Referring to the desire for great changes which the advocates of Reform manifested, he said :—

"We must watch and resist that unenquiring and undiscriminating desire for change amongst us which threatens to produce, along with partial good, a melancholy preponderance of mischief; which, I am persuaded, would aggravate beyond computation the deep-seated evils of our social state, and the heavy burthens of our industrial classes."

He professed his adherence to

"That principle on which alone the incorporation of religion with the State, in our constitution, can be defended—that the duties of governors are strictly and peculiarly religious, and that legislators, like individuals, are bound to carry throughout their acts the spirit of the high truths they have acknowledged. Principles are now arrayed against our institutions; and not by truckling nor by temporising, not by oppression nor corruption, but by principles, they must be met."

There is no uncertain note in these words. They are those of

ETON COLLEGE.

CHRIST CHURCH COLLEGE, OXFORD.

NEWARK.
Mr. Gladstone's first Constituency in Parliament.

a man desperately in earnest, who feels that he has taken his side, and must stand or fall by his colours. We have here the rudiments of his book, published six years afterwards, on the relations of Church and State. He appears to have had but little sympathy with the rigid theories of the political economists on the subjects of the poor and labour, and promised

> "A sedulous and special attention to the interests of the poor, founded upon the rule that those who are the least able to take care of themselves should be most regarded by others. Particularly, it is a duty to endeavour by every means that labour may receive adequate remuneration."

On the subject of Slavery, then so prominently before the public, he spoke rather hesitatingly. He was, in truth, in a peculiar position in reference to this matter. Bred among Liverpool merchants, "the bricks of whose stately mansions were cemented with the blood of negroes"—so the ardent Emancipationists said —he had been taught to believe that the grossest exaggeration as to the real condition of the slaves in the British colonies had been indulged in by benevolent, but ill-informed, persons; and that the evils of the system were rather theoretical than practical. Indeed, he was not sure that slavery was, in itself, unsanctioned by the highest law, although he might think that as civilisation extended it might be beneficially ameliorated, or even disappear altogether. His father owned slaves in Demerara, and he knew that his father was a thoughtful, religious, and just man; and he knew other merchants and slave-owners who conscientiously desired the well-being of the negroes on their plantations. He said:—

> "As regards the absolute lawfulness of slavery, I acknowledge it simply as importing the right of one man to the labour of another, and I rest it upon the fact that Scripture, the paramount authority on such a point, gives directions to persons standing in the relation of master to slave, for their conduct in that relation; whereas, were the matter absolutely and necessarily sinful, it would not regulate the manner."

He hoped that "an universal and efficient system of Christian instruction," set on foot by impartial and sovereign authority, would, by teaching both parties, lead to gradual emancipation. No doubt, as he gained a wider experience of human nature, he somewhat modified this utopian view. "The Duke's nominee," "the slave-driver," were epithets freely bestowed upon him by the supporters of the Whig candidate; but the Duke's influence carried the day (many of his tenants, it is said, voting as he wished, but grumbling considerably as they did so), and when the poll was declared, the numbers stood: Gladstone, 832; Handley, 793; Wilde, 719.

The first Reformed Parliament assembled on the 23rd of January, 1833, and on the 5th of February the King delivered the Royal Speech. Among the more important domestic topics referred to, was the state of the Established Church, particularly as regarded temporalities, the maintenance of the clergy, the rearrangement in a more equitable manner of the revenues, and, generally, the correction of acknowledged abuses. As to the Church of Ireland, the speech recommended "the adoption of a measure by which, upon the principle of a just commutation, the possessors of land may be able to free themselves from the burthen of an annual payment." The Speech continued, "In the further reforms that may be necessary, you will probably find that, although the Established Church of Ireland is, by law, permanently united with that of England, the peculiarity of their respective circumstances will require a separate consideration."

The subjects for discussion thus indicated, no doubt commended themselves to the serious attention of the young member for Newark; but he modestly and prudently abstained from obtruding himself on the attention of the House. He was yet an untried warrior, and was not rash enough to enter the fray until he had proved his weapons and trained his forces. The debate on the Address was signalised by one of those brilliant "duels of debate" between O'Connell and the Hon. E. G. Stanley (afterwards Lord Stanley and Earl of Derby), Chief Secretary for Ireland in the Grey Ministry, which made so many debates memorable.

Mr. Gladstone spoke only once or twice in the course of the Session, and then briefly. Indeed, he was so unimportant a personage, that "Hansard" did not take the trouble to give his proper name in the official reports of the debates. Sometimes he appears as Mr. William Gladstone, sometimes his Christian name is given as Ewart, and once as Edward. We see it stated in some biographies that his maiden speech was delivered on the 18th of May, on the subject of Slavery. This is incorrect. His first utterance in the House was on the 21st of February. Mr. Benett, the member for Wiltshire, had presented a petition from more than three thousand inhabitants of Liverpool, complaining of bribery and corruption at the recent election, and expressing their persuasion that the provisions of the Reform Act were not sufficient to remedy the abuses complained of. The members returned for the borough were Mr. Ewart and Lord Sandon. In the debate which ensued, Mr. Rigby Wason, the member for

Ipswich, said he was sure that no two gentlemen in the House would be found who would not admit that the case of the last election for Liverpool was one of the most flagrant instances of corruption which had ever taken place.

These remarks called up Mr. Gladstone, who said, " The Reform Bill had not produced at Liverpool the effect which had been anticipated from it. He would venture to say, however, that no corrupt influence had been used either by the noble Lord (Sandon) or by any of his supporters during the last election." Mr. Warburton, member for Bridport, somewhat contemptuously enquired how it could be possible in the case of Liverpool, where there was so much opposition among the parties which divided the electors, for any individual to make a positive asseveration that no undue influence had been exerted?

In the course of the debate on the Ministerial Bill for " the Abolition of Slavery throughout the British Colonies, and for the promotion of industry among the manumitted slaves, and for compensation to the persons hitherto entitled to the services of such slaves," Lord Howick (now Earl Grey), who had been Under-Secretary for the Colonies in the previous Administration, referred to the sugar plantations of Vreeden Hoop and Demerara, the property of Mr. John Gladstone, of Liverpool, where he said, " a large amount of sugar had been produced, to the great advantage of the owner, but unhappily at the price of a dreadful loss of life amongst the slaves." Three days afterwards, on the 17th of May, Mr. Gladstone made a reply to this statement, and vindicated the character of his father's manager, who had been referred to in strong terms of condemnation by Lord Howick. " He was ready to admit," Mr. Gladstone said, " that the cultivation of sugar was of a more severe character than others, and he would ask were there not certain employments in this and other countries more destructive to life than others?"

On the 3rd of June he again referred to the subject, in his first really important speech, in opposition to the Government proposition. He once more defended the manager at Vreeden Hoop, and finished a speech of moderate length and delivered with much vivacity and energy, by saying, " Let not any man think of carrying this measure by force. England rests not her power upon physical force, but upon her principles, her intellect and virtue; and if this great measure is not placed on a fair basis, and is conducted by violence, I shall lament it as a signal for the ruin of the colonies and the downfall of the empire."

c

About a month afterwards, Mr. Mark Philips, the member for Manchester, having moved for a select committee to take into consideration the petition of the inhabitants of Liverpool, Mr. Gladstone defended the freemen, and described the attempt to deprive them of their privileges as a persecution. His resistance, however, was unavailing. O'Connell gave his powerful support to the motion, and it was carried by a majority of 84.

On the 8th of July he made a speech in defence of the Irish Church, in opposition to the Ministerial Church Temporalities (Ireland) Bill :—

"He opposed the Bill because he thought it would tend to desecrate the Established Church, and the desecration of a Church must be productive of the most serious injury to the country. He was prepared to defend the Irish Church, and if it had abuses, which he did not now deny, those abuses were to be ascribed to the ancestors and predecessors of those who now surrounded him. . . . He thought it was of the utmost advantage to society to have a body capable of spreading and extending the Protestant doctrine ; and without meaning any offence to his Catholic fellow-subjects, he could not but think that it would be productive of great benefit, in a national point of view, to have the means of expounding, defending, and maintaining their doctrines in an active manner. All he asked was that such an opportunity should be given, and then, ' God defend the right.' "

Throughout the remainder of this, his first session, he remained silent, except making a very brief speech on the Slavery question, in opposition to the Bill, and defending the planters.

On the reassembly of Parliament in 1834 the Slavery question was again discussed, in connection with the proposal for the continuance of the Sugar Duties, and Mr. Gladstone contributed a short speech to the debate. He spoke somewhat more at length on the 19th of March, when the Liverpool Freemen Bill was before the House. With characteristic courage, he attempted to defend his fellow-townsmen ; but we imagine the Gladstone of later times must have smiled if the poor excuse made by him in his early days for the corrupt voters at the Municipal and Parliamentary elections of Liverpool was brought to his recollection. He said :—

"Men in the humbler walks of life could not be supposed to have very correct abstract opinions upon the nature of bribery. The utmost, perhaps, that could be reasonably expected from them would be that they should consistently adhere to one political creed. He did not mean to defend the corruption that had taken place ; but ought not the argument he had just adduced be taken as some palliation in the case of the poorer freemen ?"

These poor freemen could get drunk, fight, and deliberately sell themselves to the highest bidder, and the fact that they did not

MR. GLADSTONE DELIVERING HIS MAIDEN SPEECH IN THE HOUSE OF COMMONS,
FEBRUARY 21, 1833.

have "very correct abstract opinions" as to honesty and decency, was a strange argument in favour of not putting a stop to their amusements, and punishing those who indulged in drunkenness and window-breaking, with variations of assault and even manslaughter. The Liverpool electors appear to have been in bad case. In the course of the debate, Sir Charles Wood said he had never seen—indeed, he had never conceived —anything so gross and flagrant as the corruption in Liverpool; and Mr. Baines said it was a notorious fact that the freemen of Liverpool looked upon the return of an election, not as an occasion for the exercise of privileges conferred upon them for important political purposes, but as a saturnalia, in which they were to indulge in the most extravagant licentiousness.

On the 6th of May Mr. Gladstone supported the introduction of a Bill, by Mr. Hesketh Fleetwood, member for Preston, for the better observance of the Lord's Day; and on the 28th of July he delivered the longest and most important speech he had as yet made in the House. It was on the occasion of the motion by Mr. Hume for the third reading of the Universities' Admission Bill. His defence of slave-owners in the West Indies and Demerara, and apologies for Liverpool freemen who received bribes and broke heads, were doubtless less the result of deliberate judgment than of personal influences. Respecting the Irish Church he no doubt felt strongly, because he considered it his duty to defend a political theory which he believed to be of the highest importance to the State. But a proposition to meddle with what he believed to be the very essential principle of the great Universities touched him to the quick. He had unlimited faith in the importance of the Established Church as an element in the British Constitution on which its stability depended; and in the importance of the Universities as nurseries of the Church. That they should be deprived of that exclusive character was, in his estimation, a most dangerous and destructive proposition, to be regarded with something like horror by every true Churchman. As one who had benefited so greatly by University training, who had found in the Oxford colleges so much that he admired and loved, he felt called upon to champion them with all the vigour at his command; and, no doubt, the earnestness and impetuous eloquence of the young orator, flushed with excitement, which added a charm to his handsome countenance, produced a considerable effect on the House. It was perhaps that speech which made Southey say, "Young Gladstone, the member for Newark, is said to be the ablest person that Oxford has sent forth for

many years, since Peel or Canning." We quote the concluding
passages of the speech which summarise his argument :—

"The Universities had been spoken of as national institutions. He admitted
the term, but not in the sense with which it is generally put forth. They were
undoubtedly national institutions, but only so far as the ere connected with
the National Church. The vital principle of these collegiate foundations was
to provide a course of education which should attend to the moral character
as well as the scientific attainments of the pupils. To attain this, a certain
fixed course of study and of discipline must be observed ; but how could this
be done when, by the Bill before the House, it was proposed to throw open the
doors not only to Dissenting Christians of every sect and denomination, but
also to all sorts of persons, be they Christian or not ? . . . It was said of
the ancient Romans that they 'made a solitude and called it peace.' He very
much feared that the House, in establishing their present principle of religious
liberty, would drive from their functions men who had so long done honour
and service to their country, and thus inaugurate the reign of religious peace by
an act of the grossest tyranny."

That Mr. Gladstone was, at that time, a better orator than
prophet, is evident from the preceding passage. The professors
and tutors, the heads of houses and proctors, have not been
"driven from their functions," and, certainly, the students are not
as a body less moral, nor in scholarship less exact, because
Dissenters have been admitted to the colleges. This speech, however, added greatly to the estimation in which the young member
for Newark was held by his party, and marked him out as a recipient of official position when the opportunity should occur.

On the 13th of January, 1833, he had been admitted to the
Society of Lincoln's Inn; and he kept eleven terms between 1833
and 1837. When he had been a member for six years and three
months, he petitioned to have his name removed from the books,
on the ground of "having given up his intention of being called
to the Bar." He was not a mere "diner" at an Inn of Court,
but "performed exercises" as other students preparing for the
bar did.

CHAPTER IV.

ACCESSION TO OFFICE IN PEEL'S FIRST ADMINISTRATION.

THE most influential member of the Melbourne Cabinet—influential alike by the integrity of his private character and his business abilities—was John Charles Spencer, Lord Althorp, Chancellor of the Exchequer and leader of the House of Commons. On the 10th of November, 1834, he succeeded, by the death of his father, to the earldom of Spencer, and necessarily vacated his office in the Administration. When Lord Melbourne, the Premier, waited on the King at Brighton to communicate the intelligence, he was surprised—at least, as much surprised as a man of his calm temperament could be—to receive an intimation that the King had decided to form a new Administration. This, at least, is the generally accepted version of the story. It was suspected that Queen Adelaide, who disliked Melbourne, had influenced the King, and the opening sentence of a leader in a powerful daily newspaper, " The Queen has done it !" expressed a widespread but most unfounded impression. Mr. Thomas Raikes, who was well informed on all matters of political as well as social gossip, tells us in his " Diary," that the King's decision took place on the avowal of Lord Melbourne that he despaired of carrying on the Government, and that a dissolution of the Cabinet was inevitable before the meeting of Parliament.

On the 14th, Melbourne and his colleagues formally resigned. William the Fourth had never liked the Whig statesmen. The Reform agitation had compelled him to accept their services; and he willingly availed himself of the excuse which the changes in the Cabinet necessitated by the removal of Althorp to the Upper House would afford, to get rid of Brougham, whom he hated, and others whom he less openly disliked. He seems to have thought that the Whigs had lost public confidence—and, indeed, the general feeling of dislike at the Poor Law Amendment Act and other measures, in some degree justified his opinion—and that he could safely recall the Duke of Wellington to his councils. The Duke was sent for, but declined the task of forming an Administration, referring the King to Sir Robert Peel, who was in Rome. The Duke was gazetted as Foreign Secretary, and Lord

Lyndhurst as Lord Chancellor; and, until the arrival of Sir Robert, the Government was virtually carried on by the Duke, except in regard to legal matters in which the Lord Chancellor's aid was necessary.

On the arrival of Sir Robert Peel, on the 9th of December, he accepted office as First Lord of the Treasury and Chancellor of the Exchequer, and with some difficulty succeeded in forming an Administration. He showed that he had not been unmindful of the promise displayed by Mr. Gladstone, by appointing him to the office of Under-Secretary for the Colonies. It is worth noting that this was the first office Peel himself had occupied, twenty-three years before.

Sir Robert decided on a dissolution of Parliament, announced in the last Gazette of the year. The new Parliament opened on the 24th of February, after an exciting contest for the Speakership, in which the late Speaker, Sir Charles Manners Sutton, the nominee of the Whig party, was defeated by a majority of ten, the successful candidate being Mr. Abercromby, a member of the advanced Reform party. The contest excited considerable interest, and the coarse caricaturists of the day represented a fight between "Sooty," a sweep, and "Crummy," a baker. In the House, the contest had little to do with the comparative qualifications of the candidates for the high office, but was made a test of party strength, the result showing that the new House could not be relied on to support the new Ministers.

Mr. Gladstone entered with zeal on the duties of his office. The Earl of Aberdeen was his official chief; and the duty of representing the department in the Commons fell upon the young Under-Secretary, who had been re-elected for Newark. On the 19th of March he introduced a Bill for the regulation of emigrant ships, and the protection of poor emigrants to the colonies, who suffered great hardships, and were exposed to great dangers from overcrowding and the deficient supply of boats.

One of the earliest acts of the Opposition was to re-introduce the question of the Temporalities of the Irish Church, Lord John Russell moving for a Committee of the whole House to consider the subject. On the 31st of March Mr. Gladstone spoke in opposition to the motion, and concluded by saying:—

"If those individuals who are called upon to fill the high functions of public affairs should be compelled to exclude from their consideration the elements of true religion, and to view various strange and conflicting doctrines in the same light, instead of administering those noble functions, they would be helots and slaves. . . . If, in the administration of this great country, the element of religion should not enter—if those who were called upon to guide it in its career should be forced to look to the caprices and the whims of every body of visionaries, they would lose that station all great men were hitherto proud of. He hoped he should never live to see the day when any principle leading to such a result would be adopted in that country."

His tenure of office was of brief duration. The ministerial supporters experienced repeated defeats, and early in April were beaten by a majority of 27, on the question of the commutation of tithes in Ireland. On the 8th, Sir Robert announced that he and his colleagues, " finding it impossible to carry measures, had tendered their resignations." The King sent for Lord Melbourne, who was reinstated at the Treasury. Lord Palmerston resumed the office of Foreign Secretary ; and Lord John Russell, who had been Paymaster of the Forces in the previous Whig Ministry, took office as Home Secretary. The arrangement probably most gratifying to the King was that the impracticable and erratic Brougham did not return to the woolsack, the Chancellorship being put in commission.

Throughout the remainder of the Session Mr. Gladstone was almost a silent member. One vigorous speech he made, defending with characteristic courage the House of Peers against the vigorous attacks of the veteran Radical, Joseph Hume, and the Parliamentary giant, O'Connell. He charged them with advancing atrocious and dangerous doctrines. O'Connell's reply was the expression of "much contempt for the honourable member's argument."

Early in the Session of 1836 Mr. Fowell Buxton moved for the appointment of a committee to enquire into the working of the apprenticeship system in the colonies. Mr. Gladstone maintained that the system had worked well, that the masters had, on the whole, behaved with kindness, and that the Anti-Slavery Society had "sent forth to the public garbled statements," unfairly representing the state of things in the West Indies. The planters, he maintained, had not been enormously remunerated, for, if £20,000,000 had been granted, the value of slave property had been estimated at £45,000,000.

In the latter part of the Session, and in the early part of the Session of 1837, the affairs of Canada were prominently before the House. The dissensions between the House of Assembly in Lower Canada and the Executive Government, which had broken out fifteen or sixteen years before, had increased in intensity, and were deepened by the national prejudices of the two parties of colonists—those of French and those of English descent. Com-

missioners had been appointed by the Home Government to enquire into the causes of the dissension. Arrests were made, but
the prisoners were rescued, and serious disturbances ensued, not
subdued without the employment of the military force. The
Canadian Legislature refused to vote the money necessary for the
salaries of the ministers and executive officers. On the 6th of
March Lord John Russell, the Home Secretary and leader of
the Commons, moved a series of ten resolutions on the subject,
and Mr. Gladstone, and the members of his party, gave a general
support to the Ministers.

A leading item in the programme of the Melbourne Ministry
was the Abolition of Church Rates, and, on the 3rd of March,
Mr. Spring Rice, Chancellor of the Exchequer, moved a resolution, in Committee of the whole House, for the abolition of the
rate. On the 15th, Mr. Gladstone made a vigorous speech against
the resolution. He referred with a touch of haughty contempt to
the scruples of conscience which had been pleaded by some persons
who had persistently refused to pay the rate. "When the Legislature," he said, "made a demand on its subjects for a part of
their property, whatever might be the purpose for which it was
applied, the Legislature absolved the conscience of its subjects.
They might use every means of getting rid of it, but as long as
the payment was law, no scruple of conscience could fairly resist
it." He said an allusion had been made, in a speech delivered
on another occasion, to the grandeur of ancient Rome, and it was
attributed to her municipal institutions. He continued:—

"But it was not by the active strength and resistless powers of her legions,
the bold independence of her citizens, or the well-maintained equilibrium of
her constitution, or by the judicious adoption of various measures to the
various circumstances of her subject states, that the Roman power was upheld.
Its foundation lay in the prevailing feeling of religion. That was the superior
power which curbed the licence of undivided rule, and engendered in the
people a lofty disinterestedness and disregard of personal matters, and devotion
to the Republic. The devotion of the Romans was not enlightened by a
knowledge of the precepts of Christianity. Here religion was still more
deeply rooted and firmly fixed. Would they now consent to compromise the
security of its firmest bulwark? No ministry would dare to propose its unconditional surrender; but with the same earnestness and depth of feeling with
which they should deprecate the open avowal of such a determination, they
ought to resist the covert and insidious introduction of the principle."

The death of William the Fourth, on the 20th of June, of
course caused a dissolution of Parliament. Mr. Gladstone was
nominated for Manchester, without his consent, he preferring
to remain member for Newark, for which he was returned. At
the Manchester poll he was in a minority. The first Victorian

Parliament met on the 15th of November. The condition of
Canada was again a subject of paramount interest. The *Fils de
la Liberté*, headed by Papineau, had raised an insurrection at
Montreal, and there was the prospect of a long and arduous
contest. On the 22nd of December Mr. Gladstone took part in
the debate. The colony, he asserted, had very few real grievances to complain of, and the dissatisfaction was caused by
agitators.

In January, 1838, Mr. Roebuck was heard at the bar as agent
for the colony. Mr. Gladstone spoke at length, intimating his
opinion that some part of the blame for the disturbed condition
of the colony rested on the Home Government. He spoke again
on the 7th of March, and charged the Canadian Executive and
the Home Government with want of energy in putting down the
insurrection. In reply, Mr. Spring Rice taxed Mr. Gladstone
with a desire to govern by coercion.

As yet, indeed, respecting colonial as well as home matters,
he was a Tory of the straitest sect. He believed most absolutely in the "paternal-providential" theory of government, in the
colonies as at home; and in the Church as an integral part of
the State. Trained at home, and at Oxford, to believe that the
Church of England was a Divinely-appointed and supported
institution, he had given all his energy to support it. To attack
its right to benefit by church rates levied by the Government was,
as he said, to attack a sacred institution; and even where, as in
Ireland, it was the Church of a minority, he believed it to be a
paramount duty to make all the people contribute to its support.
In his place in Parliament he had expressed his views earnestly
and fearlessly, and in private he was devoting his leisure to the
production of a book, which he hoped would be a complete
exposition of his views, and a solid contribution to the support of
a cause he had so much at heart.

CHAPTER V.

FIRST APPEARANCE AS AN AUTHOR.

"THE State in its Relation with the Church; by W. E. Gladstone, Student of Christ Church, and M.P. for Newark," appeared in the autumn of 1838, and a second edition was soon called for.   This work (dedicated to the University of Oxford, as the "fountain of blessings, spiritual, social, and intellectual") was a statement of the author's creed respecting the union of Church and State—a methodical arrangement and completion of the arguments he had hitherto employed when speaking in the House of Commons on subjects connected with the Church.   He took high and indepen- dent ground, rejecting the argument of expediency, and resting on what he believed to be the eternal principles on which the State should be bound in its relation with the Church.   Neither Bishop Hooker nor Bishop Warburton, the popular champions of the cause, satisfied his intellectual and religious earnestness; and Paley and Chalmers, both able, but very different in mental calibre, appeared to him to fall short of the height of the argu- ment.   His fundamental propositions were that the propagation of religious truth is one of the principal duties of Government; and that a proper Government could no more perform its duties without a consideration of religious principles than an individual man could lead a righteous life without the support of religious belief and a sense of religious responsibility.   "Wherever there is power in the universe," he argued, "that power is the property of God, the key of that universe—His property of right, however for a time withholden or abused. . . . The powers, therefore, that dwell in individuals acting as a Government, as well as those that dwell in individuals acting for themselves, can only be secured for right uses by applying to them a religion." A governing body in a State should profess a religion, because it is composed of individual men who, "being appointed to act in a definite moral capacity, must sanctify their acts done in that capacity by the offices of religion." Again, "in fulfilment of his obligations as an individual, the statesman must be a worshipping man." Very explicitly he lays down the doctrine that, as the acts of statesmen are essentially public—

"They must be sanctified, not only by the private personal prayers and piety of those who fill public situations, but also by public acts of the men composing the public body.   They must offer prayer and praise in their public and collective character—in that character wherein they constitute the organ of the nation, and wield its collective force.   Wherever there is a reasoning agency, there is a moral duty and responsibility involved in it.   The governors are reasoning agents for the nation, in their conjoint acts as such.   And, therefore, there must be attached to this agency, as that without which none of our responsibilities can be met, a religion.   And this religion must be of the conscience of the governor. . . . .   A nation, having a personality, lies under the obligation, like the individuals composing its governing body, of sanctifying the acts of that personality by the offices of religion, and thus we have a new and imperative ground for the existence of a state religion."

Obviously, holding such views, Mr. Gladstone could not regard the Protestant Established Church in Ireland as a grievance. It was the duty of the State to support it, because its teachings were right and those of the Roman Catholic Church were wrong. If five-sixths of the population of Ireland refused to accept Protestant doctrines and to attend Protestant worship, then so much the worse for them.   The State had performed a duty imposed on it of taking the horse to the water (rather, perhaps, of taking the water to the horse), and if it could not make the horse drink, it had, at least, discharged its conscience.   That the horse should pay for the water, as for other matters provided by the governing power, was natural and right.

The courage with which the author enforced his principles, the lofty disdain with which he treated all considerations of mere political expediency, his rejection of Warburton's "contract" theory, and his uncompromising assertion that the care of the Church was a trust Divinely committed to Governments, no less than the remarkable talent exhibited in the book, excited the admiration of the Tory party, and arrested the attention of Whigs and Radicals.   It was recognised on both sides that the young member for Newark was destined to occupy a very prominent and influential position in the political world.   The two great Reviews, the literary champions of the opposite parties, the *Edinburgh* and *Quarterly*, devoted elaborate articles to the book.   The review in the *Quarterly*, appearing in December, 1839, extended to fifty-five pages.   The writer said :—

" If Mr. Gladstone were an ordinary character, we should be inclined to speak most strongly of the singular vigour, depth of thought, and eloquence, which he has displayed in this essay.   But he is evidently not an ordinary character ; though it is to be hoped that many others are now forming themselves in the same school with him, to act hereafter on the same principle. And the highest compliment which we can pay him is to show that we believe him to be what a statesman or philosopher should be—indifferent to his own reputation for talents, and only anxious for truth and right . . . He

has most wisely abandoned the argument for expediency, which offers little
more than an easy weapon to fence with, while no real danger is apprehended;
and has insisted chiefly on the claims of duty and truth—the only considerations
which can animate and support men in a real struggle against false principles.
Even if he stood alone, yet with his talent and position in the country, this
movement to escape from the low ethics of the eighteenth and nineteenth centuries would be of great importance."

The review in the *Edinburgh* appeared in the number for
April, 1839, earlier than that in the *Quarterly*. It was written by
Macaulay, was of great length, and in the collected "Critical
and Historical Essays" of the great Whig reviewer and historian
there are few more brilliant, incisive, and "readable" papers than
this. It begins and ends with graceful, and no doubt sincere
compliments. In the very first sentence is the since often-quoted
description of Mr. Gladstone as a "young man of unblemished
character, and of distinguished Parliamentary talents, the rising
hope of stern and unbending Tories;" and in the last sentence
of the long review Macaulay writes: "We admire his talents; we
respect his integrity and benevolence; and we hope that he will
not suffer political avocations so entirely to engross him as to
leave him no leisure for literature and philosophy."

Comparatively few persons, probably, have read, or if they have
read, remember much about Gladstone's book; but Macaulay's
review is known to thousands upon thousands of modern readers.
It is very clever, very adroit, even witty, and very characteristic
of the writer, who apparently pounced eagerly upon the book, and
began the work of dissection with a will. As an ardent Whig, he
was ready enough to take up arms against the young Tory champion; as a practised literary combatant, he delighted in encountering an opponent, younger, indeed, and less skilled in the
controversial arena than himself. It seems scarcely possible to
doubt that Macaulay was actuated, unconsciously probably, but
still considerably, by some personal motives in attacking with
so much vigour and elaboration the maiden book of a young
author. Although nine years older than Gladstone, he was still
a young man, but had already achieved a very great reputation.
He was the boast of Cambridge, as Gladstone was of Oxford.
When only twenty five years old, he had astonished the readers
of the *Edinburgh* by his marvellous essay on Milton; and his
reputation had increased with the appearance of many scarcely
less brilliant and more comprehensive articles. He was the
young literary phenomenon of the day, and would have been less
than human if he had not recognised his position and valued
the homage paid to his abilities. Cambridge was proud of him, as

Oxford was proud of Gladstone. The latter had no pretensions to rival the literary achievements of Macaulay, although in classical scholarship he was his equal; but his political promise, as the reviewer so frankly admitted, was great, and his intellectual power undoubted. As competitors in the exclusive field of letters they were not likely to meet; but Macaulay was a politician as well as an essayist, and Gladstone having ventured to fling his glove into the arena, the redoubtable champion of the *Edinburgh* picked it up, and couched his lance for the fray.

Gladstone's arguments had many weak points, which he has long since seen and acknowledged, especially in respect to the support of the Irish Church. Very skilfully Macaulay exposed these, and very skilfully, too, he maintained his own theory of the relation of the State to the Church. But he condescended to misrepresentations and even burlesques of the author's arguments, for which no excuse can be offered. The gravity and simple earnestness of Mr. Gladstone would seem to have tempted his critic, who had an almost irrepressible element of fun in his composition, to indulge a little in banter; although the sincere respect he felt for the character and abilities of the author, did not allow him to indulge the vein as he did in the case of Robert Montgomery. If, he said, according to Mr. Gladstone, the Government of a nation was to be composed of religious men— "worshipping men"—so should be the directors of the London and Birmingham Railway Company, managers of docks and banks, masters of foxhounds, committees of clubs and other associated bodies, which should "profess some one faith, and have its articles and its public worship and its tests." Macaulay must have seen clearly enough that there is very little analogy between a national government, which is a legislative as well as an executive body— which has necessarily to deal with questions affecting the morals of the community—which is called on to devise and carry out laws in accordance with religious principles—and an association, a managing committee, which has to deal solely with material interests. It is the duty of a railway company to carry passengers and luggage in the best and most convenient manner from one place to another, and, having done so much, its duty to the public ends; but it is the duty of a government, in the interests of the community whose guardian it certainly is, to provide safeguards for morality, and afford facilities for cultivating and disciplining the moral nature of the people. In short, the governing power of a nation has to deal with the social relations of many individuals among whom there is a strong tendency to immorality and disorder ; and railway or bank directors, with people who want to travel or to invest money. Macaulay would have been delighted to expose such fallacious reasoning from fictitious premises as he stooped to in his famous review, had it emanated from a Tory politician or writer. How Croker would have been annihilated, if he had criticised Sir James Mackintosh in that style!

When the article appeared in the *Edinburgh*, it of course bore no signature ; but everybody knew that Macaulay, and none other, was the author. Mr. Gladstone immediately wrote to him, and received a good-humoured and courteous reply. The letters are well worth quoting, as proofs how literary and political discussion could, even in those times of personalities and sledge-hammer controversy, be carried on by two cultivated men of high ability, who respected themselves and each other.

" 6, Carlton Gardens, April 10, 1839.

" DEAR SIR,—I have been favoured with a copy of the forthcoming number of the *Edinburgh Review*, and I, perhaps, too much presume upon the bare acquaintance with you of which alone I can boast, in thus uncere-moniously assuming you to be the author of the article entitled ' Church and State,' and in offering you my very warm and cordial thanks for the manner in which you have treated both the work and the author, on whom you deigned to bestow your attention. In whatever you write you can hardly hope for the privilege of most anonymous productions, a real concealment ; but if it had been possible not to recognise you, I should have questioned your authorship in this particular case, because the candour and single-mindedness which it exhibits are, in one who has long been connected in the most dis-tinguished manner with political party, so rare as to be almost incredible.

" I hope to derive material benefit, at some more tranquil season, from a consideration of your argument throughout. I am painfully sensible, when-ever I have occasion to reopen the book, of its shortcomings, not only of the subject, but even of my own conceptions ; and I am led to suspect that, under the influence of most kindly feelings, you have omitted to criticise many things besides the argument which might fairly have come within your animadversion.

" In the meantime, I hope you will allow me to apprise you that on one material point especially I am not so far removed from you as you suppose. I am not conscious that I have said either that the Test Act should be repealed, or that it should not have been passed ; and though on such subjects language has many bearings which escape the view of the writer at the moment when his pen is in his hand, yet, I think that I can hardly have put forth either of these propositions, because I have never entertained the corresponding sentiments. Undoubtedly I should speak of the pure abstract idea of Church and State, as implying that they are co-extensive ; and I should regard the present compo-sition of the State of the United Kingdom as a deviation from that pure idea, but only in the same sense as all differences of religious opinion in the Church are a deviation from its pure idea, while I not only allow that they are per-mitted, but believe that (within limits) they were intended to be permitted.

There are some of these deflections from abstract theory which appear to me allowable ; and that of the admission of persons not holding the national creed into office is one which, in my view, must be determined by times and circumstances.   At the same time I do not recede from any protest which I have made against the principle that religious differences are irrelevant to the question of competency for civil office ; but I would take my stand between the opposite extremes—the one that no such differences are to be taken into view, the other that all such differences are to constitute disqualifications.

"I need hardly say the question I raise is not whether you have misrepresented me, for, were I disposed to anything so weak, the w! ole internal evidence and clear intention of your article would confute me ; indeed, I feel I ought to apologise for even supposing that you may have been mistaken in the apprehension of my meaning, and I freely admit, on the other hand, the possibility that, totally without my own knowledge, my language may have led to such an interpretation.

"In these lacerating times, one clings to everything of personal kindness in the past to husband it for the future, and if you will allow me I shall earnestly desire to carry with me such a recollection of your mode of dealing with the subject, upon which we shall agree the attainment of truth so materially depends upon the temper in which the search for it is instituted and conducted.

"I did not mean to have troubled you at so much length, and I have c_.y to add that I am, with much respect,

"Dear sir, very truly yours,
"W. E. GLADSTONE.

"T. B. Macaulay, Esq."

To this letter Macaulay replied :—

"3, Clarges Street, April 11, 1839.

"MY DEAR SIR.—I have very seldom been more gratified than by the very kind note which I have just received from you.   Your book itself, and everything that I heard about you, though almost all my information came—to the honour, I must say, of our troubled times—from people very strongly opposed to you in politics, led me to regard you with respect and good-will, and I am truly glad that I have succeeded in marking those feelings.   I was half afraid, when I read myself over again in print, that the button, as is too common in controversial fencing even between friends, had once or twice come off the foil.

"I am very glad to find that we do not differ so widely as I had apprehended about the Test Act.   I can easily explain the way in which I was misled.   Your general principle is that religious nonconformity ought to be a disqualification for civil office.   In page 288 you say that the true and authentic mode of ascertaining conformity is the act of communion.   I thought, therefore, that your theory pointed directly to a renewal of the Test Act.   And I do not recollect that you have ever used any expression importing that your theory ought in practice to be modified by any considerations of civil prudence.   All the exceptions that you mention are, as far as I can remember, founded on positive contract—not one on expediency, even in cases where the expediency is so strong and so obvious that most statesmen would call it necessity.   If I had understood that you meant your rules to be followed out in practice only so far as might be consistent with the peace and good government of society, I should certainly have expressed myself very differently in several parts of my article.

"Accept my warm thanks for your kindness, and believe me, with every good wish,

"My dear sir, very truly yours,

"T. B. MACAULAY.

"W. E. Gladstone, Esq., M.P."

Macaulay could not help, it seems, indulging in a slight touch of humorous irony at the close of his letter.

As a recreation after the Parliamentary and literary labours of the early part of the year, Mr. Gladstone visited Italy and Sicily in the autumn of 1838. To him who had studied so closely and lovingly the great writers of antiquity, this was "classic ground," as Italy was to Addison, who invented the phrase. On the 30th and 31st of October he ascended Etna, a feat described with considerable minuteness in his Diary, some portions of which have been made public. At this time the volcano was in a disturbed condition. With the description by Virgil fresh in his retentive memory, he was greatly interested in watching the stupendous phenomena, and records: "We enjoyed keenly our full clear sight of the volcanic action, and even at the moment I could not help being struck with the remarkable accuracy of Virgil's account." He remembered and quoted passages describing with remarkable accuracy the thunder-clap or crack, the vibration of the ground, the smoke, the fire-shower and the column of ash. "This," he notes, "is within the compass of twelve lines. Modern poetry has its own merits, but their conveyance of information is not, generally speaking, one of them. What would Virgil have thought of authors publishing poems with explanatory notes (to illustrate is a different matter) as if they were so many books of conundrums?"

In reference to the luxuriance of vegetation on the slope of Etna, he notes, "It seems as if the finest of all soils were produced from the most agonising throes of nature, as the hardest characters are often reared amidst the severest circumstances."

With his head full of Virgil, and enforcing his comments by quotations from the *Georgics*, he comments on the primitive methods of culture practised in the island: "One finds the precepts of Virgil in some respects observed in Sicilian agriculture, contrary to modern, at least to our northern practice. Further, in some respects, Virgil's advice, if followed, would improve the aspect of Sicilian culture."

A passage in the Diary, respecting the ruined temples in Sicily, is imbued with the feeling of reverence for the antique and suggestive appreciation of the spirit of classic art which are remark-

EARLY PORTRAIT OF MRS. GLADSTONE.
From a picture by Saye, photographed by G. Watmough Webster

able characteristics of his mind, more strikingly developed in his
later studies of the Homeric age. He says:—

"After Etna, the temples are certainly the great charm and attraction of
Sicily. I do not know that there is any one among them which, taken alone,
exceeds in interest and beauty that of Neptune at Pæstum ; but they have the
advantage of number and variety, as well as of highly interesting positions.
At Segesta the temple is enthroned in a perfect mountain solitude ; and it is
like a beautiful tomb of its religion, so stately, so entire ; while around, but
for one solitary house of the keeper, there is nothing, absolutely nothing, to
disturb the apparent reign of Silence and of Death. At Selinus, the huge
fragments on the plain seem to make an eminence of themselves, and they
listen to the ever young and unwearied waves which almost wash their base and
mock their desolation by the image of perpetual life and motion they present,
while the tone of their heavy fall upon the beach well accords with the solemnity of the scene. At Girgenti, the ridge visible to the mariner from afar
is still crowned by a long line of fabrics, presenting to the eye a considerable
mass and regularity of structure, and the town is near and visible ; yet that
town is so entirely the mere phantom of its former glory, within its now
shrunken limits, that, instead of disturbing the effect, it rather seems to add a
new image and enhance it. The temples enshrine a most pure and salutary principle of art, that which connects grandeur of effect with simplicity of detail ;
and, retaining their beauty and their dignity in their decay, they represent the
great man when fallen, as types of that almost highest of human qualities—silent,
yet not sullen, endurance."

The year 1839 is memorable in the personal, rather than in the
public, history of Mr. Gladstone. By the publication of his book,
and the elaborate manner in which it had been reviewed, he had
attained a considerable literary reputation, and his position as a
politician was distinctly advanced. Macaulay, in the famous Essay,
describes the Tories as following "reluctantly and mutinously, a
leader [Peel] whose experience and eloquence are indispensable
to them, but whose cautious temper and moderate opinions they
abhor."   Gladstone, so high-minded and able, so variously
accomplished and courageous, so uncompromising in his support
of the old dogmas of Toryism—and who added to an almost
Puritan gravity and rectitude of character a spirit of reverence and
loyalty to ecclesiastical institutions with which the best and purest
of the old Cavalier supporters of Church and State might have sympathised—was, in their estimation, the "coming man," destined
to lead the party in the troublous times which the success of the
Reform party heralded.

But in another respect, 1839 was a memorable and a happy
year for Mr. Gladstone. On the 25th of July, he married Miss
Catherine Glynne, eldest daughter of Sir Stephen Richard Glynne,
of Hawarden Castle, Flintshire, whose ancestry can be traced for
more than a thousand years. Early in the ninth century, Cilmin.

Troed-D.lû, of Glyn Llhwon, in Carnarvon, was chief of the Fourth
Tribe of North Wales. His sixteenth descendant in a direct line
was William Glyn, of Glyn Llyvon (in the course of time the name
of the place had assumed that form), who married Catherine,
daughter of Thomas Mostyn, Esq, of Mostyn, Flintshire, and
became the father of two sons. From the eldest, Thomas, are
descended the Glynnes of Hawarden ; from the younger, Richard,
the Glyns, of Ewell, Surrey. From the younger branch, Richard
Glyn, founder of the great London banking-house was descended.
The grandson of Thomas Glyn, the elder of the brothers, was
Sir John Glynne (the first of the line who adopted that mode of
spelling the family name), who, as Serjeant Glynne, was an eminent
lawyer in the time of Charles the First, changed his political
opinions and obtained professional employment and preferment
under the Protectorate of Cromwell ; and after the Restoration
again "changed his spots," and rose to be Chief Justice of the
King's Bench in the succeeding reign. He was able, adroit
and unscrupulous, made money, and contrived to possess himself of a goodly estate. He and Serjeant Maynard prosecuted
Strafford, and succeeded in sending him to the block. Butler
asks in "Hudibras,"—

> "Did not the learned Glynne and Maynard
> To make good subjects traitors, strain hard ?"

He was active, also, in the impeachment of the twelve bishops,
who, in 1641, were sent to the Tower for protesting against the
legality of proceedings in the House of Lords during their enforced absence. Afterwards he was as ready to prosecute his
old colleague of the Parliamentary party, Sir Harry Vane, as he
had been to procure the conviction of Strafford.

When Charles the Second was crowned at Westminster, both
Glynne and Maynard rode in the procession as gaily as if they
had been the most ardent Royalists all the while Charles was
skulking on the Continent. Glynne's horse fell with him, and
Pepys records : "Serjeant Glynne's horse fell upon him, and is
like to kill him, which people do please themselves to see how
just God is to punish the rogue at such a time as this."
But he was fated to die in his bed, and lies buried in St.
Margaret's Church, Westminster. After the execution of James
Stanley, Earl of Derby, taken prisoner at the battle of Worcester,
in 1651, Sir John Glynne managed to get possession of one of
the Earl's Welsh estates, Hawarden Castle ; and although, after

the Restoration, forfeited estates of Royalists were ordered to be restored, Glynne contrived to retain the property.

The present Hawarden Castle was built in 1752, near the ruins of the older castle, which dates from very remote times. Sir Stephen Glynne, brother of Mrs. Gladstone, died unmarried in 1874, and the estate was bequeathed to Mr. Gladstone for life, and afterwards to his eldest son. The present heir to the estate is Master William Gladstone, only son of the late Mr. W. H. Gladstone.

Mrs. Gladstone's name has been so frequently before the public as the sympathising wife and life-companion of the great statesman, and on account of her own philanthropic exertions, in the establishment of a Convalescent Home and the constant and liberal support given to other institutions, that we shall, we trust, be acquitted of any impertinent intrusion on domestic privacy if we take this opportunity of expressing our respect for that admirable lady. Mr. and Mrs. Gladstone have had four sons and four daughters. One daughter, Jessy, died in infancy. In 1891 the eldest son, William Henry, who had represented East Worcestershire in the House of Commons, and was a musician of uncommon merit, died after a brief illness. His widow, a daughter of Lord Blantyre, resides with her children at Hawarden. The second son, the Rev. Stephen Edward Gladstone, is Rector of Hawarden, the family living; and the third, Mr. Henry Neville Gladstone, is engaged in mercantile pursuits. He married in 1890 the Hon. Maud Ernestine Rendel, daughter of Lord Rendel. The Right Hon. Herbert John Gladstone, the youngest son, has been in Parliament for several years as member for West Leeds. He was First Commissioner of Works in 1894, and is a Privy Councillor. The eldest daughter, Anne, married the Rev. E. Wickham, Head Master of Wellington College; and the third and fourth daughters, who have so frequently accompanied their father in his political progresses, are Mrs. Harry Drew, wife of the Warden of St. Deiniol's Hostel, Hawarden ; and Miss Helen Gladstone, who was till recently Vice-Principal of Sidgwick Hall, Newnham.

CHAPTER VI.

RENEWED PARLIAMENTARY WORK.—AGAIN IN OFFICE.

THE opening of the Session of 1840 was marked by a great
debate on the war with China—the "Opium War." Forty years
ago the name of the Chinese Commissioner Lin was familiar
enough, but is now almost forgotten. He was an energetic administrator, who—the trade in opium having been prohibited by
the Emperor of China—put the edict in force by attempting to
seize the opium stored in Canton by British merchants, surround-
ing the factories, and making the occupants virtually prisoners,
a condition from which they were released by Captain Elliot, the
English naval commander on the station and special commissioner.
The opium was left behind, and destroyed by order of Lin.
Many outrages were committed by the Chinese, and there was
some sharp fighting between two British frigates and armed
Chinese junks. In the first week of 1840, the Emperor of China
issued an edict interdicting all trade and intercourse with England
"for ever." A war was the inevitable result; and equally inevitable was a vigorous Parliamentary debate and attack by the Opposition on the Ministers; Lord Palmerston, the Foreign Secretary,
being the especial object of attack.

Sir James Graham moved a resolution blaming the Ministry
for the hostilities which had taken place, which, the mover said,
were mainly to be attributed to their "want of foresight and pre-
caution." The debate on this resolution was a memorable one.
Macaulay, Secretary at War, made a brilliant speech, as carefully
prepared as one of his Review articles; Sir William Follett replied; Mr. Thesiger, destined, as Lord Chelmsford, to be Lord
Chancellor, delivered his maiden speech in the Commons, apolo-
gising for his diffidence (as to which, Lord Palmeston jokingly
remarked, the House could judge for itself); and Sir George
Staunton contributed special knowledge and Chinese experience.
Sidney Herbert, Charles Buller, Gladstone, Peel, and Palmerston
made vigorous speeches. Sir James Graham's resolution was defeated by the narrow majority of 9—the numbers being: Ayes,
262; Noes, 271.

Mr. Gladstone vigorously condemned the conduct of Lord

Palmerston, whom he accused of not having read the official despatches on the opium trade, and being, in fact, culpably ignorant of the state of affairs preceding the outbreak of war. " Be the trade in opium what it may," he said, " be it right, or be it wrong, we are now called on to give an assent to a war caused by the indolence and apathy of the noble Lord." In the course of his lengthy speech, Macaulay had indulged in a little of the patriotic claptrap which he could on occasion so gracefully introduce into his speeches and writings. Captain Elliot had displayed the British flag on the balcony of the factory at Canton.

"This," he said, " was an act which revived the drooping hopes of those who looked to him for protection. It was natural that they should look with confidence on the victorious flag which was hoisted over them, which reminded them that they belonged to a country unaccustomed to defeat, to submission, or to shame; it reminded them that they belonged to a country which had made the farthest ends of the earth ring with the fame of her exploits in redressing the wrongs of her children ; that made the Dey of Algiers humble himself to her insulted consul ; that revenged the horrors of the Black Hole on the field of Plassey ; that had not degenerated since her great Protector vowed that he would make the name of Englishman as respected as ever had been the name of Roman citizen."

This very Macaulayan outburst was not likely to escape the notice of Gladstone, who now for the first time crossed swords in debate with the brilliant essayist and orator. He said :—

"The right honourable gentleman opposite spoke in eloquent terms of the British flag waving in glory at Canton, and of the animating effects which have been produced on the minds of British subjects on many critical occasions when the flag has been unfurled on the battle-field. But how comes it to pass that the sight of that flag always raises the spirit of Englishmen? It is because it has always been associated with the cause of justice, with opposition to oppression, and respect for national rights, with honourable commercial enterprise ; but now, under the auspices of the noble lord, that flag is hoisted to protect an infamous contraband traffic ; and if it were never to be hoisted except as it is now hoisted on the coast of China, we should recoil from its sight with horror, and should never again feel our hearts thrill, as they now thrill with emotion, when it floats proudly and magnificently on the breeze."

It is very probable that Macaulay was nearer the truth than Gladstone in explaining why the English at Canton were delighted to see the British flag ; and that the opium traders and their families thought very little about the flag being associated with " the cause of justice and opposition to oppression," but a great deal about it indicating the presence of a British force able to protect them against the Chinese, whether they were right or wrong.

A hasty expression in the course of his speech elicited some comment. He said : —

"The Chinese had no armament ready wherewith to expel us from Lintin. They therefore said, 'We will resort to another mode of bringing you to reason. We will expel you from our shores by refusing you provisions.' And then, of course, they poisoned the wells."

This unlucky phrase was hailed with derisive cheers from the Ministerial benches, and the speaker endeavoured to explain : " I have not asserted—I do not mean to assert—that the Chinese actually poisoned their wells. All I mean to say is that it was alleged that they had poisoned their wells." Mr. Ward, who followed him, said he had justified the poisoning of the wells. Mr. Gladstone interrupted by denying that he had done so.

Sir Stephen Lushington administered a severe rebuke to Mr. Gladstone—a rebuke which probably the latter felt keenly.

" I will discard the law of nations," said Sir Stephen—"I will look alone to the law of God and to the law of man—to those eternal principles which must exist as long as man and man have the power of conversation and intercourse with one another. The honourable member for Newark, I am distressed to say, has gone the whole length. I trust that those who follow me in this debate will not tread in the steps of the honourable member. I respect that honourable member—I admire his talents—I know the honourable gentleman to be a powerful champion in every cause he thinks to be right ; but I own I shall never cease to reprobate the argument which the honourable gentleman used, or to avow my abhorrence of the doctrines the honourable gentleman endeavoured to maintain."

Lord Palmerston said he had heard Mr. Gladstone's speech with deep regret and sincere pain. What he objected to on the part of the honourable member was that, without having ascertained whether the charge of poisoning the wells was true or not, he had assumed it in his own mind as a fact and treated it as a matter of course, and said they were justified in doing it.

On the 26th of May, Mr. Villiers introduced his annual motion on the subject of the Corn Laws, moving for a Committee of the whole House to take into consideration the Act regulating the importation of grain. Mr. Gladstone took no part in the debate, and did not vote, but "paired" against the resolution with Serjeant Talfourd. Free Traders were as yet in the minority in Parliament, and Mr. Villiers was defeated by a majority of 123.

When Lord John Russell, Colonial Secretary, introduced the Government of Canada Bill (in accordance with the recommendation of the Earl of Durham, who had been Governor-General of Canada, for the union of the two provinces), Mr. Gladstone supported the measure as " less open to objection than any other course ;" and he took occasion to explain his views of the proper relation of the Colonies to the mother country :—

" It seemed to him that the maintenance of our connection with the Colonies was to be regarded rather as a matter of duty than one of advantage. . . . He thought that, so long as we retained the Colonies as receptacles for our surplus population, we remained under strict obligation to provide for those who left our shores at least what semblance we could of British institutions. Upon this ground he should always be glad to see Parliament inclined to make large sacrifices for the purpose of maintaining the Colonies as long as the union with the mother country was approved of by the people of these Colonies. But he conceived that nothing could be more ridiculous, nothing could be more mistaken, than to suppose that Great Britain had anything to gain by maintaining that union in opposition to the deliberate and permanent conviction of the people of these Colonies themselves. Therefore, he thought, that it should be a cardinal principle of our policy to regard the union between Great Britain and Canada, and her other American Colonies, as dependent on the free will of both parties."

While the union lasted, however, he asserted the supremacy of the British Legislature—"to talk of a permanent union between two countries each possessing an independent Legislature, was one of the most visionary ideas that ever entered the mind of man."

On other matters, too, the Government received support from Mr. Gladstone and the more moderate members of the Tory party, in the course of the Session. One of these measures was the Government Bill for the Sale of the Clergy Reserves in Canada ; one-half of the proceeds to be given to the Churches of England and Scotland, and the remainder to be divided among the clergy of all denominations of Christians recognised by certain Acts of the Province. The ecclesiastical opinions of the author of " The State in its Relation to the Church " were evidently undergoing some modification.

The Colonial Passengers Bill which provided for the proper treatment of the Hill Coolies imported into the Mauritius, and the vote for National Education in Ireland, also received Mr. Gladstone's support. In June he voted against the proposition of Mr. Ewart (son of his father's old friend, Mr. Gladstone's godfather) to reduce the duties payable on foreign sugar from 63s. to 34s. per cwt. He contended that facilities for the introduction of foreign (slave-grown) sugar, would act injuriously to the interests of the British Colonies, where slavery had been abolished, and " encourage slave labour, and the slave trade." He alluded to the " sensibility on slavery," which had been expressed, but which was very slightly exhibited when mercantile considerations interfered. Mr. Ewart, in reply, said "he would remind the honourable member that there were those whose sensibilities were only of recent growth, and conveniently matured in accordance with their own interests, and with the maintenance of monoply." In the division, by which Mr. Ewart's motion was rejected, Mr. Gladstone's name appears with those of the Whig leaders, and Mr. Goulburn, Sir James Graham, Sir Robert Inglis, and other prominent members of the opposition went with him into the lobby.

Such intervals of leisure as the pressure of Parliamentary duties permitted, had been given to the production of a volume, "Church Principles Considered in Their Result"—an elaborate exposition of the principles of the Church of England, and suggestions for uniting it more closely with the religious spirit and the great awakening of thought which characterised the time. The book is a goodly volume, which a less energetic man than the author might have been disposed to rest on as a *magnum opus.* but which forms a mere episode in the unceasingly active career of Mr. Gladstone. It was, as a notice on the fly-leaf informs us, "completed beneath the shades of Hagley, and dedicated, in token of sincere affection, to the Lord Lyttelton." Hagley is in Worcestershire, and Lord Lyttelton was one of Mr. Gladstone's most intimate friends, the husband of Mrs. Gladstone's sister, and a prominent High Churchman, after whom was named the settlement in New Zealand.

Early in the Session of 1841 Mr. Divett, member for Exeter, introduced a Bill, the object of which was to do away with the declaration required by the "Municipal Corporations Act" from all persons taking corporate offices, and so admit Jews to the civic magistracy. The second reading of the Bill was carried in a thin House by a majority of 113; only 24 voting in the minority; but on the motion for the third reading, Mr. Gladstone adopted a course—very unusual when a Bill has reached that stage—and moved that it be read a third time that day six months. He appeared to consider the admission of Jews to municipal offices the necessary prelude to admitting them to Parliament; and the question, he said, "really before the House was, whether they would consent to destroy the distinctive Christianity of the constitution."

Macaulay, who never missed a chance of firing a shot at Gladstone and his High Church friends, sprang to his feet. He alluded to the "learned casuists"—meaning the Churchmen then leading the Tractarian movement at Oxford—and said, if they would teach the Jews some of their own ingenuity, then, "as those ingenious persons swallowed confession and absolution, so these tests might also be swallowed by the Jews without the slightest hesitation."

Gladstone's vigorous opposition to the measure was unavailing, the third reading being carried by a majority of 77, the opponents of the Bill only numbering 31.

The vexed question of the Sugar Duties again occupied the attention of the House when Mr. Baring, the Chancellor of the Exchequer, introduced the Budget. He proposed, almost exactly adopting the suggestion of Mr. Ewart, to reduce the duty on foreign sugar from 63s. to 36s. per hundredweight. The debate on this portion of the Budget scheme extended over nine nights. Gladstone made a long speech in opposition to the proposed reduction. He argued, as he had argued before, that to increase the facilities for the consumption of foreign sugar would be injurious to the planters in the British Colonies. We had paid heavily, after a most exciting agitation, for the suppression of slavery in our own possessions, and had of course raised the price of labour. It was clearly understood at the time, he said, that sugar produced by free labour must be increased in price, and now we were asked to allow our colonists to be exposed to a ruinous competition with foreign growers. He stated his case tersely: " Increased consumption must require increased growth; that increased growth requires that there should be more hands to produce it; and then, if we are to repair to foreign sources for our supplies, it means that more and more of the natives of Africa must be borne by the slave trade from their homes." He taunted some of the Ministers with a desire to continue the slavery which the nation had worked so earnestly and paid so dearly to abolish. Lord Clarendon, the Lord Privy Seal, had, he said, been described as " the man peculiarly qualified to effect the abolition of the slave trade, yet he is a member of the Cabinet which has proposed the present plan." He had now a chance to give a return for some of the sharp hits he had received from the Secretary at War, and he availed himself of it :—

"There is another name still more strangely associated with it. I can only speak from tradition of the struggle for the abolition of slavery ; but, if I have not been misinformed, there was engaged in it a man who was the unseen ally of Mr. Wilberforce, and the pillar of his strength ; a man of profound benevolence, of acute understanding, of indefatigable activity, and of that self-denying temper which is content to work in secret, to forego the recompense of present fame, and to seek for its reward beyond the grave. The name of that man was Zachary Macaulay, and his son is a member of the present Cabinet.'

Macaulay was absent from the House when these words were uttered; but on the following night he took the earliest opportunity of replying to them :—

"I will not say that the right honourable member for Newark, whom I will still call my honourable friend, could have intended to be personally offensive to one from whom he never received any personal provocation. I am satisfied of the contrary; and the more so as some parts of the expressions imputed to the honourable gentleman were of a nature so gratifying to my feelings that they more than compensated for the pain which was given by a censure which is not deserved."

Lord Sandon, member for Liverpool, moved as an amendment on the Sugar Duties resolution—

"That, considering the efforts and sacrifices which Parliament and the country have made for the abolition of the slave trade and slavery, with the earnest hope that the example might lead to a mitigation and final extinction of those evils in other countries, this House is not prepared (especially with the present prospect of supply from the British possessions) to adopt the measure proposed by Her Majesty's Government for the reduction of the duty on foreign sugar."

After a very energetic debate, extending over several nights, the amendment was carried by a majority of 36, the numbers being 317 against 281. Mr. Gladstone voted in the majority, as did also Mr. Disraeli.

At this time the subject which most strongly agitated the public mind was that of the continuance or repeal of the Corn Laws. Ebenezer Elliott, and other early workers in the cause of abolition, had been succeeded by men of greater political influence and higher position. In September, 1838, the Anti-Corn-Law League had been established at Manchester, supported by a large array of able, energetic and wealthy men. Richard Cobden, who entered Parliament as representative of Stockport at the beginning of this Session (1841); Charles Villiers, brother of the Earl of Clarendon; John Bright, as yet not a member of Parliament, but who had already given promise of achieving the rank of the first orator of the age; Colonel Thompson, and many others were "constant in season and out of season" advocating Free Trade doctrines; and the poorer classes, always peculiarly susceptible to the argument of the "big loaf," were greatly excited. The Melbourne Ministry were willing to make some advances in the direction of relaxing import duties, and offered a moderate fixed duty on corn, instead of the sliding scale, which had been in force since 1828; and their great opponent, Sir Robert Peel, was hesitating between the prejudices of his old Toryism, his partial acceptance, in theory, of the doctrines of

Huskisson, and the conviction growing in strength that ere long a very large measure of Free Trade must be conceded.

Before going into Committee of Ways and Means, Lord John Russell had announced his intention to move, at a later day, that the House should resolve itself into a committee to consider the Acts of Parliament relating to the trade in corn. Lord Sandon pressed him hard as to the intentions of the Ministry; and he replied that he should propose a moderate fixed duty, and he subsequently announced that it would be 8s. a quarter on wheat.

Lord John Russell's motion was fixed for the 4th of June; but on the 27th of May Sir Robert Peel brought matters to an issue by moving a resolution of want of confidence. The Ministerial majority had dwindled, and the most important propositions of the Budget had been rejected; the Irish party, led by O'Connell, were in open opposition, and the attempt to pass an Irish Registration of Voters Bill had been defeated. The debate lasted five nights, and on the division Sir Robert's resolution was carried, in a full House, by one vote ! the numbers being 312 against 311. Lord Melbourne and his colleagues declined to consider the result of the division as necessitating their resignation, the majority being so small; and Lord John Russell, the leader in the Commons, announced that Ministers had decided on appealing to the country. On the 22nd of June Parliament was prorogued by the Queen in person, and on the following day appeared the official notification of dissolution.

The elections took place amid considerable excitement. In the counties the Ministerial candidates suffered repeated defeats; and when the returns were made up, it was ascertained that the Conservatives would probably have a total majority of 76. The Whigs professed their preference of a small fixed duty on corn; their opponents adhered to the principle of the " sliding scale," which had been in operation since 1828, but with very considerable rearrangement and concessions.

The new Parliament was opened by commission on the 24th of August, and the royal speech contained some important passages which showed that the Whigs, if they had been able to continue in office, were ready to adopt, at least to some extent, the commercial and financial policy which Peel, aided by Gladstone, afterwards so vigorously carried out. It was perhaps to this that Disraeli afterwards referred in one of those famous phrases he was so adroit in hurling at Sir Robert: " You caught the Whigs bathing, and you stole their clothes." The royal speech said :—

" It will be for you to consider whether some of these duties are not so trifling in amount as to be unproductive to the revenue, while they are vexatious to commerce. You may further examine whether the principle of protection upon which others of those duties are founded is not carried to an extent injurious alike to the income of the state and the interests of the people. Her Majesty is desirous that you should consider the laws which regulate the trade in corn."

The debates on the Address were conducted with great animation, and in each House the result was a majority against Ministers: in the Lords of 72, and in the Commons of 91. On the 3rd of August, Lord Melbourne and Lord John Russell announced that Ministers had resigned. Sir Robert Peel was sent for, and undertook the task of forming an administration. When the arrangements were completed, it was seen that Mr. Gladstone was appointed Vice-President of the Board of Trade and Master of the Mint, but as yet without Cabinet rank.

When Parliament reassembled in 1842, the country was in a perturbed condition. The agitation for the total repeal of the Corn Laws was gaining strength, ard the distress which prevailed in the country added weight to the arguments employed by the vigorous orators of the League. On the 9th of February, Sir Robert Peel brought forward his proposals for the readjustment of the import duties on wheat and other grain. His scheme was known as " the sliding scale," and its leading features may be briefly explained. Since January, 1828, the import duty on wheat had been 25s. 8d. a-quarter whenever the average price of all England was under 60s.; at 62s. to 63s., 24s. 8d., and the duty was gradually reduced as the average price advanced, until it was only 1s. when the average price was 73s. and upwards. That this sliding scale gave great opportunities to the development of a gambling spirit was evident; yet Sir Robert Peel retained the principle while modifying the details. The highest duty he proposed was £1 a quarter, when the average price was under 51s.; and the scale decreased by shillings, as the price rose by shillings. The reduction was considerable; for instance, under the old scale, when British wheat was at 62s. a-quarter, the duty on imported wheat was 24s. 8d., reduced by Sir Robert's scale to 10s. Of course the farmers, and the " farmers' friends " violently denounced the plan, the League would accept nothing short of entire Free Trade, and the Whig party, attached to the principle of a moderate fixed duty, opposed the measure with all their strength in the House. Lord John Russell moved a condemnatory amendment, and was replied to by Mr. Gladstone. The public excitement was great. Anti-Corn Law delegates from all parts of the kingdom thronged the lobby of the House, and it was necessary to have them removed by the police.   Ministers were successful, and the new sliding scale was sanctioned by a majority of 202.

Early in the Session, Mr. Gladstone, in his official position as Vice-President of the Board of Trade, introduced a Bill for the better regulation of railway traffic, and to enlarge the regulating powers of the Board of Trade in the interests of the public. This was the first step in a comprehensive scheme of railway improvements, including the establishment of Parliamentary fares, and important regulations for the protection and comfort of third-class passengers, which Mr. Gladstone carried out during his tenure of office.

Meanwhile he was devoting his great energies and knowledge of commercial matters—in respect of the details of which few trained merchants could surpass, or even rival him—to the preparation of the famous revision of the Tariff, which was the crowning triumph of the Ministry of Sir Robert Peel. That sagacious statesman recognised the great financial abilities of his subordinate, and, having introduced the subject with consummate ability, left to Mr. Gladstone the general conduct of the measure through the House. Indirect taxes to the amount of nearly £12,000,000 were removed by this bold revision of the Tariff and subsequent developments of the plan. To meet the deficiency expected to be experienced at first, Sir Robert proposed an income-tax of sevenpence in the pound, and carried it, though of course not without encountering considerable opposition.

Soon after the opening of the Session of 1843, Lord Howick moved for a committee of the whole House to take into consideration the distress in the manufacturing districts. His speech was an earnest appeal to Sir Robert Peel to progress in the Free Trade course he had partially adopted. "The object of my motion," he said, "is to induce you not to cling with obstinate perseverance to the absurd and vicious system of restriction, based on an exploded theory, and of which the practical fruits are before you in a destitute and suffering people, an empty exchequer, increasing taxation, and a falling revenue."

Mr. Gladstone led the opposition to Lord Howick's motion, and took occasion to refer to the income-tax, the imposition of which had led to great public dissatisfaction. Nobody ever did, or will, like an income-tax, however it may be justified by financial or political considerations. The mass of the public are not philosophers, and indirect taxation will always find admirers. When a man pays a pound for income-tax he misses the sovereign from his purse; but he knows very little about the five sovereigns he may really have paid if the sum was spread over the retail price of fifty different articles of daily necessity. Mr. Gladstone said:—

"There are many objections fairly applicable to the imposition of an income-tax; but surely it must be allowed on all hands that at least such a tax has one great and signal merit, that it does reach what no other tax can be guaranteed to reach—that enormous accumulation of wealth which is constantly mounting upwards in this country. It is one of the most melancholy features in the social state of this country, that we see, beyond the possibility of denial, that while there is at this moment a decrease in the consuming powers of the people, an increase of the pressure of privation and distress—there is at the same time a constant accumulation of wealth in the upper classes, an increase of the luxuriousness of their habits, and of other means of enjoyment, which, however satisfactory it may be as affording evidence of the existence and abundance of one among the elements of national prosperity, yet adds bitterness to the reflections which are forced upon us by the distresses of the rest of our fellow-countrymen; and, in this point of view, I cannot help thinking that the arguments which the noble Lord has advanced upon the question of the income-tax are satisfactorily met by the fact that it is upon those accumulating riches that the weight of the impost chiefly rests."

He was still a long way from being a thorough Free Trader. He defended the Corn Laws as resting upon a peculiar basis, and by being different from other restrictions. Towards the close of his long speech he said:—

"We surely must proceed with a due regard to our industry and interests both at home and abroad; and it would be absurd indeed if we were so to regulate our trade as to leave ourselves altogether at the mercy of the policy or of the impolicy of the countries with which we trade. . . . . . If it be the intention of the noble Lord to proceed to a repeal of the Corn Laws, or to the substitution for the present law of such a plan as he has himself recommended (a small fixed duty), I must contend that the noble Lord has made out no ground for the change, that the House must be governed in that or in other commercial questions by a fair estimate of conflicting claims and considerations, and that the change is one of which the benefits would be altogether remote and indefinite, while it would be attended with the most important and serious disasters, not less to the trading than to our agricultural interests, and the general industry of the country."

Mr. Cobden spoke on the fifth night of the debate, and referred in his downright manner to Mr. Gladstone's speech:—

"The right honourable gentleman, the Vice-President of the Board of Trade, admits the justice of the principles of Free Trade. He says he does not want monopoly, but then he applies these just principles only in the abstract. Now I do not want abstractions. Every moment that we pass here which is not devoted to providing for the welfare of the community is lost time. I tell the honourable member that I am a practical man, I am not an abstract member, and I ask what have we here to do with abstractions? The right honourable gentleman is a Free Trader in the abstract."

Lord Howick's motion was lost by 306 votes against 191, showing a majority of 115.

In May, 1843, the Earl of Ripon, President of the Board of Trade, died, and Mr. Gladstone succeeded to the office, and for the first time entered the Cabinet. On the 9th of the month Mr. Villiers brought forward his annual resolution for the repeal of the Corn Laws, and Mr. Gladstone replied to his speech at great length. He defended the action of Sir Robert Peel in continuing the sliding scale of duties, and argued—

"If we agree to the motion of the honourable gentleman, we shall be guilty of a great injustice to a large portion of the community in the first place, and hereafter to the whole community, as a necessary consequence of our injustice to a part; and, beyond that injustice, we shall convict ourselves of the grossest imbecility, and, in the face of the world declare ourselves unworthy and incompetent to conduct the affairs of a great and mighty nation."

Mr. Villiers' motion was lost by a majority of 256, the numbers being 125 for and 381 against. A few weeks afterwards an attempt by Lord Howick to repeal the duty on coal, and a motion by Mr. Hawes, the member for Lambeth, for reducing the duty on foreign sugar, were both lost, and in each case Mr. Gladstone, on the part of Government, strenuously opposed them.

On the 13th of June, Lord John Russell, who secured a more favourable opportunity than Mr. Villiers' motion had afforded for developing his views in favour of a fixed duty, renewed the proposition for a committee of the whole House to consider the operation of the Corn Laws. Mr. Gladstone replied to him, defending the Ministerial policy, and expressed his opinion that the agricultural interest generally were satisfied with the law as it at present stood, believing that it afforded a reasonable adjustment of the question. The Ministerial majority was 99.

The Free Trade leaders, encouraged by the popular feeling outside, fought the battle bravely, if for the time unavailingly, within the House. The opening of the Session of 1844 found them ready for the fray. On the 12th of March, Mr. Cobden moved for a select committee to enquire into the effects of the protective duties on imports on the interests of the tenant farmers and farm labourers of the country. Mr. Gladstone again appeared as the Ministerial champion, and took occasion to have a fling at the Anti-Corn Law League, and the public meetings at which the energetic terseness of Cobden's and Villiers' addresses, and the sonorous eloquence of Bright and W. J. Fox, so greatly excited the crowds which attended. Mr. Gladstone said:—

"The honourable gentleman had said, 'Do you think the appointment of the Committee will add to the agitation on the subject of the Corn Laws?' He thought it would ; or, at least, it would add to what was of much more importance—to apprehension on the subject. With regard to agitation, th's country had the happy peculiarity of being able to bear a larger amount of agitation, without serious consequences, than perhaps any other nation in the world ; and he believed there was a strong impression upon the public mind that the exertions of the Anti-Corn Law League, with which the honourable member for Manchester was connected—however active and able and inde-fatigable its members might be—need not, at all events, under existing cir-cumstances, so long as it should please Providence to bless the country with the abundance which it now enjoyed, and so long as the Parliament and the Government were firm in redeeming the pledges—expressed or implied—which they had given, be regarded with any very serious apprehensions, and that the most important feature of the meetings was probably the parade and ceremonial with which they were attended."

Mr. Cobden's motion was rejected by 91, the numbers being 133 and 224.

Throughout the remainder of the Session Mr. Gladstone's par-liamentary utterances were mostly limited to the business of his department, to which he devoted himself with characteristic zeal and industry.

The Royal Speech, at the opening of the Session of 1845, con-tained a paragraph, not very alarming in its wording, but which led to the withdrawal of Mr. Gladstone from office :—

"I recommend to your favourable consideration the policy of improving and extending the opportunities for academical education in Ireland."

On the surface it would seem strange that Mr. Gladstone, who had himself reaped so great advantage from a liberal academical education, should be averse to the extension of the system ; but it was the knowledge that Sir Robert Peel contemplated affording State support to the Roman Catholic academies of Ireland that induced Mr. Gladstone to decline to share the responsibility of the measure. His intention to secede from the Ministry was an open secret, and in the debate on the Address, Lord John Russell paid a high compliment to his great ability, and hoped for an explanation of the reasons which had induced him to withdraw from the Ministry.

Mr. Gladstone at once rose, and, in the course of his speech, while declining to enter into all the circumstances, said :—

"I can state at least what has not been the cause of my resignation, and thus put an end to the rumours that appear to have gone abroad. I have not, as has been supposed, resigned on account of any matter connected with that department of the public service of which I had the honour of being entrusted with the charge. I have not resigned on account of the intentions of the Government, so far as I have a knowledge of its intentions, with regard to any matter affecting the Church of England or the Church of

Ireland ; the cause, then, that I am about to bring before the House is the sole cause which has led to the step I have adopted.   I am driven to the necessity of adverting to myself, and to what I have said and done in former days.   I took upon myself, some years ago—whether wisely or unwisely is not now the question—to state to the world, and that in a form the most decided and deliberate, not under the influence of momentary consideration, nor impelled by the heat and pressure of debate, but in a published treatise, the views which I entertained on the subject of the relations of a Christian State to Religion, and to the Christian Church.   Of all subjects, therefore, which could be raised for public consideration, this, in its ultimate results at least the most important, I have treated in a manner the most detailed and deliberate.   I have never, indeed, been guilty of the folly which has been charged upon me by some, of holding that there are any theories of political affairs, even in the highest department, which are to be regarded alike under all circumstances as inflexible and immutable.   But, on the other hand, I have a strong conviction, speaking under ordinary circumstances, not as a general rule, that those who have thus borne the most solemn testimony to a particular view of a great constitutional question, ought not to be parties responsible for proposals which involve a violent departure from them.   Now, sir, it cannot fail to be in the recollection of the House that my right honourable friend at the head of the Government did, towards the close of last Session, allude to enquiries he was about to make into the possibility of extending academical education in Ireland, and he indicated the spirit in which that important matter might be examined. . . . .   Those intentions pointed to measures at variance with the system which I had maintained and recommended as the best and most salutary scheme for the regulation of the relations between a Christian State and the Christian Religion, and which I still believe to be the most salutary and the best in every condition of the public sentiment that will bear its application. . . . .   It is absolutely due to my public character, due to those terms on which alone general confidence can be reposed in public men, that I should under such circumstances, and in so important a matter, place myself, so far as in me lay, in a position to form not only an honest, but an independent and an unsuspected judgment."

He professed that he entertained no animosity against the Roman Catholics :—

"I fervently and earnestly trust that if we are to change the policy of the State, and to substitute for the former practice of the Constitution one that gives a more indiscriminating support, that the Irish Roman Catholics will not be selected for proscription, but that they will be regarded as having a title to the favour of the Legislature upon a footing similar to that of other Christian professions differing from the Church."

Sir Robert Peel confirmed the statements of Mr. Gladstone, for whose abilities, he said, he entertained the highest respect and admiration—admiration equalled only by his respect for his private character.   He was responsible that Mr. Gladstone did not press his resignation (which he had intimated as possible) at an earlier period, for he was unwilling to lose, until the latest moment, the advantages derived from "one whom I consider capable of rendering the highest and most eminent services to the country, and who is a distinguished ornament of the Government."

E

After retiring from office, Mr. Gladstone gave an independent support to the Peel Administration. It was not unreasonable, however, to suppose that he would be unable to accept the proposition for the permanent endowment of the Roman Catholic College at Maynooth, an act which appeared to be opposed to his views on the duty of the State to support only what he considered the orthodox creed. There was some surprise, therefore, when he spoke and voted in favour of the Bill introduced by Sir Robert Peel on the 3rd of April. There was a division on the motion for leave to introduce the Bill, the Opposition being led by Sir Robert Inglis, member for the University of Oxford, but the Ministers had a majority of 102. On that occasion, Mr. Gladstone did not vote ; but on the motion for the second reading on the 11th, he spoke at some length and with his accustomed eloquence. He supported the measure, he said, on the ground that those who paid the taxes of a country had a right to share in the benefits of its institutions.

" After a mature consideration of the subject, in the position in which it stands, and in the position in which we stand, I am prepared, in opposition to what I believe to be the prevailing opinion of the people of England ; in opposition to the judgment of my own constituents, from whom I greatly regret to differ ; and in opposition to my own deeply-cherished predilections, to give a deliberate and even an anxious support to the measure which my right honourable friend has submitted."

These remarkable words indicate alike the sensitive conscientiousness and the moral courage which throughout his political life have been Mr. Gladstone's characteristics ; and they, in some degree, prepare us for yet more marked changes in his views respecting very important questions.

In his " Chapter of Autobiography " he refers to this period :—

" Lord Derby was one of those colleagues who sought to dissuade me from resigning my office. He urged upon me that such an act must be followed by resistance to the Government, and that I should run the risk of being mixed with a fierce religious agitation. I replied that I must adhere to my purpose of retirement, but that I did not perceive the necessity of its being followed by resistance to the proposal. Overtures were not unnaturally made to me by some of those who resisted it, but they were at once declined. My whole purpose was to place myself in a position in which I should be free to consider my course without being liable to a just suspicion on the ground of personal interest."

CHAPTER VII.

IN the autumn of 1845, the course of events produced an almost unanswerable argument in support of Free Trade. The terrible potato disease broke out, and famine stared us in the face. In Ireland the people were dying from hunger, and no method of relief appeared possible but a removal, or, at least, extensive modification, of the restrictions which kept food out of the country. Sir Robert Peel announced that, in face of the alarming prospect of the destruction of a large portion of the staple food of the labouring population, his resolution to maintain the existing Corn Laws had given way, and he was prepared at once to resign.

Mr. Gladstone, too, saw reason to modify his views, and was ready to enrol himself under the Free Trade banner. At the close of the year, he published a pamphlet, "Remarks on Recent Commercial Legislation," in which he gave an able and elaborate detail of the beneficent working of the tariff modifications of 1842, which, the writer intimated, opened the way for a greater modification of the existing system of commercial restriction.

Lord John Russell was sent for by the Queen ; but, after considerable delay and much fruitless negotiation with the leading members of his party, he announced that he was unable to form a Ministry ; and Sir Robert Peel, supported by all the members of the Cabinet, except Lord Stanley, Colonial Secretary, remained in office. A writer of the period said : "Office was resumed notoriously and avowedly for a single purpose, the accomplishment of a single measure ; this done, the disruption of the party would render his removal from office inevitable, and that, too, with a very distant, if any, prospect of return. . . . That course involved the sacrifice of each object and every feeling most dear to a political leader. It was equally fatal to the reputation of the past and the prospects of the future, and it exposed him to a storm of obloquy and reproach, under which nothing could have supported him but consciousness of having acted with a single aim for the public welfare."

Sir Robert knew and accepted his position. His separation from the Conservative party was completed, and a new and inde-

pendent party was formed, leaning towards the Liberals, but with
distinctive tendencies retaining some of the old Conservatism—
uniting an adoption of the economical theories of the former with
the determination to support the institutions of the State around
which the Conservatives rallied.   The name Peelites was popularly given to the numerically small, but intellectually powerful,
party which followed Sir Robert's lead.   It included Mr. Goulburn, the late Chancellor of the Exchequer; Mr. Sidney Herbert,
Sir James Graham, the Earl of Lincoln, Mr. Cardwell, Sir George
Clerk, the Earl of Elgin, Lord Canning, and, very far from the
least, in such a gathering of men of high ability and Parliamentary
experience, Mr. Gladstone, who succeeded Lord Stanley as Secretary of State for the Colonies.

Parliament was opened on the 19th of January, and the Royal
Speech recommended the early consideration of the expediency
of the further repeal of prohibitory, and the relaxation of protective, duties.   In the debate on the Address, Sir Robert Peel
admitted that his opinions on the subject of Protection had
undergone a great change; and on the 27th he introduced his
financial and commercial scheme, remitting the duties on many
articles of consumption.   He was not prepared to sweep away
the Corn Laws at once, as probably the Anti-Corn Law League
would have wished him to do; but he proposed that the continuance should be only temporary—three years being taken to effect
the change.   After the 1st of February, 1849, grain of all kinds
should be admitted without payment of duty, except the almost
nominal charge of one shilling a-quarter, for the purpose of register-
ing the quantity imported.   He proposed that, previously to that
date, whenever the average price of wheat should be under 48s.
a-quarter in this country, the duty should be 10s.; and with
every shilling increase in price, there should be a reduction of
1s. duty, until the price reached 54s., or more, when an un-
varying duty of 4s. would be imposed.   The duty at that time
payable on corn, regulated by the average price, was 16s., and
the proposed change would reduce it to 4s.

The debate on Sir Robert's proposals lasted twelve nights, and
nearly every man of mark in the House took part in it.   The Free
Trade leaders supported the ministerial policy, and Mr. Bright
declared that he envied Sir Robert Peel, who had delivered almost
the finest speech ever heard in the House.   Mr. Disraeli took
occasion to sneer at the suddenness of the political conversion of
some of the Peelites, and at the "Protectionist Cabinet and the
Free Trade Prime Minister."   Ultimately the resolution was

carried by a majority of 97, the numbers being 337 for and 240 against.

Mr. Gladstone could take no part in this memorable division, his acceptance of office having deprived him of his seat. His re-election for Newark was out of the question. The Duke of New-castle, whose influence was paramount in the borough, was a Tory of the old school; and his anger against the Peelites was probably intensified by the fact that his son and heir, the Earl of Lincoln, was one of their number. A writer in a local newspaper of the 9th of January, says: "Mr. Gladstone having been appointed Secretary to the Colonies, it is reported in Newark that the Duke of Newcastle and Lord Winchelsea were averse to his being again returned for that town, on account of his vote on the Maynooth question; and on Saturday week the tenants of the latter were waited upon with a command that they were not to vote for Mr. Gladstone. Notwithstanding all this, the feelings of the majority of the electors were in favour of Mr. Gladstone's re-election; but as the Lord of Clumber [the Duke] did not appear to sanction it, Mr. Gladstone's address appeared, declining the representation of Newark."

The electors were at once made to understand that Mr. Stuart, a barrister and Queen's counsel, was the Duke's nominee, and that they were expected to return him, whether Mr. Gladstone did or did not offer himself for re-election.

Mr. Gladstone did not choose to enter on a contest in which defeat was certain, and his address to the electors was a farewell to the constituency he had represented for thirteen years. He said :—

"As I have good reason to believe that a candidate recommended to your favour through local connection may ask your suffrages, it becomes my very painful duty to announce to you, on that ground alone, my retirement from a position which has afforded me so much of honour and of satisfaction."

His support of the Government by the acceptance of office, rested, he said :—

"Upon no merely apologetic plea, but upon the assertion that I have acted in obedience to the clear and imperious calls of public obligation, and with the purpose which I have ever sought to follow, of promoting the personal interests of the community, and of all classes of which it is composed."

On the 27th of June, the Peel Ministry resigned, having been defeated by a majority of 73 on the motion for the second reading of the Protection of Life (Ireland) Bill, the purpose of which was to give to Ministers powers which they deemed necessary for the repression of outrage and the protection of life in Ireland. On the same night that Sir Robert announced in the House of Commons that he and his colleagues had placed their resignations in the hands of the Queen, the Corn Law Bill passed the third reading in the House of Lords. Success and defeat were simultaneous.

Mr. Gladstone made no other attempt to obtain a seat until the general election of 1847, when he appeared as a candidate for the representation of Oxford University. Sir Robert Inglis had long been the senior member, and his seat was secure; but the second seat was contested by Mr. Round. Mr. Cardwell had been brought forward as a candidate, but withdrew, the general result of the preliminary canvass not offering a prospect of success. When Mr. Gladstone appeared in the field, Mr. Round's committee charged him with having voted for the Dissenters' Chapel Bill, and so favouring Socinianism, and with having supported the Maynooth Bill, and so opposing the Church of England. In reply, Mr. Gladstone maintained that he was " heartily devoted to the doctrine and constitution of our Reformed Church," but he added :—

" I will never consent to adopt as a test of such devotion a disposition to identify the great and noble cause of the Church of England with the repression of the civil rights of those who differ from her. I shall rather believe that it may more wisely, justly, and usefully be shown, first, by endeavours to aid in the development and application of her energies to her splendid work, and next by the temperate but firm vindication of those rights with which, for the public good, she is endowed as a national establishment."

The election was marked by great activity and excitement ; there had been no contest for the University seats for twenty years, the last having been in 1828, when Peel was rejected. There were no speeches by the candidates, it being a rule of the University that after the issue of the writ, and during the election, candidates were prohibited coming within twenty miles of the place. Dr. Richards, rector of Exeter College, proposed Mr. Gladstone in a long Latin oration. Having alluded to his distinguished academic career, and lauded him for his piety, integrity, ability, and honour, he spoke of him as an ardent advocate of the Episcopal Anglican Church throughout every part of the globe.

The result of the election was that Sir Robert Inglis was returned at the top of the poll, with 1,700 votes; Mr. Gladstone occupied the second place with 997, and Mr. Round polled 824. The number of votes was the largest ever known to have been given at an election for the University.

One of Mr. Gladstone's earliest speeches in the new Parliament, which opened in November, was in support of Lord John Russell's motion that the House should resolve itself into a committee to consider the removal of the civil and political disabilities of the Jews. Sir Robert Inglis, the senior member for Oxford University, strongly opposed the motion ; it was known that the University generally regarded it as an attack on the Christian Church of the Constitution ; and it therefore required considerable courage on the part of Mr. Gladstone to give it an open and energetic support. A weaker man, holding the same opinions on the subject, might have sought to effect a compromise between conscience and convenience by keeping silence and absenting himself from the division ; but Mr. Gladstone was at once too courageous and too honest for such a course. His speech was long, closely reasoned, and remarkable as indicating a broadening of ecclesiastical views, and a foreshadowing of the course taken very recently respecting the admission to Parliament of persons who objected to make an avowal of specific religious belief. He expressed his great respect for the constituency which had returned him, and which he knew was opposed to the Bill the Premier proposed to introduce ; but, he maintained, undoubtedly the true principle of legislation was that a member should follow the conscientious dictates of his own judgment, whether they happened to coincide in the particular case with the judgment of the constituency or not. " I should," he said, " be betraying my plain duty to my constituents, if I were to succumb to their judgment in a case where I am conscientiously convinced there is a better course to pursue."

In the course of his speech he said :—

" When it is said that we unchristianise the Parliament, while it may be true in name—and I would not deny it—I must ask, is it true in substance ? . . . If we are a Christian nation, we shall, even after removing the disabilities of the Jews, be a Christian Parliament ; if it be true that we must then cease to be a Christian Parliament, it is also true that we are not now a Christian nation. I think that Parliament will continue to derive its character mainly from the personal character of those who elect, and of those who compose it. And I must say, with regard to the speech of the noble Lord (Lord John Russell), that when he spoke of oaths and declarations as affording insufficient securities, I certainly did not understand him to signify—and I trust he did not intend—that they were to be looked upon as altogether worthless, and to be discarded from our use ; but that we were not to place upon them an exclusive reliance, and that we were to depend more, after all, upon the qualities of men than upon the letter of any regulations we could establish."

He concluded by saying :—

"If the act we have done be indeed an act of civil and social justice, then, whatever be its first aspect, it can involve no disparagement to the religion we profess, can never lower Christianity in public estimation, but must, on the con-

trary, tend to elevate the conception of Christianity in all considerate minds ;
for it will show—either now, or at farthest when some years have passed, and
when we can look back upon the differences of the present day with the aid of
those lights which after events and experience will have thrown upon them—
that the Christian religion which we professed was a religion that enabled us,
when convinced, to do an act of justice in spite of prepossessions appealing
to our liveliest and tenderest feelings—prepossessions which still attracted our
sympathy and respect, almost our veneration—in the full belief that truth and
right would vindicate themselves, and those who desired to follow them."

Mr. Newdegate, who spoke afterwards, of course in opposition to
the motion, referring to Mr Gladstone, said : " Had it been known
that the right honourable gentleman entertained such sentiments
as he had expressed on the subject of the Jews, when he offered
himself as a candidate for the representation of Oxford University,
he was certain that he never would have been returned for that
eminent seat of learning." The two members for Cambridge
University—Mr. Goulburn (Chancellor of the Exchequer in the late
Ministry, and a conspicuous member of the Peelite party), and
Mr. Law, the Recorder of London—strongly opposed the resolution, to which, however, Sir Robert Peel himself, and his friends
the Earl of Lincoln and Mr. Cardwell, gave their support.
Another eminent Peelite, Mr. Sidney Herbert, did not vote. The
motion was carried by a majority of 67 ; the numbers being,
Ayes, 253; Noes, 186.

In the Session of 1848, Mr. Gladstone afforded another instance
of the modification of the extreme views he once held, by supporting the Roman Catholic Relief Bill, introduced by Mr. Chisholm
Anstey, the object of which was the removal of certain disabilities
imposed by the existing Acts of Parliament. On the 23rd of May,
Lord George Bentinck, the leader of the Protectionist party in the
Commons, made a vigorous attack on the Free Trade policy, in
moving for returns of quantities and prices of various articles.
Mr. Gladstone replied, with equal energy, and with a far greater
mastery of facts and figures.

The vexed question of the sugar duties again cropped up in
June. On that subject Mr. Gladstone declined to accept abstract
Free Trade doctrines. The imposition of differential duties, by
which slave-grown sugar was to a considerable extent kept out of
the market, he considered as a necessary sequel of the work of
emancipation in the British colonies ; and he protested,
as many times before he had done, against subjecting British
planters, who were compelled to employ paid labourers, to
competition in the open market with the employers of slaves. It
was obvious that sugar and other articles imported—grain, for in-

stance—did not stand on the same footing, for the producers worked under different conditions. He argued :—

> " Do not let it be said that the plan of emancipation, mighty and gigantic as it was, was based upon the ruin of private fortunes, and that, while it overspread the whole world with its fame, we took the gl ry upon ourselves, that we laid the burden on the West Indies, and left the debt to posterity. Let us not shrink from the burden that our own shoulders ought to bear—let us not shrink from making the return which is due to the colonies, and necessary to complete the work of regeneration for the negro race by whom they are inhabited."

The Session of 1849 was not marked by any important speech by Mr. Gladstone ; but he took an active part in the business of the House, especially in the debate on the regularly-recurring proposition to repeal the law prohibiting marriage with a deceased wife's sister — which he strongly opposed, appealing to the Levitical and ecclesiastical law on the subject, and paying little regard to merely secular arguments.

The great Parliamentary event of 1850 was the memorable debate on the conduct of Lord Palmerston, in connection with what we know as the Don Pacifico affair. The worthy Don, a naturalised British subject, had been for several years preferring claims for compensation against the Greek Government for injuries sustained, and other British subjects had similar claims, which the Greeks delayed, or declined, to satisfy. Lord Palmerston, being appealed to, adopted a very energetic mode of obtaining reparation, by ordering Admiral Parker, in command of the Mediterranean fleet, to blockade the harbour of the Piræus ; the consequence being the immediate submission of the Greek Government. This prompt, but certainly high-handed, proceeding caused great excitement at home. In the House of Lords, Lord Stanley, afterwards the Earl of Derby, proposed and carried a direct vote of censure on the Ministry. Palmerston was not disposed to wait for attack in the Commons, but invited it by the friendly action of John Arthur Roebuck, the member for Sheffield. Mr. Roebuck's Liberalism was essentially of the combative kind. He described himself in later days as " the dog Tear'em "; and his political predilections certainly never approached (except in a hostile attitude) the doctrines of the Peace advocates. His position in the House was peculiar. Highly gifted, possessed of great Parliamentary experience, adroit in all the arts of debate, and of indomitable courage, delighting in sharp personal contests, he chose to fight, like Hal o' the Wynd, for his own hand. A philosophical Radical in theory, he was in many respects vigorously Conservative, with a considerable tendency to what, in after

days, was vulgarly known as Jingoism. In political life he would
rather knock down than argue with anyone who ventured to
oppose him. He willingly came forward, as an "unattached
friend," in support of the Palmerstonian policy, by moving a resolution of approval. Palmerston defended himself in the longest
and ablest speech he ever delivered, speaking for five hours—
"that speech," said Sir Robert Peel, who nevertheless condemned
his policy, "which made us all proud of him."

On the third night of the debate Mr. Gladstone spoke. He
had evidently nerved himself for a great effort, and he achieved a
striking success. Never before had he made so direct a personal
attack; never before had he displayed such powers of invective,
and sarcastic, almost grim, humour. Once more he maintained
principles against expediency; once more he maintained that
which would be mean or dishonourable in an individual would
be so in a nation. In his speech, Lord Palmerston had made a
great point of the famous phrase *Civis Romanus sum*, and
the comparison he drew from it. Mr. Gladstone seized on it with
avidity :—

"I will grapple with the noble Lord on the ground which he selected for
himself, in the most triumphant portion of his speech, by his reference to those
emphatic words, *Civis Romanus sum*. He vaunted, amidst the cheers of his
supporters, that under his administration an Englishman should be, throughout
the world, what the citizen of Rome had been. What then, sir, was a Roman
citizen? He was the member of a privileged caste : he belonged to a
conquering race, to a nation that held all others bound down by the strong
arm of power. For him there was to be an exceptional system of law ; for
him principles were to be asserted, and by him rights were to be enjoyed, that
were denied to the rest of the world. Is such, then, the view of the noble Lord
as to the relation that is to subsist between England and other countries?
Does he make the claim for us that we are to be uplifted upon a platform high
above the standing-ground of all other nations? It is, indeed, too clear, not
only from the expressions, but from the whole spirit of the speech of the noble
Viscount, that too much of this notion is lurking in his mind ; that he adopts
in part that vain conception that we, forsooth, have a mission to be the censors
of vice and folly, of abuse and imperfection, among the other countries of the
world ; that we are to be the universal schoolmasters ; and that all who hesitate to recognise our office, can be governed only by prejudice or personal
animosity, and should have the blind war of diplomacy forthwith declared
against them. And, certainly, if the business of a Foreign Secretary properly
were to carry on such diplomatic wars, all must admit that the noble Lord is a
master in the discharge of his functions. What, sir, ought a Foreign Secretary to be? Is he to be like some gallant knight at a tournament of old, pricking
forth into the lists, armed at all points, confiding in his sinews and his skill, challenging all comers for the sake of honour, and having no other duty than to lay as
many as possible of his adversaries sprawling in the dust? If such is the idea
of a good Foreign Secretary, I for one would vote to the noble Lord his
present appointment for his life. But, sir, I do not understand the duty of a

Secretary for Foreign Affairs to be of such a character.   I understand it to be his duty to conciliate peace with dignity.   I think it to be the very first of all his duties studiously to observe, and to exalt in honour among mankind, that great code of principles which is termed the law of nations, which the honourable and learned member for Sheffield [Mr. Roebuck] has found, indeed, to be very vague in their nature, and greatly dependent on the discretion of each particular country ; but in which I find, on the contrary, a great and noble monument of human wisdom, founded on the combined dictates of reason and experience—a precious inheritance bequeathed to us by the generations which have gone before us, and a firm foundation on which we must take care to build whatever it may be our part to add to their acquisition ; if, indeed, we wish to maintain and to consolidate the brotherhood of nations, and to promote the peace and welfare of the world.   Sir, the English people, whom we are here to represent, are indeed a great and noble people ; but it adds nothing to their greatness or nobleness that when we assemble in this place, we should trumpet forth our virtues in elaborate panegyrics, and designate those who may not be wholly of our mind as a knot of foreign conspirators.   .   .   .   It is this insular temper, and this self-glorifying tendency, which the policy of the noble Lord, and the doctrines of his supporters, tend so much to foment, and which has given to that policy the quarrelsome character that marks some of their speeches ; for, indeed, it seems as if there lay upon the noble Lord an absolute necessity for quarrelling.   No doubt, it makes a difference, what may be the institutions of one country or another.   If he can, he will quarrel with an absolute monarchy.   If he cannot find an absolute monarchy for the purpose, he will quarrel with one that is limited.   If he cannot find even that, yet, sooner than not quarrel at all, he will quarrel with a republic.   .   .   .   I, for my part, am of opinion that England will stand shorn of a chief part of her glory and her pride if she shall be found to have separated herself, through the policy she pursues abroad, from the moral supports which the general and fixed convictions of mankind afford—if the day shall come in which she may continue to excite the wonder and the fear of other nations, but in which she shall have no part in their affection and their regard."

From this fierce battle Lord Palmerston emerged a conqueror. The *Civis Romanus sum* had brought down the House.   Peel and Gladstone sought to do their best, but " England, right or wrong, against the world," was too potent for them, and a majority of 46 in favour of the resolution endorsed the action of the Foreign Secretary.

Sir Robert Peel's speech on this occasion was the last he delivered.   On the following day (June 28) he was thrown from his horse on Constitution Hill, and fatally injured.   On the evening of Tuesday, the 2nd of July, the great statesman breathed his last. When the House of Commons met on the 3rd, for the Wednesday sitting, Mr. Hume moved the adjournment of the House as a mark of respect.   No member of the Cabinet was present to second the motion, the Premier being absent from town, and the other Ministers engaged at their offices ; and Mr. Gladstone undertook the duty, for which he was so well fitted by his long

political and private friendship with Sir Robert.   His speech was
short, but graceful and effective.   In the course of it, he said :—

"I am quite sure that every heart is much too full to allow us, at a period so
early, to enter upon the consideration of the amount of that calamity with
which the country has been visited in his, I must even now say, premature
death ; for, though he has died full of years and full of honours, yet it is a
death which our human eyes will regard as premature ; because we had fondly
hoped that in whatever position he was placed, by the weight of his character,
by the splendour of his talents, by the purity of his virtues, he would still have
been spared to render to his country the most essential services.   I will only,
sir, quote those most touching and feeling lines which were applied by one
of the greatest poets of this country to the memory of a man great indeed,
but yet not greater than Sir Robert Peel :—

> Now is the stately column broke,
> The beacon light is quenched in smoke ;
> The trumpet's silver voice is still ;
> The warder silent on the hill.' "

This quotation from Scott's noble eulogy of William Pitt, delivered with admirable elocution and beauty of voice, produced a
great effect.

In the course of the Session of 1850, Mr. Gladstone supported
a motion for the revision of the Poor Laws, brought forward by
Mr. Disraeli ; and opposed the Australian Government Bill.   The
close of the year was marked by exertions in other fields, and
one fruit of the relaxation of Parliamentary work was the publication of " Remarks on the Royal Supremacy, as it is defined
by Reason, History, and the Constitution."   It was a pamphlet in
the form of a letter to the Bishop of London (Dr. Blomfield),
and was the result of the author's examination of the historical
evidence for the royal supremacy in the Church, in relation to
matters of doctrine.   The ecclesiastical world had been greatly
excited by the result of the Gorham trial, and of the subsequent
appeals.   It may be well to remind our readers—for events march
quickly, and in the course of thirty years much is forgotten—that
Dr. Philpott, Bishop of Exeter, had refused to institute the Rev.
Mr. Gorham into the living of Brampton-Speke, Devonshire,
on the ground of his want of orthodoxy, in denying that spiritual
regeneration was conferred by baptism.   Mr. Gorham brought
an action against the Bishop in the Ecclesiastical Court, which
held that the Bishop was justified in his action.   Against this
judgment Mr. Gorham appealed to the Judicial Committee of the
Privy Council, which, in March, 1850, reversed the decision of
the Ecclesiastical Court, and decided that Mr. Gorham ought
not to have been refused institution.   The Bishop was not to be
beaten easily—" Harry of Exeter " was too resolute and com-

bative for that—and application was made to each of the other Superior Courts of Common Law, successively, for a rule to show cause why a prohibition should not issue, directed to the Judge of the Arches Court and to the Archbishop of Canterbury, against giving effect to the judgment of Her Majesty in Council. The rule was refused in each Court, and in August Mr. Gorham was instituted into the vicarage.

The question of the respective rights of the secular and ecclesiastical power, of the nature and limits of the supremacy of the Crown, which all ministers of the Church acknowledged when they subscribed the Articles, was raised anew by the High Churchmen, who saw in this action of the Privy Council a renewed attack on the Establishment. Mr. Gladstone was not likely to remain silent when such a topic was exciting men's minds; and he set to work with characteristic industry and ardour, examining old statutes and the bases of ecclesiastical law, the acts of Convocation, and the Acts of Parliament bearing on the question. The result he arrived at appears to be embodied in the following extract from the letter :—

"It is an utter mistake to suppose that the recognition of the royal supremacy in matters ecclesiastical established in the Church a despotic power. The monarchy of England has been from early times a free monarchy. The idea of law was altogether paramount in this happy constitution to that of any personal will. . . . Here lay the grand cause of the success of our English revolutions, that the people never rent the web of history, but repaired its rents ; never interposed a chasm between, never separated the national life of the present and that of the past, but even when they seemed most violently to alter the momentary, always aimed at recovering the general direction of their career ; thus everybody knew that there were laws superior to the Sovereign, and liberties which he could not infringe ; that he was King in order to be the guardian of these laws and liberties, and to direct both the legislature and all other governing powers in the spirit which they breathed, and within the lines which they marked out for him. . . . I say that the intention of the Reformation, taken generally, was to place our religious liberties on a footing analagous to that on which our civil liberties had long stood. A supremacy of power in making and amending Church law as well as State law was to vest in the Sovereign ; but in making Church law he was to ratify the acts of the Church herself, represented in Convocation, and if there were need of the highest civil sanction, then to have the aid of Parliament also ; and in administering Church law he was to discharge this function through the medium of bishops and divines, canonists and civilians, as her own most fully authorised, best instructed son, following in each case the analogy of his ordinary procedure as head of the State."

This letter was reprinted in 1865, and a third edition, with a preface, in which the author said he saw no reason to modify the views he had expressed, appeared in 1877.

CHAPTER VIII.

IN THE DUNGEONS OF NAPLES.

THE winter of 1850-51 found Mr. Gladstone in Naples; and
that event furnished one of the most remarkable and interesting
incidents of his life.

Ferdinand the Second, of Naples and Sicily, was then on the
throne—a throne terribly shaken and threatened by the political
convulsions of 1848, but as yet preserved by unscrupulous false-
hood and oppression, by remorselessly shooting down rebellious
subjects, and by almost unparalleled cruelty to political opponents
and patriots who dared to advocate the rights of humanity.
" Bomba " was the popular nickname of the King; a nickname
which preserved in the popular memory the slaughter by the royal
troops in the streets of Naples, when the people had thrown up
barricades and attempted a revolution, put down by the cannon
which swept the streets and the persistent fire of the King's
soldiers. When the resistance slackened, and the dead citizens
were being borne away, and the weeping women and children
were mixed with the men who had so stoutly, but unavailingly
fought, the King gave the order to continue the firing: " The business has begun; it must end," he said brutally. " In short," says
Mr. Cayley, one of the best historians of that troubled time in the
history of modern Europe, " he slew the rabble, intimidated the people, dissolved by military force the Chamber of Deputies before it
had regularly met, and became again absolute and irresponsible."

The people of Sicily, united against their will with continental
Naples, had endeavoured to throw off the odious yoke. They
proclaimed the independence of the island, and the deposition of
Ferdinand and his dynasty, and appointed Rugero Settimo
regent until a new king should be elected. The Neapolitan fleet
bombarded Messina, directing the fire not on the defences, but
on the houses, churches, and those parts of the city most
thickly populated. The bombardment having lasted five days,
the greater part of the city was destroyed, and many of the
inhabitants buried in its ruins. It was continued two days after
resistance had ceased, and the soldiery carried fire and sword
through the city, murdering the flying inhabitants. Well had the
King earned the name of Bomba, " the bombardier ! "

At Naples he summoned Parliament when the popular pressure was too strong for him to resist, and dismissed them when, by fair means or foul, he had regained the mastery. It is said, and very probably with truth, that the Court party paid the scum of the Neapolitan population to insult the deputies as they left the Chamber, and the respectable citizens who were known to be their friends, and to raise shouts for an absolute king. "After the earlier throes of the great convulsion had subsided in Naples," says Mr. Cayley, "the King who, during the heat of the revolution had sworn to anything, and courted the mob while they were uppermost, not having either courage or power to resist, was now worrying the discomfited supporters of the constitution to which he had sworn; and, having taken in pay a set of lazy rogues, employed them in bullying and insulting the deputies who had assembled at his summons, and whom, at the moment, Ferdinand was not strong enough at once to dismiss. They complained to the King of his administration, but the administration set the Parliament at nought, prevented them from laying their complaints before the King, and finally dissolved them. Then began a series of political persecutions."

Persecutions, indeed, unparalleled in the history of the century. There are instances in the records of other nations of unjust prosecutions, fictitious evidence, mock trials, long and solitary imprisonments, executions even of political opponents of ruling powers; but the state prosecutions of Naples exceeded in atrocity all similar contemporary events. The victims were to be counted by thousands; the punishments inflicted were a revival of the tortures of the Inquisition, and the filthy abominations of the galleys. The judges were corrupted or intimidated by the King and his advisers; forgery and perjury were most extensively resorted to; laws sworn to be observed were recklessly violated; and men of culture, patriotism, and pure and honourable lives were condemned to imprisonment in loathsome dungeons, loaded with heavy fetters, chained to the vilest scoundrels that even the criminal population of Naples could furnish, and subjected to hideous torture. So foul were the dungeons that the jailors themselves hesitated to visit them, and the official doctors "dared not risk their lives by entering them."

Among the victims was Carlo Poerio, the son of a patriot who had suffered greatly for his advocacy of popular rights, and himself one of the ablest, most energetic, and high-minded of the leading spirits of the time. He had suffered imprisonment when the King was the stronger, and had been invited to accept minis-

terial office when the King was compelled to grant, and promised
to observe, a liberal constitution. Poerio was successively Director
of Police and Minister of Public Instruction, but soon resigned,
and also refused the rank of Privy Councillor offered by the
King, preferring to sit as an independent deputy in the Parliament. His ruin was resolved on as soon as the King felt that he
had the power again to defy public opinion. He was arrested,
his house ransacked, and compromising papers were produced,
alleged to have been discovered, but which were forgeries prepared by his enemies. The fraud was successfully exposed, and
then perjury was called in to do the desired work. One Jervolino,
a secret agent of the Government, was employed to swear that
Poerio was the head of a conspiracy to murder the King and
Ministers and proclaim the Republic. Poerio demanded to be
confronted with his accuser, but that was refused, and for a short
time the charge was abandoned, and another plan was resorted
to. One or two other political prisoners were induced by the
promise that their lives would be spared to make statements involving Poerio; but they were so extravagant and unsupported,
that even the unscrupulous prosecutors were ashamed to bring
them forward, and the evidence of Jervolino was again produced.
In vain Poerio proved that the man was a paid spy of the police;
the Court accepted the evidence, declared that Poerio was guilty,
and sentenced him to imprisonment in chains for twenty-four
years, and to pay a heavy fine. He was dressed as a felon, loaded
with fifteen pounds of iron, and taken from hulks to hulks at
Nisida, Procida, Ischia, Montesfasco, and Montesarchio, his com-
panions being cut-throats and miscreants, the vilest of the vile
brigands and twin scoundrels Italy could furnish.

Another eminent politician and advocate, of high public position
and honourable life, Settembrini, was condemned to be imprisoned
for life and loaded with double chains, and was tortured by having
sharp instruments thrust under his finger-nails; and others, conspicuous by their talents and position, were fellow-sufferers, sentenced to wear out their lives in indescribable misery.

The trial of Poerio was proceeding when Mr. Gladstone visited
Naples, and he was present during a part of the proceedings.
The infamous condemnation and sentence greatly shocked him,
and he was led to give great attention to the prosecutions for
political offences. He visited the prisons, exploring underground
dungeons, conversing with the prisoners, and witnessing their
sufferings. He found that of one hundred and forty deputies
returned to the Neapolitan Parliament, seventy-six were in

prison or exile, and that more than twenty thousand other subjects of Ferdinand had been thrown into prison on the charge
of political disaffection.   Burning with indignation, he published,
in the form of a "Letter to the Earl of Aberdeen," a detailed
narrative of the trials, sentences, and sufferings endured by the
wretched prisoners, and in scathing terms denounced the Neapolitan authorities.   The condemnation of Poerio, "a cultivated
and accomplished gentleman," distinguished for "obedience to
law and love of his country," had been, he said, obtained by
perjury and intimidation, in order "to obtain the scaffold's aim
by means more cruel than the scaffold, and without the outcry
which the scaffold would create."

The publication of this letter produced an intense sensation.
It circulated through Europe, and of course was immediately
answered by "official statements," which flatly contradicted him ;
and there were not wanting journalists and pamphleteers to declare
that the statements were enormously exaggerated by Mr. Gladstone's fervid imagination.   In a second letter, he corrected a few
errors of detail, and examined the replies made, the result being
that the main points of his story remained intact.

Towards the close of the Parliamentary Session of 1851, Sir
De Lacy Evans, the Liberal member for Westminster, asked Lord
Palmerston, the Foreign Secretary, if the British Minister at
Naples had been instructed to employ his good offices in the
cause of humanity for the diminution of these lamentable sever-
ities.   Lord Palmerston replied :—

"It has not been deemed a part of the duty of the British Government to
make any formal representations to the Government of Naples on a matter
that relates entirely to the internal affairs of that country.   At the same time,
I thought it right, seeing that Mr. Gladstone has done himself, as I think,
very great honour by the course he pursued at Naples, and by the course he
has followed since ; for I think that when you see an English gentleman,
who goes to pass a winter at Naples—instead of confining himself to those
amusements that abound in that city—instead of diving into volcanoes and
exploring excavated cities—when we see him going to courts of justice, visiting prisons, descending into dungeons, and examining great numbers of
unfortunate victims of illegality and injustice, with a view afterwards to
enlist public opinion in the endeavour to remedy those abuses—I think
that is a course that does honour to the person that pursues it ; and, con-
curring in opinion with him that the influence of public opinion in Europe
might have some useful effect in setting such matters right, I thought it my
duty to send copies of his pamphlet to our Ministers at the various Courts of
Europe, directing them to give to each Government copies of the pamphlet,
in the hope that, by affording them an opportunity of reading it, they might
be led to use their influence for promoting what is the object of my honourable and gallant friend—a remedy for the evils to which he has referred."

Corrupt as was the Neapolitan Government, and seared as the conscience of Ferdinand must have been, all feeling of shame was not quite extinct, and the disclosure was followed by considerable remissions of punishment, and release of some of the prisoners. Poerio was permitted to leave Italy, and reached London, where he was warmly received. Afterwards, when the Kingdom of Naples ceased to exist, and there was an Italian Kingdom and an Italian Parliament, he returned to serve his country as a statesman.

It might seem a little inconsistent that a politician who had so vehemently protested against the principle of interference in the internal government of other States, as Mr. Gladstone had done when he denounced Lord Palmerston, should have made himself so prominently the champion of a people oppressed by its Government, and should have called for official interference. In this respect, as in others, Mr. Gladstone's generous and courageous nature was in advance of his abstract political theories. He had seen with his own eyes injustice and cruelty at Naples, and as a man, the instincts of humanity were stronger than the cold maxims of the politician.

The British public generally were actuated by the same sentiment. Political partisanship was forgotten, and on all sides was expressed the praise of Mr. Gladstone's course of action.

The *Edinburgh Review* of October, 1851—an opponent of the political party to which Mr. Gladstone at that time belonged, and therefore certainly not animated by the zeal of political partiality —said :—

"Providence inspired a gentleman of unblemished character, brilliant talents, high position, uniting to the qualifications which eminently fitted him for discovering the truth, a heart that urged him on to search for it, and a will which was not to be baffled in its pursuit. Mr. Gladstone went to Naples soon after having voted against the Government on a vital question of foreign policy. Secretary of State for the Colonies in that Administration which had Lord Aberdeen for Foreign Secretary, Mr. Gladstone would have been too happy to be able to say that the Conservative Government of Naples deserved the respect and support of the great and influential party in this country of which he is an ornament and leading member. But Mr. Gladstone is not one of those who attach much importance to a name; and, having soon had reason to suspect that under the cloak of Conservatives and Conservatism may be concealed persons whose wickedness it is a duty to expose, and principles which every honest man may repudiate, he determined to enquire into the facts and get at the truth. . . . Mr. Gladstone determined on endeavouring to mitigate the horrors which he had witnessed, and to expose the infamies which he had discovered, no matter at what sacrifice. We confess we envy his party a man whose talents we have often admired, but whose generosity of feeling had not been sufficiently appreciated."

CHAPTER IX

THE ANTI-PAPAL AGITATION.—OPPOSITION TO THE
ECCLESIASTICAL TITLES BILL.

WHILE Mr. Gladstone was attending State trials and exploring underground dungeons in Naples, England was in a ferment. In a consistory held at Rome in September, a Papal edict was prepared which divided England and Wales into one archiepiscopal and twelve episcopal sees, and appointed the newly-created cardinal Dr. Wiseman, Archbishop of Westminster, with twelve bishops, who were to supersede the old vicars apostolic. On the 27th of October, Dr. Ullathorne was enthroned as Roman Catholic Bishop of Birmingham; and on the same day a Pastoral from Cardinal Wiseman, announcing the new arrangement of the sees, was read in all the Catholic chapels. The tone of this Pastoral was certainly arrogant and offensive. It spoke of England being restored to the true Church, and announced that " we shall govern and continue to govern the country," &c.

The excitement produced by the action of the Roman Church was intense. Protestants, of course, resented with indignation the assumption of episcopal titles and the formation of dioceses by Roman Catholics; and a very large portion of the public, who had little religious enthusiasm, denounced the pretensions of any foreign potentate, pope or prince, to parcel out the English soil at his good pleasure. The feeling of irritation was at once religious and rational. Shakspeare's famous phrase, " No Italian priest shall tithe or toil in my dominions," was in everybody's mouth; and when excitement was at the height, there appeared the historical letter known as the "Durham Letter," from Lord John Russell, the Prime Minister, to the Bishop of Durham, in which he announced his intention to resist to the utmost the Papal aggression. It is to be feared that the inflated tone of this ministerial manifesto (for such it really was) justified to some extent the epithets of "clap-trap" and "bunkum" applied to it. *Punch* caricatured Lord John as a naughty boy who chalked " No Popery " on the walls. The last paragraph of the letter was to this effect :—

"I have little hope that the preparers and framers of this invention will desist from their insidious course; but I rely on the people of England, and

I will not bate a jot of heart or life so long as the glorious principles and the immortal martyrs of the Reformation shall be held in reverence by the great mass of a nation which looks with contempt on the mummeries of superstition, and with scorn at the laborious endeavours which are now making to confine the intellect and enslave the soul."

It was rather a dangerous experiment upon the forbearance and self-control of the public to issue such an inflammatory letter the day before the Fifth of November; but the Englishmen of 1850 were more law-abiding and order-loving, more reasonable and less violent, than the Englishmen who took part in the Sacheverell or the Gordon riots. The effigies of Guy Fawkes carried about were outnumbered by figures presumed to represent popes and cardinals, and there was perhaps a little extra enthusiasm in the matter of fireworks; but there the open demonstrations ended. None the less was the popular indignation intense. More than six thousand public meetings were held in November and December, from which addresses were sent to the Queen calling upon her and the Ministry to resent the "usurpation."

At the opening of Parliament in February, 1851, allusion was made to the subject in the Royal Speech; and very shortly afterwards Lord John Russell introduced the Ecclesiastical Titles Assumption Bill, the object of which was to prohibit the assumption of the titles of archbishop, bishop, or dean in respect of any places within the United Kingdom by persons other than those already legally entitled. The debate on the second reading was long. That the majority of the House of Commons would support the Government was anticipated; but the opponents of the measure would not submit silently to defeat. They rested their arguments on the basis of toleration, and repudiated the idea that the loyalty of English Catholics would be affected by the assumption of episcopal functions by some of their priests. Practically, they argued, English Catholics would continue to regard the Pope temporally as a foreign prince, having no claim to any other than spiritual allegiance; and Mr. Gladstone (speaking on the second night of the debate) indeed urged that the appointment of bishops by the Papacy was a concession to the long-expressed wishes of the English members of the Roman Church, and would render them less dependent on the cardinals and priests of Rome. The Premier, Mr. Gladstone reminded him, had been foremost in supporting the endowment of Maynooth, and had then no fear that the Romish priesthood would ever be dangerous to the British Constitution. He continued:—

"The noble Lord said, in reference to the powerful opposition then offered to the Bill for the endowment of Maynooth, 'it seems that the strife upon the question of religion is never to fail, and that our arms are never to rust.' Would any man who heard the noble Lord deliver these impressive sentiments have believed that the strife with regard to religious liberty was to be revived not only with a greater degree of acerbity in the year 1851, but that the noble Lord himself was to be a main agent in its revival—that his was to be the head that was to wear the helmet, and his the hand that was to grasp the spear? My conviction is that the question of religious freedom is not to be dealt with as one of the ordinary matters that you may do to-day and undo to-morrow. The great principle which we have the honour to represent, moves slowly in matters of politics and legislation ; but, although it moves slowly, it moves steadily. The principle of religious freedom, its adaptation to our modern state, and its compatibility with ancient institutions, was a principle which you did not adopt in haste. It was a principle well tried in struggle and conflict. It was a principle which gained the assent of one public man after another. It was a principle which ultimately triumphed after you had spent upon it half a century of agonising struggle. And now, what are you going to do? You have arrived at the division of the century. Are you going to repeat Penelope's process, but without Penelope's purpose? Are you going to spend the latter half of the nineteenth century in undoing the great work which, with so much pain and difficulty, your greatest men have been achieving during the former? Surely not. Recollect the functions you have to perform in the face of the world. Recollect that Europe and the whole of the civilised world look to England at this moment, more than they ever looked before, as the mistress and guide of nations, in regard to the great work of civil legislation. And what is it they chiefly admire in England? It is not the rapidity with which you form constitutions and broach abstract theories. On the contrary, they know that nothing is so distasteful to you as abstract theories, and that you are proverbial for resisting what is new until you are assured of its safety and beneficial tendency. But they know that when you make a step forward, you keep it. They know that there is reality and honesty about your proceedings. They know that you are not a monarchy to-day, a republic to-morrow, and a military despotism the third day. They know that you are free from the vicissitudes that have marked the career of neighbouring nations. Your fathers and yourselves have earned this brilliant character for England. Do not forget it. Do not allow it to be tarnished. Show, if you will, the Pope of Rome, and his Cardinals, and his Church, that England, as well as Rome, has her *semper eadem*, and that when she has once adopted the great principle of legislation which is destined to influence her national character and mark her policy for ages to come and affect the whole nature of her influence among the nations of the world ; show that when she has done this slowly, and with hesitation and difficulty, but still deliberately, but once for all—she can no more retrace her steps than the river that bathes this giant city can flow backwards to its source. The character of England is in our hands."

The second reading of the Bill was carried in the Commons on the 25th of March by a majority of 343, the numbers being: Ayes, 438; Noes, 95. The ordinary lines of party were obliterated on this occasion, and Tories of the most old-fashioned type, and Whigs whose watchword was " Toleration," walked together into the lobby. Disraeli and Thesiger, Newdegate and Sibthorpe,

voted with Russell and Palmerston ; and the Peelites and High
Churchmen, Gladstone, Cardwell, Sir James Graham, and Sidney
Herbert, shared the defeat of the minority, with such advanced
Liberals and opponents of all ecclesiastical establishments as
John Bright, the Quaker, and W. J. Fox, the more than Uni-
tarian.

The Bill became law, and the agitation ceased.   Practically it
was almost a dead letter ; and in 1871 it was repealed.

In the debate on Supply, in July, Mr. Gladstone took occasion
to refer to the position of the Colonial bishops, who, he said,
laboured under great difficulties with respect to the government
of their dioceses.   A system of perfect religious equality prevailed, he said, in New South Wales, and all the Australian
colonies, and he contended that the House should proceed to
define the position of those bishops, clergy, and laity in communion with the Church of England, not by giving them the
status of an establishment, but by so emancipating them from the
trammels of the law in this country as to give them the freedom
that is enjoyed by other communities of Christians.   The
colonial bishops were in this position—they could not assemble
the clergy or laity from the different dioceses, and could form no
valid system of regulations to govern the Church, because they
did not know whether they would not be liable to a penalty
under an Act of the Imperial Parliament for assembling synods
or convocations without the consent of the Crown.   He hoped
the Government would take up the subject during the next
Session ; but if no ministerial measure was proposed, or if no
more competent person in either of the Houses undertook to
propose a remedy, he would do so himself.

CHAPTER X.

In December, 1851, the political world was excited by the announcement that Lord Palmerston was no longer a member of the Ministry. At a very critical time, when the *coup d'état* in France had made the relations between the two countries very delicate, the Foreign Secretary, without consultation with his colleagues, and without observing the usual practice of submitting all important despatches to the Queen, had written to Lord Normanby, the English ambassador in Paris, in terms of approval of the act of the Prince-President. The Queen highly disapproved of this conduct, and sent a memorandum on the subject to the Premier, accompanied by an expression of her wish that he should show it to Lord Palmerston. This was, of course, the preliminary to a dismissal of the Foreign Secretary, and Lord John Russell acted with promptitude. Lord Palmerston quitted the Cabinet, Earl Granville being transferred from the Board of Trade to the Foreign Office.

When Parliament met in February, 1852, the subject was prominently referred to in both Houses, in the debates on the Address. In the House of Commons, Lord John Russell said: "The noble Lord's course of proceeding in the matter he considered to be putting himself in the place of the Crown, and passing by the Crown, while he gave the moral approval of England to the acts of the President of the Republic of France, in direct opposition to the policy which the Government had hitherto pursued. Under the circumstances, he (Lord John Russell) had no alternative but to declare that while he was Prime Minister Lord Palmerston could not hold the seals of office; and he had assumed the entire responsibility of advising the Crown to require the resignation of his noble friend, who had forgotten or neglected what was due to the Crown and his colleagues."

Palmerston was ready to defend himself; and his speech was an excellent specimen of the good-humoured, dashing "sauciness," which when, as in his case, combined with great talents and associated with eminent public services, always pleases even opponents. He had, he said, only expressed his individual opinion to the

French Ambassador and the Marquis of Normanby, as the
Premier and other Cabinet Ministers had also in conversation
and other ways expressed their opinions. " It follows," he said—
and there was cheering and laughter from both sides of the
House when he finished the sentence—" that every member of
the Cabinet, whatever his political avocations may have been,
however much his attention may have been devoted to other
matters, is at liberty to express an opinion of passing events
abroad ; but the Secretary of State for Foreign Affairs, whose
peculiar duty it is to watch those events, who is unfit for his
office if he has not an opinion on them, is the only man not permitted to express an opinion ; and, when a Foreign Minister
comes and tells him that he has news, he is to remain silent, like
a speechless doll or the mute of some Eastern pacha." If anybody
had told Palmerston that, as Foreign Secretary, his utterances
on Foreign Affairs carried no more weight than those of the
Ministers in charge of other departments of State, he would have
been prompt enough to vindicate his position, and claim that his
words should carry official weight, while the words of others were
merely the expressions of individual opinion. But he would
scarcely have claimed that any opinions he might hold, on the
subject of finance, for instance, would be of as much public importance as the opinion of the Chancellor of the Exchequer. That
he *was* Foreign Secretary at the time when he chatted so unre-
servedly to the French Ambassador, and wrote so freely to Lord
Normanby, was a sufficient reason why he should have been quite
certain that his views were in accordance with those of the Ministry responsible to the country for the conduct of foreign as
well as domestic affairs.

Palmerston quitted the Treasury bench, and the Russell administration was drawing to an end. On the 9th of February the
Premier obtained leave to bring in a new Reform Bill ; and probably desired to complete—at least so far as he thought it required
completion—his great work of 1832. But the best laid schemes
of statesmen, like those " of mice and men, gang aft agee." Before the time appointed for the first reading, he was called upon
to explain the Militia scheme of the Government, and moved for
a Committee of the whole House to take into consideration the
Local Militia Acts. He proposed to revive the Local Militia,
instituted in 1808 and suspended in 1816. This force, which
during that period numbered about 213,000 men, consisted of a
force for each county six times as numerous as the proper Militia
quota ; comprising, of course, many who, from age or other cir-

cumstances, were ineligible for the regular Militia. These troops could only be marched beyond the limits of their respective counties in the event of an invasion. The regular Militia can be embodied at any time of emergency, on the responsibility of the Government, and employed as a defensive or garrison force, setting free the regular army for aggressive operations. The force is highly valued as a training school for the regular army, into which many of the best men, physically and morally, enlist.

The opposition to the Government scheme was led by Lord Palmerston, who now had his opportunity for retaliation. He moved the omission of the word "local," and advocated an increase of the regular Militia, which he thought was justified by the critical position of public affairs. "What the country wanted," he said, " was a regular Militia, a force which had existed nearly two hundred years, whereas a local Militia was an occasional force for a particular emergency." On a division Ministers were defeated by a majority of 11 ; and Lord John Russell stated that he considered the result tantamount to a vote of want of confidence. A few days afterwards he announced to the Commons, and the Marquis of Lansdowne to the Lords, that Ministers had placed their resignations in the hands of the Sovereign.

A writer in the *Annual Register* says: " The event created little surprise, the progressive feebleness of the Cabinet and its measures having for some time prepared the public mind for a change. It was generally felt that the catastrophe was a mere question of time, and that the defeat which immediately preceded the crisis was but one of the many causes which contributed to produce it."

The Earl of Derby received the royal command to form a Ministry, and by the 27th of February his arrangements. were completed. It is generally understood that he offered Mr. Gladstone a place in the Cabinet, but that the offer was declined. The Peelites, or Liberal Conservatives—of whom, since the death of Sir Robert, Mr. Gladstone had been the most conspicuous member in the lower House—were too identified with an advanced commercial and financial policy to cast in their lot with the party led by Lord Derby ; but they had not as yet joined the Whigs, and might be looked upon generally as independent supporters of the Government. Respecting Free Trade, the Government held itself in reserve. The Parliament, which had assembled in November, 1847, was dying out ; the Conservatives were in a minority, and must trust to the issue of the imminent general election for the possibility of being able to carry on public affairs. In his first speech as Premier, the Earl of Derby said that his individual

opinion was in favour of the principle advocated by Sir Robert
Peel in 1842, and which was similar to the American system--" the
freest admission of raw materials, but the imposition of duties
principally and avowedly on those articles which enter into competition with the produce of our own soil and industry." He
could, he declared, see no grounds why the article of corn should
be a solitary exception from the general system of imposing
duties on foreign imports; but he was prepared firmly to abide by
whatever verdict the country might pronounce at the forthcoming
general election on the merits of Free Trade. If that verdict were
favourable, he avowed his intention, notwithstanding his own
opinion on the subject remained unchanged, to accept and adhere
to the decision of the country. If the issue should be different,
he was equally prepared to give effect to the public wishes. In
the House of Commons, Mr. Disraeli, for the first time a Cabinet
Minister, holding the important office of Chancellor of the Exchequer, made a similar statement.

Mr. Gladstone urged the Government to make the appeal to
the country with as little delay as possible; but there was a considerable amount of necessary business to be disposed of before
the dissolution could take place.

On the 29th of March, Mr. Spencer Walpole, the Secretary of
State for the Home Department, introduced the new Militia Bill,
in which the principle of a local Militia was abandoned, and provision was made for greatly strengthening the general force. It
was in the debate on the Bill that the amiable Home Secretary,
one of those good people who take everything in earnest, adopted
as serious an after-dinner joke of the Earl of Derby's, and gravely
announced that it was the intention of the Government to confer
a Parliamentary vote on every militiaman of a certain standing in
the force—an announcement he withdrew on the following night
amid the laughter of the House. The perilous position of the
Continental Powers, just escaped from the great revolutionary
wave, and the uncertainty with regard to the action of the Prince-
President of France, whose ambition to revive the Empire was
known to all the world, made it imperative on the Government to
strengthen the military power of the country; and by increasing
and organising the Militia that end would be best obtained. The
Bill passed both Houses with little difficulty; and in the Lords,
the Duke of Wellington, in almost his last Parliamentary utterance—he died in less than six months afterwards—gave the great
weight of his unrivalled authority and experience to the ministerial
plan. He said: "We have never up to this moment maintained

a proper peace establishment—that is the real truth. . . . For the last ten years you have never had in your army more men than enough to relieve the sentries on duty at your stations in the different parts of the world."

In the spring of the year, another ecclesiastical matter had greatly excited the public mind, and in due course became the subject of Parliamentary discussion. The Rev. Mr. Bennett, whose High Church practices at St. Paul's, Knightsbridge, had alarmed the Evangelicals but had greatly pleased the Ritualists, was instituted to the vicarage of Frome, Somerset, by the Bishop of Bath and Wells, in face of very energetic protests. It was contended that the Bishop had acted in excess of his authority, and confounded the true principles of the Church of England. Mr. Horsman—a man of considerable ability, and possessed of great rhetorical power, whose supercilious and patronising manner earned in after years Disraeli's description of him as "the superior person of the House of Commons"—moved an address to the Queen, asking for "an inquiry whether respect was paid to the decrees of the Constitution and Canons Ecclesiastical of the Church of England in the recent institution of the Rev. Mr. Bennett to the vicarage of Frome."

The Chancellor of the Exchequer opposed the motion on the part of the Government, and was supported by Mr. Gladstone. The motion was negatived, but on the 8th of June, Mr. Horsman renewed the subject by moving for a Select Committee of the House to enquire into the circumstances connected with the institution of Mr. Bennett. Mr. Gladstone opposed this motion also, and defended the Bishop of Bath and Wells, who had, he maintained, done his duty. He had no objection to an inquiry into the whole subject of ecclesiastical appointments, and the state of the law on the matter generally. Such an inquiry would confer one of the greatest possible services on the country, and materially contribute to the stability of the Church of England. In his reply, Mr. Horsman said: "The right honourable gentleman, member for the University of Oxford, was a practical debater, a zealous theologian, a subtle reasoner; and he had shown himself that night to be by no means a contemptible casuist. The right honourable gentleman had addressed the House as if he held a brief upon the question, and most ably did he play the advocate for the accused." The motion was again opposed from the Treasury bench, but carried by a majority of 45, and the Committee was appointed.

On the 22nd of April, Mr. Milner Gibson, representing the Free

Traders, appeared as the champion of the movement for repealing the " Taxes on Knowledge," and introduced a resolution in
favour of the repeal of the paper duty.   The Chancellor of the
Exchequer opposed it on financial grounds, without reference to
the merits of the question ; and, after several vigorous speeches,
the debate was adjourned till the 12th of May, and then Mr
Gladstone spoke in opposition to the motion, supporting Mr.
Disraeli. " He would be heartily glad, " he said, " when the time
came for the paper duty to be repealed ; but they should have the
whole case, and the whole state of the revenue before them, before
entering on a discussion of that kind.   It was most imprudent
for members of Parliament, when they were under a strong impression of the disadvantage of a particular tax, to pledge themselves to its unconditional repeal."   He took occasion, in the
course of his speech, to attack the booksellers for keeping up the
price of books, by trade restrictions of " a most imprudent and
unwarrantable character "; and said : " I venture to say that the
whole system of the bookselling trade of this country, except so
far as it is partially neutralised by what are called cheap publications, is a disgrace to our present state of civilisation."   We read
these remarks with some surprise in these days of good and cheap
literature, when the best books can be bought for prices which
scarcely appear sufficient to cover the expense of paper and print.
    Mr. Milner Gibson's resolution was negatived by a majority of
88 (Mr. Gladstone did not vote); and resolutions for the abolition
of the newspaper stamp and the duty on advertisements were
also lost by majorities respectively of 99 and 65.
    In a similar spirit, Mr. Gladstone supported Mr. Disraeli's
Budget, which was necessarily of a temporary character, for the
real financial policy of the Derby Government could not be re-
vealed until the decision of the constituencies had been given.
The leading feature of the Budget was the continuance for another
year of the income and property tax, imposed by the last Administration.   Mr. Gladstone took occasion to compliment the
Chancellor of the Exchequer on the manner in which he had
introduced the financial statement.   He might have been suspected of a little touch of *badinage*, if not, indeed, of satire, when
praising the first appearance in the character of finance minister
of the brilliant novelist and poet, the man of imagination and
epigram, whose political career had been almost as dramatic
as any of the creations of his own brain.   But Mr. Gladstone
was always in earnest, and the faculty of humour is not a remarkably conspicuous element of his capacious intellect. He accepted

the Chancellor's statement of the financial position of the country as a proof that the commercial policy initiated by Sir Robert Peel had borne good fruit. "He should have been perfectly satisfied to have allowed the case of the commercial policy of the last few years to remain on the very able statement of the right honourable gentleman, who had, in a manner highly honourable to him, and in a manner peculiarly his own, laid before the House the result of that policy."

On another subject Mr. Gladstone opposed the Ministry and caused its defeat. St. Albans and Sudbury had been disfranchised as a punishment for flagrant electoral corruption; and the Government proposed to allot the four seats so rendered vacant to other constituencies. On the 10th of May, Mr. Disraeli moved for leave to introduce a Bill for the purpose; and in the course of a long speech, in which he weighed the claims of the metropolitan boroughs and other places, proposed to give two more members to the West Riding of Yorkshire and two to the Southern Division of Lancashire. Mr. Gladstone argued that there was no pressing necessity to enter on the question; no sufficient reason why the number of members should be fixed at what Mr. Disraeli had described as "the constitutional number of members of the House." "It appears," he said, "upon the clearest evidence, that the idea of any legal title or constitutional virtue attaching to the number 658 is as pure a fiction as ever entered the mind of man. It appears a matter of fact, patent and notorious to all the world, that, for the last eight years, during three ministries and with a general election intervening, we have fallen short of the constitutional number." He moved: "That the House do pass to the order of the day." The division showed a majority against the Government of 86, the numbers being: Ayes, 148; Noes, 234. It might have been supposed that the proposition to give four additional members to the great manufacturing districts would have received the support of representatives of commercial constituencies; but Mr. Cobden, one of the representatives of the West Riding, and Mr. Bright, member for Manchester, went into the lobby among the majority with Mr. Gladstone and the Peelites, who, on their part, rubbed shoulders with Mr. Duncombe and Mr. Wakley, the Radical representatives of Finsbury.

The Ministry, however, received Mr. Gladstone's support of the Bill for giving a responsible constitution to New Zealand, introduced by Sir John Pakington, Secretary of State for the Colonies.

A considerable amount of time was lost in the debate on a motion by Mr. Spooner, member for North Warwickshire, who

proposed the appointment of a select committee to enquire into
the system of education followed at Maynooth. He condemned
the instruction given on the ground that it tended to weaken the
allegiance of the students to a Protestant Sovereign, and incul-
cated and defended immorality. Mr. Spooner and other ultra-
Protestants declared that spiritual allegiance to the Pope must be
incompatible with temporal allegiance to the English Sovereign,
and that the practice of the confessional sapped the foundations
of morality. Mr. Spencer Walpole, on the part of the Government, supported the motion for enquiry. Mr. Gladstone, too,
supported it; but insisted that the proposed enquiry should be
conducted under the immediate superintendence, and on the
responsibility of the executive Government, and not by any individual, however great his eminence and gifts. " Respecting the
Parliamentary grant to Maynooth," he said, " if this endowment
be withdrawn, the Parliament which withdraws it must be prepared to enter upon the whole subject of a reconstruction of the
ecclesiastical arrangements of Ireland." These words greatly
alarmed Sir Robert Inglis, who understood them to indicate that
his colleague in the representation of the Oxford University was
not indisposed to reconsider the status of the Irish Church. Sir
Robert was a good man, but did not possess the gift of prophecy,
and was probably spared considerable mental anxiety by not
being able to foresee what his colleague would achieve in 1871.
On the 9th of June, after protracted debates, Mr. Spooner's
motion dropped—killed by a Wednesday sitting.

The development of Church of England principles in the British
colonies had for a long time been an object dear to Mr. Gladstone's heart; but he also entertained a clear perception that
the Church, as an institution, must be modified in its action in
the new communities, where it could not be allied with the Government, as he desired it to be in the mother country. The political
equality of sects, which he was not disposed to concede here,
must be recognised there, where all parties claimed equal privileges. As matters stood, the members of the Anglican Church
were at a disadvantage in the colonies, for they had not the power
of self-government which the Nonconformist churches possessed,
nor the parochial organisation, synodic action, and right of appeal
to regularly constituted ecclesiastical courts which Churchmen at
home possessed. Clergymen in the colonies had no defence
against the bishop of the diocese if he were disposed to make a
hasty or arbitrary use of his power; they were not parochial incumbents, but practically the curates of the bishops, and it was

doubtful if they were entitled to appeal to the Archbishop of
Canterbury. The Bishop of Tasmania claimed to be empowered
by the terms of his letters patent to establish ecclesiastical courts
in his diocese ; but the Nonconformists of the colony discovered,
to his discomfiture, that the letters patent on which he relied
were illegal, as the Queen's prerogative did not enable her to
confer that power. All the episcopal communities in the Australian
and American colonies asked for a remedy for their grievances ;
and, in the hope of affording it, Mr. Gladstone brought in the
Colonial Bishops Bill.

In moving the second reading, on the 22nd of April, he said
the principle which he had endeavoured to carry out was that of
leaving the colonies (subject to any restraints needful on imperial
grounds) to the uncontrolled management of their own local
affairs, whether for ecclesiastical or civil purposes. He said :—

"I must not attempt to disguise from the House that the principle upon which
I wish to proceed with reference to this Bill is that of religious equality. If I am
asked how I can justify such a course with my duties to a constituency formed
in great part of the clergy of the Established Church, I say at once that it is
my paramount duty to promote, by any means in my power, the interests of
that religious system to which they belong ; and I feel convinced, after not a
brief study of colonial affairs, that I should be taking a course detrimental and
ruinous to those interests if I were to refrain from recognising, or hesitate to
recognise, any measure for the Church of England in the colonies which had
for its basis the principle of perfect religious equality as the principle of
colonial legislation. . . . I will frankly state, in the face of the House
of Commons, that if any man offered me for the Church of England in the
colonies the boon of civil preference, I would reject the boon as a fatal
gift ; convinced that any such preference would be nothing but a source of
weakness to the Church itself, and of difficulty and discord to the colonial
communities, in the soil of which he wanted to see her take a free, strong,
and healthy root."

At first the Ministry seemed disposed to give the Bill a favourable consideration ; but Sir John Pakington, the Secretary for the
Colonies, wished for time to consider its provisions, and the
debate was adjourned for three weeks. When the subject again
came before the House, he strenuously opposed the Bill ; and,
yielding to circumstances, Mr. Gladstone declined to press the
Bill to a division.

In the division by which Mr. Locke King's County Franchise
Bill was lost, Mr. Gladstone's name appears in the majority.

The urgent business having been disposed of, Parliament was
dissolved on the 1st of July; and Ministers and members prepared for the great appeal to the decision of the country.
As the elections proceeded, it became increasingly evident that

there would not be such a decisive majority in favour of the restoration of Protection as would justify the Government in attempting to reverse the policy of Free Trade.

Mr. Gladstone's seat for the University of Oxford was threatened. His resolute assertion of independence as a representative, and his utterances respecting Church matters, had offended and alarmed many among his clerical constituents ; and a considerable number of members of the constituency determined to oppose his re-election. They signed a declaration that they were " compelled, by their sense of duty at the present crisis, to declare that, notwithstanding their high respect for the personal character, literary attainments, and acknowledged talents of the Right Honourable W. E. Gladstone, they considered him, since he has opposed, by his speeches and votes, the judgment pronounced by Convocation on questions of great importance, to be no longer a suitable representative of the University in Parliament." Dr. Marsham, the Warden of Merton, was requested to come forward as a candidate.

Then, as now, many practices which at other times everybody would stigmatise as dishonest, and many statements which everybody knows to be false, were resorted to as legitimate tactics. " All is fair in elections," is a principle deeply grafted in the mind of the average Englishman, who appears to think that some mysterious power gives dispensation from the observance of the rules of ordinary morality between the time of issuing the writ and announcing the result of the poll. In this instance, the Oxford University election of 1852, a wide publicity was given to assertions that Mr. Gladstone had changed his views on the relation of Church and State, and that the legitimate development of the principles he now held would lead to the abandonment of the connection between the two. Mr. Gladstone felt it incumbent on him to reply to these statements; and he did so in a letter to Mr. Greswell, of Worcester College, Chairman of his Oxford Committee. He asserted that his principles were unchanged, that he was aware of no incompatibility between the principle of full religious freedom and the maintenance of the National Church in connection with the State, to both of which he was, as ever, cordially attached. He added— and the remark was characteristic of the man—that if he had changed his opinions, he should not have left it to others to announce it to the world.

The election lasted four days, and the result was that Sir Robert Inglis, the old and honoured member, headed the poll with 1,369 votes; Mr. Gladstone polled 1,108 ; and Dr. Marsham, 758.   By a clear majority, therefore, of 350, Mr. Gladstone was again returned to the House of Commons as representative of the University.   It will be noticed that the votes given for Mr Gladstone exceeded by 111 those recorded at the previous election in 1847.

The new Parliament met on the 4th of November, and, the preliminary business of electing a Speaker and swearing-in the members having been disposed of, was formally opened by the Queen on the 11th.   The most interesting paragraph of the Speech was that which referred to the Free Trade policy—at that time the paramount question :—

"It gives me pleasure to be enabled, by the blessing of Providence, to congratulate you on the generally improved condition of the country, and especially of the industrious classes.   If you should be of opinion that recent legislation, in contributing, with other causes, to the happy result, has at the same time inflicted unavoidable injury on certain important interests, I recommend you dispassionately to consider how far it may be practicable equitably to mitigate that injury, and to enable the industry of the country to meet successfully that unrestricted competition to which Parliament, in its wisdom, has decided that it should be subject."

In the debate in the Lords on the Address, the Earl of Derby said :—" With regard to the policy of free trade, he did not hesitate to say that, after the opinion pronounced by the country, he was prepared to bow to its decision ; and, while desirous as far as possible to mitigate the injury inflicted by that policy, to adopt it, and carry it out frankly and loyally."

Mr. Disraeli spoke to the same purpose in the Commons, and their speeches were the farewell to the policy of Protection. Henceforth Free Trade was practically an item of British political faith.   The Conservative leaders accepted their defeat with grace, and manfully avowed their faithful allegiance to the new order of things.   It did not, however, suit the temper of the Free Traders, pure and simple, to accept the new adherents and their policy without an attempt to exult over the victory.   They determined, if possible, to make their former opponents drain to the dregs the cup of humiliation.

It was, of course, known to all that one of the first tasks of the Ministry must be the preparation of a Budget framed in accordance with the policy they had adopted as their own.   The Free Traders, however, determined to anticipate the discussion that must arise on the financial propositions by binding the House to an emphatic assertion of Free Trade principles, worded in such a manner that it would carry an effective condemnation of the past

G

conduct of those who had previously supported Protection. Mr.
Charles Villiers, member for Wolverhampton, one of the ablest
of the Anti-Corn Law champions, moved a resolution expressing
the approval of the House of the Free Trade policy, and asserting
that the Act of 1846, which established the free admission of
foreign corn, was a " wise, just, and beneficial measure."

A large number of members on both sides of the House felt
that these words were unnecessary, that the victory was gained,
and that it was ungenerous to hurl adjectives at the heads of
the defeated opponents of the measure ; and Lord Palmerston,
—who, as he once said, was always ready to hit as hard as he
could when engaged in a fight, but quite ready to forget all about
it afterwards—moved an amendment to the effect : " That the
improved condition of the country, and especially of the industrious classes, is mainly the result of recent legislation, which has
established the principle of unrestricted competition, has abolished
taxes imposed for the purposes of Protection, and has thereby
diminished the cost and increased the abundance of the principal articles of the food of the people." Mr. Disraeli, the Chancellor of the Exchequer, withdrew an amendment he had proposed
and accepted that of Lord Palmerston. He strongly objected to
the words " wise, just, and beneficial," employed by Mr. Villiers,
describing them as " three odious epithets." The divisions took
place in a very full House. The resolution proposed by Mr.
Villiers was rejected by a majority of 80 ; and Lord Palmerston's
accepted by a majority of 415, only 53 voting against it.

Mr. Gladstone made a long and, even for him, remarkably eloquent and earnest speech, in support of Palmerston's amendment,
which, he said, would have ensured the approval of Sir Robert
Peel ; and he proceeded to refer to the political career of that
great statesman :—

" It is our honour and our pride to be his followers ; and I say, if we
are his followers, let us imitate him in that magnanimity which was one of
the most distinguished characteristics of the man. When Sir Robert Peel
severed a political connection of thirty-five years' standing, he knew and felt
the price he was paying for the performance of his duty. It was no small
matter, in an advanced stage of life like his, to break up, and to break up
for ever, too, its habits and its associations. He looked, indeed, for his
revenge—but for what revenge did he look ? He did not seek for vindication
through the medium of any stinging speeches or motions made or carried in
favour of his policy, if they bore a sense of pain or degradation to the minds
of honourable men. His vindication was this : he knew the wisdom of his
measures would secure their acceptance ; he knew those who opposed them
for erroneous opinions would acknowledge them after competent experience ;
he looked to see them established in the esteem and in the judgment of the

country; he looked to see them govern by some degree the policy of every
nation in the civilised world; he knew he would have his reward—first of all
in the enormous good that he was the instrument, in the hand of Providence,
of effecting; and, secondly, in the reputation which he knew would be his
own appropriate desert.   And as to that aristocracy whose purposes he might
feel he was then somewhat violently thwarting, I am convinced that, with a
prophetic eye, he anticipated the day when every man who reviled him, if
they were men, as he believed them to be, of honest judgment and intention—
though perhaps using towards him opprobrious language, never so ill-deserved
—that they were men who would in the course of time see that he never
rendered them so great and solid a service as when, with the whole power of
the Government, he proposed to Parliament the repeal of the Corn Laws.
His belief was that their cause was a great and sacred cause; that the aristocracy of England were elements in its political and social system with which
the welfare of the country was inseparably bound up; and to him it was a
noble object of ambition to redeem such a cause from associations with a
policy originally adopted in a state of imperfect knowledge and with erroneous views, but which, when the clear light of the day was poured upon it,
should be found, in the daily experience, and in the light and view of the
thinking portion of the community, to bear the character of much that was
sordid and much that was false.   .   .   .   This is the vindication to which he
looked, and seeing that we are now celebrating the obsequies of this obnoxious
policy, and are now seeking to adopt a declaration admitted on all hands to
be perfectly clear in its assertion of the principle of Free Trade, if we still
cherish the desire to trample on those who have fought manfully, and been
defeated fairly, let us endeavour to put it away from ourselves, to rejoice in
the great public good that has been achieved, and let us take courage, from
the attainment of that good, for the performance of public duty in future.'

Great applause from both sides of the House greeted this
earnest vindication of the character and policy of Peel, and the
implied reproof of the indiscreet exultation of the Anti-Corn Law
party.

On the 3rd of December, Mr. Disraeli brought forward the
anxiously expected financial statement.   In his introductory
speech he said that, as the principle of unrestricted competition
had been finally adopted as the principle of our commercial
system, he desired to blend the financial system and the commercial code more harmoniously together, and to remove many well-
founded causes of discontent among the people.   The chief
alterations he proposed to make were the reduction of the light
dues on shipping, of the malt tax by one half, of the tea duty
immediately from 2s. 2½d. per lb. to 1s. 10d., and ultimately to
1s., the reduction to be spread over six years, and of the hop
duty by one half.   These remissions would involve a loss to the
revenue of more than £3,000,000, to supply which he proposed
to impose the income tax on industrial incomes above £100, and
on incomes derived from property above £50, and on funded
property and salaries in Ireland; and to extend the house tax to

houses rated at not less than £10 a year, private houses 1s. 6d. and shops 1s. in the pound.

The debate on the Budget propositions, when, after the interval of a few days, the formal resolutions were brought forward, lasted four nights. The public feeling in opposition to the house tax, especially in the metropolis and large towns, was very strongly expressed, and in the House the Opposition made it one of the strong points in their resistance to the financial scheme. Sir Charles Wood, the Chancellor of the Exchequer in the last Whig ministry, said: "The direct taxes proposed would subject large numbers of the poorer classes to taxation for the first time, and although exemptions were said to be a vice in direct taxation, the income tax was applied to Ireland with exemptions that would make it partial and odious, as well as a breach of national faith. Nothing could be so bad as the Budget, which prodigally sacrificed revenue and tampered with the credit of the country." Mr. Gladstone argued that the extension of the income tax to fundholders in Ireland was a breach of public faith with the national creditor.

On the last night of the debate, Mr. Disraeli replied to the objections raised. He said the Ministers were opposed by a coalition, but he appealed from that to the public opinion of the country. He especially referred to Sir James Graham (who, of all the Peelites, seems to have been most disliked by the Conservatives) as "one whom he would not say he greatly respected, but whom he greatly regarded."

No sooner had the Chancellor of the Exchequer resumed his seat than Mr. Gladstone rose. It was evident that he was prepared to make a great effort, and the expectation raised was not disappointed. He spoke with, even for him, extraordinary energy, beginning with a direct personal attack on Mr. Disraeli for "the license of language he had used, and the phrases he had applied to public men." The surplus on which the Chancellor of the Exchequer prided himself consisted only of the Exchequer Loan Fund, which was a surplus of borrowed money, and it was clear there was an actual deficiency. He continued:—

"I vote against the Budget not only because I disapprove upon general grounds of the principles of that Budget, but emphatically and peculiarly because, in my conscience—though it may be an erroneous belief—it is my firm conviction that the Budget is one, I will not say the most radical, but I will say the most subversive in its tendencies and ultimate effects which I have ever known submitted to the House. It is the most regardless of those general rules of prudence which it is absolutely necessary we should preserve, and which it is perfectly impossible that this House, as a popular assembly, should observe, unless the Government sets us the example, and uses its influence to keep us in the right course. Sir, the House of Commons is a noble assembly, worthy of its historical and traditional associations ; but it is too much to expect that we should teach the Executive its duty in elementary matters of administration and finance. If I vote against the Government, I vote in support of those Conservative principles which, I thank God, are common in a great degree to all parties in the British House of Commons, but of which I thought it was the peculiar pride and glory of the Conservative party to be the champions and the leaders. .   .   .   . You are now asked to vote for a Budget which consecrates, as it were, the principle of a deficiency, which endangers the public credit of the country, and which may peril our safety. . . I feel it my duty to use that freedom of speech which, I am sure, as Englishmen, you will tolerate, when I tell you that, if you give your assent and your high authority to this most unsound and destructive principle on which the financial scheme of the Government is based—you may refuse my appeal now, you may accompany the right honourable gentleman the Chancellor of the Exchequer into the lobby, but my belief is that the day will come when you will look back upon this vote, as its consequences, sooner or later, unfold themselves, with bitter, but with late and ineffectual regret. "

He concluded by moving " the previous question " as an amendment to the resolution affecting the inhabited house duty, and the Government was defeated by a majority of 19, the numbers being 305 against 286—Whigs, Peelites, and advanced Radicals uniting to defeat the Ministerial proposition. On the motion of Mr. Disraeli the House immediately adjourned.

On Monday, the 20th of December, the Earl of Derby announced in the House of Lords the resignation of the Ministry, and that the Earl of Aberdeen had undertaken the formation of a new administration. He reiterated the assertion of Mr. Disraeli that there had been a deliberate combination against the Government. " We have had," he said, "some curious revelations made to us by a right honourable baronet [Sir James Graham], a member of the other House, who has lifted the curtain, admitted us behind the scenes, shown us the actors preparing for their parts, and discussing the most convenient phrases to be adopted in order to obtain that universal concurrence which is necessary to accomplish their object, and studiously concealing their measures so as to place the Government in a minority."

The Duke of Newcastle (who, when Earl of Lincoln, in the House of Commons, had been one of the staunchest of the supporters of Sir Robert Peel, and the close ally of Mr. Gladstone) followed the Earl of Derby, and contradicted the statement respecting a combination adverse to the Ministry. What Sir James Graham had done was that, with others, he had endeavoured to prepare a resolution which should unite all the friends of Free Trade, and, at the same time, be separate from all measures of hostility, or even appearance of opposition to the Government.

On the same day, Mr. Disraeli, in the House of Commons, announced the resignation of the Ministry, and took occasion to express regret if, in the heat of debate, he had hurt the feelings of any gentleman in the House. There was a general interchange of amiabilities, Sir James Graham, Sir Charles Wood, and others retracting any strong language they might have employed, and uniting in complimenting Mr. Disraeli on the ability he had shown in discharging the duties of leader of the House.

A week afterwards the Earl of Aberdeen was able to announce that he had succeeded in forming an administration, and the Houses adjourned till the 10th of February, 1853.

The Earl of Aberdeen, who at the age of sixty-eight attained the highest of political honours, had been accepted as the leader of the Peelite section—party it could scarcely be called—which, since the death of Sir Robert, had played so remarkable a part in Parliamentary politics. It was neither Tory nor Whig, but occupied a middle position between the two parties—attached to Church and State, very averse to Radical theories, but perceptive of economical truths, and sincerely patriotic and desirous to ameliorate the condition of the country. Direct, in preference to indirect taxation, was a maxim of the Peelites; and by the remission of imposts on articles of first necessity, Sir Robert Peel and his disciple in finance, Mr. Gladstone, had conferred incalculable benefit on the industrial classes. The Earl of Aberdeen had been Foreign Secretary under the Duke of Wellington, Colonial Secretary in Sir Robert Peel's first administration, and afterwards Foreign Secretary again.

CHAPTER XI.

THE "travelled Thane, Athenian Aberdeen," of Byron's "English
Bards and Scotch Reviewers," found himself at the head of a
Ministry of a composite character, in which, however, the Peelites
were well represented. Mr. Gladstone, who had so successfully
thrown the late Chancellor of the Exchequer in the great financial
struggle, was obviously entitled, by the great ability he had displayed, to assume the vacant office. The Duke of Newcastle
was appointed Secretary for the Colonies, Sir James Graham
went to the Admiralty, Mr. Cardwell to the Board of Trade, and
Mr. Sidney Herbert became Secretary of War. The Whigs contributed Lord John Russell, who took the seals of the Foreign
Office; Lord Palmerston was Home Secretary (quite a new
position for him, but one which he filled admirably); Earl
Granville presided at the Council; the Duke of Argyll was Lord
Privy Seal; Sir Charles Wood, President of the India Board;
and Lord Cranworth, Lord Chancellor; while the veteran
Marquis of Lansdowne, holding no office, added strength to the
Cabinet. The philosophical Radical, Sir William Molesworth,
accepted office as Chief Commissioner of Public Works.

There was certainly a considerable breaking down of party ties
in the formation of the famous Coalition Ministry; and Colonel
Sibthorpe, who was more noted for comical utterances than for
political astuteness, expressed dismal forebodings as to the future,
and prophesied a speedy disruption of the discordant elements.

The re-elections necessitated by the acceptance of office
followed with as little delay as possible. On the 6th of January,
1853, the nomination of candidates for Oxford University took
place. The growing Liberalism of Mr. Gladstone had encouraged
the idea that he was not so "sound" on Church questions as the
extreme Protestant and Church and State party desired, and an
opposition candidate was brought forward in the person of Mr.
Dudley Perceval, of Christ Church, son of Mr. Spencer Perceval,
who was shot by Bellingham in the lobby of the House of
Commons.

The new candidate was proposed by Archdeacon Denison,

who said Mr. Perceval was "noted for the warmth of his opposition to the errors and superstitions of the Romish Church and
the Papal tyranny. He regretted that a sense of public duty
made it incumbent on him to call on them to reject one who had
already represented them, but the nature of the present crisis
made it of paramount importance that the University should be
represented by a man whose most strenuous efforts would be
given to the maintenance of public order, the safety of the Church,
and the advancement of its interests."

Dr. R. Phillimore supported Mr. Gladstone's candidature.
"He knew," he said, "how greatly his right honourable friend had
suffered from the etiquette which prevented him from appearing
and giving in person a truthful reply to the calumnies of which
he had been the object; but he could, better than any other
man living, afford to be deprived of the advantage he would have
gained by the prevalence of a different custom, for he had the
shield of an unblemished character, the same noble reputation
which he bore when one of the most distinguished undergraduates
of that University, the same spotless moral character, and the
same intellectual eminence, refined and improved by time and
experience. He (Dr. Phillimore) well remembered the time
when his right honourable friend, avoiding the vices incident to
youth, yet retaining unimpaired all the gentleness, sweetness,
and forbearance of his disposition, was the ornament and pride of
the undergraduates of the University. He thought he might ask,
with all confidence, was there a man living who had reflected
more credit on the system under which he was educated and the
place in which he was brought up?"

At the close of the poll Mr. Gladstone was returned by 1,022
votes, giving a majority of 124 over his opponent.

The new Chancellor of the Exchequer was soon in harness,
and ready for the financial fray in which that important political
functionary is destined to pass the greater portion of his official
existence. On the 8th of April he introduced resolutions on
the subject of the National Debt, proposing to liquidate certain
minor stocks, viz., the South Sea, Old and New South Sea
Annuities, Bank Annuities (1726), and the Three per Cent.
Annuities (1751), the total amount to be dealt with being about
£9,500,000. These stocks, differing only in denomination,
perpetuated a certain complexity in the Debt, and Mr. Gladstone
proposed that they should be converted, or paid off, at the
option of the holders; and by this plan estimated that an annual
present saving of £25,000 would be effected. He also pro-

posed to issue Exchequer Bonds, bearing interest at the rate of £2 15*s.* per cent. to September 1, 1864, and £2 10*s.* to September 1, 1874. The total amount of stock converted was not to exceed £30,000,000.

The object of the conversion of stock and the issue of Exchequer Bonds was "to lay the foundation of a permanent form of irredeemable public debt—irredeemable, I mean, at the option of the holders—bearing an interest of 2½ per cent."

Mr. Disraeli, being in opposition, no doubt felt bound to defend "the elegant simplicity of the Three per Cents.," and object to the proposed change, and probably was not personally indisposed to ridicule the first financial proposals of his rival. He compared the explanations of Mr. Gladstone to that chapter in the works of Thomas Aquinas which speculated as to how many angels could dance on the point of a needle. "Every age," he said, "has its great object ; this is the financial age, and its great object is, at all costs and by whatever means, to create a Two and a Half per Cent. Stock." The resolutions were carried, and Bills to embody them ordered to be brought in.

Some of the leaders of the Free Trade agitation now directed their energies to the work of removing what were known, in the political language of the day, as the taxes on knowledge—the advertisement duty, the compulsory stamp on newspapers, and the paper duty. On the 14th of April, Mr. Milner Gibson moved three resolutions in favour of the repeal of these imposts. It was within four days of the time when the Chancellor was to bring forward his financial statement, and he would have been most painfully embarrassed if fettered by resolutions of this kind, passed after he had prepared his Budget. He moved the previous question, and warmly condemned the passing of abstract resolutions in favour of repealing taxation without knowing the state of the finances. He said :—

"Large portions of the House had shown a very strong inclination to vote away the funds by which the public charges were to be met, at the tolerably rapid rate of £1,000,000 a week. That is a serious state of things for the House to consider. If the House was disposed to think that the best mode of managing the finances of the country were by these successive votes at the instance of individual members, regulated by all the chances and accidents that determined which motion should come first—if they thought it a safe course to encourage these motions and divisions with respect to them, then he had no more to say, except to suggest a public economy which might be very acceptable to many—a particular reduction, not a general economy—the total abolition of the office he had the honour to hold. He knew no conceivable reason why a gentleman should be appointed with a considerable salary, and decorated with a certain title, as steward of the public revenue, and guardian of the public credit, and responsible for presenting to the House, in some tolerable shape, a balance between the expenditure and the income of the year, if the House, which was supreme in all these matters, was deliberately of opinion that the best mode of dealing with them was by condemning on successive motion days one sum after another."

This vigorous remonstrance, aided by the support of the Opposition, ensured the defeat of two of the resolutions by considerable majorities ; but that respecting the advertisement duty was carried by a majority of 31.

The night of the 18th is memorable in the history of the House, and very remarkable in the history of Mr. Gladstone's political career. He occupied five hours in unfolding his financial scheme, and was, it was said, the first statesman who had made a Budget interesting, not only on account of its own financial features, but also from the method of explaining them. His speech was a brilliant success, and enhanced even his great reputation for oratorical ability and power of grasping and arranging the details of an intricate subject.

He began with an announcement of remission and reduction. The soap duty was to be taken off—a boon alike to the manufacturer (who was annoyed by the supervision of an officer of Excise prying into his vats and examining his packages) and to the public, who found cleanliness then an expensive luxury. The duty on life assurances, a tax on prudence, was to be reduced from half-a-crown per cent. to sixpence. A more startling novelty still was the substitution of penny receipt stamps for the expensive stamps which had varied in proportion to the amount paid, but the limit at which a stamped receipt was necessary was extended from £5 to £2. The duty on attorneys' certificates, on articles of apprenticeship to attorneys, and on the ordinary indentures of apprenticeship, were reduced. A concession (not very thankfully received) was made to Mr. Milner Gibson and his friends by the abolition of the stamp duty on newspaper supplements, and the reduction of the advertisement duty from eighteenpence to sixpence ; and postage to the colonies was made uniform at sixpence. Then came the tea duty, in respect of which Mr. Gladstone's proposition differed little from that of his predecessor. It was to be reduced for the coming year to 1s. 10d., and to be lowered by 3d. a year until the limit of 1s. was reached. Various fruits, cheese, butter, and eggs were to be admitted at a lower duty. Altogether there were reductions of duties on 133 minor articles of food, and an abolition of duties on 123; besides which, the duties on hackney carriages, horses, post-horses, dogs, and on other matters, were lowered.

THE HOUSES OF PARLIAMENT.

PHOTO BY

RUSSELL & SONS

These abolitions and alterations would cause a total loss to the revenue of £5,315,000, and then came the financier's great difficulty. Taking off taxation is an agreeable duty, and sure to please those who directly benefit by the proceeding; but it is a more delicate task to make up the deficiency and yet give satisfaction. The elastic income-tax was depended on to supply the greater part of the sum required, and Mr. Gladstone was eloquent in his defence of the imposition :—

"Sir Robert Peel, in 1842, called forth from repose this giant, which had once shielded us in war, to come and assist our industrious toils in peace; and if the first income-tax produced striking and memorable results, so, I am free to say, at less expenditure by far in money, but without the painful accompaniments of havoc, war, and bloodshed, has the second income-tax. The second income-tax has been the instrument by which you have introduced, and by which, I hope, ere long you may perfect the reform—the effective reform—of your commercial and fiscal system; and I, for one, am bold enough to hope and to expect that in reforming your own fiscal and commercial system, you have laid the foundation of similar reforms—slow, perhaps, but certain in their progress—through every country of the civilised world. I say, therefore, that if we rightly use the income-tax, when we part with it we may look back upon it with some satisfaction, and may console ourselves for the annoyance it may have entailed by the recollection that it has been the means of achieving a great good, immediately to England and ultimately to mankind."

He proposed to renew the income-tax for seven years (to June, 1860), the rate at first to be 7*d.* in the pound on all incomes over £150, and to be reduced after two years; but the impost was extended to incomes of £100, and between that amount and £150, the previous limit, it was to be 5*d.* in the pound throughout the whole period. The tax was to be extended to Ireland, but not limited to salaries or imposed on fundholders, as proposed by Mr. Disraeli. A very important alteration was proposed—the extension of the stamp duties payable on legacies to succession and estate after death. The duty on Scotch spirits was to be raised from 3*s.* 8*d.* to 4*s.* 8*d.*, and on Irish spirits from 2*s.* 8*d.* to 3*s.* 4*d.* There was to be a slight increase on licences for brewers and dealers in tea and coffee.

The result of these financial readjustments would be an estimated surplus for the coming financial year of £700,000.

The proposition gave rise to a long and comprehensive debate. The Income-Tax Bill was carried by 126 to 55; but the advertisement duty resolution was lost by the division on an amendment proposed by Mr. Crawford; and the advertisement duty was taken off at last.

But the "best laid schemes" of Chancellors of the Exchequer, as well as those "of mice and men, gang aft aglee." Not long after the delivery of the great budget speech, it became evident

that the Eastern troubles were ripening to a head, and that it
would be impossible for England, with a due regard to treaty
obligations, to remain neutral in the contest which appeared to
be inevitable.   A Russian army had crossed the Pruth, and
financial estimates for the coming year were of little value in the
immediate prospect of the outbreak of a contest the results of
which no one could predict.   The Ministry were determined to
support Turkey against Russia, and it was evident that "moral
support" only would avail little.   On the 12th of October Mr.
Gladstone took part at Manchester in the inauguration of the
statue of Sir Robert Peel, and in his speech in reply to an address
presented to him said : "There is a necessity for regulating the
distribution of power in Europe; and an absorption of power by
a great potentate in the east of Europe, which would follow the
conquest of the Ottoman Empire, would be so dangerous to the
world that it is the duty of Europe, at whatever cost, to set herself
against the possibility of it."

That phrase, "at whatever cost," implied a conviction in the
mind of the Chancellor of the Exchequer that he would, ere long,
be called upon to remodel his financial arrangements.   Referring
on this occasion to the late Sir Robert Peel, the memorial of
whom was the object of his visit to Manchester, and whose
political pupil he was proud to consider himself, Mr. Gladstone
said : "Great as were the intellectual powers of Sir Robert Peel,
there was something yet more admirable than the immense intellectual endowments with which it had pleased the Almighty to
gift him, and that was his sense of public virtue, his purity of
conscience, his determination to follow the public good.'

A few days before the delivery of this speech Turkey had
declared war against Russia; ten days afterwards the English and
French fleets had entered the Bosphorus ; and on the 5th of
December a protocol had been signed between Great Britain,
France, Austria, and Prussia, with the object of endeavouring to
re-establish peace between Russia and Turkey.

When Parliament reassembled in February, 1854, the aspect
of Eastern affairs was indeed formidable.   The Russians were
advancing, the Turks were straining every nerve to prepare for
the defence of the European and Asiatic frontiers.   The Greek
Government favoured an insurrection in Epirus and Albania, and
proclaimed an Hellenic Empire, encouraged no doubt by Russia,
which assumed to be the champion of the Greek Church, the
defender of the members of that communion in the Holy Places
of Syria, and to have no special designs upon Constantinople and

the Bosphorus, although the Czar, in confidential communication with Sir Hamilton Seymour, British representative at St. Petersburg, was hinting ominously at the dying condition of the " sick man," and the most convenient mode of dividing his property.

Although the formal declaration of war against Russia was not made by this country until the 28th of March, it was known to be inevitable. On the 11th of the month the Queen reviewed the Baltic fleet, to the command of which the " tough old Commodore," by that time Admiral Charles Napier, was appointed; and on the following day a treaty of alliance between Great Britain, France, and Turkey was signed. Mr. Gladstone had to provide the sinews of war, and as the Army and Navy Estimates showed a great increase, the task before him was of a peculiarly arduous character.

On the 6th of March he made his financial statement. The time was unusually early for the production of a budget, but the necessity was urgent. The Chancellor estimated that he would have in hand, when the balance was struck, on the 5th of April, a surplus of £2,864,000, notwithstanding the sums already expended in military preparations. He estimated that the revenue for the coming financial year (including this surplus) would be £53,349,000, and the expenditure £56,189,000, leaving a deficiency of £2,840,000, for which provision must be made. Hitherto his efforts had been in the direction of Peel's policy, the reduction of indirect taxation ; and he resolved, as far as possible, to adhere to that plan. He did not, he said, propose at present to add a farthing to the indirect taxation of the country, but he spoke only of the present moment—

" Should the struggle—which God forbid—be prolonged, it will not be in our power to secure for all those articles which have recently been relieved from duty a permanent continuance of that relief. I fear all I can say with respect to the objects of indirect taxation, as compared with those of direct taxation, at the present time, is but a repetition of the promise given by the Cyclops to Ulysses, that he should have the privilege of being devoured last."

He announced his determination to meet, if possible, the expenses of the forthcoming contest as they accrued by appealing to the resources of the country, and not by resorting to the expedient of a loan from British and foreign capitalists.

" It is impossible to give an absolute pledge, or to record an immovable resolution, that the expenses of a war shall be borne by additions to taxation ; but it is possible for us to do this—to put a stout heart upon the matter, and to determine that, so long as these burdens are bearable, and so long as the supplies necessary for the service of the year can be raised within the year, so long we will not resort to the system of loans."

He proposed to increase the income-tax by one half, and by that means he would have a revenue of £56,656,000, leaving a small surplus of less than half a million. He also asked for power to issue Exchequer Bills to the amount of £1,750,000, but did not expect the whole of that sum would be required. That he did not regard his budget as having an exclusively warlike character, was shown by a proposition to reduce the cost of stamps on bills, and permit the use of adhesive stamps, a great convenience to business men.

Mr. Disraeli denounced the plan of increasing direct taxation, and advocated resort to loans, taking occasion to refer to "the terrible prospect of war brought about by the combination of geniuses opposite me, and brought about absolutely by the amount of their talents and the discordancy of their opinions."

The general feeling of the country supported the financial policy of the Chancellor of the Exchequer, described by Prince Albert, in a letter to Baron Stockmar, as "manly, statesmanlike, and honest," and the resolutions were carried.

Two months afterwards, however, on the 8th of May, Mr. Gladstone was compelled to make another demand for money. So great had been the amount expended on military and naval preparations that the appeal was for £6,850,000, in addition to the sum already granted. The time, he feared, had come, and the objects of indirect taxation could no longer escape. The Cyclops was implacable, and Ulysses must prepare, if not exactly to be devoured, yet to suffer considerably. There was, however, still the wonderfully elastic and accommodating income tax—that was to be doubled; then the duty on Scotch spirits, last year reduced, was to be augmented by 1s. per gallon, and Irish spirits to the extent of an additional 8d. After the 5th of July the sugar duties would be increased by imposition of 1s. and 1s. 6d. per cwt.; and the malt tax would be raised from 2s. 9d. to 4s. The actual augmentation of the public burdens on the fiscal year would be £8,683,000, "two-thirds of which would be raised by a direct tax on the wealthier classes, and the remaining one-third by indirect taxation, affecting the whole consuming population of all classes."

No effectual opposition could be offered to the proposals; the Opposition contented itself with harmless grumbling, and the resolutions and bills founded on them were accepted by considerable majorities. Mr. Gladstone had trusted to the elasticity of trade, and the growing prospects of the country to enable it to bear the burdens imposed on it, and it seemed at the time as if he was fully justified in his expectation. Parliament was prorogued on the 12th of Augus', and it was fondly hoped that, ere it met again, peace might be re-established, and that the bountiful harvest, of which there was assurance, would compensate in some degree for the privations so cheerfully borne.

On the 14th of September the allied armies of France and England landed at Old Fort, near Eupatoria, in the Crimea ; on the 20th they carried the heights of Alma ; and a few days later came the false news of the capture of Sebastopol, which reached England on the very day of public thanksgiving for the bountiful harvest.   A few hours brought the awakening from the pleasant dream, and the intelligence that English and French were throwing up entrenchments and establishing batteries on the dismal heights, destined to be so tragical, on the south side of Sebastopol.

There had been changes in the Ministry in the course of the year.   Lord John Russell, who had first held office as Foreign Secretary, but had given place to the Earl of Clarendon, and remained in the Cabinet without office, had, in June, become President of the Council, in succession to Earl Granville, who was appointed Chancellor of the Duchy of Lancaster.   The Duke of Newcastle, who had united the offices of Colonial Secretary and Secretary of War, had become Secretary of State for War (a new office, rendered necessary by the increased magnitude of military affairs), and Sir George Grey succeeded him at the Colonial Office.

So alarming was the state of affairs in the Crimea, that Parliament met again on the 12th of December.   Sebastopol was untaken ; but Balaklava and Inkerman had been fought.   The one had nearly annihilated the Light Cavalry brigade, was "magnificent, but not war;" the other was the result of a surprise, and the British army might have been destroyed had not our French allies gallantly come to the rescue of their comrades in arms. The cold was intense, provisions were scarce, the commissariat arrangements were miserably defective, and the ranks were being daily thinned by disease, starvation, and cold.   Shakespeare's description of the English soldiers before the battle of Agincourt might, with very little modification, have been applied to Lord Raglan's army on the Crimean plateau :—

> " The poor condemned English,
> Like sacrifices, by their watchful fires
> Sit patiently, and inly ruminate
> The morning's danger ; and their gesture sad,
> Investing lank-lean cheeks, and war-worn coats,
> Presenteth them unto the gazing moon
> So many horrid ghosts."

The public at home were greatly excited by the accounts which reached them through the press, and there was an intense feeling of indignant anger with the officials, which extended to the Ministry. The cry was that our soldiers, who had exhibited an unsurpassed courage, were being sacrificed by incompetent blundering. Parliament reassembled on the 12th of December, but shortly afterwards adjourned for the Christmas holidays, and met again on the 23rd of January, 1855, when Mr. Roebuck, not in this instance the convenient friend of Ministers, but the outspoken and indomitable champion of public opinion, gave notice of his famous motion for a select committee to inquire into the condition of our army before Sebastopol, and the conduct of those departments of the Government whose duty it had been to minister to the wants of that army.

On the same night the Earl of Ellenborough gave notice in the House of Lords of a motion somewhat similar in effect; and a few nights afterwards the veteran Lord Lyndhurst gave notice that he would, on the 3rd of February, move, "That in the opinion of this House the expedition to the Crimea was undertaken by Her Majesty's Government with very inadequate means, and without due caution or sufficient inquiry into the nature and extent of the resistance to be expected from the enemy; and that the neglect and mismanagement of the Government in the conduct of the enterprise have led to the most disastrous results."

On the 25th of the month, when Mr. Roebuck's motion was to be brought forward, the House was taken by surprise by the announcement of the resignation of Lord John Russell, the President of the Council, and Lord Palmerston moved the suspension of the orders of the day in order to afford his late colleague an opportunity for explanation. Lord John Russell said he was compelled to admit that the army was in a most terrible condition, and therefore he could not resist Mr. Roebuck's motion; and that as early as the previous November he had urged the Earl of Aberdeen to recommend the Queen that Lord Palmerston should replace the Duke of Newcastle at the War Office. That suggestion had not been acquiesced in, and he had only remained in office by the advice of Lord Palmerston. Notwithstanding his representations to the Premier, he was unable to say that any arrangements had been made to remedy defects; and, as he could not give the only answer that would stop inquiry, he felt compelled to resign the office he held. In his concluding observations he said he should look back with pride to his association with every member of the Administration, and especially eulogized Mr. Gladstone's financial scheme of 1853.

When Lord John had resumed his seat, Mr. Roebuck proceeded to move the resolution of which he had given notice, but was labouring under physical weakness, and limited his speech to a few introductory remarks. The British force in the Crimea had, he said, been reduced from 54,000 to 14,000, of whom only 5,000 were fit for duty, and the country imperatively demanded that the cause of such a condition of things should be fully investigated.

Mr. Gladstone defended the Ministry, and especially the Duke of Newcastle, in a long speech. He contradicted Mr. Roebuck's statements as to the reduction of the strength of the army, and asserted that there were 30,000 available men. He added :—

> " I sincerely hope that the House, in the vote which it is about to give, will recollect its responsibility to the country, and will reflect on the mode of proceeding which it is about to adopt. For my part, I believe that mode of proceeding to be worse than useless so far as regards the army in the Crimea. Your inquiry will never take place ; or, if it does, it would lead to nothing but confusion and disturbance, increased disaster, shame at home, and weakness abroad. It would carry no consolation to those whom you seek to aid, but it would carry malignant joy to the hearts of the enemies of England ; and for my part I shall rejoice, if the motion is to be successful, that my last words as a member of the present Government were an indignant protest against it, as useless to the army, unconstitutional in its nature, and dangerous to the honour and the interest of the Commons of England."

Mr. Roebuck, in a brief reply, took strong ground :—

> "If we refuse this inquiry, we shall be abdicating our functions as the representatives of the people. But we are asked to put off this committee until the expedition to the Crimea shall be brought to a close. That means, in other terms, until not a remnant of our gallant army remains. I say, inquire at once ; inquire, and save that army which is in jeopardy. The country looks to us for aid in this extremity. Let us not disappoint the expectation of the whole English people."

Popular feeling was stronger than considerations of party, and the motion was carried by a majority of 157, the numbers being 305 for and 148 against.

The fall of the Coalition Ministry necessarily followed. On the 1st of February the Earl of Aberdeen in the House of Lords, and Lord Palmerston in the House of Commons, announced that Ministers had resigned. The Earl of Derby, and afterwards Lord John Russell, were sent for by the Queen, but the former declined the attempt, and the latter was unsuccessful in the endeavour to arrange a Ministry. On the 8th, Parliament was informed that Lord Palmerston had accepted office as Prime Minister, and a week afterwards the Cabinet was completed.

H

Many of the old Ministers retained office ; but the Earl of Aberdeen was, of course, omitted from the arrangements, and the Duke of Newcastle, against whom, as Secretary of State for War, a considerable amount of indignation had been directed, was replaced by Lord Panmure. Mr. Sidney Herbert, who had not held office in the previous Administration, took the Colonial Office, Sir George Grey being transferred to the Home Department in place of Lord Palmerston, and Mr. Gladstone resumed his official duties as Chancellor of the Exchequer.

When, on the 16th of February, Lord Palmerston announced that he had been successful in forming a Ministry, he said the great difficulty which stared him in the face was Mr. Roebuck's motion. He still retained his objection to the appointment of a committee of inquiry, as not in accordance with the Constitution, or efficient for its purpose ; and he trusted that the House would at least consent to suspend its decision, and not proceed to the nomination of the committee. The reason he would ask it to give would be its belief that the Government would of itself do all that was possible to be done. As an English king rode up to an insurrection, and offered to be its leader, so the Government offered the House of Commons to be its committee.

Even Palmerston, with all his popularity and personal influence, could not persuade the House to stultify itself. Not only did Mr. Roebuck and his supporters desire security for the future— so far as that went, probably some of them would have trusted to the Premier—but they were determined, and in that determination they were encouraged by feeling outside the walls of the House, that the causes of the past disastrous errors should, if possible, be discovered. Mr. Roebuck refused to be a party to rescinding the resolution the House had accepted, and tersely remarked, " Although there is a new Ministry, there are not new members."

CHAPTER XII.

RETIREMENT FROM OFFICE—THE IONIAN MISSION.

THE three Peelites had accepted office under Palmerston with
the expectation apparently that his popularity and confidence in
his energy and desire to remedy defects would induce the House
to reconsider the proposition for a committee of inquiry. The
determined attitude of Mr. Roebuck and his friends speedily
undeceived them, and they determined to withdraw from the
Ministry. On the 22nd of the month the Prime Minister announced that Mr. Gladstone, Sir James Graham, and Mr. Sidney
Herbert had resigned office. On the following day, previous to
Mr. Roebuck moving the nomination of the committee, the ex-
ministers made the anxiously-expected explanations, Sir James
Graham leading the way.

Mr. Gladstone said he had taken office on the supposition that
Lord Palmerston would resist the appointment of the committee ;
but finding that the Premier yielded on the subject, and would
not make it a question of confidence, he had felt it his duty,
objecting as he did on constitutional principles to the inquiry, to
resign office. He took occasion to eulogise the Earl of Aberdeen, who " had been dismissed by a blow darkly aimed from an
official hand." (Probably there was here a covert allusion to the
conduct of Lord John Russell.) "The fame of the Earl of Aberdeen," continued Mr. Gladstone, " not so much on account of
the high office he has held, as from his elevated and admirable
character, will not only live, but his name, I venture to say, will
receive the grateful recollection of his country."

An almost purely Whig Cabinet was the result of the reconstruction of the Ministry. Lord John Russell returned to office
as Colonial Secretary, and Sir Charles Wood replaced Sir James
Graham at the Admiralty. The new Chancellor of the Exchequer
was Sir George Cornewall Lewis, a man of vast ability and considerable official experience, but, as yet, untried in finance. He
was a scholarly and philosophical statesman, who said that "life
would be endurable were it not for its pleasures," and who
found his recreation, in the intervals of Parliamentary and official
labours, in writing treatises on "The Astronomy of the Ancients,"
and other abstruse subjects.

Sir George Lewis's liking for solving complex problems must have found ample scope for exercise in preparing the financial statement, which, on the 20th of April, less than two months after his appointment to office, he laid before the House. The war expenditure had been enormous; the estimates for the Army and Navy were each about £16,000,000, and there was a deficiency to be made good at which Mr. Gladstone himself, with all his financial dexterity and high courage, might have been appalled. The new Chancellor of the Exchequer began with a compliment to his predecessor's accuracy. "In the last year Mr. Gladstone had, by exercising a sort of financial second sight, estimated the produce of the taxes at £59,496,000 ; they actually produced just £154 above that sum." He (Sir George Lewis) estimated the expenditure of the current year at £86,339,000, and the revenue at £63,339,000, leaving a deficit of £23,000,000 to be provided for, and Government had resolved, he announced, to resort to a loan for a part of the required sum. He would have preferred raising money by terminable annuities, but it would be impossible to obtain all that was needed by that means, and accordingly the great bulk of the loan which had been that day effected was contracted in a permanent Three per Cent. Stock, for the gradual extinction of which it was proposed to set aside a million annually. By this new stock £16,000,000 would be raised ; £2,000,000 more would be obtained by putting 2d. more on the income-tax, raising it to 16d. in the pound, and the remaining £5,000,000 must be raised by indirect taxation. The sugar duty would be increased by 3s. per cwt. ; an additional 1d. a pound would be imposed on coffee, and 3d. a pound on tea ; bankers' cheques drawn within fifteen miles of the place where they were payable must have a penny stamp ; the duty on Scotch spirits would be raised 1s. 10d. a gallon, and Irish spirits 2s. In this way the required amount would be provided.

The country was receiving very practical instruction as to the costliness of war. Expenses of living had increased greatly within the previous twelve months. The price of bread and meat was already nearly double that at which those articles could be obtained in " the year of peaceful prophecies of smooth things," 1851, when the Great Exhibition was supposed to offer the means of solving many complex problems. Employment was scarce, for commercial and manufacturing enterprise was dormant, and the infliction of so heavy an income-tax was felt severely by all classes. We had seemed to be entering on a period of national prosperity, in which the necessaries and comforts of life

were made more obtainable by the lessening or reduction of
indirect taxation, and a limit was promised to the direct
taxation which had been resorted to. The time had come when
Peel's economic theories, which Gladstone had so energetically
supported, must be laid aside until "a more convenient season."
We had indulged in the luxury of war, and must pay its price.

It is probable that Sir George Lewis watched with some
anxiety, as with anxious care he explained his propositions, the
expression of Mr. Gladstone's face. If, however, he anticipated
severe criticism, his anticipations were not realised. Mr. Gladstone saw that the time had come when theories must be in
abeyance, and the pressure of circumstances must be paramount.
He said, although as a general principle he greatly objected to a
loan, he thought resource to it was now inevitable, and continued :—

> "I apprehend there is a limit to the application of the principle, and that
> we cannot possibly expect a free country to push the very soundest economical
> doctrines to the extreme. You must remember that you have to deal with
> flesh and blood, and that you cannot ask from flesh and blood more than they
> can reasonably bear. I go a step further, and I admit that there is a point at
> which the sudden accumulation of taxation becomes so great an evil, and so
> great a source of disturbance to all personal and social relations, that it is
> better to provide yourself with money, up to a certain limit, at a pecuniary
> disadvantage, than to carry that disturbance through all ranks of the country."

The budget resolutions were carried with slight opposition,
beyond a due amount of grumbling. The money must be provided, and nobody appeared able to suggest a better method of
providing it than the Chancellor of the Exchequer had proposed.

The Conservatives appear to have perceived an opportunity in
the recent Cabinet difficulties, and the conduct of the Vienna
negotiations, for challenging the conduct of Ministers; and on
the 22nd of May Mr. Disraeli, the leader of the Opposition in
the Commons, gave notice of a resolution expressing dissatisfaction with "the ambiguous language and uncertain conduct of Her
Majesty's Government in reference to the great question of peace
or war." The debate was opened on the 24th, when Sir Francis
Baring moved an amendment substituting for the "dissatisfaction"
sentence a regret that the conference at Vienna had not led to a
termination of hostilities.

Lord John Russell, who represented Great Britain at Vienna,
and took part in the Conference, by which it was hoped peace
would be restored, had supported propositions which, however, were unacceptable to the Ministry at home, as being too
favourable to Russia, on which it was desired to impose certain

restrictions, the most important being the limitation of her Black
Sea fleet.   Austria had suggested, as "a counterpoise," that the
sea should be open to the war navies of all nations, a proposition
which Lord Palmerston described as *une mauvaise plaisanterie*—a
bad joke.

Mr. Gladstone was strongly in favour of concluding a peace.
He said :—

> "Russia had receded from her pretence ; she had gone far to put herself
> in the right, and in war as well as in peace the great object should be to be in
> the right.   All the terms we had demanded had been substantially conceded,
> and if it was not for terms we fought, but for military success, let the House
> look at the sentiment with the eye of reason, and it would appear immoral,
> inhuman, and un-Christian.   If the war continued in order to obtain military
> glory we should tempt Him in whose hands was the fate of armies to launch
> upon us His wrath."

This speech brought up Mr. Whiteside, member for Ennis-
killen, a vigorous and showy rhetorician, whose ornate style and
dramatic elocution, although becoming old-fashioned, generally
commanded the attention of the House.   He made a tremendous
attack on Mr. Gladstone, denouncing him as "the moralist and
philosopher upon whom a new light had broken respecting the
horrors of war, and who now felt the stings of conscience so
strongly.   Who," he asked, "advised the invasion of Russia?
Who made war on the territories of Russia?   The right honourable gentleman.   Who advised the attack on Sebastopol?   The
right honourable gentleman.   Who plunged the country into the
horrors in which it was now involved?   The right honourable
gentleman."

Mr. Lowe proposed an amendment adding to Sir F. Baring's
resolution words attributing the failure of the Conference to the
refusal of Russia to restrict the strength of her navy in the Black
Sea.

Lord Palmerston made a characteristic speech in defence of
the Government.   He said one of the alternatives before the
House was that offered by Mr. Gladstone, in the name of a
party who would accept dishonourable conditions of peace ; but,
he added, "if a Government were now formed of this party, I
think that not one of them would be re-elected to serve in this
House."

Mr. Disraeli's resolution was negatived by a majority of exactly
100, the numbers being 319 against 219 ; and on the 4th of June
Sir F. Baring's amendment (then a substantive resolution) was
carried, having received Ministerial support.   Mr. Lowe's amendment was negatived.

On another important subject, which gave rise to considerable discussion, and the decision respecting which has materially affected the Civil Service, Mr. Gladstone made a decided utterance. The popular demand for administrative reform had followed that for free trade; and the new agitation, if less powerful than that which preceded it, was scarcely less demonstrative. One of the leaders of the movement, Mr. Layard, brought forward a resolution on the 15th of June, condemning the manner in which public appointments were made—"merit and efficiency had been sacrificed to party and family influences, and a blind adherence to routine."

Mr. Gladstone supported the motion, and expressed his belief that patronage was the weakness not the strength of the Executive. Lord Aberdeen's Government, he said, had first brought under public notice the principle of unrestricted competition.

The Conservatives were not unwilling to take some steps in this direction, but decidedly objected to the sweeping censure conveyed in Mr. Layard's resolution, which was described by the Chancellor of the Exchequer as tantamount to an expression of want of confidence in the Ministry. Sir E. B. Lytton, representing the Opposition benches, moved an amendment in favour of instituting "judicious tests of merit, and removing obstruction to its fair promotion and legitimate rewards, so as to secure to the service of the State the largest available proportion of the energy and intelligence for which the people of this country were distinguished."

Mr. Layard's motion was rejected by 359 against 46; and Sir E. B. Lytton's amendment, becoming a substantive motion, was accepted without a division taking place. The subject was revived on the 10th of July by a motion by Mr. Vincent Scully, member for the county of Cork, for an address to the Queen thanking her for the Order in Council appointing commissioners. In the course of the debate, Mr. Gladstone strongly supported the demand for open and unlimited competition; but the motion was defeated, the "previous question" being carried by a majority of 15.

The course pursued by Lord John Russell at Vienna, and his retention of his office, although the other members of the Cabinet did not support his views, in July formed the subject of two adverse motions, by Mr. Milner Gibson and Sir E. B. Lytton; but Lord John resigned on the 16th, and the inconvenient motions were withdrawn. The Sebastopol Committee had completed its labours and made its report, and Mr. Roebuck moved a

resolution, based upon it, to the effect that the House shou.d visit
with severe reprehension every member of that Cabinet whose
conduct led to such disastrous results.   There was a hot debate ;
but it ended on the second night by the previous question being
carried by 289 to 182, the House showing by a majority of 107 that
it was not disposed to carry the controversy to the bitter end.

There was a very strong feeling that the time had arrived wl en
hostilities might be terminated, and that enough had been done
to limit the power of Russia.   On the 3rd of August, Mr. Laing,
the member for the Wick Burghs, moved for copies of correspondence respecting the recent Conference at Vienna, and declared that the Government was "carrying on the war for no
definite object, or the miserable object of limitation versus
counterpoise."   Mr. Gladstone supported the motion in a very
energetic speech, severely blaming the Ministers for prolonging
the contest.   They had rejected the golden opportunity of
making peace, and continued to make war on account of petty
differences.   He protested against the notion that the Cabinet of
which he had been a member considered the capture of Sebastopol as the great object of the war, to be pursued at all costs,
and continued :—

> "I say that the doctrine that you never ought to forego the accomplishment
> of a great military operation when the practical objects have been attained,
> lest you should incur military odium, is both an immoral and an irreligious
> doctrine—a doctrine which will not carry you forward and onward to the
> furtherance of civilization, but backwards towards a state of savagery and
> barbarism. . . .   I remain content in the belief that, in endeavouring to
> recall the Government from that course of policy which they are now pur-
> suing, I am discharging my duty as a patriot, a faithful representative of the
> people, and a loyal subject of my Queen."

The motion had no result beyond producing an animated and
interesting debate, a motion for the adjournment of the House
being carried.

In the course of the Session, Mr. Gladstone had an opportunity of expressing his opinions on the subject of marriage with
a deceased wife's sister, respecting which he maintained that it
was contrary to Scriptural teaching, and that to permit it would
be to make an attack upon the doctrines and practices of the
Church.   The debate on the Marriage Law Amendment Bill,
introduced almost every Session, took place on the 9th of May,
and Mr. Gladstone entered at length on the religious and social
aspects of the question :—

> "When it is said that there shall be in the Church of England a law with
> respect to these marriages, then I am told that this is a question of religious

liberty. By applying this fully, what would be its result? Why, that every principle and ordinance of the Church of England may be modified and absolutely done away with under the pretence of religious liberty. . . . If the honourable member assumes that he has a right to introduce into the Church of England an anarchy, or a principle of indifference for that which is strictly commanded on the basis of Divine law, I say the principle on which he proceeds is good for abolishing every restrictive law applicable to the creed or discipline of the Church of England. The demand here made is not for persons wishing to be relieved, but for the alteration of Church and State, and in deference to the scruples of a small minority we are asked to change a position which has been clearly maintained by the voice of Christendom through all time. . . . The honourable member for Kidderminster (Mr. Lowe) speaks of the collective conscience of mankind—I interpret him in the best sense, though I think that he meant the conscience of each individual—and he maintains that this would be a proper and sufficient guide from age to age for the course of legislation on this question. God forbid that I should say a word lightly of conscience, which remains an index of the will of God even among those who have not felt as we have the fuller and blessed light of revelation. But are we, who have realised the results of Christianity, to go back from Christianity to conscience? That which is sometimes called the light of conscience, sometimes the law of nature—and there are no two ages or countries in which it has ever been alike—has been of gradual growth and training, from the infancy of mankind until it has reached the highest level on which Christianity has been placed; and if we are asked to go back from that level, I ask, where are we to stop? And I say that, while I have a superior, I should not be content to adopt an inferior standard. The law of the land, not in an arbitrary manner, but on principles based on Divine revelation, has adopted our present prohibitions in marriage; and I oppose the present measure because I see that it is part of a system, which I do not say is intended to be so, but which in its working is certain to be most pernicious to those results which the Christian religion has wrought out for mankind."

The Bill was rejected by a majority of 7. Since then, we know, a similar Bill has several times received the sanction of the House of Commons, but been rejected by the Lords.

The prorogation took place on the 14th of August, and Parliament did not meet again until the 31st of January, 1856.

Sebastopol had fallen, three weeks after the rising of Parliament; and on the day after the opening of the 1856 Session, a protocol had been signed accepting the propositions of peace which, with the consent of the allies, Austria had forwarded to St. Petersburg. On the 25th of February peace conferences were opened at Paris, and an armistice agreed on. Termination of hostilities was virtually attained, although it was not until the 30th of March that the treaty was signed at Paris.

All England rejoiced at the peace, for it was heartily sick of the war. Many thousands of brave men had been sacrificed; an almost unbearable strain had been put upon the resources of the nation; and after more than eighteen months of terrible warfare

2nd more terrible disease, we had the satisfaction of knowing that
the Sebastopol fortifications and docks had been destroyed; that
France had achieved the chief glory of the final attack; that
Russia was for a time non-aggressive, and that Turkish misgovernment was granted a few years' longer lease. There was
public rejoicing, and a million rockets were discharged in Hyde
Park, and rockets and red fire in the other royal parks delighted
the hearts of loyal subjects—and then came the reckoning.

On the 22nd of February the Chancellor of the Exchequer
was called upon prematurely to face the House with a scheme
for raising more money. He had the unpleasant task of informing the House that the financial position was worse than he had
anticipated to the extent of nearly £4,000,000. The war expenses
had, up to that date, been about £43,500,000. To meet the
deficiency already existing, and to provide funds for the remainder
of the financial year, he had that day obtained a loan of £5,000,000
in Three per Cent. Consols, and funded £3,000,000 of Exchequer
bonds. He asked the House to sanction these arrangements,
and congratulated himself on the fact that the resources of the
country were so elastic that the new additions to the debt would
not be severely felt. In support of this view he quoted Macaulay's
recently published "History of England," to show that the
country could bear a great addition to the National Debt without
serious injury. "Persons who confidently predicted that England
would sink under a debt of £800,000,000 were beyond all doubt
under a twofold mistake. They greatly overrated the pressure of
the burden, and they greatly underrated the strength by which
the burden was to be borne."

Mr. Gladstone, while offering no opposition to the proposal of
Sir George Lewis, repeated objections he had before made to the
power claimed by the Chancellor of the Exchequer of borrowing
without direct Parliamentary sanction, "a power which ought
not to be given to any executive government whatever." The
quotation from Macaulay led him to indulge in a slight "gird" at
his brilliant adversary of former years.—"I would rather have
heard Mr. Macaulay quoted in almost any other passage of his
wonderful book than in that relating to the National Debt of the
country."

In less than three months afterwards, on the 19th of May, the
Chancellor of the Exchequer had to make another financial
statement, the more formal annual Budget. Of deficiencies it
might be said as of Macbeth's foes, "The cry is still they come!"
Sir George Lewis gravely announced that, notwithstanding all

that had been asked and given, he wanted £6,875,000 more, to supply the actual deficit, and he thought it very advisable that this sum should be increased by a vote of credit of £2,000,000, as a provision for contingencies. He did not propose to make any additions to taxation, but to have recourse to a loan for the greater part of the amount, and to ask for power to raise, at a later period of the session, £2,000,000 by Exchequer bonds or bills.

There was no help for it. Mr. Gladstone saw that it would be useless to offer criticisms when the money must be had, and when it was tolerably certain that the limits of taxation, direct or indirect, had been reached; but he urged that the Navy estimates might have been reduced now that peace was assured.

Peace was proclaimed in London on the 29th of April, and on the 6th of May there was a great debate in the Commons on the subject of the Treaty. Mr. Gladstone made a memorable speech, some passages of which merit quotation as evidencing the opinions he then held regarding the government of the Ottoman empire—opinions differing very slightly from those expressed so forcibly in more recent times :—

"If I thought this treaty was an instrument which bound this country and our posterity to the maintenance of a set of institutions in Turkey which you are endeavouring to reform, if you can, but with respect to which endeavour few can be sanguine, I should look for the most emphatic word in which to express my condemnation of a peace which bound us to maintain the laws and institutions of Turkey as a Mahometan state. . . . With respect to the objects for which the war had been undertaken, it appears to me that my right honourable friend (Mr. Milner Gibson) has quite misunderstood them in the construction which he gives to the term 'independence and integrity of the Ottoman empire,' and the guarantee of that independence. I apprehend that what is sought to secure by the war was not the settlement of any question regarding the internal government of Turkey. Great Britain and France have not yet been able to afford a complete solution to the problem which has existed for six hundred or seven hundred years. . . . The juxtaposition of a people professing the Mahometan religion with a rising Christian population having adverse and conflicting influences, present difficulties which are not to be overcome by certain diplomatists at certain hours and in a certain place. It will be the work and care of many generations—if even then they may be successful—to bring that state of things to a happy and prosperous conclusion."

In the course of the Session Mr. Gladstone supported a motion by Viscount Goderich for an address to the Queen on the subject of admission to the Civil Service, and spoke warmly in favour of a system of competitive examinations. On the 1st of July he spoke in favour of Mr. Moore's resolution condemning the Government for their conduct in first covertly sanctioning a scheme of enlistment for the British army in the United States, and then repudiating the action of Mr. Crampton, the British Minister at Washington, and permitting him to be made "a scape-goat," as Mr. Gladstone expressed it.

On the 29th of July Parliament was prorogued, meeting again on the 3rd of February, 1857. Ten days afterwards the financial situation of the country was again the subject of discussion. It was then discovered that the cost of the war had been more than £76,000,000. There would probably be a surplus on the financial year ending on the 5th of April of £1,384,000; and the Chancellor of the Exchequer estimated that in the year 1857-8 there would be a revenue of £66,365,000, to meet an expenditure of £65.474,000, showing a balance on the right side of £891,000. He proposed to give the public the benefit of the reduction of some £15,000,000 in the annual expenditure by reducing the income-tax to 7*d.* in the pound for the next three years, and making a gradual reduction in the tea and sugar duties, not, however, going so far as to reduce these imposts to a " peace footing."

It was anticipated that considerable dissatisfaction would be aroused by this Budget. Ever since the time of Sir Robert Peel's great financial achievements the effort on the part of himself and successors in office had been to reduce indirect taxation, and make direct taxation supply the deficiency. Mr. Gladstone, who had done so much in that direction, had been compelled by the pressure of circumstances to acquiesce in a reimposition of some of the duties he had remitted; but now that the war was over, he desired that the added duties on tea, sugar, and other necessaries of life, really constituting a war tax, should be taken off. The partial remission proposed by Sir George Lewis, and the reduction of the income-tax at the expense of tea and sugar, were warmly opposed by him.

Mr. Disraeli also opposed the scheme of the Chancellor of the Exchequer, but on other grounds. On the 20th of the month he moved "that it would be expedient, before sanctioning the financial arrangements for the ensuing year, to adjust the estimated income and expenditure in a manner which should appear best calculated to secure the country against the risk of a deficiency in the years 1858-59 and 1859-60, and to provide for such a balance of revenue and charge respectively in the year 1860 as may place it in the power of Parliament at that period, without embarrassment to the finances, altogether to remit the income-tax."

This motion was defeated by a majority of 80 ; but, influenced perhaps by the vigorous criticism of Mr. Gladstone, the Chancellor of the Exchequer announced, on the 6th of March, a modification of the Budget resolutions so far as the tea duties were concerned, and proposed that the amount of the tax, which he had arranged for three years, should be applicable for one year only. Mr. Gladstone moved an amendment to the effect that after April 5, 1857, the duty should be 1s. 3d., and after the 5th of April, 1858, 1s. The amendment was negatived by 187 to 125, and the Chancellor of the Exchequer's resolution, fixing the duty at 1s. 5d., was carried. When the report of the committee was brought up on the 9th of March, Mr. Gladstone declared his belief that the discontinuance of the income-tax could only be effected by such a reduction of expenditure as the Government did not appear able to make. The increase of the expenditure, he said, was rapidly depriving the country of the means of doing away with the tax.

There was little probability of an immediate decrease in the expenditure, however ardently it might be desired, for another war with China had broken out, and Admiral Seymour was busily engaged in bombarding Chinese forts. What was described at the time as "the miserable lorcha dispute," had occurred in the preceding autumn, and the spark had kindled to a flame, involving, as we shall see, very considerable political consequences. On the 8th of October, 1856, a "lorcha," the *Arrow*, a small Chinese vessel, built on the European model, had been boarded in the Canton river by Chinese officials, and twelve men taken away on a charge of piracy. The owner of the lorcha declared that it was a British vessel, and appealed to Mr. Parker, the British consul at Canton, who made a formal demand on Yeh, the Chinese governor of Canton, for the release of the men, as, by treaty between the two powers, Chinese officials had no right to seize Chinese offenders, pirates or otherwise, on board an English vessel, but only to require the surrender of them by the British authorities. Governor Yeh replied that the lorcha *Arrow* was not an English vessel, but belonged to a Chinese pirate, who occasionally displayed the English flag as a means of deception. The fact was that the *Arrow* had been registered as a British vessel, but the term of registration had expired about ten days before the men were seized. It has been stated, and apparently with truth, that the British authorities were not disposed to renew the registration, having strong suspicions as to the real character of the vessel. Consul Parker, however, insisted that a breach of national rights had been committed, persisted in his demand, and, as Yeh refused to submit, sent to the British plenipotentiary at Hong Kong, Sir John Bowring, for assistance.

Sir John Bowring was a great linguist, a literary man of some eminence, and a Benthamite of the first water ; but neither his political economy nor his scholarship—his long experience in China nor his knowledge of the principles of international law— saved him from committing what at the time was considered to be, and afterwards generally recognised as, a great blunder.   He sent a peremptory demand for the restoration of the men within forty-eight hours, and an ample apology on the part of Yeh.   If the men were not restored, and if the apology were not sent, the admiral in command of the fleet in Chinese waters would "know the reason why."   Yeh sent back the men for the sake of avoiding a quarrel, but would not offer an apology, because, he maintained, the *Arrow* not being a British, but a Chinese vessel, he had a perfect right to board her if he chose.   Sir John Bowring admitted to Consul Parker that the registration had expired, but added that, as the Chinese were not aware of the fact, they were in the wrong in boarding it.   He translated Palmerston's "Civis Romanus" into Chinese, and let loose Sir Michael Seymour, the blue jackets, and guns.   Canton was bombarded, the suburbs destroyed, shot and shell showered upon the city, forts and war junks destroyed. No doubt there was a great destruction of life ; and as Chinese morals could scarcely be expected to be superior to those of English philosophers and diplomatists, Yeh offered rewards for the heads of Englishmen, and the English factories were burned.

When news of these events reached England, a strong feeling of indignation was excited.   Very shortly after the opening of Parliament, the Earl of Derby brought forward the subject in the House of Lords, in the form of a motion condemning the con- duct of the British authorities in China.   It was supported by the venerable Lord Lyndhurst, then in his eighty-fifth year, who, supporting himself by leaning on a rail placed specially for his accommodation, made a powerful speech, explaining the bear- ing of the law on the matter, and emphatically denying that the lorcha had any claim to British protection ; but, he said, "When we are talking of treaty transactions with Eastern nations, we have a kind of loose law and loose notion of morality in regard to them."   Lord Chancellor Cranworth attempted to reply to the legal arguments of "the old man eloquent," adopting, in fact, Sir John Bowring's suggestion, that as the Chinese did not know the lorcha had no right to hoist the British flag, they should have taken the nationality for granted.

The Lords rejected the Earl of Derby's motion by a majority of 36 ; but, the day afterwards, a more formidable attack on the Government was made by Mr. Cobden in the House of Commons. The Conservatives and the Free Trade and Peace party were by their very nature antagonistic; but on this occasion the followers of Lord Derby and the friends of Mr. Cobden united in attacking the ministry, and the Peelites and ultra-Radicals gave their support. On the 26th of February, Mr. Cobden moved a resolution asserting that the papers laid on the table failed to establish satisfactory grounds for the violent measures resorted to at Canton in the affair of the *Arrow*, and that it was desirable to appoint a select committee to inquire into the state of our commercial relations with China. The debate lasted four nights. Lord John Russell opposed the Government, and Mr. Roebuck, who had given Lord Palmerston such uncompromising support in the Pacific business, and defended the bombardment of the Piræus, objected to carrying out the principle in Chinese waters, and protested against the shelling of Canton.

Mr. Disraeli supported the motion, and so did Mr. Gladstone. The latter spoke at considerable length, and with his usual earnestness. He said : " If the House has the courage to assert its prerogative and adopt the resolution, it will pursue a course consistent at once with sound policy and the principles of strict justice." Religious considerations always influenced Mr. Gladstone's opinions, and he referred to them in his argument; but the House preferred to discuss the matter on its legal and international aspect, and the speaker continued :—

" As it seems to give offence, I will make no appeal to Christian principles, but I will appeal to that which is older than Christianity, to that which is broader than Christianity, because it extends in the world beyond Christianity, and to that which underlies Christianity, for Christianity chiefly appeals to it—I appeal to that justice which binds man to man. . . . With every one of us it rests to show that this House, which is the first, the most ancient, and the noblest temple of freedom in the world, is also the temple of that everlasting justice without which freedom itself would only be a name, or only a curse to mankind. And I cherish the trust that when you, sir, rise in your place to-night to declare the numbers of the division from the chair which you adorn, the words which you speak will go forth from the walls of the House of Commons as a message of British justice and wisdom to the farthest corner of the world."

Lord Palmerston put forth all his strength in reply ; but the House was less easily moved than that which, seven years

before, listened to the defence of his Greek policy. He struck
out vigorously as ever at all his opponents, but the phalanx was
unbroken.   He even reiterated the old charge against Mr.
Gladstone, that he defended the acts of retaliation committed by
the Chinese—a charge which, of course, nobody believed, and
which Mr. Gladstone again indignantly denied. When the
division took place there appeared, for the resolution, 263;
against, 247; leaving the Ministry in a minority of 16.

Lord Palmerston was not the man to take a beating in a spirit
of resignation. He had arguments to support his action which
the constituencies might accept, although they would have little
vitality in the House of Commons. He advised her Majesty to
dissolve the Parliament, then in the fifth year of its existence,
and he appealed to the country. In his address to the electors
of Tiverton, he adopted the tone of what the Americans know
as "spread-eagleism," or "high falutin'." There is an old
theatrical legend that, once on a time, at the Portsmouth Theatre,
a dull piece was dragging its slow length along, to the great dissatisfaction of the sailors in the gallery; and the leading actor,
seeing how matters went, suddenly broke off a long speech,
stepped to the footlights, and, striking an attitude, shouted,
"And did not our gallant Nelson, at Trafalgar, beat the French
mounseers?" It was not necessary to say more, for a hurricane of
applause followed. In like manner, Palmerston did not attempt
to defend the legality of the proceedings in China, but declared
that "an insolent barbarian, wielding authority at Canton,
violated the British flag, broke the engagements of treaties,
offered rewards for the heads of British subjects in that part of
China, and planned their destruction by murder, assassination,
and poison." The last words referred to a supposed attempt by
a Chinese baker named Allum to poison bread which he supplied
for the household of Sir John Bowring. He was tried for the
offence, but acquitted—a fact which did not prevent Palmerston
making the most of the incident.

The general election reversed the verdict of Parliament in the
most emphatic and decisive manner. Men who, a few months
before, had seemed to be almost the idols of their constituencies,
whose seats appeared to be assured, if ever Parliamentary seats
could be so described, were ejected in favour of supporters of
the Ministry. Mr. Cobden declined to offer himself again for
the West Riding of Yorkshire, and appeared as a candidate for
Huddersfield, but was defeated. Mr. Bright, absent from
England, suffering from severe illness, was rejected at Manches-

ter, as was his colleague, Mr. Milner Gibson. Mr. W. J. Fox met a like fate at Oldham, and Mr. Layard was left in the cold shade of defeat at Aylesbury. Mr. Lowe was elected for Kidderminster, but nearly killed in a hustings riot. Mr. Gladstone was re-elected for Oxford University without competition; but Mr. Cardwell lost his seat at Oxford. Only two members of the Administration were unseated—Admiral Berkeley at Gloucester, and Mr. Frederick Peel at Bury.

The new Parliament met on the 30th of April, and was ready to begin business on the 7th of May. Lord Palmerston found himself supported by a large majority, so successful had been his appeal to the constituencies. There were 189 new members in the House, and the party ranks showed 317 Liberals and 284 Conservatives.

When, on the 24th of June, the Divorce and Matrimonial Causes Bill came on for second reading (having passed the House of Lords), Mr. Gladstone opposed it, partly on the ground that the session was too far advanced to permit the full discussion which a measure of such importance demanded, but primarily on principle. Especially he objected to the inequality between the sexes which the Bill would establish. He said :—

"I shall always assert the principle of equal rights between the sexes with regard to a right of divorce. It is impossible to do a greater mischief than to begin now, in the middle of the nineteenth century, to undo, with regard to womankind, that which has already been done on their behalf, by slow degrees, in the preceding eighteen centuries, and to say that the husband shall be authorised to dismiss his wife on grounds for which the wife shall not be authorised to dismiss the husband."

Regarding the general scope of the Bill, he said :—

"It appears to me that by this Bill we are dealing with an unprecedented levity with matters that do not belong to us. I do not appeal simply to the conscience of the clergy—although I think the views of the clergy, as a class, are entitled to much weight, with regard to a question of this description—I speak of the religion which we entertain, and I do say that it is a matter of the deepest consequence to take care that in our legislation with respect to matrimony we do not offer profanation to that religion by making its sacred rites—designated by Apostles themselves with the very highest appellations— the mere creatures of our will, like some turnpike trust or board of health, which we can make to-day and unmake to-morrow."

The second reading of the Bill was carried by a majority of 111, the numbers being 208 against 97 ; but in committee every clause, almost every sentence, gave rise to a sharp contest. Mr. Gladstone was one of the most persistent, certainly the most formidable, of the assailants. He supported Mr. Drummond's

I

unsuccessful amendment to remove the distinction between man
and wife, and place the one on an equality with the other as to
the right to obtain a dissolution of marriage. He also spoke i ɩ
favour of Lord John Manners' amendment, to add to the grounds
on which a wife might petition for dissolution of marriage that
of adultery committed by the husband in the conjugal residence,
an amendment accepted by Lord Palmerston. Mr. Gladstone
then moved an amendment limiting the right of re-marriage of
divorced persons to a civil contract before the registrar, with a
view to avoid offending the conscientious scruples of clergymen
who might object to re-marry such persons. That amendment,
however, was withdrawn in favour of another, assented to by the
Government, which provided that no clergyman of the Church of
England should be compelled to solemnize the marriage of any
person whose previous marriage had been dissolved on the
ground of his or her adultery. The Bill passed the third reading
in the Commons on the 21st of August; but on the amendments
being referred to the Lords, the Bill narrowly escaped rejection,
for Lord Redesdale moved that the amendments should be taken
into consideration that day six months, and that motion was only
defeated by a majority of two. The amendment of Lord John
Manners, supported by Mr. Gladstone, and accepted by Lord
Palmerston, was, however, rejected; and, to that extent mutilated,
the Bill was passed, and received the Royal assent.

Parliament was prorogued on the 28th of August, soon after
the news of the incidents of the Indian mutiny had reached this
country; and for a time Englishmen forgot all minor things in
the excitement produced by that terrible event.

The new year (1858) was marked at its opening by an event
which led to memorable results in connection with the English
Administration. On the 14th of January an attempt was made
by Felix Orsini, an Italian, to assassinate the Emperor Napoleon,
by the explosion of three shells, in the streets of Paris, as the
Emperor was on his way to the Opera. Napoleon escaped un-
hurt, but two persons were killed, and many wounded. Orsini, a
man of considerable ability and of good social position, had for
fifteen years been connected with secret societies and revolutionary movements in Italy, and was associated with the chief
leaders of reactionary movements. He had twice visited England, had been well received, and had there arranged the mur-
derous plot against the life of the French Emperor. The idea
was entertained in Imperialist and military circles that the English
people sympathised with the assassin and his associates, and that

the English Government had been blameably lax in permitting the conspiracy to be arranged. A congratulatory address to the Emperor from colonels of the French army, printed in the official columns of the *Moniteur*, displayed a great feeling of irritation. Some of the addresses demanded "an account from the land of impurity which contains the haunts of the monsters who are sheltered by its laws." "Give the order, Sire," said one, "and we will pursue them even to their strongholds." Another said, "Let the infamous haunts in which machinations so infernal are planned be destroyed for ever."

Count Walewski, the French Minister for Foreign Affairs, addressed a despatch to M. de Persigny, the French ambassador in this country, for communication to our Government, in which he asked, "Ought the right of asylum to protect such a state of things? Is hospitality due to assassins? Should English legislation serve to favour their designs and manœuvres, and can it continue to protect persons who place themselves, by flagrant acts, without the pale of the common law, and expose themselves to the law of humanity?"

An address of congratulation to the Emperor on his escape having been presented by the Lord Mayor and Corporation of the City of London to M. de Persigny, the ambassador said, in the course of his acknowledgments, "If men in France were sufficiently infamous to recommend at their clubs, in their papers, in their writings of every kind, the assassination of a foreign sovereign, and actually to prepare its execution, a French administration would not wait to receive the demands of a foreign Government, nor to see the enterprise set on foot."

There was great irritation on each side of the Channel. The French Imperialists were angry with us for giving a home to political refugees, some of whom might be conspirators and assassins; and Englishmen generally warmly resented what they considered the dictatorial tone of the French despatches and the warlike blustering of the French colonels. As to the suggestion that our law was imperfect, or imperfectly administered, English feeling on the subject may be described in homely fashion, "Let them look after their own laws, and leave ours alone." There was certainly a worse feeling between the two countries than there had been at any time since the Prince de Joinville, a dozen years before, had published his remarkable pamphlet speculating on the capabilities of England to resist invasion.

When Parliament re-assembled, the indomitable Mr. Roebuck called attention to the expressions in the addresses of the French colonels and the tone of some of the speeches which had been made. He asked whether official notice had been taken of the matter, and whether any correspondence had passed between the English and French Governments with reference to any propositions for making changes in the criminal code of this country. Lord Palmerston replied that a communication had been made by the French minister to our ambassador in Paris, urging the British Government to take measures in that direction, but not pointing out any particular step to be taken. This reply was not considered satisfactory, especially as Lord Palmerston had already given notice that he should ask for leave to bring in a Bill to amend the law relating to conspiracy to commit murder.

On the 8th of February, the Prime Minister introduced the Bill, the chief provision of which was to make conspiracy to commit murder within the United Kingdom a felony, punishable with penal servitude for five years, or imprisonment, with hard labour, for three years. As the law stood, the offence was (except in Ireland) only a misdemeanour. The second clause of the Bill extended the same penalties to all who should "incite, instigate, or solicit" any other person to commit the offence. Lord Palmerston said, "I cannot but think that the provisions of the Bill will have a decisive effect in deterring those who may wish to make this country a place where they may hatch or concoct crimes of a disgraceful character, and, at all events, they will learn that they cannot do so without liability to punishment."

Mr. Kinglake, the future historian of the Crimean war, moved an amendment to the effect that it was inexpedient to legislate in compliance with the demands of Count Walewski's despatch of the 30th of January, until further information should be obtained.

Sir George Grey, the Home Secretary, said the intention of the Government was to make the law for England the same as that for Ireland, and to mitigate the latter when the offence was a felony, subject to the highest punishment. Referring to the expression of feeling in France, he read a later despatch from Count Walewski, in which it was stated that the colonels' address had been published in the *Moniteur* by an inadvertence, which the Emperor greatly regretted. Ultimately Mr. Kinglake withdrew his amendment, and the House assented to the introduction of the Bill by a majority of exactly 200, the numbers being 299 to 99.

Lord Palmerston, with all his experience and shrewdness, was perhaps a little misled by the success he had obtained so far. There was a fierce battle to come and a defeat to be sustained.

When the Bill came up for the second reading, on the 19th of February, Mr. Milner Gibson moved an amendment which, after expressing the detestation of the House of such guilty enterprises as the conspiracy against the life of the French Emperor, went on to say, " The House is ready at all times to assist in remedy ing any defects in the criminal law which, after due investigation, are proved to exist ; but it cannot but regret that Her Majesty's Government (previously to wanting the House to amend the laws relating to conspiracy at the present time) have not felt it to be their duty to make some reply to the despatch received from the French Government."

Mr. Disraeli, representing the opposition, supported the amendment ; and in the course of the debate Mr. Gladstone made a powerful speech against the Bill.   He said :

"These times are grave for liberty. We live in the nineteenth century. We talk of progress. We believe that we are advancing, but can any man of observation who has watched the events of the last few years in Europe have failed to perceive that there is a movement, indeed, but a downward and backward movement? There are a few spots on which institutions that claim our sympathy still exist and flourish. They are secondary places, nay, they are almost the holes and corners of Europe so far as mere material greatness is concerned, although their moral greatness will, I trust, ensure them long prosperity and happiness. But in these times more than ever does responsibility centre upon the institutions of England ; upon her principles, upon her laws, and upon her governors. Then I say that a measure passed by this House of Commons—the chief hope of freedom—which attempts to establish a moral complicity between us and those who seek safety in repressive measures, will be a blow and a discouragement to that sacred cause in every country in the world."

The second reading of the Bill was lost ; but not by a very large majority. Four hundred and forty-nine members went into the lobby, and the numbers were 215 for the Bill and 234 against —majority 19. The " Noes " included 146 Conservatives, 84 Liberals, and 4 Peelites—Gladstone, Graham, Cardwell, and Sidney Herbert. Mr. Gibson's amendment was carried without a division. The majority was not immense, but, like the wound given by Tybalt, in " Romeo and Juliet," it was " enough " for the Mercutio of the Ministry, and Palmerston could say, " I have it, soundly too." He had lost popularity as well as Parliamentary confidence. A few months before, when he talked about insolent barbarians violating the British flag, he was the hero of the hour ; but now when suspected of himself cringing to a foreign Emperor, at no time a favourite in this country, the popular voice was against him. On the 20th of February he announced the resignation of himself and colleagues.

The new Ministerial arrangements, entrusted to the Earl of Derby, were completed by the 25th. Mr. Disraeli resumed office as Chancellor of the Exchequer, and his great financial rival, Mr. Gladstone, was invited to enter the Cabinet as Secretary of State for the Colonies. He was not disposed, however, to cast in his lot with the Conservatives, for between their political doctrines and his the line of division was becoming more and more marked.

One of the earliest subjects which engaged the attention of Parliament was the seizure of a mail steamer, the *Cagliari*, belonging to Genoa, by the Neapolitan Government. A number of men, belonging to the revolutionary party then so active in Italy, had embarked on board the steamboat, and when well out at sea, had forcibly taken possession of it, and compelled the captain to steer for Ponza, where the Neapolitan prison was broken open, and about 400 political and other prisoners released. The desperadoes having left the vessel, the captain directed his course to Naples, with the intention of making the authorities acquainted with what had occurred ; but was met by a Neapolitan squadron. The *Cagliari* was boarded, and all hands taken into custody, among them being two Englishmen, named Watt and Park, who were imprisoned in dungeons where one became very ill, and the other lost his reason. This occurred in June, 1857, but some time elapsed before the particulars were known in England.

In March, 1858, Mr. Kinglake brought the matter before the House of Commons. He stated that two British subjects were wrongfully imprisoned, and made to suffer great hardships, on the plea that they awaited trial, and he asked if any correspondence on the subject could be produced. Shortly before Lord Palmerston quitted office, the attention of the Foreign Office had been directed to the subject, and it was at first supposed that the capture had taken place in Neapolitan waters, and that consequently the authorities were within their legal right ; and Mr. Disraeli, the Chancellor of the Exchequer in the new Ministry—not, probably, being aware at the time that it had been discovered the steamer at the time of the capture was in neutral waters, beyond the jurisdiction of Naples—could promise nothing more than that care should be taken that the men were speedily tried, and have justice. A long debate ensued ; and perhaps there were some who wished that Palmerston was once more at the Foreign Office to administer a little advice of the Piræus and Canton kind to the Government of King Bomba. Mr. Gladstone spoke at some length. He said : " I confess it will be with pain, astonishment, and shame, I shall find that the duty of vindicating the law of nations and the rights of Englishmen, even by accident, has fallen into the hands of feeble Sardinia, and has not been taken up by powerful England herself." Ultimately the Neapolitan Government released the men, giving £3,000 as compensation for their illegal detention.

Lord Palmerston had, in February, obtained permission, by 318 to 173, to introduce a Bill for transferring the government of India from the East India Company to the Crown; and it still stood for second reading. The Chancellor of the Exchequer, on the 26th of March, introduced a Government Bill having the same object. Lord John Russell suggested that the Bill should not be proceeded with, but that resolutions should be proposed in Committee of the whole House, by which means there would be a practical consultation between the Queen's Ministers and the House of Commons on the principles of the future government of India. Mr. Disraeli accepted the suggestion, which was approved of by Lord Palmerston, who said the government of India was far too important a matter to be made the shuttlecock of political parties. A few days afterwards the Chancellor of the Exchequer submitted fourteen resolutions.

Some of the resolutions were unavailingly opposed by Mr. Gladstone, who, on the 7th of June, moved as an amendment, "That, regard being had to the position of affairs in India, it is expedient to constitute the Court of Directors of the East India Company, by an Act of the present Session, to be a Council for administering the affairs of India in the name of Her Majesty, under the superintendence of a responsible Minister, until the end of the next session of Parliament." In opposing one of the resolutions he had said that, notwithstanding some errors, the Court of Directors had been practically a body protecting the people of India, and he could not see in the plan of the Government any advantages. Besides, the business of the Session would not allow sufficient time for the discussion of all the important subjects involved. He was evidently averse to the abolition of the governing power of the old Company; but his amendment was rejected by 285 to 110.

He afterwards moved the addition of a clause, accepted by the Ministry, providing that, "except for repelling actual invasion, or under other sudden and urgent necessity, Her Majesty's forces in the East Indies shall not be employed beyond the external frontier of her Majesty's Indian possessions, without the consent of Parliament to the purposes thereof." This clause was frequently referred to in after days.   An India Bill, founded on the resolutions, was brought in by Lord Stanley, passed with very little opposition, and received the Royal assent on the 2nd of August.

The first Budget of the new Ministry was introduced by the Chancellor of the Exchequer on the 19th of April.   Mr. Gladstone did not subject it to hostile criticism, but expressed a hope that Government would not lose sight of their obligations to the country in respect to the income-tax and the reduction of expenditure.

There was a remanent of the Crimean War in the position of the Danubian Principalities—Wallachia and Moldavia.   By the 22nd Article of the Treaty of Paris, 1856, the two Principalities had been guaranteed in all their privileges and immunities by the great Powers.   They now desired the privilege of self-government ; and on the 4th of May Mr. Gladstone moved that an address be presented to her Majesty expressing an earnest hope that just weight might be given to the wishes of the people, expressed through their representatives elected in conformity with the Treaty of Paris.   If, he argued, the provinces were united, a living barrier would be interposed between Russia and Turkey, and the union would not have the slightest effect upon the Ottoman Empire, which had not, and never had, the sovereignty of the Principalities.   The bonds of the people, in their relation to Turkey, were, he said, "only silken bonds, if they consisted only of the payment of a moderate sum of money, and the acknowledgment of a nominal supremacy.   Their relation to Turkey leaves about everything that a people can most earnestly desire. Their personal liberties, the power of self-government, and legislation are entirely theirs.   In the Principalities the feeling is favourable to Turkey, and the reason why it is favourable is, not that the people are inclined to the creed or the institutions of Turkey, but that the relation between the countries is one founded upon a liberal basis, and that there has been no sensible collision of interests between them."   These words were uttered only three years after the conclusion of the Crimean War, when the feeling against Russia had hardly subsided, and the "bag and baggage" theory had not been developed.   The motion for an address did not meet the approval of the House, being rejected by a majority of 178 (292 to 114).

Almost the only other occasion on which Mr. Gladstone spoke at any length in the Session of 1858 (which came to an end on the 2nd of August) was on the 1st of June, when he

supported a resolution in support of the project for making the
Suez Canal.

In the latter part of the autumn the political world was startled
by the announcement that Mr. Gladstone had accepted from
Lord Derby the appointment of Lord High Commissioner Extraordinary to the Ionian Islands.   The *Saturday Review* expressed
the astonishment very generally felt :—

> "What good is Corfu to derive from Mr. Gladstone, or Mr. Gladstone
> from Corfu? To the question of *Cui bono?* or, Who is to profit by the appoint-
> ment? Mr. Disraeli probably considers that he can give a satisfactory
> answer.   To buy off, or to seem to buy off, a dangerous rival or formidable
> opponent—effecting the purchase at the low price of a remote personal interest
> —is a transaction entirely in the spirit of that political philosophy which is
> expounded in the pages of 'Vivian Grey.' . . . Mr. Gladstone's paradoxical,
> or unexpected, determination to accept office under Lord Derby has assuredly
> not arisen from any vulgar calculation of conscious selfishness.   Romantic
> sympathy for a church which he misunderstands, and for a race with which he
> has no practical acquaintance, an intelligible longing to escape for a time from
> party struggles at home, and an honourable ambition of acquiring fame in an
> untried career, may explain a course which seems equally at variance with
> public policy and with personal interest."

The acceptance of the appointment was supposed by some to
indicate an intention on the part of Mr. Gladstone to unite with
the Conservative party ; but all such speculations were ill-founded.
It seems to have been by the influence of Sir Edward Bulwer
Lytton, who had succeeded Lord Stanley as Colonial Secretary,
that Mr. Gladstone was offered the appointment, which involved
no compromise of political opinions, but was for the purpose of
an inquiry for which Mr. Gladstone's studies, sympathies, and
eminent position peculiarly qualified him.   Some months before,
when Lord Palmerston was in office, Sir John Young, Lord High
Commissioner of the Ionian Islands (which had been, since 1815,
under British protectorate), had forwarded two despatches to the
Colonial Office, recommending the abandonment of the protectorate in all the islands, except Corfu, to be retained as a military
post.   Whatever the Palmerston Ministry might have thought
about the project, they kept their opinions to themselves, and
the despatch might have remained unknown to the public if, on
the principle, it would seem, that all is fair in love, law, and
journalism, a person, who had access to the library of the Colonial
Office, had not obtained a copy surreptitiously—"Convey, the
wise it call," said Antient Pistol—and forwarded it to the *Daily
News*, in which the despatch appeared soon after the prorogation
of Parliament, in the autumn of 1858.   The ingenious, if not

ingenuous, purveyor of information was prosecuted, and appeared at the Old Bailey, but was acquitted on a point of law, namely, that the offence did not amount to felony, as charged in the indictment.

It was a matter of notoriety that there was a strong feeling on the part of many of the inhabitants of the Ionian Islands in favour of a union with Greece, a kindred nationality; and now that it was announced to the world that official representations on the subject had been made to the British Government, it was almost a necessity that some action should be taken on the matter; and the appointment of a Commissioner of high reputation and independent position was an obvious and creditable course to pursue.

On the 29th of November, Mr. Gladstone arrived at Corfu and met with an enthusiastic reception. The popular impression seems to have been that he was empowered to make arrangements for the desired annexation with Greece. On the 3rd of December he addressed the Senate in explanation of the object of his mission, which, he said, avoided every ulterior question that could derogate from the relation in which, by the consent of so many great States, England and the Ionian Islands have been reciprocally placed. "The liberty guaranteed by the Treaties of Paris and by the Ionian law are, in the eyes of Her Majesty sacred. On the other hand, the purpose for which she has sent me is not to inquire into the British protectorate, but to examine in what way Great Britain may most honourably and amply discharge the obligations which, for purposes European and Ionian rather than British, she has contracted."

On the 27th of January, 1859, the members of the Ionian Legislative Assembly passed a resolution in favour of union with Greece. Mr. Gladstone advised the Assembly to proceed in the usual way, by petition, memorial, or representation to the protecting Power. The Home Ministry advised her Majesty to decline to grant the prayer of the petition, and Mr Gladstone, his mission ended, returned to England. General Sir Henry Storks, a soldier of great experience and administrative ability, was appointed Lord High Commissioner. The Legislative Assembly continued its agitation for annexation; and in May, 1864, the desired result was obtained.

CHAPTER XIII.

HOMERIC INVESTIGATIONS.

In one respect the visit to the "Isles of Greece" had probably an especial charm for Mr. Gladstone. From a very early age he had given himself with imaginative enthusiasm to Homeric studies. To his scholarly taste the work of textual and historical criticism was peculiarly adapted; his vigorous imagination delighted to realise the great actions and the great events of the Homeric narrative; and his religious instinct appreciated the recognition of the alliance of the divine and human which is concealed from common view behind the mythological veil. He believed in the individuality of Homer from internal evidence, although the personal poet is lost in the mists gathered around the ages which have passed away; and he sought to identify the scenes of the great epic, to trace with some approach to certainty the limits of the world known to the poet, and to tell us something of the manner in which his poems were preserved to posterity. For sixty years or more Homer has been to Gladstone what Horace was to a genial, but much inferior man, who, in one of his best moods, said—

> "In childhood I prattled about him,
> In youth he was ever my charm;
> In manhood I ne'er went without him,
> In age he lies under my arm."

If, in Sicily, Mr. Gladstone could trace the steps of Virgil, far more clearly could he recognise in the islands of the Greek sea the influences which inspired or aided the muse of Homer. The glorious skies, the Mediterranean waves, beating on rocks and sandy shores, the rich verdure, the mountains and caves, were there. A less scholastic mind than that of Mr. Gladstone, imbued so richly with classical lore that the past is almost as vivid a reality as the present, a less vigorous imagination, might have indulged a vision of the lonely Penelope of Ithaca and the wandering Odysseus, or of galleys filled with armed legions, described in the famous catalogue of the ships in the second book of the "Iliad," making way through devious channels amid the cluster of islands to the Asian Troad, where, in Ilium, the beauteous Helen, the stolen wife of Menelaus of Sparta, was a captive.

Quitting for a time the records of the remarkable political career of Mr. Gladstone, we may fitly devote a few pages to a notice of the results of his studies in "Homerology," as he styles it. A brief summary of the conclusions he has arrived at respecting the personal history of Homer, and an analysis of the great epics, are given in a little book—one of the popular "Literature Primers," published in 1878. The year before his visit to the Ionian Islands he had given to the world, "Place of Homer in Classical Education and Historical Inquiry," and in the year of his visit (1858), "Studies of Homer and the Homeric Age." In 1869 appeared "Juventus Mundi; the Gods and Men of the Homeric Age," and, so recently as 1876, when for a brief space he rested from Parliamentary labours, and hoped to pass the remainder of his life in learned leisure, appeared "Homeric Synchronism," and "An Inquiry into the Time and Place of Homer." We do not propose to attempt a close and analytical criticism of these works; it will be sufficient for our present purpose to indicate generally the conclusions the author has arrived at. He probably hopes that he may be enabled to continue the work; at any rate there is a significant hint in a passage in the "Homer" of the "Literature Primers" series :—

"Unhappily, the full contents of the poems have never yet been methodically submitted to the world, so as to allow of a comprehensive consideration of their wide range, their variety, and their very extensive coherence in detail. Even German sedulity has until the present time shrunk from this task, and the world has been contented hitherto with slight and imperfect efforts. Dr. Buckholz, of Erfurt, has at length confronted the enterprise, and has already published two volumes of *Homerische Realsen*. One *Englishman*, at *last*, *has a similar undertaking in hand*."

Mr. Gladstone, as we have stated, believes in the personality of Homer, and rejects the theories advanced by the German Professor, Frederick Augustus Wolf, and others, that the "Iliad" is a compilation of ballads by various authors, embodying national tradition, and not the work of one mind. "Over and above correspondence of tangible particulars," says Mr. Gladstone, "there is what I must call an unity of atmosphere in the poems, such as I believe has never been achieved by forgery or imitation." Homer—which he does not understand strictly as the proper name of the poet, but rather as a generic term implying author—was born, he thinks, shortly before the Trojan war, or during the war. The much vexed question of the place of his nativity, "Scio's rocky isle," or elsewhere, he leaves as unsolved

FIDE ET VIRTVTE

WILLIAM EWART GLADSTONE

NORTHBOVRNE d:d: 23 JVLY 1838
23 JVLY 1889

MR. GLADSTONE'S BOOK-PLATE.

and comparatively unimportant. In " Homeric Synchronism,"
he maintains that the historical and ethnological situation in the
" Iliad " and the " Odyssey " is such that we are able to fix the
date of the Trojan war, and also of the poems, with approximate
certainty, "to the satisfaction of all reasonable minds." This
evidence (and a confirmation is afforded by Egyptian inscriptions)
justifies him in supposing that the overthrow of Troy took
place some time between 1286 and 1226 B.C. He thinks, too,
that the site of Troy, or Ilium, was discovered by Dr. Schliemann
when (1871–3) he excavated the hill of Hissarlik.

In " Juventus Mundi," he says of Homer :—

"He has supplied us with a more complete picture of the Greek, or, as he
would probably say, of the Achaian people of his time, than any other author
—it might almost be said, than any number of authors have supplied with
reference to any other age and people. . . . He was not only the glory and
delight, but he was, in a great degree, the *poietes*, the ' maker ' of his
nation."

In the " Literature Primer," he says of the Homeric poems :—

"They, and the manners they describe, constitute a world of their own,
and are severed by a sea of time, whose breadth has not been certainly
measured, from the firmly set continent of recorded tradition and continuous
fact. In this sea they lie, as a great island. And in this island we find not
merely details of events, but a scheme of human life and character complete
in all its parts. We are introduced to man in every relation of which he is
capable, in every one of his acts, devices, institutions ; in the entire circle of
his experience. There is no other author whose case is analogous to his, or
of whom it can be said that the study of him is not a mere matter of literary
criticism, but is a full study of life in every one of its departments."

Some readers may be disposed to ask, after perusing the last
sentence, whether Shakspere is quite unknown to Mr. Gladstone.
The information contained in the Homeric poems is, he tells us,
" of the utmost interest, and even of great moment "—

"It introduces to us, in the very beginning of their experience, the most
gifted people in the world, and enables us to judge how they became such as
in later times we know them ; how they began to be fitted to discharge the
splendid part allotted to them in shaping the destinies of the world. And
this picture is exhibited with such a fulness both of particulars and vital
force, that perhaps never in any country has an age been so completely placed
upon record."

As a man of strong religious convictions, and profoundly interested in the spiritual progress of humanity, Mr. Gladstone
naturally and earnestly directed his attention to the principles
which underlay the actual faith of the ancient Greeks. Homer
lived at a time when the worship of the greater deities of the old

Pelasgian system had been superseded, and that of smaller
divinities had succeeded, and when worship was localised. He
"had to exercise his plastic power as a poet upon traditions
which he found ready at hand;" and some of these traditions he
embodied with wonderful power. The strength of the Olympic,
or highest form of localised religion,

"Lay in its beauty . . . and probably we could not name, in all human
experience, a more signal instance of the vast power of the imagination than
is to be found in the long life and the extended influences of the Greek
religion. It found a way to the mind of man through his sympathies and
propensities. Homer reflected upon his Olympos the ideas, passions, and
appetites known to us all, with such a force that they became with him the
paramount power in the construction of the Greek religion. This humanita-
rian element gradually subdued to itself all that it found in Greece of traditions already recognised, whether primitive or modern, whether Hellenic,
Pelasgian, or foreign. The governing idea of the character of deity in Homer
is a nature essentially human, with the addition of unmeasured power."

In another passage he says :—

"During twelve or fourteen hundred years, it [the Olympian system] was
the religion of the most thoughtful, the most fruitful, the most energetic portion of the human race. It yielded to Christianity alone. . . . Even within
what may be called our own time, the Olympian religion has exercised a
fascination altogether extraordinary over the mind of Goethe, who must be
regarded as standing in the very first rank of the greatest minds of the latest
centuries. The Olympian religion, however, owes perhaps as large a share of
its triumphs to its depraved accommodations as to its excellences. Yet an
instrument so durable, potent, and elastic must certainly have had a purpose
to serve. Let us consider for a moment what it may have been. We have
seen how closely, and in how many ways, it bound humanity and deity
together. As regarded matters of duty and virtue, not to speak of that
highest form of virtue which is called holiness, this union was effected mainly
by lowering the divine element. But as regarded all other functions of our
nature, outside the domain of life, and God-ward, all the functions which are
summed up in what St. Paul calls the flesh and the mind, the psychic and
the bodily life, the tendency of the system was to exalt the human element,
by proposing a model of beauty, strength, and wisdom, in all their combinations, so elevated that the effort to attain them required a continual upward
strain. It made divinity attainable, and thus it effectually directed the
thought and aim of man 'along the line of limitless desires.' Such a
scheme of religion, though failing grossly in the government of the
passions, and in upholding the standard of moral duties, tended powerfully
to produce a lofty self-respect, and a large, free and varied conception of
humanity. It manifested itself in schemes of notable discipline for mind and
body, indeed of a lifelong education : and these habits of mind and action had
their marked results (to omit many other greatnesses) in a philosophy, literature, and art which remain to this day unrivalled or unsurpassed. The
sacred fire, indeed, that was to touch the mind and heart of man from above
was in preparation elsewhere. Within the shelter of the hills that stand
about Jerusalem, the great Archetype of the spiritual excellence and purifica-
tion of man was to be produced and matured. But a body, as it were, was to

be made ready for this angelic soul. And, as when some splendid edifice is to be raised, its diversified materials are brought from this quarter and from that, according as nature and man favour their production, so did the wisdom of God, with slow but ever sure device, cause to ripen amidst the several races best adapted for the work the several parts of the noble corporeal fabric of a Christian manhood and a Christian civilisation. 'The kings of Tharsis and of the isles shall give presents : the kings of Arabia and Saba shall bring gifts.' Every worker was, with or without his knowledge and his will, to contribute to the work. And among these an appropriate part was thus assigned both to the Greek people and to what I have termed the Olympian religion."

Mr. Gladstone admits that Hebrew tradition, the expectation of a Redeemer at once human and divine, favoured the anthropo-morphic principle, and "laid a basis for the entire system, by annexing the glory of Divine attributes to the corporeal form of man." The familiar belief of the intercourse of God with the patriarchs was, he thinks, equally favourable to the principle, which "readily adapts itself to, if, indeed, it does not require, the use of a form approaching, at least, to the human type."

In the "Studies of Homer and the Homeric Age" Mr. Glad-stone lays great stress upon these points, and his views excited considerable controversy. He says :—

"The general view which will be given in these pages of the Homeric Theo-Mythology is as follows :—That its basis is not to be found either in any mere human instinct gradually building it up from the ground, or in the already formed system of any other nation of antiquity, but that its true point of origin lies in the ancient Theistic and Messianic traditions which we know to have subsisted among the patriarchs, and which their kin and contem-poraries must have carried with them as they dispersed, although their original warmth and vitality could not but fall into a course of gradual efflux, with the gradually widening distance from their source. To travel beyond the reach of the rays proceeding from that source was to make the first de-cisive step from religion to mythology. To this divine tradition there were added, in rank abundance, elements of merely human fabrication, which, while intruding themselves, could not but also extrude the higher and prior parts of religion."

In another part of the work he says :—

"Those who have found in Homer the elements of religious truth have resorted to the far-fetched and very extravagant supposition that he had learned them from the contemporary Hebrews, or from the law of Moses. . . . Few, comparatively, have been inclined to recognise in the Homeric poems the vestiges of a real traditional knowledge, derived from the epoch when the covenant of God with man, and the promise of a Messiah, had not yet fallen within the contracted form of Judaism for shelter, but entered more or less into the common consciousness, and formed a part of the patrimony, of the human race. But surely there is nothing improbable in the supposition that in the poems of Homer such vestiges may be found. Every recorded form of

society bears some traces of those by which it has been preceded ; and in
that highly primitive form which Homer has been the instrument of embalm-
ing for all posterity the law of general reason obliges us to search for elements
and vestiges belonging to one more primitive still. . . . Standing next to the
patriarchal histories of Holy Scripture, why should it not bear, how can it
not bear, traces of the religion under which the patriarchs lived?"

Whatever corruptions may have entered into the Greek mythology, even in Homer's time, "the system of government was
addressed, in the main, to good ends. It exhibited, generally
speaking, though in an imperfect, yet in a real manner, supreme
power, as real and active on behalf of truth, justice and humanity."
Referring generally to Greek literature and philosophy, Mr.
Gladstone admits that

"It is quite idle for modern theorists to suppose that we can dispense with
their (the Greeks') aid, or shake off what some would call a thraldom. This
could only be done by going back to a state which, whatever its equipments
in certain respects, would be, in essential points, one nearer to barbarism than
that which we now hold. The work of the Greeks has been done once for
all, and for all mankind. Regarding more closely their office in the great
designs of Providence for the education of man, we may say at large that it
was to supply a special school, in which the whole intellect of the individual
man should be trained."

The writings of Mr. Gladstone on this subject have been generally acknowledged by scholars to be valuable contributions to
Homeric literature ; but, of course, all his conclusions have not
been accepted, especially by German critics. At home, the
Edinburgh Review, in an article on the "Studies of Homer and
the Homeric Age," highly praised the taste and feeling displayed,
while dissatisfied with the volumes as a critical essay :—"A more
attractive composition on the one hand, so far as taste and
feeling are concerned, one more unsatisfactory, on the other, as
a critical essay, the product of accurate learning, it is scarcely
possible to imagine. Under the first point of view, the volumes
well deserve the great admiration, not to say enthusiasm, which
they have excited, especially among younger and fresher readers ;
but, in their learned aspect, we cannot regard them as anything
but monuments of ingenuity wastefully expended, and, as usual
in such cases, and with such writers, the cleverest parts are precisely the most unconvincing."

That so active a politician as Mr. Gladstone should escape a
little *badinage* respecting his classical investigations was scarcely
likely. The *Edinburgh Review* smiled at his defence of Hebe,
"that primitive Traviata," and asked, "Does not the smile
become broader still when we find the old Pagan poet pressed

into the service of the Parliamentary corps with which Mr. Gladstone has been acting during recent sessions?—when a negative authority is squeezed out of him against the 'poor invention of divorce'? or, stranger yet, when the copiousness of his vocabulary in distinguishing different degrees of relationship by affinity is shown to indicate that, if he had lived, he would have voted in decided opposition to Lord Bury on the question of marriage with a deceased wife's sister?"

Homer is not the only classical author who has enjoyed the attention of Mr. Gladstone. In 1861, in conjunction with Lord Lyttelton, he published a small volume of translations, his contributions to the book including translations of passages from the "Agamemnon" of Æschylus, the "Iliad," and the Odes of Horace and Catullus. Latin and Greek readings from Dante and Manzoni were added. In noticing this volume, the *Edinburgh* said : "In translating poetry of a high class, he takes rank, beyond the possibility of controversy, in the forefront of the very best translators."

Literature, however, is but an episode in the life of Mr. Gladstone, however much he may have desired to make it a very prominent feature. He is always scholarly, well-informed, clear-headed, and accurate ; a master of all mere forms of composition ; but seeming to lack the fine instinct, the emotional susceptibility, the unconscious mastery of language as an instrument of thought, which mark the really great writer. As in his oratory, so in his writings, there are fluency, force, rhetorical ornament, but little fancy, and few phrases that will live for ages in crystal clearness and epigrammatic vigour.

CHAPTER XIV.

THE CONSERVATIVE REFORM BILL.

THE special feature of the opening of the Session of 1859 was the introduction of the Conservative Reform Bill, by the Chancellor of the Exchequer. Mr. Gladstone had returned from the Ionian Isles, and dismissing, for a time, from his mind the blue Ægean and its poetical associations, prepared himself to examine the provisions of the new measure. Unlike Lord John Russell, he entertained no " finality " views, and did not regard the Reform Bill of 1832 as a masterpiece, to endure for all time. But, as we shall see, he felt something like a lingering respect for something that had been destroyed by that enactment.

On the 28th of February, Mr. Disraeli brought in the Bill, which he explained had a tendency to " lateral " representation ; that is, extended the suffrage sideways at its existing levels. He said, " The House ought to represent not only numbers and property, but all the interests of the country, and these interests were often analogous and competing. . . . . The object of representation was to present a mirror of the mind of the country, its agriculture, its commerce, its professional ability." Ministers, he explained, did not propose to alter the limits of the franchise, but to introduce into boroughs a new kind of franchise, founded upon personal property, and to give a vote to persons having property to the amount of £10 a year in the Funds, Bank Stock, or East India Stock. A person having £60 in a savings' bank would, under the Bill, be an elector for the borough in which he resided, as well as the recipient of a pension in the naval, military, and civil services amounting to £20 a year. Dwellers in a portion of a house, the aggregate value of which was £20 a year, should be entitled to vote. The suffrage would also be conferred upon graduates of the Universities, ministers of religion, members of the legal profession and of the medical body, and certain schoolmasters. It was proposed also to make the suffrage identical in towns and counties ; by giving to counties a £10 franchise, 20,000 voters would be added to the constituencies. Polling papers might be substituted for the present mode of voting. The Bill proposed that there should be a West York.

shire, a North-West Yorkshire, and a South Yorkshire; and that sixteen small boroughs now returning two members each, should in future return only one. The seats thus vacated would be appropriated by giving four to Yorkshire (as newly divided), two to South Lancashire, two to Middlesex (a new constituency to include Chelsea and Kensington), and eight towns—Hartlepool, Birkenhead, West Bromwich, Wednesbury, Barnsley, Staleybridge, Croydon, and Gravesend—should be enfranchised. In a genuine vein of Disraelian grim humour, the Chancellor of the Exchequer consoled the members for the small boroughs who would be deprived of their seats, by the suggestion that "it would be an admirable opportunity for a display of patriotism, an opportunity seldom offered by the circumstances and occasions of society."

The introduction of the Bill caused a split in the Cabinet. Mr. Walpole, the Home Secretary, and Mr. Henley, President of the Board of Trade, resigned, on the ground that they could not accept the lowering of the county franchise, which Mr. Walpole described as a dangerous innovation, and Mr. Henley as fatal to the Constitution of the country.

Mr. Baxter, member for Montrose, moved "That it is expedient to consider the law relating to the representation of the people in England, Scotland, and Ireland, not separately, but in one measure." One of the clauses of the Bill proposed to take away from freeholders in boroughs the franchise by which they were entitled to vote for counties. This was very unpalatable, not only to Liberals, but to many Conservatives. So strongly expressed was the feeling of opposition, that Ministers made a concession by giving notice of the introduction of a clause by which freeholders in boroughs should have the option of being placed on the borough or county register, but not on both.

When the Bill came on for the second reading, on the 20th of March, Lord John Russell moved, as an amendment, "That the House is of opinion that it is neither just nor politic to interfere in the manner proposed by the Bill with the freehold franchise as hitherto exercised in counties in England and Wales; and that no re-adjustment of the franchise will satisfy the House or the country which does not provide for a greater extension of the suffrage in cities and boroughs than is contemplated by the present measure."

Lord Stanley, on behalf of the Government, said the amendment would, if carried, be fatal to the Bill.

The debate was vigorous and prolonged. On the 29th of

March, the sixth night, Mr. Gladstone spoke in favour of the
second reading of the Bill, especially approving of that part of
it which related to the redistribution of seats. He would have
voted for the resolution proposed by Lord John Russell, but he
found only a limited agreement among the Liberal leaders, and if
the resolution were carried, the Opposition would pursue separate
courses. Previous Governments had failed to carry a Reform
Bill, and now there was a golden opportunity, which should not
be lost. He concurred in nearly everything that had been said
against the Bill; but thought amendments might be made in
committee. "I cannot," he said, "be a party to the disfranchisement of the county freeholders residing in boroughs. I
cannot be a party to the uniformity of the franchise. I cannot
be a party to a Reform Bill which does not lower the suffrage in
boroughs." It was in this speech that he made his remarkable
defence of the small nomination boroughs, which advanced
reformers described as a political scandal :—

"I must frankly own it appears to me that to proceed far in the disfranchisement of small boroughs is a course injurious to the efficiency of the
House of Commons. You must not consider in this matter the question only
of the electors. You must consider quite as much who are likely to be elected.
. . . I am no great lover of small constituencies, and it never was my lot to
sit for one. At the same time, small constituencies undoubtedly tend to
answer the great purpose of a representative system, in securing its diversity
and completeness. If you have nothing but large and populous bodies to
return your members of Parliament, then, as recent experience seems, I am
sorry to say, in a great degree to prove, local interests and local influences
will upon the whole prevail, and you will not find it possible to introduce
adequately into the House the race of men by whom the government of the
country is to be carried on. By means of small boroughs, generally considered
—I have no doubt there are objections to them, but I believe these objections
are gradually disappearing under the action of improved laws, and an improved
state of public feeling—by means of small boroughs you introduce into the
House the representatives of separate interests, who stand apart from the
great and the paramount interests of the country. You introduce here the
masters of civil wisdom, such as Mr. Burke above all, Sir James Mackintosh,
and many others who might be named—a class of men with respect to whom
nothing is less probable than that they should command to any great extent
the suffrages of large and popular constituencies. You introduce those calm,
sagacious, retired observers, who are averse from the rough contact necessary
in canvassing large bodies of electors, but who form no small part of the best
substrata of the House, and contribute greatly to the efficiency of your representative system. Many, however, have spoken on behalf of small boroughs—
of those where, from kindly interest, from ancient and affectionate recollections,
from local and traditional respect, from the memory of services received, from
the admiration of great men and great qualities, the constituencies are willing
to take upon trust the recommendation of candidates for Parliament from
noblemen or gentlemen who may stand in immediate connection with them.
[Cries of "Oh!" interrupted the speaker.] I do not complain at all of that

interruption.   I admit that there is something of paradox in such an argument
upon such a question, if it is to be considered as an argument upon paper only ;
but practice has proved that the real paradox lies with those who will allow of
no ingress into the House but one.   If that one ingress is to be the suffrages
of a large mass of voters, the consequence is a dead level of mediocrity, which
destroys not only the ornament, but the force of this House, and which, as I
think the history of other countries will show, is ultimately fatal to the liberties
of the people.   Allow me, in explanation of my meaning, to state the case of
six men in one line each—Mr. Pelham, Lord Chatham, Mr. Fox, Mr. Pitt,
Mr. Canning, and Sir Robert Peel.   Mr. Pelham entered the House for the
borough of Seaford in 1719, at the age of twenty-two ; Lord Chatham entered
it in 1735 for Old Sarum, at the age of twenty-six ; Mr. Fox, in 1764, for
Midhurst, at the age, I think, of twenty ; Mr. Pitt, in 1781, for Appleby, at
the age of twenty-one ; and Sir Robert Peel, in 1809, for the city of Cashel,
at the age of twenty-one.   Now, here are six men, every one of whom was a
leader in this House.   Here are six men whom I do not hesitate to say you
cannot match out of the history of the British House of Commons for the
hundred years which precede our own day.   Every one of them was a leader
in this House, almost every one was a Prime Minister, all of them entered
Parliament for one of those boroughs where influence of different kinds prevailed. . . . What does this show ?   It shows that small boroughs were the
nursery-ground in which these men were educated—men who not only were
destined to lead this House, to govern the country, to be the strength of
England at home, and its ornament abroad ; but who, likewise, when once
they had an opportunity of proving their powers in this House, became the
chosen of large constituencies and the favourites of the nation. . . .   It is not
too much to say that no one of those mere boys could have become a member
of Parliament if it had not been for the means of access to the House of
Commons which then existed.   You must recollect that they were nearly all
chosen when they were about twenty-one or twenty-two.   What is the case
now ?   I fully grant that you have an answer as far as regards a very limited
class of persons indeed.   Take the heir to a dukedom or an earldom, or the
son of a great territorial potentate, and there will be ready access to Parliament
for such men ; nor, I trust, shall we ever see any measures which will exclude
them.   I rejoice to see that by so limited a class so much ability and so much
promise is shown.   If you look to the young men of the day—and, after all,
it is to them we must look to carry on the business of the country in future
years—the most distinguished persons in this House are the men who owe
their seats here to territorial influence.   The cases of Canning, Fox, Pitt, and
Peel carry a moral with them.   What would have been Mr. Canning's chance
had he been dependent on that influence?   I do not know what would
have been the chances of Mr. Fox, or Mr. Pitt, or Sir Robert Peel at twenty-
one or twenty-two if they had been dependent on territorial influence.   You
cannot expect of large and popular constituencies that they should return boys
to Parliament, and yet, if you want a succession of men trained to take part in
the government of the country, you must have a great portion of them returned to this House when they are boys.   The conclusion to which this
brings me is that the matter will be a more serious one if you are prepared to
part with your whole system of small boroughs.   I am not arguing this in the
sense of one party or another ; far less am I arguing it in a sense adverse to
popular rights.   For what, let me ask, have these men whose names I
have just mentioned been ?   Have they been the enemies of popular rights ?
Is it not, on the contrary, under Providence, in a great degree to be attributed to a succession of these distinguished statesmen, introduced at an

early age into this House, and, once made known in this House, securing
to themselves the general favour of their countrymen, that we enjoy our
present extension of popular liberty, and, above all, the durable form
which that liberty has now assumed?"

On the seventh night a division took place, and the second
reading was lost; the Ayes numbering 291 and the Noes 330 —
majority 39. Mr. Gladstone was the only Peelite who voted for
the Government; Sir James Graham, Mr. Cardwell, and Mr.
Sidney Herbert voting with the opposition. Mr. Gladstone probably hoped that, if the second reading were carried, considerable
modification might be made in committee, and he was unwilling
to lose the opportunity of carrying a practically useful measure of
reform. Lord John Russell's resolution was carried as a substantive motion.

After so signal a defeat on a vital measure, Ministers had no
other course open than either to resign office or appeal to the
verdict of a general election. They preferred the latter alternative, and Parliament was dissolved on the 19th of April. In the
Royal Speech, delivered by Commission, it was stated, "Her
Majesty commands us to inform you that the appeal she is about
to make to her people has been rendered necessary by the difficulties experienced in carrying on the public business of the
country."

The new Parliament met on the 31st of May. The appeal to
the country had been made on the ground that it was desirable
to obtain the judgment of the constituencies on the Reform propositions of the Ministry; but there was apparently some disposition to allow the subject to drift over to a more convenient
season. The result of the election showed that, to say the least,
Ministers had not strengthened their hands; and, although they
could not well avoid a reference to Reform in the Speech at the
opening of Parliament, it was qualified and conditional:—
"Should you be of opinion that the necessity of giving your
immediate attention to measures of urgency relating to the
defences and financial condition of the country will not leave you
sufficient time for legislating with due deliberation during the
present session on a subject so difficult and so extensive, I trust
that at the commencement of the next session your earnest attention will be given to a question of which an early and satisfactory
settlement would be greatly to the public advantage."

The Liberal party, encouraged by the result of the elections,
determined to challenge the Ministry at once; and a meeting of
the party was held at Willis's Rooms, on the 6th of June, to make

arrangements for proposing a vote of want of confidence. Lord Palmerston, Lord John Russell, Mr. Bright, Mr. Horsman, and Mr. Sidney Herbert (representing the Peelites, now almost absorbed in the Liberal ranks), were among the speakers.

In the House of Commons, an amendment to the Address was moved by a young member, destined in after times to occupy a very prominent Parliamentary position—the Marquis of Hartington, son of the Duke of Devonshire. He was then only twenty-six years old, and had sat in the House as representative of North Lancashire for two years. He was very young to be entrusted with so important a duty, but he proved that the confidence of his friends was not misplaced. His amendment was a direct expression of want of confidence in Her Majesty's Ministers ; and he condemned their conduct in dissolving Parliament at a time when its advice was so much needed. The war between Austria and France was waging, and our position in regard to foreign complications was one which caused great anxiety ; and there was a strong feeling that the Ministry should not have considered the defeat on the Reform Bill as involving the necessity of a dissolution. The Liberal party, however, it may be observed, had no objection to the farther delay of business and the political embarrassment which the change of Ministry they were so desirous to bring about would involve.

The amendment was carried by a majority of 13—323 against 310. The ministerial minority was therefore less (13 as compared with 39) than on the division on the Reform Bill a few weeks before. Mr. Gladstone did not speak in the debate, but he voted for the Ministry, and against his old associates, Sir James Graham, Mr. Cardwell, and Mr. Sidney Herbert, who swelled the ranks of the majority.

On the 17th of June, the Earl of Derby, in the House of Lords, and Mr. Disraeli, in the House of Commons, announced the resignation of the Ministry. The Queen, apprehensive, perhaps, of a rivalry between Lords Palmerston and Russell, sent for Earl Granville ; but he declined to attempt to form a Ministry, and advised that Lord Palmerston should be entrusted with the task.

An understanding, it seems, existed between Lords Palmerston and Russell that, whichever of the two should be selected as Prime Minister, the other would give him all the assistance in his power, and the arrangement was loyally carried out. Lord John Russell took the Foreign Office ; the Duke of Newcastle, the Colonies ; Sir G. C. Lewis, the Home Department ; and Mr. Sidney Herbert became Secretary of War. Lord Palmerston was very desirous to include Mr. Cobden in the new arrangements, and kept the office of President of the Board of Trade open for his acceptance. The great Free Trader was then on his way home from America, and on his arrival declined to take office. Mr. Milner Gibson, who had been appointed President of the Poor Law Board, shifted to the vacant office, his place being supplied by Mr. Cardwell, who had previously accepted office as Chief Secretary of Ireland.

There was still one great office to be filled up—that of Chancellor of the Exchequer—in some respects the most important in the Cabinet, next to that of the Prime Minister, and all eyes were turned towards the man who, by universal consent, was best qualified to fill it. Mr. Gladstone had opposed the vote of want of confidence and had supported the second reading of the Conservative Reform Bill. That he was a Liberal in the main none could doubt; but lately he had shown more sympathy with the opposite side. There was some curious speculation as to the course he would take; but the matter was settled by his acceptance of office.

Another appeal to the University constituency was necessary. At the general election Mr. Gladstone had been returned without opposition, but now he was not permitted to retain his seat unchallenged, and an effort was made to bring forward the Marquis of Chandos, son of the Duke of Buckingham. The opposition was strongly commented on even by those organs in the public press which by no means gave an undeviating support to Mr. Gladstone. As exhibiting a very general feeling, we may quote a passage from the *Saturday Review* of the 25th of June, 1859:—

"This journal is not to be classed amongst the great admirers of Mr. Gladstone's course as a statesman; nor does it contemplate the possible ascendancy of his counsels in the Government at the moment with satisfaction. . . . . Were the representation of Oxford now a perfectly open question, and were Mr. Gladstone placed in competition with a man approaching him in genius and accomplishments, and superior to him in coolness of judgment and steadiness of public conduct, we should think the University might do the best thing for the country in giving his competitor the preference. But the present opposition to his return is utterly unjustifiable. . . . . . Lord Chandos is a man of great private worth and business-like habits, but his sense and modesty must have been under a temporary eclipse when he allowed himself to be put forward as a candidate for the representation of a great intellectual constituency, against a man of genius—a man of genius who had served Church and State in the highest offices, and with splendid distinction, through a public life begun so early that it is already long. . . . . . A doubtful and chequered fame Mr. Gladstone will assuredly leave, but he will leave a fame bright enough to gibbet the ungenerous presumption of his obscure opponent when his own faults are buried in a great man's grave."

Mr. Gladstone himself felt that some explanation of his conduct was necessary, and he addressed a letter to the Provost of Oriel on the subject. He said :—

"Various differences of opinion, both on foreign and domestic matters, separated me, during the greater part of the administration of Lord Palmerston, from a body of men with the majority of whom I had acted, and had acted in perfect harmony, under Lord Palmerston. I promoted the vote of the House of Commons in February of last year which led to the downfall of that Ministry. Such having been the case, I thought it my duty to support, as far as I was able, the Government of Lord Derby. Accordingly, on the various occasions during the existence of the late Parliament when they were seriously threatened with danger or embarrassment, I found myself, like many other independent members, lending them such assistance as was in my power ; and although I could not concur in the late Reform Bill, and considered the dissolution to be singularly ill-advised, I still was unwilling to found on such disapproval a vote in favour of the motion of Lord Hartington, which appeared to imply a course of previous opposition, and which has been the immediate cause of the change of Ministers. Under these circumstances it was, that while I had not the smallest claim on the victorious party, my duty as towards the late advisers of the Crown had been fully discharged. It is hardly needful to say that, previously to the recent vote, there was no negotiation or understanding with me in regard to office ; but when Lord Palmerston had undertaken to form a Cabinet, he acquainted me with his desire that I should join it. . . . . Were I permitted the mode of address usual upon elections, I should, after the preliminary explanation, proceed to submit with confidence to my constituents that, as their representative, I have acted according to the obligations which their choice and favour brought upon me, and that the Ministry which has thought fit to desire my co-operation is entitled in my person, as well as otherwise, to be exempt from condemnation at the first moment of its existence. Its title to this extent is perhaps the more clear because, among its early, as well as its very gravest duties, will be the proposal of a Reform Bill, which, if it be accepted by Parliament, must lead, after no long interval, to a fresh general appeal to the people, and will then afford a real opportunity of judging whether public men associated in the present Cabinet have or have not forfeited by that act, or by its legitimate consequences, any confidence of which they may previously have been thought worthy."

The 27th of June was the nomination day at Oxford University. The Dean of Christ Church proposed Mr. Gladstone, and the President of St. John's nominated the Marquis of Chandos. The polling commenced the same day, and continued till Friday, the 31st, when the voting stood—Gladstone, 1050 ; Marquis of Chandos, 859 : majority, 191.

Very soon after the Palmerston Ministry had settled down in office, Sir William Somerville introduced a Bill to remove one of the disabilities under which Roman Catholics in Ireland still suffered, that which limited the office of Lord Chancellor of Ireland to members of the Protestant Church. A vigorous opposition set in from the Conservative side of the

House; and Mr. Whiteside, representing the extreme Church
party, with all his fiery rhetoric, denounced the Bill as the "most
indecent proposition ever submitted to Parliament, because it
proposed that a Roman Catholic should decide questions touching the doctrines of the Church of England." Mr. Gladstone
replied to Mr. Whiteside with equal earnestness and certainly not
less eloquence. The Irish Chancellorship, he maintained, was a
secular office, the holder of which had no direct ecclesiastical
influence, but was only connected with Church matters as an
administrator of the law, and in connection with others who were
Protestants. Mr. Disraeli, the Conservative leader, was willing
that the Bill should be referred to a select committee, in order that
the exact functions and position of the Irish Chancellor might be
clearly ascertained and defined. At length the debate was
adjourned, and the state of public business did not permit it to
be resumed.

Mr. Gladstone had scant time—only three weeks—to prepare
his Budget; but he was ready by the 18th of July, when he made
his financial statement. The revenue of the past year had produced £65,477,000, and the expenditure had been £64,663 000,
leaving a surplus in hand of £814,000. The estimated revenue
for the current year was £64,340,000, and the expenditure,
£69,207,000. The increase of expenditure was owing to the
increase in the Army and Navy estimates, the former to the
amount of £1,280,000 and the latter £3,091,000, due to the
expectation of a possibility of European complications. Austria
had been defeated by the French and Sardinian armies at Monte-
bello, Palestro, Magenta, and Solferino. The old dynasties had
been driven out, and provisional governments established at
Florence, Parma, and Modena: there had been an insurrection
in the Papal States; and Austria, humbled, had signed the preliminaries of peace at Villafranca. There was quite enough disturbance in the air of Europe to justify England in keeping its
powder dry and strengthening its blue-jackets. But the Chancellor of the Exchequer had to provide for a deficit of £4,867,000,
and in accordance with his financial maxims, there was but one
mode by which the money could be provided. He declined to
increase indirect taxation, and so impose an additional burden on
the labouring man. "That being so," he said, "we arrive at a
point which can be easily anticipated. The divining faculty
of an intelligent audience altogether outruns either the power
or necessity of a detailed statement. It remains to consider what
we shall do with the income tax." He had, however, a minor

resource at hand; and proposed to diminish the malt-tax credits from eighteen to twelve months. Under the existing system of collection, the maltster made and sold the malt before he paid duty; as Mr. Gladstone put it, " the public found him capital." By diminishing the period of credit, £780,000 would come into the Treasury in the current, instead of the next year, so reducing the deficiency to little more than £4,000,000. He proposed to raise the income-tax from fivepence to ninepence in the pound, which would yield about the amount required; but the additional fourpence would be limited to incomes of £150 and above, and upon incomes between that amount and £100 three-halfpence only would be imposed. The whole of the addition to the income-tax would be made available to the service of the year by being charged on the first half-year's payment. On the larger incomes the increase would be considerably more than fourpence; for, as Mr. Gladstone explained, " The effect of my proposal is to place an addition of three-halfpence upon all incomes under £150, and upon all incomes above that amount an addition of sixpence-halfpenny, or at the annual rate of thirteenpence on all incomes above £150; but the first half-yearly payment for the taxpayer whose income is under £150 a-year will be at fourpence in the pound, and the remaining liability for income tax for 1859-60 will stand exactly as it does now, at twopence-half-penny for both classes." The result of this arrangement wou'd bring into the Exchequer the sum of £4,340,000, and that, with the sum obtained by reduction of the malt credits, would yield £5,120,000, leaving a surplus of £253,000.

The resolutions were much debated—nobody was particularly pleased with proposals to increase the income-tax; and the discussion of the financial proposition was enlivened by some wanderings into the region of foreign politics and other not strictly relevant matters. Mr. Disraeli especially widened the range of debate. Probably he was not prepared to suggest a better method of raising the money which everybody knew must be raised; but he could interpose some gratuitous advice to Ministers respecting the conduct of foreign affairs. Mr. Gladstone, in reply, said: " I may perhaps be permitted to observe that, considering the range of those remarks, and the extent of the topics they introduce, which carry a mere journeyman Chancellor of the Exchequer like myself out of his true regions, and require much higher flights than he can hope to reach, it might have been more convenient if the right honourable gentleman had taken a more suitable opportunity, and one chosen after due

notice to the House, for advancing those principles of his high
policy than a discussion on the finances."

The Budget resolutions were carried. Maltsters and tax-
payers were left to ease their minds by grumbling, and Parliament was free to devote its energies to the consideration of
European politics, certainly perplexed enough. The shaking of
principalities and powers had not been so great, as in the earth-
quake year, 1848; but it had been considerable. The once
great Austrian empire had been humiliated; another and a
greater power was foreshadowing its predominance in Germany;
a free and united Italy was rising on the ruins of the old and
corrupt dukedoms and of the temporal power of the Papacy,
and for a time, at least, our "faithful ally," Napoleon the Third,
was posing as the liberator and the arbitrator of southern
Europe.

On the 8th of August, Lord Elcho revived a motion, which had
been postponed, for an address to Her Majesty on the subject of
Italian affairs. The proposed address stated " that in the opinion
of this House it would be consistent neither with the honour nor
dignity of the country to take part in any Conference for the
purpose of settling the details of a peace the preliminaries of
which had been arranged between the Emperor of the French
and the Emperor of Austria." The late Government, said Lord
Elcho, had pursued a course of neutrality, and he could not
sympathise with Sardinia and France. "If we had confidence in
the Emperor of the French, let us keep out of the Conference;
if we distrusted him, *à fortiori,* let us keep out of the Conference."

Mr. Kinglake moved the previous question. Lord Elcho's
motion, he said, was intended to express distrust of Her
Majesty's Ministers, and was almost a vote of want of confidence.

Mr. Gladstone's speech in opposing Lord Elcho's motion was
manly and outspoken. He was not aware that the Government
proposed to take part in a Conference for the purpose of settling
terms of peace between the two Emperors. The details of the
peace would be settled by the belligerents themselves, and what
remained would be, not the details of the peace, but great
questions of European policy, virtually affecting the happiness of
Italy. He continued :—

"The main question we have to consider, after all, is not the abstract
question of whether diplomatic negotiations or conferences are desirable or
not, but whether under present circumstances there is a clear prospect or a

reasonable hope that the social position of a very large portion of our fellow men would be benefited by the adoption of such a course. That is the real question for our consideration, and it is in order that we may have free scope to arrive at such a decision with respect to it as we may deem most advantageous that Her Majesty's Government entreat the House of Commons to leave their hands unshackled in the matter. The hon. and learned gentleman, casting an eye over the States of Italy, saw that many questions were raised by the peace which it failed to settle. What does the declaration made at Villafranca, for instance, that certain Sovereigns should return to their territories, mean? It has received no authoritative construction, and I do not understand what it necessarily conveys beyond this—that the parties subscribing the terms of peace are perfectly willing that those Sovereigns should return to their territories, other circumstances permitting. If it means that they are to be restored by force—which interpretation, be assured, the Emperor of the French does not mean to put upon it—then is there another reason furnished why the hands of Her Majesty's Government should not be tied up, and why they should not be prevented from protesting, with all that energy which the Government of a free State can command, against a doctrine that would treat the inhabitants of the territories in question as the property of so many ducal houses, who might dispose of them, their families, their fortunes, and those of their posterity, as they pleased, without any regard to that independent will and judgment which, as human beings, they are entitled to exercise. . . . In reference to the Pope—quite apart from all sectarian differences—as a personage occupying an eminent station and possessing distinguished personal virtues, as the head of a great body of Christian believers, my wish would be to look upon him with all the respect which is due to those united titles. I, however, lament, as cordially as I could lament if I had the nearest interest in all that concerns him, when I see a Sovereign who makes pretensions to represent in a peculiar manner the majesty of Heaven reduced to become a mendicant at foreign Courts—a mendicant, too, not for the purpose merely of obtaining the means of subsistence, but with the object of procuring military armaments whereby to carry the ravages of fire and sword over the fair provinces which he governs, and to rivet on the necks of men a yoke that is detested by every one except those who have a direct personal interest in its continuance. That is a policy which is unworthy of a civilised nation."

Satisfied with having produced a discussion on the subject, Lord Elcho withdrew his motion; and it was apparent that the address to the Queen would have been superfluous, the Ministers having no intention to advise taking part in a Conference.

When Parliament was prorogued by commission on the 13th of August, the speech announced that Her Majesty " had not yet received the information necessary to enable her to decide whether she may think fit to take part in any such negotiation."

CHAPTER XV.

About the middle of January, Mr. Cobden, who had, as we have
seen, refused to take office in the Ministry, accepted the appointment of plenipotentiary to France, to negotiate a treaty of commerce with that country. Many Englishmen then believed in
Napoleon the Third. He had been our ally—"our faithful ally,"
said Tennyson, accompanying the words by a famous sneer—in
the Crimean war; and Free Traders especially were ready to
credit him with the intention of making the alliance closer by
joining with us in the peaceful achievement of uniting the two
countries by commercial bonds, to their mutual benefit. Writing
about this time, one prominent Radical and Free Trader enthusiastically eulogised the Emperor, saying, "It is already asked,
which is Napoleon the Great?" Mr. Cobden appears to have
felt a peculiar pleasure in the task of endeavouring to arrange a
treaty in the provisions and operations of which the two countries
should have a common interest, and by which they should be
alike advantaged. It has been truly remarked that "the treaty
was not altogether in accordance with the principles of political
science, of which Cobden declared himself the disciple and advocate, but he rejoiced over it, and was proud of the share he
took in effecting it, because he believed that not only would it
tend to increase the national prosperity, but also that in proportion as nations were banded together by commercial and trading
interests would peace be rendered more secure, and that as these
bonds multiplied it would become more and more difficult for
rulers to fling nations into war at their will."

Cobden was old enough to remember something of the animosity of the English nation against France, and was well read in
the history of his own and the neighbouring country from the
time of the Revolutionary panic till the "crowning victory" of
Waterloo. He knew well what blind, almost brutal animosity
existed, how right judgment and feeling were obscured in the
national vanity, and he desired to see the two nations at once
more self-respecting and less suspicious and aggressive. If the
general public feeling were more liberal than in the old war-time,
when any street ruffian could ensure being called an "honest

fellow," and treated to a pot of beer, if he only cursed the French with all the emphatic, if limited, vocabulary at his command—when Nelson instructed his midshipmen that one of their paramount duties was to "hate the French with all their heart and soul"—there had been evidence enough recently on both sides of the Channel that there were smouldering embers which a little breath might kindle into a fierce flame. In the belief, then, that his efforts might be beneficent to both countries, the great Free Trader and lover of peace—with no faith whatever in the efficacy of war as a civiliser, and a very great belief in the value of corn, coal, iron, and cotton as the best intermediary between nations—accepted the mission entrusted to him by Lord Palmerston as the head of the Government, but no doubt proposed and planned by Mr. Gladstone, who, as Chancellor of the Exchequer, was deeply interested in the financial results. Lord Palmerston had in his nature a considerable amount of the pugnacity of the old school, and was more disposed to adopt Grantley Berkeley's famous "punch his head" policy towards a foreigner than to show from price-currents and market reports that it would be to his interest to make things pleasant.

M. Michel Chevalier, who had given his life to the study and solution of economical problems, and was the leader of the small band of French Free Traders, was chosen by the French Emperor to arrange the treaty with Mr. Cobden, with whom he had long maintained a private friendship. The provisions of the treaty were arranged with little difficulty, and the signatures on behalf of the respective governments were attached in the course of February. This treaty, as we shall see, considerably affected Mr. Gladstone's great Budget of 1860.

On the 24th of January, Parliament was opened by the Queen. The Royal speech announced that the revenue was in a satisfactory condition, and also that measures would be introduced "for amending the laws which regulate the representation of the people in Parliament." In the debates on the address foreign affairs were debated with much earnestness and some acrimony. Many who did not believe in the Emperor Napoleon were greatly averse to the cession of Savoy to the French empire; and there were others who, although they could not readily defend the old Italian dukedoms of Italy, regarded with some apprehension the results of their abolition and the substitution of a kingdom of Italy, with Victor Emmanuel supreme in the entire peninsula—the king of a revolution, backed up by the purchased support of another result of revolution, the Emperor Napoleon. Neither

Lord Palmerston, the English Premier, nor Lord John Russell, the English Foreign Secretary, had any liking for the annexation; but they felt that England had no recognisable plea for interference, and accepted the fact with the best grace they could.

The bulk of the English people were more interested in the financial prospects of the year. If the middle and industrial classes had little liking for Napoleon, they liked the income-tax and the war duties on tea and sugar less; and, with so adroit a financier as Mr. Gladstone at the Exchequer, great things were hoped for. True, there had been a Chinese war entailing a heavy expense which must be met; but then a considerable amount would be available from the falling in of long annuities, and Mr. Gladstone might be trusted to make the most of the opportunity.

On the 10th of February, an unusually early period, he produced the anxiously expected Budget, speaking for four hours, with unfailing vivacity (although he was just recovering from a sharp attack of illness) and a comprehensive mastery over the arrangement of many topics. If, he said, the war with China had not involved heavy charges, the position would have been better; but there had been an addition to the Army and Navy expenditure amounting to £1,170,000, and he estimated besides that the loss on the Customs in the period up to the end of March would probably be £640,000. These deficiencies would have put them "on the wrong side of the account"; but deliverance came from an unexpected quarter. Spain had, with "a high sense of honour and duty," paid £500,000 which she owed, but was not actually compelled to pay at that time. Half of that amount would be placed to the credit of the revenue before March. With that aid there would be a surplus of £65,000, one of the smallest that a Chancellor of the Exchequer ever had to boast of. He estimated the revenue of the ensuing financial year at £60,700,000, against which he must place an estimated expenditure of £70,100,000, leaving a deficit of £9,400,000 to be provided for. He related at considerable length the financial history of the previous year, and defended his policy when previously in office, and that of Sir Robert Peel. Between the years 1842 and 1853, he said, the increase of the wealth of the country was at the rate of 12 per cent. and of its expenditure 8¾ per cent.; while between 1853 and 1859 the wealth grew at the rate of 16½ and the public expenditure, so far as it was optional and subject to the action of public opinion, at the rate of 58 per cent. He stated frankly that he was not satisfied with the rapid growth of the public expenditure, but before anything could be done there must be provision for filling up "the gap which yawns before you, represented by the figures £9,400,000." There were two alternatives which might be offered—one a "generous budget," which would, with an income-tax of one shilling in the pound, relieve tea and sugar of the "war duties"; the other a "niggardly budget," which would keep up the tea and sugar duties and leave the country liable to an income-tax of tenpence. Before stating what course he intended to adopt, he explained the provisions of the commercial treaty with France. On the 1st of October, 1861, France would reduce duties and take away prohibitions on British productions on which there was an *ad valorem* duty of 30 per cent., and there was a promise that the maximum of 30 per cent. should, after a lapse of three years, be reduced to a maximum of 25 per cent. England engaged, with a limited power of exception, to abolish immediately and totally all duties on manufactured goods, to reduce the duty on brandy from 15s. to 8s. 2d., on wine from 5s. 10d. to 3s., with power reserved to increase the duty on wine if we raised our duty on spirits. England engaged to charge upon French articles subject to excise the same duties which the manufacturer would incur in consequence of the changes. The treaty would be in force for ten years, and he epitomized the general results of it. The reduction of the duty on wine, which would afford relief to the consumer, would be £830,000, entailing a loss to the revenue of £515,000. The reduction of the duty on brandy would relieve the consumer of £446,000, but the loss to the revenue would be £225,000. The total financial result of the treaty would show that the consumer of the articles included in its provisions would be relieved to the extent of £1,737,000; but the revenue would lose £1,119,000. But, he continued, we should take other considerations into account :—

"The commercial relations of England with France have always borne a political character. What is the history of the system of prohibition on the one side and on the other which grew up between this country and France? It is simply this—that finding yourselves in political estrangement from her at the time of the Revolution, you followed up and confirmed that estrangement, both on the one side and the other, by a system of prohibitory duties. And I do not deny that it was effectual for its end. I do not mean for its commercial end. Economically it may, I admit, have been detrimental enough to both countries; but for its political end it was effectual. And because it was effectual, I call upon you to legislate now for an opposite end by the exact reverse of that process. And if you desire to knit together in amity those two great nations whose conflicts have often shaken the world, undo for your purpose that which your fathers did for their purpose, and pursue with equal intelligence and consistency an end that is more beneficial. Sir, there was once a time when close relations of amity were established between the Governments of England and France. It was in the reign of the later Stuarts ; and it marks a dark spot in our annals, because it was an union formed in a spirit of domineering ambition on the one hand, and of base and vile subserviency on the other. But that, Sir, was not an union of the nations; it was an union of the Governments. This is not to be an union of the Governments, it is to be an union of the nations ; and I confidently say again, as I have already ventured to say in this House, that there never can be any union between the nations of England and France except an union beneficial to the world, because directly either the one or the other began to harbour schemes of selfish aggrandisement, that moment the jealousy of its neighbour would powerfully react, and the very fact of being in harmony will itself be at all times the most conclusive proof that neither of them can meditate anything that is dangerous to Europe."

Objections to the treaty, he said, came rushing in from all quarters. " It was like the ancient explanation of the physical causes of a storm—all the winds, north, east, west, and south, rushing together." Some said the treaty was an abandonment of Free Trade ; and others said—an unquestionably sounder suggestion, for it was founded on facts—that it was an abandonment of the principle of Protection. The treaty *was* an abandonment of the principle of Protection—"our old friend Protection, who used formerly to dwell in the palaces of the land, and who was dislodged from them some ten or fifteen years ago, and since that period had found shelter and good living in holes and corners ; but you are now invited, if you will have the goodness to concur in the operation, to see whether you cannot eject him from those holes and corners." Referring to the relative positions of England and France, he said :—

"It is perfectly true that France is a foreign country, but she is a foreign country separated from you absolutely by a narrower channel than that which divides you from Ireland ; and while nature, or Providence rather, has placed you in the closest proximity, it has also given to these two great countries such diversities of soil, climate, products, and character that I do not believe you can find on the face of the world two other countries which are so constituted for carrying on a beneficial and extended commerce."

Mr. Gladstone predicted that great good would arise from increasing facilities for the admission of pure French wines ; and described the practice adopted in the wine trade by which African wines were used for mixing with foreign European wines, and "new composts are brought forward and delivered to a discerning public, with what results it is not for me to say." There was a duty on foreign wine of 5s. 10d. the gallon, on colonial wine of 2s. 11d., on British wine of 1s. 2d. ; the result was that the consumption of foreign wine diminished, that of colonial wine increased, and that of British wine had doubled within the previous ten years. The case, then, had all the essential characteristics of a trade

carried on, and a revenue pining, under the influence of differential duties.   There was, in some quarters, he asserted, a prejudice
against the use of French wines :—

"You find a great number of people in this country who believe, like an
article of Christian faith, that an Englishman is not born to drink French
wines.   Do what you will, they say, argue with him as you will, reduce your
duties as you will, endeavour even to pour the French wine down his throat,
but still he will reject it.   Well, these are most worthy members of the com
munity ; but they form their judgment from the narrow circle of their own experience, and will not condescend for any consideration to look beyond that
narrow circle.   What they maintain is absolutely the reverse of truth, for
nothing is more certain than the taste of English people at one time for French
wine.   In earlier periods of our history French wine was the great article of
consumption here.   Taste is not an immutable, but a mutable thing.   If you
go back to what an eminent living poet [Tennyson] has called 'the spacious
times of great Elizabeth,' you will find that the most delicate lady in the land
did not scruple then to breakfast off beefsteaks and ale.   Down to the Revolution, French wine was very largely consumed here.   . .   The importation
of French wine is absolutely increasing, as the percentage of the total consumption is relatively increasing.   Taste, I say, is mutable.   It is idle to talk
of the taste for port and sherries and the highly brandied wines as fixed and
unchangeable.   There is a power of unbounded supply of wine if you will
only alter your law, and there is a power, I won't say of unbounded demand,
but of an enormously increased demand, for this most useful and valuable
commodity."

It would be seen, he added, that the changes on the English
side would come immediately into effect, notwithstanding the
postponement of the changes intended by France.   Ministers
had acceded to this arrangement as, on the whole, advantageous
to the English people.   The speech continued :—

"I cannot pass from the subject of the French treaty without paying a
tribute of respect to two persons at least, who have been the main authors of
it.   I am bound to bear this witness at any rate with regard to the Emperor
of the French, that he has given the most unequivocal proof of sincerity
and earnestness in the progress of this great work, a work which he has prosecuted with clear-sighted resolution, not, doubtless, for British purposes, but in
the spirit of enlightened patriotism, with a view to commercial reforms at
home and to the advantage and happiness of his own people.   With regard
to Mr. Cobden, speaking, as I do, at a time when every angry passion has
passed away, I cannot help expressing our obligations to him for the labour
he has, at no small personal sacrifice, bestowed upon a measure which he, not
the least among the apostles of Free Trade, believes to be one of the greatest
triumphs Free Trade has ever achieved.   Rare is the privilege of any man who,
having fourteen years ago rendered to his country one single and splendid
service, now again, within the same brief span of life, decorated neither by
rank nor title, bearing no mark to distinguish him from the people whom he
serves, has been permitted to perform a great and memorable service to his
Sovereign and to his country."

Having stated that there was a yawning gap of nine and a half millions to be filled up, and that the French treaty would greatly increase the deficiency, the House was now prepared to listen to the great master's propositions for raising the amount; but, to the astonishment of his hearers, the Chancellor of the Exchequer proceeded to say that the plan included considerable reductions and remissions of taxation. That a Finance Minister with a large surplus at command should take off or reduce duties was intelligible enough; that a Finance Minister struggling against an alarming deficiency should be a liberal giver, greatly perplexed members on both sides of the House. Mr. Gladstone went on calmly to explain his plan. He proposed to abolish entirely the Customs duties on butter, tallow, cheese, oranges and lemons, eggs, nuts, nutmegs, pepper, liquorice, dates, and various minor articles, and those abolitions would entail a loss to the revenue of £382,000. There would be a reduction in the duties on some articles of great importance—timber, from 7s. 6d. and 15s. per ton to 1s. and 2s.; currants, from 15s. 9d. per cwt. to 7s.; raisins and figs, from 10s. to 7s.; hops (after Jan. 1, 1861), from 45s. to 14s. The direct loss to the revenue from these changes would be £1,035,000, but probably reduced by increase of consumption to £910,000. To help make up that sum he intended to resort to what had been described as "penny taxation," and impose a registration duty of one penny per package on all goods imported or exported, by which means, he thought, £300,000 a year could be raised. He would also place a moderate imposition on various operations connected with the warehousing system, such as "removals," "bottling," "vattings," &c., and this, he hoped, would yield £120,000. One new duty he would impose—6d. per cwt. on chicory or other vegetable product used with coffee—partly as a protection to the coffee revenue, and this duty, with the improvement of the revenue from coffee, would produce £90,000 per annum.

Having disposed of Customs matters, the Chancellor of the Exchequer turned to the Excise, or Inland Revenue. He proposed a tax of 1d. on notes of sale of foreign and colonial produce and on broker's contract notes; 3d. on dock warrants, and a reduction of agreement stamp from 2s. 6d. to 6d., with repeal of exemption under £20. Then came the proposition destined to arouse such a storm of opposition and vituperation from the representatives of "vested interests" as a minister is rarely doomed to encounter. The most violent of the broad-acred defenders of Protection, in the hottest times of Free Trade agitation—and they delighted in strong language—were mild in comparison with the champions of the licensed victuallers, who rushed into print and leaped on to platforms when the proposition was announced. To the ordinary mind there was nothing very terrible in it, for it was simply to the effect that licenses a⁺ a low rate should be granted to pastrycooks and keepers of eating-houses to sell wine and beer. "We think," said Mr. Gladstone, "that it is essential, in giving effect to the changes in the wine duties, that this sort of facility should be provided in connection with the sale of eatables, wherever the trade may be carried on, and we also look on it as a change favourable to sobriety, for the man who can get his glass of wine or beer at the same time with his necessary food, in an easy manner, is less likely to resort to places whither he would repair for drinking only, and where he would be tempted to drink to excess." The expense of the license would be doubled in the case of houses kept open after midnight.

A reduction would be made in the duty on game certificates, and some limited minor changes effected in connection with stamps on cheques, the probate duty, conveyances of building societies, and other matters. These remissions and abolitions would produce some diminution of expenditure as well as loss to revenue, for savings could be effected in the official Customs and Inland Revenue establishments to the extent together of £86,000. That amount, added to £896,000 to be raised by the new taxes, would produce £982,000, more than sufficient to replace the revenue he proposed to withdraw. So far, the balance stood thus: there would be a relief to the interest payable on the National Debt by the falling in of the long annuities of £2,146,000; the treaty arrangements disposed of £1,190,000, and the remissions and abolitions of £910,000, together £2,100,000; but the changes and savings would produce £982,000, so that there would still be £1,128,000 available for further remission. He proposed to devote the greater portion of this to the abolition of the excise duty on paper. The uses to which that material could be applied, but from which it was totally or partially excluded by the duty, were numerous. He had received communications from persons engaged in sixty-nine trades, in not one of which, it was commonly supposed, it could be used. Paper, for instance, was used in the construction of artificial limbs, telescopes, boots and shoes, caps and hats ; ship-builders could advantageously employ it ; it might be used in the manufacture of portmanteaus, Sheffield goods, panels for doors and decorative mouldings ; and even water-pipes of great strength, equal to a pressure of 300 lbs. on the square inch, could be made of paper. He proposed that the duty should be abolished after the 1st of July. The immediate loss to the revenue would be £1,100,000; but a saving of £20,000 would, by the abolition, be effected in the Inland Revenue establishment. Next, he proposed to get rid of the impressed stamp on newspapers, and, to meet some difficulties in connection therewith, the introduction of a three-halfpenny rate into the present scale of book postage. The Excise duty on hops would be reduced from 19s. per cwt. to 14s. The prohibition on the importation of malt to be remitted, but a Customs duty of 3s. per bushel would be imposed.

So far the Budget had relieved indirect taxation to the extent of about £4,000,000; and now he turned his attention to the mode of supplying the deficiency of £9,500,000—a difficulty the consideration of which he had for the time laid aside, but which must be encountered. He would not interfere with the tea and sugar duties. In the presence of the great deficiency they must remain as they were for fifteen months, and he had the consolation of knowing that "there never was a time when the people were so able to pay taxes as now." The income-tax must bear the greater part of the burden. He proposed to fix it at 10d. in the pound on incomes above £150, and at 7d. on incomes below that amount. He proposed also to apply in aid of the expenditure £1,400,000 to be obtained by rendering available another portion of the malt credit and the credit usually given on hops. By these means he was able to estimate the income for the coming financial year at £70,564,000, and the expenditure at £70,100,000, leaving him a disposable surplus of £464,000.

The Chancellor of the Exchequer had concluded his exposition. Hitherto, in his long speech, he had exhibited a mathematical clearness of intellect in dealing with complicated arithmetical details, and an unrivalled facility in making them intelligible and interesting to others; but he concluded with an animated appeal characteristic of the emotional side of his character, and his habit of regarding the moral influence of administrative measures. Laying aside his notes, which had assisted his memory in dealing with the figures, he concluded his speech with a power of voice and animation of gesture that showed no trace of weariness. He said:—

"I feel a hope, which amounts to a persuasion, that this House, whatever may happen, will not shrink from its duty. After all it has heretofore achieved by resolute and persevering commercial reforms on behalf of the masses of the people, and not on behalf of them alone, but on behalf of every class, on behalf of the Throne, and of the institutions of the country, I feel convinced that this House will not refuse to go boldly on in the direction in which Parliament has already reaped such honours and rewards. By pursuing such a course as this it will be in your power to scatter blessings among the people, and blessings which are among the soundest and most wholesome of all the blessings at your disposal, because in legislation of this kind you are not forging mechanical help for men, nor endeavouring to do that for them which they ought to do for themselves; but you are enlarging their means without narrowing their freedom, you are giving value to their labour, you are appealing to their sense of responsibility, and you are not impairing their sense of honourable self-dependence. There were times, now long gone by, when Sovereigns made progress through the land, and when, at the proclamation of their heralds, they caused to be scattered heaps of coin among the people who thronged upon their steps. That may have been a goodly spectacle; but it is also a goodly spectacle, and one adapted to the altered spirit and circumstances of our time, when our Sovereign is enabled, through the wisdom of her great Council assembled in Parliament around her, again to scatter blessings among her subjects by means of wise and prudent laws; of laws which do not sap in any respect the foundations of duty or of manhood, but which strike away the shackles from the arm of industry, which give new incentive and new reward to toil, and which win more and more for the Throne and for the institutions of the country the gratitude, the confidence, and the love of an united people. Let me say even to those who are anxious, and justly anxious, on the subject of our national defences, that that which stirs the flame of patriotism in men, that which binds them in one heart and soul, that which gives them increased confidence in their rulers, that which makes them feel and know that they are treated with justice, and that we who represent them are labouring incessantly and earnestly for their good, is in itself no small, no feeble, and no transitory part of national defence."

Such a Budget was not to be criticised at once, and the House took a week to think about it. Then the Opposition opened fire. The Conservatives intensely disliked the French treaty, partly because the provisions were opposed to their old notions, and partly because Mr. Cobden had negotiated it; and the House generally had no love for the increased income-tax. Even some members sitting on the Ministerial side of the House, although bound by party ties to support the Ministry, had an uncomfortable presentiment that the French had got by far the best of the arrangement. On the 17th of February, Mr. Ducane, Mr. Disraeli's colleague in the representation of Buckinghamshire, gave notice of a resolution deprecating the diminution of the revenue, and so adding to the existing deficiency and disappointing the just expectations of the country by reimposing the expiring income-tax. This resolution was postponed in favour of another, proposed by Mr. Disraeli, the leader of the Opposition: —"That this House does not think fit to go into Committee on the Customs Act, with a view to the reduction or repeal of the duties referred to in the treaty of commerce between Her Majesty and the Emperor of the French, until it shall have considered and assented to the engagements in that treaty." If, asked Mr. Disraeli, the remissions of duty under the treaty were made, how could the Government subject the treaty to the constitutional control of the House of Commons? He thought the appointment of Mr. Cobden as their secret agent to be a most unwise act on the part of the Government, and that the treaty ir dicated the idiosyncrasy of the negotiator.

Mr. Disraeli's amendment was negatived by 293 to 230, and then Mr. Ducane's postponed resolution came on for debate. It met with less favour than the other; for on a division the numbers were—For, 223; against, 339, giving Ministers a majority of 116, or 53 more than in the division on Mr. Disraeli's resolution. Afterwards, when Lord Palmerston, as Ministerial leader of the House, moved an address to the Queen thanking her for concluding the treaty, the majority was very decisive, 282 supporting the address, and only 56 voting against it, giving the Ministry a majority of 226.

The independent organs of the public press, even those least favourable to the Conservative party, were by no means favourable to the treaty. One writer said:—

"The provisions of the treaty are apparently one-sided and unfair. France gives us very little; we give a great deal. What we give is of inestimable value to France—coal, iron, raw materials of manufacture of all kinds—the means, in fact, of developing all her latent resources, and power for manufacturing industry and for warlike equipment. What we receive from France is comparatively of small importance—luxuries which afford no additional means of directly augmenting our power or resources—brandy, wine, silks, gloves, &c. And add to these the admission of our manufactures into France at a duty of thirty per cent."

Another asked in the *Saturday Review* :—

"What practical benefit will the mass of the people of the country derive from the admission at low prices of the inferior French wines? Their present beer is vastly superior for them in every respect, and the command of that at a moderate price renders the admission of inferior French wines a privilege of no real value, if not absolutely undesirable."

The most virulent attacks, however, were from the publicans. The highly respectable and influential licensed victuallers, always vigorous in defending their vested interests, were more energetic than ever. They were horrified at the idea of drinking a glass of ale or wine in any other place than the bar or the parlour of a public-house, and predicted not only the ruin of their own trade, but such an amount of public demoralisation as had never before been witnessed. To get gloriously drunk in a tavern was conduct no fine old English gentleman need be ashamed of—indeed, rather a constitutional proceeding; and the working man's æsthetic faculties were wonderfully improved by the contemplation of the gilding and gas-fittings of a gin palace. But nothing but destruction of individual and national character could result from assisting the digestion of a bun eaten at a pastrycook's counter by drinking a glass of sherry, or permitting the working man or poor clerk, who dined at a coffee-house, to wash down the cut from the joint with a draught of stout or sixpenny ale.

The licensed victuallers appointed a deputation to wait upon Mr. Gladstone, and, either by a singular chance or a happy inspiration scarcely to be looked for in such a quarter, selected as the spokesman a gentleman named Homer. Certainly, if any name would appeal to Mr. Gladstone's sympathies and claim his attention, that ought to be expected to do so.

With admirable candour, the modern Homer informed the Chancellor of the Exchequer that "the licensed victuallers thought they had a claim for consideration on account of the fact that they had invested £60,000,000 of capital in the business, and the proposed change would be highly detrimental to their interests, and it would be a gross injustice to the licensed victuallers to deprive them of vested rights and to depreciate their property." The arguments of the earnest spokesman had little effect on Mr. Gladstone. The subjects of King Priam might as well have appealed to Agamemnon not to attack Troy because such a course of action might be injurious to their vested interests ; and, it is painful to add, the arguments of the deputation were almost laughed at by some influential leaders of public opinion. The cynical *Saturday*, which a few days before had eulogised British beer at the expense of French wine, now said :— "The victuallers seem to have forgotten the duty which their name imposes. What we get at their shop is all drink, and no victuals—what the Budget promises is victuals and drink in moderation and decency. We want meat and liquor—not the public-house refreshment of oceans of drugged beer and rivers of gin, with a single mouldy biscuit."

Under the influence of panic men sometimes seek strange alliances, and, perhaps, it was scarcely surprising that the publicans implored teetotalers to help them in their time of trouble. An appeal was made to "the clergy, temperance societies, and all friends of decency, order, and morality, to avert this public calamity, which will encourage drunkenness, legalise immorality,

offer every opportunity to temptation and vice, crime and de-
bauchery, and turn London, from one end to the other, into one
huge *café.*"

The *Morning Advertiser* is, as everybody knows, the property
and daily organ of the Licensed Victuallers' Association; and
the *Morning Advertiser* of the time to which we are referring
deserves a place among the curiosities of literature. It had a
character for high morality to sustain, for the editor at that time
was a gentleman prominent in evangelical circles, who indulged
his own taste by devoting a certain portion of the paper to matters interesting to the religious world, while a sub-editor of a more
eclectic mind provided the news respecting prize-fights, racing,
ratting, betting, sporting events generally, and conviviality, which
the public-house readers of the *'Tiser* particularly appreciated.
This incongruity in the contents of the journal obtained for it, in
profane circles, the nickname of the "Gin and Gospel Gazette,"
and evil-minded correspondents occasionally procured the inser-
tion of letters abounding in classical quotations, the subsequent
translation of which by some erudite friend greatly shocked the
pure-minded, if classically untaught, editor. The Budget was
smitten hip and thigh, and a correspondent, who modestly signed
his articles with the Greek word "Delta," displayed a power of
hitting out which the pugilistic readers of the journal must have
admired. "Eating and coffee-house keepers," argued one writer,
"will gladly avail themselves of the opportunity thus presented
to them of supplying the wants of their customers from their own
cellars," and then what will become of the property of the publicans? But it was when defending public morality that the
writers shone most brilliantly. "Not only," argued one, "shall
we have the working classes degraded by these temptations to
intemperance, but our females and domestic servants, and even
the children, will be tempted to these places for their pennyworth
of wine." (The quantity of the cheapest French claret which
could be procured for a penny, and the amount of intoxication
to be obtained from it, might have afforded an interesting subject
for inquiry.) "An Englishwoman" solemnly warned the readers
of the *Advertiser:* "Let women be able to obtain wine at a pastry-
cook's as easily as they can an ice or a jelly, and, my word for it,
hundreds and thousands will avail themselves of the privilege
beyond the limit of health and refreshment." But worse remained
behind. "These houses will become the resort of all the disso-
lute men and abandoned women in London, and the facilities
which will be given to indulgence in immoral practices will make

these places the high road to ruin." Day after day columns of
this kind of writing appeared in the papers; and the subject may
be dismissed by quoting one passage from one of the letters
signed with the Delta, which has almost become classical—as
classical, at least, as the phrase "The three tailors of Tooley
Street," and some others—so frequently has it been referred to,
and so hugely has it been laughed at :—"There is a class of sin-
ners who yearn for sin, but can't afford, or don't like to be
caught in it. Mr. Gladstone is the man for them. He will be,
as he deserves to be, an immense favourite with a certain sort of
ladies.   They have a taste for stimulants which it would be
awkward to gratify at home; they cannot go into a public-house
—that would be too conspicuous.   A pastry-cook's shop of Mr.
Gladstone's stamp is the very thing they wanted.   For respectable females of easy virtue the *locale* is just as convenient, and
assignations can be decently masked under a passion for pastry.
A man, perhaps, might not unfrequently alight, in one of Mr.
Gladstone's beerhouses, on his wife dead drunk in the back parlour, or his daughter debauched upstairs." That, of course,
would be a terrible experience for any man; but the phrase "not
unfrequently" is peculiarly rich.

The publicans, however, with all their energy and rhetoric,
failed to find the vulnerable part of the Achilles of the Exchequer.
The House of Lords was more successful.   In the Commons Mr.
Gladstone had experienced more opposition to the resolution for
abolishing the paper duty than to any other part of his Budget.
At the different stages of the proposition the majority greatly
dwindled; and when the Bill was brought into the Lords, Lord
Monteagle moved its rejection.   The aged Lord Lyndhurst supported Lord Monteagle's motion, maintaining that the House of
Lords had a right to refuse assent to a repeal of taxation; and
that in the present state of European affairs it would be most unwise to reduce the revenue, which might be called upon to meet
great emergencies.   Many of the Lords disliked the extension of
the cheap press, and thought that to cheapen paper would be to
offer facilities for the dissemination of dangerous, if not absolutely
revolutionary, doctrines.   The second reading of the Bill was
rejected by a majority of 80.

Lord Palmerston at once moved for, and obtained, a committee of the House of Commons to ascertain the practice of
each House with regard to bills imposing or repealing taxes.
When the report of the Committee was presented, two months
afterwards, it was to the effect that the Lords had a constitutional

right to reject a Bill for the repeal of a tax. Mr. Bright, who was a member of the committee, dissented, and drew up a report of his own, in which he asserted that the Lords had no right to reimpose a tax which the Commons had repealed, because, if they did so, the Commons would not have absolute control over the taxation of the country. On the presentation of the report, Lord Palmerston proposed a series of resolutions, reaffirming the claims of the Commons to a "rightful control over taxation and supply." There was considerable agitation out of doors. Public meetings were held, and the cheap papers of advanced principles made the most of the chance of attacking the House of Lords. Mr. Gladstone was disposed to take much stronger ground than his leader thought necessary to assume. He protested against the "gigantic innovation," which Lord Palmerston, more easy tempered, and better acquainted, perhaps, with the inner life of the Upper House, treated with a sort of contemptuous indifference. Probably he did not care greatly whether the paper duty were repealed or not; and he knew that the Lords, when they found themselves decidedly opposed to prevalent public opinion, would be very likely to be satisfied with one attempt to assert their privileges, and the next session the repeal of the duty would be quietly permitted. Mr. Gladstone had no alternative but to yield the remission of the duty, and content himself with carrying a resolution for removing, in accordance with the provisions of the French Treaty, so much of the duty imposed by the Customs on imported paper as exceeded the Excise duty on paper made in this country.

So ends the story of the Great Budget of 1860, in some respects the most memorable of Mr. Gladstone's financial achievements, but incomplete so far as he was thwarted in carrying one of the propositions, to the advantageous results of which he had looked forward with eager expectation.

CHAPTER XVI.

POST-OFFICE SAVINGS BANKS AND REPEAL OF THE PAPER DUTY.

THE political year, 1861, opened with a demand for retrench-ment. Some members of the House of Commons, before the opening of the session, addressed a letter to Lord Palmerston on the subject. They "could not but hope," they said, "that the enormous expenditure of the current financial year was forced upon the Government against their will, by an unhappy combina-tion of circumstances." The Premier, possibly, was as little im-pressed by the opinions of the author of the epistle as by the peculiar English in which it was written. He knew that expen-diture sanctioned by Parliament must be provided for ; and that retrenchment would not be easy, indeed, scarcely possible, until the occasion for heavy expenditure had passed away. There certainly was a hope — more rational and more grammatical, be-cause it was a hope for the future, not a paradoxical hope for the past—that the new year then opening would be marked by less expensive proceedings than the last, and that some of the public burdens even might be lessened ; but any abstract resolves on the subject were certainly premature, and very little could be known of the financial position and consequent necessities of the year until at least the Military and Naval Estimates of the year had been brought forward, and the Chancellor of the Exchequer had made his statement. We shall see, as we proceed, that there were other attempts early in the session to pledge the House to resolutions which would embarrass the Chancellor of the Ex-chequer.

Parliament was opened by the Queen, in person, on the 5th of February, and several efforts to obtain fragments of reform in the representation of the people were made. The Ministry, desirous as they might be to introduce a Bill which would settle many troublesome questions, were as yet not ready for the task, and private members aired their various pet projects. On the 19th, Mr. Locke King again moved for leave to bring in a Bill to reduce the county franchise to a £10 qualification. The Bill was introduced, but the motion for the second reading, on the 13th of March, was defeated by 248 to 229. Mr. Baines's proposition for extending the borough franchise in England was also nega-

tived, and a like fate befell Mr. H. Berkeley's renewal of his
annual Ballot motion, which was lost by a majority of 125.

There was vigorous fighting over the Government Bill for
assigning the four seats vacated by the disfranchisement of Sudbury and St. Albans, brought in by Sir G. C. Lewis, the Home
Secretary. It was proposed to assign one of the seats to the
West Riding of Yorkshire, one to South Lancashire, one to
Chelsea and Kensington (to form a new metropolitan borough),
and one to Birkenhead, a town which had risen into importance
with marvellous rapidity. Of course the propositions were
objected to, and the seats were eagerly claimed for other constituencies. Mr. Bentinck, as a country gentleman and Tory of
the old school, thought all the seats should go to the counties ;
Mr. Stirling, member for Perthshire, claimed them for Scotland ;
Mr. Maguire, the eloquent representative of Dungarvan, while
willing that Scotland should have two, urged the propriety of
allotting two more members to Ireland ; and some Scotch members advocated the claim of the Scotch Universities. The second
reading of the Bill was agreed to, the consideration of the places
to which the seats should be allotted being left to the committee
of the whole House. Mr. Knightley, member for South Northamptonshire, carried, by a majority of 103, an amendment by
which Chelsea and Kensington were excluded, and left to pine
memberless for a few years more, not because the majority of the
members thought the inhabitants of these important districts less
worthy of the franchise than the voters of Marylebone or Lambeth, but because they thought the metropolis, as a whole, had a
sufficient supply of representatives. By way of a slight compensation, a proposal was made to add another member to Middlesex, but it met with little favour. After many amendments had
been discussed and many divisions taken, it was agreed that two
seats should be given to the West Riding, one to East Lancashire, and one to Birkenhead. In that modified form the Bill
passed both Houses.

Another stock subject of debate duly made its appearance
early in the session. On the 24th of February, Sir John Tre-
lawney moved for leave to bring in a Bill to abolish Church rates.
It had been rumoured that Mr. Gladstone had modified his
opinions on the subject, and was not prepared to renew his support of the rates ; but he soon dispelled the illusion, speaking
with all his wonted animation and vigour. He said he retained
his opinions ; if he had changed them, he would have felt it to be
his duty to resign the representation of the University of Oxford.

In populous parishes, he allowed, the imposition of the rate might be objectionable, and he would abandon the principle there; but in rural parishes, where the rate was paid with as much satisfaction as any other public charge, why should the ancient law be abolished? What paid the charge in rural parishes? The land; and it was proposed to force £250,000 a-year upon the proprietors of land. If the law of Church rates was an old and a good law—if it provided for Divine ordinances for the benefit of the poor, amounting to a large majority of the population, it was too much to say that we were to abolish such a law to meet, not the scruples, but the convenience of individuals. He suggested that the Legislature should begin by converting the power of the majority of the parish into a right, firmly maintaining the right of the parish to tax itself, and giving to those parishes where the ancient Church rates had lapsed the power of raising a voluntary rate. The division on the motion for the third reading of the Bill showed a rather remarkable result, the numbers being equal, 274 on each side. The decision was thus left to the casting vote of the Speaker, who gave it for the Noes.

On the third day of the session Mr. Gladstone had obtained leave to bring in a Bill for the creation of Post Office Savings Banks, one of those practical projects which are sometimes fortunate enough to be considered by both sides of the House as beyond the region of party politics, and are welcomed as promising great advantages to the public. The second reading was agreed to, without opposition, on the 18th of March, and the Bill passed the Upper House, though not without a sneer by the Earl of Derby at "the financial freaks" of the Chancellor of the Exchequer.

In anticipation of the Budget, the attempts to pass abstract resolutions, to which we have alluded, were made. Mr. H. Williams, member for Lambeth, believed by his constituents to have inherited the position in the House as an economical reformer so long occupied by Joseph Hume, moved a resolution, "That real property should be made to pay the same duty as was paid on personal property," but it was negatived by a majority of 116. Mr. Dodson, one of the members for Sussex, brought forward a resolution to the effect that provision should be made, in any financial arrangement, for removal of the duty on hops. Mr. Gladstone objected (as he had frequently done before) to abstract resolutions on matters of finance, and the motion was defeated by a majority of 92. Mr. H. B. Sheridan (member for Dudley) renewed his motion for leave to bring in a

Bill for a reduction of the duty on fire insurance, but was left in a minority of 89.

Mr. Hubbard, member for Birmingham, on whose soul the income-tax always sat heavily, moved for the appointment of a select committee to inquire into the mode of assessing and collecting the tax, and found such support in the House—many even of those who had made up their minds to accept the tax as inevitable objecting to the mode in which it was levied—that, notwithstanding Mr. Gladstone's opposition to the motion, it was carried against the Government by a majority of four votes. The Committee was appointed, but the report made did not support the views of Mr. Hubbard, and no result followed.

The Budget was looked forward to with even more than ordinary interest. Was there to be another wonderful exposition of financial dexterity by the great master? Would he make another attempt to repeal the paper duty? And, if so, would the Lords again veto the proposition? Such were the questions eagerly asked, and when, in a crowded house, on the 15th of April, Mr. Gladstone rose to make his financial statement, there was almost breathless expectation. His speech was another masterpiece of lucidity, and his manner was even more animated than usual. It was soon evident that he intended to hazard another wrestle with the House of Lords, and that he was quite "ready for the fray." It would not, at any rate, be his fault, if there was a repetition of what he had a year before denounced as "the most gigantic and dangerous invasion of the rights of the Commons which has occurred in modern times." He began by stating that the revenue of the past year had been £70,283,100, considerably less than estimated, owing to a bad harvest and other causes, and the expenditure £72,842,000. These amounts indicated a deficiency of £2,559,000; but, allowing for drawbacks on stock belonging to the account for the former year, the real deficiency was £855,000. Adverting to the effects of the commercial treaty with France, he said that the imports of articles unaffected by the legislation of the previous year had been nearly stationary, but those on which the duty had been reduced had increased 17½ per cent., and those from which the duty had been taken off altogether had increased 48½ per cent. The total expenditure for the coming financial year he estimated at £69,900,000, and the revenue at £71,823,000, the highest estimate of revenue ever made by a British Chancellor of the Exchequer. There would, therefore, be available for disposal a surplus of £1,923,000. He proposed to take a penny off the income-tax, and to abolish the paper duty, and would then have a surplus of £408,000. The tea and sugar duties would be continued for another year.

In the course of his speech, Mr. Gladstone referred to the comparative claims of direct and indirect taxation with an amusing vivacity rarely bestowed on so dry a subject. He said:—

" I take some credit to myself that I have never entered in this House into any disquisition upon such a subject. I have always thought it idle for a person holding the position of Finance Minister to trouble himself with what to him is necessarily an abstract question—namely, the question between direct and indirect taxation, each considered upon its own merits. To many people both, as is natural, appear sufficiently repulsive. As for myself, I confess that, owing to the accident of my official position rather than to any more profound cause of discrepancy, I entertain quite a different opinion. I never can think of direct and indirect taxation except as I should think of two attractive sisters who have been introduced into the gay world of London, each with an ample fortune, both having the same parentage—for the parents of both I believe to be Necessity and Invention—differing only as sisters may differ, as where one is of a lighter, another of a darker complexion, or where there is some variety of manner, the one being more free and open, the other somewhat more shy, retiring, and insinuating. I cannot conceive any reason why there should be any unfriendly rivalry between the admirers of the two damsels ; and I frankly own, whether it be due to a lax sense of moral obligation or not, that, as a Chancellor of the Exchequer, if not as a member of this House, I have always thought it not only allowable, but even an act of duty, to pay my addresses to them both."

In a similar vein he referred to the income-tax :—

" It has often been charged upon me, and I believe it is to this day alleged, that it is my absolute duty, whatever be the circumstances and whatever be the expenditure, to find means of abolishing that tax, with or without a substitute. I must confess that I think that is a hard imposition. I should like very much to be the man who could abolish the income-tax. I do not abandon the hope that the time may come—[" Hear !"]. I can assure hon. gentlemen that I am not about to be too sanguine, for in finishing the sentence I should have proceeded to quote Mr. Sidney Smith, who, in his admirable pamphlet upon the ballot, speaking, I think, of its establishment, or of something else, as a very remote result, says he thinks we had better leave the care of this subject to those little legislators who are now receiving a plum or a cake after dinner. I am afraid that some such amount of prudence may be necessary with regard to the income-tax. . . . I think it would be a most enviable lot for any Chancellor of the Exchequer—I certainly do not entertain any hope that it will be mine—but I think that some better Chancellor of the Exchequer, in some happier time, may achieve that great accomplishment, and that some future poet may be able to sing of him as Mr. Tennyson has sung of Godiva—although I do not suppose the means employed will be the same—

' He took away the tax,
And built himself an everlasting name.' "

While expressing a hope that the subject of public expenditure would be carefully considered, he deprecated rash reductions.

M

" For my own part, I say that if this country will but steadily
and constantly show herself as wise in the use of her treasure as
she is unequalled in the production of her wealth and moderate
in the exercise of her strength, then we may well believe that
England will, for many generations yet to come, continue to
hold her foremost position among the nations of the world."

The Budget resolutions encountered a strong verbal opposition, the repeal of the paper duty being especially objected to
by the Conservatives. Paper-makers did not want it, they
argued; the proprietors of cheap newspapers would be chiefly
benefited, and the public would vastly prefer other remissions.
" Take fivepence a pound off tea," urged Mr. Baring, who added,
" If I were asked to say whether the Budget is safe, politic, or
even honest to the country, I should be obliged to answer in the
negative."

In reply, Mr. Gladstone, having lightly alluded to certain
members who had expressed an opinion that it was very doubtful
if there would be any surplus at all, insisted that, in asking the
House to consent to a resolution for the repeal of the paper
duty, which would close the controversy of 1860, the Government had done that which would be approved, he believed, by
those who brought a candid mind to the question before the
House.

The income-tax resolution was agreed to without a division.
In the discussion on the resolution for continuing the tea and
sugar duties, Mr. Gladstone argued that the reduction of duty
on tea would no doubt give an impulse to labour, but it would
be foreign labour, that of the Chinese, whereas the remission of
the paper duty would stimulate British labour in the manufacture
of the article and the produce of agricultural fibre, while the
removal of the Excise regulations would relieve the trade of
restrictions that operated as a check upon it by stinting and
repressing enterprise.

Mr. Horsfall, member for Liverpool, said the House had
pledged itself to reduce the tea duty before it had pledged itself
to remove the paper duty. In every town in England, he
believed it would be said by nine persons out of ten, " Give us
the duty off tea, and not off paper." He moved to amend the
resolution by reducing the duty on tea, on and after the 1st of
October, to 1s. per pound.

Mr. Disraeli accused the Chancellor of the Exchequer of inconsistency, asserting that in 1857 he admitted the obligation of
abolishing the war duties on the ground of pledges given, and

because it was "important to the political interests of the country." The strength of the opposition to the resolution was shown by the division on the amendment, 299 voting against and 281 for it, leaving the Government the comparatively small majority of 18.

The resolution for the repeal of the paper duty was allowed to pass without a division, the decision of the House having been practically given by the previous division; but Mr. Gladstone then disturbed the passive, if somewhat sullen, attitude of the Opposition by announcing that he intended to include the chief financial propositions of the Budget in one Bill, instead of dividing them, as was generally the practice. His object in this course was evident. The Lords could not again reject the abolition of the paper duty without at the same time rejecting other items of the financial scheme. The Opposition was furious at the manœuvre. Lord Robert Cecil (now the Marquis of Salisbury), the man of "flouts and jeers," said the Ministerial course was unworthy of a sharp attorney; and Mr. Disraeli declared that the proposed method of action was an injury and affront to the other House of Parliament, and "an unhandsome mode of retaliating upon the Peers for the rejection of the paper duty."

The second reading of the objectionable single Bill was fixed for the 13th of May. Mr. Macdonogh, an eminent member of the Irish bar, who had recently taken his seat for Sligo, said the Bill raised a great constitutional question, and was an attempt to coerce the House of Lords. Sir James Graham replied effectively, expressing his belief that the power and authority of the House of Commons would be supported by a very large majority of their constituents. A long debate took place, and Mr. Newdegate moved a resolution condemning the mode of proceeding by a single Bill, which was rejected by 195 to 31. The Bill then went into committee, and another division took place when the paper duty clause came on. Mr. Gladstone said the doctrine of engagement set up by Mr. Disraeli was a perfect figment. The remission of the "so-called war duties" on tea and sugar would sacrifice £2,500,000, or twice the amount of the paper duty. Lord Palmerston wound up the debate by describing the opponents of the clause as "a fortuitous concourse of discordant atoms," and at length the clause was carried by a majority of 15, the numbers being 296 to 281. Earl Granville introduced the Bill into the House of Lords in a conciliatory manner, and it passed through the stages, not without some grumbling, but without a division.

CHAPTER XVII.

THE mission of Mr. Gladstone to the Ionian Islands, and the subsequent administration of Sir Henry Storks, had not produced the results which the annexation party in the islands desired ; and in March the local assembly declared in favour of union with Greece. They found sympathisers in probably unsuspected quarters. Mr. Maguire, the member for Dungarvan, who had warmly defended the temporal rule of the Pope and the tyrannies of the King of Naples and the Italian dukes, now appeared as a champion of the rights of the people of the Ionian Islands to choose their own form of Government. Mr. Maguire had a great command of the fervent oratory possessed by many of his cultured countrymen, and he brought forward the subject in the House of Commons on the 7th of May, in the form of a motion for papers relating to the affairs of the Ionian Islands, his chief object being, he said, to ascertain what were the recommendations Mr. Gladstone had made to the English Government. He described, in vivid language, the expectations which had been raised in the islands when it was known that so eminent and able a man had been sent to investigate and report upon the political position. "No sooner," said Mr. Maguire, "was it known that he was to come on his great mission, than a feeling of passionate hope passed like electricity from island to island, from community to community. Even before they caught one glimpse of that pale, thoughtful countenance, or heard one sweet tone of that voice which can lend enchantment even to the details of the dryest Budget, they hailed him as a political saviour, who was to free them from a detested country, and grant to them the fulfilment of their wishes—union with the mother country, Greece." The speaker quoted from a speech said to have been made by Mr. Gladstone to the Bishop of Cephalonia (reported in the *Trieste Gazette* and quoted by the *Times*), in which he said the union of the islands with Greece seemed to be "designed by Providence." Mr. Gladstone interrupted the speaker with a point-blank denial that he had ever made such a speech. In the course of the debate which ensued, he said the object of his mission was, believing that the position of this country in relation to the

islands was not altogether satisfactory, to see if it would be practicable to set England right by offering institutions unequivocally
and undoubtedly founded on principles of freedom.   He concluded by saying :—

> "If it is deemed even ridiculous that I should have undertaken so small
> and limited a mission, and that I should have been obliged to retire from it
> baffled and disappointed, without any visible result, I am willing to bear with-
> out complaint any comments, any conclusion, or any ridicule that may attach
> to my finding myself in that predicament.   The object which I had in view,
> if it has not been gained so far as the advantage of the Ionian Islands is con-
> cerned, has been gained at least in one respect—namely, that we have
> effectively placed England in her right position as the friend of free and
> constitutional laws and institutions, and have thus enabled ourselves to look
> Europe in the face, and say that if evils and abuses still prevail in the Ionian
> Islands, they prevail not by our fault, but in despite of our honest endeavours
> to cure and remove them."

The motion for the production of Mr. Gladstone's report was
opposed by Ministers, Lord Palmerston saying they were actuated
by a due sense of the best interests of the people in steadily
refusing to comply with the request for union with Greece.   Mr.
Maguire withdrew his motion for the production of papers; and
very little more was heard about the Ionian Islands until the end
of May, 1864.   Lord Palmerston and Earl Russell no longer
seeing any reason for " steadily refusing to comply," the islands
were formally annexed to Greece.

The cession of Savoy to France, and the dominance in Italy of
the King of Sardinia, supported by the then powerful Emperor of
the French, was keenly felt by the Roman Catholic politicians of
this country, who feared, not without reason, that the temporal
power of the Pope was threatened.   Tuscany, Parma, a considerable portion of Lombardy, and the kingdom of Naples, had been
added to the dominions of Victor Emmanuel, and his assumption of the title of King of Italy was imminent (indeed, it was
formally conferred about three weeks afterwards), when Mr. Pope
Hennessy, the member for King's County, Ireland, called attention to the conduct of Lord John Russell in promoting the
" Piedmontese policy," although he had previously made a profession of neutrality.   Mr. Hennessy charged the Foreign Secretary
with having committed a breach of international law, and with
destroying the confidence of European statesmen in the honour
and integrity of the British Foreign Office.   Sir George Bowyer,
an enthusiastic and almost fanatical admirer and defender of the
Papacy as a temporal power, followed Mr. Hennessy.   About
two years before, Europe had been shocked by an account of the

cruelties practised by the Papal troops, under General Schmidt, in suppressing an insurrection in Perugia. Sir George Bowyer denied that the massacre had taken place, and went on to eulogise " the gallant young King of Naples fighting for his rights."

Mr. Gladstone replied to Sir George Bowyer, and gave a history of the sufferings of the people of Naples, which he had himself witnessed, and established by documentary evidence the truth of the statements respecting the murders at Perugia, and the executions ordered by the Duke of Modena, notwithstanding that the victims were not legally liable to capital punishment.

Deviating a little from the chronological order of events, it may here be mentioned that in the following session (April 11, 1862) Sir George Bowyer again ventilated his opinions on the recent events in Italy, and attacked the Government for encouraging revolutionary movements, which, he asserted, were promoted by foreign adventurers, and received little sympathy from the mass of the people, who were well satisfied with the government of the old rulers. Mr. Gladstone replied in a powerful speech, indulging in a little banter at the expense of the fervid Sir George :—

" I do not wish to use unparliamentary language ; but if I may be permitted—as I believe I may without being open to the charge—to accuse an honourable member of indulging in paradox, and being the victim of credulity, I would appeal to my honourable and learned friend himself, and, at all events, with great confidence to the House generally, to say whether his speeches are not distinguished by astonishing powers of paradox, as well as by a capacity for credulity which is absolutely marvellous. . . . He tells us that 4,000 people in a corner of Italy, who, he says, are regarded as strangers by all the rest of the people of the country, and are detested by the Neapolitans, have, by their own unprincipled agency, succeeded, not, indeed, in uniting in the bonds of friendly alliance, and fully incorporating with themselves, but in subjugating to their sway, some 15,000,000 or 20,000,000 of Italians. . . . Let me take a particular instance—the downfall of the late King of the Two Sicilies, in bringing about which my honourable and learned friend was so kind—I do not know whether he meant it as a kindness or not—as to speak of so humble an individual as myself as having had some infinitesimal share ; and let me observe, that if he could prove to me that I have been in the smallest degree instrumental in assisting to cause the removal from a world in which there is wickedness, and misery, and sorrow enough, of one great and gigantic iniquity, I should accept that proof as another favour conferred upon me. I do not, however, assume to myself any credit of that character. But what, according to the representation of the honourable and learned baronet, has happened in the case of the King of the Two Sicilies, to which I am referring? Here was a kingdom in which, he tells us, the whole population, with the exception of a few busybodies belonging to the middle classes—in which the aristocracy, the educated classes, the peasantry, as well as the great bulk of the middle classes—were attached to the expelled dynasty. That being so, what takes place? An adventurer named Garibaldi, clad in a red shirt, with a certain number of followers, also clad in red shirts, lands upon the southern point of the Italian peninsula, marches through Calabria, and, with those few men in red shirts, faces a Sovereign with a well-organised army of 80,000 men, and a fleet perhaps the best in Italy, and the Sovereign at once disappears before him like a mock king of snow. Then comes my honourable and learned friend, and with the evident sincerity and earnestness which mark all he says and does in this House, seeks to persuade us that such events as these can occur in a country where the feelings of the people are not alienated from the throne, and where misgovernment does not prevail—thus exhibiting, in addition to the power of paradox to which I have already referred, a credulity which is almost incomprehensible, and in which he asks us to receive his statements on this head as a kind of political gospel."

Reverting to the year 1861, it is only necessary to note that Parliament was prorogued on the 8th of August, and that, before the year closed, the Prince Consort was laid in his grave, and with him departed the brightness of the British Court. The "fierce light that beats upon a throne" showed a broken-hearted widow, whose tears were sympathised with by the entire nation. About a month earlier a circumstance occurred which caused great excitement both in Great Britain and the United States, and at first seemed to presage an open rupture. The Southern Confederation, as they styled themselves—the "rebels," in the language of the Northern States—sent two Commissioners, Messrs. Slidell and Mason, to England. They embarked on the West India mail steamer the *Trent*, which was stopped on the open seas by Captain Wilkes, of the *San Jacinto*, a vessel of the United States navy. Messrs. Slidell and Mason, and their secretaries, were forcibly taken away, notwithstanding the protest of the captain of the *Trent*, and carried to Boston as prisoners of war. The United States Government, however, after the receipt of a firm demand from the English Government, restored them to British protection and disavowed the action of Captain Wilkes, and so, probably, avoided a serious result; for the British public was in no humour to concede the right of search, and many of the people of the Northern States were not unwilling to pick a quarrel with this country. Congress gave a vote of thanks to Wilkes for an action which the Executive Government admitted to be illegal, and the captain was invited to a public dinner at Boston, at which the Governor of Massachusetts declared that "every American heart thrilled with pride when he read that Captain Wilkes had fired a shotted gun across the bows of a vessel surmounted by the British lion." Our Government had made vigorous preparations for war, in case of an adverse reply from Washington.

CHAPTER XVIII.

THE AMERICAN WAR OF SECESSION.—POSITION OF THE SOUTHERN
CONFEDERATION.

PARLIAMENT was opened by commission on the 6th of February. The Queen, stricken down by her great sorrow, was unable to appear personally ; and necessarily one of the leading topics of the Address voted in reply to the Royal Speech was an expression of condolence with her Majesty, and a reverential eulogy of the departed Prince.

One of the earliest subjects which occupied the attention of Parliament was National Education.   Earl Granville in the House of Lords, and Mr. Lowe in the House of Commons, made elaborate statements respecting the new Minute of the Committee of the Privy Council.   Although 2,200,000 children ought to have been brought into the inspected schools, only 920,000 actually attended, and less than a third of that number received adequate instruction in the elements of reading, writing, and arithmetic.   The new Minute substituted for the numerous grants of the old system a capitation grant of one penny for each attendance over a hundred, subject to a favourable report of the inspector. Children, grouped according to age, would pass examinations, and their failure in any one branch—reading, writing, or arithmetic—would subject the school to the loss of one-third of the allowance, and, in case of failure in all, the allowance would be altogether withdrawn. The discussions on the subject occupied a considerable time.   Ultimately Ministers made some concessions.   The early part of the session was chiefly occupied with debates on this topic, Church rites and ceremonies, Maynooth, and other matters which led to no great result, and in which Mr. Gladstone did not take a conspicuous part.

On the 1st of April Mr. Sheridan introduced his motion— expected each year, as a matter of course—for leave to introduce a Bill to reduce the duty on fire insurance. There was a majority against the Government of 11, and the Bill was introduced, but rejected at a subsequent stage. Two days afterwards, the Chancellor of the Exchequer made his financial statement for the year.   He was in possession of a surplus of £355,000, and

estimated the expenditure for the coming financial year at
£70,040,000, and the revenue at £70,190,000, leaving him the
small surplus of £150,000 to deal with.   He occupied three
hours in making his statement to the House, exhibiting his
wonted power of securing the interest of his hearers, although he
had little of an exciting nature to communicate.   The Budget,
indeed, was remarkably simple.   It was impossible, he said, to
make any very important remissions, but he proposed some alterations and readjustments.   The hop duty would be repealed,
and the scale of brewers' licenses rearranged.   A license for
private brewers was included in the scheme, but abandoned in
deference to the expressed opinion of the House.   The result of
these alterations would be a loss of £451,000; and if, he said,
it was hoped to effect a reduction of taxation, it would be necessary to apply to every department the principles of true economy.
The resolutions passed the House of Commons, but when the
Bills founded on them were presented to the House of Lords
they were unfavourably received, some of the Peers (among
them Lord Overstone), who usually supported Ministers, expressing disapprobation of the financial policy of the Chancellor of the
Exchequer.   The Bills, however, passed the House.

Although direct opposition to the Budget provisions was unavailing, there was still some dissatisfaction in the House of
Commons on the subject, not confined to the Conservative
benches; and on the 13th of May Mr. Hubbard introduced a
resolution, "That the incidence of the income-tax should not
fall upon capital or property, and when applied to the annual
products of invested property should fall upon the net income
arising therefrom, and that net profits and salaries should be subject to such an abatement as may equitably adjust the burden
thrown upon intelligence and skill as compared with property."
Mr. Craufurd, member for the City of London, seconded the
resolution, which, after a speech in opposition to it by Mr. Gladstone, was lost by a majority of 37.

On the 3rd of June Mr. Stansfeld, the Radical member for
Halifax, recalled the attention of the House to financial matters
by moving, as a resolution, "That the national expenditure is
capable of reduction without compromising the safety, the independence, or the legitimate influence of the country." Mr. Baxter,
member for the Montrose Burghs, who had already made a reputation as an economist, seconded the resolution, to which Lord
Palmerston moved an amendment, to the effect that the House,
while deeply impressed with the necessity of economy, was, at the

same time, mindful of its obligation to provide for the security of
the country. Mr. Stansfeld's resolution was defeated by a very
large majority (367 to 65), and Lord Palmerston's amendment
agreed to without a division. Mr. Gladstone, as guardian of the
public purse, was bound to make provision for the public service,
but certainly, neither by nature nor political training, was he disposed to be extravagant, and was perfectly willing that the
strongest light should be thrown on the details of his financial
administration ; and he moved the appointment of a standing
Committee of Public Accounts, for the examination of the
accounts, showing the appropriation of the sums granted by
Parliament to meet the public expenditure.

The powerful speech on Italian affairs, delivered in reply to
Sir George Bowyer, on the 11th of April, has already been
noticed. The session came to an end on the 7th of August, and
after a few weeks of necessary leisure, Mr. Gladstone paid a visit
to the North of England, making one of those political " progresses" which are now so familiarly associated with his career,
and in the course of which he has delivered some of his most
effective speeches.

On the 7th of October he paid a visit to Newcastle-on-Tyne,
where he was most enthusiastically received. A banquet was
given in his honour in the New Town Hall, the Mayor presiding.
All men's minds were then turned to the terrible civil war raging
in America, and the effects so painfully felt in Lancashire, where
the cotton trade and manufactures were nearly paralysed, and
hundreds of thousands of workpeople were thrown out of employment and reduced to the utmost extremity. The attitude of
the English Ministry was eagerly watched, and any utterance on
the subject by a Cabinet Minister anxiously looked for. Would
England endeavour to exert its influence to obtain a pause in the
terrible hostilities, for the purpose of arranging, if possible, terms
of peace? Would it recognise the Southern Confederation as a
belligerent power? Such were the questions asked, although
little hope was entertained that a direct reply would be given, for
it was believed that within the Cabinet there were differences of
opinion which would stand in the way of definite action. In
replying to the toast of the day, Mr. Gladstone made a long
speech, in the course of which he spoke in the highest terms of
appreciation of the manly, patient, and excellent conduct of the
suffering factory hands in Lancashire. Referring to the Southern
Confederacy, he uttered a remarkable phrase, much quoted and
commented on : " We may have our own opinions about slavery,

we may be for or against the South, but there is no doubt, I think, about this—Jefferson Davis and the other leaders of the South have made an army ; they are making, it appears, a navy ; and they have made, gentlemen, what is even of more importance, they have made a nation." These words elicited an outburst of cheering, and the speaker continued : " We may anticipate with certainty the success of the Southern States, so far as regards their separation from the North. I, for my own part, cannot but believe that that event is as certain as any event yet future and contingent can be. But it is from feeling that that great event is likely to arise, and that the North will have to suffer that mortification, that I earnestly hope that England will do nothing to inflict additional shame, sorrow, or pain upon those who have already suffered much, and who may probably have to suffer more."

This outspoken expression of opinion—false prophecy, as it afterwards proved to be—excited much attention. Mr. Gladstone's high position in the Ministry encouraged the supposition that the sympathy of the British Government was with the Southern States—that it was prepared to recognise the Confederation as an independent power, and that the time when it would do so could not be far distant. The "Southern Association" at Liverpool agreed to memorialise the Government for the immediate recognition of the Confederate States, and the members of the Liverpool Chamber of Commerce took into consideration the propriety of presenting a similar memorial.

In reply to Mr. Mozley, of Manchester, who wrote on behalf of many shippers of cotton, Mr. Gladstone said that his words at Newcastle were no more than the expression, in rather more pointed terms, of an opinion which he had long ago stated in public, that the efforts of the Northern States to subject the Southern ones was hopeless by reason of the resistance of the latter. This decided expression of opinion, and of sympathy by implication, called forth a vigorous attack from Professor Francis Newman, in the form of a letter to the *Morning Star*, a daily newspaper long since defunct. The writer declared that it was an offence against public morality for a statesman of Mr. Gladstone's position to speak at all of the Southern Confederation "without declaring abhorrence of it ; or, at least, to speak in such a tone that he can for a moment be suspected of desiring its success."

While at Newcastle Mr. Gladstone made an excursion down the Tyne, described by the *Newcastle Chronicle* at the time as

resembling a royal progress. The report of the trip published
in that journal is really worth quoting :—

" What was intended at first as a visit of inspection, to show him to what
use the Tyne Commissioners were putting the £100,000 they lately borrowed,
expanded into a triumphant display of the wealth and industry of the Tyneside. It was not possible to show to royal visitors more demonstrations of
honour than were showered on the illustrious commoner and his wife. The
procession of vessels which followed his were regal in their multitude and
splendour of enthusiasm. Some of the works upon the Tyneside, lifting their
grim and lofty piles high in the air, crowned with clouds of densest, blackest
smoke, out of which forks of sulphureous flames darted, revealing hundreds of
living men surmounting roofs and pinnacles, cheering in ringing tones above,
while cannon boomed at their feet below, was a sight to see, which [the reporter proceeds, with rather remarkable taste, to say] resembled one of
Martin's famous pictures of the exultation of Pandemonium when Lucifer
ascended his throne. [Recollecting himself, however, the gushing reporter
continued :] We do not intend by any means to apply the latter part of this
comparison to the Chancellor of the Exchequer ; but we are sure he must have
been reminded of Martin's celebrated mezzotint by what he saw at some points
of his triumphal progress. At every point, at every bank, and hill, and
factory, in every opening where people could stand or climb, expectant crowds
awaited Mr. Gladstone's arrival. Women and children in all costumes, and
of all conditions, lined the shores, and these waved their hands who had
nothing else to wave as Mr. and Mrs. Gladstone passed. Cannon boomed
from every point : the Chancellor was nearly shot to death, as far as violence
of reverberation could go to it. Such a succession of cannonading never
before greeted a triumphant conqueror on the march. It never ceased throughout his whole progress, and recommenced as he returned, and continued until
the shades of evening fell."

Mr. Gladstone afterwards visited Sunderland, Middlesborough,
and York, and at each place his presence was made the occasion
of a most hearty demonstration of welcome.

The year 1863 opened well, except for the sad condition of
Lancashire. There was—but for that calamity, which had its
origin in external causes—a condition of general prosperity ; and
the sufferings produced by the cotton famine had been greatly
alleviated by the exertion of a noble spirit of generosity. It was
estimated by Mr. Bazley, a very competent authority, that the
loss to the labouring class was at the rate of £12,000,000 a-year,
and near £30,000,000 in addition was lost to the employing
classes. In Lancashire alone 315,000 persons were dependent
on the cotton manufacture, and, as the result of the stoppage
in the supply of the raw material, nearly every mill was wholly
or partially closed. About 163,500 persons were receiving
scanty parochial relief in the Lancashire district at the opening of
the year, although assistance in money and food to the amount
of £1,800,000 had been given. The intense desire for the restora-

tion of peace on the other side of the Atlantic can be readily understood ; and when Parliament assembled early in February Mr. Disraeli took the opportunity offered by the debate on the Address to refer to the conduct of various members of the Ministry in making different statements as to the recognition of the Confederated States.   Mr. Gladstone's utterances at New-castle, of course, did not escape severe comment, not because Mr. Disraeli himself had much sympathy with the Northern States, the reverse being the case ; but because he blamed a leading Cabinet Minister for encouraging the South by words which the Ministry were not prepared to follow up by action, and to induce the public to suppose that his individual opinion expressed the unanimous policy of the Administration.   "If the speech meant anything, it meant that the Southern States would be recognised ; because, if it be true that they have created armies, navies, and a people, we are bound by the principles of policy and of public law to recognise their political existence."

It is remarkable that Mr. Disraeli, like Mr. Gladstone, believed that the Southern Confederation had practically achieved inde-pendence, and that separation was inevitable, for in the course of this speech he said: "I cannot conceal from myself the conviction that whoever in this House may be young enough to witness the ultimate consequence of the Civil War, will see, whenever the waters have subsided, a different America from that which was known to our fathers, and even from that of which this genera-tion has had so much experience.   It will be an America of armies, of diplomacy, of rival States and manœuvring Cabinets, of frequent turbulence, and probably of frequent wars."   It is well for the western world that both Mr. Disraeli and Mr. Glad-stone proved to be false prophets.

CHAPTER XIX.

FINANCIAL SUCCESSES.

THE speech from the throne announced that the Treaty of
Commerce with France had "already been productive of resu ts
highly advantageous to both the nations to which it applies";
and that statement, although, as might have been expected, a
little cavilled at in the course of the debate on the Address, was
not seriously impugned. The Budget was introduced on the
16th of April, and Mr. Gladstone was able to make the agreeab'e
announcement that he had a good surplus in hand. The
revenue for the coming year he estimated at £71,490,000, and
the expenditure at £67,749,000, leaving £3,741,000 at his
disposal. He proposed to equalise the duty on chicory and
coffee, remove some anomalies in respect to licences, and make
clubs liable to the duties payable for the sale of wines and spirits.
Railways were to pay 3½ per cent. on passenger receipts, without
exemption, for excursion trains, instead of the 5 per cent., with
exemptions, previously paid, and there were to be some slight
changes in the hackney carriages dues. Then came the proposition
for a charge which, as we shall see, gave rise to considerable
opposition—no less than the withdrawal of the exemption of
corporate trust property and charitable endowments from
the provisions of the Income Tax Act. These charges
would add £133,000 to the annual revenue, and so raise the
surplus to £3,874,000. He would then be enabled to take
twopence off the income-tax, and equalise the tax on annual
incomes between £100 and £200, by making the former sum the
limit of liability to taxation, and allowing a deduction of £60 on
amounts between the two sums; the tea duty would be reduced
to 1s. a pound, and then he would have a surplus of £534,000,
which the Government proposed to keep in hand.

Of course the clubs were up in arms; so were the patrons,
trustees, and officials of the great hospitals and other charitable
institutions, who found support in the press. One influential
organ of opinion described the proposition as "a tax on the
convalescence of the poor"—not a very intelligible phrase; and
it was stated that St. Bartholomew's Hospital would lose a
thousand a year, "which is now wholly spent in relieving the

very poorest at the most helpless moment; and the other metropolitan hospitals will lose sums of proportionate amount." The extravagant assertions of the licensed victuallers, when it was proposed to give wine licences to pastrycooks, were almost rivalled by the statements made on this occasion. It was gravely asserted that the proposition "has been chiefly adopted on the professed ground that the clerks at Somerset House are weary of the calculations which so many exemptions force on them. . . . The sufferings of the mechanic, whose broken limb cannot be healed because Mr. Gladstone has impoverished the hospitals, are amply balanced by the joys of the Inland Revenue clerk on discovery that he has escaped three sums in decimals out of a dozen rules of three."

Mr. Gladstone, on his own showing, proposed to remove the exemption, "partly on account of the altered position of the State, and the heavy charge it undertakes for charitable purposes; partly on account of the difficulty and confusion encountered in the attempt to give effect to the exemptions, and partly on account of the sound general principle that all property ought to contribute to the taxes of the country, which, if they are justly and wisely imposed, ought not to be regarded as a penalty on property, but as the necessary means of rendering property available for the effective use and enjoyment of the owner."

On the 4th of May, a very influential deputation waited on the Chancellor of the Exchequer for the purpose of submitting reasons why he should not persevere with the scheme. The Duke of Cambridge, the Archbishop of Canterbury, the Bishop of London, and other bishops, the Earl of Shaftesbury, and many members of both Houses of Parliament attended; and the result was that the Chancellor of the Exchequer withdrew the objectionable clause in the Customs and Inland Revenue Bill. The proposed alterations in the hackney carriage dues and the licences for clubs were also withdrawn.

One of Mr. Gladstone's most conspicuous political utterances in this session was in reference to the condition of Ireland; and, in connection with later events, it is interesting to preserve a record of his views in 1863. On the 12th of June, Colonel Dunne, member for Queen's County, moved for a select committee on the condition of Ireland, "to inquire into the causes of the depressed condition and the effect of the taxation which it now bears." Mr. Gladstone, on the part of the Government, declined to concur in the motion, and made a long speech on the subject. To open an inquiry, he said, at a period of the session when no effectual progress could be made with it, could only have the effect of exciting hopes simply to disappoint them. He did not see how the House could interfere to correct the evil of absenteeism, except by endeavouring to do everything in its power to improve the social and economical condition of Ireland, and give its people equal rights and advantages with the rest of the kingdom in regard to the security, confidence, and freedom of their enjoyment and disposal of their property. He demurred to the assertion of—

"A right in the various parts of the kingdom to have public money expended on what I may call geographical principles ; that the taxes raised in Ireland is to be computed, and against that taxation a counter claim is to be lodged on behalf of Ireland for the expenditure of the money so levied within her own limits. If that doctrine is good, it will be difficult to confine it to Ireland. It will travel into Scotland, it will come back into England, and we shall have the south, the north, the west, and the east making their separate claims. . . . I cannot assent to the general proposition that the taxation of the country is to be like a local shower, drawn for a while from the surface of the earth by evaporation, and then descending on it again with fertilising effect at the very spot from which it first rose."

Ireland, he said, was not illiberally treated in respect to public expenditure for local purposes. Ireland had less than double the population of Scotland ; but the special votes amounted to three times as much as for Scotland. "Is there," he asked, "any form of taxation among all those varieties which the ingenuity or necessity of financiers has caused them to invent, under which Ireland is subjected to a higher charge than England?" Incomes went further in Ireland than in England. Not a shilling of duty was levied on hackney coaches, railways, or stage carriages in Ireland, although these duties were levied in England and Scotland. In adjusting the income-tax very considerable mitigations had been granted to Ireland. The landowners there had the advantage of considerable reductions not allowed in England. "We must look," he continued, "to the influence of good laws, liberal legislation, and thorough and hearty equality in our endeavours to apply the principles of justice and freedom to all three countries, for the only means by which we can really confer benefit upon Ireland. All real and permanent benefits which Ireland is to derive must be, not administered like a dose of physic, but must be gained by the exercise of her own energies and her own powers."

These are pregnant words and deserve thoughtful consideration. Colonel Dunne, satisfied apparently with having raised discussion and elicited opinion, withdrew the motion ; but a few days afterwards Irish affairs again furnished subject of debate, in which, however, Mr. Gladstone did not take part. Mr. Maguire, member for Dungarvan, moved an address to the Queen, asking for the appointment of a Royal Commission " to inquire into and report upon the state of the agricultural classes of Ireland, and to suggest such improvements on the relations between landlord and tenant as may seem necessary and expedient." The motion was opposed by the Government, and negatived by a majority of 79.

It was impossible that the position of the country in relation to the American States could escape discussion in Parliament. We have already noticed Mr. Disraeli's speech in the debate on the Address in reply to the Royal Speech. On the 30th of June Mr. Roebuck brought the subject definitely before the House. By that time there had been more than two thousand battles and skirmishes since the outbreak of the war, in the spring of 1861 ; and it appeared to many others besides Mr. Gladstone and Mr. Disraeli, that the Southern States were able to achieve independence. The prolongation of a war so disastrous to America, and the effects of which had been so painfully felt in our own manufacturing districts, was certainly most heartily to be deprecated. In the field, successes were nearly equally balanced. Ulysses Grant, the Federal general, had made a successful advance into Tennessee, but had been repelled in a tremendous assault on the strongly fortified Vicksburg. The great Confederate leader, Stonewall Jackson, had been killed in action, but his opponent, General Hooker, had been forced to recross the Rappahannock, and had been superseded in his command ; and Lee, a chivalrous and dauntless general of the Confederates, had invaded Maryland and Pennsylvania, and taken several towns. One result only of the terrific struggle could be clearly foreseen, and that was an appalling sacrifice of human life and a paralysis of the national energies.

Mr. Roebuck moved " that a humble address be presented to Her Majesty, praying that she will be graciously pleased to enter into negotiations with the great Powers of Europe for the purpose of obtaining their co-operation in the recognition of the Confederate States of North America." " If," said Mr. Roebuck, " we take time by the forelock, we shall be so much the greater people ; and London will be the imperial city of the world. But if we abstain from availing ourselves of the opportunity, it will go away at once to France." He added : " The cry about slavery is hypocrisy and cant." Lord Robert Montagu, member for

Huntingdonshire, moved an amendment in favour of an impartial neutrality.

Mr. Gladstone spoke in opposition to Mr. Roebuck, and suggested reasons why direct intervention would be unadvisable. Referring to the terrible war then raging, he said :—

"Her Majesty's Ministers, I do not think, have ever professed to feel indifferent on the question. It is impossible for anyone with the feelings of a man within him to be indifferent upon it. Moreover, I believe that a very general union of sentiment and opinion exists in the country—not upon every matter relating to the present war, but upon this great question—whether we wish that this war should continue or should cease. My belief is that at least nineteen out of every twenty men in this House, perhaps I might say ninety-nine out of every hundred—I do not know, indeed, that there is a single exception—earnestly and fervently desire that it should terminate. Why, sir, was there ever a war of a more destructive and more deplorable—I will venture to add, of a more hopeless character? Measure it by the enormous absorption of human life, which counts, not by thousands, nor by tens of thousands, but by hundreds of thousands. Was there ever a more deplorable absorption of human treasure, which has brought debts upon countries which heretofore were happily, in practice, free from them, such as not only threaten to depress permanently, or for a long course of years, the condition of the population, but even, perhaps, to involve the greatest political difficulties throughout the whole of what was once the flourishing and happy American Union? Well, if these are common to both parties, is it possible that we, as Englishmen should regard otherwise than with deep pain the special consequences entailed by this war upon each party severally? Look at the embittering and exasperation of the relations between the black man and the white man in the South. Look, again, at the suspension of constitutional liberty in the North—the utter confusion of all the landmarks that separate between right and power—the danger into which the very principle of freedom has been brought in that which used to boast itself the great, and which we, perhaps most of us, admit to have been, at any rate, one of the freest nations of the earth. Look at the discredit to liberty abroad—the discredit not only to democratic, not only to popular, but, I venture to say, to all liberal and constitutional principles—which has been caused, in the eyes of the rest of the world, by the contemplation of the transactions of the last two or three years, and especially of the last twelve months, in North America. I trust there are few of us here who have ever suffered narrow, unworthy jealousies of the American Union to possess our minds. But I believe, if there be such a man —if there be those who have taken illiberal or extreme views of what is defective in the American character, or in American institutions, who close their eyes against all that is great and good and full of promise to mankind in that country—surely all alike must have felt sentiments of compassion and concern absorbing every other sentiment. And the regret and sorrow which we feel at the calamities brought to our own door by this miserable contest are almost swallowed up when we consider the fearful price—more fearful, I believe, than in the history of the world was ever paid, I do not mean in money, by a nation in a state of civil war—a price not alone in the loss of life, not alone in the loss of treasure, but in the desperate political extremities to which the free popular institutions of North America have been reduced. Why, sir, we must desire the cessation of this war. No man is justified in wishing for the continuance of a war unless that war has a just, an adequate, and an attainable object. For no object is adequate, no object is just, unless it be also attainable. We do not believe that the restoration of the American Union by force is attainable. . . . . I will go one step further, and say I believe the public opinion of this country bears very strongly on another matter upon which we have heard much—namely, whether the emancipation of the negro race is an object that can be legitimately pursued by means of coercion and bloodshed. I do not believe that a more fatal error was ever committed than when men—of high intelligence, I grant, and of the sincerity of whose philanthropy I, for one, shall not venture to whisper the smallest doubt—came to the conclusion that the emancipation of the negro race was to be sought, although they could only travel to it by a sea of blood. . . . . I know of no benefit or advantage that would attach to any intervention, arbitration, recognition, or interference of any sort, unless it was actually free from all suspicion of partial or separate interest, or peculiar views. An act of recognition proceeding from England, an act of recognition proceeding from any State which, either from tradition or other circumstances of that kind, is placed in critical relations with America in matters pertaining to its own interests, not only might have, but probably would have, a result precisely opposite to that anticipated by the honourable and learned gentleman. It would assume the character of an interference in the, so to speak, private, at any rate particular, affairs of the American nation. . . . . I confess I have more faith in the gentle action of public opinion, as it grows and is gradually matured in Europe, than I have in diplomatic acts which may tend to assume an appearance of undue interference in American affairs, and especially those diplomatic acts which may justly be suspected of interested motives.''

The debate was adjourned, and, on its resumption, Lord Palmerston appealed to Mr. Roebuck, for political reasons, to withdraw the motion, especially as he (Mr. Roebuck) had had an interview with the Emperor of the French on the subject. The request was complied with, and both motion and amendment fell to the ground.

Parliament was prorogued on the 28th of July, by Royal Commission. The Speech announced, in reference to the civil war in America, that Her Majesty saw no reason to depart from the strict neutrality which she had observed from the beginning of the contest.

In the autumn of the year, Mr. Gladstone collected and republished his Budget speeches. The *Saturday Review*, certainly not an undiscriminating admirer generally of the Chancellor of the Exchequer, did him no more than justice in saying : " No similar statements have been more remarkable for clearness, for fulness, or for judicious distribution of topics. Hearers have been known to mark the termination of one of Mr. Gladstone's speeches, though it had extended over the length of ten sermons, with a sigh, not of relief, but regret, and almost of disappointment. The easy play of a powerful intellect rendered visible is one of the most attractive of spectacles."

In October Mr. Gladstone visited Burslem, in the Stafford-shire Potteries, for the purpose of laying the first stone of the Wedgwood Memorial Institute, or school of art, free library, and museum, intended to commemorate Thomas Wedgwood, a native of that town, whose beautiful productions so greatly ad-vanced the ceramic art in this country. Mr. Gladstone, an enthusiastic collector of porcelain, was quite at home with his subject, and delivered an eloquent address advocating the union of beauty and utility in articles of daily use. A love of beauty, he insisted, is the best correction of sordid and avaricious pro-pensities. He was particularly hard upon the "crane-necked water-jugs" for dressing-rooms, insisting that wide-mouthed ewers were at once more useful and more beautiful. Certainly water is poured out more freely from wide-necked than from narrow vessels, but Mr. Gladstone appeared to forget that the latter expose a smaller surface of fluid to atmospheric effects during the night, and that therefore the water is purer and cooler in the morning. A few years afterwards Mr. Gladstone sold his collection of old china and chimney ornaments.

The opening of the session of 1864 is memorable for the attack made by the Earl of Derby, in the Lords' debate on the Address, on the foreign policy of Earl Russell, and his professed advocacy of non-intervention. "As to non-intervention in the internal affairs of other countries," said Earl Derby, scornfully, "when I look around me I fail to see what country there is in the internal affairs of which the noble Earl has not interfered. The foreign policy of the noble Earl, as far as the principle of non-interven-tion is concerned, may be summed up in the homely words, ' meddle and muddle.'"

A few days after the House met, Mr. Gladstone introduced a measure to extend the operations of the Post Office Savings Bank. The object of the Government Annuities Bill was to amend the law relating to the purchase of annuities, by making use of the savings bank machinery, and to authorise the granting of life insurances by the Government. In introducing the Bill Mr. Gladstone explained that, as the law stood, only large amounts could be received for the purchase of deferred annuities, and it was proposed to facilitate the reception of smaller amounts through the medium of the Post Office Savings Bank. Govern-ment could grant life insurances, but only to the amount of £100, and then only to persons who purchased deferred annuities, and it was proposed to abolish that restriction. Some opposition was made. There was, of course, an outcry that Government was exceeding its proper functions; but the Bill was carried through both Houses

Another plan proposed by Mr. Gladstone, early in the session, was less successful. He proposed to alter the mode of collecting land-tax, assessed taxes, and income tax, by adopting the method practised in Ireland and Scotland, by which the collection of taxes are intrusted to the department of Inland Revenue, instead of employing unofficial collectors. The Bill was defeated by a small majority on the motion for second reading.

On the 16th of March, Mr. Dodson, member for East Sussex, introduced a Bill to abolish the tests required on taking degrees at the University of Oxford, and so putting it on the same footing in that respect as the Universities of Cambridge and Dublin. Sir William Heathcote, Mr. Gladstone's colleague in the representation of Oxford University, moved as an amendment that the Bill should be read a second time that day six months. On such a subject Mr. Gladstone could not, as a Churchman and member for the University, be silent He said he would support the second reading, though he was not prepared to accept the Bill unless considerable alterations were made in committee. He could not agree that no test should be applicable to the divinity degree, and he thought that the governing body of the University should not be thrown open irrespective of religious distinctions. The education given at Oxford had always been, and, he trusted, would continue to be, a strictly and formally religious education ; and although the University had endeavoured to provide that the liberal enactments of the Act of 1858, in relation to Dissenters, should be carried out, it had resolved that in no respect should the course of its tuition with regard to members of the Church of England be affected. He warned churchmen, however, against a policy of indiscriminate resistance to proposals of change. He said :—

" Lately it has been too much the fashion to adopt a policy of indiscriminate resistance. I cannot conceal my own opinion on that subject. If you look back upon history you will find that the greatest vice and misfortune of the Church of England has been that, for many generations past, on questions not of temporal, but spiritual interest, her friends, or those who thought themselves her friends, have shown a great tenacity in clinging to their privileges to the very last moment that it was practicable, and at length only had them positively wrenched from their grasp when concession had lost all possible grace and value, and when consequently nothing could be obtained in return. Sir, if I take my present course, it is not because I believe that this is an easy time for the Church of England, or a time without its dangers. On the contrary, as regards the religion of that Church, I admit that these are days when it is subjected to peculiar and perhaps unprecedented dangers.

But these dangers will not be averted, or even mitigated, by declining to make concessions which do not touch her faith, but indicate her desire to live in goodwill with every branch and section of the community—to consult, as far as possible, the feelings of all Christians, and all persons, be they Christians or not, to whom it is possible for the Universities to impart a portion of their benefits, and thus to show that, when she does take a course of resistance, it is from no narrow or hasty impression, but because she is convinced that the vital interests are at stake of that faith which is committed to her charge. That is the policy upon which I desire to act."

The Bill was read a second time by a majority of 22, the numbers being 211 against 189. Mr. Gladstone did not vote. On the motion for committal the majority was reduced to 110. The division on the motion for the third reading resulted in equal numbers, and the Speaker, being called on for his casting vote, gave it for the Ayes, in order that the measure might not be dropped, but that the House might have another opportunity of voting. When that opportunity was afforded, by the division on the question that the Bill do now pass, it was rejected by a majority of two, the numbers being 173 to 171. In each of these divisions Mr. Gladstone voted against the Bill, and, in doing so, separated himself from most of his colleagues.

Another Bill, having to some extent the same object—proposing the repeal of those portions of the Act of Uniformity which required subscription from persons who sought fellowships at universities—was afterwards brought in by Mr. Bouverie, but rejected by a majority of 56.

The Budget was introduced early in the session, on the 7th of April. The Chancellor of the Exchequer had a surplus in hand, after allowing for extra expenditure on fortifications, of £2,352,000. He took occasion, in introducing the statement, to refer to the financial progress of the country in the five years during which he had held office. The revenue had increased at the rate of more than a million a year, and the advance in trade had been surprising. The aggregate value of imports and exports in 1861 was £377,000,000; in 1862, £391,000,000; and in 1863, £444,000,000. He was entitled to refer to this result with some feelings of pride, for he had encountered enough prophecies of disaster resulting from his financial policy to have alarmed a weaker man :—

"The present amount of trade is about three times the trade of the country as it stood at a period comparatively recent—namely, in the year 1842, when Parliament first began deliberately and advisedly to set itself to the task of reforming our commercial legislation; and, in the second place, the same may be taken to represent, as nearly as possible, £1,500,000 for every working day in the year, a magnitude of industry and of operation so vast that if it did not stand upon incontrovertible figures, it hardly could receive belief. But, in my judgment, not only are these figures remarkable when we consider them as the produce of the energy of Englishmen and of the strength of the country, which is dear to all our hearts ; they mean much more than that—though that, too, of itself were much—they mean that England is becoming more and more deeply pledged from year to year to be the champion of peace and justice throughout the world ; and to take part, with no view to narrow or selfish interests, but only with a view to the great object of the welfare of humanity at large, in every question that may arise in every quarter of the globe. . . . I find that if I select several years, in which Parliament has, with firm and unsparing hand, addressed itself to the business of liberating commerce, these operations have been immediately followed by striking augmentations in the trade and industry of the country. . . . I think we may conclude that we have not been feeding ourselves by an empty dream when we have held that, in giving freedom to the energy, capital, and skill of Englishmen, we were adopting the true means of extending our commercial prosperity."

Referring to the treaty of commerce with France, he said that in 1859, immediately before the treaty, our imports from that country amounted to £16,870,000, and in 1863 they had risen to £24,024,000. The value of the exports in 1859 was £9,561,000; in 1863, £22,963,000. Mr. Gladstone added : " I am very glad to say that the French manufacturers are beginning to discover the futility of their alarms, just as the traders of this country have so frequently found it by experience on their side." In fact, the trade of the country had not been swamped by a deluge of French wine, and the publicans were still "lusty gentlemen." Both countries had prospered by the increased facilities of commercial intercourse ; and it was as obvious as figures could make it that in the course of the five years of Mr. Gladstone's administration of the finances, very notable results had occurred. In 1859 we exported to France very little more than half what we received from that country, and to that extent the balance of trade was against us. In 1863 the imports and exports were very nearly equal, and the former had increased about 50 per cent., and the latter more than 130 per cent. If the commercial community was not thankful to Mr. Gladstone, it should have been so.

An estimated expenditure for the year 1864–5 of £66,890,000, against an estimated revenue of £69,460,000, gave promise of a surplus of £2,570,000. Against the alliterative "meddle and muddle" of Lord Derby, the Minister might have pitted another alliterative phrase—"surprises and surpluses"—as descriptive of Mr. Gladstone's Budgets. A reduction of the sugar duty to one shilling per hundredweight disposed of £1,330,000 ; the fire insurance duty on stock-in-trade was diminished by one-half; the duty on malt used for the consumption of cattle was taken off, and altogether taxation was lightened to the amount of more than £2,000,000, leaving a surplus of £238,000 to be carried forward to the next account. An unsuccessful struggle was made on behalf of a total repeal of the malt-tax, and later in the session (June 24) Mr. Morritt, member for the North Riding of Yorkshire, moved a resolution, " That in case of any modification of the indirect taxation of the country the excise on malt requires consideration." Once more Mr. Gladstone objected to pledging the House to abstract financial resolutions, and the motion was lost by 166 to 118.

The session of course produced the accustomed motions connected with Parliamentary representation. Mr. Berkeley again advocated vote by ballot, and was again defeated, Lord Palmerston opposing the motion. Mr. Locke King revived the proposition for extending the franchise in counties to occupiers of the value of £10. Lord Palmerston, on the part of the Government, did not oppose the introduction of the Bill, because he did not wish it to be thought that the Government were averse to any change in the county franchise; but he gave notice that in Committee he should vote against the particular franchise the Bill provided, and added that he thought it was hardly expedient on the part of Mr. Locke King to bring it in at a time when, from the course of foreign affairs, and other causes, there was very little desire on the part of the people for organic change. The Bill was rejected.

A more vigorous debate on the subject of the franchise was begun on the 11th of May, when the Borough Franchise Bill, introduced by Mr. Baines, member for Leeds, came on for discussion. The object was to extend the franchise in boroughs by substituting a £6 rental for the existing £10 standard. Mr. Cave, member for New Shoreham, met the Bill by moving "the previous question." Mr. Gladstone, representing the Ministry, opposed the Bill. It was not a time, he said, for Government to deal with the question, and even the party which represented the liberal opinion of the country was not unanimous in respect to it. Yet, as the subject had been introduced, he would not vote for the amendment, which went to deny that the question of the franchise ought to be discussed, and, if possible, settled. In the course of his speech he made a memorable declaration respecting the extension of the franchise to the working-classes :—

" I will not enter into the question whether the precise form of franchise and the precise figure which my honourable friend has indicated is that which, upon full deliberation, we ought to choose ; whether the franchise should be

founded on ratepaying or on occupation; neither will I consider whether or
not there should be a lodgers' franchise. I put aside every question except
the very simple one which I take to be at issue, and on this I will endeavour
not to be misunderstood. I apprehend my honourable friend's Bill to mean
(and if such be the meaning, I give my cordial concurrence to the proposition) that there ought to be, not a wholesale, nor an excessive, but a sensible
and considerable addition to that portion of the working-classes—at present
almost infinitesimal—which is in possession of the franchise. I
apprehend that I am correct in saying that those who possess the franchise
are less than one-fiftieth of the whole number of the working-classes. Is
that a state of things which we cannot venture to touch or modify? Is there
no choice between excluding forty-nine out of every fifty working-men on the
one hand, and on the other a 'domestic revolution'? [Mr. Cave had made
use of that phrase in moving the amendment] . . . . . We are told
that the working-classes do not agitate for an extension of the franchise ; but
is it desirable that we should wait until they do agitate? In my opinion,
agitation by the working-classes, upon any political subject whatever, is a
thing not to be waited for, not to be made a condition previous to any Parliamentary movement, but, on the contrary, it is a thing to be deprecated, and,
if possible, anticipated and prevented by wise and provident measures. An
agitation by the working-classes is not like an agitation by the classes above
them—the classes possessed of leisure. The agitation of the classes having
leisure is easily conducted. It is not with them that every hour of time has
a money value; their wives and children are not dependent on the strictly
reckoned results of those hours of labour. When a working-man finds himself in such a condition that he must abandon that daily labour on which he
is strictly dependent for his daily bread, when he gives up the profitable
application of his time, it is then that, in railway language, 'the danger
signal is turned on,' for he does it only because he feels a strong necessity
for action, and a distrust in the rulers who, as he thinks, have driven him to
that necessity. . . . . *I venture to say that every man who is not
presumably incapacitated by some consideration of personal unfitness, or of
political danger, is morally entitled to come within the pale of the Constitution.* . . . . . As a general rule, the lower stratum of the middle
class is admitted to the exercise of the franchise, while the upper stratum of
the working-class is excluded. That, I believe, to be a fair general description of the present formation of the constituencies in boroughs and towns. Is
it a state of things, I would ask, recommended by clear principles of reason ?
Is the upper portion of the working-classes inferior to the lowest portion
of the middle? That is a question I should wish to be considered on both
sides of the House. For my own part, it appears to me that the negative of
the proposition may be held with the greatest confidence. Whenever this
question comes to be discussed, with the view to an immediate issue, the conduct of the general body of the operatives of Lancashire cannot be forgotten.
What are the qualities which fit a man for the exercise of a privilege such as
the franchise? Self-command, self-control, respect for order, patience under
suffering, confidence in the law, regard for superiors ; and when, I should
like to ask, were all these great qualities exhibited in a manner more signal, I
would even say, more illustrious, than under the profound affliction of the
winter of 1862? I admit the danger of dealing with enormous masses of
men ; but I am now speaking only of a limited portion of the working-class,
and I, for one, cannot admit that there is that special value in the nature of
the middle class which ought to lead to our drawing a marked distinction, a
distinction almost purporting to be one of principle, between them and a select

portion of the working-classes, so far as relates to the exercise of the franchise? . . . . . I believe that it has been given to us of this generation
to witness, advancing, as it were, under our very eyes from day to day, the
most blessed of all social processes ; I mean the process which unites together,
not the interests only, but the feelings of all the several classes of the community, and which throws back into the shadows of oblivion those discords
by which they are kept apart from one another. I know of nothing which
can contribute, in any degree comparable to that union, to the welfare of the
commonwealth. It is well, sir, that we should be suitably provided with
armies, and fleets, and fortifications ; it is well, too, that all these should rest
upon and be sustained, as they ought to be, by a sound system of finance, and
out of a revenue not wasted by a careless Parliament or by a profligate administration. But that which is better, and more weighty still is, that hearts
should be bound together by a reasonable extension, at fitting times, and
among selected portions of the people, of every benefit and every privilege
that can justly be conferred on them."

The " previous question " was carried by 272 against 216 ;
majority against the second reading, 56. In this division neither
Mr. Gladstone nor Lord Palmerston voted, unwilling, it would
seem, either to support the Bill or to place on record a Ministerial opinion that the subject should not be discussed. Mr.
Gladstone's speech was described at the time as having " afforded
great delight and encouragement to the reforming party, but as
having also produced considerable dismay and consternation
among the Conservative benches." It was certainly a very near
approach to an approbation of the principle of universal suffrage,
and was generally accepted as the first step in a new political
departure. Mr. Gladstone was evidently not desirous that his
words should be too literally interpreted ; for he immediately
published the speech, with a preface, in which he said : " Candid
minds ought to find an explanation of general statements in the
context of the speech which contains them." The already famous
sentence was " drawn forth on the moment, by a course of argument from the opponents of the measure." He fully admitted that
candidates for the franchise might rightly be rejected "if it should
appear that though no present unfitness can be alleged against
them, yet political danger might arise from their admission."
"As the opinion of an individual," wrote Mr. Gladstone, "the
whole matter is of trifling consequence." But when that individual happened to be the Chancellor of the Exchequer, one of
the most able and influential of members, and a probable Prime
Minister in the future, his expressed opinion was of no trifling
importance. In offering the explanation, Mr. Gladstone committed the same error that Lord Palmerston did, when, being
Foreign Secretary, he asserted that the expression of his views on

a question of foreign policy had no greater weight than the utterances on the subject of any other member of the Cabinet. As a writer of the time properly observed, "The consequence which attaches to the opinion of an individual depends on the preliminary consideration who the individual is."

In October Mr. Gladstone visited Lancashire, and spoke at length at Liverpool, Bolton, Farnworth, and other places. He avoided political topics likely to arouse party feeling. He described the growing prosperity of England, fostered by prudent legislation, congratulated his hearers on the diminution of political disaffection, and on the better understanding between the various classes of the community. He spoke of England's high place among nations, and her privileges at home. But all this was to lead up to the moral that this place and these privileges imposed duties which must be manfully undertaken and performed. He enlarged upon our recent progress, but it was less our progress in wealth and comfort than our progress in intelligence and morality. "In one word," said a contemporary writer, "Mr. Gladstone's theme has been the rise of a sense of brotherhood in our land. It has sprung up as soon as the burden of physical want has been removed, through the operation of the wise measures which, since the Reform Bill, have been inaugurated, but its effects have been moral even more than physical."

On the 7th of November Mr. Gladstone attended at the closing of the North London Industrial Exhibition, at the Agricultural Hall, Islington, and delivered a genial and instructive address, some passages of which may well be read in connection with his presumed encouragement in Parliament of the principles of manhood suffrage. He told his hearers, presumably working men, that although legislation had done much for them, there was much remaining which they must do for themselves : "It is not possible, in a well-organised society, that any one class should make essential progress in any way, except through its own exertions. The mere mitigation of abuses will never give energy and dignity of character to a class, and especially to the great labouring classes of the community ; it is upon themselves they must depend, in order to exhibit in the face of their fellow-countrymen those characteristics which constitute the true basis of greatness."

CHAPTER XX.

THE session of 1865—the last session of the sixth Victorian Parliament—was opened on the 7th of February. Mr. Gladstone's first speech of importance was on the 28th of March, in the debate on a motion by Mr. Dillwyn, member for Swansea, "That the Irish Estab'ishment is unsatisfactory, and calls for the early attention of Her Majesty's Government." There was nothing very novel in the arguments of the mover of the resolution. Then, as before, "the church of the minority" was the main point relied on; but Mr. Gathorne Hardy, in his earnest and impetuous manner, speaking on the Conservative side, had imparted a little unwonted spirit into the debate, declaring that the maintenance of the Protestant Church in Ireland was part of the contract made at the Union, and that if the resolution were carried the House would violate the principles of the Reformation, the Act of Settlement, the Act of Union, and the Settlement of 1829. Mr. Gladstone did not support the motion, but replied to Mr. Hardy. He said :—

"I am bound to say that I must differ from the doctrine to which the honourable member appears to incline, that the Protestants in Ireland, or the members of the Established Church in any one of the three kingdoms—for I believe them all to be on the same footing—are solely entitled to have provision made for their spiritual wants, without any regard being paid to the requirements of the remaining portion of the population. Neither our constitution nor our history will warrant such a conclusion. There is not the slightest doubt that if the Church of England is a national Church, and that if the condition upon which the ecclesiastical endowments are held was altered at the Reformation, that alteration was made mainly with the view that these endowments should be intrusted to a body ministering to the wants of a great majority of the people. I am bound to add my belief that those who directed the government of this country in the reign of Queen Elizabeth acted in the firm conviction that that which had happened in England would happen in Ireland ; and they would probably be not a little surprised if they could look down the vista of time and see that in the year 1865 the result of all their labours had been that, after three hundred years, the Church which they had endowed and established ministered to the religious wants of only one-eighth or one-ninth part of the community."

The House was not called on to vote on the motion, for an adjournment of the debate was carried by 221 to 106, and it was not resumed. Mr. Gladstone's words were naturally much canvassed. They were something like an open advocacy of disestablishment in Ireland; and they certainly considerably affected the decision of the Oxford University constituency four months afterwards. Public and private remonstrances were addressed to the speaker, and he felt it necessary to make some explanation of his position in relation to the question. On the 8th of May he replied to a letter from Dr. Hannah, who, as principal of a Church of England college, had forwarded to Mr. Gladstone a letter he had received on the subject :—

"It would be very difficult for me to subscribe to any interpretation of my speech on the Irish Church like that of your correspondent, which contains so many conditions and bases of a plan for dealing with a question apparently remote, and at the same time full of difficulties on every side. My reasons are, I think, plain. First, because the question is remote, and apparently out of all bearing on the practical politics of the day, I think it would be for me worse than superfluous to determine upon any scheme, or basis of a scheme, with respect to it. Secondly, because it is difficult, even if I anticipated any likelihood of being called upon to deal with it, I should think it right to take no decision beforehand on the mode of dealing with the difficulties. As far as I know, my speech signifies pretty clearly the broad distinction which I make between the abstract and the practical views of the subject. . . . One thing, however, I may add, because I think it is a clear landmark. In any measure dealing with the Irish Church, I think (though I scarcely expect to be called on to share in such a measure) the Act of Union must be recognised, and must have important consequences, especially with respect to the position of the hierarchy."

Notwithstanding that, in May, 1865, he "did not expect to be called on to share in such a measure," less than five years afterwards, he introduced a Bill to disestablish the Irish Church.

In anticipation of the financial statement, the familiar attempts were made to pledge the House, by abstract resolutions, to remit or reduce certain taxes. The Conservative "friends of the farmer" made a desperate effort to score a success by carrying a resolution in favour of the abolition of the malt duty, moved by Sir Fitzroy Kelly and seconded by Sir B. Lytton. Neither law nor literature, however, was able to command a majority of the House. The "previous question" was carried by a majority of 81.

Mr. Sheridan was more fortunate. In the previous session he had, by dint of perseverance, obtained a partial remission of the fire insurance duty, and he now moved to extend the remission to houses, household goods, and all description of insurable property. Mr. Gladstone did not wish to place on record an absolute refusal to make the desired reduction ; but he decidedly objected to being pledged to anything in advance of his Budget. He met the proposition by moving the "previous question," but was defeated, and the resolution was carried by a majority of 72.

The 27th of April was Budget night; and as it was very confidently anticipated that the Chancellor of the Exchequer would have a good surplus to dispose of, and, that being the case, would be in good spirits, and make a capital speech, even more than the usual interest was excited. In that respect, indeed, he did not disappoint his hearers. The actual expenditure for the past year had been £66,462,000 (less than the estimate), and the revenue £70,313,000 (more than the estimated sum), and there was therefore a surplus of £3,851,000, or, if the expenditure on fortifications sanctioned by the House were taken into account, of £3,231,000. Comparing the financial position of the country with that in previous years, he said that from 1859 (the year in which he took office) to 1865, the balance of taxes repealed over taxes imposed might be taken at £6,713,000. During the same period the increase of the revenue had been £3,968,000. A total of £10,681,000 was thus obtained, and dividing the sum among the six years, he arrived at the remarkable result that the rate of annual growth in the income of the country from the same sources was, in that time, £1,780,000. In 1864 imports and exports amounted to £487,000,000, or an increase of more than £219,000,000 since the comparatively recent period of 1854. The absolute increment of trade in that period was nearly 30 per cent. more in England than in France. This country had experienced an increase of 71 per cent., while Belgium had advanced only 43 per cent., and Holland only 25 per cent. Having referred to the magnitude of our railway system, the large amount of capital invested in it, and the facilities it offered for increasing the wealth of the country, Mr. Gladstone continued :—

"After all that has been said on the subject of machinery and locomotion, all these figures go to place it beyond doubt that immense advantages have also resulted from the apparently simple, but in practice sufficiently difficult business of removing the bars, fetters, and obstructions devised by the perversity of man himself from the processes of human industry, and of trusting to the simple expedient of freedom for the development of the productive power of a country. And, sir, it is no small honour to the kingdom of the Queen that, as in regard to locomotion, so in regard to the freedom of trade and industry, it has been given to them to lead the vanguard and bear the banner of civilisation. In the words of one of our own poets [Tennyson], used to describe the establishment of justice and order after barbarous anarchy, and not less justly applicable to the changes we have now in view with all their long train of consequences, it may be given to our acts—

> ' To serve as model for the mighty world,
> And be the fair beginning of a time.

To be the beginning of a time richly fraught not only with economical advantages—not only with results which can be exhibited in statistical tables—but fraught more richly still with results which promote and confirm the union of class with class among ourselves, and even, as we may hope, of nation with nation throughout the wide surface of the earth."

Diverging for a few moments to eulogise the great public services of Mr. Cobden (at whose funeral he had been present ten days before), Mr. Gladstone, then proceeded to his estimates of income and expenditure for the coming financial year. He calculated that the revenue would amount to £70,170,000, and the expenditure to £66,139,000, leaving a surplus of £4,031,000. Having given notice of some slight alteration in stamp duties, he referred to the attempts which had been made to obtain a remission of the duty on malt. Ministers had, he said, been reproached with having done nothing for the agriculturists; but they disclaimed any design of looking to the interests of classes; they looked to the interest of the community—the revenue of the country was the public property of the country. He examined the reasons brought forward to justify the abolition or the reduction of the duty. "The total abolition of the duty would," he said, "be the death warrant of our whole system of indirect taxation, and transfer of the burden to property." He proposed, however, to give the maltster the option of having the amount of duty estimated according to weight instead of measure, the latter mode being unfair to barley of different qualities. The tea duty would be lessened by 6d. per pound, and that reduction would involve a loss to the revenue for the year of £1,868,000; the income tax would be reduced from 6d. to 4d., equivalent to a loss on the year of £1,650,000. As the House had assented to a resolution in favour of reducing the duty on fire insurance, he was bound to accept the decision, and proposed to impose a uniform duty of 1s. 6d., and substitute a 1d. stamp on the policy for the 1s. duty previously paid. Allowing for all these reductions, the estimated surplus for the current year would be £253,000.

The Budget resolutions were carried, though not without a running fire of adverse comments from the Opposition benches; but the reduction of the income tax and of the tea duty were too generally acceptable advantages to allow a very strong fight to be made by the opponents of the malt duty.

Early in May, Mr. Baines once more brought in a Bill for reducing the borough franchise, which, however, was rejected, on the motion for the second reading, by a majority of 74. Lord Palmerston, the Premier, was ill from an attack of the gout when the Bill was introduced—too ill even to see and advise with his colleagues; and a Tory contemporary writer tells us: "When Mr. Baines rose to address the House, nobody on the Ministerial benches knew either what he was to do or what was expected of him. Then was seen on the Cabinet bench a spectacle such as, in modern times, has rarely astonished the Senate. The Ministers spoke together, not in quiet whispers, but with eagerness, much gesticulation, and warmth. The Chancellor of the Exchequer made a movement as if to get upon his legs, and was with difficulty restrained; and the Lord Advocate jumping up, nobody would hear him."

Before the time came on for the resumption of the debate, Palmerston was able to pay a little attention to public affairs, and a Cabinet Council was summoned to meet at his private residence, Cambridge House. Mr. Gladstone's disposition to extend the franchise was well known, and the Premier's objection to extension was also a familiar fact: and if we may believe statements made at the time, a serious Ministerial crisis was imminent. *Blackwood's Magazine*, the High Tory organ, gave its version of what occurred: "Lord Palmerston, we understand, informed Mr. Gladstone that, if he was determined to speak in favour of Mr. Baines's motion, he must resign the seals of office. Mr. Gladstone, proud and irritable, and full of self-conceit, at once accepted the alternative, and was with difficulty prevailed upon to give way rather than break up the Cabinet. Hence his silence during the second debate. He held his peace when his friends of Leeds, Manchester, Liverpool, and Bolton expected him to speak, and submitted to be marched out, a silent and disgusted voter, into the same lobby with Sir George Grey, Mr. Milner Gibson, and Mr. Baines.

The attempt to abolish tests in the University of Oxford was renewed in June, when Mr. Goschen obtained leave to bring in another Tests Abolition (Oxford) Bill, which Mr. Gladstone opposed in an earnest speech, and voted against in the division. The second reading was carried by a majority of 16; but the session was too far advanced to permit a hope that the Bill could be passed through all its stages, and it was withdrawn.

The Parliament died a natural death in July, and on the 6th of the month a Royal Commission dismissed the members to make their preparations for a general election. Mr. Gladstone had represented the University of Oxford for eighteen years; but his growing Liberalism, and especially his expressed opinions on the subject of the Irish Church, had alienated the affections of many of his supporters in the constituency, and made the renewed tenure of his seat doubtful. In view of the probability of his rejection, the Liberals of South Lancashire nominated him as candidate for their division of the county.

Before the dissolution of Parliament, Mr. Gladstone made a speech at Chester in support of the candidature of his son, Mr. W. H. Gladstone, for the representation of that city; and by doing so, laid himself open to severe comments from the Tory party. In his famous speech in defence of small nomination boroughs, on account of the facilities they offered for introducing young men of great talent into Parliament (see *ante*, page 138), he had adduced instances of the eminent services rendered to the country by states-men who in very early manhood had been introduced into Parlia-ment; and that speech was remembered when he introduced his son, as admittedly an inexperienced and very young man, to the electors of Chester. *Blackwood* made a fair and telling hit in an article, "Mr. Gladstone at Chester":—

"It is quite true, as Mr. Gladstone urged, that many of our leading states-men were introduced early into Parliament upon what he calls the principle of trust, and more than justified that selection by the talents which they subse-quently displayed. But he was most careful not to tell his audience that, in almost every case, these young men had won distinction at the universities, or had otherwise given such proofs of their genius and mental capacity as entitled them to come forward in the capacity of political aspirants. Peel, Macaulay, Mr. Gladstone himself, were eminent instances of this. The honours which they gained at the university were their passports into public life. They were marked men before they ever crossed the threshold of St. Stephen's. . . . If Mr. Gladstone could have pointed to any such achievements on the part of his son—to any indication, however faint, of his talents—we should have been inclined to pass over, leniently at least, the extraordinary demonstration which he has made, and have abstained from censuring an indiscretion which paternal fondness might excuse. But no such apology can be preferred."

It was certainly an error of judgment on Mr. Gladstone's part to indulge in remarks about "the youth and imperfect knowledge" of Mr. Raikes, the Conservative candidate. It was in this speech he declared that "the principle of the Conservative party was mistrust of the people, tempered by fear."

The nomination for the University of Oxford was fixed for the 13th of July. The Warden of All Souls proposed Sir William Heathcote (whose return was secure); the Dean of Christ Church proposed Mr. Gladstone; and the Public Orator nominated

o

Mr. Gathorne Hardy. Votes for the latter were given rapidly. Mr. Gladstone's supporters lagged behind, and on the third day of polling he was 230 behind. Sir J. T. Coleridge, chairman of Mr. Gladstone's committee, issued a circular to the electors still unpledged, announcing that there was reason to fear the seat was in danger, and pressing upon them the duty of recording their votes in his favour: "The committee do not scruple to advocate his cause on grounds above the common level of politics. They claim for him the gratitude due to one whose public life has for eighteen years reflected a lustre on the University herself. They confidently invite you to consider whether his pure and exalted character, his splendid abilities, and his eminent services to Church and State do not constitute the highest of all qualifications for an academical seat, and entitle him to be judged by his constituents as he will assuredly be judged by posterity."

This appeal was unavailing to save the seat. At the close of the poll, which Sir W. Heathcote headed, Mr. Hardy occupied the second place by a majority of 180 over Mr. Gladstone, the numbers being respectively, 1,904 and 1,724. It was a notable circumstance that Bishop Wilberforce, of Oxford, and Bishop Baring, of Durham, voted, as members of the University, for Mr. Gladstone, although it is certain that, in case of a scrutiny, the votes would have been rejected, on the ground that, as spiritual peers, they could not legally interfere in the election of a member to the House of Commons. The total number of voters who polled, either in person or by proxy, was 3,850, a number nearly double that on any former occasion. Mr. Gladstone received 415 plumpers, and, although rejected, polled 674 more than at the previous election, when the seat was contested by the Marquis of Chandos.

The result at Oxford was so clearly foreseen from the daily state of the poll that Mr. Gladstone had no hesitation in accepting the candidature for South Lancashire, and he was addressing the electors at Liverpool at the very time when the poll at Oxford closed. He had borne his defeat with a dignity which his most virulent opponents recognised and respected. Even the combative and often truculent *Blackwood* could not deny that the University had sustained a loss : "The feeling towards him of the great bulk of the constituencies was rather that of brother for brother than anything else. All were proud of his scholarship, of his eloquence, of his great ability, of the place which he had won for himself in public estimation. Probably there are not a dozen among all who have recorded their votes against Mr. Gladstone but lament now

SKETCHES OF HAWARDEN CASTLE.

By S. H. Scott.

as they lamented when their minds were, after a severe struggle, made up, that they had no choice in the matter."

Mr. Gladstone himself said, when addressing the electors of Liverpool :—

> "I have endeavoured to serve that University with my whole heart and with the strength or weakness of whatever faculties God has given me. It has been my daily and my nightly care to promote, as well as I could, her interests, and to testify to her, as well as I could, my love. Long has she borne with me— long, in spite of active opposition, did she resist every effort to displace me. At last she has changed her mind. If I have clung to the representation of the University with desperate fondness, it was because I could not desert that post in which I seemed to have been placed. I have not abandoned it. I have been dismissed from it, not by academical, but by political agencies."

He told his hearers that it had been his ardent desire, and his earnest labour, to unite that which is represented by Oxford and that which is represented by Lancashire ; to establish and main-tain a harmony between the past of England and the future that is in store for her. To the University constituency he said, in a farewell address :—

> "After an arduous connection of eighteen years, I bid you respectfully farewell. My earnest purpose to serve you, my many faults and short-comings, the incidents of the political relations between the university and my-self, established in 1847, so often questioned in vain, and now at length finally dissolved, I leave to the judgment of the future. It is one imperative duty, and one alone, which induces me to trouble you with these few parting words —the duty of expressing my profound and lasting gratitude for indulgence as generous, and for support as warm and enthusiastic in itself, and as honour-able from the character and distinction of those who have given it, as has, in my belief, ever been awarded by any constituency to any representative."

" Henceforward," exclaimed the *Times*, " Mr. Gladstone will belong to the country, but no longer to the University." " The loss to the University bids fair to be the gain of the people of England," said a writer in another journal of the time. The Liberal party believed that he had been relieved from restraints which impeded his political development. " Those Oxford in-fluences and traditions which have so strongly coloured his views, and so often interfered with his better judgment, must gradually lose their hold on him," said the *Times*.

The *Saturday Review*, commenting on the result of the election, said : " No harm has been done to Mr. Gladstone, who will be a more powerful man in the House of Commons as the representa-tive of a great commercial constituency. . . . Few people will take the trouble to analyse the majority and minority, and to weigh as well as to count. Otherwise it would be easily seen that

it is not by the academical, but by the non-academical element
of the constituency that Mr. Gladstone has been turned out.
He had an immense majority among the residents, and the
lists of his two committees show that not only almost all the
academical eminence, but the great body of those who take any
active interest in academical or literary matters, were upon his
s·de. On the other side were the men whose names ' are on
the books,' and no small number of whom were persuaded to put
their names upon the books solely that they might give a party
vote at the election. It was, in fact, a battle between the
University, struggling for its independence, and the Carlton
Club; and the University—for the time, at least—has gone under
the yoke."

Mr. Gladstone himself appears to have felt that the University
connection imposed certain restrictions ; for, speaking at Manchester, in the Free Trade Hall, he told the electors that he came
among them "unmuzzled." He spoke freely on Church questions. He denounced as misguided folly any endeavour to promote the interests of the Establishment by maintaining odious
stigmas on Dissenters and Roman Catholics, and said :—

> "If the Church of England is to live amongst us, she must flourish, and
> she must grow ; and God grant that she may do so by making herself bene-
> ficially known in the discharge of her apostolic offices, by the faithful custody
> of the word which she has received, by making her ministration the friend and
> consoler of every man in every rank of life, by causing herself to be felt by
> each one of you in those actions wherein her assistance can be available."

On the subject of Parliamentary Reform he spoke with plain-
ness and boldness ; though, of course, he declined to pledge his
colleagues in the Ministry to any particular course of action. But
he blamed successive Governments for trifling with the question
—taking it up when it was forced upon them, and laying it aside
as soon as they could escape from their pledges. Such conduct,
he said, was attended with " loss of credit, loss of dignity, loss of
confidence in the powers and institutions of the country in relation to the mind of the nation at large."

In the course of the electoral campaign Mr. Disraeli had taken
occasion, in addressing the Buckinghamshire voters, at Aylesbury,
to make a vigorous attack on Mr. Gladstone's financial arrangements, and his last Budget speech especially. The Chancellor
of the Exchequer, according to Mr. Disraeli, had appeared to
claim, as results of his financial arrangements, benefits which
came from the bounty of Providence. "I don't believe," he
went on to say, in that drily humorous manner which he could

adopt so effectively, "the good harvest we enjoy has been produced by any Cabinet Council whatever.   I don't think the gold
discoveries, nor the wonderful construction of railroads which
now interline the country, are due to Downing Street, nor that
these enterprises have been carried on by the capital or enterprise of the Government."   The Conservatives, he maintained,
had originated, but were unable to carry out, the most important
of the financial changes which Mr. Gladstone prided himself on
effecting.   He, Mr. Disraeli, had been the first to grapple with
the tea duties; he had advocated the repeal of the paper duties,
and, indeed, pledged the House to the remission at the first convenient opportunity; and Lord Derby's Government, as far back
as 1852, had entered into negotiations with France respecting
the establishment of a treaty of commerce.   The Conservatives
had reduced the income-tax ; and, as to the surplus which Mr.
Gladstone had announced, the surplus was " obtained by the adoption of the policy which we have been urging year after year."   In
dealing with the terminable annuities Mr. Gladstone had performed
a feat of legerdemain.   "He took one million and turned it into
ducks, then he took another million and turned it into drakes, and
for half an hour those ducks and drakes flew cackling about the
House of Commons."   As to the claim of having reduced public
expenditure, made by the Liberals, the whole thing, said Mr.
Disraeli, "has been a genteel imposture from beginning to end,
and if the ' parties,' as the phrase has it, did not move in eminent
circles, and occupy a distinguished position in life, they would be
taken before the Lord Mayor and punished for obtaining applause
under false pretences."

Mr. Gladstone replied to these assertions.   When he entered
office he had found that the actual expenditure was rapidly
advancing beyond Mr. Disraeli's estimate for the year.   The six
millions of money spent on the Chinese War, in 1859, had been
caused by the mismanagement of affairs by the Conservative
Government, and as to the negotiations for the treaty of commerce with France, Mr. Disraeli and his friends had endeavoured
to arrange a treaty which should "carry out Free Trade in the
abstract, while protecting every important English interest in the
concrete."

There were six candidates for South Lancashire, and three
members to be elected.   Mr. Gladstone came in third, with 8,768
votes, two Conservatives, Mr. Egerton and Mr. Turner, being
ahead.

CHAPTER XXI.

LORD PALMERSTON died on the 18th of October, 1865, and Earl Russell succeeded to the Premiership, being succeeded at the Foreign Office by the Earl of Clarendon, transferred from the Chancellorship of the Duchy of Lancaster. Mr. Gladstone was the only Minister of sufficient prestige to fill the vacant position of leader of the House when it should reassemble in February, and no attempt was made to dispute his supremacy. There were some who doubted whether his acute sensitiveness and impulsiveness of temperament fitted him for a position requiring peculiar tact and that self-control which enables a man to control others; but the admiration of his great abilities, and respect for his high character far outweighed other considerations, and a cordial allegiance to the new chief was promised, not only by the lieutenants, but by the rank and file of the party.

Nearly four months, however, would elapse before he would be called on to take his place in Parliament; and, as his custom was, Mr. Gladstone occupied himself during the vacation by hard intellectual work. Some brains require to lie fallow for a time; others find refreshment and recreation in (to employ an agricultural figure) a change of crops. Sir George Cornewall Lewis turned from hard Parliamentary work to astronomical calculation, and Mr. Stuart Mill from political economy to the Hamiltonian philosophy. When Mr. Gladstone laid aside for a time the preparation of Budgets, he found a delightful recreation in investigating the problems presented by the Greek mythology, and the effect of the Homeric poems on human civilisation, varied by occasional recurrences to the political arena, in the way of addressing popular gatherings in the provinces.

His term of office as Lord Rector of the University of Edinburgh was about to expire, and it was arranged that he should deliver a parting address to the students. Availing themselves of his visit to Scotland for that purpose, the good folks of Glasgow resolved to present him with the freedom of that city;

and, of course, there would be other demonstrations of welcome to the commercial capital of Scotland.

On Wednesday, the 1st of November, an address was presented to him in the Trades' Hall, Glasgow, from the Parliamentary Reform Union. Mr. Graham, one of the members for the city, presided. The address expressed a hope that a comprehensive measure of reform, extending the franchise both in boroughs and counties, and providing for the redistribution of seats, would be carried through by the Government. Mr. Gladstone made only a brief reply, reserving for another occasion a more complete exposition of his views, and carefully avoidirg pledging the Ministry to details. Mr. Gladstone, who was accompanied, as usual on such occasions, by his wife and daughters, then proceeded to the City Hall, where the Lord Provost formally presented him with the freedom of the city, inclosed in a massive gold box. In the course of his reply, Mr. Gladstone made a touching allusion to the losses the country had sustained by the death of men eminent in the political world. "I confess to you," he said, "that a painful, perhaps a predominant, feeling in my mind at the present juncture is a feeling of solitariness in the struggles and in the career of public life." He mentioned Palmerston, the great leader, who had so recently been removed, Cobden, Lord Elgin, Lord Dalhousie, Lord Canning, Lord Herbert, Sir G. C. Lewis, and the Duke of Newcastle. An eulogium of the abilities and public services of Earl Russell was followed by a review of the great material progress made by the country in the course of the preceding thirty or thirty-five years; and a denunciation of the evils inflicted by many of the great wars in which, especially during the past century, England had been engaged, due, in a great measure, to a thirst for territorial acquisitions :—

"Had our forefathers known, as we now know, the blessings of free commercial intercourse, all that bloodshed would have been spared. For what was the dominant idea that governed that policy? It was this—that colonising, indeed, was a great function of European nations; but the purpose of that colonisation was to reap the profits of exclusive trade with the colonies which were founded; and, consequently, it was not the error of one nation or of another, it was the error of all nations alike. All the benefits of colonisation were summed up as these—that when you had planted a colony on the other side of the ocean, you were to allow that colony to trade exclusively and solely with yourselves. But from that doctrine flowed immediately all these miserable wars; because if people believed, as they then believed, that the trade with colonies must, in order to be beneficial, necessarily be exclusive, it followed that at once there arose in the mind of each country a desire to be possessed of the colonies of other countries, in order to secure the extension of the exclusive trade.   Such was the perversity of the misguided ingenuity of man, that during the period to which I refer he made commerce itself, which ought to be the bond and link of the human race, the cause of war and bloodshed, and wars were justified both here and elsewhere—justified when they were begun, and gloried in when they were ended—upon the grounds that their object and effect had been to obtain from some other nation a colony which previously had been theirs, but which now was ours, and which in our folly we regarded as the sole means of extending the intercourse and the industry of our countrymen."

Adverting to the working of the commercial treaty with France, Mr. Gladstone said :—

"Human beings on the two sides of the water are coming to know each other better, and to esteem one another more ; they are beginning to be acquainted with one another's common interests and feelings, and to unlearn the prejudices which make us refuse to give to other nations and peoples in distant lands credit for being governed by the same motives and principles as ourselves. We may say that, labelled upon all these parcels of goods there is a spark of kindly feeling from one country to the other, and the ship revolving between those lands is like the shuttle upon a loom weaving the web of concord between the nations of the earth. . . . . . It is the quiet unassuming prosecution of daily duty by which we best fulfil the purpose to which the Almighty has appointed us ; and the humble task, as it may appear, of industry and commerce, contemplating it in the first instance as little more than the supply of our necessities and the augmentation of our comforts, has in it nothing that prevents its being pursued in a spirit of devotion to higher interests ; and if it be honestly and well pursued, I believe that it tends—with a power, quiet and silent, indeed, like the power of your vast machines, but at the same time manifold and resistless—to the mitigation of the woes and sorrows that afflict humanity, and to the acceleration of better times for the children of our race."

He concluded a really remarkable speech, and one very illustrative of his mental character, so greatly influenced by a sense of religious obligation, by saying :—

"We have little to complain of—we have much indeed to acknowledge with thankfulness—and most of all we have to delight in the recollection that the politics of this world, are perhaps very slowly—with many hindrances, many checks, many reverses, yet that upon the whole they are gradually—assuming a character which promises to be less and less one of aggression and offence, less and less one of violence and bloodshed, more and more one of general union and friendship, more and more one connecting the common reciprocal advantages and the common interests pervading the world, and uniting together the whole of the members of the human family in a manner which befits rational and immortal beings, owing their existence to one Creator, and having but one hope either for this world or the next."

In the evening, after dining with the Lord Provost, Mr. Gladstone received, in the Scotia Hall, an address from the working men of Glasgow. Mr. Dalglish, member for Glasgow, presided, as his colleague in the representation of the city, Mr. Graham,

HAWARDEN CHURCH.

had done in the morning in the Trades' Hall. Mr. Gladstone made another long speech. One speech a day is generally considered a creditable achievement for an ordinary orator ; but Gladstonian powers are not of an ordinary kind, and the speaker was as fresh and eloquent as in the earlier part of the day. He spoke of the recent legislation on behalf of the working classes, and the benefits they had derived from financial changes ; and deprecated any course of action that would tend to diminish the freedom of labour and sow dissension between classes of the community.

On the following morning, at Edinburgh, Mr. Gladstone, as Rector of the University, received from the Provost a bust of Prince Alfred (now the Duke of Edinburgh), to be placed in the University buildings. Friday, the 3rd, was appointed for the delivery of the address to the members of the University. The Music Hall, in George Street, one of the largest, if not the largest, public hall in Edinburgh, capable of accommodating more than two thousand persons, was densely crowded. For the time the speaker divested himself of the character of the politician, and appeared, robed in academic gown, as the scholar and historian. The subject chosen was " The Place of Greece in the Providential History of the World." The address was a development of the theories suggested in his "Studies on Homer and the Homeric Age." (See *ante*, the chapter on " Homeric Investigations," p. 129.) So marked, indeed, was the advance in the argument, that some critics maintained that the later theories contradicted the former. In the earlier essay he considered the ancient Greeks as the transmitters of a " traditional knowledge, derived from the epoch when the covenant of God with man, and the promise of a Messiah, had not yet fallen within the contracted form of Judaism for shelter, but entered more or less into the common consciousness, and formed a part of the patrimony of the human race." In the Edinburgh address he claimed for ancient Greece " a marked, appropriate, distinctive place in the providential order of the world, not in the general, ordinary, and elementary way, but in a high and special sense—the rearing and training of mankind for the Gospel. The Greeks," he argued, "had their place in the providential order, aye, and in the evangelical preparation, as truly and really as the children of Abraham themselves." This " evangelical preparation " consisted of two principles—the first " a humanistic element," which led the Greeks to represent their deities in a human form, and invest them with the noblest human attributes, a principle that reached its culmination in the incarnation of Apollo, a type of the incarnation of the Saviour; and, secondly, the almost perfect development of bodily and mental excellence which was given to Greece beyond other nations, " so as to lift up man's universal nature to the level upon which his relation as a creature to his Creator, and as a child to his father, was about to be established."

No wonder Scottish Puritanism was rather startled by this announcement of the discovery of a second " chosen people ; " and that classical scholars inquired at what period the Greek mythology and history possessed such credentials. The anthropomorphism of Olympus was considerably below the ideal; if the Pelagic ancestors of the Hellenes had clearer views, the evidences of their mission were unknown to scholars ; if polished Athens knew much about the matter, historians, and its own poets and philosophers, must have been greatly misrepresented by modern critics ; and certainly St. Paul found very scanty traces of the preservation of primitive knowledge in the "altar to the unknown God," and apparently believed very little in it when he said the Gospel was " foolishness to the Greeks." The oration, however, was enthusiastically received by the vast audience, ready enough to be delighted with the voice and elocution of the brilliant speaker, and not very curious to inquire into the validity of his theories. One of the publications of the day, which ranked among the warmest admirers of Mr. Gladstone, probably expressed the verdict of the majority of the reading public when it said: " As an oration, this performance has certainly a rhetorical value of a high degree ; as an historical or religious essay, its value is worthless, for the principles on which it rests have no solid foundation."

Very shortly after the delivery of this oration, Mr. Gladstone and his colleagues found it necessary to give all their energies to the preparation for very practical and difficult work. The closing months of 1865 and the opening of 1866 were made painfully memorable in this country by the ravages of the cattle plague. From six thousand to eight thousand animals were dying weekly, graziers were nearly ruined, and food was scarce and dear. There was reasonable ground for fear that the dreaded cholera might again visit these shores, and that human beings might be subjected to as terrible an enemy as that which had attacked the cattle. The Fenian conspiracy, with its attendant outrages in Ireland, kept the public in a state of anxiety, and offered a topic for the immediate consideration of Parliament when it met. The condition of the money market gave rise to unpleasant anticipations; and during the year there had been an unhealthy development of limited liability companies, which suggested to cool-headed and prudent observers the remembrance of the results which had followed similar growths of the mania for speculation.

The General Election of the preceding summer had resulted in the return of 367 professed Liberals and 290 Conservatives. On the surface, therefore, there was a good ministerial majority; but " Liberal" then, as before and after, was a designation which covered many variations of opinion; and it was not long before discordant elements of great potency exhibited themselves. Earl Russell was deficient in some of the qualities which made Palmerston so popular, and Mr. Gladstone was as yet an untried leader, and his power of leading a new Parliament, containing many members sitting in the House for the first time, remained to be tested. Legislation of a coercive character for Ireland appeared to be certain; but it was almost as certain that many of the more advanced members of the Liberal party would be unwilling to accede to it, even if they did not openly oppose it. Earl Russell considered himself and his colleagues pledged to introduce yet another Reform Bill; and on that rock previous Ministries had split and ignominiously come to grief. No hint had been given of the manner in which Ministers proposed to deal with the subject. It was known, however, that there was enough of difference of opinion in the Cabinet to make it probable that concessions would be made to avoid secessions; and it was generally expected that the Bill, when introduced, would be found to be of a half-hearted and tentative character.

On the 6th of February the Queen opened Parliament in person, for the first time since the death of the Prince Consort; and that was a popular proceeding to begin with. The Royal Speech promised the introduction of a Reform Bill, and, of course, invited attention to the alarming condition of Ireland. In the debate on the Address, Mr. Gladstone strongly condemned " the folly, the madness, and the deep guilt " of the Fenian conspiracy; but he added, "the existence of, and the emerging from, a conspiracy like this—so far from taking away any duty, any obligation of the Legislature and the Government to examine into Irish evils with a sincere desire to improve the condition of the country—on the contrary, raised that obligation to its highest point."

Very little time elapsed before an attempt was made to extort from the Government some declaration of its intentions as to

Reform. On the 20th of February, Mr. Clay, member for Hull, obtained leave to bring in a Bill to extend the elective franchise for cities and boroughs in England and Wales. The chief object appeared to be to "force the hand" of Ministers; but Mr. Gladstone said he intended, when the proper time came, to make a proposal to the House on the subject, and he resolutely declined to give any forecast of the details of the promised measure.

About three weeks afterwards, on the 12th of March, he introduced the Reform Bill, and it proved to be, as had been anticipated, a fragmentary scheme. From the brief time at the disposal of Parliament, Government, said Mr. Gladstone, had been compelled to restrict their labours to dealing with the elective franchise alone, excluding the subject of redistribution of seats and other matters. The Bill proposed to extend the occupation franchise in counties from houses of £50 rental to £14 rentals; to create savings-bank franchises, place compound householders on the same footing as ratepayers, abolish tax and ratepaying clauses, and to make the gross estimate rental from the rate-book the measure of the value, thus making the rate-book the register. A lodger franchise was to be established, and it was proposed to follow the example of the Conservatives, and introduce a clause disabling from voting persons employed in the Government dockyards. Altogether, about 400,000 new voters would be added to the electoral lists.

On the 20th of March, Earl Grosvenor gave notice that he would, on the motion for the second reading of the Bill, move as an amendment a resolution to the effect that "it is inexpedient to discuss a Bill for the reduction of the franchise in England and Wales until the House has before it the entire scheme contemplated by Government for the amendment of the representation of the people." On the 23rd, Mr. Gladstone intimated that the Government would consider this amendment as a vote of want of confidence, but promised that, before going into committee, Ministers would be prepared to state their intentions with respect to the franchise for Scotland and Ireland, and also as to the redistribution of seats.

A division in the Liberal ranks was at once apparent. Mr. Bright said the Bill did not go far enough to give him unqualified satisfaction, but he would support it as, so far, a simple and honest measure. He addressed great meetings at Birmingham, urging the constituencies to support Ministers, and recommended immediate organisation for meetings and petitions. In the House the most violent opposition had come from the Liberal side of

the House, led by Mr. Horsman and Mr. Lowe, who, said Mr.
Bright, had succeeded in forming a party of two, which reminded
him of a "Scotch terrier that was so covered with hair that you
could not tell which was the head and which was the tail." Mr.
Lowe, in language which was long remembered against him, denounced the working men who, under the Bill, would be so largely
added to the constituencies, as unfit for the franchise. "You
have had," he said, "the opportunity of knowing some of the
constituencies of the country, and I ask, if you want venality,
ignorance, drunkenness, and the means of intimidation—if you
want impulsive, unreflecting, and violent people, where will you
go to look for them, to the top or to the bottom?" In concluding his speech, which, as a mere specimen of animated
rhetoric, he has never surpassed, Mr. Lowe said : "If the Bill is
passed, I covet not a single wreath of the laurels that may
encircle the brow of the Chancellor of the Exchequer. I do not
envy him his triumph. His be the glory of carrying it ; mine, of
having, to the best of my poor ability, resisted it."

The "party of two" was increased by the adhesion of Earl
Grosvenor, Lord Elcho, Mr. Laing, and several other prominent
Liberals, whose action gave occasion for a saying by Mr. Bright
which has taken a permanent place in the literature of political
controversy. Mr. Lowe, he said, had entered "into what might be
called his political Cave of Adullam, to which he invited every one
who was in distress or discontented." The allusion was, of course,
to David's hiding in the Cave Adullam, as recorded in the First
Book of Samuel. Lord Elcho accepted the comparison : "No
improper motive has driven us into this cave, where we are a most
happy family, daily—I may say hourly—increasing in number and
strength, where we shall remain until we go forth to deliver Israel
from oppression."

Mr. Gladstone was entertained by the Liberal electors of the
town at a great banquet at Liverpool, at which the Duke of
Argyll, Mr. Goschen, Lord Clarence Paget, and many of the
leading merchants and residents were present. The dinner was
followed by a public meeting at the Amphitheatre, at which a
resolution approving of the Bill was unanimously carried. In
Mr. Gladstone's speech, he said : "We stake ourselves, we stake
our existence as a Government—whether it be much or little, is
not for us to say—but such as it is, we stake it, and we also stake
our political character on the adoption of the Bill in its main
provisions. You have a right to expect from us that we should
tell you what we mean, and that the trumpet which it is our

business to blow shall give forth no uncertain sound.   Its sound
has not been, and I trust will not be, uncertain.   We have passed
the Rubicon, we have broken the bridge and burned the boats
behind us.   We have advisedly cut off the means of retreat;
and, having done this, we hope that, as far as time has yet permitted, we have done our duty to the Crown and the nation."
It is well that when Mr. Gladstone was staking so much, he did
not stake his credit as a classical scholar on the Rubicon
allusion.   Cæsar crossed that familiar little stream on horseback ;
there was no bridge to be broken, and there were no boats to be
burned.

On the 12th April the Bill came on for the second reading, and
Earl Grosvenor's resolution was moved as an amendment.   The
debate lasted eight nights, and was carried on with indomitable
vigour on both sides of the House, nearly all the leading speakers
taking part.   Mr. Lowe, roused apparently into unwonted animation by Mr. Bright's allusion to Scotch terriers and Adullam
caves, and the storm he had aroused outside the House by his
vituperation of working-class voters, made a fierce attack on
Ministers: "they had laid on the grave of Palmerston, as a
mortuary contribution, all their moderation, all their prudence,
and all their statesmanship."   On the last night of the debate
Mr. Disraeli, the leader of the Opposition, spoke.   The Bill, he
asserted, would swamp the county constituencies, and put the
government of the country into the hands of one class of the community.   He bitterly attacked Mr. Gladstone, and was betrayed
into the pettiness of recurring to the records of the Oxford Union
Debating Society, for the purpose of showing that, thirty-five
years before, Mr. Gladstone had, when an undergraduate of
Christ's College, spoken, at a meeting of the Society, against the
Reform Bill introduced by Lord John Russell.   This inex-
cusable attack was replied to by Mr. Gladstone, and the reply has
a special interest as a fragment of autobiography :—

"The right honourable gentleman, secure, I suppose, in the recollection of
his own consistency, has taunted me with the political errors of my boyhood.
The right hon. gentleman, when he addressed the honourable member for
Westminster [Mr. Mill], took occasion to show his magnanimity, for he
declared that he would not take the philosopher to task for what he wrote
twenty-five years ago.   But when he caught one who, thirty-five years ago,
just emerged from boyhood, and still an undergraduate at Oxford, had expressed an opinion adverse to the Reform Bill of 1832, of which he had so
long and bitterly repented, then the right honourable gentleman could not
resist the temptation that offered itself to his appetite for effect.   He, a
Parliamentary champion of twenty years' standing, and the leader, as he
informs us to-night, of the Tory party, is so ignorant of the House of Com-

mons, or so simple is the structure of his mind, that he positively thought he would be obtaining a Parliamentary advantage by exhibiting me to the public view for reprobation as an opponent of the Reform Bill of 1832. Sir, as the right honourable gentleman has done me the honour thus to exhibit me, let me, for a moment, trespass on the patience of the House to exhibit myself. What he has stated is true. I deeply regret it. But I was bred under the shadow of the great name of Canning ; every influence connected with that name governed the first political impressions of my childhood and my youth ; with Mr. Canning I rejoiced in the removal of religious disabilities from the Roman Catholic body, and in the free and truly British tone which he gave to our policy abroad ; with Mr. Canning I rejoiced in the opening he made towards the establishment of free commercial interchange between nations ; with Mr. Canning, and under the shadow of that great name, and under the shadow of the yet more venerable name of Burke, I grant my youthful mind and imagination were impressed with some idle and futile fears which still bewilder and distress the mature mind of the right honourable gentleman. I had conceived that very same fear, that ungovernable alarm at the first Reform Bill, in the days of my undergraduate career at Oxford, which the right honourable gentleman now feels, and the only difference between us is this—I thank him for bringing it into view by his quotation—that, having those views, I, as it would appear, moved the Oxford Union Debating Society to express them clearly, plainly, in downright English, while the right honourable gentleman does not dare to tell the nation what it is that he really thinks, and is content to skulk under the shelter of the meaningless amendment which is proposed by the noble Lord. And now, Sir, I quit the right honourable gentleman ; I leave him to his reflections, and I envy him not one particle of the polemical advantage which he has gained by his direct reference to the proceedings of the Oxford Union Debating Society in the year of grace 1831."

Mr. Disraeli had hinted that the Ministers were endeavouring to coerce the House, and force it, by a threat of resignation, to support the measure, because Earl Russell had pledged himself to introduce it. Mr. Gladstone said, after a splendid tribute to the political career of the Prime Minister :—

"Sir, I am not Earl Russell. My position in the Liberal party is in all points the opposite of Earl Russell's. Earl Russell might have been misled, possibly, had he been in this place, into using language which would have been unfit coming from another person. But it could not be the same with me. I am too well aware of the relations which subsist between the party and myself. I have none of the claims he possesses. I came among you an outcast from those with whom I associated, driven from them, I admit, by no arbitrary act, but by the slow and resistless force of conviction. I came among you, to make use of the legal phraseology, *in pauperis formâ.* I had nothing to offer you but faithful and honourable service. You received me as Dido received the shipwrecked Æneas. You received me with kindness, indulgence, generosity, and, I may even say, with some measure of confidence. And the relation between us has assumed such a form that you can never be my debtors, but that I must for ever be in your debt. It is not from me, under such circumstances, that any word will proceed that can savour of the character which the right honourable gentleman imputes to the conduct of the Government with respect to the present Bill."

He concluded an especially animated speech with an especially animated peroration, which produced a storm of cheers :—

"You cannot fight against the future. Time is on our side. The great social forces which move onward in their might and majesty, and which the tumult of our debates does not for a moment impede or disturb, those great social forces are against you ; they are marshalled on our side ; and the banner which we now carry in the fight, though, perhaps, at some moment, it may droop over our sinking heads, yet it soon again will float in the eye of heaven, and it will be borne by the firm hands of the united people of the three kingdoms, perhaps not to an easy, but to a certain and to a not distant victory."

At 3 o'clock in the morning the division was taken, the House being greatly excited. The number for the second reading was 318, and against it 313, giving Ministers the small majority of 5. So many members had never before voted in one division, and only two paired.

On the last day of April Mr. Gladstone announced that the Government did not see in the result of the division any reason or warning against persisting in the efforts they had engaged in to amend the law for the representation of the people. Their present duty was a very simple one—it was, to lose no time in producing the plan for the redistribution of seats, and the Reform Bills for Scotland and Ireland. By the expression "stand or fall," he had meant while the Bill stood the Government stood, and the Bill had not fallen.

Amid all this turmoil of debate, all this excitement within and beyond the walls of the House, the Chancellor of the Exchequer had found time to arrange the details of the Budget. Perhaps he found in financial details a relief from the labour of discussing the franchise ; and during the sitting of Parliament the income tax and the results of the commercial treaty afforded refreshment to his wearied brain, as, in the autumn recesses, did the Homeric mythology. Endeavours to anticipate the financial arrangements had, as usual, been made; but with less success than Mr. Sheridan had achieved in the preceding session, in the matter of the fire insurance duty. Mr. White, one of the members for Brighton, moved a resolution in favour of an early and large reduction of the Government expenditure ; and Sir Fitzroy Kelly made another gallant effort to pledge the House to an "immediate reduction and ultimate repeal" of the malt tax. Both motions were opposed, as a matter of course, by Mr. Gladstone, and both were unsuccessful.

The Budget was brought forward on the 3rd of May ; and once more the favourite of financial fortune announced that the revenue of the past year had exceeded the expenditure. He had a surplus of £2,338,000 to begin with ; and his estimates for the coming year left him with even a slightly larger amount on the right side of the balance sheet. He anticipated a revenue of £67,575,000, against an expenditure of £66,225,000, showing a surplus of £1,350,000. He proposed to remove the duty from timber and pepper, to modify the duty on wine in regard to the proportion of alcohol, and to reduce the stage-carriage and post-chaise duty from a penny to a farthing a mile. These reductions would absorb £562,000, almost one-half of the surplus ; and the remainder he proposed to apply to the reduction of the National Debt, the capital of which then stood at £799,000,000. Mr. Gladstone had often enough shown that he was a Chancellor of the Exchequer *sui generis*, and had, in that capacity, said many unexpected things, and opened up many unexpected views ; but he fairly astonished his hearers when he invited them to accompany him, in imagination, to the subterranean coal fields, and estimate the probability of the extent of the continuance of the supply ; and still more, when he undertook to show that his financial plans for the present year took into account the interests of their descendants yet unborn—the Englishmen of a century hence. Probably some of the members mentally repeated the testy exclamation of the worthy politician who objected to looking too far ahead, " Let posterity take care of itself ! " According to the most carefully prepared estimates of the highest authorities, said Mr. Gladstone, in less than a hundred years, at the present annually increasing rate of consumption, the supply of coal in this country would be exhausted ; probably in a much shorter time, for some of the known beds lay so far beneath the surface that it was impossible to work them. The final disappearance of coal in this country would put an end to our power of cheap production. " Suppose coal to fail, and to carry away this pre-eminence of cheap production of ours across the Atlantic, I ask you what will happen ? There will be a decline of rent, profits, and wages. At that period, when rent, profit, and wages decline, the charge on the National Debt will remain a permanent mortgage on the land and durable property of the country. I wish I could convey to the committee my own sense of the importance of these considerations."

To provide against this alarming, if remote, catastrophe, he proposed to convert £24,000,000 of the savings bank stock into terminable annuities, to expire in 1885, and to reinvest the spare dividends. By these means he hoped to extinguish by the year

P

1905 nearly £50,000,000 of the debt, at an annual increased charge of a little more than one million.

Legislation for a distant future was not recognised by some members as a very distinct duty incumbent on them to perform ; and they reasoned on the good old-fashioned principle that " a bird in the hand is worth two in the bush," especially when the bush is so far off that it would take a century to reach it. The annual charge of a little more than a million represented a penny in the pound on the income tax, and that was a practical matter. Sir Fitzroy Kelly objected to burdening the country, whether there was a surplus or not, to pay more than a million sterling for the next forty years. Mr. Fawcett (then a young member, sitting for Brighton) also objected, but from a different point of view. It was proposed, he argued, to throw upon the next generation a greater burden than the present generation was able to bear. The House should adopt measures for creating a surplus, and then follow the old-fashioned method of cancelling stock. Mr. Henley described the operation as a revival of the old sinking fund.

The Bill passed its second reading, but made no further progress. A Ministerial crisis was not far off; and before the end of the session there was a new Chancellor of the Exchequer—Mr. Disraeli—who abandoned the Bill, and appropriated the balance of Mr. Gladstone's surplus, intended to go towards the relief of the coal-less Englishmen of the twentieth century, to provide for Supplementary Army Estimates. Mr. Gladstone, then leading the Opposition, made no objection ; but intimated that, if the opportunity offered, he should revive his project for reducing the National Debt.

On Thursday, the 16th of May, three days after the introduction of the Budget resolutions, came the terrible crash which made commercial London tremble to its foundations. Since the winter of 1825 there had been no such catastrophe.

Over speculation in limited liability companies, the manœuvres of desperate and unscrupulous promoters and wreckers, had produced their fruit, and bitter fruit it was. The announcement of the suspension of the great discount house, Overend, Gurney and Co., was followed by the stoppage of other establishments of a similar kind, and of private and joint stock banks. There was an unprecedented rush of depositors, and bank after bank closed their doors. Friday, the 11th of May, " Black Friday," is sadly memorable, not only in City annals, but in the history of thousands of ruined families. The depositing public was frantic

with excitement, and scarcely less so bank directors and man: gers.
Appeals for assistance to the Bank of England were incessant :
but the extent of the aid that could be afforded was strictly
limited by the provisions of the Bank Charter Act. In the
course of the day the governor and directors, and directors of
joint stock and private banks, had interviews with the Chancellor
of the Exchequer, and at midnight he announced to the anxious
and excited House of Commons that Government had taken
upon itself the responsibility of authorising the suspension of the
Act. The assistance was given, and the panic was allayed; but
the disastrous effects were felt long afterwards. In one day,
" Black Friday," the resources of the Bank of England were
reduced to the extent of nearly £6,000,000. One of the great
joint stock banks paid over the counter two millions of money in
the course of the day, and other banks were drawn upon for
nearly as large amounts. " Another day of similar panic," remarked a writer of the time, "and every bank and monetary
establishment in London must have stopped payment."

A prominent feature of the session was the introduction of a
Bill for the abolition of Church-rates, by Mr. Hardcastle, member
for Bury St. Edmunds. The motion for the second reading of
the Bill was made on the 7th of March, and Mr. Walpole met
it by moving that it be read a second time that day six months.
Mr. Gladstone spoke in the debate, not in his ministerial capacity,
but as an individual member. He was not prepared to consent
to the simple and unconditional abolition of Church-rates. To
abolish the rates, he argued, and at the same time to allow
Dissenters to interfere with the disposal of funds to which they
did not contribute, would be the introduction of a new injustice
in the removal of the old one. He invited Mr. Hardcastle to
consider whether, by an equitable compromise, Dissenters ought
not to be exempted from paying Church-rates, and at the same
time disqualified from interfering with funds to which they had
not contributed.

Mr. Hardcastle refused to withdraw the Bill. Mr. Walpole's
amendment was rejected, and the second reading was carried by
a majority of 33 in a full House. Before, however, any further
progress was made, Mr. Gladstone himself (on the 8th of May)
obtained leave to bring in a Compulsory Church-rate Abolition
Bill, the leading provisions of which were that no suit or proceedings could be taken to compel the payment of Church-rates
in England and Wales; except in parishes where Church-rates
were provided for by endowments or fixed funds, parishioners in

vestry might assess a voluntary rate for the purpose; persons who declined to pay the rate should, after a certain lapse of time, be ineligible to fill the office of churchwarden, but if they changed their minds and made a tender of the amount of their proper proportion, they should be entitled to vote. The second reading of the Bill was agreed to on the 1st of August, and on the same day Mr. Hardcastle withdrew his Bill, and Mr. Newdegate adopted the same course with a Church-rates Commutation Bill to which he stood sponsor. By that time, however, Mr. Gladstone had ceased to be a Minister, and the prorogation of Parliament following so soon afterwards, the Bill failed to reach the Lords.

It is time now to take up the dropped thread of the narrative of the fortunes of the Reform Bill and of the Ministry. On the 7th of May, Mr. Gladstone brought in the promised measure for the redistribution of seats. The Bill proposed to withdraw one member from every borough with a population under 8,000, and by that plan thirty seats would be placed at the disposal of Parliament. It was also proposed to group as many of the boroughs as could be joined together with geographical convenience. When the population of a group was under 15,000, there would be one member, and when above that number, two members. Altogether there would be 49 seats available for redistribution. Of these, 26 were to be given to English counties—first, by dividing the southern division of Lancashire, and giving to each division three members, and 23 seats would be disposed of by giving an extra member each to counties, or divisions of counties, previously returning two members. Liverpool, Manchester, Birmingham, and Leeds were each to have a third member, and Salford a second member. The Tower Hamlets would be divided; Chelsea and Kensington united into a borough with two members; and the large towns, Burnley, Staleybridge, Gravesend, Hartlepool, Dewsbury, and Middlesborough were to be constituted Parliamentary boroughs, returning one member each. One seat would be given to the University of London, and the remaining seven seats would be transferred to Scotland; the counties of Ayr, Lanark, and Aberdeen receiving an additional member each; Edinburgh and Glasgow each a third member, Dundee a second, and the Scotch Universities one representative.

On the same night the Lord Advocate and Mr. Chichester Fortescue respectively brought forward the Scotch and Irish Bills. The Scotch Bill followed the lines of the English measure in proposing a £7 borough and a £14 county franchise, and the property franchise was reduced from £10 to £5, with the condition, however, of personal residence. The Irish Bill reduced the rating occupation franchise from £8 to £6, and lodger and savings bank franchises, as in the English Bill, were proposed. Dublin City and Cork County were each to have another member, and one would be given to Queen's University. To provide these seats some of the smaller boroughs would be grouped.

The second reading of the three Bills was not actively opposed; but Mr. Disraeli satirically advised Mr. Gladstone to recross the Rubicon and reconstruct his boats. He had a majority in the House, and could afford to accept advice. His best course would be to withdraw the Bill, and prepare for a better considered measure in the next session.

When the House went into committee, on the 28th of May, after the Whitsuntide holidays, the Representation of the People Bill and the Redistribution of Seats Bill were considered together. Sir R. Knightley, representative of South Northamptonshire, moved "that it be an instruction to the committee to make provision for the better prevention of bribery and corruption at elections;" and that resolution was carried against the Government by a majority of 10, notwithstanding Mr. Gladstone's opposition. Captain Hayter, member for Wells, then moved: "That, in the opinion of this House, the system of groups proposed by the Government is neither convenient nor equitable, nor sufficiently matured to form the basis of satisfactory legislation." The debate on the resolution occupied four nights, and ultimately Captain Hayter withdrew the motion. In committee Mr. Gladstone expressed himself willing to make some slight concessions, and various amendments were proposed, but negatived. On the 18th of June, Lord Dunkellin, member for Galway County, aimed a deadly blow at one of the vital points of the Bill, by moving the substitution of rateable value instead of clear yearly value. The discussion was most animated, and the excitement was intense. When the division was taken the number in favour of the amendment was 315, and against it 304. Ministers were defeated by 11. The Bill had now really fallen, and they must fall with it. The scene which followed the Speaker's announcement of the numbers has rarely been equalled, even in the British House of Commons. Conservatives, Adullamites, thirty-two Liberals, and the floating balance of "independents," whose action can never be predicted with certainty, had united to swell the ranks of the victors, and they again united to swell the chorus of cheers

and counter-cheers.   Members rushed into the lobby to acquaint
their anxiously waiting friends with the result, and " Bob Lowe
has done it " was uttered by more than one voice.

On the following day, the 19th, the announcement was made
in both Houses that Ministers had made a communication to
Her Majesty, and on the 20th the resignation of the Russell
Ministry was announced.

The Earl of Derby accepted the task of constructing a new
Administration, and Mr. Disraeli was again Chancellor of the
Exchequer, and leader in the Commons. That one of the earliest
duties of the Conservative Ministry would be to prepare a Reform
Bill was evident.   The public were considerably excited on the
subject.   On the 29th of June there was a Reform demonstration
in Trafalgar Square, attended by about 10,000 people.   Earl
Russell was censured for not having appealed to the country by
a general election, but the name of Gladstone was received with
enthusiastic cheers.   From Trafalgar Square the collected thousands marched in orderly procession to Carlton Gardens, where
Mr. Gladstone resided, shouting " Gladstone for ever."   They
evidently expected an address from the ex-Minister ; but he was
absent from home, and Mrs. Gladstone and some members of
the family having appeared on the balcony, by request of the
police, who feared a disturbance might take place, the concourse
of admirers dispersed in tolerably good order, stopping in front
of the Carlton Club, however, to give a few yells.

On the 23rd of July occurred the famous Hyde Park riot, when
the railings were pulled down, Ministers having refused to permit
a Reform meeting to be held in the Park, and ordered the gates
to be closed.   The meeting, presided over by Mr. Beales, was
held, and the right of the people to the use of the Park established.   A Reform meeting, chiefly composed of working-men,
was held in the City, under the presidency of Lord Mayor
Phillips, on the 8th of August, and there were colossal demonstrations at Birmingham and Manchester in August and September,
at each of which Mr. Bright was the most prominent speaker.

CHAPTER XXII.

TWO YEARS OF OPPOSITION—THE REFORM BILL OF 1867.

THE political world was in a state of considerable anxiety and uncertainty previous to the opening of the Session of 1867. The public demand for a Reform Bill—that is, if excited demonstrations at all fairly represented general public opinion — had increased rather than slackened during the recess, and the programme of the new Administration was awaited with no ordinary interest. The country generally was dissatisfied and alarmed. The harvest of 1866 had been poor, the cattle plague was by no means stamped out, the Fenians were gaining head in Ireland, and the closing months of the year had amply justified the description of a writer of the time as " a gloomy and unprosperous period."

Parliament opened on Tuesday, the 5th of February, and one paragraph of the Royal Speech announced : " Your attention will be again called to the state of the representation of the people in Parliament ; and I trust that your deliberations, conducted in a spirit of moderation and mutual forbearance, may lead to the adoption of measures which, without widely disturbing the balance of political power, shall freely extend the elective franchise."

On the 11th, Mr. Disraeli, the Chancellor of the Exchequer, moved that on the 25th the House should resolve itself into a Committee, and take into consideration the Act 2 and 3 Will. IV., cap. 45, by which formula, of course, the famous Reform Act of 1832 was meant. This method of procedure, superseding the ordinary practice of asking for leave to introduce a Bill, intimated that the Ministry were about to adopt an unusual course. On the 25th, Mr. Disraeli, instead of bringing forward a Bill, moved thirteen resolutions laying down bases on which a Reform Bill could be constituted. If these were carried, the House would be to a certain extent pledged to the principles of the measure, and Mr. Disraeli, in his speech, described the chief provisions of the Bill, which, if the resolutions were approved, he would bring forward. There would be four new franchises con-ferred, by which the power of voting would be given to persons who had taken degrees, ministers of religion, and others; to

depositors of £30 for one year in savings banks; to holders of
£50 in the public funds; to payers of 20s. annually of direct
taxation.   In conformity with the decision of the House on
Lord Dunkellin's amendment in the last session, rating, not
rental, would be the basis of the occupation franchise.   A £6
rating franchise would be fixed for boroughs, and the occupation
franchise in counties reduced from £5 to £20.   The Bill would
contain provisions for the punishment of bribery; and it would
be proposed to disfranchise four boroughs which had been unfortunate enough to be found out—Great Yarmouth, Lancaster,
Totnes, and Reigate—and to transfer the seven seats thus
vacated to towns which had risen into importance since 1832.
The Tower Hamlets would be divided, and new county divisions
formed, while, to find the required seats, a certain number of
small boroughs would be deprived of a member each.

Mr. Lowe and Mr. Bright vigorously attacked the Ministry
for proceeding by resolution instead of at once bringing forward a Bill.   Mr. Gladstone, although he would have preferred
a Bill, was not unwilling to consider the resolutions.   The Liberal
party, however, were so evidently opposed to that course that,
on the following day, there was a very large gathering at Mr.
Gladstone's residence on Carlton Terrace, and, yielding to the
wishes of the meeting, the leader of the Opposition agreed to
move an amendment which, if carried, would set aside the resolutions, and call upon Ministers to proceed at once with a Bill.
There was a crowded House that night, and a very animated
debate was expected.   The Liberals were united in their determination to support Mr. Gladstone's amendment, and it was
reasonably expected that the Conservatives would strain every
nerve to "stand at the right hand" of the Chancellor of the
Exchequer.   To the surprise of the Liberals, and very probably
to the surprise and astonishment of the greater number of the
Conservative members as yet not in the secret, Mr. Disraeli
announced that the Government had decided to withdraw the
resolutions, and that, in the course of the following week, he
would introduce a Bill.   It was inexplicable that Ministers, with
a solid majority at their back, could have feared the success of
Mr. Gladstone's amendment, supported by a minority notoriously
composed of incohesive elements; more inexplicable still that,
in the course of twenty-four hours, Ministers should have changed
their views of the proper mode of proceeding.   There had been
either strange timidity or strange vacillation in Downing Street.
It is not easy to keep even Cabinet secrets, when so many eager

eyes and ears are at work to find out a mystery. Rumours of dissensions were soon flying about, and speculation was at an end when, on the 4th of March, it was announced that Lord Cranborne (Secretary of State for India), the Earl of Carnarvon (Secretary for the Colonies), and General Peel (Secretary for War), had resigned office. Sir John Pakington was transferred from the Admiralty to the War Office, and, re-election being necessary, told the story of the Cabinet quarrel and the mysterious resolution in the course of a speech to his constituents at Droitwich. In that speech and the Ministerial explanations, a few days afterwards, we have the materials of a strange and rather amusing chapter of political history.

The Cabinet met on Saturday, the 23rd of February, and the resolutions which were to form the basis of a Bill were almost unanimously agreed on, and the draft of a Bill approved. One Minister, General Peel, found it difficult to accept the estimate of the number which would, according to Mr. Disraeli, be added to the constituencies by the new franchise, but offered to resign, if his dissent would embarrass his colleagues. He was persuaded by the Premier not to take that extreme course, but to accept the decision of the majority ; and the Cabinet Council broke up, apparently, in a very pleasant spirit of accord and good-humour.

La nuit porte conseil, says a French proverb ; and when Lord Cranborne woke on the morning of Sunday, the 24th, he began to think that probably General Peel was right and Mr. Disraeli wrong. He set to work with the official returns and other blue books which his well-stocked Parliamentary library contained, passed a pleasant arithmetical Sunday, and on the following morning communicated with Earl Carnarvon, the result of their deliberations being that the estimates of Mr. Disraeli were untrustworthy, and that the proposed franchise would be exceedingly disastrous to the political balance so essential to the proper working of the British Constitution. The two Ministers —to whom General Peel, thus encouraged, joined himself— called on the Premier, and, in a few words, shattered the harmonious fabric reared on the Saturday. A Council was hastily summoned, but the Ministers were scattered. Some were busy at their offices, some did not arrive in town until the middle of the day, and although half-past one was the time announced for the meeting, a Council was not formed till after two o'clock. That very afternoon the Earl of Derby had arranged to address a meeting of his supporters, and Mr. Disraeli to introduce to the

House of Commons the thirteen resolutions, and to sketch the measure to be founded upon them. That, in the face of the secession of three very prominent Ministers, the Bill agreed to on the Saturday could be proceeded with, was, it seemed, out of the question. But another Bill of a less alarming character had been sketched out, and it was resolved, the three troublesome Ministers agreeing, that that should be the Ministerial measure. Only ten minutes were occupied in coming to this decision, and with the rough draft of the Ten Minutes Bill (as it came to be named) in his pocket, Mr. Disraeli, who had not even had time to snatch a luncheon, and could only fortify himself with a glass of wine in Downing Street, hurried to meet the expectant Commons.

A few hours of reflection convinced the Earl of Derby that a false step had been taken. For once in his life the dashing Rupert had erred on the side of timidity; but his old spirit revived, and he resolved to retrace his steps, and, if the three Ministers adhered to their decision, accept a reconstruction of the Cabinet. So came it that, on the evening of Tuesday, the 26th, the Chancellor of the Exchequer withdrew the resolutions, the Ten Minutes Bill was consigned to oblivion, and another Bill promised. The Cabinet was not much the worse for the change. Sir John Pakington was quite as useful at the War Office as at the Admiralty; the Duke of Buckingham was, perhaps, a little weaker in administering the affairs of the Colonies than was Earl Carnarvon; and if Sir Stafford Northcote was less energetic and autocratic than Lord Cranborne at the India Office, he was clear-headed, industrious, able, and conciliatory— very good qualities in an Indian Secretary.

When the personal explanations of the causes of the Ministerial rupture were made in Parliament, the Earl of Derby said " It very shortly became obvious that on neither side of the House would the propositions of the Government meet with a satisfactory concurrence, and therefore it became necessary to consider whether they should adhere to the second proposition or revert to the first. They resolved on taking the latter course, and the scheme would in a short time be laid before the other House of Parliament." Mr. Disraeli made a statement to the same effect in the House of Commons, and announced that he would bring in the new Reform Bill on the 18th of March. " It is our business," he said, " to bring forward as soon as we possibly can the measure of Parliamentary Reform which, after such difficulties and sacrifices, it will be my duty to introduce to the

House. Sir, the House need not fear that there will e any
evasion, any equivocation, any vacillation, or any hesitation in
that measure.   The measure will be brought forward as the definite opinion of the Cabinet, and by that definite opinion they
will stand."

On the date mentioned, the Chancellor of the Exchequer
explained the provisions of the proposed measure.   Three days
previously the Earl of Derby had called a meeting of the Conservative party, and described the scope of the Bill, which he,
not very hopefully, it would seem, styled " a leap in the dark."
Speaking at a later date, Mr. Disraeli modestly said that since
1859, when his earlier Reform Bill was so unsuccessfully introduced, he had " educated his party " to the belief that if the
borough franchise was to be dealt with at all, it must be in the
boldest manner.   The Bill now introduced proposed that all
householders within boroughs who were rated for the payment of
poor-rates should be entitled to vote ; but two years' residence
and the personal payment of rates were necessary.

That troublesome person, the "compound householder" (that
is, a tenant whose landlord paid rates for him, charging them in
the rent), might obtain the franchise if he claimed to be personally
rated—a claim to be made only at the expense of some time and
money, and probably without the lessening of the rent he paid to
his landlord ; and payers of £1 yearly of direct taxation (not to
include licences), depositors in savings banks to the amount of
£50, or investors to that amount in the public funds, educated
persons who had taken degrees, and ministers of religion, would
also be entitled to the franchise.   Then there came a remarkable
proposition, the "dual vote," by which every possessor of one of
these "fancy franchises " would, in virtue of it, have a vote in
addition to that which, if he were a rated householder, he would
possess.   For counties, the Bill proposed a £15 rating franchise,
all existing franchises remaining untouched.   By the disfranchisement of the guilty, if impenitent, boroughs named in the
preceding Bill, and by taking away one member each from
boroughs having less than 7,000 inhabitants, thirty seats would
be available for distribution, and it was proposed to give a representative each to Hartlepool, Darlington, Burnley, Stalybridge,
St. Helen's, Dewsbury, Barnsley, Middlesborough, Wednesbury,
Croydon, Gravesend, and Torquay ; to form a new borough, with
two representatives, out of the immense metropolitan borough,
the Tower Hamlets ; to divide North Lancashire, North Lincoln-
shire, West Kent, East Surrey, Middlesex, South Staffordshire,

and South Devon, giving two members to each of the new constituencies, and to give an additional member to South Lancashire, which, already returning three members, was to be divided
into two constituencies, each returning two members.   It was also
proposed to allot a seat to the University of London.   There
was also a provision for permitting the use of voting papers, instead of personal voting.

Mr. Gladstone at once expressed a vigorous dissent from the
provisions of the Bill.   He began his speech by censuring the
conduct of the Earl of Derby in calling a meeting of his supporters, and acquainting them with the details of a measure
which would be submitted to Parliament a few days afterwards.
To the compound householder clause he strenuous'y objected.
It would give to parochial officers, many of whom might not
unfairly be supposed to be political partizans, the power of
enfranchising or not whom they pleased.   Vestries had the option
of adopting or not the Small Tenements Act, which provided
for owners paying rates instead of the occupiers of houses ; and
as vestries were mainly composed of the proprietary classes, they
could withhold the franchise from hundreds of occupiers of small
houses whose known opinions might be disapproved.   Mr.
Gladstone also suggested the propriety of introducing a lodger
franchise.

When the motion for the second reading was made on the
25th of March, Mr. Gladstone criticised the scheme more
minutely, and enumerated the alterations the Bill would require
to make it an acceptable measure of reform ; among the most
important being the introduction of a lodger franchise, the
abandonment of the tax-paying franchise and the dual vote, and
of the plan for voting papers.   The redistribution scheme must
be enlarged and the proposition of voting papers dropped.

Mr. Disraeli said he was willing to accept the lodger franchise
and to abandon the dual vote—in fact, to make considerable
concessions ; and on the 1st of April, in the adjourned debate
on the second reading, announced that he would move in committee that the dual vote clause be struck out.   Probably his
ingenious mind did not consider that the withdrawal of that
clause was a symptom of vacillation or hesitation, or that the
proposition of dual voting represented "the definite opinion of
the Cabinet" by which they would stand.

On the 5th of April another meeting was held at Mr. Gladstone's residence.   As before, the members assembled in the
spacious hall, and Mr. Gladstone addressed them from the stair-

case, none of the rooms in the house being large enough to accommodate the 259 Liberal representatives who attended. It was agreed that Mr. Coleridge, the member for Exeter (now Chief Justice Coleridge), should move an amendment on the motion for going into committee, " That it be an instruction to the committee that they have power to alter the law of rating, and to provide that in every Parliamentary borough the occupiers of tenements below a given rateable value be relieved from liability to personal rating, with a view to fix a line for the borough franchise, at and above which all occupiers shall be entered on the rate-book, and shall have equal facilities for the enjoyment of such franchise as a residential or occupation franchise."

Mr. Coleridge duly gave notice of this amendment; but before he had the opportunity to exert his persuasive eloquence in its favour, discord appeared in the Liberal ranks, and Mr. Gladstone once more was made aware of the fact that his nominal following was anything but a compact phalanx. A considerable number of Liberal members assembled in the Tea-room of the House of Commons, and resolved that they would not support the amendment, as worded. The result was that Mr. Coleridge limited his resolution to the first few words, " That it be an instruction to the committee that they have power to alter the law of rating." In that form it was accepted by Mr. Disraeli, and adopted. The Tea-room party was now almost as great a cause of perplexity to the Liberal leader as the Adullamites had been in the previous session. The Bill was allowed to be read a second time without a division.

On the 11th of May a deputation from some provincial Reform Associations waited on Mr. Gladstone, at his residence, for the purpose of presenting addresses expressive of confidence in him as leader of the Liberal party. In his reply, after referring to the unfortunate dissensions among the Liberals, Mr. Gladstone spoke of the delusive character of the Government scheme of reform, especially condemning " the absurd, preposterous, and mischievous distinctions of personal rating," which he held to be a totally unfit basis for the franchise, and to which he would continue to offer an unqualified and unhesitating opposition. Three days afterwards Mr. Disraeli took occasion to refer to the deputation, and, in his customary style of polite sneering, to Mr. Gladstone's reception of the addresses:—" I should have been very glad if these spouters of stale sedition had not taken the course they have done. It may be their function to appear at noisy meetings, but I regret very much they should

have come forward as obsolete incendiaries of that character to
pay homage to one who, wherever he may sit, must always be
the pride and ornament of this House—

> ' Who would not smile if such a man there be ?
> Who would not weep if Atticus were he?' "

In the course of the debate Mr. Gladstone slightly alluded to
this sneer, with a touch of contempt best fitted to reply to such
a splenetic breach of good taste.

In committee Mr. Gladstone moved an addition to the personal payment clause, " Whether he in person or his landlord be
rated to the relief of the poor." He said there were two results
which it was desirable to attain—one, the passing a Reform Bill ;
and the other, passing it that year, and without a change in the
Government ; but he was not prepared to sacrifice the first to
the second. The Bill, as it now stood, opposed great barriers
to enfranchisement. In boroughs, the rates of two-thirds of the
houses under the value of £10 were compounded for ; and
as the occupiers of these houses would practically remain
disfranchised, the Bill would do little towards enfranchising the
working classes in towns. It was an error to say that by paying
the rates the occupiers might get the votes ; for, besides
the expenditure of money, there would be the expenditure of
time to take the necessary steps. If they passed the Bill in
the form in which it stood, an agitation would commence, as its
true character was seen, which would never cease till the last
vestige of such legislation was swept away. The amendment
was lost by a majority of 21, and the division list showed that
many Liberals had voted with the Government. Other amendments stood in Mr. Gladstone's name, but, in reply to a letter of
inquiry from Mr. Crawford, one of the members for the City of
London, representing many Liberal members, Mr. Gladstone
announced that he should not proceed with the amendment, nor
give notice of others.

By the time the Bill had got through committee, passed the
third reading, and been sent up to the Lords, it was changed
indeed. " Bless thee, Bottom ! bless thee ! thou art translated ! "
might have been the exclamation of many a Quince on the Conservative benches ; but probably Mr. Disraeli satisfied himself
and his colleagues that the "definite opinion " of the Cabinet was
an elastic material, and that a little stretching would not hurt the
fabric. The savings-bank and public funds clause had vanished,
in company with the dual franchise ; the interesting compound

householder was swept away altogether, and the franchise was conferred upon all householders except those excused from paying rates on the score of poverty. Mr. Ayrton, member for the Tower Hamlets, had obtained the reduction of the period of residence from two years to one, and Mr. M'Cullagh Torrens, one of the representatives of Finsbury, had obtained the franchise for lodgers who paid £10 a-year for unfurnished apartments. The county franchise was reduced from £15 to £12 rating, and copy or leaseholders of property of the free annual value of £5 were to be entitled to vote, and to that extent put on an equality with the old forty-shilling freeholder. Some other attempts at amendment were rejected, among them Mr. Lowe's proposal for cumulative voting—that is, allowing a voter, when more than one candidate was to be returned, to "cumulate" his votes in favour of one candidate; and Mr. Stuart Mill's amendment in favour of extending the suffrage to women; a proposition which obtained seventy-three supporters.

The scope of the redistribution scheme was greatly enlarged. The limit at which boroughs then returning two members should hereafter return only one was raised from 7,000 inhabitants to 10,000. This gave thirty-eight seats to be distributed, making, with the seven seats forfeited by corruption, forty-five available for distribution. West Kent, North Lancashire, East Surrey (already having two members each), and South Lancashire (already with three members), were subdivided, and two members given to each division; and the counties of Chester, Derby, Devon, Essex, Lincoln, Norfolk, Somerset and Stafford, together with the West Riding (all already in two divisions, with two members each), were divided into three parts, each represented by two members. Middlesex got no more members; but two new metropolitan boroughs within the county, Hackney (a division of the Tower Hamlets), and Chelsea (including Kensington), were created. Birmingham, Leeds, Liverpool, Manchester, Salford, and Merthyr Tydvil were each to have an additional member, and some new boroughs, with one member each, were formed.

When the Bill reached the Lords, Lord Cairns introduced, supported by a large majority, a clause providing for the representation of minorities. This clause provided that in counties and boroughs where three members are returned, a vote can only be given for two, and in London, where four members are returned, for three only. A similar proposition had been made in the House of Commons by Mr. Lowe, but rejected, Mr. Bright being in the majority against it. The idea was not original, for

Lord John Russell had included it in the provisions of his Bill in 1854. When the amendment came down from the Lords it was accepted. The Bill received the Royal assent on the 15th of August. It cannot be spoken of in political history as a Conservative or a Liberal Bill, as Disraeli's or Gladstone's. It was the result of an accommodating Ministerial conscience and Liberal disunion, and yet was a very good measure, the result of the eclectic wisdom of all parties and floating balances of parties. The compound householder had been politically extinguished, but the compound Reform Bill remained and throve.

In an interval of the discussion, on the 4th of April, the Chancellor of the Exchequer made his financial statement, and his Budget received the general support of Mr. Gladstone. The only noticeable feature was, that, having a surplus of £1,206,000 to dispose of, Mr. Disraeli adopted to some extent the scheme of Mr. Gladstone for creating terminable annuities, and so reducing the National Debt.

On the 20th of March Mr. Gladstone voted in the majority for the second reading of Mr. Hardcastle's Church-rate Abolition Bill. On the 7th of May the greater ecclesiastical question, the status of the Irish Church, was once more the subject of discussion. There had been a debate on the subject in the Lords, and on the day named, Sir John Grey, member for the borough of Kilkenny, moved, in the Commons, that the House would, on a future day, resolve itself into a committee to consider the temporalities and privileges of the Established Church in Ireland; and the motion was seconded, in a very earnest speech, by Col. Greville-Nugent, member for the county of Longford. Mr. Gladstone said he felt a difficulty in supporting the motion, because he thought they ought not to pass a resolution on the subject without being prepared to give effect to it; but he agreed with much that had been said by the mover and seconder. One of the grounds on which the State support of the Irish Church might be defended was that the Church maintained the truth. But such a plea would be inconsistent, as the State also supported the College of Maynooth, where priests were educated to teach that the doctrines of the Protestant Church were false. A second ground might be that the Established Church represented the faith of the bulk of the people; but that notoriously was not the case. A third ground might be that it was the Church of the poor; on the contrary, it was the Church of the rich. Neither Englishmen nor Scotchmen would tolerate being treated in ecclesiastical matters as the Irish were. We should apply to Irishmen

the same measure by which we would ourselves be treated.   He
thought the time was not far distant when Parliament must look
the question fairly and fully in the face.   " I confess that I am
sanguine enough to cherish a hope that, though not without
difficulty, a satisfactory result will be arrived at, the consequences
of which will be so happy and pleasant for us all that we shall
wonder at the folly which has so long prevented it being brought
about."

The Attorney General for Ireland (Mr. Chatterton) opposed
the motion, and described Mr. Gladstone's speech as full of the
Socialist and Communistic element.   In his time Mr. Gladstone
has had to endure many hard words, but there was a striking
novelty in this description of his opinions which was decidedly
amusing.

Sir Frederick Heygate, member for the county of Londonderry,
had met the resolution by moving the previous question, the
result being that Sir John Grey's motion was lost by a majority
of 12, Mr. Gladstone voting in the minority.

In the course of the session Mr. Gladstone spoke on one or
two subjects of some importance.   He supported, but unsuccessfully, a clause in the Officers and Oaths Bill, introduced by Sir
Colman O'Loghlen, member for Clare county, which would enable
a Roman Catholic to be Lord Lieutenant of Ireland.   The Secretary for Ireland could, he argued, by the existing laws be a
Roman Catholic, and why should the Lord Lieutenant, whose
political functions were less important, necessarily be a Protestant?   He spoke and voted in favour of Mr. Fawcett's instruction to the committee on Mr. Coleridge's Bill for the
Abolition of Religious Tests at Oxford, by which the provisions
of the Bill would be extended to Cambridge.

On the 10th of July Mr. Bruce, member for Merthyr Tydvil,
who had been Vice-President of the Committee of Council on
Education, introduced a Bill on the subject of the Education of
the People.   He had no hope that it could be carried in the
present session, but laid it on the table with the view of eliciting
opinions on the subject, and paving the way for future legislation.   Mr. Gathorne Hardy, who had succeeded Mr. Walpole
at the Home Office, said the Government would not support the
Bill, nor would he pledge Ministers to bring in a Bill on the
subject next session.   Mr. Gladstone expressed dissatisfaction
with the statement, and said a comprehensive measure was
required which would effect a national object.

In the course of the Reform agitation outside the House

Q

Mr. Bright took occasion, in a speech delivered at Birmingham on the 22nd of April, to pay a splendid compliment to Mr. Gladstone. "Who," he asked, "is there in the House of Commons who equals him in knowledge of all political questions? Who equals him in earnestness? Who equals him in eloquence? Who equals him in courage and fidelity to his convictions? If these gentlemen [referring to the Tea-room party] who say they will not follow him have anyone who is his equal, let them show him. If they can point out any statesman who can add dignity and grandeur to the stature of Mr. Gladstone, let them produce him."

Shortly before the end of the session Mr. Gladstone addressed a letter to a correspondent at New York respecting his memorable statement at the Newcastle banquet, that the South had made itself a nation. There was a characteristic conscientious candour in this acknowledgment of an error of judgment :—

"I must confess that I was wrong; that I took too much upon myself in expressing such an opinion. Yet the motive was not bad. My sympathies were then—where they had long before been—with the whole American people. I probably, like many Europeans, did not understand the nature and working of the American Union. I had imbibed conscientiously, if erroneously, an opinion that twenty or twenty-four millions of the North would be happier, and would be stronger (of course assuming that they would hold together), without the South than with it, and also that the negroes would be much nearer to emancipation under a Southern government than under the old system of the Union, which had not at that date (August [October] 1862) been abandoned, and which always appeared to me to place the whole power of the North at the command of the slaveholding interests of the South. As far as regards the special or separate interest of England in the matter, I, differing from many others, had always contended that it was best for our interest that the Union should be kept entire."

Parliament was prorogued by commission on the 15th of August, but assembled again on the 19th of November, for the purpose of sanctioning the Abyssinian expedition, and providing for the necessary expenditure. Mr. Disraeli, the Chancellor of the Exchequer, was ill, and the duty of proposing an additional penny on the income-tax devolved on Mr. Ward Hunt, the Secretary of the Treasury. That uncomfortable proposition having been assented to, the Houses adjourned. The Royal Speech was delivered in November, the new session beginning then; and in it the subject of the education of the people was especially recommended to the consideration of the Houses, showing that Mr. Hardy was not quite correct in saying that the Government were not prepared to take action in the matter.

A few days after the meeting of Parliament in February it was announced that the Earl of Derby had resigned his high office on account of failing health, and that, on his recommendation, Mr. Disraeli had been raised to the dignity of First Lord of the Treasury. Rather singularly, the duty of officially announcing the resignation of the Premier to the House of Commons devolved on his son, Lord Stanley, Foreign Secretary, the acceptance of the new office by Mr. Disraeli having vacated his seat. Mr. Gladstone took occasion to eulogise the high character and great ability of the Earl of Derby, and to express a sincere sympathy on account of the illness which had incapacitated him for political work. The new Premier made some ministerial rearrangements. Lord Chelmsford was not reappointed Lord Chancellor, Lord Cairns taking his place on the woolsack, and Mr. Ward Hunt, Secretary to the Treasury, was promoted to the dignity of Chancellor of the Exchequer, with, of course, Cabinet rank.

On the 19th of February Mr. Gladstone moved the second reading of the Compulsory Church-rates Abolition Bill, a similar measure to that which had been partially accepted in the previous session, but had not gone through all its stages when the close of the session extinguished it. Mr. Hardcastle, whose Bill for the entire abolition of the rate had been rejected in the House of Lords by a majority of 58, reintroduced it; and two other Bills on the subject were before Parliament. Mr. Gladstone's Bill, however, was the most important, as most likely to receive support. It abolished all legal process for the recovery of Church-rates, except in cases of rates already made, or where money had been borrowed on the security of the rates; but permitted voluntary assessments to be made, and all agreements to make such payment on the faith of which any expenditure had been incurred would be enforcible in the same way as any other contract would be. No person who had not paid the rate would be able to vote on any question relating to voluntary assessment.

The Bill offered a compromise, but it obtained an amount of support which a more thorough measure would probably have failed to secure. In committee, Mr. Henley made an unavailing attempt to defeat the first clause, which contained the pith of the measure; but the numbers on the division in favour of the clause, 167 to 30, showed that the principle of the Bill was satisfactory. The third reading was carried by 131 to 28; and after some slight cavilling in the House of Lords, it passed, and received the Royal assent.

An early discussion of Irish affairs was inevitable. More and more was it becoming evident that the condition of Ireland was the great problem to the solution of which the Government, from whichever side of the House it was chosen, must speedily address itself. On the 16th of March, Mr. Maguire, one of the members for Cork, moved that the House should resolve itself into a committee to take into immediate consideration the condition of Ireland. In a strain of impassioned eloquence he dwelt on the decaying condition of his country, and the miserable condition of the peasantry, starving in their native land and straining every nerve to expatriate themselves to other lands where the means of subsistence could be obtained. Absentee and oppressive landlords and an alien Church were grievances to the consideration of which Parliament was morally bound to apply itself.

The Earl of Mayo, Secretary for Ireland, opposed the motion on the part of the Government, and denied that Ireland was exhibiting the symptoms of decay spoken of. In respect of the Church, he reminded the House that a committee, appointed at the instance of Earl Russell, was then sitting, and Government, therefore, thought it would be impolitic to endeavour to deal with the question immediately.

The debate lasted four nights, most of the prominent members taking part in it. Among those who spoke were Mr. Lowe, Mr. Mill, Mr. Hardy, Mr. Chichester Fortescue, Mr. Bright (who made one of the most effective and brilliant speeches he has ever delivered), and Sir Stafford Northcote. Towards the close of the fourth night's debate Mr. Gladstone rose. Ireland, he said, had an account with this country which had endured for centuries, and in the opinion of every enlightened nation in the world, much as we had done, we had not done enough to place ourselves in the right. He thought that the great political changes introduced into the constitution of the representation by the Reform Bill of the previous session had produced a considerable effect in imparting an impetus to the public mind, and in quickening the temper, that for many years had been somewhat sluggish, to grapple closely and resolutely with the problems and the necessities of legislation. He recommended Mr. Maguire to withdraw the motion, because it embraced many Irish questions which had better be dealt with separately, and in respect to some of which the Government had promised action. On the subject of the Irish Church he spoke out boldly :—

" If we are to do any good at all by meddling with the Church in Ireland it must, in my judgment, be by putting an end to its existence as a State

Church.   No doubt it is a great and formidable operation—I do not disguise it—to constitute into a body of Christians united only by a voluntary tie those who have for three centuries and a half been associated more or less closely with the State—and by the Act of Union, seventy years ago, brought still more closely into relation with the civil power. This is a great and formidable task, yet my persuasion is that, in removing privilege and restraint together, in granting freedom in lieu of monopoly, a task will be proposed to us that is not beyond the courage and the statesmanship of the British Legislature. . . . I recognize the fact that the time has come when this question ought to be approached, and when, if approached, it ought to be dealt with once for all."

Mr. Gladstone concluded a long and animated speech in these words :—

"We remember the words, the earnest and touching words, with which the noble Earl the Chief Secretary for Ireland closed his address, when he expressed a hope and uttered a call inviting the Irish people to union and loyalty.   Sir, that is our object too, but I am afraid that, as to the means, the differences between us are still profound ; and it is idle, it is mocking, to use words unless we can sustain them with corresponding substance. That substance can be supplied by nothing but by the unreserved devotion of our efforts now, in, perhaps, the last stage of the Irish crisis. to remove the scandal and mischief which have long weakened and afflicted the Empire. For that work I trust strength will be given us.   If we be prudent men, I hope we shall endeavour, so far as in us lies, to make provision for the contingencies of a doubtful and, possibly, a dangerous future.   If we be chivalrous men, I trust we shall endeavour to wipe away the stains which the civilized world has for ages seen, or seemed to see, upon the shield of England in her treatment of Ireland.   If we are compassionate men, I hope we shall now at once, and once for all, listen to that tale of sorrow which comes from her, and the reality of which, if not its justice, is testified by the continuous migration of her people ; that we shall

> ' Raze out the written troubles from her brain,
> Pluck from her memory a rooted sorrow.'

But, above all, if we be just men, we shall go forward in the name of truth and right, bearing this in mind : that, where the case is proved and the hour is come, justice delayed is justice denied."

Mr. Disraeli's reply, as customary with him, was rhetorically effective and bristled with personalities. How was it, he asked, that Mr. Gladstone, at this period of his long political career, had only just discovered that there was a crisis in Irish affairs. which nothing but the disestablishment of the Church could relieve. Government were preparing carefully considered remedies for admitted Irish grievances, and " they ought not to be deterred from a moderate and a judicious course by those monstrous inventions of a crisis in Ireland, got up by the right honourable gentleman opposite for the advantage of his party." He hit hard when he continued, " The right honourable gentle-

man, who has had the power of the Crown in a large proportion
for a quarter of a century, has never done anything but make
speeches—make speeches in favour of the Irish Church. . . .
At the last general election the Liberal party had been seven
years in power, but not one word during those seven years had
ever issued from any person in authority—certainly not from the
right honourable member for South Lancashire—as to his having
doubted the wisdom of the cardinal principle upon which our
whole social system is founded." That cardinal principle the
speaker had previously explained to be, ecclesiastical endowments.

Mr. Maguire's motion was withdrawn, Mr. Gladstone's significant speech being considered satisfactory evidence that he
was prepared to take the lead in attacking the giant evils of
which the Irish complained. He redeemed his implied promise
by giving notice, on the 23rd, of March of three resolutions, to
be proposed in a committee on Acts relating to the Established
Church of Ireland. These memorable resolutions were to this
effect :—

" 1. That, in the opinion of this House, it is necessary that the Established
Church of Ireland should cease to exist as an establishment, due regard
being had to all personal interests and to all individual rights of property.

" 2. That, subject to the foregoing considerations, it is expedient to prevent
the creation of new personal interests by the exercise of any public patronage, and to confine the operations of the Ecclesiastical Commissioners of
Ireland to objects of immediate necessity as involving individual rights, pending the final decision of Parliament.

" 3. That an Address be presented to Her Majesty, humbly to pray that, with
a view to the purposes aforesaid, Her Majesty be graciously pleased to place
at the disposal of Parliament her interest in the temporalities of the arch-
bishoprics, bishoprics, and other ecclesiastical dignities and benefices in
Ireland and in the custodies thereof."

It was arranged that the resolutions should be moved on the
30th of March ; and on the 27th Lord Stanley, on the part of the
Government, took up the glove, in a somewhat feeble fashion, by
giving notice that he would move as an amendment, on the motion
for immediately going into committee—

" That this House, while admitting that considerable modifications in the
temporalities of the Established Church in Ireland may, after pending inquiry,
appear to be expedient, is of opinion that any proposition tending to the
disestablishment or disendowment of that Church ought to be reserved for
the decision of the new Parliament."

The fact seems to be that Ministers were apprehensive and
disunited. In the present temper of the House of Commons a

defeat was more than probable ; and some of the Cabinet were disposed to hope that another House, elected under the new conditions, might strengthen their hands. There were, however, one or two bolder spirits—notably Mr. Gathorne Hardy, the Home Secretary—who were eager for the fray, and ready to respond to Mr. Gladstone's challenge *à l'outrance*.

On the 28th, the day following that on which Lord Stanley had given notice of his amendment, the leading members of the Liberal party entertained at a banquet Mr. Brand, the devoted and clever Whip of the party, and in later times the much-enduring Speaker, and presented him with a testimonial in recognition of his long and valuable services to the party. Mr. Gladstone occupied the chair, and, as the occasion was essentially political, the great topic of the day—the Irish Church resolutions—was alluded to. "Having put our hand to the plough," said Mr. Gladstone, "we shall not look back. Now is the time to address ourselves, not as to a trivial work, but as to one demanding every exertion we can make, and with a firm determination that, so far as depends on us, efforts shall not be wanting to establish throughout the civilised world the good name of England in her relation to her sister Ireland, and to make the kingdom united, not merely by the paper form of law, but by the blessed law of concord and harmony which is written in the heart of man."

When, on the 30th of March, the order of the day for moving the resolutions was reached, Colonel Stuart Knox, member for Dungannon, a Tory of the old school, moved that the 5th Article of the Act of Union be read. In the belief of many persons this article made the maintenance of the Irish Church as an establishment an essential element of the union between the two countries, and to disestablish the one would be to destroy the other. The article was read by the Clerk at the table, as was also, on the motion of Mr. H. E. Surtees, member for Hertford-shire, the formula for the administration of the Coronation Oath, prescribed for use by the Statute of William and Mary. By this oath the Sovereign promised to support and defend the Protestant Church in Ireland "as by law established;" but Mr. Gladstone, and others who wished to alter the status of the Church, naturally understood by these words that the Sovereign's promise only extended to the Church so long as it *was* by law established, and would cease to be operative if the Church was "by law" disestablished. At any rate, the reading of the article of the Union and of the extract from the Coronation Service was listened to

with about as much respect and attention as formal readings by
the Clerk of the House generally are, and did not appear to
exercise the slightest influence on the course of the debates.

Mr. Gladstone spoke for an hour and a half. He sketched
the history of the Protestant Church in Ireland, and of the
influence in the country generally of British domination. He
anticipated the accusation of inconsistency which he knew would
be brought against him, and was quite prepared to encounter the
storm of quotations from his early book on "The State in its
Relation with the Church," which he reasonably guessed was
preparing. A change, he said, which extended over a quarter
of a century could hardly be deemed a sudden change. In 1846
he, having then lost his seat on account of the Corn Laws, was
invited to oppose a member of Lord Russell's cabinet, and obtain
for himself a seat in Parliament; but he refused, because they
had both voted on the same side as to Free Trade, and because
the question of the Irish Church was then likely to come forward.
His proposed opponent was averse to the maintenance of the
establishment, and he (Mr. Gladstone) felt it impossible to pledge
himself to maintain it. In the following year he had a contest
for the University of Oxford. Application was then made to
him to know his views as to the Irish Church, and he replied
that he did not anticipate the proposal of any plan which would
lead him to vote for a change in the ecclesiastical establishment
of Ireland, but that to maintain it in principle he must entirely
decline. In 1865 it appeared to him that the coming Parliament
would probably have to deal with the question, and he at once
took the opportunity, for the fair warning and notice of his constituents, of making a speech, and detaching himself wholly and
absolutely from the maintenance of the Irish Church, either on a
large or more contracted scale. Having given this notice, the
constituency, as they were perfectly entitled to do, took advantage of it, and in consequence he was not now member for Oxford
University, but for South Lancashire.

"For my part," he said, referring to the frequent coercive
legislation for Ireland, "I know not what is worse than tranquillity purchased by the constant suspension of the Habeas
Corpus Act, unless it be that last extremity of public calamity—
civil war." He continued—

"That being the state of things, I, for one, Sir, am not willing to wait.
It appears to me that our responsibility is quite sufficient for having waited
thus long, and that it befits us now to do all that the time will permit towards
clearing our account with Ireland. I know there is a feeling in this matter

FROM THE PAINTING BY SIR J. E. MILLAIS, BART., R.A.

THE RIGHT HON. WILLIAM EWART GLADSTONE.

which I admit it is difficult to get over.   There are many who think that to
lay hands upon the national Church Establishment of a country is a profane
and unhallowed act.   I respect that feeling.   I sympathise with it.   I sympathise with it, while I think it my duty to overcome and repress it.   But if it
be an error, it is an error entitled to respect.   There is something in the idea
of a national establishment of religion, of a solemn appropriation of a part of
the commonwealth for conferring upon all who are ready to receive it what we
know to be an inestimable benefit ; of saving that portion of the inheritance
from private selfishness in order to extract from it, if we can, pure and unmixed advantages of the highest order for the population at large—there is
something in this so attractive that it is an image that must always command
the homage of the many.   It is somewhat like the kingly ghost in *Hamlet*, of
which one of the characters of Shakespeare says—

> ' We do it wrong, being so majestical,
> To offer it the show of violence ;
> For it is, as the air, invulnerable,
> And our vain blows malicious mockery.'

But, Sir, this is to view a religious establishment upon one side—only upon
what I may call the ethereal side.   It has likewise a side of earth ; and here
I cannot do better than quote some lines written by the present Archbishop of
Dublin [Dr. Trench] at a time when his genius was devoted to the Muses.
He said, in speaking of mankind—

> ' We who did our lineage high
> Draw from beyond the starry sky,
> Are yet, upon the other side,
> To earth and to its dust allied !'

And so the Church Establishment, regarded in its theory and in its aim, is
beautiful and attractive.   Yet what is it but an appropriation of public
property, an appropriation of the fruits of labour and of skill, to certain purposes, and unless those purposes be fulfilled that appropriation cannot be
justified.   Therefore, Sir, I cannot but feel that we must set aside fears
which thrust themselves upon the imagination, and act upon the sole dictates
of our judgment."

The debate extended over four nights, and the speech of
Lord Cranborne was certainly one of the most effective delivered.   Much as he disliked Mr. Gladstone's resolutions, he
scarcely less disliked Lord Stanley's amendment, which he denounced as half-hearted.   He pledged himself to support the
principle of establishment to the last extremity, and expressed a
feeling of great disappointment that a principle had not been
laid down for which the Conservative party could fight, and
appeal to the tribunal of public opinion.   The amendment, he
declared, gave no clue to the policy of Ministers, but its
ambiguity indicated that the object was merely to gain time, and
to enable the Government to keep the cards in their hands fo
another year, and shuffle as they pleased.

General Peel, another Conservative of the antique sturdy school
who did not believe in the good old Tory trumpet emitting an

uncertain note, also condemned the amendment. As a ministerial blast, the note was uncertain indeed, but at least one Minister, Mr. Gathorne Hardy, who made a vigorous speech. on the second night of the debate, was ready at once to enter into the fray, and support the Protestant Establishment, although willing to admit that the Irish Church needed reform and modification. General Peel avowed that so long as Mr. Hardy sat on the Treasury bench he should feel perfectly secure.

Sir Stafford Northcote, another of the Ministers, though not so fiery as Mr. Gathorne Hardy, gave promise of being quite as resolute. Ministers, he said, would vote with Lord Stanley on the question of time, but, if beaten on the amendment, would oppose the resolutions on principle. The object of Mr. Gladstone and his supporters, he said, was less to benefit Ireland than to turn out the Government.

As Prime Minister and Ministerial leader in the Commons, Mr. Disraeli, of course, spoke at length. He defended the course the Government had taken in meeting the resolutions by Lord Stanley's amendment. They might have met them by a direct negative, but then it would have been said that Ministers were of opinion that no change, no improvement, no modification was necessary, expedient, or desirable in the condition of the Church in Ireland, and Government did not wish that inference to be drawn. The amendment they had adopted had been drawn in strict accordance with Parliamentary experience and precedent—a precedent sanctioned on more than one occasion by the practice and advice of Sir Robert Peel and Lord John Russell. The former statesman had said, " If you are obliged to have an amendment, never attempt to express your policy in it. Your amendment should never be inconsistent with your policy, but you must fix on some practical point which, if carried, would defeat the motion of your opponent." When the present Parliament was elected, the question of the Irish Church was not before the country, and the constituencies had had no opportunity of expressing an opinion on the subject ; and " when a fundamental law of the country was called into question, though technically and legally this House had a right to do anything within the sphere of the House of Commons, it was not morally competent to decide such a question if those who had elected it had not, in the constitutional course of public life, received some intimation that such a question was to come before it." Therefore the terms of the amendment had been arranged with the view of deferring the consideration of the matter until the assembling of a new Parliament. The Prime Minister took the opportunity of giving a good "dig" to Lord Cranborne, who, a few months before, had hit him very hard in the *Quarterly*. Mr. Lowe, too, came in for a castigation in the true Disraelian manner :—

"The hon. gentleman the member for Calne is a very remarkable man. He is a learned man, though he despises history. He can chop logic like Dean Aldrich; but what is more remarkable than his learning and his logic is that power of spontaneous aversion which particularises him. There is nothing that he likes, and almost everything that he hates. He hates the working-classes of England. He hates the Roman Catholics of Ireland. He hates the Protestants of Ireland. He hates Her Majesty's Ministers. And until the right hon. gentleman the member for South Lancashire placed his hand upon the ark, he seemed almost to hate the right hon. gentleman the member for South Lancashire."

The speech ended with a personal innuendo respecting Mr. Gladstone :—" High Church Ritualists and the Irish followers of the Pope have long been in secret combination, and are now in open confederacy. I know the almost superhuman power of this combination. They have their hand almost upon the realm of England. Under the guise of Liberalism, under the pretence of legislating in the spirit of the age, they are, as they think, about to seize upon the supreme authority of the realm. But this I can say, that so long as, by the favour of the Queen, I stand here, I will oppose to the utmost of my ability the attempt they are making. I believe the policy of the right hon. gentleman who is their representative, if successful, will change the character of this country. It will deprive the subjects of Her Majesty of some of their most precious privileges, and it will dangerously touch even the tenure of the Crown."

In replying, Mr. Gladstone described some parts of Mr. Disraeli's speech as the result of a heated imagination, and explained the calculations by which he had arrived at the conclusion that his scheme would leave the Protestants in possession of three-fifths of the present value of the Church property.

The insinuation of Mr. Disraeli respecting Mr. Gladstone's supposed Ritualistic and Papistical tendencies led to a letter from Mr. Gladstone, which appeared in the principal daily newspapers on the 24th of April. The writer replied categorically to statements made to the effect that, when he visited Rome, he had made arrangements with the Pope to destroy the Church establishment in Ireland, being himself a Roman Catholic at heart; that he had publicly condemned all support to the clergy in the three kingdoms from Church or public funds; that

he had refused, when at Balmoral, to attend Her Majesty at
Crathie church; that he had received the thanks of the Pope
for his proceedings respecting the Irish Church; and that he
was a member of a High Church Ritualistic congregation. Mr.
Gladstone declared that these statements were " one and all
untrue, in the letter and in the spirit, from the beginning to the
end." Violent political opponents are not always squeamish as
to accusations, and Mr. Gladstone's sensitiveness would not permit him to treat them with silent contempt.   Indeed, before the
year was over, speaking at Bootle, in Lancashire, he gravely and
emphatically denied that there was any truth in a charge made
by somebody that he had misappropriated pew rents and other
Church moneys.

When the division was taken on Lord Stanley's amendment
it was negatived by 60; the numbers being 270 for, and 330
against.   Mr. Gladstone's motion for going into committee was
then put, and carried by 328 against 272.   In each division
exactly 600 members voted.   Lord Cranborne did not go into
the lobby in the amendment division, but voted in the minority
when the second division was taken.   The House having gone
into committee, the Chairman was ordered to report progress,
and the debate was adjourned till the resumption of the House
after the Easter holidays.

The greater number of members hastened to enjoy such rest
and rural enjoyment as early April could afford, but there were
politicians enough left in town to attend two large meetings held
in St. James's Hall, one presided over by Earl Russell, to support Mr. Gladstone's resolutions, and the other, with Mr. Camp-
bell Colquhoun in the chair, called for the purpose of denouncing
them.   At the former, the Earl, then in his seventy-sixth year,
eulogised Mr. Gladstone's political sincerity.   At the opposition
meeting, Mr. Colquhoun expressed great alarm at the prospect of
the results which might be expected from "the selfish madness of
politicians and the blindness of party."   The inevitable consequence of disestablishing the Irish Church, as proposed by
Mr. Gladstone, would be that we should have, "within six
hours of our shores, four millions and a half of men, led
by fanatical priests, hating England with an undying hatred,
detesting her political principles, and detesting as odious her
Crown."   The Tory *Blackwood*, which had been in a fright-
ful state of despondency, and preparing for the crack of
doom ever since Mr. Gladstone had given notice of his resolutions, plucked up courage, and, indeed, became quite

jubilant when Mr. Colquhoun uttered his "masterly appeals" and "solemn sentences."

Earl Russell said Mr. Gladstone "had indeed changed his opinions," and then asked, "what statesmin had not?" As a commentary on this inquiry, the *Times* said :—"The resolutions, as explained by their author, contemplate a course of action altogether different from that proposed by Lord Russell two short months since. Lord Russell anticipated the session by a letter to Mr. Chichester Fortescue, recommending a redistribution of the revenues of the Irish Church Establishment among the principal religious bodies in Ireland. Three or four weeks later, Mr. Gladstone pronounced this proposition antiquated and impracticable, and submitted to the House of Commons the pure and simple disestablishment and disendowment of the Irish Church, and last night the veteran Whig went to Piccadilly to declare for Mr. Gladstone and against himself."

The ultra-Conservative press teemed with denunciations of the "wicked act," the "iniquity" of which Mr. Gladstone had been guilty in proposing the resolutions; and the Earl of Derby recovered sufficiently from the indisposition which had compelled him to retire from office to be able to appear in the House of Lords on the 27th of April, and make an endeavour to obtain the expression of an adverse opinion, in advance of the renewal of the debate in the House of Commons.

The first resolution, that which expressed the opinion that "the Church of Ireland should cease to exist as an establishment," was carried against Ministers by a majority of 65, the numbers being 265 against 230. As this resolution involved the main principle in dispute, and as the majority was so considerable, Ministers were evidently called upon to consider their position, and Mr. Disraeli moved an adjournment till the following Monday. On that night, the 4th of May, the announcement was made in both Houses that the resignation of Ministers had been submitted to the Queen, who had declined to accept it, but was prepared to dissolve the existing Parliament whenever the state of public business would permit. Mr. Bright and other Liberals blamed Ministers for not pressing their resignation; and it appeared, by subsequent statements, that Mr. Disraeli had first advised a dissolution, and that the offer of resignation was only an alternative.

It was not likely that the prelates of the English Church would view with indifference an attempt to disestablish the Irish

Church; and a largely attended meeting, at which the archbishops, bishops, and many of the dignified clergy attended,
supported by peers and members of the House of Commons,
passed resolutions protesting against the course taken by Mr.
Gladstone.

The debate on the resolutions in committee was resumed on
the 7th of May, and the second and third were carried; and
then Mr. Aytoun, member for Kirkaldy, proposed another,
which, after considerable discussion, was accepted in this amended
form :—" That when legislative effect shall be given to the first
resolution of the committee respecting the Established Church of
Ireland, it is right and necessary that the grant to Maynooth and
the Regium Donum be discontinued, *due regard being had to all
personal interests.*" The words in italics were added on the motion
of Mr. Gladstone, who would, he said, have preferred that the
resolution had not been brought forward.

The Address to the Queen, prepared in conformity with the
third resolution, having been presented, a royal reply was received, expressing the willingness of Her Majesty, in accordance
with the spirit of the resolution, to place at the disposal of Parliament her interest in the temporalities of the Irish Church.
The next step to be taken was to introduce a Bill to prevent, for
a limited time, new appointments in the Irish Church, and to
restrain, for the same period, the proceedings of the Ecclesiastical
Commission for Ireland. When Mr. Gladstone moved the second
reading of the Bill, on the 23rd of June, Mr. Gathorne Hardy
moved as an amendment that it be read a second time that day
six months; but, on a division, the Government was beaten by a
majority of 54—312 voting for the second reading, and 258
against it.

So far Mr. Gladstone had been successful, and, if the ultimate
decision had rested with the House of Commons, the Irish
Church would have been practically disestablished in 1868.
But the ordeal of the Lords was to be encountered; and probably
when Lord Granville introduced the Bill, on the 25th of June,
neither he nor Mr. Gladstone supposed it would be easily
accepted, if, indeed, they were not decidedly of opinion that it
would be rejected. The Earl of Derby, notwithstanding the
state of his health, which incapacitated him for great exertion,
earnestly opposed the measure; and Lord Cairns, the Lord
Chancellor, made a very powerful speech, one of the ablest he
ever delivered, and generally considered to be the best defence
of the Establishment which the Parliamentary discussion had

produced. The Bill was rejected by the Lords by a majority of very nearly two to one—the numbers being 192 against 97.

So, for that session, ended the attempt to deprive the Protestant Church of Ireland of the support of association with the State. Mr. Gladstone, however, was convinced that the great result was only deferred for a time, and that the great and compact majority which had supported him in the Commons was not likely to be lessened in the new Parliament, and to that majority, he believed, the Peers must ultimately give way.

The financial business of the session may be briefly disposed of. Mr. Ward Hunt produced his first Budget on the 23rd of April, and was compelled to make the unpleasant announcement that he found himself in a deficiency of £1,636,000; besides which, the war in Abyssinia would involve an expenditure of £3,722,000. His estimates of revenue and expenditure for the coming year, however, promised a surplus of nearly a million, and by putting twopence more on the income-tax, he hoped to be able to provide for the expenses incurred in giving a lesson in good manners to King Theodore, and to be in possession of a surplus of £722,000. Mr. Gladstone, the great financial authority and critic, as well as leader of the Opposition, did not object to the Budget plan—indeed, as the House had voted the money in the previous November, objection would have been useless; and the resolutions were carried. True patriots were, of course, very well satisfied that Sir Robert Napier had led his Indian warriors, with elephants, camels, many thousand mules and many donkeys, over the mountains to Magdala, which he had stormed; that Theodore had committed suicide; and that we could enjoy all that amount of national glory at the trifling cost of another two-pence on the income-tax.

Parliament was prorogued on the last day of July, and on the 11th of November was dissolved by proclamation. Preparations were eagerly made for the electoral campaign. There were many new constituencies, the effect of which on the strength of parties had as yet to be seen. The great question before the electors was that of the Irish Church, and that subject was the one in respect of which the most explicit declarations were required from candidates. The election addresses of the leaders of the opposite parties almost assumed the importance of State papers. The Prime Minister addressed the Buckinghamshire electors at great length. He recounted the work of the dead Parliament in the style of a Royal speech, but with much greater prolixity; and then he made an appeal to the Protestantism of the county by

declaring that the movement for the disestablishment of the
Church in Ireland had been fostered by the Papacy to further its
own ambitious ends :—" Amid the discordant activity of many
factions there moves the supreme purpose of one power. The
philosopher may flatter himself he is advancing the cause of
enlightened progress ; the sectarian may be roused to exertion
by anticipations of the downfall of ecclesiastical systems. These
are transient efforts—vain and passing aspirations. The ultimate triumph, were our Church to fall [he had previously expressed his conviction that the assault on the Irish Church was
only a prelude to an attack on the English Establishment],
would be to that power which would substitute for the authority
of our Sovereign the supremacy of a foreign prince."

Mr. Gladstone was freely attacked, not only by direct political
opponents, but by some of those who professed independence
of any party. He was charged with having laid aside his own
opinion for the sake of a political triumph over a rival, and
violated his own convictions in an attempt to regain a seat on
the Treasury bench, and to attain the Premiership, for which he
had now no competitor in the Liberal ranks. His opponents
were unceasing in their open attacks and covert insinuations—
attacks and insinuations as inconsistent as such outbreaks of
vituperation generally are. He was at once a Papist in disguise
an agent of the Jesuits, a Ritualist, a Nonconformist, a Leveller,
and a turncoat. He was to be fought in the new constituencies,
the boroughs and county divisions enfranchised by the Reform
Bill. Mr. Gladstone offered himself as a representative of South-
West Lancashire, and there stupendous exertions were made to
insure his defeat. His address to the electors, issued from
Hawarden on the 9th of October, contained a dignified defence
of his Parliamentary conduct. After referring to the discussions
on the Reform Bill, economy in the public service, primary
education, and some other of the subjects which had been actually
debated since he had obtained their suffrages three years previously, Mr. Gladstone adverted to the Irish question, then so
prominently before the political public :—

" At this time one question, or group of questions, overshadows all the
rest. The state of Ireland, and the actual temper of no small portion of its
people towards the Throne and Government of the United Kingdom, imperatively demand the care of all public men and of all good citizens who would
seek not merely to live by expedients from day to day, but, looking onwards
into the future, to make provision, so far as human means avail, for the
strength, concord, and stability of the empire. . . . We thought that ministers
had mistaken alike the interests and the convictions of the country ; we

refused to open a new source of discord through the establishment by the State of any denominational university ; we repudiated the policy of universal endowment ; but, agreeing with the Government that the subject was ripe, we proposed a counter plan of disestablishment of the existing Church, with strict regard to the rights of property and to vested interests, but without establishing any other Church, and with a general cessation of State endowments for religion in Ireland.

"The Church of Ireland is the Church of a minority, insignificant in numbers. True, while insignificant in numbers, that minority is great in property, in education, and power. All this does not mend but aggravate the case ; for if a national Church be not the Church of the nation, it should at least be the Church of the poor. Every argument which can now be used in favour of civil establishments of religion is a satire on the existence of the Church in Ireland. But while that Establishment is thus negative for good, it misapplies the funds meant for the advantage of the nation at large. It remains as the memorial of every past mischief and oppression ; it embitters religious controversy by infusing into it the sense or the spirit of political injustice ; and it carries the polemical temper into the sphere of social life and public affairs. Nor need we feel surprise when we find that since the penal laws began to be repealed, the relative number of Protestants in Ireland appears to have declined.

" In the removal of this Establishment I see the discharge of a debt of civil justice, the disappearance of a national, almost a world-wide reproach, a condition indispensable to the success of every effort to secure the peace and contentment of the country ; finally, relief to a devoted clergy from a false position, cramped and beset by hopeless prejudice, and the opening of a freer career for the sacred ministry.

" Rest as we are by common consent we cannot. Endowment of all, after the events of the last session, is out of the question. Retrenchment or mutilation of the existing Church, by reduction of its spiritual offices, has been proposed by a Royal Commission ; but I do not learn, from the latest and most authentic declarations of the Ministry, that they adopt that, or indeed any other method of proceeding. We of the Opposition, gentlemen, have done our part ; the matter now rests with you. One path, at least, lies before you—broad, open, and well-defined. One policy has advocates who do not shrink from its avowal. It is the policy of bringing absolutely to an end the civil establishment of the Church of Ireland. It has received the solemn sanction of the representatives whom the nation chose in 1865. For this line of action, the only one just, and the only one available, I confidently ask your approval."

Mr. Gladstone appeared to be very confident of the success of his candidature. In a speech made in support of his friend and Parliamentary supporter, Lord Hartington, who was in the field for North Lancashire, he said :—" I tell you, upon a minute and careful examination of the promises of the men in South-West Lancashire, that if there is truth in man—and there is truth in man—and apart from any strange and unforeseen accidents, this day week, please God, I shall be member for South-West-Lancashire."

He was destined to experience a great disappointment. When

R

the time came, the Conservatives were above him on the poll,
which was headed by Mr. R. A. Cross (then untried as a politician,
but who afterwards made his mark as a very able Home Secretary
in Mr. Disraeli's second administration). Mr. Turner, a gentleman of considerable local influence, was the second successful
candidate, and he obtained 7,676 votes, 261 more than were
given for Mr. Gladstone.

Anticipating that the prodigious efforts to insure his rejection in Lancashire might be successful, his admirers in one of
the metropolitan boroughs had proposed him as a candidate,
and carried his election. The advanced Liberals of Greenwich
were an able and energetic body, had established an active association, and many less impulsive members of the constituency,
less disposed to take extreme views, united with them in the
desire to secure Mr. Gladstone as a representative of the borough.
Canon Miller, the vicar, was among his supporters, by the side
of most of the Dissenting inhabitants; and Dr. W. C. Bennett,
an ardent Radical, but better known for his charming poetry,
a resident in the borough, was unceasing in his advocacy. The
result was that, though defeated for South-West Lancashire, Mr.
Gladstone was returned for Greenwich, as the colleague of Alder-
man Salomons.

On the 23rd of November, two days before the formal acceptance of the Greenwich seat, appeared "A Chapter of Autobiography," in which Mr. Gladstone explained the reasons which
had induced him to appear as the antagonist of the Irish Establishment. It was natural, he admitted, that, as the author of
"The State in its Relations with the Church," he should be exposed
to the charge of inconsistency; but he professed that "the great
and glaring change in his course of action, with respect to the
Established Church of Ireland, was not the mere eccentricity,
or even perverseness, of an individual mind, but connected itself
with silent changes which were advancing in the very bed and
basis of modern society; and that the progress of a great cause,
signal as it had been and was, appeared liable, nevertheless, to
suffer in point of credit, if not of energy and rapidity, for the real
or supposed delinquencies of a person with whose name, for the
moment, it happened to be specially associated." The appearance of this "Chapter of Autobiography" gave rise to several
"Replies," "Commentaries," &c., which soon passed into
oblivion.

The results of the general election showed that in the English
boroughs generally the Liberals had been successful, but that in

NO. 10, DOWNING STREET.
The residence of the First Lord of
the Treasury.

NO. 16, JAMES STREET, PICCADILLY.

NO. 21, CARLTON HOUSE GARDENS.

NO. 1, CARLTON HOUSE GARDENS.

SOME LONDON HOMES OF MR. GLADSTONE.
Photographed by W. H. Bunnett.

the English counties the Conservatives had gained many victories. When the balance-sheet of political profit and loss was made out, it was estimated that the new Parliament would include nearly 380 Liberals and 270 Conservatives. Several very prominent Liberals lost their seats.

Mr. Disraeli did not wait for the assembling of the new Parliament (fixed for the 10th of December) to accept the verdict of the constituencies, but on the first of the month submitted to the Queen the resignation of himself and his colleagues, and, following constitutional precedent, advised that Mr. Gladstone should be sent for.

The boyish admirer of Canning, the political pupil of Peel, the colleague of Palmerston and Russell, had at length attained the distinguished position which those great statesmen had held. In this country the highest honours are seldom attained by leaps. Step by step the topmost round is reached, and each stage in the journey is long. Canning was fifty-seven years old when he was called on to form an administration; Peel was Premier at forty-six, but first held office twenty-four years before; Palmerston had been forty-eight years a member of Parliament when, in 1855, in his seventy-first year, he became the head of the Ministry; and Russell was fifty-four when he attained the same position. Mr. Disraeli was sixty-two when "Vivian Grey" was sent for; and his great opponent, the victor in the electoral struggle which unseated him, wanted a few days only to complete his fifty-ninth year when he became Prime Minister of England.

Before concluding this chapter, it may be noted that the exciting political contests of the year, the arduous Parliamentary debates, and the work of a great electoral campaign, did not hinder Mr. Gladstone from performing with characteristic ardour literary and theological work. The "Chapter of Autobiography" has been mentioned; and in the course of the year he contributed a series of papers to "Good Words," referring to the book "Ecce Homo," which, from the boldness of its views, had attracted so much attention in the religious world. These articles were collected and published in the form of a little book towards the end of the year. Mr. Gladstone generously defended the writer of the freely-attacked volume, and showed that the position he had taken had been misunderstood and misrepresented; that in describing the beautiful human nature of the Saviour he had not, as imputed, overlooked the union with the Divine nature. Mr. Gladstone's small volume is an admirable piece of sympathising, but not undiscriminating, criticism.

CHAPTER XXIII.

PRIME MINISTER—LEGISLATION FOR IRELAND.

MR. GLADSTONE and his colleagues in the Ministry received the seals of office on the 9th of December. The Cabinet was strong in talent, though some of its more conspicuous members were new to office. Mr. Bright, who rivalled—some persons think surpassed—his chief as an orator, gave the aid of his brilliant powers in debate, and his experience as a manufacturer and leadership in the free-trade movement specially qualified him for the office of President of the Board of Trade. Mr. Lowe, who had opposed Mr. Gladstone quite as often as he had supported him, the Adullamite and the Tea-room leader, always combative and always clear, who was Mr. Disraeli's match in sarcasm, and Mr. Gladstone's in classical reference, undertook to manage the Exchequer, frame budgets, and sit at the council board peaceably and pleasantly with John Bright, who had compared him to one end of a Scotch terrier. The most eminent of the Liberal lawyers could not be secured for the high office of Lord Chancellor, for Sir Roundell Palmer, staunch Liberal as he was, was a staunch Churchman too. He would have laboured willingly enough to amend the Irish Establishment, but help to disestablish and disendow it he would not; and not even the seat on the woolsack and a peerage could lure him from his allegiance to the principle of the union of Church and State. An excellent Chancery lawyer, and a sound, but not very profound politician, Sir William Page Wood, became Lord Chancellor and Baron Hatherley. The Earl of Clarendon resumed his old position at the Foreign Office, Earl Granville was Secretary for the Colonies, the Duke of Argyll for India, and Mr. Cardwell for War. Mr. Austen Bruce was Secretary of State for the Home Department, and, very fitly, Mr. Chichester Fortescue was appointed Chief Secretary for Ireland. Mr. Childers and Mr. Goschen, both men of acknowledged ability, became respectively First Lord of the Admiralty and President of the Poor Law (afterwards Local Government) Board.

The new Ministers who were members of the House of Commons of course vacated their seats, and there was no difficulty about their re-election; but as the new writs could not be

ordered until Parliament was properly constituted, they could not
be present when the House met in December. The only business transacted, however, was the election of a Speaker, and the
swearing-in of members, and the House then adjourned till the
16th February, when it met for the dispatch of business.

On the evening of the 10th the new Ministers were entertained
at a banquet by the Fishmongers' Company. In acknowledging
the toast " Her Majesty's Ministers," Mr. Gladstone, while declining to anticipate official announcements of the leading business which would occupy the coming session, assured his hearers
that not a moment would be lost in the maturing of those
measures which, when produced and explained, would, he believed,
be gratifying to all. He asked, with great earnestness of manner :

" What can be an object dearer either to the understanding or the heart of
man than to endeavour to bring about, through the whole of this vast community, that union of feeling and interest which, even in the degree in which
we have hitherto possessed it, has been the source of our strength and glory,
but which still presents to view, here and there, some points in which it is
unhappily defective, and which we wish to bring up to that condition in which
every man will almost forget whether he is a Scotchman, Englishman, or
Irishman, in the sense and consciousness of his belonging to a common
country ? "

The Royal Speech, at the opening of the session, was disappointing to those who had anticipated a revelation of the details of the
Ministerial plans. The reference to Ireland was slight ; the Church
was not even mentioned, and there was no announcement of special
legislation of any kind. The Address speeches brought forth
no announcements from Ministers ; but before the mover of the
Address in the House of Commons rose, Mr. Gladstone gave
notice that on the 1st of March he would move that the Acts
relating to the Irish Church Establishment and to the grant to
Maynooth College be read, and also the resolution agreed to by
the House in the previous session ; and that the House should
resolve itself into a committee " to consider of the said Acts and
resolution."

There was a very full attendance on that memorable 1st of
March. Members who could not find seats in the body of the
House took up their positions in the galleries ; Peers were present in their own gallery ; and strangers who had waited for many
hours about Westminster Hall thronged into the place reserved
for them. In the lobby, and around and about the House,
were eager crowds waiting for the revelations expected to be
made. The formal motion as to reading the Acts and resolution,
and going into committee of the whole House, having been agreed

to, the Prime Minister proceeded to disclose the leading pro
visions of the Bill which he was about to ask leave to introduce.
The existing Ecclesiastical Commission was to be wound up, and
a new Commission appointed, to exist for ten years, in which the
property of the Irish Church should be vested.   The union of the
Irish Church with the Church of England would terminate on the
1st January, 1871.   The Irish ecclesiastical courts would cease
to exist, and the ecclesiastical law be no longer binding.   In the
interval between the passing of the Bill and the date named,
appointments were to be made in a provisional ard temporary
manner, and not to convey with them freeholders' vested interests.
The Convention which prevented assemblings of the clergy and
laity would be at once repealed, and power would be taken by
the Queen in Council to recognise any governing body which
the clergy and laity of the disestablished Church might agree on,
as actually representing both, and which body would be incorpo-
rated.   So much for the Church in the abstract ; then the interests of the clergy had to be considered, and the clergy were
naturally much interested in the matter.   The Commission to be
appointed would ascertain the amount of each incumbent's income, deducting what he paid for curates, and, so long as he continued to discharge his duties, that income would be paid to him ;
but the option was reserved to him, if he thought fit to exercise
it, of applying to have the annual income commuted into an
annuity for life.   The tithe and the tithe-rent charge would be
vested in the Commission, and the freehold of churches wholly
in ruins would be taken from the incumbents.   Irish bishops
would no longer be Peers, and to that extent they would suffer in
dignity.   Curates were not overlooked in preparing the clauses
of the Bill, but compensation—or, if they preferred it, commutation—was provided.   Personal endowments would be respected ;
but the term was limited to money contributed from private
sources since the year 1660.   Churches intended to be preserved
for public worship would be handed over to the governing body,
and burial-grounds adjacent to the churches would go with them.
Glebe-houses, also, would become the property of the Church on
payment of building charges.

It would have been obviously illogical and unfair to continue
State aid to other denominations ; and therefore the Regium Donum
and the Maynooth grant must be dealt with.   Compensation would
be made to Presbyterian ministers for the abolition of the former,
and the grants to Presbyterian colleges and to Maynooth would
be commuted by payment of fourteen years' value of the money

annually voted.   As the financial result of the disestablishment scheme, there would remain a surplus of nearly £8,000,000, and that would be devoted to the relief of unavoidable calamities and suffering not provided for by the operation of the Poor Law, and be given to asylums for lunatics, the blind, deaf, and dumb, associations of nurses, infirmaries, reformatories, and similar institutions.

Mr. Gladstone concluded his long speech by saying :—

"This measure is in every sense a great measure—great in its principles, great in its multitude of dry, technical, but interesting detail, and great as a testing measure ; for it will show for one and all of us of what metal we are made.   Upon us all it brings a great responsibility ; great and foremost on those who occupy this bench.   We are especially chargeable—nay, deeply guilty—if we have either dishonestly, as some think, or even prematurely or unwisely, challenged so gigantic an issue.   I know well the punishment that follows rashness in public affairs, and that ought to fall upon those men, those Phætons of politics, who, with hands unequal to the task, attempt to guide the chariot of the sun.   But the responsibility, though heavy, does not exclusively press upon us—it presses on every man who has to take part in the discussion and decision upon this Bill.   Every man approaches the discussion under the most solemn obligations to raise the level of his vision and expand its scope in proportion with the greatness of the matter in hand.   The working of our constitutional government itself is upon its trial, for I do not believe there ever was a time when the wheels of legislative machinery were set in motion, under conditions of peace and order and constitutional regularity, to deal with a question greater or more profound.   And more especially, Sir, is the credit and fame of this great assembly involved.   This assembly, which has inherited through many ages the accumulated honours of brilliant triumphs, of peaceful but courageous legislation, is now called upon to address itself to a task which would, indeed, have demanded all the best energies of the very best among your fathers and your ancestors.   I believe it will prove to be worthy of the task. . . . I think the day has certainly come when an end is finally to be put to that union, not between the Church and religious association, but between the Establishment and the State, which was commenced under circumstances little auspicious, and has endured to be a source of unhappiness to Ireland, and of discredit and scandal to England.   For my part, I am deeply convinced that when the final consummation shall arrive, and when the words are spoken that shall give the force of law to the work embodied in this measure—the work of peace and justice—those words will be echoed upon every shore where the name of Ireland or the name of Great Britain has been heard, and the answer to them will come back in the approving verdict of civilised mankind."

The Opposition knew it would be useless to attempt to oppose the introduction and first reading of the Bill.   Mr. Disraeli said the general election had showed that it was the opinion of the country that Mr. Gladstone should have the opportunity of dealing with the question of the Irish Church, and he would therefore not oppose the introduction of the Bill ; but he and his friends had not changed their opinion, and still looked upon disesta

blishment as a great political error, and the disendowment of a
Church, particularly when its property was to be applied to secular
purposes, as " mere and sheer confiscation."

Thursday, the 18th of March, was fixed for the second reading.
Before that time the Opposition had resolved to make a fight,
even if they could not hope for victory. The whips on either
side could have told, with almost absolute precision, how each
member would vote, for nearly every member had been pledged
by his election address ; but it was necessary for Conservatism to
display its colours, and show a compact front, even if defeat were
certain ; and Mr. Disraeli gave notice that he should move as an
amendment that the Bill be read a second time that day six months.

The debate on the motion for the second reading extended
over four nights, the division being taken on Tuesday, the 23rd.
In moving his amendment, Mr. Disraeli exerted his great powers
to the utmost ; very effective opposition to the Bill was given by
Dr. J. Ball, who had been Attorney-General for Ireland in the
late Ministry, and one of the Commissioners appointed to inquire
into the revenue and administration of the Irish Church, and was
therefore peculiarly well qualified to deal with the statistics of
the question. Mr. Bright made a great speech in support of the
Bill—and when Mr. Bright makes a great speech it is an event
worth remembering—and especially defended the application of
the surplus funds to works of charity ; " for, after all," he said,
" I hope it is not far from Christianity to charity, and we know
that the Divine Author of our faith has left us much more of the
doings of a compassionate and loving heart than of dogma."

Much interest was aroused by the speech of Sir Roundell
Palmer. His secession on this question from the Liberal
phalanx—a secession involving the sacrifice of the realisation of
a legitimate professional and political ambition—was an unquestionable loss to the Ministry. He opened the third night's debate with a long speech against the Bill, dwelling particularly on
the legal questions involved, and was replied to by Sir John
Coleridge, Solicitor-General, who said Sir Roundell had brought
the Court of Chancery into the House, and had argued the question as if before a tribunal which interpreted the law, and not
before one which made it.

The debate was marked by a brilliant speech by Mr. Lowe, a
mild but well-argued protest against the Bill by Mr. Spencer
Walpole, and a slashing speech by Mr. Gathorne Hardy, the
beau sabreur of the Opposition benches. Mr. Gladstone having
replied, the division was taken, and there appeared a majority of

118 against the amendment, and in favour of the second reading. The numbers were 368 against 250. The number of members who voted, including the four tellers, was 622, and 14 paired. After so fierce a strife repose was welcome, and the House adjourned for the Easter holidays.

On the 15th of April, the date fixed for the motion to go into Committee, Mr. Newdegate, the unflinching Tory member for North Warwickshire, moved that the House go into Committee that day six months, but was beaten by a majority of 126. The Speaker having left the chair, the battle of the clauses began. Many amendments were proposed, and lost by large majorities; and with very little alteration—none that essentially affected the principle of the measure—the Bill passed through Committee on the 7th of May, not, however, without a sharp fight on the Maynooth clause.

The motion for the third reading was made on the 31st of May, exactly three months after the introduction of the Bill into the House: and on that motion a "this day six months" amendment was moved by Mr. Hill, member for North-Eastern Lancashire, and seconded by Lord Elcho. The attempt to stop the further progress of the Bill in that House was, of course, hopeless, but it enabled some Conservatives to make a last protest. Mr. Disraeli, in a very solemn vein, declared that the passing of the Bill might lead to the entire repeal of the Union, and the tendency of it would be to provoke a civil war. The Papal power would instantly attempt to gain ascendency, and, he asked, was it likely the Protestants would submit without a struggle? Must England again attempt to conquer Ireland? Was there to be another battle of the Boyne? another siege of Derry? another treaty of Limerick? The policy of the Government, argued Mr. Disraeli, with portentous gravity, would inevitably lead to such results.

Mr. Gladstone replied with much energy, and apparently without any fear of the recurrence of such a catastrophe; and the division being taken, it appeared that 361 had voted for the third reading, and 247 against it, the majority being only four below that which carried the second reading, so compact and well looked after were the Ministerial forces.

What will the Lords do? was a question generally asked. On the 9th of June, five days before the Bill was introduced into the Upper House, Mr. Bright, who at no time found himself much restrained by the fetters of official life and ministerial reticence, addressed a letter to the secretary of a political meet-

ing about to be held at Birmingham, in which he alluded to the
House of Lords in very disrespectful fashion. "Instead," he
said, "of doing a little childish tinkering about life peerages, it
would be well if the Peers could bring themselves in a line with
the opinions and necessities of our day. In harmony with the
nation, they may go on for a long time; but by throwing themselves athwart its course they may meet with accidents not
pleasant for them to think of." Earl Granville found it rather
difficult in the House of Lords, when Earl Cairns called attention to this certainly "bumptious" epistle, to explain that his
too impetuous and outspoken colleague did not intend to make a
threat—used the words, indeed, only in "a Pickwickian sense."

The House of Lords presented an unusually animated scene
when Earl Granville, Secretary for the Colonies and Ministerial
leader in the Upper House, moved the second reading of the
Bill. He is always a clear and pleasant, but not an impassioned
or very energetic speaker, and failed to produce a very striking
effect. The debate warmed considerably as it proceeded. The
Earl of Harrowby moved that the Bill be taken into consideration
that day three months. The Earl of Carnarvon gave a modified
support to the Bill, thought it ought to go on to a second reading, but that considerable amendments were required. The
Archbishop of Dublin (Dr. Trench), spoke in pitiful strains of
"the unfortunate Church, threatened to be cut adrift without
warning." It was a grand field-day for some of the Bishops, and
two of the most eminent prelates greatly distinguished themselves by speeches on opposite sides. Dr. Connop Thirlwall,
the historian of Greece, Bishop of St. David's, supported the
measure in words which showed that, at seventy-two, his old fire
was not exhausted; and the eloquent, witty, incisive Irishman,
Dr. Magee, Bishop of Peterborough, a prelate of only a year's
standing, resisted the Bill in a speech which, to use a theatrical
phrase, brought down the house, bursts of applause frequently
coming even from the strangers' gallery. He defended the
establishment of the Church for the sake of the principle of
establishment. He did not consider the Bill as involving a
violation of the coronation oath, or of the Act of Union, or as an
attack on private property; but he warned the House not to be
moved by menaces. "The measure had," he asserted, "been
put forth as a magnanimous specimen of national repentance for
English injustice to Ireland, but the remarkable thing was that
the Bill placed the sackcloth on the Irish Church."

The excitement caused by his speech—excitement very unusual in that placid assembly—was succeeded by a deep hush when the Earl of Derby rose to speak. He looked ill, and spoke at first with some feebleness, but soon rose to the occasion, and there were more than occasional flashes of his wonted fire in his protest against the Bill. It was his last great effort. Four months afterwards the vigorous and eloquent Parliamentary orator, before whom, in his young days of debate, even O'Connell quailed, the Rupert who feared no odds, the proud, open-handed Lord of Knowsley, and representative of the great race of Stanley, closed his eyes on the world.

The Marquis of Salisbury, the Lord Cranborne of a year before, did not object to the second reading, trusting, like Earl Carnarvon, to introduce several amendments in committee. Old Earl Russell, nearly at the close of his seventy-seventh year of life, who had first entered Parliament fifty-six years before, spoke in support of the second reading of the Bill, while strongly objecting to some of its provisions ; and then, towards the close of the debate, came the lawyers, Lord Westbury, the Lord Chancellor, and Lord Cairns. The second reading was carried by 179 against 146, giving the Ministers a clear majority of 33. It was noticed that many Peers who usually ranked with the Conservatives voted in the majority. Both the English Archbishops abstained from voting, as did the Bishop of Oxford, who was present in the House. The Bishop of St. David's was the only prelate who gave his vote in favour of the measure. Thirteen bishops voted against the second reading. The third reading took place on the 12th of July. Some of the amendments passed in Committee were accepted by the House of Commons, but others were rejected, and not insisted on by the Lords. The Royal assent was given on the 26th of July, and the first great measure of Mr. Gladstone's first administration was an accomplished fact.

During the progress of the measure through Parliament, Mr. Gladstone was exposed to unmeasured abuse from the ultra-Protestants of the country and the Orangemen of Ireland. There was a great demonstration at Exeter Hall, at which Mr. Charley (afterwards Common Serjeant of the City of London) said thousands of Protestants considered Mr. Gladstone " a traitor to his Queen, his country, and his God," and that " he ought to be excluded from power for having dared to put his hand on the ark of God." Another speaker, a clergyman, described Ministers as "a Cabinet of brigands." At an Orange demonstration at Tannimore Hall, Tyrone, the Chairman said they (the Orangemen) were ready to take their rifles and march to the Boyne ; and another speaker described the pleasure he should experience in seeing "Gladstone and his co-conspirators hanging as high as Haman." A third speaker prophetically intimated that, if the Bill passed, "they would give the Union an Irish wake and a Protestant burial."

While the Bill was under discussion in the House of Lords, Mr. Gladstone attended a banquet given by the Lord Mayor, and, replying to the toast, "Her Majesty's Ministers," said they had pledged themselves that the surplus of Church property should be applied for the benefit of the Irish people, and not for the support of a Church or a clergy. That was a covenant the terms of which were tendered "when we sat in the exile of opposition, and we shall not forget it now that we are installed in the seat of power."

Although Mr. Gladstone did not personally prepare the Budget of the year, that task having devolved on Mr. Lowe, it was a worthy pendant to the former series of Gladstonian financial statements. The estimates of revenue and expenditure for the coming year showed a surplus of £3,382,000, and a remission of taxation to the amount of more than £3,000,000 was arranged.

Parliament was prorogued by commission on the 11th of August. The paragraph in the Speech referring to the Irish Church Act expressed a hope that this "important measure may hereafter be remembered as a conclusive proof of the paramount anxiety of Parliament to pay reasonable regard, in legislating for each of the three kingdoms, to the special circumstances by which it may be distinguished, and to deal on principles of impartial justice with all interests and all portions of the nation."

The Royal Speech at the opening of the Session of 1870, on the 8th of April, promised more legislation for Ireland, and "a measure which would be calculated to bring about improved relations between the several classes concerned in Irish agriculture, which collectively constitute the bulk of the Irish people." On the 15th Mr. Gladstone asked for leave to bring in the Land Bill for Ireland, and spoke for three hours. At the close of his speech, he said, with that peculiar turn of thought—perhaps, it might be said, of over-subtle speculation—which so frequently influences his reasoning :

"The measure had reference to evils which have been long at work ; their roots strike far back into bygone centuries : *and it is against the ordinance of Providence, as it is against the interest of man, that immediate reparation should in such cases be possible ;* for one of the main restraints of misdoing would be remedied if the consequences of misdoing could in a moment receive a remedy. For such reparation and such effects it is that we look from this Bill; and we reckon on them not less surely and not less confidently because we know they must be gradual and slow, and because we are likewise aware that if it be poisoned by the malignant agency of angry and bitter passions, it cannot do its proper work. In order that there may be a hope of its entire success, it must be passed—not as a triumph of party over party, or class over class; not as the lifting up of an ensign to record the downfall of that which has once been great and powerful—but as a common work of common love and goodwill to the common good of our common country."

The motion for leave to bring in the Bill (which bore the names of Mr. Gladstone, Mr. Chichester Fortescue, and Mr. Bright) was agreed to, and it was read the first time. The most important provisions, so far as tenants were concerned, were that the Ulster tenant-right custom, and similar customs in other parts of Ireland, received a legal status; new rights were conferred with reference to compensation for disturbance by the acts of landlords; compensations were given for improvements, and the respective liabilities of landlord and tenant were defined. One leading object of the Act was to facilitate the creation of a tenant proprietary. A landlord would be enabled, subject to the approval of the Landed Estates Court, to agree with the tenant for the purchase by the latter of his holding, and Government was to be empowered to advance to the tenant a sum not exceeding two-thirds of the purchase money, repayable, with interest, by instalments. The Landed Estates Court was directed, on the ordinary sale of estates under the Court, to afford, by the formation of lots, reasonable facilities for tenants to purchase their holdings.

The Bill, as has been remarked, was "a compromise, a step in advance, which committed the English Parliament and Government to two principles: the principle of tenant-right, and the expediency of a tenant proprietary."

The second reading was moved on the 7th of March, and the debate lasted four nights. Dr. Ball, member for Dublin University, made a powerful speech—indeed, the most powerful speech on his side of the House that the discussion produced; Sir Roundell Palmer described the Bill as "a humiliating necessity;" and Mr. Disraeli, on the fourth night of debate, delivered himself in a diffuse and somewhat random manner. He disposed of the Ulster custom by saying no such thing existed—the custom varied, and had no prescription of antiquity; the proposed tribunal would be ineffectual, and advances of public money would do more harm than good. "Do not," he said, "let us vote upon the subject as if we had received a threatening letter, as if we expected to meet Rory of the Hills when we go into the lobby."

Mr. Gladstone's concluding speech was marked by a brilliant peroration :—

"For a hundred years Ireland has been engaged in almost a continuous conflict with the governing power—I will not say of the nation, but with the governing power of this island. She has engaged in the conflict with all the disadvantages of a limited population, of inferior resources, of backward political development, and yet she has been uniformly successful. Strength and weakness have grappled together in almost incessant conflict, and on every occasion, in a succession of falls, strength has been laid prostrate on the ground, and weakness has waved the banner of victory over it . . . The career of Ireland has ever been onward, her cry has ever been Excelsior ! because she has had justice for her cause, and has been sustained in it by that which is the highest earthly organ of justice, the favouring opinion of the civilized and Christian world . . . We have been invoked to-night in solemn terms, from both sides of the House, to be just and fear not. It is our desire to be just, but, to be just, we must be just to all. The oppression of a majority is detestable and odious—the oppression of a minority is only by one degree less detestable and less odious. The face of justice is like the face of the god Janus—it is like the face of those lions, the work of Landseer, which keep watch and ward around the record of our country's greatness. She presents one tranquil and majestic countenance towards every point of the compass and every quarter of the globe. That rare, that noble, that imperial virtue has this above all other qualities, that she is no respecter of persons, and she will not take advantage of a favourable moment to oppress the wealthy for the sake of flattering the poor, any more than she will condescend to oppress the poor for the sake of pandering to the luxuries of the rich."

Mr. Disraeli did not attempt to oppose the second reading ; on the contrary, he led his party to vote for it, reserving power to deal with it in committee. When the division took place, there appeared for the second reading, 442 ; against it, only 11, mostly Irish members, but aided by the presence of that stout, uncompromising old Tory, Mr. Henley.

Before the time came for going into committee, Ireland was in such a disturbed condition—armed bands visiting farmers in county Mayo, compelling them to take oaths to break up the pasture lands, and committing other outrages—that another and very stringent Peace Preservation Bill was hurried through both Houses, prohibiting the possession of arms, and giving power to suppress newspapers if found necessary, and to trace out the authors of threatening letters.

Notice had been given of about three hundred amendments to be proposed in the committee on the Irish Land Bill, but many were withdrawn or otherwise disposed of. The most important amendment, over which a sharp fight took place, was

proposed by Mr. Disraeli. The third clause of the Bill pro
vided for compensation for eviction, and it was known that
Ministers intended to propose an alteration in that clause in committee, establishing the right of an evicted tenant to compensation
for the loss which the Court shall find to have been sustained by
him in quitting his holding. Mr. Disraeli contended that this
alteration would change the entire character of the Bill as first
introduced, and which he and his friends had been willing to
support. His amendment proposed to limit the compensation to
cases in which it was claimed for unexhausted improvements, or
on account of interruption in the course of husbandry. This
amendment was lost by a majority of 76; and the Government
alteration of the clause was adopted by a majority of 111. A
writer of the time, referring to the division on Mr. Disraeli's
amendment, said, " This vote, in effect, rescinded the policy of
two hundred years, and acknowledged generally that, in the great
question in dispute between England and Ireland, the tenure of
Irish land, Ireland had been right and England wrong."

The Bill was read a third time and passed in the Commons,
without having sustained any other material alteration, on the
30th of May. In the Lords some amendments were made in
committee, but, on going back to the Commons, a spirit of concession prevailed, and the Bill received the Royal assent on the
1st of August.

Two sessions had produced two great measures for Ireland,
but Mr. Gladstone was already meditating another. He had disestablished the Church and established (as he thought—it proved
too hopefully) a peasant proprietary; the next difficulty to be
grappled with was connected with the Irish Universities, almost
a necessary complement to the ecclesiastical reform.

The next most important achievement of the Session of 1870
was the passing of the Elementary Education Act. Mr. Forster
had charge of the Bill, and gallantly he fought clause by clause.
Churchmen, Dissenters, Secularists, all had their hobbies to ride.
Some insisted that the Bible should be read to the children,
others that it should not. Churchmen feared that the character
of her special schools would be altered; Dissenters objected to
Churchmen teaching their children; Secularists wished to exclude
all kinds of religious teaching, and against them were arrayed
the whole force of Church and Dissent. Mr. Gladstone did not
take a very active part in the excited debate, but made one
memorable unpremeditated speech. Mr. Miall, member for
Bradford, a man of great mark among the Nonconformists,

attacked Ministers for not having, as he asserted, sufficiently deferred to the views of Dissenters. Speaking in a style which a
sensitive man might easily mistake for an exhibition of arrogant
assumption, Mr. Miall said the Dissenters had mainly contributed at the last election to place the Administration in power—
" they were the heart, and, he might say, the hand of the Liberal
cause in this country," and they thought they were entitled to be
consulted, in some respects, as to the great principles and drift of
legislation which grated harshly on their sympathies; but they
had been made to pass through the Valley of Humiliation.
There was scarcely a Dissenting congregation in the country that
had not pronounced condemnation of the Bill. The Dissenting
community were " elbowed out " of their rights; and almost all
the measures in which they were interested had been cast out
with something like contumely; but, " once bit, twice shy."

Directly Mr. Miall sat down Mr. Gladstone sprang to his feet.
He had not intended to speak at that stage of the debate; but
he was evidently moved to the quick, and with animated gestures
and, even for him, amazing fluency, proceeded to administer a
rebuke which perhaps even Mr. Miall felt to be severe, and which
many present thought to be well deserved—

"'The speech of my honourable friend amounts to a reproach on the
Government for not having fulfilled the expectations under which they were
brought into power. To this I say fearlessly, in the face of my honourable
friend and of those who have made use of similar language, that if, in 1868,
we made bold professions to the country—professions involving, as we well
knew then, and as we know now, the greatest responsibility—we have laboured
to the utmost to fulfil them, and the whole of our energies and the whole of
our influence have, in no spirit of common calculation, been devoted to the
purpose of redeeming those pledges. I am not here, therefore, to be told,
with nice analysis, of what elements was made up that large degree of national
support to which we owe the position we hold. I am not prepared to admit
that my honourable friend, great as is the weight of his character and the
respect to which he is justly entitled, speaks in this matter the sentiments of
all those with whom he is connected by religious opinions, because there are
others in this House, who have sat on these benches for many years and who
have earned the respect of all who know them, who have not participated in
the severe judgment passed upon us by my honourable friend. My honourable friend thinks it worthy of him to resort to a proverb, and to say that the
time has come when he is entitled to use the significant language, ' once bit,
twice shy.' But if my honourable friend has been bitten, by whom is it? If
he has been bitten it is only in consequence of expectations which he has himself chosen to entertain, and which were not justified by the facts. We have
been thankful to have the independent and honourable support of my honourable friend, but that support ceases to be of value when accompanied by reproaches such as these. I hope my honourable friend will not continue that
support to the Government one moment longer than he thinks it consistent
with his sense of duty and right. For God's sake, Sir, let him withdraw it the

moment he thinks it better for the cause that he has at heart that he should do so.   So long as my honourable friend thinks fit to give us his support, we will co-operate with him for every purpose we have in common ; but when we think he looks too much to the section of the community which he adorns, and too little to the interests of the people at large, we must then recollect that we are the Government of the Queen, and that those who have assumed the high responsibility of administering the affairs of this Empire must endeavour to forget the parts in the whole, and must, in the great measures they introduce to the House, propose to themselves no meaner or narrower object—no other object than the welfare of the Empire at large."

The clause of the Bill which provided for the election of members of School Boards by ballot, encountered considerable opposition, but was at length agreed to by the Commons ; but when the Bill reached the Lords, the Duke of Richmond moved an amendment, afterwards accepted by the other House, which limited the operation of the clause to the metropolitan district.

The Irish Land Act and the Elementary Education Act were considerable achievements for one session ; and the fact, in addition, that the Chancellor of the Exchequer (Mr. Lowe) was able to announce an estimated surplus of £4,357,000; and the consequent reduction of taxation to that amount, added to the general satisfaction.   It is just worth noting that halfpenny postage-cards were instituted, because Mr. Gladstone is popularly credited with a peculiar liking for these cheap and convenient means of transmission.

Earl Clarendon, the Foreign Secretary, died on the 27th of June, and Earl Granville succeeded to the vacant office.   As customary, he consulted the officials of the Foreign Office as to the state of affairs, and was informed by the Permanent Under-Secretary of State, Mr. Hammond, an official of the old school, industrious, precise, courteous, but very "official" and not particularly far-seeing, that the world had never been so profoundly at peace.   If the late Earl of Clarendon had seen elements of disturbance very near the surface, he had kept his opinions to himself, and death had erased whatever might have been written on the tablets of his mind.

In the first week of July angry speeches were made in the French Chamber by the Duc de Grammont, Minister for Foreign Affairs, respecting the support given by the Prussian Government to the proposal that Prince Leopold of Hohenzollern-Sigmaringen should be a candidate for the throne of Spain.   A few days sufficed for the embers of a quarrel to break out into a great flame.   France demanded guarantees from Prussia, and Prussia, irritated, refused to give them.   King William snubbed the French Ambassador, M. Benedetti, and on the 15th

S

of July, France proclaimed war against Prussia. In about a fortnight after Earl Granville had been assured that Europe, indeed the world generally, was enjoying peace, with no probability of being alarmed by the blast of war, the most terrible contest of modern times began, not to be concluded till the French empire had been destroyed, the French Emperor made a prisoner, and Paris had been so terribly besieged. Belgium was imperilled, and we were bound by treaty to support Belgium. Mr. Gladstone was eagerly questioned as to the course England would take, and at first his replies amounted to little more than vague professions of neutrality. In fact, the English Ministers, like the world generally, were taken by surprise, but soon recovered themselves, and on the 9th of August a treaty with Prussia, and two days afterwards with France, was arranged, by which the security of Belgium was assured.

The Session of 1871 was opened on the 9th of February, by the Queen in person. The Royal Speech announced a Bill for the better regulation of the Army and auxiliary forces, and another for the adoption of the Ballot in Parliamentary election ; and recommended that attention should be directed to the subject of primary education in Scotland.

The introduction and management of the Ballot Bill was entrusted to the indefatigable Mr. Forster, who had fought so well in the fierce educational battle; but it was cruelly mangled in the Commons, and the Lords rejected it. Mr. Cardwell, Secretary of State for War, by virtue of his office took charge of the Army Regulation Bill, and as that measure included a provision for the abolition of the purchase of commissions, a tremendous storm arose. The House of Commons passed the Bill by 289 to 231, on the 4th of July, and on the 13th of that month it was introduced into the Lords, receiving the support of the Duke of Cambridge. But the Lords "would have none of it ; " and at the close of an unusually long sitting (protracted until 2 o'clock in the morning of the 18th of July) the motion for the second reading was lost by a majority of 25.

Mr. Gladstone had set his heart upon carrying the measure, and resolved on taking a very bold course. He advised the Queen to cancel the Royal warrant authorising the purchase of commissions, and issue a fresh one, which would make purchase illegal. His peremptory mode of setting aside the verdict of the House of Lords produced no little excitement. It was described by the Tory peers as a *coup d'état*, a flagrant outrage offered to the House of Lords. *Blackwood* declared that Mr. Gladstone deserved to be impeached, and that he had "struck such a blow at Parliamentary government as it has not received since the days of Strafford and Laud. Nor is this all: the blow is struck by the hand of the Queen. The Queen's signature is attached to the deed or warrant which deliberately reverses a decision of the House of Lords; and the Queen can do no wrong. But the Minister who advised the Queen is responsible." The discussion of the subject in both Houses turned on nice distinctions between the Royal prerogative, or the special power of the Sovereign in right of pre-eminence over all persons and laws, and the discretion conferred on the Crown by statutory enactment. Mr. Disraeli said Ministers had fallen back on prerogative, and put it in conflict with Parliament; and Mr. Gladstone replied, "We have had no recourse to prerogative, and we have had no conflict with Parliament." The Earl of Granville, in the House of Lords, said Ministers had advised her Majesty "not to make any use of her Royal prerogative, because there is no question of that in the matter, but in the exercise of that discretion which is conferred on the Crown by statutory enactment, to take the only means which is possible, and put an end to the illegal practice." The Opposition flatly denied that any statutory power of the kind mentioned existed, and charged Ministers with having obtained the Royal signature by false representations.

A vote of censure on the Administration was carried in the House of Lords by a majority of 80, on the 24th of July, but the Ministers bore it with equanimity, strong in the support of the Commons; and the Regulation of the Forces Act, arranging the compensation to be given for the loss of the price of commission, passed both Houses, though not without some opposition. The Royal warrant was a fact which even the Lords were compelled to accept; but Lord Cairns, at the close of an eloquent speech, summed up the anger of the Peers on his side of the House. "Read your Bill a second time, but take with it the mark of censure and condemnation of the House—censure and condemnation which I am persuaded will be approved by the deliberate opinion of the country, and confirmed by the verdict of history—censure and condemnation, that, at a crisis which demanded the wisdom and the forbearance of statesmen, you, with the petulance and fickleness of children, in order to obtain an apparent and casual triumph at the last moment, pre-eminently violated and wantonly strained the constitution of your country."

This was altogether a busy session. Soon after it opened, the Westmeath Commission was appointed, in consequence of

the outrages in that part of Ireland, resulting in the passing of a
very stringent measure, the Protection of Life and Property
Act, popularly known as the Westmeath Act.   It was the year,
too, of the Match Duty Budget, which damaged the reputation of
Mr. Lowe as Chancellor of the Exchequer.   His estimates for
the year (chiefly owing to the effect on trade of the great
war raging on the continent) showed a deficiency of £2,713,000,
to be supplied by the increase of taxation.   Mr. Lowe hit upon
the brilliant idea of stamping match-boxes, the result being a
universal outcry, and a procession of match-makers from Bethnal
Green and Shoreditch and Westminster, to protest against a proposition which would lessen the demand for matches, deprive them
of their wretchedly-paid occupation, and drive them over the
narrow line which separated abject poverty from actual starvation.
Mr. Gladstone came to the rescue, modified the obnoxious
Budget, which was ultimately withdrawn altogether, and put
twopence on the income-tax, by way of getting out of the
difficulty.

There was a strong party who held that the disestablishment
of the English Church was a necessary corollary of disestablishment in Ireland.   But Mr. Gladstone by no means accepted that
view.   Mr. Miall brought the matter to an issue on the 9th of
March, by moving " That it is expedient, at the earliest practicable
period, to apply the policy introduced by the disestablishment
of the Irish Church by the Act of 1869 to the other Churches
established by law in the United Kingdom."   Just as Mr. Miall
was on the point of rising, some amusement was created by the
presentation, by Mr. Gathorne Hardy, of a petition from Bradford (represented by Mr. Miall) against the reception of the
resolution, with 24,700 signatures, genuine or otherwise — " very
much otherwise," the Committee on Petitions afterwards seemed
to think. The debate was vigorously conducted — few subjects could
be found better adapted to promote an exciting debate in the
House of Commons.   Sir Roundell Palmer, a devoted son of the
Church, editor of " Hymns Ancient and Modern," eloquently
opposed the motion ; Mr. Richard, a Nonconformist of renown,
formerly a Congregational Minister, eloquently defended it.   Each
side had able champions.   Mr. Disraeli, as leader of the Opposition, spoke against the motion, " in the interest of civil and religious liberty, more for the sake of the State than of the Church,
more for the sake of society than of the congregation, because I
believe, in resisting that policy, we are maintaining the best
interests of all, of civilisation and of pure religion."   Mr. Glad-

stone spoke with moderation and dignity in opposition to the
resolution, explaining that the positions and histories of the two
Churches were unlike ; and the division resulted in the resolution
being lost by a majority of 285—the numbers being 374 against
89.

When the end of the session came—Parliament was prorogued
on the 21st of August—the Prime Minister could congratulate
himself on some successes ; but there was a reverse to the medal.
He had vanquished the Lords on the University Tests Bill and
the Abolition of Purchase in the Army, but they had thrown out
the Ballot Bill, and had passed a vote of censure on the Ministry,
which had not been met by a vote of confidence in the Commons.
Russia had been permitted to violate the Black Sea clause of the
Treaty of Paris ; the Budget had been a failure, and Mr. Gladstone had offended many of his working-class supporters by
opposing the scheme for securing Epping Forest as an open space
for the inhabitants of the metropolis.   Some evidence of his declining popularity appeared when, in the autumn, he addressed his
constituents from a platform erected on Blackheath.   At least
20,000 people assembled, and when the Prime Minister came forward a considerable amount of hissing mingled with the cheers.
Nothing daunted, he made a long speech, covering the whole
field of political discussion, and before he had concluded, his
earnestness and eloquence had reinstated him in the estimation
of his hearers as " The People's William," the most popular of
statesmen, the most effective of orators.

There were other extra-Parliamentary utterances.   At Aberdeen,
on the 26th of September, speaking on the occasion of receiving
the freedom of the city, he referred to the Irish demand for Home
Rule.   He had been accused of trifling with the agitation, and
now he spoke out.   " What," he asked, " are the inequalities of
England and Ireland ?   I declare that I know none, except that
there are certain taxes still remaining which are levied over
Englishmen and Scotchmen, and which are not levied over Irishmen ; and likewise that there are certain purposes for which public
money is freely and largely given in Ireland, and for which it is
not given in England and Scotland."   There was a higher law
than the law of conciliation, good as that might be, and that was
the law of duty.

There was a scare that autumn about our national defences,
especially the condition of the army.   The wonderful achievements of the Germans, who had " made hay " of the gallant
French *corps d'armée*, the perfection of her military system, had

invited unpleasant comparisons.   What could we do to resist an
invading army, led by a Red or Black Prince and manœuvred by
a Moltke?   Our army, brave as were the men individually, was
but a handful compared to the legions our neighbours could hurl
against us.   Colonel Chesney, a clever writer and cap'tal soldier,
added no little to the panic by describing, in *Blackwood's Magazine*, an imaginary Battle of Dorking, in which he showed how
futile would be any attempt on our part to prevent the march of
an invading army on London, supposing it had effected a landing
on the south coast.   "After the first stand in line," wrote the
fictitious volunteer, supposed to be relating the story of the
defeat, "and when once they had got us on the march, the
enemy laughed at us.   Our handful of regular troops was sacrificed almost to a man in a vain conflict with numbers ; our volunteers and militia, with officers who did not know their work,
without ammunition or equipment, or staff to superintend, starving in the midst of plenty, we had soon become a helpless
mob, fighting desperately here and there, but with whom, as a
manœuvring army, the disciplined invaders did just what they
pleased.   Happy those whose bones whitened the fields of Surrey ;
they at least were spared the disgrace we lived to endure."

In a speech at Whitby, after the recess, Mr. Gladstone took
occasion to utter a warning against the spread of the spirit of
"alarmism."   "The power of this country," he said, "is not declining.   It is increasing; increasing in itself, and, I believe,
increasing as compared with the power of the other nations of
Europe.   It is only our pride, it is only our passions, it is only
our own follies, which can ever constitute a real danger to us."

Obscure writers and speakers had not unfrequently hinted that
Mr. Gladstone was a Roman Catholic at heart, if not, indeed, a
Jesuit in disguise, but perhaps the only person of the grade of a
member of Parliament who would have ventured openly to give
publicity to such a suspicion was good, one-idead, simple-minded
Mr. Whalley, the member for Peterborough, that grown-up Alice
in the Wonderland of politics.   In all innocence of heart and
sincerity he addressed a letter of inquiry to Mr. Gladstone at
Hawarden, stating that it would be very satisfactory if the Premier
would kindly say whether he really was a Roman Catholic who
declined to avow his faith for reasons of convenience.   Mr. Gladstone replied politely but cuttingly, "I am entirely convinced
that, while the question you have put to me is in truth an insulting one, you have put it only from having failed to notice its true
character."

The great achievement of the session of 1872 was the passing of the Ballot Act. The year before the Lords had thrown out the Bill, and once more Mr. Gladstone had to express his determination that he would not consider the decision of the Upper House as final on any important question. If a measure approved by the House of Commons was rejected by the House of Lords, he determined it should be reintroduced, and so their verdict directly challenged. Walter Scott's literary motto, " If it is nae weel bobbit, we'll bobbit agen," was practically adopted. One of the first Ministerial acts of the session was the revival of the Ballot Bill; and the second reading passed the House of Commons, on the 15th of February, by 109 to 51, and the third reading by 271 to 216. The whirligig of time does, indeed, bring about strange changes. Not many years before, Mr. Grote was looked upon by steady-going politicians, both Tory and Whig, as little better than a revolutionist, and, after him, Mr. H. Berkeley as a political crotcheteer, because they made annual motions in favour of vote by ballot; but the House of Commons in 1871 and 1872 adopted the principle by large majorities, and for several years past Englishmen have recorded their votes on slips of paper dropped into a ballot-box, and we are no more the worse for it than we are for the prophecies of Mother Shipton. The Lords seemed to think they must concede a little. When the House of Commons keep "pegging away," as Abraham Lincoln expressed himself, the Lords not unfrequently look at matters in a new light. As a body, they disliked Reform, but they gave in; they intensely disliked the disestablishment of the Irish Church, but they passed the Act; Protection was a pet, but Protection came to an end; Church-rates were dear to them, but they were given up; they nailed their colours to the mast in the Army Purchase contest, and there they remained nailed, but purchase was got rid of nevertheless; they vowed to maintain the paper duty, yet the paper duty disappeared, thanks to the daring and adroit management of Mr. Gladstone; and now, for the second time, the ugly phantom of secret voting intruded itself into the gilded chamber, and the Lords arrived at the prudent conclusion that they had better not attempt to turn it out again, but do their best to mutilate and make it as little harmful as possible. The second reading was passed; but, in committee, an amendment, making secret voting optional instead of imperative, was carried by 162 to 91. The amendment would have taken the life out of the measure; for, in boroughs where family or territorial interest is paramount, an elector asking to record his vote secretly would be a marked man, because it would be understood that he intended to vote against the favoured candidate. The third reading was passed on the 25th June, and the Bill was sent back to the Commons, who rejected the amendment. The Lords accepted the decision of the " other place," and, the Royal assent being given on the 13th of July, Vote by Ballot, which had been advocated by Andrew Marvell a hundred and eighty years before, which had been approved by the Commons, but rejected by the Lords, in 1710, which had figured in the first draught of the great Reform Bill of 1832, and the discussion of which had troubled the Parliamentary waters for about forty years, was added to the achievements of the Gladstone Administration.

An appointment made by Mr. Gladstone at this time was seriously animadverted on. Sir Robert Collier, Attorney General, was selected for the office of one of the Judges of the Judicial Committee of the Privy Council. As a preliminary qualification, he was, in November, 1871, appointed a Judge of the Court of Common Pleas, and, a few days afterwards, transferred to the Judicial Committee. This procedure was strongly objected to by the members of the legal profession, and Lord Chief Justice Cockburn remonstrated on behalf of the Bench and the Bar, describing the appointment as a subterfuge and evasion of the Act regulating the appointment. When Parliament met, the subject provoked warm discussion, and votes of censure on the Ministry were proposed in both Houses, but lost by a majority of 2 in the Lords, and of 27 in the Commons.

One of the most serious imputations made upon the Ministry in the course of the year was that they had too tamely submitted to the demands of the United States in the matter of the *Alabama* damages. In May, 1862, a powerful steam vessel, constructed by Messrs. Laing, at Birkenhead, had been launched. There was good reason to believe that she was intended for the service of the Confederate States of America, and on the 28th of July the British Government telegraphed to detain her in the Mersey. The message was a day too late; the *Alabama* had started on its voyage, and soon afterwards became notorious under the command of the famous Confederate sailor, Captain Semmes, for attacks on the mercantile navy of the United States. She was, in June, 1864, attacked and destroyed by the Federal ironclad, *Kerseage* in the British Channel. The Government of the United States claimed reparation from the British Government for the losses sustained in consequence of the depredations committed by the *Alabama*, on the ground that she was built in an English dockyard, and that the Government ought to have interfered. It is not necessary to relate in detail the history of the correspondence between the Governments, the Joint Commission at Washington, the Arbitration Tribunal at Geneva, and the final payment of about £3.330,000 (about one third of the amount claimed, and very probably considerably more than should have been paid) as damages to the United States.

The more violent opponents of the Ministry made the most of the transaction; and even now, when the subject is referred to in the Press or on the platform, charges of "cowardice," "trickery," "disgracing the British flag," if not of acting disrespectfully to the British lion, are freely made. The "peace at any price" party, we are told, submitted abjectly to be kicked, and so disgraced England. Other writers and speakers, however, have argued, with greater reason, that by submitting the matter to arbitration, and abiding by the decision of the chosen tribunal, instead of provoking a conflict which might have been productive of almost inconceivable bloodshed and misery, the Ministry acted wisely and patriotically. One of the greatest blessings possible to the world would be a great cosmopolitan tribunal for the settlement of quarrels between nations far too ready to blow one another's brains out, even if the big guns were melted down to supply metal for statues of Peace and Justice and medals to commemorate the fact that the world is coming to its senses.

The damages awarded at Geneva may have been excessive; but the tribunal was one chosen by all parties to the dispute, and by submitting to its adjudication the British Government set a good example, and marked an epoch in civilization. A similar course, similarly reviled, was adopted when the San Juan dispute, involving the question of the exact boundary between the English possessions on the north-west coast of America, and those of the United States, was submitted to the arbitration of the Emperor of Germany, and his decision was accepted. There were Englishmen enough ready to fight about that, but the Ministry would not give them the chance.

On the 21st of December Mr. Gladstone addressed the students of Liverpool College, and strongly condemned the writings of Strauss and the German Rationalists, advising his hearers not to adopt too readily the prevalent notion that this age is vastly superior to all that have gone before it.

The Session of 1873 was opened on the 6th of February, and the Royal Speech announced the introduction of a Bill dealing with the subject of University Education in Ireland. This was to complete the triad of measures by which Mr. Gladstone hoped to " satisfy the unsatisfiable," and put Ireland at peace. Certainly he was not so popular outside the House as he had been. The British public is rather fickle in its hero worship, and in the course of a few years is rather disposed to listen to the Outs who want to be the Ins, and who lose no opportunity of insinuating that " Codlin's your friend, not Short." In the House, too, the bye-elections had transferred fourteen seats to the Conservatives.

A week after the meeting of Parliament Mr. Gladstone introduced the Irish University Bill, by which he proposed to abolish the exclusive connection of the University of Dublin with Trinity College, and transfer the Theological Faculty to that college, as the representative body of the Disestablished Irish Church. The University of Dublin, with the Queen's Colleges (" the godless colleges" as they were termed by ardent sectarians), were to be converted into a university, which was to be a teaching as well as an examining body, though, in deference to the feelings of various religious denominations, theology, modern history, and moral and metaphysical philosophy, were not to be included in the curriculum. The University funds were to be furnished in different proportions by Trinity College and the Consolidated Fund.

The Bill pleased very few; and on the motion for the second reading, after a debate of four nights' duration, it was, on the 11th of March, rejected by a majority of 3, the numbers being 287 against 284. Thirty-six Irish members voted in the majority.

This defeat on a question which Mr. Gladstone had made a vital point of policy left him no other course open but to tender his resignation of office; and, on the 13th, Earl Granville in the Upper House, and Mr. Gladstone in the Commons, announced that the Minstry only held office until the appointment of their successors.

Mr. Gladstone afterwards described the defeat as having been effected, " if not by a combined, yet by a concurrent effort of the leader of the Opposition and of the Roman Catholic prelacy of Ireland."

In accordance with constitutional precedent, the Queen sent for Mr. Disraeli, the leader of the Opposition. He declined to undertake the task of forming an Administration with the existing House of Commons; for, although the Ministry had suffered a defeat on one particular question, there was still a majority which might be generally relied on, and there appeared to be no hope that if the country were appealed to a Conservative majority would be obtained.

The Gladstone Ministry consequently remained in power. In England the question of the reconstruction of the Irish University excited but moderate interest, and as Mr. Lowe's budget was, compared with that of the preceding year, very satisfactory, showing an estimated surplus of £3,146,000, permitting a reduction of the income tax and sugar duties, and some minor ameliorations, the British public, if not enthusiastic, were tolerably well satisfied, especially when it was officially stated that between April, 1869, and April, 1873, the four years of Liberal administration, the funded and unfunded debt had been reduced by more than £20,000,000. The *Alabama* compensation had been paid partly out of the ordinary revenue and partly by Exchequer bonds or bills.

On the 16th of May Mr. Miall, undismayed by former defeats, renewed his attack on the strong fortress of the Established Church by moving a resolution, "That the establishment by law of the Churches of England and Scotland involves a violation of religious equality, deprives these Churches of the right of self-government, imposes upon Parliament duties which it is not qualified to discharge, and is hurtful to the religious and political interests of the community, and therefore ought no longer to be maintained."

It is very noticeable that throughout the political career of Mr. Gladstone in his advance from Tory to, in some cases, almost extreme Liberal views, he has never faltered in his attachment to the Church of England, and his belief that the best interests of the country are—at present, at least—bound up with its retention as an establishment. He vigorously opposed the resolution, and made a most earnest defence of the Church :—

"It is all very well to complain of the Church, and I might, perhaps, complain of the particular course that some of its leading members may have taken upon this question or upon that, but the Church of England has not only been a part of the history of this country, but a part so vital, entering so profoundly into the entire life and action of the country, that the severing of the two would leave nothing behind but a bleeding and lacerated mass. Take the Church of England out of the history of England, and the history of England becomes a chaos, without order, without life, and without meaning. . . . . I once made a computation of what sort of allowance of property should be made to the Church of England if we were to disestablish her, upon the same rules of equity and liberality with respect to property which we adopted in the case of the Irish Church, and I made out that between life incomes, private endowments, and the value of fabrics and advowsons, something like £90,000,000 sterling would have to be given in the process of disestablishment to the ministers, members, and patrons of the Church of

England. That is a very staggering kind of arrangement to make in supplying the young lady with a fortune and turning her out in life to begin the world."

Mr. Miall's resolution was rejected by a majority of 295, ten more than the majority on the resolution in the previous session.

An incident of the session was the debate raised by Mr. Mowbray, the member for Oxford, on the appointment by Mr. Gladstone, of the Rev. Mr. Harvey to the rectory of Ewelme, Oxfordshire. That living had been attached to the Regius Professorship of Divinity of Oxford, until a few years previously, when an Act of Parliament separated the appointments, but provided that the incumbent should be a member of the Convocation of Oxford. Mr. Harvey was a Cambridge man; but, on being offered the appointment, applied to become a member of the Oxford Convocation. The necessary formalities were not completed when he became Rector of Ewelme, although the Royal Warrant appointing him described him as a member of the Oxford Convocation. Mr. Henley said Mr. Harvey could no more be made an Oxford man than a blackamoor could be washed white. The appointment was unquestionably a mistake on the part of Mr. Gladstone.

The prorogation of Parliament took place early in August, and Mr. Gladstone retired to Hawarden to read Homer, cut down trees, and indulge for a brief space in such other congenial pastimes as his considerate fellow-countrymen will permit an eminent man who nearly works himself to death in the public service to enjoy. An active politician, who has been for several months working by night as well as by day, in his office and in his place in Parliament, is expected to recreate his wearied mind and body by addressing public meetings, travelling at express speed from one end of the country to the other, lecturing at literary institutions, and presiding at all kinds of commemorations and festivals. He must always hold himself in readiness to take the chair at a dinner or a public gathering, or to unveil a statue, and on every opportunity to speak for two hours at a time. (It is noticeable, by the way, how successfully Mr. Gladstone has avoided the dinner ordeal, the occasions on which he has officiated as chairman being few indeed.) On the 19th of August Mr. Gladstone presided at the Welsh National Eisteddfod, at Mold, in Flintshire. The old Welsh bards were the national orators, and Mr. Gladstone, besides his supreme claims as an orator, was to some extent a bard too; that, coupled with the fact that his wife's remote ancestor was a Welsh prince, entitled

ST. DEINIOL'S CHURCH AND THE LIBRARY, HAWARDEN.

MRS. GLADSTONE'S HOME FOR BOYS AT HAWARDEN.

him to the privilege of listening to poetical effusions in a language which, with all his accomplishments, he has admitted he does not understand.

In the course of the autumn Ministerial rearrangements were announced. Mr. Bruce was raised to the Peerage, Mr. Lowe taking his place at the Home Office, and Mr. Gladstone adding the office of Chancellor of the Exchequer to the Premiership. Mr. Ayrton, the Chief Commissioner of Works, a very able man, but who contrived to be unpopular, and so damaged the Administration, was removed from office.

The session of 1874 was to have begun on the 5th of February, but the daily papers of the 24th of January published a manifesto from Mr. Gladstone, in the form of a letter to his Greenwich constituents, informing them that her Majesty had been advised to dissolve Parliament. The announcement caused some surprise, but the Liberal majority had greatly dwindled, and Mr. Gladstone was unwilling to enter on a new session with weakened resources. The Prime Minister's letter was lengthy. He alluded to the efforts he had made to carry the three great Irish measures, and the failure of his attempt to place the Irish University on a new footing, and he expressed a hope that a new appeal to the constituencies would result in such a strengthening of his hands that another attempt to complete his Irish programme would be more successful than the last. The first two measures had been carried by large majorities—the House of Lords not especially favouring them, but submitting to the irresistible force of public opinion. The third measure had met with disfavour on the part of the Roman Catholic priesthood, in spite of the concessions made to their Church; and it was defeated, to use Mr. Gladstone's own words, "if not by a combined, yet by a concurrent effort of the leader of the Opposition and of the Roman Catholic prelacy of Ireland." The financial position of the country, due in no small degree to his administration, would, he believed, constitute an irresistible claim to renewed confidence; and he so far anticipated the ordinary Budget announcement as to affirm that he believed it would be possible, with the surplus at his command, to abolish the income-tax.

The result of the general election was to give the Conservatives a majority of 60. It may be observed that this was the first general election in which vote by ballot was adopted. On the 17th of February Mr. Gladstone and his colleagues resigned office, and Mr. Disraeli, being now supported by a majority, undertook the responsibility he had declined a few months before.

CHAPTER XXIV.

RESIGNATION OF THE LIBERAL LEADERSHIP.—INCESSANT

LITERARY ACTIVITY.

PARLIAMENT met on the 5th of March, and Mr. Brand, who for
many years had been the Liberal Whip, was elected Speaker.
The business of the session began on the 9th, and the debate on
the address was marked by rather an unfortunate occurrence.
Sir William Stirling-Maxwell, member for Perthshire, but better
known in connection with literature and art than with politics, on
moving the address, commented with some asperity on the
" elaborate surprise of the dissolution," and said : " It is obvious
that the right honourable gentleman, the late Prime Minister, by
the dissolution and by his manifesto, was determined to astonish
the country. The country, not to be outdone, seemed also bent
on astonishing the right honourable gentleman."   Mr. Gladstone,
in reply, stated that the bye-elections having gone against the
Government, their position was " very considerably worsted " in
the month of January, and that he had felt it right to appeal to
the country before the meeting of Parliament.

Mr. Disraeli mildly but firmly rebuked his too zealous follower,
who, he said, in deference to his previous Parliamentary experience, had not been advised as to the tone of his speech, and who
" had made some general observations without consultation with
anybody." The new Premier, moreover, took occasion to pay a
very high compliment to his distinguished opponent.   " The
Liberal members," he said, " even if they might think that the
action of their leader had been precipitate, refrained from com-
plaint, and," he continued, " if I had been a follower of a Parliamentary chief as eminent as the right honourable gentleman, even
if I had thought he had erred, I should have been disposed rather
to exhibit sympathy than to offer criticism.   I should remember
the great victories which he had fought and won ; I should remember his illustrious career, its continuous success and splendour, not its accidental or even disastrous mistakes."

Early in the session Mr. Gladstone had expressed his desire to
resign, at no distant time, the position of leader of the Liberal
party.   He felt the need of rest, and could not undertake to give
more than occasional attendance in the House during the session.

His friends, however, were not disposed to select another leader, and the proposed resignation was deferred. There was, in the aspect of political affairs, no demand for a very vigorous opposition, and Mr. Gladstone remained nominally the head of the party in the Commons, although not taking a very active part in the debates.

The large surplus left by the late Government had made the preparation of the Budget a comparatively easy task. The estimate by Mr. Gladstone, although at first received with some incredulity, was found to be far below the actual result, and the surplus really approached the sum of six millions. In introducing the financial statement, Sir Stafford Northcote referred to the late Prime Minister as "one of the very highest financial authorities, perhaps I may say, of the century." The total estimated revenue for the financial year 1874-5 was £77,995,000, and the estimated expenditure £72,583,000, leaving a surplus of £5,492,000. But as interest on advances ought to be included in the revenue of the year, although not so reckoned hitherto, another half million was added to the surplus. Mr. Gladstone had promised, if he remained in office, to abolish the income-tax; but the Conservative Chancellor of the Exchequer resolved to apply the magnificent amount in another manner. The half-million interest on advances he proposed to set apart for the reduction of the National Debt; the sugar duties were to be abolished, a penny taken off the income-tax and the house duty; the horsedealer's licence duty and the race-horse duty were remitted. A surplus of £462,000 then remained.

One of the most important debates of the session arose on the introduction to the House of Commons, by Mr. Russell Gurney (the Recorder of London), of the Public Worship Regulation Bill, which had passed the House of Lords. The second reading was moved on the 9th of July. Mr. Gladstone opposed the Bill with great vehemence, maintaining that "in different parts of the country, and in different congregations, various customs had grown up in accordance with the feelings and usages of the people, and they ought not to be rashly and rudely rooted out." He placed on the table six resolutions, which he conceived might be the basis of legislation which might control the eccentricities of individuals without proscribing all varieties of opinion and usage. This speech, one of Mr. Gladstone's most fervid utterances, produced a great effect, and Sir William Harcourt, who followed, supporting the Bill, said, "We have all been under the wand of the great enchanter to-night, and have listened with rapt attention as he

poured forth the wealth of his incomparable eloquence." Mr.
Disraeli spoke in favour of the Bill, and flung a famous phra.e
at the Ritualists—"mass in masquerade."

The second reading was agreed to without a division. Mr.
Gladstone withdrew his resolutions; and after a slight squabble
with the Lords respecting amendments, the Bill passed on the
5th of August.

Mr. Gladstone spoke at some length in opposition to the En
dowed Schools Bill, brought in by Lord Sandon on the 2nd of
July. The object was to reverse the policy sanctioned by the
late Parliament, and transfer to the Charity Commissioners the
power exercised by the Endowed Schools Commission. The
second reading was carried in the Commons by 291 against 209;
but in committee the Liberals were resolute and compact, and out
of doors the excitement was considerable. Lord Sandon offered
some concessions, which were rejected. The debate lasted two
days, and then Mr. Disraeli announced that, partly in consequence
of the state of public business, and partly because he desired to
have more time to consider some of the "perplexing" questions
to which the "restoration clause" of the Bill gave rise, any
attempt to amend the existing law would be postponed to another
session.

Parliament rose on the 8th of August, leaving a very blank
record of important public business.

Previously to the opening of the session of 1875 Mr. Gladstone
formally resigned the leadership of the Liberal party in the
House of Commons. He wished, he intimated, to devote more
attention to literary work and the investigation of social and
theological questions than the hurry and drive, the incessant
work and worry, of an active political career would permit. Satisfied with the political greatness he had achieved, he apparently
desired to give the remaining years of his life to the production
of some work which would achieve for him a distinguished position in the world of letters. In his own words, the desire to
retire from the leadership was "dictated to me by my personal
views as to the best method of spending the closing years of my
life."

The Liberal members probably anticipated—certainly the
public press did—that the retirement would be more nominal
than real. So long as Mr. Gladstone remained a member of the
House, his influence would be paramount with his party, whoever might discharge the routine functions of leadership, and be
the spokesman when Ministers were to be questioned or formal

opposition offered.   There were good men and true on the Opposition benches, men who had held high office with credit, whose ability was great and fidelity unquestionable.   Lord Hartington's industry, clear views, tact, and temperate firmness, his familiarity with official and Parliamentary business, and his social position marked him out as a fitting candidate for the dignity of leader of his party.   Mr. Bright, one of the greatest and most popular orators the country has ever possessed, was a doughty champion, but fitter to be an active combatant than a general, and, besides, his delicate health was a disqualification for a position demanding incessant work.   Mr. Lowe possessed extraordinary talents as a debater of the highest rank, but, unfortunately, his talents included a great ability for seceding from his party on peculiarly inopportune occasions, and a leader who might at any time develop a tendency to retire into an Adullamite cave would be the cause of considerable inconvenience.   The real choice lay between Lord Hartington and Mr. Forster, whose management of the Elementary Education Bill had greatly advanced his reputation, and established him in the confidence of the Liberals.   Mr. Forster waived his claim in favour of Lord Hartington, who, at a meeting of the party presided over by Mr. Bright, was unanimously selected to succeed to the leadership.

Mr. Gladstone loyally accepted the choice of his party, and to a considerable extent withdrew from Parliamentary work ; but his ardent temperament and the deep interest he felt in ecclesiastical and financial questions would not permit him to remain inactive when such subjects were under discussion ; and when he spoke it was to him that the Liberal members looked as their guide. One of the writers of the time remarked, " It was all very well of the Liberals to elect Lord Hartington leader, *vice* Mr. Gladstone, retired from politics.   It would have been just as efficacious for the solar system to meet and elect the moon to rule the day, *vice* the sun, resigned.   Mr. Gladstone's erratic appearances in the political firmament were sufficient temporarily to dispose of the titular leader of the Liberals, and it set the whole system once more revolving round himself."   Lord Hartington discharged the duties of his position with great ability and admirable tact, and Mr. Gladstone never consciously obtruded his personality, but it was impossible that its influence should not be felt.

The record of the ensuing five years of Mr. Gladstone's life is a narrative of incessant intellectual and polemical activity.   Occasionally he appeared in Parliament, occasionally his fervid oratory once more stirred the languid blood of Her Majesty's faithful

T

Commons. But criticism and controversy, examination of the validity of Papal pretensions, and, latterly, courageous and uncompromising championship of the oppressed nationalities subjected to the atrocious misrule of the Turkish Government, gave scope for the exercise of all his power. When he laid down the pen, he took up the woodman's axe, and having demolished an opponent who held heretical opinions respecting the hero of the Iliad or the genuineness of the Homeric epic, with equal vigour attacked a mighty tree in Hawarden Park. One beech tree, thirteen feet in circumference, fell before his axe, after six hours of stupendous exertion; and the vigorous amateur woodman, nearly seventy years old, could scarcely have felt greater pleasure had he demolished the root and branches of a Conservative budget.

When, on the 6th of August, 1877, the members of the Bolton Liberal Association, including many ladies, went to Hawarden to present an address, they probably expected a formal reception and a political speech. Mr. Gladstone, however, invited them to enjoy themselves in the park, while he and his son cut down a tree. Resting now and then from his work, he chatted with his visitors, and shook hands with the ladies; but there was no set speech, and the Bolton Liberals probably were quite as pleased at seeing the great leader in his shirt-sleeves, axe in hand, at home, enjoying his usual occupation, as if he had hurled thunder-bolts at the Conservative management of finance and foreign affairs.

About this time there was a remarkable development of periodical literature. A few years before, Mr. George Lewes had started the *Fortnightly Review*, and the example was followed by the issue of the *Contemporary Review*, and, later, the *Nineteenth Century*. The peculiarity of these publications is that they invite the contributions of men of eminence, holding different literary, political, and theological opinions. The articles are signed, and the publication, as a publication, has no individuality, in that respect unlike the other reviews and magazines. A certain subject is frequently discussed from all points of view by many writers, high-class ability being the only condition insisted on by the editors. In the lists of contributors may be found Tennyson, Gladstone, Archbishop Manning, Freeman, Froude, Lowe, Harrison, Tyndall, the Morleys—Ritualists, Positivists, and men of the highest rank in literature, science, philosophy, and politics. Mr. Gladstone's activity and variety as a contributor were prodigious. Between 1874 and 1879 his name appears in the *Contemporary Review*, appended to long and elaborate articles entitled, " Is the Church of England Worth Preserving ?"

"Ritualism and Ritualists," "The Place of Honour in History," "The Course of Religious Thought," "Russian Policy and Deeds in Turkistan," "The Iris of Homer and her Relation to Genesis ix. 11–17" (the announcement of the rainbow covenant with Noah), and "The Sixteenth Century Arraigned before the Nineteenth : A Study of the Reformation" (a comment on a paper in a previous number, "What Hinders the Ritualists from Becoming Roman Catholics?" by the Abbé Martin).

His contributions to the *Nineteenth Century* were even more diverse in subjects :—"The County Franchise," "The Peace to Come" (having reference to the Eastern Question and India), "England's Mission," "The Slicing of Hector," "Electoral Facts," "The Friends and Foes of Russia," "On Epithets of Movement in Homer," "Probability as the Guide of Conduct," "Greece and the Treaty of Berlin," "The Olympian System *versus* the Solar Theory," and "The Country and the Government." One paper, which appeared just before the assembly of the Berlin Conference, "The Paths of Honour and of Shame," attracted great attention. It was a vigorous attack on the Ministerial policy, and concluded with these words :—

"I am selfish enough to hope, in the interest of my country, that in the approaching Conference, or Congress, we may have, and may use, an opportunity to acquire the goodwill of somebody. By somebody I mean some nation, and not merely some government. Neither in personal nor in national life will self-glorification supply the place of general respect, or feed the hunger of the heart. Rich and strong we are ; but no people is rich enough or strong enough to disregard the priceless value of human sympathies."

The contributions to the *Fortnightly* included "Free Trade, Railways, and the Growth of Commerce," "Russia and England," "Religions, Achaian and Semitic," "On the Influence of Authority in Matters of Opinion" (which produced a reply from Sir James Fitzjames Stephen, to which Mr. Gladstone made a rejoinder), "Montenegro : A Sketch," "Aggression in Egypt and Freedom in the East," "The Colour Sense," and two articles on "The County Franchise," in reply to Mr. Lowe's arguments.

It will be seen from the titles of some of these articles that the unhappy disputes in the Church of England greatly exercised Mr. Gladstone's mind. A staunch Churchman, and attached to the High Church section, he is strongly opposed to Ritualism, with its vestments and genuflections, which seem to him, as they seem to many others, an imitation of the ceremonies and a symbolising of the doctrines of the Romish Church, unaccompanied

on the part of the imitators by the courage of their convictions.
When at home at Hawarden he generally reads the lessons of
the day in the church, of which his son is incumbent—an office
which a layman may discharge ; and when in town he usually
attends a church where the service is somewhat "high" and
choral ; but to walk in a procession carrying a taper or a banner,
following priests wearing embroidered stoles and birettas, would
be an act entirely opposed to Mr. Gladstone's notions of Protestant Churchmanship.   His greatest literary achievement at that
period was a vigorous protest against Papal pretensions to
exercise a dominion over the consciences of British Catholics.
"The Vatican Decrees in their Bearing on Civil Allegiance : A
Political Expostulation," was published, and at once made a sensation.   In the course of a few weeks Mr. Murray, the publisher,
disposed of 120,000 copies, edition following edition.

Writing in the *Contemporary Review* for October, 1874, in the
article headed "Ritualism and Ritualists," Mr. Gladstone, referring to "the question whether a handful of the clergy are or
are not engaged in an utterly hopeless and visionary effort to
Romanize the Church of England," went on to say—

"At no time since the bloody reign of Mary has such a scheme been possible.
But if it had been possible in the seventeenth or eighteenth century, it would
still have become impossible in the nineteenth ; when Rome has substituted
for the proud boast of *semper eadem* a policy of violence and change in faith ;
when she has refurbished, and paraded anew, every rusty tool she was fondly
thought to have disused ; when no one can become her convert without re-
nouncing his moral and mental freedom, and placing his civil loyalty and
duty at the mercy of another ; and when she has equally repudiated modern
thought and ancient history."

The comments and expostulations which this passage excited
induced Mr. Gladstone to repeat and enlarge upon them, to
"expostulate in his turn ;" the result being the pamphlet.   He
denied that his remarks were an attack upon, or an insult to
Roman Catholics generally—"they constitute generally a free
and strong animadversion on the conduct of the Papal Chair, and
of its advisers and abettors."   At considerable length he defended
the four allegations contained in the paragraph quoted, and
maintained that in the third chapter of the *Constitutio Dogmatica
Prima de Ecclesiâ Christi,* issued by the Vatican Council,—

"Absolute obedience, it is boldly declared, is due to the Pope, at the peril
of salvation, not alone in faith, in morals, but in all things which concern the
discipline and government of the Church. . . .   On all matters respecting
which any Pope may think proper to declare that they concern either faith or
morals, or the government or discipline of the Church, he claims, with the

approval of a Council undoubtedly œcumenical in the Roman sense, the absolute obedience, at the peril of salvation, of every member of his communion.
It is well to remember that this claim in respect of all things affecting the
discipline and government of the Church, as well as faith and conduct, is
lodged in open day by and in the reign of a Pontiff who has condemned free
speech, free writing, a free press, toleration of nonconformity, liberty of conscience, the study of civil and philosophical matters in independence of the
ecclesiastical authority, marriage unless sacramentally contracted, and the definition by the State of the civil rights of the Church; who has demanded for
the Church, therefore, the title to define its own civil rights, together with a
divine right to civil immunities, and a right to use physical force. . . I submit, then, that my fourth proposition [that Rome has equally repudiated modern
thought and ancient history] is true ; and that England is entitled to ask, and
to know, in what way the obedience required by the Pope at the Council of
the Vatican is to be reconciled with the integrity of civil allegiance ? "

The sixth section of the pamphlet answered a question which
Mr. Gladstone probably felt would very likely come to the front,
" Were the propositions proper to be set forth by the present
writer ? "   So long as he continued to be Prime Minister he should
not have considered a broad political discussion on a general
question suitable to him ; but now the limitations of official
position had been removed.   In fact, he was once more " un
muzzled."   The reason why he now took up the questions are
given :—

" For thirty years, and in a great variety of circumstances, in office and as
an independent member of Parliament, in majorities and in small minorities,
and during the larger portion of the time as the representative of a great constituency, mainly clerical, I have, with others, laboured to maintain and
extend the civil rights of my Roman Catholic fellow countrymen.   The
Liberal party of this country, with which I have been commonly associated,
has suffered, and sometimes suffered heavily, in public favour and in influence
from the belief that it was too ardent in the pursuit of that policy ; while, at
the same time, it has always been in the worst odour with the Court of Rome
in consequence of its (I hope) unalterable attachment to Italian liberty and
independence.   I have sometimes been the spokesman of that party in recommendations which have tended to foster, in fact, the imputation I have
mentioned, though not to warrant it as a matter of reason.   But it has existed
in fact.   So that while (as I think) general justice to society required that
these things which I have now set forth should be written, special justice as
towards the party to which I am loyally attached, and which I may have had
a share in thus placing at a disadvantage before our countrymen, made it, to
say the least, becoming that I should not shrink from writing them."

It may be necessary, as a key to this controversy, to recall the
fact that on the 8th of December, 1864, the tenth anniversary
of the declaration of the dogma of the Immaculate Conception,
the Pope issued an Encyclical Letter, accompanied by an appen-
dix of eighty propositions, enumerating the principal modern
errors which the Pope, as head of the Church, condemned.

Among other opinions widely entertained and advocated, but which were condemned as heretical, were these :—

"That the Pope can and ought to become reconciled to progress, Liberalism, and modern civilization."

"That it is not fitting that in the present day the Catholic religion should be the exclusive religion of the State."

"That it is untrue that civil liberty to worship and freedom of the press conduce to the corruption of morals and to propagate indifference."

The appearance of Mr. Gladstone's pamphlet produced a host of replies, and among the most eminent of those who entered the controversial lists were Dr. Manning, Dr. Newman, and Monsignor Capel. These replies and comments—Mr. Gladstone enumerates twenty-one, books, pamphlets, and articles in reviews and magazines—were met by the appearance of another and larger pamphlet from Mr. Gladstone's pen, "Vaticanism; or, Answer to Reproofs and Replies." It displays great research and scholarship, and amply proved—if proof were necessary to anybody who had any acquaintance with the range of the author's studies—that if he had not been a great politician and financier, he might have occupied an eminent position among controversial theologians and ecclesiastical scholars. The pamphlet concluded eloquently :—

"I am not one of those who find or imagine a hopeless hostility between authority and reason, or who undervalue the vital moment of Christianity to mankind. I believe that religion to be the determining condition of our well or ill-being, and its Church to have been, and to be, in its several organisms, by far the greatest institution that the world has ever seen. The poles on which the dispensation rests are truth and freedom. Between them there is a holy and divine union, and he that impairs or impugns either is alike the enemy of both. To tear or beguile away from man the attribute of inward liberty is not only idle, I would almost say it is impious. When the Christian scheme first went forth, with all its authority, to regenerate the world, it did not discourage, but invited the free action of the human reason and the individual conscience, while it supplied these agents from within with the rules and motives of a humble, which is also a noble, self-restraint. . . . As freedom can never be effectually established by the adversaries of that Gospel which has first made it a reality for all orders and degrees of men, so the Gospel never can be effectually defended by a policy which declines to acknowledge the high place assigned to Liberty in the councils of Providence, and which, upon the pretext of the abuse that, like every other good, she suffers, expels her from its system. Among the many noble thoughts of Homer, there is not one more noble or more penetrating than his judgment upon slavery. 'On the day,' he says, 'that makes a bondman of the free, wide-seeing laws take half the man away.' He thus judges, not because the slavery of his time was cruel, for evidently it was not, but because it was slavery. What he said against servitude in the social order, we may plead against Vaticanism in the spiritual sphere, and no cloud of incense which zeal or flattery, or even love, can raise, should hide the disastrous truth from the vision of mankind."

Many as were Mr. Gladstone's contributions to English literature, they did not, it would seem, afford scope enough for his
mental activity. In the autumn of 1878 he contributed to the
North American Review an article, " Kin beyond Sea," in which
he described with great minuteness the political working of the
British Constitution, and, as some of his critics thought, instituted
a comparison between British and American institutions, very much
to the disparagement of the former. Some went so far as to accuse
him of disloyalty and disrespect to the Sovereign, because the
American printers, as is their custom, spelled Queen with a
small " q."

The various articles we have mentioned display great scholarship, close reasoning, many graces of style, and much vigour
of expression, with an almost pedantic care for accuracy. If the
writer uses a Shakspearian phrase--or even two words, such as
"sucking dove"—in a familiar manner, a footnote gives the exact
reference to the act and scene of the play. He is convinced
that Shakspeare apparently misunderstood the character of Hector
of Troy, because, in the *Merry Wives of Windsor*, the Host
of the Garter speaks of " Bully Hector," not remembering that
the word was a familiar prefix ; that Bully Hercules is also spoken
of, and that Bottom the Weaver is addressed as Bully Bottom.
These are little matters, but they indicate the fastidious desire for
accuracy characteristic of the writer.

Mr. Gladstone earnestly but unsuccessfully opposed the Bill
introduced by Mr. Disraeli in the Session of 1876, by which the
title of Empress of India was added to the style of the Queen
of Great Britain.

In 1876 Europe was horrified by the narrative of the massacres and other atrocities in Bulgaria. We need not dwell on the
details. Mr. Gladstone questioned Ministers on the subject, but
received cold and unsatisfactory answers. He then published a
pamphlet, " Bulgarian Horrors and the Question of the East,"
urging that England was grossly neglecting her duty, and ought
to " put a stop to the anarchical misrule, the murdering which
still desolated Bulgaria." The Turks should be expelled from
the province " bag and baggage." He made a great speech on
the subject to his constituents at Blackheath; and when in December a great meeting or "conference " was held at St. James's
Hall, he spoke at great length. At various smaller meetings, at
railway stations when travelling, and at other places, he spoke
strongly on the subject. In vain Mr. Disraeli, speaking at City
dinners and on other occasions, sneered at the " hare-brained

chatter of irresponsible frivolity," Mr. Gladstone had once more got the ear of the majority of the public and the sympathy of the great mass of the nation.

Parliament assembled on the 8th of February, 1877. Throughout the session the debates on the Eastern Question excited the greatest amount of interest. On the 30th of April Mr. Gladstone introduced five resolutions, which he afterwards reduced to one, complaining of the conduct of the Porte with regard to the despatch of the Earl of Derby relating to the massacres in Bulgaria; but after several nights' discussion it was lost by a majority of 151. The debate was memorable for a direct attack on Mr. Gladstone by Mr. Chaplin, the Conservative member for Mid-Lincolnshire, and the crushing reply given:—

"The time is short; the sands of the hour-glass are running out. The longer you delay, the less, in all likelihood, you will be able to save from the wreck of the independence and integrity of the Turkish empire. If Russia should fail, her failure would be a disaster to mankind, and the condition of the suffering races, for whom we are supposed to have laboured, will be worse than it was before. If she succeeds, and if her conduct be honourable—nay, even if it be but tolerably prudent—the performance of the work she has in hand will, notwithstanding all your jealousies and all your reproaches, secure for her an undying fame. When that work shall be accomplished, though it be not in the way and by the means I would have chosen, as an Englishman I shall hide my head, but as a man I shall rejoice. Nevertheless, to my latest day I will exclaim, Would God that in this crisis the voice of the nation had been suffered to prevail! Would God that in this great, this holy deed, England had not been refused her share."

During the session he delivered an important speech on the same topic at Birmingham.

In the autumnal recess Mr. Gladstone, for the first time, paid a visit to Ireland, but only in a private capacity, and steadily declined all invitations to make political speeches. He was presented with the freedom of Dublin. On his return the Anglesea folk received him at Holyhead, and he indulged them with a speech.

Comparatively unimportant incidents of this period were, that on the 16th of February, 1876, Mr. Gladstone was presented with the freedom of the Worshipful Company of Turners; and that on the 30th of January, 1878, he addressed a meeting of Oxford undergraduates, on the occasion of a meeting to celebrate the opening of the Palmerston Liberal Club.

CHAPTER XXV.

THE GREAT MIDLOTHIAN CAMPAIGN.

THE ninth Victorian Parliament was dying out. It met on the 5th of March, 1874, and few people believed that the full legal term of seven years would be reached, and the only question was whether the dissolution would take place in the autumn, or that Ministers would try the hazard of another session. There was not only a black cloud in the horizon, but the whole atmosphere was gloomy. The handsome surplus of nearly six millions which, in 1874, Mr. Gladstone had bequeathed as a legacy to his successor had disappeared, and Sir Stafford Northcote's financial arrangements showed at the end of the session a deficiency of £1,163,000, besides which there was an increase in the debt of £5,350,000, the payment of which was deferred till better times. What the attainment of a "scientific frontier" meant, on the Afghanistan side of British India, no man knew, and the Indian officials were very anxious that no man should know—at any rate, for the present. The Zulu account was yet to be settled, and any impartial observer must have been sanguine indeed if he supposed that South African difficulties were ended by the capture and imprisonment of King Cetewayo. Very hopeful, too, must he have been if he expected that the Treaty of Berlin, the partition of the provinces of the Turkish empire, and the promise of reform, had settled the Eastern Question.

The energy with which Mr. Gladstone had denounced the apathy of the Ministers in respect to the Bulgarian atrocities, and the reaction of public opinion which had been stimulated and dazzled for a time by the loud talk about "peace with honour," had materially weakened the position of the Beaconsfield Administration; and strenuous efforts were made by the Liberal party to prepare for the inevitable, and probably immediate, general election. It was resolved to attack the counties, where the Conservatives were strongest; and the boldest attempt in that direction was undertaken by Mr. Gladstone.

He was then in his seventieth year. He had been a member of Parliament for forty-seven years, for nearly twenty years had sat in the Cabinet, and had attained the summit of political ambition when, eleven years before, he became Prime Minister.

He had professed himself weary of politics, and desirous of peaceful literary pursuits ; but that dream—for dream it was, in the case of a man so acutely sensitive and sympathetic—had been dispelled, perhaps almost forgotten, in the excitement of the last three years. He might be desirous to tell the world more about Homer, he might wish to disentangle some ecclesiastical complexities, to help to disperse some of the shadows which darkened the fair picture of his beloved Church ; but there, in the far East, loomed the phantom of the " unspeakable Turk," most unwilling to be driven out "bag and baggage;" and at home there were financial difficulties, rapidly increasing distrust in the Ministry, and the opportunity once more to hold the helm and guide the vessel of the State.

Mr. Gladstone had found Greenwich convenient, and he appreciated the trust the constituency reposed in him, but he desired to represent a county rather than a metropolitan borough. He determined to lead the movement against the predominance of Conservatives in the counties by attacking the metropolitan county of Scotland, Midlothian, the representation of which had come to be looked on almost as part of the property of the Buccleuch family. While to win the county would be a great political achievement, it would also be a great personal gratification to Mr. Gladstone, who prided himself on his Scotch ancestry, and who had so many family associations with that part of Scotland.

On Monday the 24th of November, 1879, Mr. Gladstone started on one of the most arduous expeditions ever undertaken— not, of course, arduous in the sense in which the word is applied to a walk across Africa, or a search expedition in the Arctic regions, but as involving a strain upon the mental powers which very few young men, even those most gifted with intellectual and bodily vigour, could have successfully encountered. The old man of seventy, who for nearly half a century had been incessantly at work by night and by day, to whose capacious brain and indomitable energy, rest, except the nightly sleep, seemed almost unnecessary, undertook and achieved a feat, occupying just two weeks, the like of which was probably never performed by mortal man.

Accompanied by Mrs. Gladstone and his daughter, he quitted Liverpool *en route* for Scotland. At every station at which the train stopped crowds assembled, and he was loudly cheered. At Carlisle many Liberal Members of Parliament and other gentlemen awaited his arrival, and Mr. M'Laren, Vice-President of, and representing the East and North of Scotland Liberal Association, was there to welcome him. In the hall of the County Hotel there was a representative gathering of more than 500 Liberals, and probably there would have been many more if accommodation could have been afforded. Addresses were presented from Langholm, Dumfriesshire, accompanied by a present of cloth manufactured in the district; from the Carlisle Liberal Association, the Newcastle-on-Tyne Liberal Association, the Newcastle Liberal Club, and the Gateshead Liberal Association. In his reply he described the existing condition of political affairs as a crisis of an extraordinary character, such as alone could "induce me at my time of life, when every sentiment would dictate a desire for rest, to undertake what may be called an arduous contest."

At Hawick there was a crowd at the station, to whom Mr. Gladstone, at the invitation of the Provost and other leading Liberals, addressed a few words, hailing them as "fellow soldiers in a common warfare, who had in their charge a cause which is the cause of liberty, which is the cause of honour, and which in the hands of the people of this country, by the blessing of God, will not fail."

As the train dashed past St. Boswell's and Melrose loud cheers rose from assembled crowds, and at Galashiels, where a halt was made, there was an enthusiastic reception. There stood the Provost of the busy town, that day *en fête*. Addresses from the Galashiels Liberal Committee and the Selkirk Liberal Association were presented, and there were packages of the tartans and tweed fabrics, the staple manufacture of the town, awaiting Mr. Gladstone's acceptance. A long speech was made here, and then the carriage was re-entered, and the train went swiftly on its way to Edinburgh.

Those who are familiar with "stately Edinburgh, throned on crags," know the large railway station in the depression between the old and new towns, and the splendid Princes Street which skirts it on the northern side. That broad thoroughfare was densely thronged, every available spot at the station was occupied by privileged spectators, and on the platform, waiting to receive the distinguished visitor, were the Earl of Rosebery, President of the East and North of Scotland and of the Midlothian Liberal Associations, many members of Parliament, nearly all the members of the Midlothian Executive Committee, a deputation from the Trades Council, and a considerable number of the members of the Corporation. There were no addresses or

speeches—the hour was late, and it would have been unkind to
impose additional fatigue on Mr. Gladstone; besides, on the
morrow he was to make his first great Midlothian speech. Lord
Rosebery was his host, and, bowing in acknowledgment of the
storm of cheers, Mr. Gladstone entered an open carriage and rode
to Dalmeney Park, where he rested for the night.

The Music Hall in George Street, Edinburgh, is the most
capacious building in the city; and there, on Tuesday, an
immense audience assembled. Three hundred ladies occupied
the gallery, the platform was crowded with political and local
notabilities, and nearly two thousand persons were massed in the
great hall. The speech was of great length, and referred chiefly
to the action of the Government in relation to foreign affairs,
especially the Eastern Question. The financial position of the
country he reserved as a topic for another opportunity. At the
opening of his address he took occasion to explain that he contested Midlothian solely on public grounds, and with no feeling
of personal animosity against the dominant ducal family.

"I will begin this campaign, if so it is to be called—and a campaign, and
an earnest campaign I trust it will be—I will begin by avowing my personal
respect for my noble opponent, and for the distinguished family to which he
belongs. Gentlemen, I have had the honour—for an honour I consider it—to
sit as a colleague with the Duke of Buccleuch in the Cabinet of Sir Robert
Peel. That is now nearly forty years ago. I render to the Duke of
Buccleuch as freely as to Lord Dalkeith this tribute, that he—given and pre-
supposed the misfortune of his false political opinions—is in all respects what
a British nobleman ought to be, and sets to us all an example in the active
and conscientious discharge of duty, such as he believes duty to be, which we
shall do well, from our very different point of view, to follow."

On the following day, the 26th, he addressed a meeting, at
which nearly 3,000 persons attended, in the Corn Exchange,
Dalkeith. The foreign policy of the Ministry, the desire for
annexation, and the engagements entered into, which, he said,
bound this country as the Liliputians bound Gulliver, with a
multitude of small threads and pins; the inadequate representation of Scotland—a subject sure to enlist the sympathies of a
Scotch audience, and an allusion to the law of hypothec, also a
purely Scotch topic, and disestablishment of the Church—which
he said was not for him, but for the people of Scotland themselves
to decide on—were then noticed, and the land laws and the laws of
entail and settlement came under notice. Respecting the latter
laws he was particularly outspoken:—

"It appears to me that if there is one law written more distinctly than
another upon the constitution of human society by the finger of the Almighty,

it is this, that the parent is responsible for making sufficient provision on behalf of the child ; but the law of England is wiser than the Almighty. It improves upon Divine Providence. It will not trust the father to make provision for his son. It calls in the aid of the grandfather, commits to him the function of the parent, introduces a false and, in my opinion, a rather unnatural relation even into the constitution of that primary element of society, the sacred constitution of the family. Not only, then, to liberate agriculture, gentlemen, but upon other grounds—and I will say upon what I think still higher grounds —I am for doing away with the present law of settlement and entail."

Local Government and the Irish demand for Home Rule were then touched on. Subject to the supreme authority of the Imperial Parliament, he thought a very considerab'e amount of local government, and even of Home Rule, might be conceded. At present Parliament was overweighted, he might say overwhelmed by business, and the man who should devise a machinery by which some portion of the excessive and impossible task laid upon the House of Commons would be shifted to the more free and therefore more efficient hands of secondary and local authorities, would confer a blessing upon his country that would entitle him to be reckoned among the prominent benefactors of the land.

After the meeting at the Corn Exchange, a visit was paid to the Foresters' Hall, where a presentation was made to Mrs. Gladstone by the ladies of the place. Mrs. Gladstone herself acknowledged it with a few earnest words, and her husband addressed the ladies in a very graceful speech, in the course of which, however, he made a slip of memory, which excited some amusement, and which, with his usual sensitiveness, he felt it necessary to explain in a letter to the newspapers. He quoted Lady Nairne's beautiful epithet, "the land o' the leal," as if she meant Scotland, not heaven. When the speech was published in the revised collection the slip was corrected.

A third speech was delivered on the following day at West Calder, fifteen miles to the west of Edinburgh, in a temporary building specially erected. The route from Dalmeney Park to West Calder was decorated with triumphal arches, and the town was brilliantly illuminated at night. Agricultural matters, the price of land, legislative restraint, small proprietaries, and similar topics, formed the staple of his speech, and the free trade and "reciprocity" doctrines were dilated on ; a very comprehensive view of foreign affairs ; and then came a scathing exposition of the real value of Lord Beaconsfield's famous quotation, "Imperium et Libertas."

"The Prime Minister quoted certain words, easily rendered as ' Empire

and Liberty'—words (he observed) of a Roman statesman, descriptive of the
state of Rome—and quoted by him as capable of legitimate application to the
position and circumstances of England.   I join issue with the Prime Minister
upon that subject ; and I affirm that nothing can be more fun lamentally unsound, more practically ruinous, than the establishment of Roman analogies
for the guidance of British policy.   What, gentlemen, was Rome?   Rome
was, indeed, an Imperial State, you may tell me—I know not, I cannot read
the counsels of Providence—a State having a mission to subdue the world ;
but a State whose very basis it was to deny the equal rights, to proscribe the
independent existence of other nations.   That, gentlemen, was the Roman
idea. . . .   We are told to fall back upon this example.   No doubt the word
'Empire' was qualified with the word 'Liberty.'   But what did the two
words 'Liberty' and 'Empire' mean in a Roman mouth?   They meant simply
this—'Liberty for ourselves, Empire over the rest of mankind.'   Gentlemen, it is but in a pale and weak and almost miniature form that such ideas
are now set up, but you will observe that the poison lies—that the poison and
the mischief lie—in the principle and not the scale.   It is the opposite principle, which, I say, has been compromised by the action of the Ministry, and
which I call upon you, and upon any who choose to hear my views, to vindicate when the day of our election comes ; I mean the soun I and the sacred
principle that Christendom is formed of a band of nations who are united to
one another in the bonds of right ; that they are without distinction of great
and small ; there is an absolute equality between them : the same sacredness
defends the narrow limits of Belgium as attaches to the extended frontiers of
Russia, or Germany, or France.   I hold that he who by act or word brings
that principle into peril or disparagement, however honest his intentions may
be, places himself in the position of one inflicting—I will not say intending to
inflict—I ascribe nothing of the sort—but inflicting injury upon his own
country, and endangering the peace and all the most fundamental interests of
Christian society.'

A little rest from oratorical exertion was taken on Friday, the
27th, at Dalmeney Park, but an address was presented by the
Corporation of Leith, and of course suitably and briefly replied
to ; and in the afternoon the Countess of Rosebery gave a reception to the Executive Committee of the Midlothian Liberal
Association.

Two important speeches were delivered at Edinburgh on Saturday, one in the Corn Exchange, and the other in the Waverley
Market.   At the former, Lord Rosebery took the chair.   These
great meetings were not directly connected in any way with the
Midlothian election, and therefore Peers felt themselves at liberty
to be present, and at the first meeting eleven were on the platform.
At the Corn Exchange about 4,700 persons assembled from all
parts of the country, under the auspices of the East and North
of Scotland Liberal Association, to hear Mr. Gladstone, and more
than one hundred Scotch Liberal Associations were represented.
At the Waverley Market a vast gathering of more than 20,000
people met for the same purpose, under the direction of a com-

mittee of working men representing the different trades of Edinburgh.   At the Corn Exchange meeting the financial state of
the country was the chief subject of comment.   The Tory
Government, he asserted, had raised the annual expenditure by
£8,000,000.   They had imposed nearly £6,000,000 of taxation,
in order to produce £6,000,000 of deficiency; and in India the
deficiency was about the same in amount.   The speaker was quite
happy when dealing with figures in this fashion.   His examination
of the financial situation was like the preludes to half a dozen
Budgets rolled into one.

The meeting in the Waverley Market was attended by, it is
said, more than 20,000 persons.   Various addresses were presented, and the speech, though short, chiefly referred to foreign
affairs, especially the position of the provinces of the Balkan,
and the possible intentions of Austria respecting them.   "It
is not Russia alone whose movements ought to be watched
with vigilance.   There is too much reason to suspect that some
portion of the statesmen of Austria will endeavour to extend her
rule, and to fulfil the evil prophecies that have been uttered, and
cause the great change in the Balkan peninsula to be only the
substitution of one kind of supremacy for another."

These words gave rise to some unpleasant comments in the
Austrian press, and official explanations were made.

Sunday, the 30th of November, was passed in privacy, Mr.
Gladstone attending divine service and the communion at one
of the Episcopal churches.   On Monday morning he took his
departure for Taymouth Castle, on a brief visit to the Earl and
Countess of Breadalbane, previous to going to Glasgow.   The
commercial capital of Scotland is not within the limits of Midlothian; but Friday, the 5th of December, was the day fixed for
his installation as Lord Rector of Glasgow University; and it
was not to be expected that he would be permitted to visit the
great town without being called upon to make a political speech.
The eyes of all Scotland were fixed upon him, and the "Glasgow
bodies" were not likely to allow the students to have him all to
themselves.

On the way from Dalmeney Park to Taymouth Mr. Gladstone
crossed the Forth at Queensferry, and went thence by train to
Inverkeithing, where he received an address from the magistrates
and town council.   The next stopping-place was Dunfermline,
and there a crowd, estimated at 9,000 strong, was waiting for
him.   The Provost presented an address, to which Mr. Gladstone
replied; and then beautiful specimens of the manufactures of the

town, in the shape of sets of damask table linen, were presented to Mrs. Gladstone.

When the train reached Perth a halt was made. The Lord Provost and magistrates were ready to give a welcome, and on their invitation Mr. Gladstone proceeded to the City Hall and received the freedom of Perth. In replying, he made a feeling allusion to the late Mr. Roebuck, of whose death he had just heard. The party then returned to the railway station, near which a platform had been erected, and addresses from the City and County Liberal Associations were presented. In his speech Mr. Gladstone summarized the charges he had made against the Ministry, and certainly it was a very copious and tremendous indictment :—

"I charged them with the mismanagement of finance; secondly, with an extravagant scale of expenditure ; thirdly, with having allowed legislation, which is always in arrear in this country, from the necessary pressure of the concerns of so vast an empire—with having allowed that legislation to come into such a state that its arrears are intolerable and almost hopeless. I charged them with a foreign policy which has gravely compromised the faith and honour of the country. I charged them with having, both through their ruinous finance and through their disturbing measures, broken up confidence in the commercial community, and thereby aggravated the public distress. I charged them with having contributed needlessly and wrongfully to the aggrandizement of Russia. I charged them with having made an unjust and dangerous war in Afghanistan, and I further charged them in these terms : ' By their use of the treaty-making and the war-making powers of the Crown, they have abridged the just rights of Parliament, and have presented prerogative to the nation under an unconstitutional aspect, which tends to make it insecure.'"

There were other speeches at railway stations. At Dunkeld an address was presented and replied to; and at Aberfeldy an address was presented from the inhabitants of the town and district, in reply to which he said, " It really seems as if, under the present sway, our business was not to regulate the concerns of our own land and of our own firesides, but the concerns of the people of Europe, Asia, Africa, and the rest of the world." He denounced the " theatrical displays and tricks," the " high-sounding discourses about the great position of England, and the necessity that England should become the teacher and the instructor of every nation in the world, while we are in danger of falling into a condition in which we shall be conspicuous for the neglect of our own affairs."

At Aberfeldy the railway was quitted, and the party drove through the village of Aberfeldy on the way to Taymouth Castle. Bonfires blazed upon the hills, and rows of torch-bearers lined the approach to the castle, where "fireworks and rejoicings closed the eventful day," in the course of which Mr. Gladstone had been presented with four addresses, made a freeman of Perth, and delivered two lengthy speeches and several brief replies.

The address to the students of the University of Glasgow was delivered on the 5th of December. It dealt with subjects far apart from political strife, and urged the students to be mindful of the great duties and responsibilities imposed on them by their opportunities for intellectual culture. "Be thorough in all you do, and remember that though ignorance often may be innocent, pretension is always despicable. Be you, like men, strong, and the exercise of your strength to-day will give you more strength to-morrow. Work onwards and work upwards, and may the blessing of the Most High soothe your cares, clear your vision, and crown your labours with reward."

In the evening of the same day Mr. Gladstone addressed a meeting in St. Andrew's Hall, attended by nearly 6,000 persons. It was one of the longest and most elaborate addresses he delivered in Scotland ; and although some short speeches were delivered in reply to addresses, it virtually concluded the Midlothian campaign. At the conclusion of the speech, having summarized the proceedings of the Government, he said :—

"I will use the fewest words. We have finance in confusion ; we have legislation in intolerable arrear ; we have honour compromised by the breach of public law ; we have public distress aggravated by the destruction of confidence ; we have Russia aggrandised and yet estranged ; we have Turkey befriended as we say, but mutilated, and sinking every day ; we have Europe restless and disturbed. . . . To call this policy Conservative is, in my opinion, a pure mockery, and an abuse of terms. Whatever it may be in its motive, it is in its result disloyal, it is in its essence thoroughly subversive. There is no democrat, there is no agitator, there is no propounder of anti-rent doctrines, whatever mischief he may do, who can compare in mischief with possessors of authority who thus invert and who thus degrade the principles of free government in the British Empire. Gentlemen, I wish to end as I began. Is this the way, or is this not the way, in which a free nation, inhabiting these islands, wishes to be governed ? Will the people, be it now or be it months hence, ratify the deeds that have been done, and assume upon themselves that tremendous responsibility ? The whole humble aim, gentlemen, of my proceedings has been to bring home, as far as was in my power, this great question to the mind and to the conscience of the community at large. If I cannot decide the issue—and of course I have no power to decide it—I wish at least to endeavour to make it understood by those who can."

In the course of the fortnight he spent north of the Tweed he addressed upwards of 75,000 persons.

CHAPTER XXVI.

THE GENERAL ELECTION OF 1880—AGAIN PRIME MINISTER.

As the appeal to the country was inevitable, it was thought that
the Ministry might resolve on a dissolution at once; but they
decided to meet Parliament. A temporary Budget was presented, showing a further deficiency. The great impression
made by Mr. Gladstone's speeches, and his vigorous denunciation of the foreign policy of the Government, had greatly affected
public opinion, and the shout of disapprobation which greeted
Mr. Cross's Bill for purchasing the stock of the Metropolitan
Water Companies at a price inordinately beyond tne real value,
completed the discomfiture of the Ministers. Without any previous intimation, it was announced in both Houses, on the 8th of
March, that a dissolution would take place, and on the 24th of
March, 1880, the ninth Victorian Parliament came to an end.

Mr. Gladstone made another visit to Midlothian to address his
constituents previous to the election. His exertions were almost
as great as on the previous occasion, for he made long speeches
at Edinburgh on the 17th of March, at Corstorphine March 18,
at Ratho on the same day, at Dalkeith on the 19th, at Peni-
cuik on the 24th, at Storm on the 30th, and at West Calder on
the 2nd of April. At the close of the last speech he said,
referring to the victories of the Liberals at the elections:—

"Great things have been done in the last three days, and these things,
gentlemen, are not done in a corner. The intelligence, limited, but yet intelligible, has been flashed over sea and land, and has reached, long before I
address you, the remotest corners of the earth. I can well conceive that it
has been received in different countries with different feelings. I can believe
that there are one or two Ministers of State in the world, and possibly even
here and there a Sovereign, who would have eaten this morning a heartier
breakfast if the tidings conveyed by the telegraph had been reversed, and if
the issue of the elections had been as triumphant for the existing Administration as it has been menacing, if not fatal, to their prospects. But this I know,
among other places to which it has gone, it has passed to India—it has before
this time reached the mind and the heart of many millions of your Indian
fellow-subjects—and I will venture to say that it has gladdened every heart
among them. They have known this Government principally in connection
with the aggravation of their burdens and the limitation of their privileges;
and, gentlemen, I will tell you more, that if there be in Europe any State or
country which is crouching in fear at the feet of powerful neighbours with

gigantic armaments, which loves, enjoys, and cherishes liberty, but which at the same time fears lest that inestimable jewel should be wrenched out of its hands by overweening force—if there be such a State, and there may be such a State in the East and in the West—then I will venture to say that in that State, from the highest to the lowest, from sovereign to subject, joy and satisfaction will have been diffused by the intelligence of these memorable days. The great trial, gentlemen, proceeds. It is a great trial. You have great forces arrayed against you. . . . The nation is a power hard to rouse, but when roused harder still and more hopeless to resist. I believe from the indications that crowd upon us from hour to hour that it is now roused. It is impossible for a nation—for the mass of a community—to make politics its daily task. It can be but occasionally and rarely that you can afford to draw aside your minds from the pursuits and exigencies of life and to concentrate them upon public interests. But one has arrived, gentlemen, of those great occasions on which it is alike your interest, your duty, I would even say your necessity, to concentrate your attention, now when this great trial is proceeding, in which I figure to myself those who have constituted the majority of the late House of Commons as the persons arraigned, and the constituencies of the country as those who are called together in the solemn order of the Constitution to hear the evidence and to pronounce the verdict. That evidence has been pretty largely given. That verdict we await. We have none of the forms of a judicial trial. There are no peers in Westminster Hall, there are no judges on the woolsack ; but if we concentrate our minds upon the truth of the case as apart from its mere exterior, it is a grander and more august spectacle than ever was exhibited either in Westminster Hall or in the House of Lords; for a nation called to undertake the discharge of a great and responsible duty, a duty which is to tell, as we are informed from high authority, on the peace of Europe and on the destinies of England, has found its interests mismanaged, its honour tarnished, its strength burdened and weakened by needless, mischievous, unauthorised, unprofitable engagements, and it has resolved that this state of things shall cease, and that right and justice shall be done."

The election took place on Monday, the 5th of April. The result of the poll showed votes for Gladstone 1,579; Lord Dalkeith, 1,368; majority, 211. On receipt of the intelligence, Mr. Gladstone thanked his constituents from the balcony of Lord Rosebery's house in George Street, Edinburgh.

To guard against the consequences of a possible, though improbable defeat, Mr. Gladstone had been nominated and returned for Leeds ; but as he elected to sit for Midlothian, his son, Mr. Herbert Gladstone, who had unsuccessfully contested Middlesex, was put in nomination and returned.

The final elections showed that the tide had turned. Day by day appeared the record of Liberal gains. When the final return was made, it appeared that the Liberals had a majority, including the Irish Home Rulers, of 175, and of 53 over Conservatives and Home Rulers combined. In the list of Liberal gains there were no less than 54 constituencies in which the verdict of 1874 had

been wholly or partia'ly reversed.   The Conservatives, for their
part, succeeded in wresting back from the Liberals only two seats
gained by the latter in 1874.   The counties closely competed
with the boroughs in swelling the Liberal gairs.   Of the 219 seats
for county constituencies, 45 were gained, and the Liberal representatives of the counties (94 in number) are more than they
have ever been since the general election of 1835.   The total
number of Conservative votes recorded in 1874 was 1,217.806 ;
in 1880, 1,412,956.   The total number of Liberal votes recorded
in 1874 was 1,431,805 ; in 1880, 1,877,290.

The Earl of Beaconsfield placed his resignation in the hands
of the Queen when the result of the elections was known, and the
Queen sent first for Lord Hartington, the Liberal leader in the
House of Commons, and then for Earl Granville, the leader of
the party in the House of Lords.   Both these statesmen knew
that the victory was due to Mr. Gladstone, and declined to undertake the task of forming an administration; and on the 23rd of
April Her Majesty sent for Mr. Gladstone, who accepted the
office of First Lord of the Treasury, combining with it that of
Chancellor of the Exchequer.

CHAPTER XXVII.

THE new Parliament was opened by Royal Commission on the
29th of April; but the Royal Speech was not read until the 20th
of May, the intermediate time being occupied in the House of
Commons by the election of the Speaker and the swearing in of
the members. This generally formal proceeding was interrupted
by the first mutterings of a storm which greatly disturbed the
House in this and the ensuing session. Mr. Bradlaugh, who
had been many years before the public as a propagator, in the
press and on the platform, of atheistic opinions, had been
elected for the borough of Northampton, and presented himself
at the table, claiming to make a declaration, or affirmation, instead of taking the oath in the usual form. He had been permitted to do so by magistrates and by the Judges of the Superior
Courts, on the ground that, as he did not believe in the existence
of God, the form of oath could not be specially binding on his
conscience. The Clerk at the table and the Speaker himself
were perplexed by the claim. Parliament had generously made
provision for accommodating the consciences of Quakers and
Jews; but "Turks and heretics" had not hitherto claimed
exemption from the ordinary form. Mr. Bradlaugh was certainly
not a Jew, and he repudiated Quakerism as emphatically as he
did any other form of Christianity. If he had been content to
follow the example of many, and repeat the words of the oath
without attaching any meaning to them, or with any amount of
mental reservation he might have thought fit to employ, he could
have taken his seat quietly; but he stood out for the right of
making an affirmation, and the House could not see its way clear
to any other course than the appointment of a committee
of nineteen members to enquire whether he was or was not
entitled to affirm only. When the report was presented, it appeared that, by a majority of one only, the committee denied
Mr. Bradlaugh's right to affirm.

On the 20th of May the Royal Speech was read by the Lord
Chancellor. The position of affairs in Afghanistan and South

Africa was of course referred to ; but the most important announcement was that the Peace Preservation Act for Ireland,
the operation of which expired on the 1st of June, would not be
renewed. In the debates on the Address, in both Houses, this determination was vigorously commented on ; and beyond the walls
of Parliament the opinion was freely expressed that, in presence of
the elements of disorder so abundant in Ireland, the Ministry
exhibited an undue amount of confidence in divesting themselves
of the power given by the Act. In the Commons, Mr. O'Connor
Power, member for Mayo, moved, and Mr. R. Power, member for
the city of Waterford, seconded, an amendment, but it was
rejected by a majority of 253, and the Address was carried.

Mr. Gladstone met Parliament with a strong array of Minis-
terial colleagues—some veterans of proved power, others
recruits of more than ordinary promise. Lord Selborne and
Earl Granville had resumed the offices they had previously held ;
Lord Hartington was Secretary of State for India, the Earl of
Kimberley for the Colonies, the Duke of Argyll Lord Privy Seal,
and Earl Spencer President of the Council; Lord Northbrook
was at the Admiralty, and Mr. Childers at the War Office ; Sir
William Harcourt was at the head of the Home Department;
Mr. Forster, whose administrative capacity was so well established.
undertook what proved to be the most arduous position in the
Ministry, that of Secretary for Ireland ; and Mr. Bright, in the
comparatively easy office of Chancellor of the Duchy of Lancaster,
gave the prestige of his great reputation to the Cabinet. The most
conspicuous of the new men were Mr. Fawcett, whose physical
infirmity was an insurmountable objection to his becoming a
Cabinet Minister, but who undertook the office of Postmaster
General; Mr. Mundella, Vice-President of the Council; Mr.
Chamberlain, the colleague of Mr. Bright in the representation of
Birmingham, who entered the Cabinet as President of the Board
of Trade, and Sir Charles Dilke, who, as Under-Secretary, represented the Foreign Office in the Commons. The two appointments last mentioned were a recognition of the abilities of the
leading members of the advanced Liberals. Of Mr. Gladstone's
colleagues in his previous administration, two eminent members
had no place in the new arrangements. Lord Cardwell apparently
had no desire to resume office, content to be an unattached
member of the Liberal party ; and Mr. Lowe, with the title of
Viscount Sherbrooke, transferred his great abilities and uncertain
support of the Premier to the Upper House.

The House had scarcely settled down to work, when Mr.

Bradlaugh again appeared upon the scene. The committee having decided against him on the affirmation claim, he presented himself at the table on the 21st of May, and offered to take the oath.   Here was a change of front involving an embarrassing dilemma.   About a fortnight before, he had objected to take the oath because he did not believe in the assumption it involved, and to which he would appear to assent; now he demanded to take it, admittedly as a fictitious ceremony—an affirmation in disguise. A large number of members of the House were unable to appreciate the subtle train of reasoning which had apparently been satisfactory to Mr. Bradlaugh. To some, taking the oath with an avowed expression of disbelief in its obligation seemed a profanation ; to others, an audacity. Sir H. Drummond Wolff, member for Portsmouth, brought the matter to an issue by moving a resolution to the effect that Mr. Bradlaugh could not be permitted to take the oath, as he had publicly declared it was not binding on his conscience. A two-nights' debate ensued, in the course of which much irrelevant matter was introduced, and it is to be hoped that Mr. Bradlaugh benefited by the criticisms on his character and contributions to his biography. Mr. Gladstone, anxious that any action of the House should be deliberately taken, moved, as an amendment to the resolution, that a select committee should be appointed to consider and report upon the question whether an avowed atheist could legally take the oath. This amendment was strongly objected to, the Opposition insisting that the House was competent to decide upon the matter at once. A division was taken, and Sir H. Wolff's resolution being negatived by 289 to 214, the committee was appointed. On the 16th of June, Mr. Walpole reported that the committee had arrived at the conclusion that the oath ought not to be administered to an avowed atheist. A few days afterwards, Mr. Henry Labouchere, Mr. Bradlaugh's colleague in the representation of Northampton, moved that he should be allowed to make a declaration or affirmation ; but, after an exciting debate, the motion was negatived by a majority of 45.   On the following night Mr. Bradlaugh presented himself at the bar of the House, and having been permitted to make a speech in support of his claim to take his seat, was ordered to withdraw. He refused to do so, on the ground that he was a duly elected member of the House, and resisted the Sergeant-at-Arms, wherefore he was, on the motion of Sir Stafford Northcote (Mr. Gladstone, the leader of the House, having declined to interfere), taken into custody and committed to an apartment in the clock-tower, where he

remained a prisoner in comfortable quarters until the following
evening, when Sir Stafford Northcote, thinking that the dignity of
the House had been sufficiently vindicated, moved that he be
released from custody—a motion to which nobody objected.   On
the 1st of July Mr. Gladstone moved a resolution permitting
Mr. Bradlaugh to affirm, "subject to any liability by statute."
The words quoted made the resolution different from that proposed by Mr. Labouchere and rejected by the House; and many
members who hesitated to accept the responsibility of coming to
a decision, the legality of which might afterwards be questioned,
saw, in the words introduced by the Prime Minister, a saving
clause by which any responsibility would be made to rest on Mr.
Bradlaugh himself, and not on the House.   The resolution was
carried by 303 against 249.

The course adopted by Mr. Gladstone was much criticised at
the time; and some of his habitual supporters and admirers
fancied they had discovered a concession to the opinions of the
advanced Radicals in the Cabinet.   It may be well, therefore,
for the purpose of showing that the Prime Minister acted in
accordance with his own views of political duty, to quote his
words :—

"It is not well that any person duly elected, and tendering himself in the
terms of the Act of Parliament at the table to swear or affirm, should be precluded from taking his place in the House—subject to the liabilities incumbent
on him by statute—through any question put to him on behalf of the House.
That, sir, is the simple issue which I present to the mind of the House, and
I detach it altogether from the specialties of Mr. Bradlaugh's opinions.
There might have been other opinions which might have been elicited by
questions from persons in other circumstances.   I care not what the
opinions were; we stand upon this point—that where the law has laid down
a rule, where the constituency have exercised their privilege, where the proceedings are unimpeachable in form and substance, and where the man whom
they have chosen neither says nor does anything in this House, of his own
accord, spontaneously deviating either to the right or left from the line pointed
out by the Act of Parliament—we say that it is not well for the general
interests of the country, it is not well for the interests or character of this
House, that such a person, whatever his opinions, on presenting himself should
be stopped on his road to his seat by the act of any person proceeding to
question him on the part of the House.   It is well that he should be left to
be tried by the tribunals of his country, which have full means for conducting
his trial, and which will acquit or condemn him according to law."

One of the earliest duties incumbent on Mr. Gladstone was the
preparation of a new Budget.   Sir Stafford Northcote, previous
to the dissolution of Parliament, had made a comfortable financial arrangement, to which Mr. Gladstone had assented; but
neither of them then knew what soon became very unpleasantly

apparent, that Sir John Strachan, the Military Accountant-General in India, had, "by mistake," under-estimated the cost of the war in Afghanistan to the extent of about £9,000,000! As some portion of the expense must devolve on the Imperial Government, and a supplemental estimate had not only absorbed the small surplus on which Sir Stafford had relied, but created a considerable deficiency, Mr. Gladstone was compelled to confine his financial arrangements within narrow limits. It was not a time for a sensational Budget. In expectation of the renewal of the expiring Commercial Treaty with France, he proposed some modifications of the wine duties, but subsequently withdrew the resolution, in consequence of the difficulties attending the negotiations for the renewal of the treaty. The malt-tax—that *bête noir* of so many Chancellors of the Exchequer—was at length to be abolished; but a tax on beer was substituted, a duty of 6s. 3d. being made payable on every barrel (with allowance for waste); and private brewers would be required to take out a licence. Another penny would be added to the income-tax, and that was all. Lord George Hamilton and Sir Stafford Northcote objected to the abolition of the malt-tax at the expense of the payers of income-tax; but no formal opposition was made to the passing of the resolutions.

On Sunday, the 1st of August, Mr. Gladstone was prostrated by a severe attack of congestion of the lungs; and for several days was in great danger. An intense sympathy was aroused, and all political differences were forgotten in the anxiety respecting the condition of the Prime Minister. The excellent constitution of the patient and the skill of his medical attendants obtained the mastery in the struggle between life and death; and when sufficiently recovered to be removed from Downing Street, a cruise round Great Britain, on board one of Mr. Donald Currie's magnificent steamers, restored Mr. Gladstone to health and comparative strength. It is not too much to say that all England rejoiced when, on the 28th of August, exactly four weeks after the first attack, Mr. Gladstone resumed his place in the House of Commons.

During the enforced absence of the Prime Minister, Lord Hartington occupied the position of leader of the House; and seldom has a most arduous duty been more ably discharged. Firmness, discretion, and good temper were qualities pre-eminently necessary under the circumstances, and all these qualities Lord Hartington exhibited. Previous to Mr. Gladstone's illness, the Compensation for Disturbance Bill, introduced by

Mr. Forster, had been carried through the House, with no little difficulty, some of the Irish members doing their best to obstruct it at every stage. The Bill reached the House of Lords on the 27th of July, and was rejected by their lordships on the 3rd of August by 282 against 51. Once more the Lords had defeated the Ministerial policy ; but, this time, Mr. Gladstone reserved his strength for another opportunity.

The Irish members were not the only obstructors. A small " Fourth Party," as it was named, consisting of three members, Lord Randolph Churchill, Sir H. Wolff, and Mr. Gorst, professedly Conservatives, but dissatisfied with the mild-mannered Sir Stafford Northcote, and fighting "for their own hand," in Hal-o'-the-Wynd fashion, were indomitable and irrepressible. If their philosophy was not Socratic, their power of putting questions on all possible occasions was quite in accordance with the Socratic method ; and their speech-making proclivities were equally active. Lord Hartington, while acting as leader, summed up in an amusing manner the performances of the Fourth Party and the Irish members. Up to that time (August 20)—exactly three months from the beginning of business—Mr. Gorst had asked 85 questions and made 105 speeches ; Sir H. Wolff, 34 questions and 68 speeches ; Lord R. Churchill, 21 questions, 74 speeches ; Mr. Biggar, 14 questions, 58 speeches ; Mr. Finigan, 10 questions, 47 speeches ; Mr. A. O'Connor, 2 questions, 55 speeches. Six members, said Lord Hartington, had made 407 speeches, and, allowing ten minutes for each speech, occupied a fortnight of the working time of the House.

The prorogation took place on the 7th of September. Little, indeed, had been done in legislation ; and absolutely nothing in respect to Irish difficulties, which were assuming alarming dimensions. Early in the year Mr. Parnell had visited America with the view of organizing an Irish party there, who would assist to provide funds for carrying on the political objects of his party, and for the relief of the distress suffered by the Irish peasantry. There was distress indeed, but it was mitigated as the summer came on. The Land League then advised the tenants to refuse to pay rent, and then followed evictions and outrages. That peculiar form of opposition known as Boycotting, from the name of Captain Boycott, the most conspicuous victim, was pursued with indomitable tenacity of purpose. It consisted in isolating the objectionable person from all kinds of social intercourse. No shopkeeper would supply him with food or other necessaries ; his labourers left the crops to rot in the ground ; no one would speak

to him, or to any member of his family. If he himself drove a
few cattle to the public market, there was no purchaser to be
found. His life was in such peril that he wandered about his
farm or pastures guarded by policemen with loaded rifles, and his
house was converted into a small garrison. Captain Boycott
appealed to the authorities for help, and, a party of Ulster
Protestants having volunteered to cut and house his crops, a
strong military force escorted them to the estate near Lough
Mask, and remained on guard till the harvest was got in. Then
the relief party returned, guarded as before, greeted in every
village they passed through with muttered execrations and malignant jeers. Outrages increased ; evictions were resisted or the
evicted tenant was replaced in his holding by silent, but determined parties of angry men, whom the landlord dared not attempt
to resist. Cattle and sheep were cruelly mutilated in a spirit of
revenge. Process servers, unless guarded by soldiers, were
assaulted, sometimes nearly killed ; sheriff's officers performed
their duties accompanied by an imposing array of armed constabulary. There were open assassinations of unpopular landlords and others. The ordinary operations of law were suspended ;
and virtually, if not legally, a large portion of western Ireland was
under martial law, and that very inadequate to the work of maintaining order and suppressing crime. The Land League agitators
travelled through the country, making inflammatory speeches and
encouraging the ignorant, violent peasantry to continue in their
work of intimidation and outrage.

By their refusal to renew the Peace Preservation Act, which
expired in June, Ministers greatly weakened the arm of the
executive ; and it became evident that some strong measures
must be taken. Irish noblemen and gentlemen urged the Lord
Lieutenant and the Chief Secretary to adopt some steps by which
they would be protected, not only in executing processes of law,
but in the ordinary peaceful and secure enjoyment of life and
property. The known aversion of some members of the Cabinet
to coercive measures, the acknowledgment of the Ministry
generally that Ireland had great grievances, which they were
bound in reason and justice to endeavour to redress, encouraged
the agitators, who believed that the terrorism they aroused would
induce Ministers to make great concessions. Mr. Forster,
the Chief Secretary, visited Ireland several times during the
session, and it was believed that he advocated strong measures
of repression ; but, on the other hand, Mr. Bright and Mr.
Chamberlain, Cabinet Ministers, in addressing their Birmingham

constituents, had maintained that "force is no remedy." The
Irish members believed, perhaps the Opposition members hoped,
that there were dissensions in the Ministry. If so, they must
have been disappointed when Mr. Gladstone, at the Lord Mayor's
banquet, on the 9th of November, speaking, of course, as Prime
Minister, with full authority, said :—

"Anxious as we are for the practical improvement of the land law, I
assure your lordship, and all who hear me, as well as those who may become
acquainted with the proceedings of this meeting, that we recognise also the
priority of the duty above any other of enforcing the law for the purposes of
order. We hold it our first duty to look to the law as it stands, and to
ascertain what fair and just administration means. But the obligation incumbent upon us to protect every citizen in the enjoyment of his life and property
might, under certain circumstances, compel us to ask for an increase of
power ; and, although we will never contemplate such a contingency, nor
imagine it to exist, until it is proved by the clearest demonstration, yet if that
contingency were realised, if the demonstration were afforded, you may rely
on it we should not shrink from acting on the obligation it would entail."

The demonstration and clear evidence were not far to seek.
The Judges of Assize supplied them. "Mr. Justice Fitzgerald
in Cork, and Mr. Baron Dowse in Galway," we are told, " drew
an alarming picture of the prevailing lawlessness in Munster and
Connaught, while Justices Barry and Lawson bore testimony to
the progress of the contagion in Leinster and even in Connaught.
Not one case of outrage in ten led to a prosecution, and the trials
at the assizes proved that, even of this small proportion, very few
could be expected to end in the punishment of the guilty. Mr.
Justice Fitzgerald complained that both witnesses and jurors had
been driven by menaces to forget or forego the obligations of
their oaths. Prisoners were acquitted against whom conclusive
evidence had been taken before the magistrates. The judges
themselves were threatened if they persisted in doing their duty."

Nearly thirty years ago, Mr. Griffiths had made an official
valuation of land in Ireland ; and the Land League orators now
advised the tenants to refuse payment according to any other
valuation, and to resist any consequent proceedings. Thirty years
make a considerable change in most things ; but, according to
the agitators, not in the value of Irish land. At any rate,
Griffiths' valuation was a convenient pretext for resisting authority
Very strong language was used ; and the Government decided on
indicting Mr. Parnell, some other Members of Parliament, and
some officials of the Land League, for seditious conspiracy. The
trial at Dublin began on the 28th of December, and resulted in
the acquittal of the accused.

The year ended in gloom. There was little repose for Ministers. Not Ireland only occupied their thoughts. They felt the necessity of reviewing the decision of their predecessors in respect of Afghanistan and South Africa. The former must be evacuated by British troops, and the Ameer and his rivals left to fight their own battles; the Transvaal must be restored to the Boers, and the restoration of annexed territory was an idea not agreeable to British traditions, and certainly very disagreeable to pugnaciously disposed persons. It may be added that intelligence early in the year of defeats of the English troops, by the Boers, and the death of Sir George Colley, the British general, did not make the project of restoration one whit more acceptable.

Parliament was summoned to meet on the 6th of January. The Royal Speech referred to the alarming social condition of Ireland. Agrarian crimes had multiplied far beyond the experience of recent years; the administration of justice had been frustrated by the impossibility of procuring evidence; and an extended system of terror had been established in some parts of the country which paralyzed almost alike the exercise of private right and the performance of civil duties. Propositions, it was announced, would be submitted for additional powers necessary for the vindication of order and public law, and to secure protection for life and property and personal liberty of action. Parliament was recommended to undertake the further development of the principles of the Land Act of 1870 in a manner conformable to the special wants of Ireland, both as regards the relation of landlord and tenant, and with a view to effective efforts for giving to a large portion of the people by purchase a permanent proprietary interest in the soil. A measure was also promised for the establishment of county government in Ireland, founded upon representative principles, and framed with the double aim of conferring popular control over expenditure, and of supplying a yet more serious want by extending the formation of habits of local self-government.

Then commenced a session the records of which will form one of the strangest chapters in the history of the Parliament of the United Kingdom. The Irish members decided on a policy of obstruction, the like of which had never before been encountered. The previous Parliament had tasted the pleasures of an all-night sitting, and had enjoyed some little experience of the ability of the Irish members to impede business. But the session of 1881 was unique. The motion for the Address in reply to the speech produced a vigorous debate in the House of Lords, in which the

Earl of Beaconsfield defended the Afghan policy of the late Ministry, and referring to Ireland, said: "I am not using exaggerated language when I say that Her Majesty's executive in Ireland have absolutely abandoned their functions."

The debate on the Address in the Commons occupied eleven nights. Mr. Parnell, Mr. Justin M'Carthy, Mr. Dawson, Mr. Sexton, Mr. O'Kelly, and others proposed amendment after amendment, nothing daunted by the fact that they were all rejected by large majorities. Time was wasted, and that was all the obstructionists desired. Ultimately the Address was carried by 435 to 57. On the 24th of January Mr. Forster moved for leave to bring in a Bill for the Protection of Person and Property in Ireland. The Bill would confer on the Lord Lieutenant the power by his warrant to make arrests of persons reasonably suspected of having been, either before or after the passing of the Act, guilty, as principal or accessory, of treason-felony, or treasonable practices, or of having incited acts of violence or intimidation The Act was to be in force until the end of September, 1882. On the following night Mr. Gladstone moved that the Bill, and the Bill which was to follow, should have precedence over all other Bills. It cost the House twenty-two hours of continuous sitting to carry this motion, although only thirty-three members voted against it. But when some thirty members, gifted with fluency of speech and good lungs, persist in moving amendments and adjournments, and make speeches on every motion, they can easily amuse themselves for twenty-two hours by working in relays.

It was not until the 25th of February that the Bill passed the Commons, by a majority of 245, the numbers being 281 to 36. It was carried in the Lords and received the Royal Assent on the 2nd of March, the day after Sir William Harcourt had moved in the Lower House for leave to bring in the Peace Preservation (Ireland) Bill. According to his wont, the Home Secretary was very outspoken. "Pikes, revolvers, and dynamite," he said, "are not the instruments of legitimate reform; but in such a state of society as has been created in Ireland, they are the secret armouries of treason and revolution, of the midnight brigand and the skulking assassin. It is against such persons that the Bill is directed."

The debate—if by any stretch of ordinary language the obstructive talk can be considered a debate—on the motion for leave to bring in Mr. Forster's Bill, extended over five nights, and involved a continuous sitting of the House for forty-two hours. At length, the Speaker, exercising an authority which, however

desirable, was perhaps a little open to question, refused to hear
any more speeches and put the question of the first reading. On
the following night a very remarkable scene was enacted.
Ministers and the regular Opposition were alike agreed that some·
thing must be done to prevent hindrance to public busine:s
by the Irish members taking advantage of the existing rules of
the House. Mr. Gladstone introduced a resolution giving power
to the Speaker to frame new rules; and Mr. Dillon, persistently
out of order with his interruptions, and refusing to defer to the
Speaker, was at length suspended from taking any further part in
the sitting, and ordered to leave the House. Other Irish
members sprang to their feet, defied the Speaker, and were
ordered out. Altogether, thirty-five, the whole body of the
obstructors, marched out, one after the other, escorted by the
Sergeant-at-Arms. Relieved of this troublesome contingent, the
House then agreed to a resolution that when a Bill was declared
urgent by a majority of three to one in a House of 300 members,
on the proposal of a Minister of the Crown, the power of the
House for the regulation of all business should be in the hands of
the Speaker. The resolution worked well, with the assistance of a
code of rules devised by the Speaker and sanctioned by the House.

Mr. Gladstone introduced his Budget (it might be, he said, his
last Budget) on the 4th of April, before the Easter holidays. It
was simple in its arrangements, and did not excite much interest.
The penny added to the income-tax in 1880 was taken off, and
some alterations were made in the surtax on foreign spirits and
wines, and in the legacy and probate duties. A surplus of about
£300,000 would be in hand. He avoided complex arrangements, which might produce long debate, for his great object was
to introduce the promised Land Bill for Ireland, on the success
of which he had staked his Ministerial fortunes.

On Thursday, the 7th of April, Mr. Gladstone rose to move
for leave to bring in the Irish Land Bill. A rumour of dissensions in the Cabinet, and the consequent retirement of the Duke
of Argyll from the office of Lord Privy Seal, had reached the
members, and before the sitting had ended was confirmed. In his
introductory remarks, Mr. Gladstone admitted that the Bill of
1870 had failed to realize the results proposed. Having referred
to the two commissions which had been appointed, one by the
late and one by the present Government, he proceeded to sketch
the leading provisions of the Bill. He went on to say :—

"I feel that I have led the House through a wilderness of detail, and I
will now try to sum up in a very few words the effect of what I have said.

What we propose to do is this. To set up, on one hand, a system of limited and regulated freedom of contract between the landlord and the tenant, wherein, in consideration of the circumstances of Ireland, the tenant shall, notwithstanding, be fortified by certain provisions of the law as to his right of sale, and as to guarantees against arbitrary increase of rent. That we offer on the one side. On the other side, we offer freely the entrance into a Court passing under a public authority, so that no matter relating either to tenure, assignment, or to rent, can escape the supervision of the Court. The Court must act upon general principles of justice. Improved general law may keep the tenant out of the Court; but if it does, it is only because it is his interest to remain out. I must say that I think in any country of which the agricultural relations were established on a tolerably happy footing, it would indeed be an extremely sorry offer either to landlords or tenants to tell them they might have the privilege of going into a court of justice, with all the incidents attaching to such a proceeding, for the purpose of making their bargain. Still, in this peculiar case that is what we deliberately and advisedly make an essential part, and indeed the very core of the measure. On the morning after this Bill passes every landlord and tenant will be subject to certain new provisions of the law of great importance. In the first place increase of rent will be restrained by certain rules. In the second place, compensation for disturbance will be regulated according to different rates; and in the third place—more important probably than any—the right to sell the tenant's interest will be universally established. What I am now saying is outside the Court. But there also remains free power to go into the Court, to authorise application to the Court for a judicial rent, which may be followed by a judicial tenant right; that judicial rent to entail a statutory term of fifteen years, and the renewal of it *toties quoties* to be provided so long as the present tenancy exists, and the present tenancy not to be determined by the mere change of tenant. Eviction will hereafter, as I trust, be only for default, and resumption by the landlord, apart from the default of the tenant, will disappear in Ireland, except it be for causes both reasonable and grave, the which causes may be brought into question before the Court. Well, we are sometimes told that it is a hopeless business to legislate for Ireland. I am not of that opinion. Let me consider what has happened in Ireland in our time. For half a century Parliament has been intermittently—but still, on the whole, not without resolution and not without good intention, engaged in bringing into Ireland better, larger, and more liberal systems of policy and legislation. And what has happened in Ireland within that time? No country has reaped greater benefits. Ireland had, from the great transition between Protection and Free Trade, reaped benefits absolutely unmixed. The price of everything Ireland produced was raised. In England the tenant farmer had to face a decrease in the price of his principal commodity, on which he had always mainly and unduly relied for the payment of his rent, namely, his wheat. But to Ireland, a country which imports more wheat than she grows, the benefit from that has been unmixed, and from other causes it has been abundant. Look at the improved condition of the people. What old man is there in Ireland now who can compare the condition of the people in almost every part of Ireland with what it was half a century ago, and not thank God for the transformation which has passed over that country. . . . . There may be other facts disheartening enough, but there are circumstances which should teach us neither to despair nor to despond. But there is a higher encouragement and nobler encouragement yet than these; and that is one that is to be enjoyed by all men who have faith in certain principles of action. It is said that we have failed in Ireland. I do not admit failure. I admit success to be incomplete. I am asked how it is to be made complete. I say by patient persistence in well-doing—by steady adherence to the work of justice. Then we shall not depend on the results of the moment. It will not be what to-day may say, or to-morrow may say. It will be rather what fruits we are to reap in the long future of a nation's existence, and with that we have a reckoning which cannot fail. Justice, sir, is to be our guide. It has been said that love is stronger than death, and so justice is stronger than popular excitement, than the passion of the moment, than even the grudges and resentments and sad traditions of the past. Walking in that path we cannot err. Guided by that light—that Divine light—we are safe. Every step we make upon our road is a step that brings us nearer to the goal; and every obstacle, even although it seems for the moment insurmountable, can only for a little while retard, and never can defeat, the final triumph."

The Bill having been read a first time, the House adjourned for the Easter vacation. Mr. Gladstone's health had been somewhat impaired in consequence of severe contusions on the head he had received by a fall as he was stepping from his carriage on to the pavement coated with ice, a result of the intense frost. He needed repose, and a few days of rest and country air at Hawarden were welcome. The second reading was proposed to be taken on the 25th of April. Sir Stafford Northcote, leader of the Conservative Opposition, declared that the Bill contained principles so intrinsically unjust, and so open to objection from an economic point of view, that he and his friends could not conscientiously vote for the second reading. After seven nights' debate, Lord Elcho moved an amendment to the effect that the House, while willing to consider any just measure founded upon sound principles that would benefit the tenants of land in Ireland, was of opinion that the provisions of the Bill were in the main economically unsound, unjust, and impolitic. The amendment was defeated by 352 to 176, exactly two to one, and the second reading was carried.

Then came the committee, and the consideration of the clauses occupied thirty-two sittings of the House. Upwards of a thousand amendments were placed on the paper; and although many were withdrawn, there was fierce fighting over the remainder. At length, on the 29th of July, the third reading was carried by 226 to 14, and the Bill went up to the Lords. It was introduced by Lord Carlingford, who had succeeded the Duke of Argyll as Lord Privy Seal, and who, when Mr. Chichester Fortescue, had enjoyed peculiar opportunities of becoming acquainted with Irish matters. On the motion for the second reading, the Marquis of Salisbury attacked the Bill with great energy, and the Duke of Argyll made a characteristic speech, in which he compared his

X

late colleagues in the Ministry to jelly-fishes, brilliant and interesting, but with no backbone. Several important amendments were made, nearly all of which were rejected when the Bill returned to the Commons. The Bill was then sent back to the Lords, who restored some of their amendments which had been struck out. The Bill went " downstairs " once more. The Commons would not yield, and a crisis was imminent. There was talk about an autumnal session, and the introduction of a new Bill, if the Lords would not accept this. Evidently the Conservative Peers desired to avoid a collision, and a meeting was held, the result of which was that when the Lords met on Tuesday, the 16th of August, the Marquis of Salisbury announced that his party would offer no further opposition, and expressed a hope " that the Bill might be of great benefit to the Irish tenant, and not of much harm to the landlord."

The contest was over, and the great Bill, not materially altered, though modified in a few details, passed the House, and received the Royal assent on the 22nd of August. The leading principles of this important measure may be briefly summarized. The complex details must be studied in the Act itself, which consists of forty-four pages. Subject to certain regulations, a tenant may sell his tenancy for the best price that can be got for it, the landlord having the right to pre-emption, or of objection, on specific grounds. A tenant disturbed in his holding by the act of a landlord after the passing of the Act, shall be entitled to compensation, according to a revised scale. The law as to compensation for improvements is amended. If the landlord demands an increase of rent, the tenant may apply to the Civil Bill Court of the county, and that Court will have the power, after hearing both parties, to fix the fair rent. The Court has also power to act equitably between the landlord and tenant, where either has made unreasonable demands. The ordinary tenancy may be converted into a fixed tenancy, the rent subject to re-valuation after a period of not less than fifteen years. The Land Commission (appointed by the Act) is empowered to advance money on security, to tenants, for the purpose of enabling them to purchase their holdings ; to purchase estates and re-sell them in parcels to tenants ; and to advance money for the reclamation of land, or to enable poor families to emigrate. A new Land Commission, to act as a superior Court and Court of Appeal for the Civil Bill, or County Court, is appointed, with a judicial commissioner, a barrister with the rank and pay of a Judge of the Supreme Court, and two other commissioners, each of whom is to receive a salary of £3,000 a year.

An official statement, in language unencumbered by legal technicalities, of the provisions of the Act, issued by the newly-appointed Commissioners, for the information of the parties interested, thus summarises the clauses which refer to security of tenure and define the position of the tenant :—

"Whenever a fair rent is fixed either by the Court or Commission, or by agreement, or by arbitration, the rent cannot be raised or altered for fifteen years, nor can the tenant be disturbed during that period. In the last year of the fifteen years the tenant can again get the rent settled and a new term of fifteen years granted, and so on. It is not, therefore, merely a term of fifteen years which the tenant gets, but practically a term renewable every fifteen years. It amounts to this, that the tenant paying a fair rent and treating the land in a proper tenantable way, and not subdividing or sub-letting his farm, will be safe from eviction or arbitrary increase of rent, and his rent cannot be increased by reason of his own improvements."

The much desired "three Fs" were nearly conceded by this Act. The tenant gains something undistinguishable from fixity of tenure, and something almost approaching to free sale, and the Act confers, in the most positive terms, a means of getting a fair rent fixed.

The Irish measures almost monopolized the business of the session. Two hundred and twenty-five public Bills were introduced into the House of Commons, but not many survived the embryo stage. Government Bills on the subjects of Bankruptcy, Educational Endowments in Scotland, Merchant Shipping, Corrupt and Illegal Practices at Parliamentary Elections, Rivers Conservancy, and Floods Prevention, were one and all withdrawn; and, of course, private members were in worse case than the Government.

One of the most important of the few measures passed—the Army Discipline and Regulation Act—made great changes in the organization of the army. The Bradlaugh difficulty cropped up again. The Law Courts having decided that the member for Northampton could not sit without taking the oath, the seat was declared vacant, and a new writ issued. Mr. Bradlaugh was re-elected, and presented himself in the House, demanding to be sworn. This the House would not allow, and Mr. Bradlaugh received an intimation that he would not be permitted to enter the House. On the 3rd of August he attempted to force his way, but was opposed in the lobby by the assistants of the Sergeant-at-Arms, aided by the police. A fight ensued, Mr. Bradlaugh was considerably hurt, and one of the ushers was nearly strangled. That, however, was only one strange episode of this strange session.

Debates on the conduct of Afghan and South African affairs
were of course inevitable. Mr. Gladstone bravely defended the
retrocession of the Transvaal, taking high ground. The occasion
was the debate on a resolution introduced on the 25th of July
by Sir Michael Hicks Beach, censuring the Government. With
the concluding passage of Mr. Gladstone's speech, so loftily
maintaining the supremacy of principle over mere political
expediency and false prestige, the subject may be left, and the
administration of the great statesman sketched in a connection
nearer home.

"Our case is summed up in this. We have endeavoured to cast aside all
considerations of false shame, and we have felt that we were strong enough
to put aside those considerations of false shame without fear of entailing upon
our country any sacrifice at all. We have endeavoured to do right, and to
eschew wrong, and we have done that in a matter involving alike the lives of
thousands and the honour and character of our country. And, Sir, whatever
may be the sense of gentlemen opposite, we believe that we are supported,
not only by the general convictions of Parliament, but by those of the country.
We feel that we are entitled to make that declaration, for from every great
centre of opinion in Europe, from the remotest corners of Anglo-Saxon
America, have come back to us the echoes of the resolution which we have
taken, the favouring and approving echoes, recognising in the policy of the
Government an ambition higher than that which looks for military triumph or
for territorial aggrandisement, but which seeks to signalise itself by walking
in the plain and simple ways of right and justice, and which desires never to
build up empire except in the happiness of the governed."

It may be added that the vote of censure was rejected by a
majority of 111 in a house of 519 members, and that the ratifica-
tion of the convention restoring the Transvaal to the Boers was
regarded by the country with approval. The death of Lord
Beaconsfield had occurred earlier in the year, and Mr. Gladstone's
tribute to the memory of his old opponent was a noble and an
ungrudging eulogy.

CHAPTER XXVIII.

SUPPRESSION OF THE LAND LEAGUE.—IMPRISONMENT OF

MR. PARNELL.

THE Land Act had excited extraordinary interest in Ireland; the relief it promised in one direction and the benefit it was calculated to confer in another were too obvious to be disguised, and it was felt that if fairly administered it would go far to remove the worst features of the agrarian trouble. The Roman Catholic Bishops had earnestly urged the people to accept and give the measure a trial, and this the latter were disposed to do, when Mr. Parnell interfered. He told them to hold back from the Act, "not to use it," until they had tested it. It was believed, and on reasonable ground, that the Act would not be fairly tested, that the test cases would be those of fair and moderate rents, that the Land Court would reject these cases, and that in this way Mr. Parnell would be provided with a cry that the Act and the Court had been tried and found alike worthless. Mr. Parnell was at the head of the Land League, and it had been stated by Mr. Dillon that if the Act were tolerated "it would in a few months take all the power out of the League:" there was, therefore, good reason to assume that Mr. Parnell was determined to defeat the object of the Act in order to save the League, and thus prevent his own power from collapsing.

That Mr. Gladstone thought so is evident from his language at Leeds. Mr. Parnell, he said, desired to "arrest the operation of the Act—to stand as Aaron stood, between the living and the dead, but to stand there not as Aaron stood, to arrest, but to spread the plague." In a week after the Leeds meeting, Mr. Parnell was lodged in Kilmainham gaol; and a circular having been issued by the Land League directing the tenants to pay no rent until Mr. Parnell was released, that organisation, which Mr. Justice Fitzgerald had declared illegal, was vigorously suppressed and the more prominent and active members were imprisoned.

Mr. Gladstone's responsibility as Prime Minister for these steps has been made the basis of a charge of inconsistency. Though clearly enough, in suppressing the Land League and in imprisoning Mr. Parnell at that time, he was acting as constitutionally as

he has acted since in opposing the imprisonment of Irish members and the suppression of the National League.   And for these
reasons.   In 1881 Mr. Parnell's following in the House of Commons was less than a third of what it became later.   It was only,
said Mr. Gladstone at Leeds, "a handful of men;" the smaller
section of the Home Rule party of that year, with no right or title
to speak for the Irish people as a whole.   Nevertheless this
"handful of men" stood between the people and the Land Act,
and in direct antagonism to the bulk of the representatives of
Ireland.   This was the position in 1881, when Mr. Parnell and
some of his followers were imprisoned; or rather it should be
said detained—and the distinction should be noted—for they
were subjected to none of the indignities of prison life.

Five years later, and the Irish representation had entirely
changed.   The nominal Home Rulers had disappeared, and the
"handful" of Parnellites increased to 85, representing five sixths
or the vast majority of the people of Ireland.   Their constitutional
right to be heard as the collective organ of the Irish people was
recognised by Mr. Gladstone, and he sided with them in resisting
coercive legislation, and in condemning excessive severity and
illegality in the administration of that legislation.   But obviously
this was not because they were Parnellites, or that he sympathised
with their trespasses on legality, or approved of their plans or
methods.   And this should be clearly understood.   But it was
because the Parnellite party were the duly elected members for
Ireland, entitled to protest in the name and with the authority of
the Irish people.

As in 1881, Mr. Gladstone, since 1885, has been with the
majority of the Irish representatives, consistently upholding the
rights of the people of Ireland and as consistently expostulating
against cruelty and illegality.   The change is not in his position,
but in that of the Parnellite party.   From a revolutionary league
in 1881, they had become the constitutional party of Ireland,
and, as a constitutional statesman, Mr. Gladstone supported their
reasonable demands.   On the other hand, the Government of Lord
Salisbury in their coercive legislation acted as directly antagonistic to the bulk of the Irish people—and consequently uncon-
stitutionally—as the Parnellite members acted in 1881.   And in
opposing that administration, in seeking to displace them, Mr.
Gladstone acted as consistently as he acted in 1881, when he
determined to remove the man who had stood not to arrest but
"to spread the plague."

CHAPTER XXIX.

DIFFICULTIES IN EGYPT.—MURDERS IN PHŒNIX PARK.

THOUGH reform was in the air early in 1882, and Mr. Gladstone was anxious to broaden the base of representation, it was soon manifest that no extension of the franchise could then be undertaken in Parliament. Useful agitation, however, in promotion of this object was going on in the country, and at Hawarden the Prime Minister announced that, with a view to reform legislation later, procedure in the House of Commons would in the opening Session be dealt with. So that what it was possible to do to help forward the movement, and clear the way for the promised Franchise Bill, was being done.

The difficulties of administration in Ireland were increasing, and in Egypt affairs were becoming complicated and embarrassing. The engagements of Lord Beaconsfield's administration, which were the source of our perplexities in Egypt, had made active interference in that country's affairs necessary, and in a joint note the English and French Governments declared their intention to support the Khedive Tewfik, against internal or external attack. This subsequently led to the bombardment of Alexandria by the British fleet. For this step Mr. Gladstone has been blamed, though it was practically unavoidable, the alternative being to repudiate honourable engagements and leave Egypt, with its Christian and Moslem population, to the rebels. England had removed one Khedive, and set up another, "and by setting him up," said Mr. Gladstone, "we became morally bound to support him; and not only so, but we entered into an actual covenant with the French to support him—to support the native government of Egypt. The consequence was, having in our hands the effectual control of the Government, and having on the throne a Sovereign whom we had put there, and who had not violated any of his duties, we were bound to sustain him." Bearing this in mind, and also that these engagements were entered into, not by Mr. Gladstone's administration, but by that of Lord Beaconsfield, it is difficult to see how Mr. Gladstone can be reasonably reproached, or what escape there was from the course Ministers felt it necessary to take when Arabi the Egyptian was in revolt, and in possession of Alexandria.

Nearer home the Government had their hands full. The area of discontent in Ireland had increased alarmingly, and it was evident, judging from the outrages which were taking place, that in imprisoning the Irish members the Government had made a mistake. They had removed the wrong men. They had removed those whose influence had restrained the more violent of Irishmen, and in doing so the Government turned the agitation from the constitutional path into that of disorder and lawlessness. The rackrenting that went on exasperated the people, and they were drawing within "measurable distance of civil war" when Mr. Parnell was released.

This step has been made the subject of a good deal of controversy. The Conservatives denounced it at the time and since, as the outcome of a discreditable bargain. The "Kilmainham Compact," it was called. It has since been disclosed that shortly before this the Conservatives were manœuvring to secure Mr. Parnell's release, and a vote against the Government for imprisoning him. And abundant evidence of this exists in the motion of Sir John Hay, and the questions put to Ministers in the House of Commons in regard to the detention of the Irish members. The truth is that the opposition were so bent upon discrediting the Government that it mattered very little to them whether they attempted it by denouncing Mr. Parnell's release, or by condemning his detention.

About this time the Cabinet had reconsidered their Irish policy, and with their sanction Mr. Chamberlain invited Mr. Parnell to assist them in restoring order. And he, being willing to do this, was set at liberty. Mr. Forster, though he took no part in the negotiations, acquiesced in what his colleagues had done, but he objected to a reversal of his policy, or to any slackening of his powers, and resigned. Lord Cowper adopted the same course, and in their vacant offices Mr. Gladstone placed Lord Spencer and Lord Frederick Cavendish. The Cabinet had decided that their coercive legislation had failed, and that the new Ministers entrusted with the Government of Ireland should enter Dublin with a message of peace. The Whig members of the Cabinet, Lords Hartington, Selborne and Northbrook, shared the responsibilities of their colleagues for the adoption of a conciliatory instead of the maintenance of a coercive policy. Yet when Mr. Gladstone attempted to embody it in practical measures they deserted him, and harked back to coercion.

On the 6th of May, Lord Frederick Cavendish and Mr. Thomas Burke, the Under Secretary of State, were assassinated in Phœnix Park. The horror this created in the public mind was not greater than that in the minds of Ministers. To Mr. Gladstone it was a sore and heavy blow. Of the younger Ministers Lord Frederick was his favourite, and besides was almost one of his own family by marriage with Lord Lyttelton's daughter. Mr. (now Sir George) Trevelyan was appointed chief secretary and, in a few days after, the Prevention of Crimes Bill was introduced.

This measure Mr. Gladstone's opponents have said is more severe than the Conservative Crimes Bill of 1887. But in 1882 criminal conspiracies were in active existence, whereas in 1887 there was no, or at any rate very little, exceptional crime. The Act of the latter year was aimed at a political party, and at combinations formed to resist injustice, and the administration of this Act created rather than removed disorder ; while, on the other hand, the Act of 1882 was administered with discriminating statesmanship; and, in extinguishing exceptional crime, restored order. It is admitted by a Nationalist writer, that in 1882 "a wild and horrible wave of crime passed over the country," and obviously a strong measure was then absolutely necessary ; but no such violence has since been witnessed in Ireland, nor is it possible while the people are hopeful. Then it should be added that to the drastic legislation of his Government Mr. Gladstone attached a healing measure, passing an Arrears Bill, which was urgently required and in consequence strenuously opposed in the House of Lords.

The length to which debates had been dragged had greatly impeded the legislative activity of the House of Commons ; and in the October Session procedure resolutions were carried, which to some extent minimised the opportunities of the obstructionists. In support of these resolutions Mr. Gladstone took the leading part ; and it may be pointed out as remarkable in parliamentary history that while thus engaged—the leader of the House, and the Prime Minister of England—he was entering upon the fiftieth anniversary of his introduction to parliamentary life. He had entered Parliament half a century before, "the rising hope of the Tories"—nay more—he had been put in by the Puseyites. He was then an earnest Oxonian, and after fifty years of public work, was still an earnest and enthusiastic student, but an advanced Liberal, filled with abiding trust in the people, and incomparably the greatest force in British politics.

CHAPTER XXX.

In forming his ministry in 1880, Mr. Gladstone, in addition to the duties of First Minister, undertook those also of the Chancellor of the Exchequer. This gave great satisfaction to the country, his skill in finance being unrivalled and his authority in this department of Government unquestioned; but obviously this arrangement involved too great a strain to be long continued, and early in May he placed the Exchequer under the care of Mr. Childers. This Minister—perhaps the most capable financier, excepting Mr. Gladstone and Sir Stafford Northcote, in the House of Commons—was placed at a great disadvantage. Mr. Gladstone had accustomed the public mind to brilliant budget speeches, in which the driest details of statement were luminously set forth, and in which also there was much to arrest and captivate the attention. Sir Stafford Northcote, his old pupil, showed wonderful lucidity in statement, but he was far short of his master in fertility of resource and in balancing or grouping the facts and figures of the budget. Mr. Childers contented himself with clearness in exposition, and, though his financial statements were interesting, they were bare and dry compared with those of Mr. Gladstone. The latter's political master was Sir Robert Peel, and he would be the first to acknowledge his indebtedness to that great man early in public life. Indeed, it would be no disparagement to Mr. Gladstone to say that, in the greatest of his financial achievements, in the most far-reaching of his fiscal measures, the grasp of Peel may be traced.

Being relieved of the work of the Exchequer, Mr. Gladstone was enabled to give his attention to much-needed legislation in other directions, and more particularly in that of agriculture. An Agricultural Holdings Bill had been passed in 1875 by the Conservatives, but its most useful clauses were, in the interest of the landowners, made permissive, and in consequence the farmers found the Act worthless. A new Bill, making the operation of the clauses compulsory, was carried by Mr. Gladstone's ministry, and the farmers gladly accepted it as affording the protection they needed. This and other Liberal measures, which the Conservatives stubborn'y resisted, recognised the tenant farmer's rights in

his improvements, and provided remedies which had been withheld by his professing friends.   So great, however, is the hold
of the landed interest on the farmers that they have been unable
to avail themselves, to the extent they desire, of the benefits of
Liberal legislation.

The counties were still exercising a limited franchise, and the
squire and the parson still ruled in the village and parish ; but it
was manifest that a new revolution was impending, such as would
reverse the old order of things and give to the county cottage-
occupier his long-deferred rights.   As yet, however, there were
difficulties in the way of parliamentary action.   The administration of the Crimes Act in Ireland was discussed in detail in the
House of Commons, absorbing the greater part of the Session ;
and in the autumn Mr. Gladstone found it necessary to recruit his
health by taking a sea voyage.   The *Pembroke Castle* was placed
at his disposal by Sir Donald Currie.   The trip was extended to
Copenhagen, where Mr. Gladstone met the Emperor of Russia ;
and it is not improbable that some interchange of views took
place in regard to the Russian advance in Central Asia.   At any
rate Merv had been occupied by Russian troops, and so obvious
would be the advantages of ascertaining at first hand what the
views of the Czar were that it may be inferred that the opportunity
was not lost by Mr. Gladstone.   Recruited in health, he returned
to his official duties, and to the consideration of the great
measure of reform which he had resolved to introduce in the next
Session.

CHAPTER XXXI.

It has been said that no man should be expected to be a progressive force in politics after fifty; and perhaps in most politicians their vigour begins at this stage to slacken, but some of the best work in English political life has been done after fifty. Not to go farther back than to the lives of living statesmen, this may be readily instanced. Lord Spencer, who is sixty-two, has both in administration and in opposition done his best work since his fiftieth year. Sir William Harcourt, who is seventy, has surpassed his own earlier record, and is now considered the greatest debater in the House. Lord Ripon did good service in India, and is still in the forefront of Liberalism. But among neither the senior nor the younger statesmen is there a progressive force in British politics, even approximately near that of the personalty of Mr. Gladstone; and his greatest and most advanced work has been done after seventy.

He had turned his seventy-fourth year when he introduced the last great Reform Bill, the measure in which he proposed to add two million voters to the electorate of the United Kingdom. Eighteen years before, he had invited the House of Commons to pass a Bill which Mr. Bright characterised as one of "a singular and most honest simplicity," and his defeat then, as has been told in these pages, was the result of a Whig and Tory combination formed for the purpose. But though the Bill was rejected, the reform movement was so far advanced in the country by Mr. Gladstone's advocacy that Mr. Disraeli saw that it was irresistible, and determined to turn it to his own account. Accordingly he executed a manœuvre which was virtually a surrender to Mr. Gladstone, though nominally it was a triumph for the Tories. The Household Suffrage Bill of 1867, as introduced by Mr. Disraeli was his own; but so many demands of Mr. Gladstone were complied with that if the scheme of redistribution had been left out, and in particular the three-cornered arrangement, the Reform which passed might reasonably have been described as Mr. Gladstone's.

Extensive, however, though the scope of the measure was, it fell far short of the country's needs. The cottage occupiers in the agricultural districts were left precisely where they were, with undiminished electoral disability. They were excluded from the franchise, while the cottage occupiers in the boroughs were enfranchised. The extraordinary anomaly manifested itself, of the labouring population in one place being denied electoral rights which in another place they possessed ; and one of the objects of Mr. Gladstone's Franchise Bill of 1884 was to remove this inequality, by assimilating the borough and county franchises.

Mr. Gladstone based his proposals on this principle :—" That the enfranchisement of capable citizens, be they few or be they many—and if they be many so much the better—gives an addition of strength to the State." And who are, he asked, the capable citizens ? An answer had been given to this question by the enfranchisement of borough householders. But they formed only one part of the capable adult population. The minor tradesmen in the country, the skilled labourers and artizans engaged in mining industry, were surely capable citizens ; and the peasant, though " not in the highest, but in a very real sense a skilled labourer," was also entitled to rank as a capable citizen.

It was pointed out by Mr. Chamberlain that out of "eight and a half millions of adult males, of grown men who directly or indirectly contributed to the taxes" there were "just three millions " on the register for voting ; and if, he added, you deduct for dual and plural qualifications, for deaths and for removals, " I doubt very much whether there are at the outside more than two and a half millions who would be able to vote at a general election." So manifest indeed was the injustice under which large bodies of industrious and intelligent workmen suffered that it seemed scarcely possible that reasonable opposition could be offered to Mr. Gladstone's proposals. All that could be said in disparagement of the labouring classes had been said in 1866, when Mr. Lowe (afterwards Lord Sherbrooke) reached high-water mark in animadverting on the vices of the wage earners. And since then the tendency, on the platform and in the press, has been all the other way. It may be that there was more sincerity in the outspoken invective of the defenders of privilege than is to be found in the compliments which politicians are never tired of paying the British workman; but the fact remains that since the Household Suffrage Bill became law the language used towards labour has vastly improved, has become kindlier and more respectful, and that it is no longer disfigured by offensive epithets.

It was clear that the Conservatives were in a dilemma in

regard to the new Franchise Bill. Mr. Gladstone had placed
them in it, in the speech in which he asked leave of the House to
introduce the Bill. If they opposed it and contended that the
workmen of the counties were incapable of exercising electoral
rights wisely, it might be asked why had they in 1867 enfranchised
the same class—the workmen in the boroughs? Obviously no
such contention was available; and if, on the other hand, they
acquiesced in the proposals, they would alienate their friends, the
squire and the parson, and create deep and mortifying dissatisfaction among their own followers in the House. It should be stated
that there were Conservative members who threw off all disguise
and declared honestly their objections to the Bill ; but the Official
Opposition refrained from outspoken hostility, and instead, resorted to expedients to gain time. They doubted whether the
Bill was really wanted by the country. Sir Michael Hicks-Beach
went so far as to say that the Bill had *absolutely passed from the
thoughts of the country.* Mr. Gibson (afterwards Lord Ashbourne)
denied that the Parliament of which they were members had been
summoned to deal with electoral reform; Lord Randolph Churchill
urged that the subject was only of secondary importance ; and
Lord John Manners moved an amendment that the House declines to proceed with the measure. Questions were raised in
regard to foreign policy, delays were interposed for the discussion
of Egyptian affairs, and other subjects were introduced, simply
with a view to stave off Reform. But it was all to no purpose.

Briefly summarised, the provisions of the Bill were as follows :—
In boroughs the " ancient rights " franchises would be left untouched ; the household franchise of 1867 and the lodger franchise would also be undisturbed ; the £10 clear yearly value
franchise would be extended to land held without houses or
buildings ; and there would be created a new franchise which
Mr. Gladstone called a " Service Franchise," intended for persons
who were the inhabitants of a legal house, but neither occupiers
nor tenants. This would leave four kinds of borough franchises
—the £10 franchise, the lodger franchise, the service franchise,
and the household franchise of the Act of 1867. With regard to the
county franchise, the £50 franchise would, in the first instance,
be abolished ; the £12 rateable value franchise of 1867 would be
reduced to £10 yearly value ; and the service, lodger and household franchise of the boroughs would be imported into the
counties.

These changes which were described for England would, said
Mr. Gladstone, be imported into Scotland and Ireland. The

borough and county franchises would thus be placed on an identical footing in the three kingdoms; and in each of the three the occupation franchise would be four-fifths of the whole. In Scotland, every one would be left to enjoy all the peculiarities of borough representation there already possessed; as in England, the £50 land-owning franchise would be abolished; whilst the £14 occuparion franchise would be reduced to £10 clear annual va'ue, as in force in England. In Ireland the Bill would abolish the £14 rating franchise, and substitute in its place a county franchise of £10 of clear annual value; and extending to Ireland the lodger franchise, the service franchise, and the household franchise, as exercised in the sister kingdoms.

These, as Mr. Gladstone sketched them in his exhaustive exposition, were the provisions of the Bill, and it may well be imagined what a difficult task that of the Opposition was to put together a case against the measure.

Lord John Manners moved, as an amendment to the second reading, that the House do not proceed with the Bill until the whole of the Government scheme was before the House. And although it was lost, the substance of this amendment formed the groundwork of the Opposition until the agreement was arrived at to which we shall later on refer. Practically there was no case against the measure. It was admitted that the voting was irresistible; but Lord Salisbury, grudging the greatness of Mr. Gladstone's triumph, cynically suggested at Manchester that it was because the Irish had been squared.

A speech by Mr. Raikes drew from Mr. Gladstone a reply which appears to have latterly escaped attention, though singularly applicable to the obstructive tactics of the Conservatives in the Home Rule and subsequent debates. The former had moved that it be an instruction to the committee to make provision for a redistribution of seats, and for the representation of popular urban districts. This Mr. Gladstone pointed out was only wasting time, and advised his supporters to take no part in the discussion.

"I myself was once," he said, "so bold, and perhaps so rash, as to frame a general definition of what might be called obstructive speaking, and I defined it to be, 'speaking which is not addressed to carrying conviction to the minds of the House.' But though it is not addressed to that end, it occupies the time of the House, and is therefore naturally construed and taken to be adopted and addressed for the purpose of consuming that time. I frankly own that this is the construction which I for one, and others on this side of the House, have placed on the speech of the right hon. gentleman, and I think very possibly some members sitting on the other side may do the same."

The determination of the Liberals to refrain from feeding a

discussion promoted so obviously to waste time, seriously embarrassed the Opposition. Lord Randolph Churchill protested against what he styled the mandate to silence discussion. And Lord John Manners accused the Premier of having himself, when a member of the Tory party, been concerned in obstruction to reform. But this Mr. Gladstone repudiated.

"I was not," he said, "concerned in any of these proceedings. I belonged to that party when it was a different party indeed—when it was a party under Sir Robert Peel, the Duke of Wellington and Lord Aberdeen. I have never been ashamed before Liberal audiences to refer to my connection with that party. I have always said, though I may have given votes at that period which I may regret, that that party in its high and honourable conduct, in its contempt for unparliamentary proceedings, in its incapability of condescending to unworthy ends, was as pure and high-minded a party as ever sat in this House."

But perhaps the passages in his speeches in which he referred to Ireland are those which carried the most significance, considered in connection with his subsequent proposals. The extension to Ireland of the franchise was stoutly opposed by the Tories. They thought that, however weak their case might be against the English and Scotch parts of the Bill, it was strong against the inclusion of Ireland in the measure. Accordingly they denounced vehemently this part of it, declaring that it was the result of another Kilmainham compact, and that they should be no party to it. They treated it indeed as though it were an entirely new and unheard-of proposition, whereas, as shown by the Premier, the Liberals had for ten years previously been trying to put the Irish franchise on a footing of equality with that of Great Britain. The passages to which in particular we invite the reader's attention are these—

"Let us," he said, "be as strong in right as we are in population, in wealth, and in historic traditions, and then we shall not fear to do justice to Ireland."

"For myself I will never consent to divide the people of Ireland into a loyal minority and a disloyal majority . . . . There is one way of making England weak in the face of Ireland, and that is to apply to Ireland principles of inequality and injustice. As long as we endeavour to do you justice (at this point he turned to the Home Rulers) you cannot, if you are ever so evil disposed, touch or mar or prejudice in any respects the interests of the United Kingdom. It is equal justice that will determine the issue of the conflict, if conflict there is to be, and there is nothing we can do, except the imprudence of placing in your hands evidence that we were not acting on principles of justice towards you, that can for one moment render you formidable in our eyes should the day unfortunately arrive when you shall endeavour to lay hands upon the great structure of the British Empire."

In these passages clearly embodied were Mr. Gladstone's views in regard to Ireland at a time when no one dreamt that two

years later he would formulate proposals conceding to Ireland
self government. And it should be noted that these views are
in perfect harmony with those which he has since enunciated.
Then and since, his policy has been shaped to do justice to
Ireland, not only as her right but as the best security against
rebellion.

CHAPTER XXXII.

WHEN the House rose for the Whitsuntide recess, the Opposition had virtually dropped their case. They found that their object was seen through by the country, and that further resistance would cause a recoil which would be disastrous to their party at the polls. The Bill, however, they knew would be strongly resisted in the House of Lords, the Marquis of Salisbury at Plymouth having urged the Peers to throw out the measure. And though they could scarcely gather much comfort from this, still something might happen to divert the attention of the country from the Bill, and perhaps in a postponement they would be able to get it permanently shelved.

But all their hopes and calculations proved vain. The people were not to be deceived; the meetings in the country increased in number and volume, and the resolutions passed at these were warmly condemnatory of the Opposition and the arts and devices to which they had resorted. The final stage of the Bill was reached towards the end of June, and in a speech of great power Mr. Gladstone moved the third reading. His felicity in quotation was never more marked than in the closing passage. He warned the Lords of their danger in a conflict with the people, and stated what the attitude of the Government was. It was that which is expressed in Shakespeare's words : "Beware of entrance to a quarrel; but, being in, bear't that th' opposed may beware of thee." At the close of the debate the Bill was read a third time, *nemine contradicente.*

The scene of conflict was now transferred to the House of Lords. Earl Cairns practically moved the rejection of the measure. He said the scheme was incomplete, that it was wanting in all the guarantees which should accompany it, and that without these it would be unwise to assent to the second reading. In short it was a renewal of the Opposition thinly disguised, and it need not be referred to at any length. An observation, however, which fell from Lord Chancellor Selborne may, perhaps, be usefully recalled. He designated Lord Salisbury's policy as that of the ostrich, " a creature which seems to think that by concealing danger from itself, it conceals itself from danger." The

MR. GLADSTONE, SPEAKING IN THE HOUSE OF COMMONS ON THE
FRANCHISE BILL, IN 1884.

From a drawing by T. Walter Wilson, R.I.

division was in favour of Earl Cairns's amendment, 205 voting for it and 146 against, and although it was not destructive of the Bill, it barred further progress.

At a meeting of the supporters of the Government, held at the Foreign Office, Mr. Gladstone state 1 that there would be an Autumn Session. This would afford the Lords time to re-consider their position, and the Government an opportunity to consult the country. The renewal of the agitation set in strongly, and the feeling against the Peers rose high. And when Mr. Gladstone in the second Midlothian campaign explained in a series of speeches that the pretended reasonableness of the Peers was only disguised hostility, that they were scheming to destroy the Bill, and that they were standing between the people and their rights, the indignation of the country boiled over. It was then seen that the Lords, with all their bravery, would give way rather than provoke a conflict with the people, and this they did. But they were let down gently. A compromise was arrived at to this effect:—An assurance was given that the Franchise Bill should be passed by the House of Lords as soon as a Redistribution Bill, satisfactory to all parties, was framed, and the principles of it approved by the House of Commons. The assurances and pledges on both sides were redeemed, the Franchise Bill was passed into law, and in the new year the Redistribution measure was carried in both Houses.

The Premier throughout the struggle was most loyally supported by his colleagues. But perhaps to Sir George Trevelyan is due the credit of advocating the extension of the franchise long before it was actually conceded. He prepared the ground for Mr. Gladstone, and hastened, no doubt, the triumph of 1884. But those who would deny to Mr. Gladstone the credit of initiation should remember that this was not his first venture in reform. It was simply another stage reached. He had promoted it in 1866 and 1867, and what is good in the Household Suffrage Bill of the latter year was due to him. The great measure, however, of 1884 is his work, framed and carried by him in the teeth of the most determined hostility. It required all his parliamentary skill, all his great authority, and all his eloquence, before it could be added to the statute book; and if his work had been finished then, it was enough to entitle him to the foremost place among the statesmen of the century.

CHAPTER XXXIII.

THE EXPEDITION TO KHARTOUM.

THE suppression of the revolt in Lower Egypt enabled the Khedive's Government to introduce and carry out some useful and much needed administrative reforms. They were prompted and encouraged to undertake these by the British Minister at Cairo, and it was hoped that the withdrawal of the English troops might soon be safely ordered. The occupation, prolonged as it had been beyond expectation, was a cause of anxiety to Ministers in London, which they were anxious to remove; for, as Mr. Gladstone repeatedly declared, they had no wish to remain in Egypt a day longer than was necessary for the secure re-establishment of the Khedival authority.

While, however, affairs were settling in an orderly fashion in Lower Egypt, a rising in the Soudan under Ahmed Mohammed, or the Mahdi, was threatening to become formidable. An army under General Hicks he had destroyed, and a force led by Baker Pasha had almost met the same fate. To attempt his overthrow with Egyptian troops was out of the question, and the British Government advised that the garrisons in the Soudan be withdrawn and that region abandoned. The authority of the Khedive had been practically extinguished in Khartoum and the four other strongholds, and it would be simply a waste of blood and treasure to try and restore it by force of arms.

It was felt, however, that some assistance should be sent to secure the withdrawal of the garrisons; and General Gordon being invited to undertake this mission, it was believed that his personal influence and intimacy with the Soudanese would effect what an armed force would find impossible. He was pointed out as the man especially well fitted for the work, and without hesitation he undertook it. He was appointed Governor-General of the Soudan; and, with instructions from the British Government to confine himself to the task of rescue, he set out for Khartoum. When he arrived he found the influence of the Mahdi increasing, and the tribes hitherto subject to in revolt against the Egyptian Government. Indeed so swiftly and wildly had the rebellion spread that, within a short time of his arrival, General Gordon found it necessary to fortify Khartoum and devote his attention to its defence.

The Mahdi, now virtually master of the Soudan, denounced Gordon as a traitor, and ordered an assault on the town. This and other attacks the General was able to resist, and for some time he held out heroically. But practically he was a prisoner, and on it becoming known in England, public feeling ran high in favour of his rescue. An expeditionary force under Lord Wolseley was ordered to proceed to Khartoum and rescue Gordon, and after what seemed an interminable delay, Khartoum was reached —but too late. The enemy, admitted by treachery, had surprised the town, and killed Gordon.

The profound sorrow of the country when the news came caused grave reflections to be made on the conduct of the Ministry. The delay was attributed to them, and the Opposition, seeing in it political capital, declared that Gordon had been sacrificed. It was even asserted that Mr. Gladstone was insensible to the great loss the country had sustained; it was stated that he was present at the play on the evening after the death of Gordon was known, and this calumny some people believe to this day. The facts are these :—The fall of Khartoum became known on the morning of Thursday, February 5, 1885, but not early enough to enable the morning journals to give the news. Mr. Gladstone was staying at a country house, where the intelligence reached him ; he returned to town immediately to meet his colleagues and arrange the necessary steps. So far from being insensible, he was greatly disquieted, and Lady Dalhousie, who happened to call on Mrs. Gladstone in the afternoon, proposed a visit to the theatre in the evening in order to afford him some distraction from the engrossing trouble of the day. It was not, however, until next day that General Gordon's death became known, if indeed it can be said that even then the lamentable news had the authoritative character that belongs to knowledge.

These facts are from the *Manchester Guardian*, whose correspondent found it necessary, as late as September, 1888, to refute the calumny ; it may be added that the Duke of Cambridge and Lord Hartington were present at the play on the same night on which the news was known. Lord Hartington, moreover, was the Minister responsible for the relief expedition, but although he attended the theatre when he knew Gordon was dead no reflection is cast upon him ; it is reserved for Mr. Gladstone.

Indeed, all the Egyptian business, in its civil, military and financial aspects, is said to be his, and he is blamed for not only the errors of his own administration but for those also of his predecessors. It is beginning, however, now to be seen where the responsibility really does lie; and when all the facts of the case are accessible, it will probably be found that Lord Wolseley's unfitness for the work caused the failure of the expedition. Had he showed the energy, the gallantry and the resource manifested by General Roberts in his famous march in relief of the Ameer, Gordon it is believed would have been rescued and the Mahdi crushed.

Mr. Gladstone has been reticent in regard both to Lord Wolseley's conduct of the expedition, and to General Gordon's departure from his instructions; these were to take no step in- volving war, to abstain entirely from provocative action, and to confine his attention to the relief of the garrisons. The gallant General, however, cut out for himself other business; he appealed to the millionaires for money to raise a great army. He aimed at the reconquest of the Soudan; in short, he ignored his instruc- tions. But has Mr. Gladstone ever charged this to his memory? Has he ever explained how little his own share of responsibility is? He has no word of reproach for Lord Wolseley, bearing with singular patience reproach for the failure of others.

The relief force was withdrawn from the Soudan as soon as it could possibly be got away. The Government were determined to enter upon no offensive engagements, and their aim was to retire from Egypt with clean hands, if with heavy hearts. Lives had been lost and money spent; but let those who blame Mr. Gladstone's administration look closely into the transactions of the Beaconsfield administration, and they will find therein ample proof that to the errors of the latter Government, the losses in men and money, both in Lower and Upper Egypt, may be attributed; if against the value of the Suez Canal shares are put the costs of war and of preparations for war since the shares were bought, it will be found that they have been a dear bargain. But for these shares there would have been no excuse to interfere in Egypt, and the entanglement of the Dual Control would have been avoided.

CHAPTER XXXIV.

EARLY in the year, the anxieties of the Cabinet were increased by the movement of Russian troops in the direction of the Afghan frontier; and at Penj-deh fighting took place between the Russians and the Afghans. The dispute as to the line of frontier was unsettled, and so great a source of danger that Mr. Gladstone determined to get rid of it. Accordingly, an arrangement was arrived at with Russia for the delimitation of the frontier. This was denounced by Lord Randolph Churchill as a surrender to Russia, though, subsequently, when he and his party were placed in office, they regarded the arrangement as perfectly satisfactory, and, carrying it out, put an end to the dispute.

The peril, however, had been averted by the Prime Minister. He had firmly declared the intentions of the Government, and these were to stand loyally by the Ameer; and, while affording to Russia no excuse for a hostile movement, to leave no doubt in her mind as to the resolution and capacity of the British Government to resist it. The vigour and firmness of the Prime Minister at this juncture gave great satisfaction to the country. His speech was strong, and the effect of it was to restrain Russia and bring about the settlement afterwards arrived at.

About this time, it was rumoured that there were differences in the Cabinet, that the Radical members were in antagonism to the Whig, and that, feeling age creeping on him, Mr. Gladstone was anxious to resign. The reported dissensions were believed, and that Mr. Gladstone wished to resign was regarded as probable. He had, however, expressed a similar wish before. No doubt, the perplexities of the Government had largely increased during this and the previous year, and there was a strong temptation to seek relief from official work; but the budget was due, and there were financial proposals to submit to the House, which, as first Minister, Mr. Gladstone felt would require his support. Mr. Childers, it is true, was Chancellor of the Exchequer, and in his judgment and ability the Premier reposed great trust; but it might be doubted whether he had the debating power to defend successfully his proposals against the threatened hostility; and more particularly from the hostility of a Cabinet colleague. Mr. Chamberlain's criticism was very keen. He advocated the substitution of an extra duty on spirits, for the proposed increase of the tax on beer. To this Mr. Childers objected, and, in the course of the debate, informed the House that the increased duty on spirits would be one shilling per gallon, instead of two, as originally proposed. Sir Michael Hicks-Beach resisted any increase in the beer and spirit duties, without a corresponding increase in the wine duties. But his more serious objection was to an increase of the duty on real property. He pleaded that so long as the resolutions in regard to local taxation remained unfulfilled, it would be unfair to add to the load already borne by the land.

This was a very thinly-disguised defence of the country party —the landowners and parsons—and it was thought that it would break down at the division. Mr. Gladstone, speaking for the Government, said they would stand or fall by the budget proposals. These were reasonable, and what the country had demanded. It was better to tax beer and spirits than tea and sugar, and fairer to put upon real property a duty for revenue purposes higher than it had borne than levy it on incomes or personal property, already sufficiently taxed. The Opposition, however, having secured the vote of the Irish members, insisted upon going to a division; and this resulted in the defeat of the Government by a majority of twelve.

On June 12 Mr. Gladstone announced that he had tendered his resignation to the Queen, and, in a few days after, his second administration was brought to a close. The country could scarcely realise the news, and it was suspected that some of the Ministers had contributed to the defeat. The divisions in the Cabinet, and the rumours that the Government had been riding for a fall, seemed to confirm the suspicion. The truth is that on the night of the division the Whips made no effort to bring up absent supporters of the Ministry. They were singularly inactive, and it is alleged that they even told Liberals leaving the House that they need not return. Indeed, it may be stated frankly that the defeat was planned by two of the Ministers, with a view to going to the country, and excluding from the Cabinet in the next Liberal Government their Whig colleagues.

Soon after the accession to office of Lord Salisbury, Mr. Gladstone addressed a letter to the chairman of the Midlothian Liberal Association, in which he said that "although a vote of the representative chamber had put an end to the late Cabinet, he wished to record his deep and grateful sense of the fidelity of the majority of 1880, and he could no more forget than he could repay its confidence and kindness." To this he added: "I am not at this moment released from my duties to the party which has trusted me, and the first of these duties is to use my strongest and most sedulous efforts to prevent anything that can mar the unity and efficiency of that great instrument which, under Providence, has chiefly and almost wholly made our history for the last half-century."

Obvious as it is that Mr. Gladstone had then no thought in his mind of retiring, it is curious that there was some talk of the leadership being transferred to a younger man. It is not known whence this suggestion originated, but it seems probable that it was of smoking-room manufacture. It failed, however. Lord Rosebery, at a meeting over which he presided, maintained that Mr. Gladstone was the only possible leader. "As for Lord Hartington," he said, "he is a Whig; Mr. Chamberlain is a Radical; and I, gentlemen, am satisfied to be a Liberal: yet we are all content to stand under Mr. Gladstone's umbrella."

The first-fruits of the understanding which the Conservatives had arrived at with the Parnellite party were shown in the debate on a resolution moved by the Irish leader in July. It was a motion censuring Lord Spencer in regard to the Barbavilla and Maamtrasna murders. Mr. Parnell demanded an inquiry, and although his motion was negatived, it was obvious that he had obtained some promises of support from the Conservatives, in return for his aid in defeating the Liberal Government. In the same month he had met Lord Carnarvon, then the Lord-Lieutenant of Ireland, and at the interview discussed Irish affairs, with a view to some concessions. There are different accounts of this interview, Lord Carnarvon's being that he only acquainted himself with Mr. Parnell's views and opinions—giving no assurances, making no promises, and entering into no understanding. On the other hand, Mr. Parnell states that Lord Carnarvon sought the interview for the purpose of ascertaining his views in regard to a constitution for Ireland, and that they practically agreed as to the need of a "Central Legislative Body" for Ireland—a Parliament in name and in fact—to which should be left the consideration of whatever system of local government for the counties might be found necessary. Lord Carnarvon admits that Mr. Parnell "spoke much on the character and functions of a central legislature," but repeats that he "said nothing which could imply any concurrence on the part of the Government to a proposal to give a Statutory Parliament, with power to protect Irish industries."

It is impossible to reconcile the two accounts of the interview;

but it may be inferred that Lord Carnarvon was in favour of an
Irish legislature, because he admitted subsequently in the House
of Lords that he thought the national aspirations of the Irish
people should be satisfied.   The fact, however, that, as Viceroy
and a Cabinet Minister, he discussed the situation with the Irish
leader will satisfy a good many people that an understanding
between them existed; and when to this is added the fact that
at the General Election in the winter the Irish party and the
Conservatives were in alliance, it becomes clear that the latter
had agreed to pay in some way for Irish support.

This should be borne in mind, so that the inconsistency of the
Conservative party may be seen when we reach the stage at which
their hostility to Mr. Gladstone's Irish Bills was declared.   In
September, Mr. Gladstone issued a manifesto from Midlothian, in
which he passed in review the different acts of his administration.
He pointed out that they had caused some of the clauses in the
Treaty of Berlin to be carried into effect; that they had made
Afghanistan united and independent; that they had brought about
peace in Africa; and that they had cemented the union between
the dependencies and the British Crown.   The programme,
in dealing with domestic affairs, would include reform of procedure, in order that the legislative action of the majority should
not be unduly impeded.   In regard to local government, he was
not as yet sure that the mind of the country had fully ripened.
He thought that the first objects to be obtained were—to rectify
the balance of taxation as between real and personal property ;
to put an end to the gross injustice of charging upon labour,
through the medium of the consolidated fund, local burdens
which our laws had always wisely treated as incident to property.
Then, in regard to the land laws, he averred that he belonged to
the school which had faith in economic laws, and, consequently,
disapproved of entails.   He would maintain freedom of bequest
and establish freedom of possession, and expressed a desire to
deal freely with the transfer, regulation, and taxation of land
during life and upon death, and, with the question of primo-
geniture in cases of intestacy.   The disestablishment question he
thought should be left until it had grown familiar to the public
mind by thorough discussion.   On the subject of free education
he desired to reserve a final judgment ; and with regard to
Ireland, he held the following views: "In my opinion," he said,
"not now for the first time delivered, the limit is clear within which
any desires of Ireland, constitutionally ascertained, may, and
beyond which they cannot, receive the assent of Parliament.   To

maintain the supremacy of the Crown, the unity of the empire, and all the authority of Parliament necessary for the conservation of that unity, is the first duty of every representative of the people. Subject to this governing principle, every grant to portions of the country of enlarged powers for the management of their own affairs is, in my view, not a source of danger but a means of averting it, and is in the nature of a new guarantee for increased cohesion, happiness and strength."

These were Mr. Gladstone's views in 1885, and in spirit they are perfectly in harmony with those he subsequently expressed. The country welcomed them ; for in the election which took place in December, Mr. Gladstone was returned to power, with a following of 333 Liberals against 251 Conservatives. The latter were still in office, sorely mortified at their defeat, which they had thought their alliance with the Irish party would render impossible. They now determined to throw off that alliance, and reverse their conciliatory policy towards Ireland.

CHAPTER XXXV.

1886.—HOME RULE.

IT is said that Lord Randolph Churchill frankly told the Irish members that, having done all he could for them and failed, he would now do all he could against them ; and certainly the action of the Government, of which his lordship was a member, as good as confirmed the story. The speech from the throne referred significantly to increasing intimidation in Ireland, and to repressive measure which Parliament would be asked to grant if the existing law failed. This of course meant a return to the old coercive policy and all that it involved. Sir Michael Hicks-Beach, the leader of the House, indicated this design. It was to suppress the National League. This aroused, as well it might, the indignation of the Parnellites ; and at a division in January on Mr. Jesse Collings' amendment on small allotments the Government were defeated by a majority of seventy-nine.

For the third time Mr. Gladstone was called upon to form an administration. There had been rumours that he had drafted at Hawarden proposals for the settlement of the Irish question : indeed it was asserted that he had drawn up a scheme of Home Rule. Beyond, however, these reports nothing was known. In the formation of the Ministry, he met with unexpected hesitation on the part of former cabinet colleagues, and the reason assigned was that they were unable to acquiesce in his Irish proposals. Lord Hartington declined to take office, and Sir Henry James, to whom the Lord Chancellorship was offered, also declined. Mr. Chamberlain and Sir George Trevelyan accepted office, to withdraw, however, subsequently. Their places were filled by Mr. Stansfeld and Lord Dalhousie, and the Ministry entered upon the consideration of measures for the better Government of Ireland.

It was a period of great excitement, and as the news leaked out that it would be proposed to establish a Statutory Parliament in Dublin, curiosity was wrought up to a high pitch. Mr. Gladstone's age seemed almost prohibitory of the exertion required for such an effort, but on April 8, when he asked leave to amend the provision for the future Government of Ireland, there was no sign of decaying strength, no indication of waning

powers. The House of Commons was crowded. Perhaps at no
other time within the generation had so brilliant an audience
filled the House—peers and ambassadors, ladies of high rank,
and almost the full complement of members were present.

So great indeed was the interest in the event that in order to
secure seats members arrived at the House as early as six in the
morning, and by eight or nine o'clock every seat in the House
was taken. Crowds had assembled outside Parliament long
before the arrival of the Premier, and as he passed through the
masses the great cheering was taken up, until it swelled into
deafening volumes as he passed into the House. There a splendid reception awaited him. As he took his seat, the Liberals
rose and cheered again and again—giving themselves up entirely
to the enthusiasm of the moment.

The speech was a marvellous effort. The variety of the topics,
the breadth of argument and wealth of language held the House
from the beginning to the end in rapt attention, broken only by
the cheering as each proposal was explained. The vague notions
of an Irish Parliament were quickly dispersed, and in their place
rose in the mind's eye a new structure, fitting perfectly in each
part, clear and beautiful in detail; and apart from the object
sought, the political art in the scheme, as it was unfolded, was
wonderful. As an example of constructive skill in legislation, it
was perfect.

The main provisions of the Bill were clearly summarised by
Mr. Sydney Buxton, from whose handbook we take the following :—

(1) The Bill provides for the constitution of an Irish Parliament sitting in
Dublin, with the Queen as its head. (2) The Parliament—which is to be
quinquennial—is to consist of 300 members, divided into two "orders," 103
members in the first "order," and 206 in the second "order." (3) The
"first order" is to consist of such or all of the 28 Irish representative Peers
as choose to serve ; the remaining members to be "elective." At the end of
30 years, the rights of peerage members will lapse, and the whole of the
"first order" will be elective. (4). The elective members will sit for 10
years ; every five years one half their number will retire, but are eligible for
re-election. They do not vacate their seats on a dissolution. (5) They will
be elected by constituencies subsequently to be formed. The elective member
himself must possess a property qualification equivalent to an income of £200
a year. The Franchise is a restricted one, the elector having to possess, or
occupy, land of a net value of £25. (6) The "second order" is to be elected
on the existing franchise, and by the existing constituencies, the representation of each being denoted. For the first Parliament, the Irish members now
sitting in the House of Commons will, except such as may resign, constitute
one half the members of the "second order" of the new House.

The Lord Lieutenant would be appointed by the Crown, and

neither his office nor his functions could be altered by the Irish Parliament. The responsible executive would be constituted as in England, and all constitutional questions would be referred to and decided by the Judicial Committee of the Privy Council. Further, the prerogatives of the Crown were to remain untouched, and the following matters were reserved to the Imperial Parliament:—The succession to the Crown, the making of peace or war ; all foreign and colonial relations ; matters relating to trade, navigation and so forth ; and the affairs of the army, navy, militia, volunteers, or other military or naval forces.

The Irish Parliament would be forbidden to make laws establishing or endowing any religion; but, with the exception of the matters reserved to the Imperial Parliament, all others, legislative and administrative, were left absolutely to the power and to the discretion of the Irish Parliament. The responsible Government could levy, with the authority of Parliament, such internal taxes as they pleased; they could raise loans, create local bodies, undertake public works, and manage their own Post Office, Telegraph, and other like establishments.

Then with regard to representatives, it was proposed that the Irish members should no longer sit at Westminster. It should be noted also that the Act constituting the Irish Parliament could not be "altered in any way, except by an Act passed by the Imperial Parliament, and assented to by the Irish Parliament ; or by an Act of the Imperial Parliament passed after there have been summoned back to it, for that especial purpose, 28 Irish representative Peers, and 103 ' second order ' members."

In respect of financial obligations, Ireland was to pay one-fifteenth as her portion of the whole existing imperial charge for debt, and in addition a small sinking fund. Also she was to pay one-fifteenth of the normal charge for army and navy and for Imperial Civil charges. The imposition and collection of customs duties and excise duties would remain in the hands of the British Treasury.

These briefly were the provisions of the Bill, and it may be gathered therefrom that they amply safeguarded British interests. This Bill, however, formed only one part of Mr. Gladstone's plan, and later he moved to introduce the second part under the title of the Irish Land Purchase Bill. The object of this measure was to give Irish landlords the option of selling their agricultural lands on certain terms. On a fairly well conditioned estate, the normal price would be 20 years' purchase of the net rental ; or if the land be exceptionally good, 22 years' purchase; or if worth less than 20 years, the price to be fixed by the Land Commission.

The money necessary for the purchase to be advanced by the British Treasury, but not to the purchaser. The money would be advanced to the Irish Parliament, and, as security against loss, the collection of the whole of the Irish revenues would be in the hands of a Receiver-General appointed by the British Government. From the revenues collected this official would first deduct the amount due for interest and repayment of capital, and what remained over he would hand to the Irish Executive. The total liability under the Bill was limited to £50,000,000.

The animated debates which followed the introduction of these measures were the beginning of an agitation for, and a movement against, Home Rule from the English point of view. It was at this stage that the Liberal party was split—Lord Hartington, Mr. Bright, Mr. Chamberlain and Sir Henry James heading the dissentients, and Mr. Gladstone, Sir William Harcourt and Mr. John Morley heading the main body, the Premier being the chief. The Government had of course the support of the Irish party, and Mr. Parnell declared that he would accept the Bills as a satisfactory settlement of the Irish question.

The Opposition, however, being reinforced by the Liberal Unionists, assumed an attitude of the strongest hostility, which was maintained until the morning of June 8. It was then that the division on the Irish Government Bill was taken. Mr. Gladstone had wound up the debate with unimpaired vigour, closing with a magnificent peroration, in which he appealed for justice to Ireland. The appeal failed. The division list showed that the Government were defeated by a majority of 30. The fact, however, that 311 votes were cast in the British Parliament for Home Rule, was in itself extraordinary evidence of the progress the question had made in the public mind. The Opposition counted 341 votes against: 94 being Liberal and 247 Conservative. It was the largest division that had ever taken place in the House of Commons.

In consequence of their defeat, Ministers decided at a Cabinet Meeting to advise the Queen to dissolve Parliament, and this course Mr. Gladstone subsequently announced to the House would be taken. It was a step, however, which placed him at a disadvantage. The country had been disturbed by a general election only six months previously and that another should so soon be ordered created dissatisfaction. The split too in the Liberal party had widened, and the leaders of the Unionist section were in the field against their former colleagues; they had the enormous advantage of Mr. Bright's great influence with them; they had also almost inexhaustible resources, and, what was even of greater consequence, a cry that the Empire was in danger.

Against these odds and the full strength of the Tory party, Mr. Gladstone had to contend. Yet obviously, if the nature of his Irish proposals had been fairly stated, if his Bills had been honestly criticised, and if the issue had not been obscured by misrepresentation, there is every reason to believe that the verdict of the country would have been with him.

This is proved by the results of the general election in July. The total poll in Great Britain was—

For Liberals	1,344,000
For Liberal Unionists...	379,000
For Conservatives ...	1,041,000

For Conservatives and Liberal Unionists 1,420,000

The Liberals of the main body were within 76,000, or only four per cent., of the united strength of the Unionists. This, as Mr. Gladstone pointed out, was a remarkable result, demonstrating beyond a doubt that the misrepresentation to which he had been subjected had barely escaped being a failure.

CHAPTER XXXVI.

THE HOME RULE CONTROVERSY.—THE LIBERAL UNIONISTS.

In the previous chapter we stated in short outline what Mr. Gladstone's Irish Bills contained. They, in a word, were framed to give a subordinate legislature to Ireland, and to settle the land question on a basis which would satisfy the Irish landowners and their tenants. The Parliament it was proposed to create would have power vested in it to deal only with local affairs in Ireland, and power was reserved to the Imperial Parliament to alter the Act constituting the Irish legislature, should any change be deemed necessary. The proposed settlement by purchase of the Agrarian difficulty had been drawn up to secure to the landowners a reasonable price for their property, and also to relieve the new legislature of a large and thorny question. Mr. Gladstone, Lord Spencer, and Mr. Morley considered that the landowners, as a body, were entitled to the safeguards which the Land Bill contained, and having provided against loss to the British Treasury, it was felt that no reasonable objection could be raised to this part of the plan.

The Opposition, however, raised the objection that the fifty millions proposed in the Bill would be insufficient ; that if the measure were passed, from one hundred and fifty to two hundred millions would be required, and that if this money were advanced it would never be repaid. It was represented that this loss would fall upon the British tax-payers ; and, without considering whether security had been provided or not, many of the electors concluded that the scheme was unsafe, and on this ground either voted against, or withheld their support from, Mr. Gladstone's followers.

The hostility, however, of the Opposition was mainly directed against the Irish Government Bill. It was contended that it involved the disruption of the Empire ; and upon this contention the resistance then and since of the Conservatives and the Liberal Unionists was based. It should be explained that the section of Liberals headed by Lord Hartington was now standing apart from the main body. They had determined to support the Conservatives in resisting Mr. Gladstone's proposals, and having, as we have already said, the advantage of Mr. Bright's influence

Z

with them, they ensured the defeat of their old colleagues in July, 1886.

The new Ministry which Lord Salisbury had formed entered upon their duties, pledged to adopt conciliatory rather than coercive measures. They talked of the requirements of England and Scotland, and endeavoured to divert the attention of the country from Home Rule ; but they found this impossible. Mr. Gladstone, though in his 77th year, headed the movement in the country, and before the close of the year it had assumed formidable proportions. The electors were beginning to realise that the nature and scope of the Irish measures had been misrepresented, and that the Conservatives had been returned to office on pretences which were discreditable.

MR. GLADSTONE.

CHAPTER XXXVII.

1887.—THE HOME RULE AGITATION.—MR. GLADSTONE'S VIGOUR.

EARLY in the year it was evident that the tide had turned, and was again flowing with the Liberal party. The bye-elections at Liverpool, Burnley, Ilkeston, and later at Coventry and Spalding, were successes it was impossible to disguise ; and Liberals rejoiced that their Leader was still spared to note them. His wonderful vigour stimulated the party to redouble their efforts at each contest. He himself, though now in his 78th year, seemed to have thrown off the physical weaknesses of age, and renewed the strength of middle life. The length and diversity of his speeches, the voluminous character of his correspondence, and his presence in heated halls, sustaining the burden of platform duty, were a source of surprise to friends and opponents.

An attempt was made to bring about the reunion of the party, by discussing the points of difference at a friendly meeting in Sir William Harcourt's house. Mr. Chamberlain and Sir George Trevelyan represented the Unionists, and Sir William Harcourt and Mr. John Morley the Liberals of the main body ; Lord Herschell presided. But the conference was fruitless. The truth is, the Unionists were unable to reconcile themselves to a Parliament in Dublin in which the Irish Nationalists would probably be in power. There was one exception. Sir George Trevelyan rejoined his old comrades ; he had satisfied himself that Mr. Gladstone had drawn no hard and fast line in regard to the retention of the Irish members, and a vacancy taking place at Glasgow he was returned to support his old chief.

Lord Hartington appeared to be irreconcilable from the very beginning of the agitation, and perhaps his attitude from a personal point of view was not altogether unreasonable : his brother had been murdered in Phœnix Park. Still, in his address to his constituents in 1886, he stated certain conditions which, if fulfilled, would, in his judgment, make a plan of Home Rule acceptable. " Parliament," he said, " ought to continue to represent the whole, and not merely a part, of the United Kingdom. The powers which may be conferred on subordinate local bodies should be delegated, not surrendered, by Parliament. The subjects to be delegated should be clearly defined, and the right of Parliament to control

and revise the action of subordinate legislative or administrative
authorities should be equally clearly reserved.   And lastly, the
administration of justice ought to remain in the hands of an
authority which is responsible to Parliament."

Now, in no respect has Mr. Gladstone been in resistance to
these conditions.   On the contrary, he has been ever willing to
accept any conditions, provided that the supremacy of the Imperial
Parliament was maintained, and that the reasonable aspirations of
the Irish people were satisfied.   The exclusion of the Irish Members from Westminster was never a vital part of his plan, and he was
willing that it should be dropped out of it.   The Land Bill
practically died.

It was deplored that Mr. Gladstone and Lord Hartington were
apart; and the more so that, though at that time sitting on
the same front bench, one assisted the Tories in their coercive
legislation, while the other strenuously opposed it.   Mr. Gladstone's indictment of the Government in the House and at Nottingham made their policy intolerable to the country, and it was
simply because they were propped up by Lord Hartington that
they remained in office.

CHAPTER XXXVIII.

It has been sometimes said that Mr. Gladstone's colleagues found it difficult to realise, at this time, that their chief had become an old man, nearly eighty, and that he had been for half a century in public life. He was still the greatest orator and the foremost debater in the House. He was accessible to deputations whose zeal and requests would have trespassed on the strength of younger men. He pursued inquiries in science, in literature, in commerce, with amazing zest ; and where his presence was desired in furtherance of some common good, there he was to be heard delighting his hearers.

The early part of the year he spent in Italy, adding to his immense stores of knowledge, and on his return he electrified the House by the vigour of his speeches and the energy of his advocacy of the Irish cause. So far from showing the infirmities of age, he manifested something of the elasticity of youth. Indeed, so abundant were the proofs of his intellectual strength, that people ceased to marvel. They saw his great hand in the reviews ; they saw his acknowledgments or answers to correspondents in the newspapers ; they read columns of his speeches ; they saw the man himself championing a nation with extraordinary fulness of knowledge and accuracy of statement. They saw all this from day to day, and it would have been hardly surprising if they had come to think that his powers were beyond the reach of decay.

Even in the dullest times, Mr. Gladstone is less open to the suggestion of apathy than any of the public men on his own side, or on that of his opponents. While others were taking holiday in the autumn, Mr. Gladstone was addressing his countrymen in long and important speeches. One of these resulted in a sharp controversy. A handsome vase had been presented to him by the Burslem Liberals, and on it were emblematic figures of Ireland and Poland. Referring to these, Mr. Gladstone said he doubted whether in Poland they could adequately parallel the condition of Ireland. Objection was subsequently raised to this, and Mr. Gladstone, after explaining that he had not desired to institute a general comparison, frankly added that Austria, by the timely concession of Home Rule, had secured the affections of the Poles of Galicia, and consequently in this respect was rather in advance of the United Kingdom.

It was in the following month (November) that the old states-man found an enthusiastic welcome in Birmingham. He was there brought face to face with 18,000 persons in Bingley Hall, and his remarkable energy and vitality were naturally matter for much congratulation. It was mainly to Irish subjects he devoted attention. He attacked both the Government and the Liberal Unionists, contending that no Government during the past half-century had shown so unblushing and unscrupulous a contempt for the law as that of Lord Salisbury. He again declared that the Union had been carried by the "foulest and wickedest means; that it was not a true Union; and that there could be no true Union until Ireland had the right to manage her own domestic affairs." Though on the subject of the maladministration of Ireland Mr. Gladstone said nothing new, he aroused great enthusiasm in the Midland capital. In his frequent passages through the streets, and especially in the famous drive through the "Black Country," there were great manifestations of popular rejoicing.

It is interesting to note that the veteran statesman, so far from showing the crippling signs of old age, continued to make advances on the lines of popular freedom. He formally declared himself in favour of "one man one vote," and also against the obstructive character of the Septennial Act. He thought the time had come for making such arrangements as would increase the number of working men in Parliament; but it should be stated that he was not in favour of the payment of members in any general sense. Those whose services would be useful in Parliament, but who could not enter it without sacrificing their means of subsistence, were, he thought, entitled to payment; and this, probably, is as far as reasonable people are prepared to go. The taxpayer, it may be said, is not prepared to add to his burdens by acquiescing in the payment of members all round—not, at any rate, so long as educated Englishmen of high character are found willing to take Parliamentary duties without payment.

It seemed, at this period, to some of Mr. Gladstone's Scotch

THE OPPOSITION BENCHES IN THE HOUSE OF COMMONS.

supporters, that the time had come for him to take up the question of Home Rule for Scotland. Accordingly they wrote him a letter on the subject, in which they hinted that though professing to be an ardent Scotchman, he had done nothing to advance Scotland's claim for Home Rule. In reply, Mr. Gladstone refused to admit that in any particular had he shown any lukewarmness to Scottish claims. He had not, he said, witnessed the production of a serious plan of Home Rule for Scotland approved by any large body of the people. Much light, he thought, ought be thrown on the question, of which Scotland might fully avail herself, before arriving at a decision. And although, no doubt, there are numerous advocates and supporters of the idea in Scotland, it can hardly, in truth, be said that any great body of the people has shown an interest in its promotion.

The close of the year was spent by Mr. Gladstone in Naples; and it need hardly be said that Mrs. Gladstone accompanied him; indeed, in all his undertakings Mrs. Gladstone has been a powerful factor. Whenever he has journeyed, she has gone; in whatever work he has been engaged, she has been at his side, mastering details and keeping pace with him, so that it may be said she has been his comrade in all things. And Mr. Gladstone at all times and on every fitting occasion pays tribute to the mind and heart of his wife, and attributes to her companionship and encouragement the stimulus and the solace without which he could not have undertaken the tasks he has performed. Always at his side ministering to him, and diverting his mind by steady cheerfulness, she has made his life an exceptionally happy one. She alone has shared alike in his labours and his recreations, his triumphs and defeats; and beyond all the incidents of their united lives, her unselfish devotion has been ever conspicuous.

Mr. Gladstone was now in his 79th year, and wonderfully vigorous for his age. Someone * speaking to John Bright, observed that Mr. Gladstone must have a strong constitution; "No, I don't think so," said John Bright, "Gladstone takes great care of himself in some ways—and his wife takes great care of him. Last November," he added, "I was at Hawarden, and Mrs. Gladstone and I went out for a walk round the house and grounds. We came to some trees, where there was a man cutting down one with an axe. 'There's our woodman!' said she, and it turned out to be the Prime Minister. He had neither coat nor

* From " A Girl's Recollections," in *The Speaker.*

waistcoat on, his braces hung down to his heels, and the perspiration was running down his face. I tell him it is too violent exercise for his age—and I am satisfied it is so. We started out for a walk, and went four or five miles. It was raining heavily. I had a great coat and an umbrella. He had no great coat and no umbrella, only a stick ; but he didn't seem to mind. Of course he changed his clothes when he got in."

CHAPTER XXXIX.

1889 —THE SOUTH-WEST CAMPAIGN.—THE GOLDEN WEDDING.

THE ex-Premier's literary activity seemed to have increased rather than slackened with age. In a delightful article in the *Nineteenth Century*, speaking of Daniel O'Connell, Mr. Gladstone says : " At all times he was most kindly and genial to one who had no claim to his notice, and whose prejudices were all against him. He had, however, without doubt, more religion than theology, and was in truth thoroughly and affectionately devout. I will not inquire whether his duel with D'Esterre requires any qualification of this statement, as applicable to the date of its occurrence. It may be said, however, that an Irishman who either then, or for some time after, was not a duellist, must have been either more or less than a man." In another passage, in the same article, Mr. Gladstone alludes to the stately figure of an Irish gentleman (a noted duellist), then a Member of the House of Commons, " who is conspicuous among all his contemporaries for his singularly beautiful and gentle manners." The allusion is to The O'Gorman, probably the last of the famous Irish duellists.

It is worth recording here that, although Mr. Gladstone has not found himself able to accept the often repeated invitations to visit the United States, his voice has been heard there for some years past. The explanation, of course, is that his voice has been phonographed. Standing one day before one of Mr. Edison's machines, in Northumberland Avenue, Mr. Gladstone, addressing the inventor in the United States, said :—

DEAR Mr. EDISON,—I am profoundly indebted to you for not the entertainment only, but the instruction and the marvels of one of the most remarkable evenings which it has been my privilege to enjoy. The request that you have done me the honour to make—to receive the record of my voice—is one that I cheerfully comply with so far as lies in my power; though I lament to say that the voice which I transmit to you is only the relic of an organ the employment of which has been overstrained. Yet I offer to you as much as I possess, and so much as old age has left me, with the utmost satisfaction, as being at least a testimony to the instruction and delight that I have received from your marvellous invention. As to the future consequences, it is impossible to anticipate them. All I see is that wonders upon wonders are opening before us. Your great country is leading the way in the important work of invention. Heartily do I wish it well ; and to you, as one of its greatest celebrities, allow me to offer my hearty good wishes and earnest prayers that you may live long to witness its triumphs in all that appertains to the well-being of mankind.—WILLIAM EWART GLADSTONE.

While enjoying his visit to Naples, one of his friends suggested, in a jocular vein, that they should make the ascent of Mount Vesuvius. This recalled to Mr. Gladstone's mind the incidents of an ascent of Mount Etna he had made fifty years before. That was in 1838, and he was one of the first spectators of the great volcanic action of that year. He wrote a description of his travels, which for some years remained unpublished; ultimately, it found its way into "Murray's Guide to Sicily." On leaving Naples, Mr. Gladstone spent a few days with Lord Acton, at La Madelaine, and afterwards returned to London.

About this time it was alleged by some of the ex-Premier's opponents that, notwithstanding his denunciations of the evictions in Ireland, cruel and unfair evictions had taken p'ace on the Hawarden estate. Need it be said that the allegation was quite untrue. That notices had been sent to tenants at Hawarden was true enough, but it was only to those tenants who were hopelessly in arrear. The tenants of Hawarden themselves recorded a protest against the charges of harshness which had been published, and the matter then dropped.

It had been so long forgotten that Mr. Glad-tone had a brother older than himself, that the news of the death of Sir Thomas Gladstone, of Fasque, came upon the public somewhat as a surprise. Early in life, Sir Thomas was returned to Parliament as a Conservative, and, unlike his more famous relative, held Conservative opinions for the rest of his life. The difference of political views did not, however, lead to the slightest estrangement between the brothers, though, on the occasion of the Oxford University election, Sir Thomas voted against Mr. Gladstone, showing that his convictions were stronger than the ties of kinship.

Shortly after, the death of Mr. John Bright severed another of Mr. Gladstone's friendships; for although the Irish question divided them politically, their mutual regard was unbroken to the last. In no letter or speech of Mr. Gladstone's will be found a word calculated to give his old friend pain; and on Mr. Bright's part, he always carefully refrained from giving utterance to anything that might wound or grieve Mr. Gladstone. "He has been kindness itself to me," said Mr. Bright, on one occasion, "and I feel most kindly towards him; indeed, he has never ceased, almost, to urge me to go into his Ministry again."

On another occasion, Mr. Bright* was asked what exercise

* From "A Girl's Recollections," in *The Speaker.*

does Mr. Gladstone take in London ? " I don't know," he replied,
" He rides sometimes, but not very often. He told me, once,
that for five-and-twenty years he had made it a habit, never
to let his mind dwell on Parliamentary or political matters after
getting into bed ; and he has acquired such a control over his
thoughts, that he can do it. I have gone on a different principle,
and I believe it is a bad one. When I was in London, I used to
sit up for half an hour, after I came from the House, reading
poetry or something quiet, to calm my mind. When I am going
to make a speech on a subject I care about, I lie awake three
or four hours every night for several nights, thinking about it."

" But, then, you must remember how different your speeches
are from Gladstone's."

"No ; the only difference is that he takes twice as long to say
a thing as I do, and that he says twice as many things. ' People
say my mind's subtle,' he said once to me, and seemed to think
it an unjust charge. 'I don't know what you mean by subtle,' I
replied, ' but I know what other people mean by it. Here is the
chart of an argument. There are three or four prominent headlands. I dwell on them at length, and so do you—but you go
into all the little creeks and bays and inlets, and enlarge on them
with equal detail and elaboration, instead of bringing out the
great promontories of your argument forcibly ; and so your
audience lose sight of them. When you use so many small
arguments, people think you have no big ones. Those are not
the arguments that convince people. I leave out the little creeks,
and dwell on the projecting headlands only. If I can convince
a hearer on one of them, I have got him. But you dwell on
small and great arguments alike.' "

" Did he make any improvement after that?" someone
inquired.

"I did not notice any ; but I have heard him make many very
good terse speeches—as good as ever were made. I think he is
the most wonderful speaker of whom we have any record in the
House of Commons. The Tory Governments of sixty or seventy
years ago, in Pitt's time, had large and subservient majorities,
and the Prime Minister had not to make anything like so many
speeches on different subjects, in the course of a Session, as he
has now. A few weeks since, I had a letter from Gladstone.
In the times of slavery, he said, the worst crime a man could
commit was to steal himself, and I had done it. In these
days, Gladstone added, the only remnant of slavery in the
Empire was the Ministry. I dare say he feels so at times."

Some interest was excited in a correspondence between Mr.
Gladstone and a man named Freeman, who was alleged to have
shot one Kinsella near Arklow, in September, 1887. Freeman
complained that Mr. Gladstone had in a speech accused him of
this deed, in spite of the fact that a jury had given a decision to
the contrary. Mr. Gladstone replied stating that when he
accused Freeman of murder, he was merely quoting from a
pamphlet written on the subject by an Irish priest. He could
not deny the matters recited, he said, until this pamphlet had
been answered ; then he would carefully consider the charge and
the defence, and would be anxious to do all that justice might
require. In reply Freeman said : " I am only a humble man, and
how could I write a book agin the priest who twisted everything
about to suit the National Leaguers, and to gull ignorant Englishmen. As your honour thinks a book written to help the plan
of campaign better to be trusted than the sworn jurors of
Dublin, I must try and live it down without your honour's help."
Subsequently a correspondence passed on the subject between
Mr. Gladstone and Mr. G. N. Curzon, M.P., in the course of
which the former declared that he had not stated, nor even
thought himself justified in supposing, that Kinsella had been shot
by Freeman.

In the House of Commons, Mr. Gladstone clearly intimated
that he thought the sum demanded for the Naval Defence
scheme by the Government was excessive in amount, but as they
asked for it on their responsibility as ministers, and with full
information, he declined to support some of his friends who
attempted to reduce it. One other matter, in which Mr.
Gladstone took part, may be mentioned. This was Dr. Clark's
motion on Scotch Home Rule. It was dismissed, and the
great influence against it was undoubtedly the speech of Mr.
Gladstone. He declared that the question was not ripe ; that
Scotland had not any concrete idea on the subject, and, in
brief, that it would be time enough to discuss the matter when
there was a definite scheme.

It was suggested by some political friends that Mr. Gladstone
should, in taking a holiday, visit some of the towns on the
south-west coast. Nothing loth, he consented and as the tour
developed into what is known as the South-West Campaign, it
may be useful and interesting to sketch an outline of it here. It
was delightful midsummer weather when Mr. and Mrs. Gladstone
arrived at Southampton, where they received an ovation which,
though it perhaps lacked a little of the heat and fire of a north-

country welcome, bore evidence of cordial kindliness.   On the platform were representatives of Liberal organisations from many distant parts of Hampshire.   Mr. Evans, M.P., on behalf of the Liberal Association of Southampton, welcomed Mr. Gladstone to the borough.   As Mr. Gladstone stood to reply, bare-headed, before the assembled thousands, a roar of cheering rose, and was followed by absolute silence, as if the people who had come to hear were anxious not to miss a word that fell from him. After drawing some cheerful auguries of future successes, and marshalling statistics, enforced by some sly hits and homely illustrations, he paused; then roused his audience to eager attention, by force of voice and gesture, when he spoke of the great feud between England and Ireland alienating hearts that ought to be united, and bringing shame and discredit to England throughout the whole world.   Loudly he was cheered when he said that the Liberals believed themselves to be engaged in a work that was patriotic in the deepest and most significant sense of the word, and more loudly still when he concluded with a hope that their efforts would be crowned with one of the brightest triumphs which in the whole course of their history they had been permitted to achieve.   His voice had ceased to ring, but under the spell of it the vast audience stood silent for a space after he had finished.

A long-promised visit was then paid to Sir William Harcourt; and a more delightful place for summer rest than Sir William Harcourt's interesting house in the New Forest could hardly be desired by any lover of picturesque woodland scenery.   Malwood Lodge, built by Sir William Harcourt, only a year or two ago, is fixed upon by local tradition as the site where stood the royal hunting-box of William Rufus.   Of the Norman building, it is needless to say, not a stone remains, but tradition has located it in the midst of scenery fair enough for any king to choose.   The dining-room, which is in a cool corner, has its broad bow window opening on to a glade where bowers nestle and rose-trees bloom.   The library, where Mr. Gladstone spent his morning in dealing with the inevitable corrrespondence, has a circular window that is almost a room in itself, and this room looks on verdant lawns, where tame storks and gulls wander at their will.   About every mullion of every window roses cluster.   Making the most of his one real holiday, Mr. Gladstone accompanied his host and hostess and other guests in exploring many beautiful bits of the forest round about.   They drove over the open moors to Brotley Hill, where they lunched under gnarled oaks, and feasted their

eyes on a panorama which is bounded only by the sea mists that
hang like a filmy veil over Bournemouth.   Thence they drove
to Boldrewood, and afterwards continued their journey to Lyndhurst, along a road every turn of which opens up some fresh
delightful scene.   At Lyndhurst, Mr. Gladstone, with Sir William
and Lady Harcourt, rested for a while in the Queen's House,
the official residence of the deputy surveyor of the forest.

After leaving Sir William Harcourt's modest domain, Mr.
and Mrs. Gladstone drove to Romsey.   In the square there is
a statue of Romsey's chief celebrity, Lord Palmerston.   As
Mr. Gladstone's carriage turned into the market place, cheers
burst out, and again as Mr. Gladstone rose to receive an address.
This was read by the Town Clerk.   As the borough had
honoured Mr. Gladstone when he came to pay a tribute of
respect to a great Englishman, whose statue had been unveiled
the day before that visit twenty-one years ago, so it desired to
honour him again while he was a guest in the neighbourhood.
This feeling was expressed in loud and prolonged cheers when,
having received the address from the Mayor, Mr. Gladstone
began to respond.   After a few sentences in a low voice, he
threw aside his overcoat, and prepared for more vigorous exertion.
Then it could be seen that he had carefully refrained from
wearing any flower that could be taken as a party emblem.
Only one spray of white heather adorned the button-hole, and
it completely symbolised the speaker's wish to keep all party
colour out of his speech.   "We meet here on national grounds,"
he began, and then came a series of apt historical references,
without one word to give occasion for hostile demonstration.
A single person in the crowd did attempt to interrupt with some
question, the meaning of which just escaped by thickness of
utterance, and an incoherence caused apparently by too many
precautions against the effects of external damp.   To him Mr.
Gladstone simply smiled good-humouredly, but as the hazy inter-
rogator persisted in being heard, he was gently removed to a spot
where he could not interfere with the desire of the others to hear.
A few cries were raised against the party represented by this
solitary champion, but Mr. Gladstone made a sign for silence, and
then, with an inimitable touch, he said that, believing himself to
be "governed like other men by upright motives," he desired to
extend the benefit of this belief to others of his countrymen,
whether they agreed with, or differed from him.   Then in a concluding sentence, spoken with warmth, and in a voice that
rang through the market-place, he said, "Every man who does

his best for the welfare of his country quite deserves to meet with
the largest and most generous interpretation of his motives."

Proceeding, the distinguished party were received with great
enthusiasm at Torquay. As they passed along Torquay Road,
which on one side is separated from the sea by a low wall, the
spectacle was very attractive. It was said that never were so
many people seen together in Torquay. In spite of some rain,
Mr. Gladstone was bareheaded a great part of the way. The
meeting in the Public Hall was a great success. It was crammed
with more than 3,000 people, including many ladies. The first
loud cheers were given when the chairman referred to Mr.
Gladstone's "eminent and able wife." There was much
sympathy when he spoke of "the damp upon the meeting,"
caused by the absence of Sir Arthur and Lady Hayter; and
again, when the spokesman of the Brixham fishermen referred to
the reception of William Prince of Orange in 1683, and to the
equal pride they felt in welcoming the Grand Old Man, William
Ewart Gladstone, in 1889. There then came forward a Torquay
workman, to present a casket of his own workmanship, and
following him came a man of few words and 90 years, who
distanced Mr. Gladstone as the oldest Liberal present. The
feeling in the streets was so enthusiastic as to justify Mr. Gladstone in the question, "Where are the Tories?"

Cornwall gave Mr. Gladstone a splendid welcome. When the
yacht came into Falmouth Harbour, there was nothing to show
what was in store. Presently the old statesman came on deck,
and received the formal address of the Mayor, Mr. Webber, as
well as the informal but extremely hearty greeting of one of the
Corporation, who, insisting on shaking hands, shouted "I am
am glad to see thee. I have known thee all my life, though I
never saw thee before." On shore the popular greeting was
repeated with great intensity. The inevitable procession, with band
ahead, was in attendance, and there was one more triumphal
progress through the streets of a very enthusiastic town. At
the place chosen for the address, Mr. Gladstone found himself
not only in front of a grand stand crowded with people, but completely surrounded by eager and enthusiastic admirers, and in
great embarrassment as to which way he should turn in order to
commence his reply. The speech was vigorous, as usual, and put
the audience into splendid humour all the more readily because
it was so well adapted to the circumstances of the constituency.

The chief excitement was at Redruth. There the whole of
the mining division offered welcome on triumphal arches. The

most extravagent computations as to the size of the crowd were
indulged in, their only value being to show that everybody was
being impressed by its proportions.   It was certainly to be
reckoned by tens of thousands, but by how many tens I will not
hazard the conjecture.   A fairly long speech was made in spite of
difficulties, and then a way was marvellously opened up in the
midst of the multitude, to enable Mr. Gladstone to drive on to view
the further decorations of the town, and to receive still further
homage.   The splendid, though somewhat embarrassing, proofs
of affection and confidence, given by thousands at Redruth, will
probably not find a parallel in any gathering outside Plymouth ;
but in some respects, the triumphs achieved have been even more
emphatic in their promise of future victories for the cause of
political freedom in every part of the United Kingdom.   Even
during Mr. Gladstone's progress up the River Fal, evidences were
not wanting of the interest his visit excited.   The people of Falmouth assembled to give him a parting cheer as the yacht slipped
her moorings and steamed away.   Two pleasure-boats laden with
excursionists accompanied the yacht, and skiffs put out from many
secluded creeks, bearing villagers who were anxious to join in the
general acclamations.   At King Harry's Ferry, just below Lord
Falmouth's beautifully-wooded domain of Tregothran, a little
crowd filled every part of the quay, and others clustered on the
hillside to give gratifying proofs of their faith in the Liberal
leader.

At Truro, when Mr. Gladstone landed, all along the route to
the cathedral city people stood to give the illustrious visitor a
welcome.   In the Guildhall there was not a vacant seat or
standing space unoccupied.   All of them rose as Mr. and Mrs.
Gladstone entered, accompanied by their friends, among whom
was Lord Brassey ; and the reception given by this meeting to
Mr. Gladstone was one of the most brilliant incidents in this
memorable campaign.   The audience broke into cheers when
their great leader rose, but having paid that tribute, they settled
down to listen, and thenceforward were silent, as if afraid of
losing a word that fell from his lips.   Mr. Gladstone devoted the
greater part of his speech to Home Rule in its possible relations
to religion.

Half-an-hour's journey by rail brought the party to Bodmin.
By the way glimpses were gained of many simple preparations,
made by villagers and farmers, to celebrate the occasion with
such pomp and ceremony as were within their means.   A waggon,
wreathed in laurels, or a flag fluttering from the gable window,

was enough to show that the owner was not indifferent to Mr.
Gladstone's presence.   One farmer had all his children grouped
together in a field, where, as the train flitted past, they made a
picture that would have made a fitting subject for Randolph
Caldicott's pencil.   At the St. Austell Station some half-hundred
sturdy yeomen, wearing sashes of the local colours, were drawn
up as a guard of honour, and the lusty cheers they raised when
Mr. Gladstone emerged from his carriage, gave earnest of the
heartiness with which St. Austell welcomed his advent.

The Union Jack, floating high above the grey castle keep that
for seven hundred years has guarded the main gate into Cornwall,
was the first sign that greeted Mr. Gladstone's eyes as a symbol
of the reception which the inhabitants of Launceston were
preparing for him.   Miles away, as he crossed the battle ground
on which " Blameless Arthur " fought his last fight against the
Saxons, that flag could be seen flaunting its blue field, embla-
zoned with the crosses of St. George, St. Andrew, and St. Patrick,
above the ruined tower of Dunheverd.   That national flag was
raised as a token that the townsmen did not show the sinister
forebodings of those who persist that Home Rule for Ireland
would mean the disintegration of the mighty British Empire.   In
the words of their own address, they welcomed him in the name
of " the Liberals and inhabitants " of the ancient borough of
Launceston.   That part Mr. Gladstone subsequently took up as
the key-note of a passage half playful, half pathetic, in which he
evoked loud cheers by the statement that since he had come into
the county of Cornwall he had seemed to be in contact, not with a
party, not with a portion merely, but with the whole population.
When the ivied ruins and rugged keep of Launceston came into
sight, after a beautiful drive over wide-stretching moors, one gets
some odour of the sea, whether the wind blows from the Atlantic
or from the English Channel.   Here again was an outburst of
enthusiasm.

Mr. Gladstone arrived in good time at Plymouth, and the
collection of addresses in this town would fill a small port-
manteau.   Bareheaded all the way, bowing right and left, he
passed through the crowded streets.   Few would have supposed
that Sir Thomas Acland, who sat opposite to him in the carriage,
was his senior in age, for the President of the Devon Federation
has no grey hairs, and is very hale and hearty in appearance.
The Hoe, a splendid green traversed with asphalte roads and
paths, is famous as the position from which the Spanish Armada
was first sighted, more than three hundred years ago.   The

A A

granite pedestal of the national monument to commemorate the Tercentenary, then completed, was the most conspicuous object, beyond the statue of Drake, from Mr. Gladstone's windows. Here the South-West Campaign ended.

The 25th July was the fiftieth anniversary of Mr. and Mrs. Gladstone's wedding. It was their Golden Wedding, and was duly honoured. A reception was held at the National Liberal Club, and a portrait of Mr. Gladstone, which had been subscribed for by women of the three sister countries, was presented to the distinguished couple. The portrait — the work of Sir John Millais—was finished just in the nick of time, Mr. William Agnew arriving at 16, James Street, with the picture, at eight o'clock on the morning of the jubilee. He expected to hear that Mr. and Mrs. Gladstone had not left their room, and that he would be able to hang the picture before they came down. As a matter of fact, they were away at church, and Lady Aberdeen and Mr. Agnew succeeded in getting the picture hung, leaving some orange blossoms about the breakfast-table, and slipping away unseen by the family. When Mr. and Mrs. Gladstone came home from church, there was the picture. In acknowledging it, Mrs. Gladstone wrote : " Now that the picture is arrived, it calls for fresh and new words of gratitude. We cannot express all our feelings, but the kind donors—those who have joined in this beautiful gift—will care to know that it has brought joy and deepest gratitude. Will you make known to them that their gift has brought joy and gladness to our dear old home? We shall never look at it, blending as it does the present and the future, without thankfulness." There were 3,000 subscribers to the fund.

About this time the interminable Silver Question again excited attention, and Mr. Gladstone was invited by Mr. R. L. Everett, of Rushmere, to explain his views thereon. In reply, the ex-Premier said that the "standard of value which is the great instrument of exchange, is itself a commodity, and being such, is itself subject to fluctuation. Such fluctuation is economically an evil, and every wisely governed State should seek to have for its standard of value the commodity which is the least subject to fluctuation. That commodity, as I conceive, is gold, and to adopt any other standard, or to add to gold any other metal more subject to fluctuation than gold, would be to increase that fluctuation, and therewith the consequent inconvenience or distress. If a change were made which should of itself lower the value of sterling money in which debts are

BY F. ROWLANDS, HAWARDEN.

MRS. GLADSTONE.

payable, this would be an additional and most formidable mischief." The bimetallists, on the other hand, say that the effect would be beneficial, not mischievous ; and so far as the theory of bimetallism goes, there is a good deal to be said for it ; but the working of it would be impracticable, and, if the proposal were adopted, it is feared that it would be as Mr. Gladstone describes it, a "formidable mischief."

The part taken by Mr. Gladstone in the debate on the Royal Grants is often referred to ; but justice has hardly been done to his courage on the occasion. The facts are these. After much communication with Windsor, Mr. W. H. Smith, then First Lord of the Treasury, was able to tell the Committee on the Royal Grants that Her Majesty, whilst holding that precedent gave her a claim upon Parliament to provide for every member of the Royal family without exception, was willing to waive her rights save as regards the family of the heir apparent. Mr. Gladstone thought that these rights, being founded mainly on precedents which were anterior to the last settlement of the Civil List, were not satisfactorily established, but as they were largely waived, he was not prepared to enter upon a barren conflict concerning them. Indeed, to get rid of all further applications whatever during this reign, he proposed to create a trust fund out of which the Prince of Wales should himself provide for his children. The Government fell in with this view, and fixed the sum at £40,000 a year. Mr. Gladstone cut this down to £36,000 a year, and again the Government agreed. But whilst Mr. Gladstone had the support of Sir H. Vivian and of Mr. Parnell, the Radicals, headed by Mr. John Morley, who had made their assent to the trust fund conditional upon an absolute waiver of all further claims of any kind, held that this condition was not satisfied. Accordingly they voted against it, with Mr. Labouchere and Mr. Burt, who from the first had taken up an attitude of uncompromising hostility to any grants whatever for the third generation of the Royal family. This division of opinion reappeared, of course, in the House of Commons. When it was proposed to go into committee to consider the Queen's message asking for provision for Prince Albert Victor and Princess Louise of Wales, Mr. Labouchere moved an amendment declaring that the funds granted to the Royal family "were adequate without further demands upon the taxpayers." Mr. Gladstone opposed this, and though it brought him in conflict with the vast majority of his immediate followers, he gave the Government an energetic support. His speech has been greatly praised both by friends and opponents, and it need only be said here that he affirmed with great emphasis that the Queen's waiver put an end to all further applications from the Crown during the present reign, just as certainly as if the House had a formal contract sealed, signed, and delivered. Ultimately, Mr. Labouchere's amendment was rejected by 398 votes to 116 votes.

Some points of interest may be noted before entering upon another year. It was in October, soon after the North Bucks election, that Mr. Gladstone, in a correspondence with the defeated candidate, declared himself in favour of the retention of the Irish members at Westminster in the event of Home Rule being granted to Ireland. It is true that a year or two before, he had recognised the necessity of modifying his views on the subject, but it was in his letter to Mr. Hubbard that he finally declared himself. Later, at Saltney, Cheshire, in speaking on the condition of the "working classes," he enumerated the advantages which they possessed over their predecessors of past ages. He advised those in search of mental improvement to read history—the, history especially of England, France, America, and Ireland. He pointed out also the danger of calling upon the State to do what might be done by individuals, and he trusted they would preserve a spirit of self-reliance and manly independence in the minds of all classes of the people. Towards the close of the year, Mr. Gladstone was visited by Mr. Parnell, and it was at Hawarden, according to Mr. Parnell, that the ex-Premier discussed the changes he proposed to make in his new Home Rule scheme.

CHAPTER XL.

MR. GLADSTONE was able to be present at the rent dinner, in January, on the Hawarden estate. One of the oldest tenants made some touching and kindly allusions to the long residence of Mr. and Mrs. Gladstone in the neighbourhood, and the regard in which they were held by the Hawarden tenantry. Mr. Gladstone made a charming speech in reply. He sketched the state of agriculture during the last half-century, and complimented the farmers of his district on the success with which they managed their farms. He hoped that the existing good relations between landlords and tenants would be found to prevent the agricultural labouring population from emigrating to towns.

The marriage of the ex-Premier's third son, Mr. Henry Nevill Gladstone, to Miss Maud Rendel, was a social event in which the country took no small interest. Mr. Henry Gladstone has as yet taken no active part in politics, being an East Indian merchant engaged in the affairs of a large business. The marriage was at St. Margaret's Church, and the scene there and at Carlton Gardens was a very striking one. The stalls on either side of the Communion table were reserved—the right hand ones for the Gladstone family, the left for the Rendels. Mr. Gladstone, looking extremely well and active, accompanied by Mrs. Gladstone, beautifully dressed in red velvet and white lace, came in immediately before the bride. The rest of the church was full to overflowing, and, with the exception of Lord Ripon and Mr. Morley, all the Liberal leaders were there.

Another interesting event, though of a different character, was an interview given by the ex-Premier to a deputation of miners, on the Eight Hours Question. The right hon. gentleman entirely agreed with the miners that eight hours are sufficient for any man to spend underground. But how was that limit to be attained? was the question they had to answer. "Whatever may be the inconvenience of strikes," said Mr. Gladstone, "and the roughness of the method of their operation, I should hesitate before assenting to this: That where an object could be gained by the working men themselves by their own independent action, with resort to strikes if necessary—that method of proceeding was less to be desired than the interference of Parliament by a positive prohibition. I must own that." In deciding this question, added Mr. Gladstone, there are two points needing consideration. "First of all, consider the case of the working man who wishes to work more than eight hours a day; he may be in a small minority, but consider his case, and consider what difficulty might arise, or whether difficulty would arise from putting him in the position of a person whose action was to be repressed and punished by law. The other point that you should consider, largely, I think, is how far you feel certain that your case is a case that can be distinguished from other cases of what is called an Eight Hours Bill, because I think that, as far as I can judge, public opinion is reasonably opposed to fixing generally the limit of eight hours to the labour of men who may be willing to labour more, and who may think it for their interests to labour more." Before the interview closed, Mr. Gladstone said that he would carefully consider the subject, reserving, however, freedom to act in the way his judgment and sense of right dictated.

The report of the Special Commission, appointed to inquire into the charges and allegations made against Mr. Parnell and others, having been laid on the table of the House, Mr. W. H. Smith moved a resolution approving the report, and instructing that it be entered on the records of the House. Then Mr. Gladstone rose, and, in a speech of an hour and forty minutes duration, addressed the House. His argumentative force was no less a theme of admiration than his matchless eloquence on the occasion referred to. He did not, he said, thank the judges, in his amendment, for the reason that it would be hazardous to introduce the practice of rendering formal thanks for the performance of judicial functions. He ungrudgingly acknowledged their "zeal, ability, assiduity, learning, and perfect and absolute good faith." And he thought that, viewing their political sentiments—he would not say prepossessions—the judges had fulfilled the best expectations that could have been held in regard to them. The report embodied a number of opinions upon issues in no sense and no degree judicial. For instance, dealing with the years 1879-80, the Commissioners laid it down that evictions were not the cause of crime ; or, if they were the cause of crime, still the evictions themselves were the results of agitation against the landlords. Distress and extravagant rents had, he supposed, nothing to do with the creation of these crimes. Again, the report declared that the rejection by the Peers of the Compensation for Disturbance Bill, in 1880, had nothing to do with the increase of crime. That was an astounding assertion, in defiance of all the first elements of common sense and of all probability. Again, it was alleged before the Commission that the land legislation of Parliament had been the great cause in instigating the condition of Ireland, and procuring a decrease of crime. "Nothing of the sort," said the Commissioners. And in like manner they rejected the same proposition with respect to the Arrears Act of 1882. This was entirely untrue, but the House was asked to subscribe to it, as to the other declarations just alluded to. As an example of "a disproportionate and ill-balanced judgment," Mr. Gladstone mentioned the heavy reprobation of certain extracts from the *Irishman* newspaper—not pardonable, but insignificant from their obscurity—and set in contrast the fact that in respect of "the grand and capital offence of the *Times*" there was not a word in all the report. Another objection to adopting the report was that essential portions of the evidence were, on the statement of the Judges themselves, entirely excluded from the consideration of the Commission. This did not prevent them from passing censure upon certain acts which could only be properly appreciated in the light of all the circumstances of the case. Further, the House could not separate the conclusions from the evidence on which they were founded, and they had not got the evidence. For all these reasons the House ought not to accept the motion of Mr. Smith.

Speaking of the hostile findings, Mr. Gladstone dismissed contemptuously that of disseminating newspapers tending to incite to crime, and that also of relieving persons who were said to have been engaged in outrage. He thought the latter, based upon an expenditure of £6 to £12, was a trumpery charge. The other matters against the Nationalists were mainly three. Seven of the respondents were said to have joined the Land League, with the ulterior object of separating Ireland from Great Britain. The judges did not point out that this offence occurred ten years ago, when desperate distress prevailed in Ireland, when she was on the brink of famine, and when unjust and impossible rents largely prevailed. Then to deny the moral authority of the Act of Union, was for Irishmen no moral offence whatever. To treat it as such in 1890, in a sanctimonious vote of the House of Commons, was a monstrous proceeding. The other two censures of the judges were more to the purpose; and these summed up the assumed guilt of the Irish members. As to the first, that they incited to intimidation by speeches, with the knowledge that intimidation led to crime, Mr. Gladstone quoted from the report, to show that the judges did not mean murder—that, in fact, they declared that the charge of inciting to murder had broken down.

Mr. Gladstone pointed out, further, that this crime happened in 1880-81, and reminded the House that Mr. Parnell had frankly told them that much was done in the early days of the League which was questionable or improper. The other great offence was that the Nationalist members never placed themselves on the side of law and justice ; that they did not assist the Administration. and did not denounce the party of physical force. Passing from this, Mr. Gladstone observed that what was done in 1880-82 was not done in a corner. The facts were known ; they were not disguised—indeed, they were the subject of incessant discussion in Parliament, and of denunciation also. There was nothing new affirmed against the Irish members which was not affirmed by Mr. Foster, in part by himself and by others. Why, if these things deserved condemnation, were they not so condemned at the time? Was it not because, in the opinion of the Liberal party, there was not a rag of reason for a vote of condemnation? Nor was the Tory idea at the time more severe. They climbed into power upon the strong shoulders of the member for Cork ; they did what the Parnellites did with the physical force party—"took full advantage of their good disposition, while declining association with their criminal proceedings."

Passing to another phase of the subject, Mr. Gladstone put forward with great earnestness what he called the counter-allegations of the Nationalist party—that the agitation of 1879-81, when it was roughest and wildest, prevented more crime than it caused ; that Mr. Parnell's aim had always been to draw off agitation from violence to Parliamentary methods and the like. And he declared, with vehemence, that "condonation was given the amplest, in the most solemn manner conceivable, when in 1885, a Viceroy of Ireland, with the knowledge and sanction of the head of the Government, entered into close, private, and confidential communication with the leader of the Irish party, for the purpose of devising a scheme and a policy for the government of Ireland." This action ought, said Mr. Gladstone, to close the book of controversy with respect to all former acts. As to "whether the conduct of which the respondents are accused can be palliated by the circumstances of the time, or whether it should be condoned in consideration of the benefits alleged to have resulted from their action," Mr. Gladstone briefly reviewed the condition of Ireland at the beginning of the League agitation. He declared, incidentally, that but for agitation the Land Act of 1881 would never have been passed, and he contended generally that the acts with respect to which the Parnellites had been censured, were not fit matter for censure, because they were so involved with other circumstances which must also be brought into view.

When this was done, said Mr. Gladstone, they found that the acts were such as were invariably incidental to periods of natural crisis, struggle, and revolution. "In all great movements of human affairs, even the just cause is marked and spotted by much that is detestable." Finally, he touched upon the matters wherein the Nationalist had been acquitted, and the conduct of the *Times* in regard to the forged letters. The most striking passage of the great speech was the peroration, with its subtly conceived notion of appealing to the Conservatives, not as a party, but as individuals. They sat silent as Mr. Gladstone, leaning across the table, in beseeching voice begged each man to put himself in the place of Mr. Parnell, and to give his judgment as it would bear the scrutiny of the heart, of the conscience, as each man took himself to his chamber. One who was present says that the House at this moment was solemnly still, breaking out, in a few minutes later, into enthusiastic cheers as the great orator resumed his seat.

This speech was the chief feature of the seven days' debate, and though the division resulted in the rejection of Mr. Gladstone's amendment by 339 to 268, there is no doubt that a great impression was made, not only on the Liberals alone, but on the Conservatives.

In May, we find Mr. Gladstone engaged in a speech-making campaign in East Anglia. He made speeches at Ipswich, Norwich, and Lowestoft, denouncing the action of Parliament with regard to the Special Commission as unconstitutional and unjust, and condemning the use of the Closure by the Government. He denied that there had been any obstruction, or that the Cabinet had passed any legislation which would entitle the Ministry to a place in the list of really great administrations. He thought that the Septennial Act should be changed, so as to make appeal to the constituencies more frequent. Later, Mr. Gladstone dealt with the subject of Party Nomenclature, as to which some bitterness had been aroused. A letter had appeared in the papers suggesting that a club in Battersea should be named the "Gladstonian Liberal," and on Mr. Gladstone's attention being called to it he said:—" It is true that I deprecate (respectfully

and with due reserve) the use of the term, not as offensive, but as
unduly flattering to myself. But this is not, in my view, the
main consideration. There is the old and venerated name of
Liberal. Why is this name to be put aside? Are we not fairly
entitled to retain it? Nineteen-twentieths (perhaps ninety-nine-
hundredths) of the old Liberal party think one way; one-
twentieth think the other way. I cannot perceive that this small
majority, which exists to support a Tory Government, ought to
make us change our name." It may, perhaps, be useful to point
out here that those who had parted from Mr. Gladstone on the
question of Home Rule were referred to by Home Rulers as
" Dissentient Liberals," and by those in opposition to that policy
as " Liberal Unionists." The latter is the designation more
familiar to the country.

In visiting his Midlothian constituents in February, the ex-
Premier covered the whole field of politics, domestic and foreign,
from the beginning of the last Parliament. It need hardly be
said that Ireland received a large share of attention. The Irish
members, he said, again would be retained at Westminster in the
new Home Rule Bill. Public opinion had declared for it, and he
bowed to public opinion, though he did not hesitate to say, what
is very true, that the thing could not be done without much
public inconvenience. His allusion to the Plan of Campaign as
"a device to keep the people from starving," due to the refusal
of the majority in the House of Commons to accept Mr. Parnell's
Arrears Bill, gave immense satisfaction in Ireland, and has been
much in discussion since. Passing from Ireland, he dealt with
certain Scottish questions. He thought Home Rule for the
northern kingdom, though expressing dissatisfaction with the
present state of things, was as yet only an initial feeling,
unformed, undeveloped, and undefined. He had never been
a worshipper of the union between England and Scotland, nor
had he ever felt an eager desire to unsettle it. It had brought
some advantages to Scotland, but it had, on the other hand,
removed from the centres of national life in Scotland some
valuable social influences, and it had brought about a state of
things in which Scottish legislation at Westminster was liable to
be moulded, not by Scottish, but by English ideas.

Passing to the question of Disestablishment, Mr. Gladstone
expatiated in characteristic fashion upon the possibility of fusing
the three Presbyterian Churches of Scotland, which, though
separate, had the same Church government and the same confession of faith. He seemed to hint that this would be facilitated

by Disestablishment.   It was not his business to tell the people
of Scotland what to do about Disestablishment; it was rather
their business to tell him,   He pleaded that if it were undertaken, Disestablishment should be carried equitably, and even
tenderly.   "Every life interest of a legal character should be
respected; questions in regard to fabrics and manses ought to be
approached in a liberal spirit, and it must be remembered that
the principal part of the property—the teinds—is not in the
nature of funds to be cast at once into the Treasury, but partakes
largely of the nature of a local asset, in which the people of the
several localities have a special interest, and in the ultimate
application of which they ought to have a certain amount of
discretion."   Obviously, Mr. Gladstone does not himself expect to
deal with Disestablishment, but in the passage quoted he points
out the way in which it should be carried out.

Perhaps the most powerful of the Midlothian speeches was that
addressed to the mining population at West Calder.   Mr. Gladstone told the working man that on the great questions which
largely stirred the public mind he was now the master.   The vote
made him all-powerful   So far, the judgment of the labouring
population had been far more just, equitable, and enlightened
than the judgment of the educated classes.   The true test of a
man, of a class, and of a people was power, and now that the
masses of our people had this supreme power, they would have
temptation, and be subject to a deep and searching moral trial.
They must preserve the balance of their mind and character, and
if they should become stronger than the capitalist, than the
peerage, than the landed gentry, and stronger even than the
mercantile classes, there would still be one glory to attain—to
"continue to be just."   This is the language of a great leader,
and will never be forgotten.

While holding that while the working man had been in the
main right, Mr. Gladstone warned his audience against preferring
the rigid action of Acts of Parliament to that judicious use of the
power of free combination which had won the bulk of what
labour had gained from capital.   He asked for a wider trial
of co-operation as a valuable means of strengthening the position
of the labouring class, without harm to anyone.   He attached to
freedom a value, he said, he could not describe.   He had a
considerable veneration for things ancient, and he detested
gratuitous change; but he deeply valued liberty (individual and
national), without which there was nothing sound, healthy, or
solid, or that could move onward in the sense of progress.

We now come to an event which was a source of great trouble, anxiety, and confusion, namely, the disclosure in the Divorce Court of Mr. Parnell's relations with Mrs. O'Shea. That Mr. Gladstone was shocked and grieved, goes without saying, Mr. Parnell having been his guest at Hawarden in the previous winter. The political consequences of the divorce were soon man'fest, and proved far reaching. In order that Mr. Gladstone's action may be explained, it is necessary to state what took place after the decision in the Divorce Court was made known.

Two days after—that is, on November 20th—there was a National League meeting in Dublin. It was held at the Leinster Hall, and a unanimous declaration was made that "in all political matters Mr. Parnell possesses the confidence of the Irish nation." No voice was raised against him. All agreed that the verdict in the divorce action in nowise affected his public position. The American delegates—Messrs. Dillon, O'Brien, T. P. O'Connor, T. D. Sullivan, T. Harrington, and T. P. Gill—announced that they stood firmly by Mr. Parnell's leadership, not only out of gratitude for his unparalleled services in the past, but "in profound conviction that Mr. Parnell's statesmanship and matchless qualities as leader are essential to the safety of our cause." Five days later he was re-elected chairman of the Irish Parliamentary party, the unanimity of the party remaining unbroken. The proposition was Mr. Sexton's, and it was agreed to amid applause. It is only fair to say that those who subsequently voted for the deposition from the leadership of Mr. Parnell, stated that his re-election in the first instance was a merely formal honour, and that he was not expected to accept the office tendered him. In other words, their version of the story is that they wished to let their old leader down easily. On the other hand, it should be stated that no hint of this appears in the report of the meeting. It is distinctly stated that Mr. Parnell "promised that he would continue to discharge the duties of leader," in response to the "unanimous desire" of the party. Judging from the report, Mr. Parnell took the re-election seriously, and no dissent seems to have been expressed from his view.

Bearing this in mind, it is evident that Mr. Gladstone concluded that it was the determination of the Irish Parliamentary party to ignore the proceedings in the Divorce Court. These proceedings, he said later, he felt "would destroy entirely the moral weight and the moral force" of Mr. Parnell. He did not at once communicate his opinion to Mr. Parnell. He waited for a week. "I determined," he subsequently explained, "to watch the state of feeling in this country, and I very soon found that the Liberal party had made up its mind to draw a broad distinction between the national cause of Ireland and the person and the personal office of Mr. Parnell." It has been asserted that "considerations of political expediency alone, and not of outraged morality," wrung from Mr. Gladstone his condemnation of the Irish leader. And, strange to say, this accusation was found in a speech delivered by Sir Charles Russell, at Braintree. "It was not," he said, "until Mr. Gladstone saw the rising, overwhelming tide of public opinion, that he felt bound, in the interest of the party he led, and of the cause he advocated, to convey to the leader of the Irish people that his continued leadership must have a chilling effect upon the enthusiasm of many staunch friends." The more reasonable explanation, considering Mr. Gladstone's character and views, is that he was reluctant to take any step that might seem interference in a matter of so much consequence to the Irish people as the leadership of the Parliamentary party. Since they had chosen him and supported him, it was their duty, and not that of an English statesman, to deal with him.

The country, in the meanwhile, let its opinion of Mr. Parnell be known very plainly; and at the National Liberal Federation meeting, held at Sheffield, there was a very decided manifestation of opinion that Mr. Parnell had forfeited confidence. The Nonconformists were greatly stirred. In their view, Mr. Parnell had acted treacherously towards his friend, and they would have neither part nor lot with him. It was said, on the other hand, that inasmuch as Mr. Parnell had been re-elected by the Irish party, and was assured of support at a great public meeting in the Irish capital, the Nonconformists of England had no title to object to his continued leadership. But they had surely a title to express their opinion of his conduct, and they were strictly within their own right in saying what their own line of action would be. Nor could their voice be ignored by the statesman they followed.

On the day previous to that on which Mr. Parnell had been re-elected, the following letter was addressed by Mr. Gladstone to Mr. John Morley:—

> 1, Carlton Gardens,
> November 24th, 1890.

MY DEAR MORLEY.—Having arrived at a certain conclusion with regard to the continuance at the present moment of Mr. Parnell's leadership of the Irish Party, I have seen Mr. M'Carthy on my arrival in town, and have enquired from him whether I was likely to receive from Mr. Parnell himself any communication on the subject. Mr. M'Carthy replied that he was unable to give me any information on the subject.

I mentioned to him that in 1882, after the terrible murder in the Phœnix Park, Mr. Parnell, although totally removed from any idea of responsibility, had spontaneously written to me, and offered to take the Chiltern Hundreds, an offer much to his honour, but one which I thought it my duty to decline.

While clinging to the hope of communication from Mr. Parnell, to whomsoever addressed, I thought it necessary, viewing the arrangements for the commencement of the Session to-morrow, to acquaint Mr. M'Carthy with the conclusion at which, after using all the means of observation and reflection in my power, I had myself arrived. It was that, notwithstanding the splendid services rendered by Mr. Parnell to his country, his continuance at the present moment in the leadership would be productive of consequences disastrous in the highest degree to the cause of Ireland. I think I may be warranted in asking you so far to expand the conclusion I have given above as to add that the continuance I speak of would not only place many hearty and effective friends of the Irish cause in a position of great embarrassment, but would render my retention of the leadership of the Liberal Party, based as it has been mainly upon the prosecution of the Irish cause, almost a nullity. This expansion of my views I begged Mr. M'Carthy to regard as confidential, and not intended for his colleagues generally, if he found that Mr. Parnell contemplated spontaneous action; but I also begged that he would make known to the Irish Party, at their meeting to-morrow afternoon, that such was my conclusion, if he should find that Mr. Parnell had not in contemplation any step of the nature indicated.

I now write to you in case Mr. M'Carthy should be unable to communicate with Mr. Parnell, as I understand you may possibly have an opening to-morrow through another channel. Should you have such an opening, I beg you to make known to Mr. Parnell the conclusion itself, which I have stated in the earlier part of this letter. I have thought it best to put it in terms simple and direct, much as I should have desired, had it lain within my power, to alleviate the personal nature of the situation. As respects the manner of conveying what my public duty has made it an obligation to say, I rely entirely on your good feeling, tact, and judgment.

Believe me, sincerely yours,

W. E. GLADSTONE.

Right Hon. John Morley, M.P.

When the contents of Mr. Gladstone's letter was known, the Irish members held a meeting the same evening, which was adjourned in Mr. Parnell's absence. He was present the following day, and was pressed to resign. There was again an adjournment, and on the 29th Mr. Parnell published his Manifesto. In this he alleged that the integrity and independence of a section of his party had been "sapped and destroyed by the wire-pullers of the English Liberal party"; that Mr. Gladstone's letter claimed "a right of veto" on the Irish party's choice of their own leader, and contained a menace that resistance to this claim would involve an indefinite postponement of Home Rule. To enable the Irish people to measure the loss wherewith they were threatened unless they threw him (Mr. Parnell), their leader, "to the English wolves," Mr. Parnell purported to describe the kind of Home

Rule Mr. Gladstone was ready to grant. Mr. Parnell declared that he had obtained his information from Mr. Gladstone himself, when on a visit to Hawarden in November, 1889. He said that Mr. Gladstone told him that, in his own opinion, and in that of his colleagues, the Irish representation in the Imperial Parliament must be reduced from 103 members to 32, that the land question must be reserved from the control of the Irish legislation, that the Irish constabulary must remain under Imperial control for an indefinite period, and that the appointment of judges, resident magistrates, etc., should be kept in the hands of the Imperial authority for some ten or twelve years. Stating next his views upon these alleged proposals, Mr. Parnell concluded his Manifesto by declaring his belief that Home Rule could be obtained only by an Irish party which was independent of any English party; that Home Rule would be neither endangered nor postponed by any action of the Irish people in supporting him; and that even a postponement of Home Rule would be preferable to a compromise of Ireland's national rights, by the acceptance of a measure which would not realise the aspirations of the Irish race. On the following day, Mr. Gladstone's reply appeared in the newspapers, and it is given here in full :—

REPLY OF MR. GLADSTONE.

November 29th.   On Saturday, Mr. Gladstone issued the following reply :—

SIR,—It is no part of my duty to canvass the manifesto of Mr. Parnell, which I have received this morning, and I shall not apply to it a single epithet, for I am not his judge in any matter, and I believe myself to have shown in the matter of the Pigott Commission that I had no indisposition to do him justice. But the first portion of the document consists of a recital of propositions stated to have been made by me to him, and of objections entertained by him to those propositions. The Irish, as well as the British public, has a right to know whether I admit or deny the accuracy of that recital, and in regard to every one of the four points stated by Mr. Parnell I at once deny it.

The purport of the conversation was not to make known "intended proposals." No single suggestion was offered by me to Mr. Parnell as formal, as unanimous, or as final. It was a statement perfectly free, and without prejudice, of points in which either I myself or such of my colleagues as I had been able to consult inclined generally to believe that the plan of 1886 for Home Rule in Ireland might be improved, and as to which I was desirous to learn whether they raised any serious objection in the mind of Mr. Parnell.

To no one of my suggestions did Mr. Parnell offer serious objection ; much less did he signify in whole or in part that they augured the proposal as " a measure which would not satisfy the aspirations of the Irish race." According to his present account he received from me, in the autumn of 1889, information of vital changes adverse to Ireland in our plans for Home Rule, and kept this information secret until in the end of November, 1890, and in connection with a totally independent and personal matter, he produces it to the world.

I deny, then, that I made the statements which his memory ascribes to me, or anything substantially resembling them, either on the retention of the Irish members, or on the settlement of the land or agrarian difficulty, or on the control of the constabulary, or on the appointment of the Judiciary. As to land in particular, I am not conscious of having added anything to my public declarations, while as to County Court judges and resident magistrates, I make no suggestion whatever.

The conversation between us was strictly confidential, and, in my judgment, and, as I understood, in that of Mr. Parnell, to publish even a true account of it is to break the seal of confidence which alone renders political co-operation possible.

Every suggestion made by me was from written memoranda. The whole purport of my conference was made known by me in the strictest confidence, when it had just taken place, to my colleagues in the Cabinet of 1886, and I assured them that in regard to none of them had Mr. Parnell raised any serious difficulty whatever.

Neither Mr. Parnell nor I myself was bound by this conversation to absolute and final acceptance of the principle then canvassed ; but during the year which has since elapsed, I have never received from Mr. Parnell any intimation that he had altered his views regarding any of them.

I have now done with the Hawarden conversation, and I conclude with the following simple statement :—

1. I have always held in public, as well as in private, that the National party of Ireland ought to remain entirely independent of the Liberal party of Great Britain.

2. It is our duty, and my duty in particular, conformably to the spirit of Grattan and O'Connell, to study all adjustments in the great matter of Home Rule which may tend to draw to our side moderate and equitable opponents ; but for me to propose any measure, except such as Ireland could approve on the lines already laid down, would be fatuity as regards myself, and treachery to the Irish nation, in whom, even by the side of Mr. Parnell, I may claim to take an interest.

I remain, Sir, your very obedient servant,

W. E. GLADSTONE.

London, November 29th, 1890.

It need only be said that this letter practically closed Mr. Parnell's public career.

CHAPTER XLI.

1891-1892.—HIS FOURTH ADMINISTRATION.

Two days before the new year, 1891, Mr. Gladstone entered upon his 81st year. He was able to look back, through fifty-eight years of public life, on a long and illustrious career. No other English statesman has ever taken part in the arena of active politics at the same age. Lord Palmerston was within two days of completing his 81st year when he died; but even when he was little over 70, those who knew him well say that he was far less capable for the transaction of public business than Mr. Gladstone was eleven years later. Mr. Gladstone began the new year with a sustained vigour, intellectually and physically, that was one of the marvels of the time. Seventeen years before, he talked of withdrawing from public life. He pleaded the need of rest—that he was growing old. Yet five years after, in Midlothian, he raised a storm that swept his opponents from power and place. And later—in the beginning of 1883—it was thought that he would again visit Midlothian, but he was unable to do so, and this was regarded as a warning that his retirement from public life was at hand. It was then asked, who would be to the next half, or even to the next quarter century, what Mr. Gladstone had been to the previous half? And this question, though asked nearly eight years ago, still remains unanswered. Lord Hartington at the time pointed out that not one of Mr. Gladstone's colleagues stood in front of his contemporaries as having exhibited by personal achievement, or by wide-reaching popularity, his right to step into Mr Gladstone's place. And this is as true to-day as it was when it was expressed. In these years, Mr. Gladstone seems to have grown younger and stronger, and in February last (1890), when it might be reasonably supposed that his labours had ended, he throws off his political cares, and runs down to Oxford to study Homer, in college rooms; and though a veteran in his country's service, over fourscore years of age, how wonderfully he enjoyed that visit! Modern Oxford delighted to do him honour, and at each festival—and there were many—he charmed everyone. His animation and good humour, his kindly interest

B B

in everything and in everybody he saw, his inexhaustible recollections and marvellous activity, excited an extraordinary interest not less in the country than at the University.   He addressed the Union Society, the famous debating club over the meetings of which he presided sixty years ago.   He was then the rising hope of the stern and unbending Tories, to be, however, "driven from them," as he himself said in his *Apologia* of 1866, "by the slow and resistless force of conviction."   Nearly two generations pass away, and the old statesman returns to his college and to the Union, and divesting himself of his political cares, rears, with all the enthusiasm of youth, a wonderful fabric in support of his views on the Homeric legend.

To social, rather than political subjects, Mr. Gladstone for some months turned his attention in his public addresses.   At Hawarden, he contrasted the condition of the people then with that of fifty years ago, showing the extraordinary progress that had been made.   Next we find him opening a new free public library in St. Martin's Lane, London, and interesting all who heard him, with delightful comments on the subject of free libraries. At Eton College, he delivered an address on the character and attributes of the goddess Artemis, as represented by Homer in the *Iliad* and *Odyssey;* and at Hastings he returned with amazing zest to the subject of Ireland.   On recovering from an attack of influenza, which caused no little public anxiety at the time, he took part, in St. James's Hall, in the jubilee celebration of the Colonial Bishopric Fund, moving a resolution of congratulation; and, although not present at the jubilee of Mr. Thomas Cook, he found time to write a letter expressing regret at being unable to attend, and speaking in flattering terms of Mr. Cook's public services.

Returning to the political arena, Mr. Gladstone addressed a great meeting at Newcastle, dealing with proposed reforms in the Liquor Traffic laws, with Scotch and Welsh disestablishment, with reform of the House of Lords, and of the Registration laws, also with the payment of labour representatives, and with Ireland. He approved the foreign policy of the Government, though he expressed a hope that it would soon be possible for Lord Salisbury to relieve Great Britain from the burdensome and embarrassing occupation of Egypt, which so long as it lasted must be a cause of weakness and a source of embarrassment. These observations, more especially those referring to Egypt, caused some sensation.   It was reported from Egypt that the old retrograde Turkish party rejoiced at this prospect of the with-

MR. GLADSTONE IN 1892.
From a photograph by Lord Battersea, taken at Aston Clinton.

drawal of the army of occupation, and of their subsequent
reacquisition of power.   But they rejoiced in too great a
haste, as they must have found out on Mr. Gladstone's return
to office.

At Newcastle, the ex-Premier was presented with the honorary
freedom of the city of Newcastle.   Later in the autumn he
visited the soap works at Port Sunlight, in Cheshire, and in his
speech there dealt with the relations of capital and labour, on
profit-sharing, and on co-operation.   Subsequently, at Spital,
en route, he denied Lord Salisbury's charge against him with
regard to the concealment of the Home Rule policy.   He also
combated the Premier's assertion that the proposal of Home
Rule was made in defiance of the course of things which was
taking place in every country in the world.   The union of Spain
had, he said, not been accomplished in our time.   In France,
every wise man thought that France was too much centralised.
Italy, it was true, had had such a number of bad Governments,
that being an historical unity from ancient times, it did unite
itself together.   Lord Salisbury saw that Mr. Gladstone had not
looked at Austria.   Mr. Gladstone replied that "emancipated
Hungary has given the most astonishing example of decentralisa-
tion and local autonomy that the world has ever seen."

Mr. Gladstone's views on Rural reforms were given at a
conference of special representatives of rural industry, held in
London.   It was at the breakfast on the second day of the conference that he addressed the delegates.   The main points with
which he dealt were those of labour, the immigration into the
towns, the condition of the rural population, land for labourers,
and parish councils.   On the subject of taking land compulsorily,
he said :—"It may be that the parish council would not in every
case be strong enough to wield those compulsory powers without
some assistance from a higher authority."   This simply means
that the taking of land should not be a power exercised by the
authority in a small area, but by that of a larger area, such as the
County Council or the proposed district authority.   It would be
a mistake, obviously, to add responsibilities to the parish council,
such as would be likely to involve it in litigation, thus exposing a
small body of ratepayers to loss should legal decisions be adverse.
It is right that the parish council should have the initiative in all
matters connected with health and parish charities ; also, in the
maintenance and management of a system of allotments.   It
should have power, moreover, to maintain a reading room and
form a library, and to do, in a word, what would help to promote
the welfare of the village, and brighten village life.   The scheme

of rural reform sketched by Mr. Gladstone delighted the delegates, and his presence amongst them aroused great enthusiasm.

After the conference, the ex-Premier left London for Biarritz. Some time after his arrival, it was suggested that he be made a member of the English club there; but a small clique of ill-natured persons so contrived it that he was refused admission. It soon became evident, however, that this decision did not meet with the approval of the whole body of members, for a requisition was not long afterwards signed by nearly all, requesting Mr. Gladstone to become a member.

Returning to London with renewed vigour, the ex-Premier began to make preparations for the dissolution of Parliament, which could not be far distant. In the spring, he addressed a letter on the subject of female suffrage to Mr. Samuel Smith, M.P. At the time, the Woman Suffrage Bill of Sir A. Rollit's was before the House; and Mr. Gladstone, in his letter, advised the House to reject it. He contended that the Bill placed the "individual woman on the same footing in regard to Parliamentary elections as the individual man," and that as "a fair and rational, and therefore morally, necessary consequence," she must be allowed to become a member of Parliament, and if allowed to become a member, must be allowed to fill any office in the State. Can we, then," he writes, "determine to have two categories of members of Parliament; one of them, the established and the larger one, consisting of persons who can travel without check along all the lines of public duty and honour; the other, the novel and the smaller one, stamped with disability for the discharge of executive administration, judicial, or other public duty? Such a stamp would, I apprehend, be a brand. There is nothing more odious, nothing more untenable, than an inequality in legal privilege which does not stand upon some principle in its nature broad and clear. Is there here such a privilege, adequate to show that when capacity to sit in Parliament has been established, the title to discharge executive and judicial duty can be withheld? Tried by the test of feeling, the distinction would be offensive. Would it stand better under the laws of logic? It would stand still worse, if worse be possible." Mr. Gladstone maintains that the "difference of social office" between the two sexes is part of the structure of things; that it does not rest upon custom or convention, or any action of the stronger sex, but "upon causes not flexible and elastic, like most mental qualities, but physical, and in their nature unchangeable. I, for one, am not prepared to say which of the two sexes has the higher, and which has the lower, province; but I recognise the subtle and

profound character of the difference between them, and I must
say again, and again, deliberate before aiding in the issue of what
seems an invitation, by public authority, to the one, to renounce as
far as possible its own office, in order to assume that of the other."
This argument should be final—that is, if it be possible to close
by argument controversy on the question of Woman Suffrage.

With a view to strengthen the Liberal party in London, Mr.
Gladstone made a great speech in the Memorial Hall, in June,
before the dissolution of Parliament. He declared that the
general election would give effect to the desire of London for a
great municipality, in which the City Corporation and the Guilds
and Companies, with their wealth, would be merged. The
municipality should have all the poweis given anywhere to any
municipal body, including the control of the police; should be
enabled to tax ground-rents; and should make any rules they
liked for the payment of the labourers employed by the con-
tractors, the ratepayers being trusted to avoid extravagance.
The Government, thought Mr. Gladstone, could not hire labour
except in a free market; but corporations and monopolies and all
limited companies could, in return for their privileges, be justifi-
ably compelled to adopt the eight hours rule. The speech gave
a great impetus to the Liberal and Radical electioneering forces
in the Metropolis.

The Ulster Convention, at Belfast, had aroused attention far
and wide. There were 11,879 delegates present, representing
every class and division of Protestants, and thousands of Roman
Catholics besides. Their declarations that an elected Parliament
in Dublin would be unworkable and impolitic, and their decision
that they have nothing to do with Home Rule, were talked of all
over the country. At a gathering of Nonconformists at the house
of the Rev. Guinness Rogers, Mr. Gladstone replied, arguing that
there were substantial grounds for the fears of the Ulster Protestants. The lay Catholics in Ireland, he said, were not to be dreaded,
for they had exercised all the powers they possessed rather in
favour of Protestants than against them. "They have obtained
powers of electing men to Parliament. Whom do they elect?
Protestants whenever they can get them, and usually there have
been a majority of Protestants ; and if they fail to be a majority,
at any rate it will be because they find greater difficulty in getting
them. By whom have they been led? Almost entirely by
Protestants, and, down to the latest moment of a great catastrophe, by a Protestant who was a very remarkable man, and who
was even in his day—not so very long ago—a diocesan repre-

sentative of the ex-Established Church in his own diocese in the
county of Wicklow. But they have got some local powers, they
have got some corporations. Well, it is perfectly notorious that
they elect corporations in perfect freedom from religious distinctions. They have Protestant Lord Mayors of Dublin, and Mayors
of other places ; they have Boards of Guardians, and they elect
Guardians who are Protestants when they can get them, and when
they are competent."

In reply to this, it has been said that what the Ulster men dread
is not what the Catholic laity will do when left to themselves, but
what they will do when under the guidance of clerics possessed, as
events have shown, of absolute control over the elections. And
this point is not one that can very well be ignored in the face of
evidence such as that given at the hearing of the North and
South Meath petitions in the election courts.

For some time the interest of the country had been directed
elsewhere than to the expiring House of Commons. Half the
members were away among their constituents, preparing for the
struggle. And when the Dissolution took place, on the 28th
June (1892), the contests were in full swing. Mr. Gladstone,
who had issued an address to his constituents, followed it up
by visiting Midlothian. But before setting out, an assault was
committed upon him at Chester, which aroused no little indignation throughout the country. A wretched woman flung a
gingerbread-nut, which struck the ex-Premier in the eye, causing
for a time acute pain, but, fortunately, without injuring his eyesight. In a few days after, he travelled to Midlothian, and
opened his election campaign amid the greatest enthusiasm.
His speeches were mainly founded upon the need of shaping
the policy of the Government by the principles of justice. He
pointed out the extreme importance to the cause of labour of
political reform, suggesting in regard to the eight hours question
that, perhaps, the principle of local option might be found applicable. We need not follow him through the campaign, which
closed with his re-election. His majority, however, was considerably less than he gained in 1885. There was no contest in
1886. The reduction of the 1885 majority from 4,631 to 690
caused much surprise. It is believed that the opponents of Disestablishment mustered stronger than had been thought likely ;
but even this would not account entirely for so great a falling off
in the majority. There is no doubt that the fall of Mr. Parnell,
and the split in the Nationalist camp, had given rise to misgivings,
even among some of Mr. Gladstone's supporters, for it is quite

certain that many of them never went to the poll. The majority, too, of Mr. Herbert Gladstone, at Leeds, sinking from 3,175 to 353, added significance to the reduction in Midlothian.

After three weeks' electioneering the new Parliament was duly elected. Mr. Gladstone's immediate followers numbered 270; the Labour members, not attached to party, 4; the followers of Mr. Justin McCarthy (Irish Nationalists), 72; and those of Mr. John Redmond (Parnellites), 9; making a total of 355 Home Rulers, against 268 Conservatives and 47 Liberal Unionists, or a total of 315 against Home Rule; Mr. Gladstone's majority, including the independent Labour members and both sections of the Irish Nationalists, being 40. It may be useful to add to the record by stating that while the returns for the United Kingdom showed a majority of 40 Home Rulers, the elections in England alone returned a majority of 71 against Home Rule, and in Great Britain a majority of 17 against Home Rule It was the large number of Home Rulers returned for the Irish constituencies that gave Mr. Gladstone his majority of 40.

Lord Salisbury having determined to meet Parliament before resigning, the Session opened on August 4. An address of No-confidence in the Government was moved by Mr. Asquith, and after three nights' debate the division was taken in the fullest House on record, and the result showed a majority against the Ministry. Lord Salisbury, of course, resigned, and in about a week the new Government was constructed, with Mr. Gladstone for the fourth time Prime Minister. He was then within four months of his eighty-third birthday. In forming previous administrations the Premier had always a large majority at his back. He now found himself with a small majority, and that dependent on the Irish Parliamentary Party. The right hon. gentleman's resources, however, being well-nigh inexhaustible, it was felt that if his strength and vigour remained, there was no reason why he should not govern as well with a small majority as a large one. There had been some very disquieting rumours in regard to his health. It was stated that he had had a fit, and the apparently feverish uneasiness of those who were behind the scenes lent some colour to the story; but it turned out, when all was known, that the aged statesman had caught cold, and his family insisted upon his taking care of himself within doors.

That he quickly recovered, and was rejoicing again in his good health, soon after his return to office, may be inferred from the fact that in September he ascended Snowdon, as the guest of Sir E. Watkin, to whom the mountain now belongs, and beside a

convenient boulder addressed a Welsh audience. He complimented Wales on returning so many good Liberals at the
election ; he approved the Welsh desire for disestablishment and
lower rents ; but reminded his audience that Home Rule for
Ireland must be conceded, so as to be got out of the way first. He
told his audience to read Welsh history, so as to understand the
condition in which their country was kept until the accession of
the Tudor House, which, he implied, abolished her oppressions.
Turning to the question of rents, he told the farmers that the
rents they were paying were too high. The landlords in England, he said, had reduced rents by 24 per cent. on the average ;
but the landlords of Wales, as he heard from Mr. Ellis, had
only reduced theirs 7 per cent., while there were actually Welsh
counties where rents had been increased. Subsequently it was
pointed out by Lord Sudeley, in the *Times*, that only permanent
reductions were noted in the returns from which Mr. Gladstone
had taken his figures. Temporary reductions do not appear at
all. Moreover, it was only on large farms that reductions were
given as permanent reductions. In the case of small holdings,
they were almost invariably given as temporary abatements, the
landlord hoping for a change of fortune, and the tenant being
willing to carry on somehow so long as the whole of the old rent
would not be expected from him. These temporary reductions,
Lord Sudeley observed, were often as high as 10, 15, and 20 per
cent., and made in addition to smaller permanent reductions. It
is not improbable that Mr. Gladstone was led into error by his
informant.

Owing to the impenetrable mist in which Snowdon was
wrapped, Mr. Gladstone was unable to reach the top; but he was
able, soon after, to make up for any disappointment he felt on that
occasion by appearing in the University of Oxford, and displaying
his astonishing intellectual and physical vigour. He delivered
the first Romanes lecture on the history of Universities, more
especially of the two great English Universities of Oxford and
Cambridge. He attributed much importance to the influence of
lay men in the origination of the two Universities. Some hold
that the Universities are purely ecclesiastical foundations, but
Mr. Gladstone observes " that according to the principle of the
old English law, the University, as such, is a lay and not an
ecclesiastical foundation, and that this principle is a deep
principle, and is also a just principle." The lecturer paid
eloquent tribute to the poets and theologians of both the
Universities, and in a noble passage deprecated that view of

a University which makes it its duty to prepare its students for professional success.   Its true ideal, he said, is to train men who are greater than their work, and who do not merge themselves in practical life.

Early in December the Premier was presented with the freedom of Liverpool, the highest honour in its gift; and although there are probably more political opponents of Mr. Gladstone there than in any other provincial city in the three kingdoms, the reception he met with must have touched him very deeply.   The whole city rejoiced in paying homage to his many splendid qualities, and in thus honouring the most famous of her sons the great seaport added to her own fame.   In acknowledging the honour conferred upon him, Mr. Gladstone referred to the past history and remarkable commercial progress of Liverpool.   Referring to the great plague of drunkenness, which had so long existed in the land, he believed that in no place had stronger special efforts been made to deal with this mischief than in Liverpool.   With regard to the Manchester Ship Canal, and the suggestion that it might be injurious to the commercial pre-eminence of his native city, Mr. Gladstone said that such an idea was utterly visionary.   He predicted that the success of the undertaking would for Liverpool be large, be an enormous gain, and that its material progress would go on unchecked.   He urged on the inhabitants to strive to win for their city a name as distinguished in arts and letters as it had in the history of commercial enterprise.   In freshness and vigour the old statesman was wonderful, and it will be long before his feat of oratory in St. George's Hall is forgotten.

Mr. Gladstone left England for Biarritz before the close of the year, returning in January, looking wonderfully well, to prepare for the meeting of Parliament.

CHAPTER XLII.

1893.—THE SECOND HOME RULE BILL.

IN the House of Commons, on Thursday, February 13th, Mr. Gladstone asked for leave to introduce a Bill to amend the provision for the Government of Ireland. In all parts of the House there was a crowded representative gathering, recalling to the mind of the Parliamentary spectator the memorable scene in 1886, when the Prime Minister, seven years younger, unfolded his first Home Rule plan. Many distinguished men have passed away since then. Many old colleagues and friends of the veteran statesman, unable in advanced life to stand the strain and stress of political warfare, were absent; and younger men, to whom Cabinet office had seemed a possibility too distant to be even dreamt of, were now sitting with some of the old Parliamentary hands on the Treasury bench. Members, gathered from all the constituencies in the United Kingdom, crowded the now too confined chamber. The floor, the benches, the gangways, the steps of the Speaker's chair were occupied. Indeed, every available foot of space within the arena was taken up by honourable members; while in the galleries, peers, and foreign ministers, and strangers privileged and unprivileged, had assembled indifferent to the discomfort of close packing. The Prince of Wales and his son, the Duke of York, were there, attentive observers of the scene below; while through the bars of the ladies' "cage" could be seen the wives and daughters of ministers and peers.

As the hour drew near, and Mr. Gladstone entered the House, almost the whole assembly rose and cheered. The cheering was not the tribute merely of partisanship, but rather of that of a great body of Englishmen who saw in the old white-haired statesman one whose genius and renown they were all proud of, whatever their views on points of policy might be. Then the House settled down, and in a few minutes more Mr. Gladstone was at the table delivering in a clear, ringing voice, the great speech in which he unfolded his new scheme of Home Rule for Ireland. And it was truly a great speech, worthy of a great occasion. None there grudged the orator the expressions of admiration which so marvellous a physical, no less than an intellectual effort called forth.

For the two hours and a-quarter during wh'ch the speech flowed from the statesman's lips, the closely crowded chamber listened attentively, while every now and then cheers from the Ministerial and Nationalist benches accentuated the more remarkable passages. In the exordium he dwelt upon the relations between Great Britain and Ireland, stating that there was a distinct breach of the promises on the faith of which the Legislative Union had been obtained. He passed from that to an analysis of opinion in England since the rejection of the Home Rule Bill of 1886, and drew therefrom the conviction that a change favourable to the principle of Home Rule had taken place. "In July, 1886," he said, "while out of 465 members there were 127 returned favourable to our way of thinking, there were no less than 338 opposed to us. The time that has passed since that year is not very long, but now the 127 have already swollen to 197, and the 338 are sunk to 268. There was a majority from England adverse to the Irish claims in 1886 of 211. That majority has declined to the more modest figure of 71."

Proceeding, Mr. Gladstone said that he could not undertake to supply a table of what the Bill he asked leave to introduce contained. He feared it would only bewilder his hearers, and completeness would be much more than balanced by practical obscurity. What he desired was to present to the notice of the House the principal and salient points of the Bill, and leave, if he could, some living impression of its character on the minds and memories of those who heard him.

Mr. Gladstone said he had endeavoured to adhere closely to the five cardinal principles of the Bill of 1886. The object of that measure was to establish a legislative body, sitting in Dublin, for the conduct of both legislation and administration on Irish as distinct from Imperial affairs; secondly, the equality of all the kingdoms was to be borne in mind; thirdly, there was to be an equal repartition of Imperial charges; fourthly, there were to be practicable provisions for the protection of minorities; and fifthly, the plan to be proposed was to bear the character of a real and a continued, if not a final, settlement. On that basis they continued to stand, and the supremacy of the Imperial Parliament would be expressly acknowledged in the preamble of the Bill. Dealing with the executive power, Mr. Gladstone said the Vice-royalty would be divested of its party character, and the appointment would be for the term of six years, subject to the revoking power of the Crown, and would be free from religious disabilities. Religious disabilities he said may have been, and were, improper and inadvisable even before the abolition of the Irish Church as an establishment, but since that abolition they have become nothing less than preposterous. Then there came an important provision for the appointment of an executive committee of the Privy Council, which might be called the Cabinet of the Viceroy, on whose advice the Viceroy would give or withhold his assent to the Bills; subject, however, to the instructions of the Sovereign in respect to any given measure.

As to the question of a Legislative Council, the Government had decided that there ought to be such a body, and that it should be elective, and not nominated. Then came the question how they were to differentiate the Council from the popular Assembly. In the first place they would take the number of councillors it was proposed to appoint, namely, 48; and in the second place they would take the term of the Council, which it was proposed to fix at eight years, the term of the Assembly being a lower one. The constituencies of the new Council would be associated with a value above £20 rent, and that figure would secure an aggregate constituency approaching 170,000 persons. In that constituency owners are included as well as occupiers, but subject to the provision that no owner or occupier is to vote in more than one constituency. With regard to the popular Assembly, the Bill left the number of members at 103, who will be elected for Irish legislative business by the constituencies in Ireland, and fixed the term at five years. In order to meet what was called the deadlock, the Bill provided that where a Bill had been adopted by the Assembly more than once, and where there had been an interval between the two adoptions of either two years, or else marked by a dissolution of Parliament, then upon the second adoption the two Assemblies might be required to meet, and the fate of the Bill would be decided in the General Assembly. All appeals were to be to the Judicial Committee of the Privy Council, and not the Privy Council of the House of Lords. Next, the Privy Council may try a question of invalidity of an Irish Act, and try it, of course, judicially, and in a reasoned judgment of what sometimes is called the question of *ultra vires*—not, however, upon the initiation of irresponsible persons, but upon the initiation either of the Viceroy, or the Secretary of State. The Judicial Committee as now recognised is the only approach we can get to the Supreme Court of the United States; and, of course, in the composition of the Judicial Committee due regard must be paid to the different elements of nationality. Two Exchequer Judges would be appointed under the Great Seal

MR. GLADSTONE DURING HIS LAST PREMIERSHIP.
From a drawing by S. Begg.

of the United Kingdom, for the purpose mainly of financial
business, and such business as was Imperial, and it was provided
that for six years all judges should be appointed as they were
now, and not removable except in pursuance of an address from
the two Houses of the Legislation in Ireland.

With regard to the Constabulary, it was proposed to abolish
the force gradually.   There would be full recognition and
discharge of every obligation to them.   During the period of
transition it would be under the control of the Viceroy, as the
representative of the Crown, and it would be eventually replaced
by a force owing its existence to the Irish authority.

Adverting next to the retention of the Irish members at
Westminster, he said he had never regarded it as vital to the
Bill, though it was undoubtedly a very weighty detail, and he still
adhered to the opinion that it would pass the wit of man to devise
a plan which should be free from practical objections.   After
reviewing at considerable length the arguments for and against
the retention, the right hon. gentleman said it was proposed that
Ireland should be represented in the House of Commons by
eighty members with limited powers of voting.   First of all, they
would be excluded from voting upon any motion or Bill expressly
confined to Great Britain ; secondly, they were not to vote for any
tax not levied in Ireland, nor for any appropriation of money
otherwise than for Imperial services—the schedule to the Bill
naming the services—nor on motions or resolutions exclusively
affecting Great Britain, or things or persons therein.   With
reference, however, to the first restriction, it seemed to the
Government that there should be some way of raising the question
whether or not the Bill or motion ought to be extended to Ireland,
and therefore Irish members would not be excluded from voting
for a motion "incidental to" such Bill or motion.   "The conclusion," said Mr. Gladstone, "we have come to, is that the whole
business is full of thorns and brambles."   "But," he added, "the
object of this Bill is autonomy and self-government for Ireland in
matters properly Irish.   The Irish did not raise this difficulty.
They were ready to accept that autonomy, and take your terms,
whatever they might be, as to sitting here or not sitting here.
True, we for our own purposes have thought it right that there
should be provisions for retaining them.   Could there be anything
more unstatesmanlike or ungenerous than to avail ourselves of our
own wrong, when they had met us freely and frankly and accepted
exclusion from this House of Commons, and when we have
insisted on their remaining, to make difficulties of detail a reason

for objection. This is the state of the case, and their retention or non-retention, important as it is, is secondary in comparison with the great purposes that we have in view, and secondary to the aim which is the main principle of our measure. Well, we offer this plan, which after much labour, is the best plan we can give."

As to the question of finance, the key-note was to be found in the provision that there was to be one system of legislation for all the kingdoms in regard to it. This might be considered as taxing legislation or regulative legislation. Under the former head might be included Customs duties, Excise duties, the Post Office and Telegraphs. By adopting this scheme they were likely to avoid any clashing or friction between the agents of the Imperial and Irish Governments, and a larger and more liberal transfer would be made to Ireland for the management of her own affairs than could be otherwise effected. The principle to which they were bound to give effect was that Ireland should bear her fair share of Imperial expenditure. The plan of a lump sum or "tribute," adopted in 1886, had disappeared, in consequence of the retention of the Irish members; and the method of "quota" had not been now adopted. It was proposed to appropriate a particular fund, and to say that that fund should be taken by us, and should stand in fulfilment of all obligations of Ireland for Imperial purposes. This amount might be represented at £2,430,000 gross a year, and subtracting from that sum £60,000 a year for collecting, £2,370,000 was the sum to be contributed, which was between the two points of 4 per cent. and a charge of 5 per cent. The Irish balance-sheet stood in this position :—On the credit side there would be a total of £5,660,000, and on the other side, the Irish Government would take over the whole of the Civil Government charges of the country, except the Constabulary charges.

These Civil Government charges amounted to £5,210,000. Then there would be the collection of the revenue, and the Postal charges, and two-thirds of the charge for the Constabulary which Ireland would be required to bear. These things would bring the Irish charge up to £5,160,000, and thus Ireland wou'd have a clear surplus of £500,000 with which to start on her own account. "Then," said Mr. Gladstone, " one would say, at whose expense does that surplus come? Well, sir, undoubtedly in the whole, or in the main, it would fall on the British taxpayer. You may be shocked at this, but there is much more reason to be shocked at what is going on. And what I want to urge is this : that by arriving at this settlement with Ireland, you will escape the

impending and constantly accruing increment of Irish charges."
The right hon. gentleman then proceeded to state what these
have been. The Irish grants from 1833 to 1837 averaged
£762,000. From 1889 to 1892 the Irish grants on the average
were £4,042,000. In fifty-five years there was an increase of
£3,300,000, or a regular increment of £66,000 a year. Re-
leasing the House from the consideration of detail, he expressed
a wish that the plan the Government presented were worthy of its
object, which was no less than to redeem the fame and character
of this country and its political genius from an old and
flagrant dishonour, and to increase and enhance and magnify
the strength, the glory, the union of the Empire. The peroration
greatly moved the House. "Sir, the sooner we stamp and seal
the deed which is to efface all former animosities, and to
open an era, as we believe, of peace and good will—the sooner
that is done the better. For my own part, I must say, I never
will, and I never can be a party to bequeathing to my country
the continuance of this heritage of discord, which has been
handed down from generation to generation without hardly a
momentary interruption through seven centuries, this heritage of
discord, with all the evils that follow in its train. Sir, I wish to
have no part or lot in that process. It would be a misery to me
if I had omitted, in these closing years, any measure possible
for me to make towards upholding and promoting the cause
which I believe to be the cause not of one party or another, one
nation or another, but of all parties and all nations inhabiting
these islands. To those nations, viewing them as I do, with all
their vast opportunities, under a living union for power and for
happiness; to those nations I say, let me entreat you—and if
it were with my latest breath, I would entreat you—to let the
dead bury its dead—to cast behind you every recollection of
bygone evils, and to cherish, to love, to sustain one another
through all the vicissitudes of human affairs in the times that
are to come."

Mr. Gladstone then resumed his seat. His voice had become
hoarse and low, and the silence deepened as he approached the
end. A roar of cheers followed. The House was now released,
and the old statesman, after an interval of seven years, had
fulfilled his pledge--he had introduced his new Bill for the
better government of Ireland.

CHAPTER XLIII.

THROUGHOUT the protracted debates which followed the second reading stage of the bill, Mr. Gladstone's mastery of Parliamentary tactics was magnificently shown. The defence of the measure was conducted mainly by himself. His colleagues, more particularly Mr. John Morley and Mr. Asquith, assisted at moments when the aged statesman needed rest, but the most part of the fighting was done by the Premier, and he never seemed happier than when in the thick of the fight he was found combatting the arguments and replying to the strictures of the Opposition. This duty, contrary indeed to the wishes of his colleagues, he took upon himself, and from the first to the last stage his whole energies and his inexhaustible fertility of resource were devoted to his arduous task. And when his historic achievement was accomplished—the passing of the Home Rule Bill through the House of Commons—'t was felt on all sides that he had not only won the honours of the Session, but had done what no other statesman of the day could do. On the 1st of September, 1893, the bill was sent up to the Lords, and after four nights' discussion it was rejected by the large majority of 419 to 41.

It might be supposed that the aged statesman had need of rest after so long and exhausting a Session, but in barely three weeks' time from the date of the rejection of the bill by the Lords, Mr. Gladstone was in Edinburgh making a great speech to his constituents, in which the peers were warned that they had "raised a greater question than they were aware of." And although Mr. Gladstone refrained from naming the greater question to which he referred, it was felt that his warning pointed

to the abolition of the hereditary chamber.   He expressed a
hope that wiser counsels would prevail, and proceeded to ex-
pound with his usual vigour and energy the measures it was
proposed to introduce in the next Session of Parliament.   These
briefly were a bill to complete local government in the English
Councils, bills to disestablish the State Churches in Scotland
and Wales, and measures relating to the hours of labour in
workshops, and to the question of Local Option.   His own
share in the promotion of the programme of legislation he out-
lined with so much zest could not, however, be large.   At his
advanced age it was inevitable that he must soon seek release
from the cares of his great office.   Still his wonderful vitality
encouraged the hope that he might be able to retain the leadership of the House of Commons and remain at the head of the
Government for some little time longer.

The winter was spent at Biarritz.   Late in January it was
announced in the columns of the *Pall Mall Gazette* that Mr.
Gladstone had "fully decided to resign office almost immediately."   This, as may well be imagined, caused a great
sensation in the country, and though corrected from Biarritz by
Sir Algernon West, who was with Mr. Gladstone, and had his
authority to correct the report, the terms in which this was made
left no doubt that resignation was contemplated by the Prime
Minister.   In the first place it was said that "the statement that
Mr. Gladstone has definitely decided, or has decided at all, on
resigning Office is untrue."   Then in the second place it was
stated, "It is true that for many months past his age and the
condition of his sight and hearing have in his judgment made
relief from public cares desirable, and that accordingly his tenure
of office has been at any moment liable to interruption from these
causes in their nature permanent."   This alarmed his supporters
in the country, and though the organs of the Government
endeavoured to show that there need be no uneasiness just then,
it was pretty generally felt that Mr. Gladstone's resignation would
not long be delayed.

Early in February he returned from Biarritz, and received at
Charing Cross a welcome home that delighted him.   The road-
way and the pavements of the station and the Strand were
crowded with people waiting to see him.   When he resumed his
seat in the House of Commons all sorts of rumours were current.
These were soon set at rest.   After a fighting speech of astonishing vigour, in which he accepted the Lords' amendments to the

Local Government Bill, he formally resigned his offices of First
Lord of the Treasury and Privy Seal. This was on the 3rd of
March. His speech on the previous Thursday was therefore his
last from his place on the Treasury Bench. It has been remarked that in withholding the fact that he intended to retire he
kept the country unnecessarily in suspense. But the truth is
that it was only when the state of his eyesight made it imperative
that an operation should be performed he arrived at the conclusion that his resignation could no longer be delayed. He had
visited the Queen at Buckingham Palace previous to the formal
visit at which his resignation was placed in her hands, and it is
not improbable that the veteran statesman's retirement from
public life was then touched upon. Subsequently her Majesty
offered her old minister a peerage, but this was declined.

When the news of Mr. Gladstone's resignation became known
it was the subject uppermost in the public mind. It was the close
of sixty years' distinguished service to the State. It will be some
time yet before it is understood what it means—it is quite
impossible to take a true measure of its effect now. It will be so
for years to come. For although the close of his great career
could not in the natural order of things be far distant, the
realization that it has actually come is very difficult: that the
illustrious man, who for so long has resisted the encroachments
of old age has stepped aside from high office, and that a minister
little more than half his years is now ruling the Empire in his
stead—it seems as though it were all a dream. Mr. Gladstone's
vigorous personality, as manifested in his last speech as Prime
Minister, lent no countenance to the rumours set flying about
through club gossip, yet in a few hours after his great figure disappears from ministerial life.

It is hardly any wonder that people felt surprised as well as
grieved. They were grieved to the heart that it was found all
too true that his eyesight was in peril—and the pathos of it was
in his own confession—and they were surprised that they were not
enabled sooner to manifest their sympathy. Somehow it had come
to be thought that whoever went he would be always to the fore;
that in his life decay had been arrested; and that so far from
enfeebling him, the exercise of power increased the strength and
flexibility of his intellect. Nor can it be said that old though he
be his powers are losing their exceeding brilliancy. He is equal
still to many a great effort, and it may be that what Parliament is
losing the whole country outside politics is gaining. Mr. Glad-

stone's leisure has always enriched us with new gifts. To literature, religion, art, the social life of the country, labour, agriculture—to all these subjects he has given something imperishable, and about which no political party can quarrel. May we not then look for another harvest of good things now that his back is turned on politics? But whether his leisure be now given to complete some new legacy for his countrymen, or whether it be passed in rest, the country will ever regard him as one of her great sons—the greatest of the century.

The tributes of respect paid to Mr. Gladstone by the leaders in both Houses of Parliament left nothing to be desired. Party politics were put on one side. And if the Lords remembered that they were to be ended or mended, they at any rate bore no grudge. They followed full of interest and sympathy the splendid eulogy on the character and career of the great ex-minister pronounced by the Marquis of Salisbury. "It was not possible," said his lordship, "for Mr. Gladstone's opponents in that House to speak of his policy and his measures on that occasion without introducing controversial elements, but at least they could pay this passing tribute to one of the most brilliant figures who had served the State since Parliamentary government in this country began, and also to the resolution, the courage, and the self-discipline which he had exhibited down to the latest period of the longest public life ever granted to any English statesman." In the House of Commons the leaders on both sides of the House were not less felicitous, all recognising the advantage of the example set by Mr. Gladstone as the greatest of members of Parliament.

CHAPTER XLIV.

IT might be said truly of Mr. Gladstone's political life that nothing became him so well as the leaving of it ; for even his adversaries bore testimony to the restraint, often most difficult for so strong a partisan to exercise, which he showed in refusing to be entangled in the various debateable questions of the period which followed his retirement.

It was not that he was less keen in hearing and discussing the events which transpired, but that he was fearful of interfering in matters now removed from his guidance. On the subject of the Armenian atrocities alone did he allow himself the satisfaction of uplifting his voice in honest indignation. The first public utterance which he made since his resignation of the Premiership was his magnificent oration delivered at Chester on August 6, 1895. The occasion was interesting for several reasons, one being on account of the reconciliation between the Duke of Westminster and Mr. Gladstone. At the time of the Home Rule crisis the Duke took so strong a view of his former leader's action that he parted with the portrait of Mr. Gladstone which Millais had painted, and in other ways showed his cleavage with the Liberal party and its leader. But the Duke was a warm friend of oppressed nations, so when the troubles befalling the Armenians at the hands of the Turks thrilled the civilised world he took a prominent place at the head of a committee formed to aid the downtrodden Armenians. This interest united the Duke once more with his neighbour at Hawarden Castle, and one of the outward and visible signs of this reunion of old friends was in the presidency of the Duke over the great gathering convened to hear Mr. Gladstone in the Town Hall of Chester.

Among the distinguished audience were Lord Kenyon, the Bishop of Chester, the Bishop of Hereford, Mr. F. S. Stevenson, M.P., who was President of the Anglo-Armenian Association, Mr. Herbert Gladstone, M.P., Dr. Clifford, and some well-known members of the Armenian community in this country. As usual Mrs. Gladstone accompanied her husband to the meeting, which was held in the afternoon for his special convenience.

Mr. Gladstone, who was awarded a wonderful reception in the handsome hall, crowded in every part by an enthusiastic multitude, began by disavowing any political aspect of the meeting. "This meeting is not called in the interests of any party, or having the smallest connection with those differences of opinion which, naturally and warrantably in this free country, will spring out in a complex state of affairs, and divide, on certain questions, man from man." He then traced in vivid language, studiedly moderate in tone, the history of the treatment of the Armenians, and made various suggestions, based on his acquaintance with Eastern affairs. This was the peroration which he uttered with great solemnity, and it was heard in hushed silence, and followed by tumultuous applause :—

"If only men like Fuad Pasha and Ali Pasha, who were in the Government of Turkey after the Crimean War, could be raised from the dead, and could inspire the Turkish policy with their spirit and their principles, that is, in my opinion, what we ought all to desire ; and, though it would be more agreeable to clear Turkey than to find her guilty of these terrible charges, yet if we have the smallest regard to humanity, if we are sensible at all of what is due to our own honour after the steps which have been taken within the last twelve or eighteen months, we must interfere, we must be careful to demand no more than what is just, but at least as much as is necessary ; and we must be determined that, with the help of God, that which is necessary and that which is just shall be done, whether there will be a response or whether there be none."

So much interest was taken in this reappearance of Mr. Gladstone in the political arena that it was stated that the Sultan of Turkey had a special verbatim report of the speech telegraphed to his palace ar Yildiz. The ideas promulgated by Mr. Gladstone were discussed by most public men who spoke on the question, and there is no doubt a great impetus was given for a while to the cause of the Armenians. Large sums were subscribed to the Duke of Westminster's Fund, and a Home for certain Armenians who had escaped was founded in London.

Previous to this interposition in national affairs Mr. Gladstone had enjoyed a pleasant voyage on board the *Tantallon Castle*, with Sir Donald Currie as his host, and accompanied by a group of friends. He was busy with literary work in any intervals of leisure, and an amusing sketch appeared in *Punch* showing the Grand Old Man reading industriously and quite oblivious of the crowd of inquisitive spectators who watched his every movement. One result of his literary studies was a Commentary on the Psalter, which was published about this time, and displayed all its author's well-known knowledge and interest in theology. The earliest fruits of his release from political chains had been a volume of translations of the Odes of Horace, which gave rise to a very clever series of parodies by Mr. C. L. Graves, after republished as "The Hawarden Horace." Mr. Gladstone was as delighted as anybody with these parodies.

The annual fête of the Hawarden Horticultural Society, which had in past years been the occasion of so many speeches from Mr. Gladstone, was this summer specially interesting by reason of a suggestive address from him on the value of small holdings.

Parliament was dissolved in July, and Mr. Gladstone adhered to his determination not to seek re-election. His long Parliamentary career thus definitely terminated. He addressed the following graceful letter to Sir John Cowan, of Beeslack—a name which will always be linked with Mr. Gladstone's in Midlothian :—

"HAWARDEN CASTLE, *July* 1, 1895.

"MY DEAR SIR JOHN COWAN,—The impending Dissolution brings into its final and practical form the prospective farewell which I addressed last year to the Constituency of Midlothian. I now repeat it, with sentiments of gratitude and attachment for the treatment I have received during fifteen happy years, which can never be effaced. I then ventured to express my good wishes for the excellent candidate who aspires to represent the county on principles conformable to the striking manifestation of 1880 and subsequent years.

"Though in regard to public affairs many things are disputable, there are some which belong to history, and which have passed out of the region of contention. It is, for example, as I conceive, beyond question that the century now expiring has exhibited, since the close of its first quarter, a period of unexampled activity, both in legislation and in administrative changes, which, taken in the mass, have been in the direction of true and most beneficial progress ; that both the condition and the franchises of the people have made, in relation to the former state of things, an extraordinary advance ; that of these reforms an overwhelming proportion have been effected by the direct action of the Liberal Party, or of Statesmen such as Peel and Canning, ready to meet odium and to forfeit power for the public good ; and that in every one of fifteen Parliaments the people of Scotland have decisively expressed their convictions in favour of this wise, temperate, and, in every way, remarkable policy.

"The Metropolitan County of Midlothian has now for a long time given it the support of her weighty example. As one earnestly desiring that she may retain in the future all the honour that she has won in the past, I trust she may continue to use her great influence as beseems her position, and may in the coming and in many future Parliaments lead the people of Scotland in their deliberately chosen course.

"Offering you personally once more the assurance of my highest esteem and regard, I remain, my dear Sir John Cowan,

"Sincerely yours,
"W. E. GLADSTONE."

Sir John Cowan also read at the meeting in Edinburgh, called to consider the choice of a candidate, the following letter, which had not been previously published, from Mr. Gladstone :—

"DOLLIS HILL, *July* 25, 1894.
" MY DEAR SIR J. COWAN,—I learn with great satisfaction the promptitude which has been shown by my constituents in the appointment of a Liberal candidate to succeed me in the representation of Midlothian, and also the choice they have made of Sir Thomas Gibson-Carmichael as the person designated. I believe he will pursue a just, true, and straightforward policy, and will be worthy of the countenance of your important county as the champion of the Liberal cause. It may be said that this is a posthumous opinion, and that for me to give it is an act of impertinence, but I rather hope, on the contrary, it will be taken as a sign that my earnest interest in the political well-being of the Constituency does not lapse with my own political relations to it.—Believe me, with great regards, sincerely yours,
" W. E. GLADSTONE."

The Chairman then moved a resolution thanking Mr. Gladstone for his unparalleled and distinguished success in the cause of liberty, declaring their unabated and affectionate interest in his future well-being and happiness, and earnestly hoping that he might be long spared, in the midst of his other avocations, to continue his life-long work in the cause of freedom throughout the world. The resolution was unanimously adopted.

The following letter from Lord Rosebery was also read :—

"THE DURDANS, *July* 2, 1895'
" MY DEAR SIR,—I am sorry that I cannot be with you to-morrow, but I am detained in the south this week. You meet at a critical time. The Government to which Scotland, Ireland, Wales, and the North of England gave their confidence has been overthrown by a Vote of Censure--petty, but fatal. It is, then, for Scotland, Ireland, Wales, and the North of England to determine whether they will renew that confidence, and replace Liberalism in power. More specially is it for them to consider whether they shall allow their interests and their aspirations to remain in permanent subjection to the hereditary and irresponsible Chamber, or whether they will strengthen the hands that would restrain that domination. With the echoes of Mr. Gladstone's eloquent and venerable voice still ringing through the Lowlands, I cannot doubt their response.—Believe me, yours faithfully,
" ROSEBERY."

The meeting afterwards agreed to support Sir Thomas Gibson-Carmichael, the Liberal candidate, in succession to Mr. Gladstone.

It may be added that the result of the election in Midlothian was that Sir Thomas Gibson-Carmichael polled 6,090 votes,

against 5,631 cast for his Conservative opponent, the Hon.
Major Dalrymple. Considering the reaction in other parts of
the country this result was considered satisfactory, especially
in view of the withdrawal of so great a personality as Mr.
Gladstone from the constituency where he had delivered his
most famous speeches. The new Member for Midlothian's
ambition was to have given his first vote in Parliament to Mr.
Gladstone, just as his first vote for a candidate at an election had
been given to him. But it was not to be, and the greater honour
of succeeding Mr. Gladstone fell to him.

At this moment in his career, when the last link with politics
was severed, it is interesting to recall a letter which Mr. Gladstone
wrote to Tennyson six years previously, when the anxieties of his
position were pressing upon him. After some other remarks he
concluded : " Wish for me, I pray you, a speedy deliverance,
if God's will may so be, from the life of turmoil and contention
which I have pursued for fifty-seven years and part of a fifty-
eighth." This throws some light on the lessened interest which
was already becoming evident long before Mr. Gladstone laid
down the burden of official duties.

Early in 1896 he went to Biarritz, where the fine weather did
a good deal to invigorate his health. While he was in the
Riviera Monsieur Faure, the President of the French Republic,
called upon him, and an interesting conversation in French
ensued, the President being much impressed with the warm
interest of the ex-Premier in the affairs of the Republic. On
Mr. Gladstone's return from the Continent there was the customary crowds in London at the railway terminus and in the streets,
showing that there was still a very affectionate interest in his
movements. He spent the next few months at Hawarden,
engaged in close study of Butler's " Analogy," and other works
of an engrossing nature.

Mr. Gladstone, who throughout his life had taken a great
interest in railway enterprise, and had known most of the mag
nates of the railway world, was persuaded to open in March the
new line of railway between Liverpool and North Wales. In the
course of a speech full of reminiscences, he said :—

" I remember when, as a little boy, I used to stroll upon the sands of the
Mersey, now occupied for the most part by Liverpool Docks. It is quite true
this enterprise has for me a particular interest, for in Liverpool, which may be
considered one of its termini, I first drew the breath of life and saw the light
of heaven. With Hawarden, if it please God, my last acquaintance with the
light and with the air is likely to be connected."

Towards the end of June Mr. Gladstone was a participant in a pleasant ceremony at Aberystwith. The Prince of Wales had accepted, appropriately enough considering his title, the Chancellorship of the new Welsh University, and among the recipients of honorary degrees was Mr. Gladstone. He was hailed with immense enthusiasm, redoubled after the charming allusions made to him by the Prince. Addressing the audience, which included the Princess of Wales and Mrs. Gladstone, the Prince said: "You will all join with me, I am sure, in thanking the veteran statesman and eminent scholar, Mr. Gladstone, who, notwithstanding his advanced age, has undertaken a journey necessarily fatiguing in order to pay a compliment to the University of Wales, and to myself as its Chancellor. I may truly say that one of the proudest moments of my life was when I found myself in the flattering position of being able to confer an academic distinction on Mr. Gladstone, who furnishes a rare instance of a man who has achieved one of the highest positions as a statesman, and at the same time has attained such distinction in the domain of literature and scholarship. His translation of the Odes of Horace would alone constitute a lasting monument to him, even had he not accomplished so much besides which has rendered him illustrious. Nor do we extend a less warm welcome to Mr. Gladstone's ever-faithful companion and helper during the many years of his busy life." At this function Master William Gladstone, son of the late Mr. W. H. Gladstone, and heir to the Hawarden estates, was train-bearer to the Prince of Wales, so that the oldest and well-nigh the youngest scions of the family were present.

On July 22nd he and Mrs. Gladstone travelled to London to be guests, by special invitation of the Queen, at the wedding in Buckingham Palace Chapel of Princess Maud of Wales with Prince Charles of Denmark. The aged couple were regarded with almost as much interest as the Royal Family, and Mr. Gladstone had the pleasure of conversing with not a few of his old friends after the ceremony. Next day he returned to Hawarden, in no way over-tired by the excitement.

Once more the crying wrongs of the Armenians, whose cause possessed Mr. Gladstone's heart as much as years before he had been stirred by the Bulgarian atrocities, led him to speak in public. This time, with great appropriateness, Liverpool was selected for the meeting. It was pathetic to think of Liverpool's greatest son' coming out of well-earned retirement to voice the sorrows of the Armenians, and the city was stirred to great excitement by Mr. Gladstone's visit. Everything was done to ensure his comfort, and the railway arrangements were admirably made to convey Mr. Gladstone with a minimum of trouble from Hawarden to the city where, eighty-six years before, he had been born in Rodney Street. He delivered an impassioned oration, denouncing the Turkish misrule, and calling for more strenuous methods than velvet-gloved diplomatists seemed prepared to use on behalf of the victims of the Sultan's fierce hatred. The speech was far stronger in note than that which Mr. Gladstone had given in the previous year at Chester, but the circumstances had meanwhile been aggravated. An echo of warm support to the old orator was aroused, and a corresponding growth of detestation of the Turk. The Sultan again manifested his impatience at criticism and his craven fear of his own suppression by having a *communiqué* circulated traversing certain of Mr. Gladstone's statements. Lord Salisbury was much reproached at this time for not having faced the question with due strength of purpose, although for a period it looked as if he was combining with the great Powers of Europe to prevent a repetition of the shocking incidents which had once more stained the record of Turkey.

The visit of Li Hung Chang, in August, was a pleasant variant in Mr. Gladstone's now uneventful life. The two great statesmen —one as representative of Western politics as the other was of Eastern—spent a very enjoyable time at Hawarden, conversing on many topics with lively volubility. Li Hung Chang had looked forward with keen anticipation to the meeting, and was not disappointed in the realisation of his hopes. He and his host were photographed together, and Li Hung Chang wrote his wonderful autograph in the visitors' book, to the delight of the younger members of the household, who regarded the grave old Chinaman with awe and astonishment. Hawarden did honour to the visit by decorating the village a little, and the only flaw in the day's proceedings was the late arrival of the volunteers who were to have formed a guard of honour.

One Monday morning in October every one was startled by the news that Dr. Benson, Archbishop of Canterbury, who had been on a brief visit to Mr. Gladstone, had died suddenly while attending service at Hawarden Church on the previous Sunday morning. A long friendship had existed between the Archbishop and Mr. Gladstone, and the tragic death of Dr. Benson was felt acutely. The body of the prelate was removed to Canterbury, where it was buried. Not long afterwards a memorial to the archbishop's memory was erected by the Gladstone family in the church where he had been smitten fatally.

This year saw the publication of a new edition of Butler's Works arranged and annotated by Mr. Gladstone, and this was followed with a volume entitled "Studies Subsidiary to the Works of Bishop Butler." Both the editions led to an increased interest in Butler, and to considerable discussion in the religious Press. Every reviewer was agreed as to the painstaking care and scholarly erudition shown by the veteran author. An absolute contrast to his ecclesiastical studies was an article on Sheridan which appeared from Mr. Gladstone's pen in the *Nineteenth Century* for June. This showed his continued interest in biography, which always possessed such a charm for him. Another article, written about this time, dealt kindly with certain minor poets. A long statement on the vexed question of the unity of Christendom and the validity of Anglican Orders was published in June also by Mr. Gladstone. Partly in response to this important document, which was published by its compiler's consent by the Archbishop of York, the Pope issued an Encyclical dealing with the subject, which was creating much controversy in ecclesiastical circles.

One of the few signs of Mr. Gladstone's great age was, however, becoming manifest in the eye trouble, which was approaching the point of serious inconvenience to one so fond of writing and reading. Christmas was spent quietly at home amid his family circle, and an especial number of kindly remembrances from past opponents and colleagues arrived on December 29th, when he celebrated his eighty-seventh birthday.

CHAPTER XLV.

EARLY in 1897 it was thought advisable that Mr. and Mrs. Gladstone should escape from the cold winds then prevalent and seek the sunshine of the South of France. Accordingly, on the 29th of January they departed, after a flying visit to London; and in the kind care of friends like Mr. Armitstead and Lord Rendel they soon were able to spend much of each day out of doors, to the decided advantage of their health. Mr. Gladstone was reported as following with close attention all foreign affairs, which were giving considerable anxiety at this period to her Majesty's Ministers. A special compliment was paid to the oldest servant of the Crown when the Queen, who was also recruiting her health in the South, called and spent an hour or more conversing with her ex-Premier. This visit gave rise to a rumour that the Queen had renewed her offer of a peerage to Mr. Gladstone, and it was also stated that, on his declining it, she had expressed a wish to raise his grandson to the peerage on the occasion of the celebration of her Jubilee. Whether there was any foundation for these reports or no is not certain, but at all events the Jubilee passed without any honour being conferred on the Gladstone family.

In the *Daily Chronicle* of March 26th there appeared in full a splendid and memorable appeal to the conscience of his countrymen from Mr. Gladstone in the form of a letter to the Duke of Westminster. It was dated from Lord Rendel's villa, the Chateau Thorenc, Cannes, as having been written on March 13th. It was full of fine phrases, which lingered in the ear and thrilled the heart. One particular passage was much criticised, and possibly Mr. Gladstone regarded it afterwards as somewhat ill-advised. He referred to the German Emperor and the Czar of Russia in these words :—

"It is time to speak with freedom. At this moment two great States, with an European population of 140,000,000 or 150,000,000, are under the government of two young men, each bearing the high title of Emperor, but in one case wholly without knowledge or experience, in the other having only such knowledge and experience, in truth limited enough, as have excited much astonishment and some consternation when an inkling of them has been given to the world."

This historic document was published by Mr. John Murray in pamphlet form, and excited great interest, even though the friends of Armenia had lost all hope of ameliorating its condition.

On May 10th, Mr. and Mrs. Gladstone were honoured by a visit paid to them by the Prince and Princess of Wales, who had been the guests of the Duke of Westminster. The Royal party drove to Hawarden, and were interested greatly in the various contents of Mr. Gladstone's study. The Princess was specially affectionate in her greeting of Mrs. Gladstone, and altogether the visit was a charming success. Hosts and guests were photographed together, and the portrait is a pleasant memorial of a delightful occasion.

Much disappointment was felt and expressed in the Press that no invitation was apparently extended to Mr. Gladstone to take part in the Jubilee celebrations, and, although no slight was evidently intended—as room was not found for many other most eminent subjects of the Queen—our colonial and foreign guests were sorry not to have seen the veteran statesmen figuring in the procession. Mr. Gladstone was at Hawarden on the great day, and spoke a few words of heartfelt eulogy of the Queen and loyal aspirations for her continued health and prosperity.

Four distinguished colonial guests of the nation—Sir Wilfrid Laurier, Premier of Canada; Hon. R. J. Seddon, Premier of New Zealand; Hon. G. H. Reid, Premier of New South Wales; and Sir Lewis Davies, ex-Premier of Prince Edward Island—visited Hawarden for the purpose of paying their respects to the oldest living ex-Premier in the world. They had a long and most delightful time with Mr. Gladstone, whose memory was at once their astonishment and pleasure. He was almost perplexing in the multitude of questions which he asked his guests, and they left Hawarden with their veneration for Mr. Gladstone doubled. A charming photograph was taken of host and guests seated on the trunk of a tree in Hawarden Park. Mr. Gladstone's agility in conducting his visitors through the grounds was a subject of continual remark by the Premiers afterwards.

A pathetic premonition of his approaching death was shown in a touching letter which Mr. Gladstone sent to his old friend, Dr. J. Guinness Rogers, in acknowledgment of the latter's volume of sermons. "As the day of parting draws nearer, I rejoice to think how small the differences between us have already become as compared with the agreements," wrote Mr. Gladstone, alluding, of course, to the divergences between his position as a High Churchman and Dr. Rogers's standpoint as a Congregationalist.

In November the *British Medical Journal* issued an interesting authoritative statement on the subject of the veteran's health :—

"It is a fact that his health has been somewhat less satisfactory than usual. Mr. Gladstone has always had a remarkably slow pulse, a characteristic very often observed in persons destined to attain an advanced age. This autumn it has increased from the usual rate of sixty-two to about seventy-two, and on two or three occasions it has been for short periods very rapid. The pulse, however, is soft and elastic, and in general perfectly regular ; he is quite free from those most serious changes in the great organs often associated with old age. On his return to Hawarden from Perthshire some time ago his left cheek was red and swollen as the result of cold, and he also suffered from nasal catarrh. Under suitable treatment, however, the inflammatory symptoms have subsided, and it is believed he will completely recover in Cannes. Before leaving Hawarden Mr. Gladstone was seen by Dr. Carter, of Liverpool, in consultation, and the opinion of his medical advisers was that his general condition was wonderful in a man of nearly eighty-eight years of age."

Once again, his birthday—this time the eighty-eighth—was spent abroad, as the guest of Lord Rendel at the Villa Thorenc, Cannes. He was in fairly good spirits, and was gladdened by the receipt of at least fifty telegrams from friends during the day. Mrs. Gladstone drove out with her husband in the afternoon, and at dinner in the evening the Grand Old Man—more than ever entitled to that name—conversed quite cheerfully of some of the events in his life. The weather in the South of France had been anything but warm, and the sudden cold undoubtedly retarded the convalescence of both Mr. and Mrs. Gladstone, although they braved the elements as often as possible. They saw a good many friends, for Cannes was full of those who had tried to escape the rigours of winter in England, only to experience very similar climatic trials abroad.

A message from Mr. Gladstone was a feature of the birthday banquet held at the National Liberal Club, and ran as follows : "Cannes, Christmas Day, 1897.—I think your appeal to me a great honour, and in reply I heartily wish that the coming and every subsequent meeting may be addressed to the purposes of truth, justice, honour, peace, good faith, and to all that is of good report." Afterwards, a phonograph repeated a portion of the last speech delivered by Mr. Gladstone in the House of Commons.

The *Daily Telegraph*, which, though it differed from the later policy of the ex-Premier, allowed itself to bear constant witness to his remarkable powers and personal character, published a particularly fine example of his literary work on January 5, 1898.

This was called "Personal Recollections of Arthur H. Hallam," and had been commissioned by the *Youth's Companion*, which had aforetime been fortunate enough to obtain contributions from the same pen. All who read this latest product of Mr. Gladstone's critical ability agreed as to its splendid rhetoric and exquisite balance of delicate appreciation. There was a postscript, written after the publication of the Life of Lord Tennyson, containing this true reflection on the volume: "That remarkable work must, by this time, have convinced a reading world that the great poet of his age was likewise full of greatness as a man."

Very soon after this new evidence of Mr. Gladstone's interest in current matters came the alarming news, stated in the most positive manner by the *Pall Mall Gazette*, of a serious relapse in his health. The fact that this newspaper had issued in 1894—four years previously to the very month—the information of Mr. Gladstone's approaching resignation, lent colour to this exclusive news, and caused quite a sensation throughout the country in the afternoon and evening. Countless telegrams were despatched to Lord Rendel's villa at Cannes asking for confirmation or contradiction, with the result that next morning's papers contained reassuring statements as to there being no immediate cause for alarm. But public sympathy was aroused, and a number of special correspondents continued for several days to chronicle the movements of the family at Cannes. One was pleased to read that Mr. and Mrs. Gladstone were still able to take outdoor exercise, and that though pain in the venerable statesman's face was at times agonising, he still bore up with praiseworthy patience.

Lord Rendel was inundated with all manner of inquiries during the remainder of the stay at Cannes, and the arrival of two or three members of the Gladstone family gave rise to renewed reports of the serious nature of the illness. Mr. Herbert Gladstone gave the following explanation to a correspondent: "When Mr. Gladstone reached Cannes he suffered from rheumatism, which has now disappeared. His sight is not good; he writes but little, and depends upon his secretary for his correspondence. It is this which makes him nervous and agitates him. At his age feebleness is not to be wondered at. Apart from this Mr. Gladstone retains his energy and ability for work."

In the *New York World* of January 30th there was printed the report of an interesting conversation with Mr. Gladstone at Cannes from the pen of the London correspondent of the well-known journal. "His only allusion to current politics," the writer said, "showed that the Irish Home Rule cause still, to use his own famous phrase, 'holds the field' with him. When preparing to depart he asked one of the guests: 'Tell me how are affairs going on in Ireland? Is there any chance of the parties becoming united?' The reply being, 'it was hoped that they would,' he said solemnly, 'By unity and perseverance they can secure all they want.' These words he uttered with impressive feeling."

A very touching incident was reported early in February. The special correspondent of the *Daily News* thus wrote :—

> "CANNES, *Sunday Night.*
>
> "The weather here is finer than ever after the extraordinary break up. On Saturday Friday night's mistral was followed by a slight snowfall in the morning. Then, after an interval of sunshine, clouds came lowering from the north, and the weather was cold and overcast, windy and showery for the rest of the day. This in the north of Europe would have meant a week's bad weather, and residents here prophesied a three days' spell of rain.
>
> "Mr. Gladstone kept indoors, but took exercise walking up and down the halls of the Chateau Thorene after his usual after-dinner rest. He had a good sleep last night, awaking to-day much refreshed and agreeably surprised to see sunlight flooding his room. The weather had recovered as suddenly as it had broken up, and although in shady lanes I found a crust of ice about the thickness of an egg-shell, the rest of the day was warm and genial, and the mistral had gone. Mr. Gladstone, speaking to a friend, remarked that he had grateful recollections of Cannes, as it was here that he recovered sleep years ago when Prime Minister."

Another recorder of the day's events wrote :—

> "This morning Mr. and Mrs. Gladstone received the Holy Communion at St. Paul's Church. Mrs. Gladstone and her daughter attended the morning service at 11, but Mr. Gladstone went only for the Celebration, leaving the Chateau in the carriage at 11.45. The right hon. gentleman, who was warmly wrapped up in an overcoat with a cape over it, entered the church just as the Rev. W. M. Wollaston was reading the opening sentences of the Communion Service, and took a vacant seat to the right of Mrs. Gladstone in one of the chairs which had been specially placed for them in front of the ordinary seats. Mr. Gladstone was able to kneel during all the prayers, and when he walked to the altar had only the support of Miss Gladstone's arm, on which he appeared to lean but slightly. Mrs. Gladstone followed immediately behind, and the aged husband and wife received the Holy Communion kneeling side by side. There were not more than twenty people in the church, and the service was over by 12.35, when Mr. Gladstone walked down the aisle with no support but that of his umbrella. A short drive was taken before the return to the Chateau which was reached at a quarter after one. Mr. Gladstone looked pale, though not more so than usual, but now and again a shade passed over his face as if of pain."

As Mr. Gladstone did not seem to be gaining much advantage

from his sojourn at Cannes, it was decided that he should return and try some English seaside resort. Dr. Arthur Habershon, who had succeeded the late Sir Andrew Clark as physician to the family, went to Cannes to see his patient, and consult with Dr. Frank, who had been recently attending him, on the developments of the case, with a view to settling as to what atmosphere would be likely to do good. The mistral had begun to make itself keenly felt in the South of France, and the neuralgia which had been troubling Mr. Gladstone was consequently very painful. Accordingly the party from the Villa Thorenc returned to this country on February 18th, having travelled slowly and broken the journey at Calais, where they spent the night, previous to crossing the Channel. Arrangements had been made for conveying Mr. Gladstone from the railway carriage to the Terminus Hotel at Calais in a hand-chair, but to this proposal Mr. Gladstone was averse. So, leaning heavily on the arms of two friends, he walked to the building, though the effort seemed to try his strength. He was under the care of Dr. Habershon, and a nurse was also in attendance in case of need. The other members of the party besides Mrs. Gladstone and Mr. Henry Gladstone were Miss Helen Gladstone and Miss Phillimore.

A correspondent of the *Daily Chronicle*, who accompanied Mr. Gladstone across the Channel from Calais, wrote :—

"When he emerged from the Terminus Hotel yesterday morning to join the steamer *Invicta*, it was at once noticed that he looked wonderfully well. He had had the benefit of a good night's rest, and had slept well. Rain was falling, and it was very unpleasant, but this did not prevent a good number of people assembling on the gangway to witness the departure of the venerable statesman. Many of these spectators raised their hats, the courtesy being acknowledged by Mr. Gladstone.

"Taking Mr. Armitstead's arm, Mr. Gladstone, who was wearing a long fur overcoat, walked quite firmly across the quay to the boat. He was conducted on board by Captain Blomefield, the London and Chatham Company's representative, who had the state saloon reserved for the party. Mr. Gladstone retired at once to the cabin, and was very soon made comfortable for the journey. A moderately calm passage was made across the Channel.

"On reaching Dover Mr. Gladstone was conducted ashore to the special South Eastern Railway saloon attached to the boat express. Mrs. Gladstone, who seemed to be in very good health, followed, accompanied by Mr. Henry Gladstone. A cheer was raised as the G.O.M. walked along the gangway, and upon reaching the landing he stopped to shade hands and exchange a few words with Mr. J. L. Bradley, the chairman of the local Liberal party.

"Mr. Gladstone's train arrived at Charing Cross at half-past five precisely. Canon Wilberforce, Sir Walter Phillimore, and others friends were gathered on the platform. As soon as the train had stopped the door of a first-class carriage opened and Mr. Gladstone appeared.

" He was assisted to step down from the carriage by Mr. Henry Gladstone and the station-master. He walked, with hardly any sign of feebleness, across the platform. He used his stick slightly as a support, but he gave one the impression that he still possessed remarkable vigour. Mr. Gladstone was at once surrounded by the friends who had come to meet him. He shook hands all round, smiling cheerfully. His winter overcoat was buttoned around him, but he was not ' muffled up' in the ordinary acceptation of the term. Then, a brown felt hat gave an almost sprightly appearance to his figure.

" Mr. Gladstone, with Mr. Henry Gladstone, drove off to Whitehall Court. Mrs. Gladstone, Miss Helen Gladstone, and Dr. Habershon followed in another carriage. A considerable number of people had gathered to see the arrival, and Mr. Gladstone got a most cordial welcome. The journey from Cannes, with very little stoppage by the way, was certainly a trying ordeal for so aged a traveller. Yet Mr. Gladstone not only stood it well, but was positively better when he reached London than when he left Cannes."

Thus did the Grand Old Man arrive once more in London, where so much of his eventful life had been spent.

CHAPTER XLVI.

THE last visit which Mr. Gladstone was destined to pay to
London—his home in so many Februaries—was full of interest, despite its brevity and the ill-health which precluded
his going out of doors. What a contrast to his customary way
of spending the time in London was this quiet residence in
Whitehall Court, so near to Westminster and Downing Street,
with their memories of political life! In former days, when Mr.
Gladstone paid a flying visit to the metropolis, it was with the
definite object of study at the British Museum on the particular
subject which was then engaging his attention. His notable
figure would be seen striding quickly up the steps of the Museum,
and wending its way to that quiet home of scholars, the Library.
Soon he would be engrossed in a pile of volumes, examining them
with the speed born of long practice and intimate knowledge of
books. He would make notes for some hours with unwearied
industry, and then, with courteous thanks to the officials at the
Library, who were only too pleased to put their almost inexhaustible information at the disposal of a man who never tired of learning,
Mr. Gladstone would walk briskly home. In the evenings a few
special friends, such as Mr. Morley, Lord Acton, Lady Frederick
Cavendish, and others, would spend a delightful time under the
spell of Mr. Gladstone's brilliant conversation. And, when they
were gone, he might be induced to play a game of backgammon
until the time arrived to retire to rest. Briefly, that was a picture
of his usual experience during a visit to London.

But in February, 1898, he had to resign himself to a programme
much simpler and restricted. Much of his time was spent in his
bedroom, where he received at least one distinguished visitor—
Dr. Nansen, who, accompanied by stalwart, blue-eyed Lieutenant
Johansen, his sole companion farthest North, gave Mr. Gladstone much pleasure. He asked a good many questions of the
intrepid explorers, and left an impression of marvellous vitality
upon both men. All day long people called on the Gladstone
family, with a view of learning how the Grand Old Man pro-

gressed.   Mr. Morley dined with his old leader, and thought that
he was looking decidedly better than prior to his departure for
Cannes.   Lord Rosebery and Sir William Harcourt both had a
few minutes' conversation with him, and the latter told him he
was going to speak at Bury, asking him for a message.   One very
touching message from the veteran was mentioned by his former
confidential secretary, Sir Algernon West, at a meeting in Marylebone.   Sir Algernon told a sympathetic audience that Mr. Gladstone had said to him, "You must pray for me," and Sir Algernon
added : "I know, if I do, my prayer will be mingled with
thousands of prayers that go up to the Eternal Throne for his
happiness."

On February 21st there was a series of special callers.   The
Prince of Wales, who always went out of his way to show respect
for the aged servant of the Crown, spent quite a long while with Mr.
Gladstone, asking most kindly after his ailments.   The call was
all the more appreciated because it took place on Levée Day,
when the Prince might have been excused from visiting personally.
Then came the Ladies Sybil and Peggy Primrose, daughters of
Lord Rosebery and favourites with Mr. Gladstone from their
childhood when he had seen them at Dalmeny in the stirring
days of the Midlothian Campaigns.   These charming young
ladies made their *début* in society on the very same day as
their call on Mr. Gladstone, at a grand ball given in their honour
at Lord Rosebery's house in Berkeley Square, when the presence
of the Prince of Wales and other members of the Royal Family
lent *éclat* to a very brilliant occasion.

The next day Mr. and Mrs. Gladstone, with Miss Helen
Gladstone (who had resigned some months previously the Vice-
Principalship of Sidgwick Hall, Newnham, in order to devote her
time to the care of her aged parents), and Mr. Henry Gladstone,
left London for Bournemouth.   Mr. Gladstone had stopped for a
few minutes on the way to Waterloo to record his name and that
of his wife in the visitors' book at Marlborough House.   A few
friends, including Lord Welby and Dr. Habershon, were on the
platform to bid the travellers goodbye.   The train which conveyed them to Bournemouth was one which had come thence in
the morning, and the heavy layer of snow on the tops of
the carriages bore testimony to the severity of the storm which
had been raging there.   It was curious and unfortunate that in
Bournemouth, as it had been previously in Cannes, the weather
was the direct opposite of what might usually be expected in
these places.   The heaviest fall of snow which Bournemouth had

experienced for some time lay on the ground when the train arrived. There a large number of people assembled to catch a glimpse of the distinguished passengers, who drove off to Forest House on the East Cliff. Mrs. Harry Drew had been there, preparing the house, which was in a pleasant situation overlooking the bay, for her parents, who bore the trying journey exceedingly well.

For the next month Mr. and Mrs. Gladstone remained at Bournemouth, but the change did not effect so much good as was expected, and the right hon. gentleman was seldom able to take outdoor exercise. The neuralgic pains in his face gave him considerable trouble, and his doctor, who visited him often deemed it unwise for him to risk the cold air. Mrs. Gladstone was, however, able to derive not a little strength during her visit, and was often to be seen attending services at a church in the neighbourhood.

Everything possible was done to relieve the tedium of the enforced inactivity of Mr. Gladstone, who was forbidden by his medical adviser to read or write—deprivations which so industrious a reader and writer could not help feeling keenly. Conversation and listening to music were his chief pleasures during this trying time. Fortunately, members of his family have a great love for, and a real ability in, vocal and instrumental music. It may be recollected that Mr. Gladstone's eldest son, the late Mr. W. H. Gladstone, composed several beautiful hymn-tunes ; Mrs. Drew is a charming pianist ; and Mr. Herbert Gladstone is one of the pillars of the Handel Society. Various friends lent their skilful aid in alleviating the weary hours of the sufferer with choice music. Lady Halle came one evening with her sister, Mdlle. Olga Neruda, to Forest House, and played exquisitely, to Mr. Gladstone's great delight. Then, on another evening, that fine pianist, Mdlle. Natalie Janotha, who was a special friend of the Tennysons, gave quite a recital, which met with much appreciation.

Writing to a correspondent on the subject of Mr. Gladstone's health, Mrs. Drew said :—

" In Mr. and Mrs. Gladstone's condition of health it is impossible to have anything fresh to say day by day. At their age it is not likely that they should be very strong, but there is really nothing to chronicle from week to week. The extravagant paragraphs that appeared some time ago as to Mr. Gladstone's 'critical condition' were about as true as the very rosy-coloured accounts that subsequently appeared as to his recovery and present freedom from the neuralgic pain. The neuralgia continues much as it was, and, this being the case, it is not advisable to drive out in the very cold weather that has prevailed since we came to Bournemouth. But his general health, strength, appetite, &c., continue to be very good. He slept very well last night, and it seems to be rather a mistake to have daily bulletins as if he was suffering from some severe illness instead of the more ordinary and perhaps chronic ailments incidental to his time of life. In this weather it is hardly to be expected there could be much improvement, but the doctor says the cause of the neuralgia (the nasal catarrh) being so much improved, there is good hope that the pain will wear off in time."

Mr. Gladstone, in company with Mrs. Gladstone and Mrs. Drew, drove in a closed carriage to St. Swithin's Church for the afternoon service on one Sunday.

Fresh anxiety was caused among friends by the news that Sir Thomas Smith, the famous surgeon, had been down to Bournemouth to consult with Dr. Habershon as to the possibilities of a successful operation on Mr. Gladstone. The fact of his visit was kept quite private for some days, and Sir Thomas mentioned that his patient had particularly requested that he should say nothing of the case "unless the Queen asks."

The air of Bournemouth having failed to achieve much betterment in the condition of Mr. Gladstone, it was thought that he would be all the happier at home, whither his thoughts had been tending for some time. So on March 22nd the party left for Hawarden. A correspondent gave the following account of the journey, which was *via* Basingstoke, Oxford, and Chester : "One of the Royal saloons had been placed at the illustrious statesman's disposal. Arrangements had been made for a special from Wrexham to Chester, so as to arrive at the latter place at about seven o'clock in the evening. Mr. Henry Gladstone and Dr. Habershon had left Bournemouth previously ; but in addition to Mrs. Gladstone, Mr. Herbert Gladstone, Miss Helen Gladstone, and the Rev. Stephen Gladstone remained to accompany Mr. Gladstone on his journey.

Mr. Gladstone arrived at Bournemouth exactly a month before in a snowstorm, accompanied by a frosty air and the sky thick with dark clouds. He left Bournemouth in perfect summer-like weather, with bright sunshine, a cloudless sky, and a light westerly breeze. The right hon. gentleman had slept fairly during the night and, according to habit, rose early. The party drove to the East station, about three-quarters of a mile distant, in a closed carriage. The station was shut to all except passengers, and the saloon in which the party were to travel was drawn up at the platform an hour before the train was timed to start. A number of persons assembled along the road to the station to witness the departure of Mr. Gladstone, who had been so little seen during his visit to Bournemouth. The arrangements at the station to prevent any inconvenience to the family of the right hon. gentleman were admirably carried out by Mr. Harvey, the station-master. The right hon. gentleman walked firmly to the railway carriage, but looked pale.

As Mr. Gladstone walked across the platform there were frequent cries of " God bless you, sir," and " God's richest blessings rest on you " ; and in response the right hon. gentleman, as he was entering the train, turned round, and in a clear voice exclaimed : " God bless you all in this place and the land you love."

Already many expressions of sympathy had reached the right hon. gentleman and his family from many quarters. It was reported that a very warm and friendly message was sent from some of the leading members of the Irish party.

Hawarden Castle was reached at half-past seven in the evening. A considerable assemblage of residents of Hawarden awaited at the station the arrival of Mr. and Mrs. Gladstone, who were so much beloved by their neighbours ; but, by the expressed wish of members of the Gladstone family, the villagers and others who were present retired from the platform, in order to prevent any crushing or crowding near the train, and to ensure Mr. Gladstone as little inconvenience as was possible on his leaving the station. The platform was reserved for the members of the family, who anxiously awaited the arrival of the special train, which steamed into the station at twenty-eight minutes past seven o'clock. Mrs. Gladstone and party were comfortably ensconced in the saloon, but Mr. Gladstone was not observed for a few moments. The Rev. Harry Drew and Mrs. Stephen Gladstone immediately entered the saloon, and the welcome was of a most touching description, Mr. and Mrs. Gladstone embracing the various members of the family. Mrs. Gladstone, who seemed somewhat fatigued by the eight-and-a-half-hours' journey, was assisted from the saloon by the Hon. Mrs. W. H. Gladstone and Mr. Herbert Gladstone, M.P., and supported and conducted to a brougham. Then the aged statesman, who was warmly clothed in a long overcoat, and was wearing a brown felt hat, was observed emerging from another portion of the saloon, where he had been resting. It was discerned that the right hon. gentleman, who was on the arms of the Rev. Stephen Gladstone and the Rev. Harry Drew, was walking with some difficulty, and was very cautious in alighting. Whether he was dazed by the station lights it is impossible to state, but certain it is that he was unable to see a portion of the raised platform, and was led to the waiting-room, through which he passed to the carriage, chatting freely as he walked. He joined Mrs. Gladstone in the carriage, and Dr. Biss and the nurse also entered the vehicle, and proceeded with them to the Castle, which was reached at a quarter to eight o'clock. The fervent hope was expressed by all who witnessed Mr. Gladstone's return home that with the family surroundings and the beautiful spring-like weather usually experienced at Hawarden Mr. Gladstone's sufferings would be alleviated, notwithstanding his advanced years.

CHAPTER XLVII.

"CROSSING THE BAR."

IT was with manifest pleasure that Mr. Gladstone found himself once more at Hawarden Castle, after an absence of four months. It was natural that he should pass his first night there somewhat restlessly owing to the excitement and weariness of the journey on the preceding day; and the next morning the weather was anything but cheering for the invalid, as rain was falling heavily, and snow lay on the mountains. His doctor came down from London a day or two afterwards and met in consultation Dr. Dobie, of Chester, and Dr. Biss. They were fairly satisfied with the condition of the patient, who already showed signs of improvement, owing doubtless to the joy of being amid familiar surroundings once more.

Mr. Gladstone had just sustained one of those sorrows which every lover of animals will understand. During his absence from Hawarden Castle, Petz, the little black Pomeranian dog who had been so faithful a follower of the Grand Old Man for nearly ten years, had gone to Buckley Vicarage, the home of the Rev. Harry and Mrs. Drew, whose little daughter Dorothy was an especial playmate of his. But the dog seemed to feel the absence of his old friend and master, and ran back to Hawarden Castle again and again. Then, just before Mr. Gladstone's return, he began to decline food, and moped. On the actual day of his arrival Petz was taken back to Hawarden, but it was too late. The little dog died, surely of a broken heart.

A very beautiful tribute to his old leader was paid by Mr. John Morley in a speech delivered at Chester on March 23rd. Having alluded to Home Rule, Mr. Morley proceeded:—

"Gentlemen, how many memories does all this recall to us? The chairman referred to it, and to that great leader of ours who first awoke the conscience of England to the strength of the Irish case. Ah! What stirring of unalterable affection do we all feel to-night, as we think of him overtaken in the evening of that long day of so many interests, so many glories, so many triumphs, so many grand public services—overtaken by suffering and by pain. How he has elevated politics, how in the Irish Question, and every other to individual responsibility, individual conviction, individual conscience his appeal has always lain! We can bring him little succour as he lies, but let us, at all events, lay to heart the grand and splendid lessons which his career has taught us."

Another eloquent tribute to Mr. Gladstone about this time was published in the *Vossische Zeitung*, which spoke of him as "the glorious man, in whom the proudest traditions of English Liberalism are embodied, and to whom the Liberals of all nations of both hemispheres look up with veneration." One of the last evidences of Mr. Gladstone's interest in current political affairs was shown by his little message—sent by him on the subject of the *Maine* disaster—"I am deeply grieved at the sad loss which the American people have suffered."

In many places of worship in the kingdom there were allusions to Mr. Gladstone's illness, and of two of these special mention may be made. On the last Sunday in March, at the Greek Church of St. Sophia, Bayswater, the Archimandrite Paraschis, who was the celebrant at the Holy Eucharist, made an eloquent appeal to the congregation in reference to the subject. Addressing the worshippers, he said, with great feeling :—

"Brethren, this morning I desire that you will join with me in praying that our Heavenly Father may in His great mercy relieve from suffering and restore to health an illustrious Englishman, eminent in many walks of life, distinguished in the Senate and at the university, but throughout a long career one who has always been a true-hearted servant of God and a loyal soldier of the Cross. William Ewart Gladstone is bound to our nation by a thousand ties of affectionate regard and service. But he is more than the friend of Greece. He is the champion of all that is noble, and pure, and humanising. His magnanimity has shone forth in a dark world like a bright ray of sunshine. Let me, therefore, invite you not merely as an Orthodox priest, but as a man speaking to men, to pray that he may be spared to his family, to his country, and to mankind."

The Archimandrite then proceeded with a special prayer for the veteran statesman, the congregation betraying signs of deep emotion. True to all his old love for Greece, Mr. Gladstone had lately sent to a gathering of Phil-Hellenes in London a message of continued sympathy with the cause.

Archbishop Walsh, having been informed that influenza prevailed to a great extent in his diocese, issued a letter removing the obligation of fasting during the remainder of Lent, except on certain specified days. In the concluding part of his letter he said that he had been asked to remind the faithful of the diocese of a duty they owed to the aged and suffering statesman to whom Ireland was mainly indebted for more than one great measure of justice. The letter proceeded :—

"Withdrawn for ever from the connections of public life, Mr. Gladstone in his present state of patient suffering attracts the sympathy not only of those who

PHOTO BY VALENTINE, DUNDEE.

REV. STEPHEN GLADSTONE.

PHOTO BY MENDELSSOHN.

MRS. WICKHAM
(née ANNE GLADSTONE).

PHOTO BY WEBSTER, CHESTER.

MRS. HARRY DREW
(née MARY GLADSTONE).

PHOTO BY WEBSTER, CHESTER.

MR. HENRY NEVILLE GLADSTONE.

PHOTO BY WINDOW & GROVE.

MISS HELEN GLADSTONE.

PHOTO BY RUSSELL.

RIGHT HON. HERBERT J. GLADSTONE,
M.P.

THE SURVIVING SONS AND DAUGHTERS OF MR. GLADSTONE.

in his years of energetic public service venerated him as a political leader, but also, and perhaps even more especially, of others who in public offices were his strenuous opponents. From a respected Irish Catholic gentleman the thoughtful suggestion has come within the last few days that if any opportunity presented itself I should ask the faithful of the diocese to discharge some portion of the debt of gratitude which we owe to Mr. Gladstone by now remembering him in our prayers before the Throne of Mercy. I feel grateful for the suggestion. Doubtless through this letter it will be the means of obtaining for our venerable benefactor of former years many prayers, and in particular a prayer that God in whom he always trusted may now in his hour of suffering be pleased to send him comfort and relief to lighten his heavy burden, and to give him strength and patience to bear it, in so far as in the designs of Providence it may have to be borne for his greater good."

It was a comfort to learn that the aged sufferer was serene and peaceful ; and, after learning the probable course of his illness, he was perfectly resigned. In his last days he was wonderfully calm and was only desirous of settling all important matters in which he was concerned. He would sit quite still, with eyes closed— the pallor of his face suggesting death—and enjoy the pleasures of reverie until a sudden spasm of pain awoke him. Sometimes, when he was sleeping placidly, his lips would be heard murmuring passages from his favourite classics. At other times he would imagine he was once more back in Parliament, and would, in his slumber, repeat various sentences on public questions, as though he were addressing the House of Commons. But, chiefly, his thoughts turned heavenwards in these days, and he longed to depart and be at rest. Once or twice, indeed, his lips could not restrain the utterance " Would God all were over ! " But this natural impatience at the agony was short-lived, and he would soon regain his tranquillity.

He was much touched at the frequent inquiries made by the Queen and other members of the Royal Family, as well as by the hosts of friends all over the world. Not a few kindly suggestions for the alleviation of his pain were sent to his family from those who united with Mr. Gladstone " in the fellowship of suffering."

Allusions were made in the House of Commons to his illness, and they were received sympathetically by all sections of parties, who could still say, in the words of the late Lord Iddesleigh, " We are all proud of him." On all hands there was the deepest interest in the bulletins published daily concerning the aged patient.

These feelings of esteem were shared by politicians in other countries as was exemplified by the fact that in the Italian Senate Signor Artom said he thought the Senate would not be maintaining its noble traditions if, before suspending its labours, it did not give expression to its solicitude regarding the health of Mr. Gladstone. Mr. Gladstone had had so illustrious a career, and his name was one which so justly commanded the sympathy of Italy, that a demonstration of such a sentiment by the Senate would certainly represent the feeling of all Italians. He proposed that the President and Vice-Presidents should send Mr. Gladstone a telegram expressing the sentiments he had mentioned, and conveying to him the sincerest wishes for his recovery. The motion was agreed to. The President remarked that he and the Vice-Presidents would feel it an honour to transmit the Senate's vote to Mr. Gladstone, for the latter was a man who did not belong to one nation alone, but to the whole of the civilised world. Mr. Gladstone had an especial claim on Italy, since at certain critical moments he had raised in her favour a voice which had found an echo in the consciences of all.

To this graceful expression of sympathy the President of the Italian Chamber received the following reply through the Italian Ambassador in London to the telegram of inquiry : " Mr. Gladstone's family are profoundly grateful for the kind message of the Italian Chamber of Deputies. There is no great change in Mr. Gladstone's condition, though he has latterly experienced great relief. He wishes me to tell you that he preserves unchanged his interest in all that touches the happiness and prosperity of Italy."

From bluff old President Kruger in South Africa there came a message condoling with Mr. Gladstone in his great affliction, and "trusting that the Lord will support and strengthen him." And the Pope, who was born only three months after Mr. Gladstone, was also concerned to learn of his contemporary's illness, which could not fail to interest the veteran Leo especially.

On March 29th the weather was sufficiently pleasant to induce Mr. Gladstone to go out in the garden for a short time. The sun was shining, and he was able to remain on the terrace for a brief period enjoying its warmth. His eldest daughter, Mrs. Wickham, wife of the Dean of Lincoln, joined the family at Hawarden. It was stated that Mr. Gladstone had been lately enjoying the reading of some of Sir Walter Scott's novels, which had always stood high in his favour, and from which he had quoted often in his public addresses. He liked listening, too, to the hymns played by the Rev. Stephen Gladstone ; among them " Rock of Ages," " Lead, kindly Light," and " Jesu, Lover of my Soul," seemed to give him special pleasure.

At the annual meeting of the three Nonconformist Boards, held under the presidency of Dr. Parker at the Memorial Hall, the following resolution was adopted unanimously: "We unite in sympathy with Mr. Gladstone in his present sufferings, and in earnest prayer that he may be granted full relief, and may be spared yet awhile for usefulness in the world, which, during his long career, by high character and eminent services in many ways, he has done so much to benefit."

In reply to this resolution, the Rev. Stephen Gladstone wrote the following interesting letter :—

"DEAR SIR,—Yesterday I had the opportunity of naming the subject of your kind letter to Mr. Gladstone. He desired me in emphatic terms to thank you and all those members of the General Body of Protestant Dissenting Ministers of the Three Denominations who joined in sending such a welcome and affectionate message to him in the hour of his suffering, and to say that he is most cordially grateful for their prayers at this time. You may like to associate with this message of his the fact that he repeated, with his own emphasis, the words of the last verse of the 150th Psalm, on the same occasion. I need not say that Mrs. Gladstone, and all the family also, deeply appreciate this very practical sympathy of earnest intercession."

The *British Medical Journal* stated that Sir Thomas Smith was unable, having regard to Mr. Gladstone's advanced age, to advise any operation for the local condition, which was, unfortunately, of such a nature that the resources of medical art could not do more than afford relief. Happily it was possible to do a great deal to mitigate the neuralgia by which the nerves of the face had been affected for some time past. His strength was still maintained, appetite was good, and he was happy to be once more amid the familiar surroundings of his home.

At a large meeting held in the Mansion House in aid of the social work of the Salvation Army, Mr. Herbert Gladstone presided, and several allusions were made to the sickness of his father. In the course of her eloquent speech, Mrs. Bramwell Booth said :—

"I thank you, Mr. Gladstone, for the words you have spoken, especially when your thoughts and heart must be burdened with great anxiety. I am sure we all share with you the desire, if it may be so, that it may yet pass away, if God will. God bless dear Mr. Gladstone. Amen."

A fervent "Amen" was repeated by the entire audience. Sir Algernon West, in moving a vote of thanks to Mr. H. Gladstone, said with the father of their chairman now at the close of his honoured life, was the love, the affection, the blessing, and the prayers of every Englishman in the country.

A specially delightful tribute to Mr. Gladstone appeared about this time in a new literary journal called the *Outlook*, from which we are glad to quote some of its passages. " 'God bless you all . . . and the land you love': that kind and brave farewell was spoken at Bournemouth to a few, but it was meant for all of us, and for all this land. The full meaning of it cannot as yet be stated, can hardly as yet be grasped; but it cannot be mistaken. An old warrior full of years and honours has spoken his farewell to the field of endeavour and embattled causes and high hope. So, with bowed heads, we accept the benediction, making obeisance to a great Englishman passing to his Home. Mr. Gladstone has been ever a fighter. And in all the pageant of humanity there is nothing more moving than the supreme surrender of a brave man's sword, not to a foe, but to the last and greatest friend of the brave. Full of thankfulness he is treading the royal road of his peers towards the vast tranquillity. For him all is well. But for us there must be human regret, and human desire that the stages of his golden pilgrimage may be prolonged and that the sunset-light may for a time yet linger about him."

It must have been almost embarrassing to the Gladstone family to receive daily so many expressions of sympathy and so many letters of inquiry concerning the condition of the patient. During this sad period Mrs. Gladstone was sustained marvellously in health, and was able to take drives daily in the neighbourhood of Hawarden. A few special friends visited the Castle, including the Bishop of St. Andrews, who had some happy conversation with Mr. Gladstone. His mind was most calm and resigned, facing the prospect of his departure with the joy and hope which can only distinguish a truly religious man. From day to day there were the slight variations of the patient's condition to be chronicled, and one was glad to note that the severe neuralgic pains somewhat lessened their violence.

A very quiet Easter was spent by the family at Hawarden, and Mr. Gladstone seemed hardly so well on Easter Monday. It was notified that a statue of the right hon. gentleman was to be erected in Athens, where his name was held in such high honour as the friend of Greece. Dr. Habershon had another consultation with a view to lessening the pain which his patient was suffering. Continual expressions of sympathy from public meetings were received, and in acknowledging one of these Mr. Gladstone's daughter wrote that they gave her father great happiness in the thought that others were praying for him. To multitudes the chief item of the day's news was undoubtedly the bulletin concerning Mr. Gladstone.

And thus, with blessing and farewell upon his lips, the day of Mr. Gladstone's death drew near. In May he was less and less inclined to take nourishment, or indeed to show any interest in things earthly. Occasional and very brief visits were paid to him, as the dying warrior "fought his one fight more—the last, the best," by personal friends such as Lord Rosebery, Canon Scott Holland, Mr. John Morley, and others. These intimates of the dying statesman were all impressed with the pathetic beauty of his last days. "The great soul," said one of the family, "was resting on the Rock of Ages." His pain was mitigated by injections of morphia ; and, though day by day his strength lessened, he was spared much of the pain which distressed him in March and April.

His doctors were assiduous in their attentions, but everyone felt that death to one so weary of life would come as a merciful release.

It came at last, that Conqueror over the mightiest. After a day of sunshine, which had brightened the room in which Mr. Gladstone lay, there was a sudden ebb of vitality. The pulse, which was never very rapid in the case of the patient, became hardly noticeable ; and from the village of Hawarden went forth, on the afternoon of May 17th, the news that "Gladstone was dying." His son, Mr. H. N. Gladstone, hurried home from London by special train, and rapidly the members of the family gathered round the bedside of the departing veteran.

And thus, in the home he loved, and amid those who were dearest to him, died William Ewart Gladstone on May 19th, Ascension Day. The partner of his joys and sorrows was at hand to say Good-bye, and, amid all the sad trial of her fortitude, was brave and comforted.

As the tidings flashed across the continents there was a world-wide regret, which must have solaced the widow and children of the greatest statesman of the century. The Queen and many other Royal personages sent their condolences ; and in the hearts of millions, less exalted but no less sincere, there was the consciousness of a noble life ended, a hero fallen in the fight, "a warder silent on the hill."

Both Houses of Parliament unanimously resolved to pay to Mr. Gladstone's memory the highest honour in their power. On the motion of his old opponents—the Marquis of Salisbury in the Lords, and Mr. Arthur Balfour in the Commons, both of whom delivered eloquent appreciations of the great statesman's genius, magnanimity, and public services—it was decided that his remains should be buried in Westminster Abbey, and that a memorial of him should be erected in that National Walhalla at the public expense. The body was removed from Hawarden on the evening of May 25th, and for two days lay in state in Westminster Hall. Vast crowds of people passed through the venerable building to pay their last tribute of reverence to one who for so many years had been the idol of the people, and who had played so large a part in the history of the century. The funeral took place on Saturday, May 28th, amid a scene of national mourning, which will never be effaced from the memory of those who witnessed it. The line of route from Westminster Hall to the West door of the Abbey was densely packed with a sorrowing multitude, and within the Abbey itself a remarkable gathering, representative of all nations and all sorts and conditions of men, assembled to witness "the last sad scene of all." The coffin was preceded by members of both Houses of Parliament, and the pall bearers included the Prince of Wales and the Duke of York, Lord Salisbury and Lord Rosebery, Mr. Balfour and Sir William Harcourt, the Duke of Rutland and Lord Kimberley. The burial service, conducted by the Dean of Westminster and the Archbishop of Canterbury, was made all the more impressive by the singing by the whole congregation of Mr. Gladstone's favourite hymns—"Rock of Ages," "Praise to the Holiest in the Height," and "O God, our Help in Ages past." Mrs. Gladstone was present at the grave, and at the conclusion of the solemn ceremony the Prince of Wales approached her, bowed low, and took her hand and kissed it. The rest of the illustrious pall-bearers followed His Royal Highness's example, and then the mourners and the vast assembly filed past the grave, and with a last fond look upon the simple inscription on the coffin-lid, bade the greatest Englishman of the Queen's reign a silent and reverent farewell.